Reckless

Also by S. C. Stephens

Thoughtless
Effortless

Reckless

S. C. STEPHENS

GALLERY BOOKS

New York   London   Toronto   Sydney   New Delhi

Gallery Books
A Division of Simon & Schuster, Inc.
1230 Avenue of the Americas
New York, NY 10020

First Gallery Books trade paperback edition March 2013

GALLERY BOOKS and colophon are registered trademarks of Simon & Schuster, Inc.

For information about special discounts for bulk purchases, please contact Simon & Schuster Special Sales at 1-866-506-1949 or business@simonandschuster.com.

The Simon & Schuster Speakers Bureau can bring authors to your live event. For more information or to book an event contact the Simon & Schuster Speakers Bureau at 1-866-248-3049 or visit our website at www.simonspeakers.com.

Designed by Nancy Singer

Manufactured in the United States of America

10 9 8 7 6 5 4 3 2

Library of Congress Cataloging-in-Publication Data is available.

ISBN 978-1-4767-1820-0
ISBN 978-1-4767-1821-7 (ebook)

To my friends for always being there for me,

my family for always supporting me,

and my fans for always believing in me.

I adore you all!

Reckless

Chapter 1
TEMPORARY BLISS

I was stirred from sleep by a hand running up my thigh. Smiling, I stretched my tight limbs and placed my palm over the wandering fingers. The hand was warm and soft, and clasped mine, cinching tight. A cool ring of hard metal dug into my skin as he held me in his firm grasp and I smiled wider, fingering the matching band on the ring finger of my hand.

I'd gotten married last night . . . in the spiritual sense, at least. A soul-filled pledge of undying devotion was enough for us right now. And really, a formal ceremony and a piece of paper wasn't what made a marriage. It was the feeling bursting apart my chest—the overwhelming sensation that I'd been cleaved in two at birth, and, miraculously, I'd managed to find my other half. And even more miraculously, he felt the same.

Soft lips touched my shoulder, and I snuggled further into the body seeking my solace. The sheets wrapped around us were the finest linens I'd ever slept in, but their luxuriousness paled in comparison to the man beside me. With his warm legs tangled around mine, his broad chest flush against my back, and his arms circled over and under me cradling my body to his, he was far more comfortable than the overpriced bed.

Pulling the fingers laced with mine up to my lips, I kissed the promise ring on his left hand. A low chuckle escaped him, then those sensuous lips of his worked their way up my neck. Warm and content, my skin instantly pricked with goose bumps as small bolts of electricity shot right through me.

When he got to my ear, he whispered, "Mornin', Mrs. Kyle."

My heart was instantly thudding in my chest. I twisted in his embrace until I could see him. Eyes the color of a twilight sky stared back at me, and a small smile curved his mouth as he searched my features. His face was perfect—the angle of his jaw, the slope of his nose, the fullness of his lips. At the moment, I couldn't recall anything quite as beautiful as the man who'd just given me his name.

"Good morning, Mr. Kyle."

A small giggle of disbelief escaped me, and Kellan's smile widened. The contentment in his eyes was nearly palpable. It warmed my heart that I made him feel that way. He'd had enough pain in his life; he deserved peace. It was all a little surreal to me, the depth of his love, the fact that I inspired it. Sometimes, I didn't feel worthy of him, but I was grateful for him, every day.

"I can't believe we just did that, Kellan."

He cocked an eyebrow, his grin instantly mischievous. "What? Have mind-blowing sex? That really shouldn't surprise you." His expression softened into adoration. "Every time with you is incredible."

Biting my lip, I forced the flush he was making me feel aside. "I wasn't talking about that." Reaching up with my free hand, I stroked his jaw with my finger. "I meant getting married."

Kellan propped himself up on his elbow and looked down at me. His gaze slid down to our hands locked together, to the ring encircling his finger. The look of contentment on his face shifted to outright bliss. I'd never seen him happier. "'Til death do us part," he whispered.

Running my fingers down his chest, the hills and valleys of his absurdly defined body starting to ignite mine, I murmured, "My parents won't accept you as my husband until you walk me down the aisle, you know."

Remembering that I'd left them a vague message on the answering machine at Kellan's place, since they were still in town for my graduation yesterday, I frowned. They were going to be so pissed when they woke up and heard that I'd run off and gotten married without including them. Honestly, I was a little surprised that my phone hadn't rung yet . . . or that the hotel room door hadn't been beaten down.

Kellan laughed and repositioned our bodies so that he was lying on top of me. Giving him a soft smile, I ran my fingertips down his back. He shuddered. "And I will. . . ." Leaning down, he placed a kiss on my neck, then my collarbone. My heart sped up. "I will give them the ceremony they want. . . ." Looking up at me, he let his lips trail from my collarbone to the top of my breast. I struggled to not squirm. "I'll give you the wedding of your dreams, Kiera."

His lips closed over my nipple then, and all of last night's passion flooded back to me. As satisfying as our first union as husband and wife had been, I wanted more, I wanted him again. I didn't think I'd ever stop wanting him in every way that that implied.

Just as my fingers drifted up to thread through his hair, my breath long past casual, his lips left the erogenous zone that they'd found. I looked down at him right as he looked up at me. Crooking a grin, he kissed between my breasts, then down my belly. Just the thought of him continuing on his southern path had me instantly aching for him. His grin turned cocky, like he knew it.

"I'll give you everything, Kiera, but, until I can do it properly . . ." His tongue dipped into my belly button before trailing down my abdomen. I groaned and closed my eyes, simultaneously shifting my hips up and pushing his head down. I heard a throaty laugh escape him as his lips traveled down my thigh. His breath hot against my skin, he finally finished his sentence, ". . . we may as well enjoy the perks."

Then his tongue brushed over my core and I lost all pretense of control.

It was several hours later that we were finally dressed and ready to leave our swanky hotel room. A quick inspection of my cell phone showed me that Kellan had turned it off sometime last night. I guess that explains why we hadn't had any interruptions. Smirking at him as he grabbed his jacket from the plush bench in front of the vanity—a bench that we'd christened last night—I turned my cell phone back on. A new voicemail alert chirped at me; I was sure there were several of them.

Considering the fact that we'd be seeing my very unhappy parental units soon, I didn't bother listening to the voice mails. I was pretty sure I knew what they all said anyway. "What were you thinking? You can't marry him, Kiera. Get your ass back here so we can fly you home!" Etcetera. They were going to take a while to accept this union.

They were going to take even longer to accept the fact that I was soon to be hitting the road with my new husband. Even I was still in shock. Touring around the country with Kellan had been out of the question while I was still enrolled at school, but I was a graduate now, and I was free. I could do whatever I wanted. And I wanted to be with Kellan, wherever that may be.

My dad was kind of old school—go to college, graduate, and get a good job. Kellan hadn't even gone to college. He'd run away from home right after high school and fallen into the Los Angeles music scene with Evan, Matt, and Griffin. He'd been playing with them ever since. Dad was mystified by Kellan's life choices. And he was going to be furious with mine.

But it was my life to live, and I was going to do what felt right. And being with Kellan felt . . . amazing. There was no place I'd rather be than by his side. I wasn't giving up on my dreams to live vicariously through Kellan's, though. No, I was going to strive to make my dreams come true too, and it just so happened that my dream job lined up perfectly with his.

I wanted to be a writer, and that gave me a certain amount of freedom since I could do it anywhere so long as I had a bit of privacy. That might be tricky in a tour bus full of rowdy boys, but I was certain I could carve out a few hours every day to put something meaningful down on paper. I was in the middle of writing my first book, which was autobiographical in a sense, since it was based on actual events. It was a detailed, intimate depiction of everything that had happened between Denny, Kellan, and me. The love, the lust, the betrayal—it was all in there.

Writing it was torturous, but therapeutic. Taking a step back and looking at the situation through critical eyes, it was easy to see my many mistakes. There were points when I had been whiny, clingy, petty, wishy-washy . . . downright annoying. Seeing all of my flaws laid bare was a humbling experience. The book was so personal, I almost wasn't sure if I could let anyone else read it. Especially Kellan. But he'd asked, and I'd told him he could. I didn't want to go back on my word, so I would just have to reassure him with each painful page that I wasn't that weak, pathetic girl anymore. I knew what I wanted, and it was him.

Scanning the room to make sure I wasn't forgetting anything, my eyes swept over the messy bed. The rich, red comforter was a jumbled mess, and the creamy, satin sheets beneath it were twisted as well. Kellan and I had made good use of the king-sized space, rolling around over every inch of it as we'd explored each other. Our moans and cries of ecstasy were still reverberating through my head, and for the millionth time I was grateful that Kellan had agreed with my idea of renting a hotel room for our honeymoon. I couldn't imagine doing the things we'd done last night at our place, with my parents in the next room.

Coming up behind me, Kellan wrapped his arms around my waist. I inhaled deeply, savoring the fresh, invigorating scent that was uniquely his. Kissing my ear he murmured, "We should go. I told Gavin I would have breakfast with him today, and we're already really late. . . . It's more like brunch now."

Looking over my shoulder at him, I couldn't contain my smile. Gavin Carter was Kellan's biological father. Kellan had put off meeting the man for months; he'd been terrified to see him. But they'd finally met yesterday, and now Kellan was going to try and have a relationship with the person who'd helped create him.

Twisting in his arms, I slung mine around his neck. Running my fingers through the back of his hair, I gave him a soft kiss. "I'm sure he'll understand that your wedding night ran a little long."

Kellan sighed and cinched me tight to him. His body flush to mine was hard and unyielding. My fingers itched to feel the curves of his defined physique, but that always led to him exploring mine, which usually led to a long, drawn-out lovemaking session . . . and we really did have to leave. Practicing as much restraint as I could, I kept my fingers tightly tangled in his hair.

Kellan kissed my head. "I still can't believe you're my wife."

Nuzzling my face against his chest, I felt like my heart was going to burst open onto the floor. God, I loved him. Desire for him started building in me as we held each other, and I again had to repress the urge to express my love for him physically. Pulling back, I frowned. "You're right, we should go."

Kellan smirked at my expression. "You want to have sex again, don't you?"

Flushing, I pushed his chest away from me. "I think we broke enough records last night . . . and this morning." I felt the heat in my cheeks and averted my eyes.

Squatting in front of me, Kellan grabbed my chin and made me look at him. "Do you want to have sex with me?" he asked, not a hint of a tease in his voice.

His question was so direct that I found it difficult to keep my eyes trained on his. I instinctively wanted to look away. I didn't, though. I made myself stare into his dark blue depths as I whispered, "Yes."

Kellan gave me a prideful grin. "Was that so hard to admit?" he asked, a gleam in his eyes.

I started to close my eyes, but stopped myself. He wanted me to not be embarrassed around him. And he wasn't trying to tease me right now; he was trying to help me grow. Locking gazes with him, I nodded again. "Actually, yeah, that was a little mortifying."

Pursing his lips, Kellan shifted away from me. "I want you to ask me to have sex with you . . . right now."

My mouth dropped open. "Kellan . . ." Feeling self-conscious, I covered my chest with my arms. As I was still wearing the tight, slinky dress my sister, Anna, had let me borrow for my graduation ceremony, there was a lot of skin to cover up. "I've asked you for sex before. . . . Why are you purposely embarrassing me?"

Sighing, he leaned down again to meet my eye. "You've asked me in the heat of the moment, when we were heading in that direction anyway. I want you to feel comfortable enough to ask me anytime, anywhere."

I cocked an eyebrow at him. "Anywhere?"

Kellan gave me an impish smile. "*Any*where."

Knowing he wasn't going to drop this, I huffed out a disgruntled breath. Dropping my hands to my sides, I counted to ten. Really, this wasn't so hard. I should be able to ask him to have sex with me. I've certainly used my body to ask him on several occasions. Bluntly saying it was different, though. It made me feel a lot more vulnerable.

Lifting my chin, I confidently asked, "Kellan, will you have sex with me?" Well, I meant to say it confidently, but my voice came out high and squeaky—anything but sexy.

But by the look on Kellan's face, you'd think I'd just given him a lap dance. His burning eyes slid down my body, igniting me. They lingered on my lips, my chest, my hips, and even though he wasn't touching me, my body responded like he was. When his bedroom eyes finally returned to mine, he took a step forward. His hip brushed against me and I gasped. Leaning down, his breath hot against my skin, he murmured in my ear, "That is the hottest thing I've ever heard you say."

My eyes fluttered closed. I felt like I was vibrating, waiting for him to touch me. Every sensitive spot on me buzzed with anticipation. All he had to do was touch his lips to mine, brush a thumb over my breast, or cup my backside, and I would explode . . . I was sure.

His lips closed over my earlobe and a low moan escaped me. "But we have to go." With those words he grabbed my hand and yanked me forward. Startled at the sudden movement, my eyes flew open. His grin was amused as he backed toward the exit . . . and not the bed.

I frowned at him as he laughed. "I'm sorry, Kiera, but you'll just have to be unsatisfied for a while." Cocking his head, his smile grew wider. "That's sort of . . . karma . . . for all the times you've left me aroused and alone."

Guilt crept toward me, but I pushed it back. Our past wasn't relevant anymore. "You're mean," I muttered.

He kissed my cheek. "Hmmm, maybe I am." Stepping into me, he grabbed my backside and pulled my hips into his. Fire swept through me instantly and I groaned a little before I controlled myself. Running his nose along my jaw, he husked out, "Because I'm really looking forward to teasing you all day."

Irritated at how turned on I was, I pushed him back. "You suck."

He laughed as he opened the door. Grabbing my purse, I looked back at the rumpled bed that screamed *A passionate romp happened here!* "Wait, Kellan. Should we make the bed before we go?"

Kellan bunched his brows as he looked between my face and the twisted sheets. Shaking his head at me, he murmured, "You're so adorable." His loving grin turned into amusement as he looked back at the bed. "No, we're leaving the room like it is. I want the world to know what happened here . . . on the night we consummated our marriage," he said, returning his eyes to mine.

I sighed, moved by his words. Then he added, "Besides . . . it's hot."

Rolling my eyes, I followed him out of our hotel room.

The woman at the front desk kept her eyes on Kellan the entire time he checked us out. I saw her gaze flick down to his wedding ring when he handed her his credit card, but by the sparkle of interest in her eyes, I don't think she much cared that Kellan was married.

Kellan was a breathtaking man, and gorgeous men attracted attention when they walked into a room. I was used to the reaction by now, and it didn't really bother me anymore. Well, at least it didn't bother me as much as it used to.

The eager hotel employee frowned as she handed Kellan his receipt. By the flash of disappointment in her eyes when Kellan thanked her without even looking at her, I think she'd been hoping he would ask her to join him upstairs. I refrained from smiling when her eyes finally shifted to me. She may have been hoping for a quick hookup with the hot man about to exit her lobby, but Kellan didn't do hookups anymore.

Snuggling into Kellan's side, I politely thanked her for the pleasant stay. I giggled after I said it, still a little high from my wedding night. Kellan kissed my head as he turned us toward the exit. "When we get home, I'll call Gavin and have him come over to our house for brunch. Might as well have our two families formally meet, right?" he said.

Kellan's smile was content and it warmed my heart. He'd referred to his father as "family." That was a far cry from when he hadn't wanted anything to do with him. "Yeah, sounds great." I cringed. "My parents are going to kill me, though." I flashed my ring. "And then kill you."

Kellan only shrugged at my comment as he led us to his car in the parking lot. Gallantly opening my door for me, he gave me a peck on the cheek as I slid inside the Chevelle. He sprinted around to the driver's side with a huge grin on his face. He looked so happy to finally have me as his wife, to know that I was his and I wasn't going anywhere. I'd always hoped that the man I married would love me beyond reason, but Kellan . . . loved me beyond anything. The depth of his love sometimes overwhelmed me, but my love for him was just as powerful. He was everything to me.

As he stepped into the vehicle, I moved across the bench seat so I could be as close to him as possible. He grinned as he draped his arm over my shoulder. "Miss me?" he asked, his voice low and husky.

Nodding, I leaned up to kiss him. Kellan eagerly returned my affection, his hand coming up to cup my cheek. I lightly flicked my tongue against his and he groaned, then pushed me back. "Hey, I'm supposed to be teasing you today, not the other way around."

He had an adorable pout on his face, and I couldn't stop the giggle that escaped me. "Sorry, I learned from the master."

Kellan let out a dramatic exhale and removed his arm from around my shoulder so he could start his car. "Serves me right, I suppose." The hearty engine growled to life, and Kellan's content expression returned.

My face was a mirror image of his as I lay my head on his shoulder. Even though the hotel receptionist had blatantly ogled my husband, even though my dad was going to try and ground me when I saw him again, and even though Kellan's newly discovered father was going to be dropping by for a visit this afternoon, today was a perfect day; nothing was going to squelch my happiness.

We turned onto Kellan's cramped street, and a feeling of homecoming came over me. I had enjoyed our night away, but I was glad to be back at our place. And I was *really* glad that I had moved back in a few weeks ago. When Kellan pulled up to his white, two-story home, a car was parked in the driveway. Kellan glanced over at the bright red sporty Jetta and frowned. Curious about who was here, I looked over as well; the car didn't belong to anyone I knew.

Shutting off the Chevelle's engine, Kellan muttered, "Hmmm," and cracked his door open. I opened mine as well, wondering if maybe Gavin and his kids were here. He was visiting from out of town. Maybe he'd rented the car? Although I found it hard to believe that Gavin would show up without asking Kellan if he could come by first. Plus, he would have needed directions to Kellan's house. And I really doubted that a rental car would have a bumper sticker on it that read: *If you're gonna ride my ass, at least pull my hair.*

Knowing the driver was female and probably one of Kellan's many, many ex-whatevers, I reluctantly followed Kellan to the front door. God, if some chick had shown up wearing only a long coat while my parents were here . . . I was going to die.

The front door was unlocked and Kellan stepped through. Reaching back for my hand, he escorted me into our entryway. Kellan's home wasn't the largest. From the front door you could turn right to go upstairs to the bedrooms, turn left to head into the kitchen, or go straight ahead to the living room. My parents were currently sitting on Kellan's lumpy living room couch, a deep scowl fixed on my father's face. My mother was trying to contain it, but I could tell she wasn't happy either.

I wasn't sure if their disappointment was over my impromptu elopement or if they were irritated by the person lounging on Kellan's comfortable chair, a chair that held a large amount of sentimental value for me since Kellan had given it to me when we'd broken up. It meant a lot to me that Kellan had cared enough to think of me at a time when I really didn't deserve his kindness. Some strange girl sitting on it sideways, dangling her high heeled legs over the armrest, made my stomach tighten.

Hearing our entrance, the girl tilted her head back so she could see the door. When Kellan got a good look at her, he muttered, "Shit," and glanced down at me with a worried expression. The tightness in my stomach shifted to ice as I wondered who this girl was.

Clenching my hand, Kellan walked into the living room so we could greet the new arrival. When we came into her view, she looked up at Kellan and narrowed her eyes. She had long black hair with equally dark eyes. She made them seem even darker by covering her lids with smoky gray eye shadow. Her lips were painted bright red and were pursed in an irritated, but erotic, pout. She was gorgeous, but I'd been expecting that. Most of Kellan's conquests were.

Her face full of contempt, her voice low and husky, she bit out, "Well, fuck me, Kellan Kyle." Amused at herself, she smiled and added, "Oh, wait, you already did." As her scowl returned, my expression darkened; I already disliked this person.

Ignoring her comment, Kellan acknowledged my parents first. "Martin, Caroline." Then he shifted his gaze back down to the rude girl lounging on my favorite chair. "Joey."

My brows shot up my forehead as I stared at the girl glowering at Kellan. Joey? As in, the ex-roommate Joey? The girl who had lived here just a few weeks before Denny and I had moved in . . . over two years ago? I never thought she'd come back. What the heck was she doing here now?

Face tight, Kellan echoed my thoughts, "What are you doing here?"

She hopped to her feet. Crossing her arms over her ample chest, she lifted her chin. Eyes fiery, she snarled, "Where the hell is all my stuff, Kellan?"

Kellan's mouth dropped a little and some anger seeped into his expression. Holding my hand a little tighter, he replied, "You've been gone for two years. I tossed it."

I bit my lip to stop myself from cringing. *I* had actually tossed her stuff. Joey had run off in a huff after Kellan had slept with her then immediately slept with someone else. He wasn't always the sweet, loyal lover that he was now. Kellan had insisted that Joey didn't care for him, that she was just possessive. He'd offended her by sharing his bed with another woman . . . even though she'd been sharing her bed with other men.

Denny and I had used her furniture when we'd moved in. After our bad breakup, the furniture had felt tainted to me, like the ghost of my ex-relationship had somehow infused into the dark wood. To purge the home, I'd had all of her stuff taken away. Maybe I shouldn't have done that, since it wasn't mine to toss, but I'd wanted it gone so Kellan and I could start fresh. I probably should have expected that decision to bite me in the ass.

Her face theatrically outraged, Joey shoved Kellan's shoulder back. "You what? That wasn't yours to get rid of, asshole!"

Face heated, Kellan took a step forward. "You ran out. It's not my problem if you left everything behind!" Eyes disdainful, he scanned her face. "My house isn't your personal storage unit."

She scoffed and raised a hand dismissively. "Whatever, Kellan. I don't need your temperamental crap. If you don't have my stuff, then you can just pay me for it." She smirked. "Fifteen hundred should cover everything."

I made a strangled noise and Joey twisted her head to glare at me. "Who the hell are you?" She raised an eyebrow. "Kellan's flavor of the hour?"

My dad rose to his feet, his cheeks flaming bright red. "I don't know who you are, missy, but you cannot talk to my daughter that way!"

I was worried that my father might have a heart attack, he seemed so angry, but his rage was nothing compared to Kellan's. Dropping my hand, he stepped up to Joey and stared her down. "Be very careful, Josephine. That's my wife you're talking to."

Joey looked intimated by Kellan for a moment and backed up a step. Then his words hit her. Her dark eyes bugged out and she openly gaped at me. Then she started laughing. "Oh my God, are you serious? You, the biggest man whore I know, actually got married? What a joke."

Kellan crossed his arms over his chest while my dad sighed and sank back down to the couch. He *really* wasn't pleased about this whole marriage thing. I thought I heard my mom sniffle, but I was too focused on Joey to look. My own temper was quickly rising, ready for this intrusive little bitch to leave.

Kellan was too. Indicating the door, he told her, "Fine. I'll get you fifteen hundred for the furniture. Now get the hell out."

Joey shook her head. "Oh, I don't think so . . . not anymore, Kellan."

He cocked his head, not understanding. I didn't either. Hands balled into fists, I stormed up to her. "You heard him! You'll get your money." I shooed her off with a hand. "Now go back to whatever hole you crawled out of."

Joey drilled daggers into me with her eyes. She kept her gaze on me, but spoke to Kellan. "I have something of yours that I'm re-turning"—she looked up at him—"since I have no use for it." Kellan bunched his brows and Joey smirked at his confused expression. "And if you want it back . . . sweetheart . . . then you'll double my price."

"You're nuts, lady!" I snapped.

Joey ignored me, turning her eyes to Kellan. Then she leaned over and grabbed her bag off the chair, her short skirt exposing almost all of her thigh. Opening the bag, she pulled out a tiny, rectangular media card, the kind that fits into digital cameras, camcorders, and some cell phones. Kellan's eyes widened when he saw it. He snapped his eyes to hers, and before I could ask what the hell was going on, he quickly told her, "Fine, I'll give you three thousand."

Throwing me a victorious smile, Joey handed Kellan the SD card. My mind was spinning over just what was on that card that Kellan was willing to pay so much money for. The fire in my belly shifted to nausea. Kellan clenched his hand around it, then pointed at the door. "I'll get it to you tomorrow."

Joey patted his cheek. "You better . . . 'cause I will make your life a living hell if you don't." She glanced back at me with a wicked grin.

Kellan closed his eyes. "Get the hell out of my house, Joey." Reopening them, he added, "And don't ever come back here."

Waggling her fingers at my parents, Joey sauntered to the front door. No one moved or spoke as she left the house. When the sound of her car starting filtered in through the door, Kellan finally seemed to relax. Turning to my parents, he discretely tucked the card he was holding into his pocket.

"I'm sorry about that. I hope she didn't give you too much trouble while we were gone."

My dad's posture turned rigid as he looked up at Kellan. I could have sworn his graying hair was getting grayer by the second. "I'm more concerned about what the two of you were doing last night than your tawdry friend." Cheeks flushed, he looked between my new husband and me. "What's this about you running off and getting married?" He focused his warm brown eyes on me. "Have you lost your mind, Kiera?"

Mom sniffled again, and Dad patted her hand. I wanted to sit and talk with them about last night, but I was still shell-shocked. What the hell did Kellan have in his pocket? And why was it worth three grand to him?

As Dad patted the couch insistently, Kellan looked back at me. His face was a mixture of amusement, resignation . . . and fear. I wasn't sure if he was doing it purposely, but he'd angled his hips in such a way that I couldn't see his card-holding pocket anymore. I still knew that damn thing was in there, though.

Kellan indicated that I should sit in the empty space beside my father, then pointed at the front door. "I'll be right back. I want to go check on my car, make sure Joey didn't mess with it." Giving me a tight smile, he added, "If she keyed my baby, you may need to restrain me, 'cause I might kill her." He laughed as he started to move toward the door.

My words stopped him cold. "What's on the SD card?"

The amused smile instantly left Kellan's face. Swallowing, he shook his head. "It's nothing. Don't worry about it, Kiera."

Ignoring my parents for a moment, I stepped close to Kellan. I tried to reach around him, to grab his pocket, but he nimbly stepped away from me. Trying very hard to control the anger roiling my stomach, I repeated, "What's on the card?"

Seeing that I wasn't going to back down, Kellan leaned in and whispered, "Can we talk about this later . . . in private?"

I wanted to nod my head and sit down to explain my "symbolic" marriage to my worried parents, but I couldn't get the smirk on Joey's face out of my mind. Aware that I sounded like a broken record, but not able to stop myself, I asked again, "What's on the card?"

Irritated at me now, Kellan narrowed his eyes and snapped, "What do you think it is, Kiera? We filmed ourselves screwing!" Instant remorse crossed his face once he realized what he'd just crassly told me. Kellan sometimes lost the filter on his mouth when he got annoyed, and Joey confronting him had put him on edge. I guess my incessant questions pushed him over it.

My mouth dropped open and I felt like he'd just doused me with ice water. I knew that's what he was going to say, I really did, but hearing him confess it hurt. My whole body felt cracked, torn. Eyes quickly watering, I murmured, "You made a sex tape with her?"

My mom cleared her throat and shifted on the couch. That's when I suddenly remembered that Kellan and I weren't alone. No, I stupidly hadn't been able to wait until we were in private to start this conversation. I really wished I'd been able to squelch my curiosity. I'd give anything to not know that my new husband had a documentary of him banging another girl in his pocket. And I'd really give anything for my parents to not know that too.

Seeing my pain, Kellan came toward me, arms extended. "Kiera, I can explain."

I held my palms up to him as tears dropped to my cheeks. I didn't want an explanation right now. I just wanted to be alone. Turning from him and my parents, I darted up the stairs. I heard Kellan asking me to wait and my mom calling my name, but I ignored them. Slamming the bedroom door behind me, I tossed my shoes across the room, collapsed onto my bed, and let the tears flow freely.

So much for nothing ruining my happiness.

Chapter 2
Falling in Love

Once the tears were expelled I felt better about the situation. I knew I was overreacting; it wasn't as if Kellan had just made the tape recently or anything. The shock of it had thrown me, was all. And the disgust. I couldn't stand the idea of another woman's hands on him, regardless of when it had happened. Having the memories of hearing him please other girls while I was across the hall was bad enough. The idea of watching it made me want to throw up. In fact, I held my hand over my mouth just in case.

When my sobs subsided, I heard murmuring downstairs. Dad was probably giving Kellan a piece of his mind. Knowing I needed to get over this, I tried to think of anything but Joey's yellow high heels wrapped around Kellan's torso. It was really difficult to push that image from my head, though.

Needing some help from the present, I slipped off my promise ring and stared at the tiny diamonds lining the sides. As I studied each diamond, I recalled all of the romantic and touching things that he had said to me and no one else.

I'd rather hold a beautiful girl than be all bruised tomorrow. I need to be close to you. Every girl is you to me. You're all I see . . . you're all I want. We could be amazing together. You wreck me. Stay. Stay with me. Work it out with me. Just don't leave me . . . please. I'm sure that

I want my life to always have you in it. We're married . . . you're my wife. I love you.

By the time I heard a light rap on the door, my emotions and my stomach had leveled. I actually felt a little silly about the whole thing. Kellan cracked open the door but didn't enter the room. "Kiera . . . can I come in?"

Rolling over to face the door, I wiped my eyes dry and readjusted my short dress. "Yeah," I croaked out, my voice scratchy.

The door didn't open right away, and I frowned at the closed wood. After another pause, Kellan asked, "You're not gonna . . . throw anything at me, are you?"

A chuckle escaped me, and hearing it, Kellan pushed the door open. I smiled up at his worried expression and shook my head. "No, it's safe."

Kellan quietly closed the door behind him, then walked over to the bed. His eyes locked onto the ring in my hand that I was still fingering. His steps slowed and his eyes glassed over. Not able to pull his gaze from my jewelry, he whispered, "Are you leaving me?"

As I searched his troubled face, I considered what my fidgeting probably looked like to him. I'd gotten upset, dramatically run away from him, and then he'd found me holding my wedding ring like I didn't want to wear it anymore. I immediately slid it back onto my finger. His eyes, still heavy with unshed tears, lifted to mine. My heart broke as I held my arms open for him. "No, of course I'm not leaving you."

He still seemed unsure, so I sat up on my knees and grabbed his T-shirt. Pulling him into me, I flung my arms around his neck. He instantly relaxed as he wrapped his arms around me. Inhaling his scent, I whispered in his ear, "I was remembering all of the reasons why I love you so much. I was appreciating everything you do, and everything you are. I was falling in love with you, all over again."

Kellan pulled back, amazement on his face. "You find out, the day after we get married, that I have a sex tape with another girl . . . and *that* makes you fall in love with me again?" He felt my forehead, like he was sure I was ill.

I laughed again and pulled him onto the bed with me. "Well, no, the tape doesn't thrill me, but"—resting my head on his shoulder, I stared up into his deep blue eyes—"there is so much about you that does, and I won't let this one thing ruin it . . . ruin us."

Kellan smiled and kissed my forehead. "Have I told you today how much I love you?"

Nestling into the crook of his arm, I tangled my legs with his and rested my cheek on his chest, right over the spot where my name was etched on his skin. "Probably, but I'll never get tired of hearing you say it."

Fisting his shirt in my hands, I took a moment to enjoy his comfort. His deep voice rumbled in my ear as he broke the silence. "I'm really sorry, Kiera. I never meant for you to find out about that."

I glanced at his hip, wondering if he still had the card in his pocket, then peeked up at his apologetic face. "I don't want you to hide things just because you think the truth will make me unhappy. We've gotten into trouble too many times that way already."

Kellan nodded, his eyes contemplative. "You're right. And I think I would have told you eventually . . . although, definitely not the morning after our wedding night. But, to be honest, I kind of forgot about the tape with Joey." His pursed his lips, clearly unhappy that Joey had un-fortuitously shown up and reminded him.

Fixing my gaze on his strong, clean-shaven jaw, I asked, "How do you forget making a sex tape with your roommate? I would have thought something like that stood out."

Kellan tensed underneath me, and I shifted my focus to his eyes. Before I could ask the question that was filling me with dread, Kellan sighed and shook his head. "I really am sorry, Kiera. She asked . . . I didn't care. I didn't really say no to a whole lot back then and she—" He clamped his mouth shut and closed his eyes. When he reopened them, he whispered, "I wasn't thinking about the future, about what I was leaving behind . . . and I'm sorry."

Getting a really bad feeling, I sat up. "That's not the only tape you made, is it?"

Kellan cringed, and I immediately had my answer. "I'm so sorry, Kiera," he whispered again.

Crossing my arms over my chest, I shook my head in disbelief. "Oh my God . . . I married Ron Jeremy."

Kellan struggled to keep his expression neutral, but he couldn't for very long. I smacked his shoulder when he laughed out loud. Grabbing my hands, he sat up and pulled my arms around his waist. Pulling me into his chest, he soothingly rubbed my back. My brief spark of anger died as he held me. Then a feeling of melancholy washed over me.

"They'll never all stay hidden, Kellan. Not once your band hits the airwaves. Not once your name is well-known. Once people know they can make money off of you"—I peeked up at his face—"those tapes will be everywhere."

His smile a sad one, he nodded. "I know . . . and I can't apologize enough."

Examining his expression, sympathy welled in me. "It's not *my* body being peddled, Kellan. You don't need to apologize for something you did years ago. I just . . . I feel bad that your intimate life is going to be so . . . public."

Kellan shrugged. "I don't care about that." He cupped my cheek. "I just don't want it to hurt you."

Leaning into his hand, I let out a long exhale. "Well, at least I'll be prepared for it." I smirked at him. "And it's not like I'm *ever* going to watch them." Kellan laughed, and I shook my head and closed my eyes. It stung a little that the world would eventually see my husband in all of his glory, but it didn't really matter. He wasn't that man anymore. He was *my* man.

Opening my eyes, I gazed at his concerned face. Wanting to ease his fear that I would reject him for this, I playfully muttered, "You're such a whore."

Shaking his head at me, he pulled me back down to the bed with him. After a moment, I remembered that we both had things to do today, people waiting for us. Just when I stirred, to remind Kellan that he needed to call Gavin, our bedroom door was tapped on. My mother's concerned voice asked, "Kiera, honey, is everything okay?"

Kellan stirred beneath me, moving me aside so he could stand up. Wishing I could pull him back into my arms, I sat up and adjusted my tight dress. "Yeah, come on in."

As she walked into the room, she glanced at Kellan with mixed emotions. I could tell she wasn't thrilled about what she'd heard downstairs. Mom liked Kellan a great deal, but she was just as protective as Dad, and Kellan made her nervous. Attractiveness, fame, youth, and monogamy didn't usually mix well. Even though she tried her best to have faith in my beau, she was certain he'd eventually stray from me.

But she didn't know Kellan like I did. And I was sure he wouldn't. He'd had that life already, and he was looking for something more. He was looking for a lifetime . . . with me.

I threw on a bright smile as she walked toward me. Kellan looked between us, then leaned over and kissed my cheek. "I'm going to go call Gavin . . . and check on my car. I'll see you in a minute." I nodded at him and kissed his fingers before he left.

Mom watched him go, then sat on the bed with me. She didn't ask me anything, but her earlier question was still clear in her green eyes. Putting a hand on her knee, I repeated my earlier answer. "I'm fine, Mom, really."

She seemed baffled by my response. "How can you be fine with him and that girl . . . ?"

She didn't finish her question and I shrugged. "It was ages ago, long before he met me. That tape doesn't have anything to do with me, and now that the shock of it has worn off . . . I'm fine."

Mom wore a look of confusion, and I laughed a little as I laid my head on her shoulder. "He's not that guy anymore and . . ." I paused, my own failings suddenly hitting me. "I can't hold his past against him."

Hearing my tone, Mom pulled back so that I had to look at her. "What about *your* past?" She scanned my face. "Do you want to tell me what really happened with you and Denny, honey?"

I blinked, taken aback. Mom and Dad had both accepted it when I'd told them that Denny had left me for a job in his home country. But Mom was observant, concerned, and curious, and had no doubt melded together guilty looks and hushed comments to form a Denny-Kellan-Kiera puzzle that was much bigger than the tiny piece that I'd admitted to her. I was sure she suspected the truth. Feeling my eyes well, I started to shake my head. No, I didn't want to tell her how horrible a human being I was, that she'd raised *that* sort of girl, that I was even more flawed than the man who'd made a sex tape with his ex-roommate. I would prefer it if she continued to think of me as sweet and innocent. But then . . . I would be a liar if I let her keep thinking that way.

Hanging my head, I whispered, "I had an affair with Kellan. Denny found out and . . . left me." Guilty tears coursed down my cheeks. Peeking up at her, I choked out, "I'm so sorry, Mom."

Her eyes were glossy as she watched my pain. I waited for her biting words of condemnation, but they didn't come. Instead, she tossed her arms around me and hugged me tight. That only made me cry harder. Resting my cheek on her shoulder, I let go of the dam holding back my remorse. I sobbed in her arms as she soothingly cooed in my ear and rubbed my back.

My tears subsiding, I lifted my head. "Do you hate me?" My throat closed up with my words.

Mom dried my tears with her thumb. A soft smile on her lips, she shook her head. "No, of course I don't hate you."

I shook my head at her. "Aren't you going to yell? Tell me how awful I am?"

I started to lower my head and she grabbed my chin. She held my gaze for long seconds before answering. "There's nothing I could say to you that would punish you more than you've already punished yourself." She shook her head, her long brown locks swishing around her shoulders. "Now, if you had no regret, then your father and I would take turns tearing you a new one." She smiled wider and cupped my cheek. "But this is obviously something that has torn you up inside, and I can't imagine that you would ever do this to yourself again."

I violently shook my head. No, I didn't want to ever go through that torture again. She grinned at me as she dropped her hand. "I'm actually more upset that you got married behind my back." Crossing her arms over her chest, she pursed her lips and raised an eyebrow. "You want to explain that?"

I sighed, knowing I wouldn't get out of this one quite so easily.

It took me a while, but I finally convinced Mom that I'd really only gotten engaged last night. Kellan and I considered our moment at the bar a marriage, but I knew the outside world wouldn't see it that way, and it definitely wasn't a legally binding ceremony. My message to Mom and Dad had been pretty short, with no explanations. I'd basically only told them that Kellan and I had gotten married and I wouldn't be home until the morning. It really was a miracle that Dad hadn't sent S.W.A.T. out after me.

Once Mom understood what we'd done, she laughed in relief. "Oh good, I was afraid you'd taken the red eye to Vegas and had some Elvis impersonator marry you." She shook her head as she grabbed my hand to examine my promise ring wedding band. "That's not a proper way to start a life together . . . if you're sure you want to spend the rest of your life with him?"

I nodded emphatically. That was one thing I was absolutely certain of.

A deep resolution marked Mom's features, then she smiled. "I guess we better get started on planning this wedding, then?" Her eyes brightening even more, she clasped her hands together. "We could do it in December, after Anna has her baby . . . oh, or in the spring, when everything is in bloom?"

My mind spun as Mom started ticking off things we would need to do between now and the wedding date. She would surely pick out for me: my dress, my bridesmaid dresses, a guest list, invitations, flowers, music, the venue, a caterer, the wedding cake, tuxes . . .

The list went on and on and I put my hands over hers to stop her from continuing to ramble. "Mom, I don't need anything fancy." I smiled in a lovesick way. "Kellan and I are already married. We just need to make it legal."

Mom gave me a blank look, then asked, "Do you want to have it here in Seattle, or back home in Athens? Because all of our family is back there, and making them fly out to you wouldn't be very nice."

I sighed. Mom wasn't going to let this one go. I was going to be dolled up and paraded down a rose-lined aisle whether I wanted it or not. It twisted my stomach into knots just thinking about it.

Wanting to change the focus, I murmured, "I should go talk to Dad, calm him down." He was probably still a little thrown by the whole sex-tape thing, as well as the marriage thing. Poor Dad. Today was just not his day.

I decided to change into some comfortable clothes before I faced my father. This dress tended to hike up my thighs, and I didn't want to be constantly readjusting it as he scolded me. It also didn't allow for a bra thanks to its square, super-low-cut neckline; a perk on my wedding night, but not so great for a one-on-one with Pops.

Mom was perky as she watched me throw on some jeans and a T-shirt; she was still planning the wedding details, going on and on about the ideal floral arrangement. Once dressed, I headed down-stairs. Mom's description of my wedding ceremony never ceased, and her words filtered into my head with each step I took. As I plod-ded down the steps, I pictured myself walking down the aisle to my husband. When I reached the bottom step, Kellan was standing by the windows, nodding at my father with a solemn expression on his face. I imagined Kellan in a tux and me in a satin gown. In my mind, he was stunning, as usual, and I, for once, was beautiful. The thought of the room full of people made me a little nauseous, so I instead imagined that Kellan and I were alone. Butterflies started to tickle my stomach as the wedding march played in my head.

Kellan looked over at me and cracked a smile. I was pretty sure he wasn't having the same vision I was having, but the expression on his gorgeous face was filled with just as much love and wonder as mine. Flushing with the anticipation of how wonderful our wedding ceremony could be, I walked over to Kellan and wrapped my arms around his waist. Grinning down at me, he enclosed me in his arms and kissed my head. We were dopily staring at each other when my dad cleared his throat.

I snapped out of my romantic vision as I looked over at him. His brow scrunched in confusion, he asked, "Everything . . . okay?"

I smiled and nodded, and Dad sighed, clearly not understanding how I'd gone from one extreme to another in a span of twenty minutes. I giggled as I let go of Kellan and gave my dad a hug. Mood swings were just a fact of life around Kellan. He could lift me up or crash me to the ground. While I sometimes enjoyed the swings, finding balance with him was something I really wanted. We would need that calm if we were going to maintain a long-term relationship. And marriage was pretty long-term. For me, at least.

When I pulled back to look at Dad, he looked over my shoulder at Kellan. I clearly saw the division in his heart. Dad wanted me to be happy, but he wasn't thrilled about me being with a rock star. A rock star with a sex tape in his pocket. Leaning in, he said, "Kellan told me about your . . . marriage . . . at the bar." He frowned and glanced at Kellan. "Are you sure about this, Kiera?"

Smiling bright, I kissed my dad on the cheek. "Absolutely, Dad."

My response didn't brighten Dad's features any. In fact, he seemed to age right before my eyes. Seeing the sullenness in his frown lines, I clutched his arms. "Did Kellan tell you his father was going to come by for brunch?" Looking back at Kellan, I asked, "Did you get a hold of him?"

Kellan lifted the cell phone in his hand. "Just got off. He'll be here in a half hour." Kellan's deep blue eyes sparkled with joy. Positive feelings for a family member were a new emotion for him, and he'd been reluctant to let himself feel it. I think a part of him was still hesitant, like he was bracing himself for the inevitable emotional implosion that was coming. But, for the moment, he was being optimistic about it.

Still beaming, Kellan pointed at the front door. "My car's fine, too." I laughed at his relieved expression. He probably would have tracked Joey down if she'd damaged his baby.

While we waited for Kellan's family to arrive, Mom asked me about color themes for the wedding; the daggers coming from Dad lengthened with each question she asked. Kellan held my hand with an amused smile on his face as he listened to my mom. I was sure he would agree to whatever outlandish ceremony she proposed. He didn't mind being the focal point of everyone's attention, and he certainly didn't mind watching me be at the center of it either. He was constantly pushing me to be more confident and outgoing. While embarrassing, I loved that Kellan cared enough about me to gently encourage me to grow.

Gavin rang Kellan's doorbell right on time. Exhaling a slow, controlled breath, Kellan stood and wiped his palms on his jeans. I didn't see a bulge in his pocket when his hand brushed over it, and I thought maybe Kellan had thrown his sex tape away. I hoped so. I didn't ever want to see him being with another woman, but I knew, if I came across it, the curiosity would kill me. It was possible that it would drive me crazy enough that I would watch it. And there are some things you can't ever unsee. Kellan making his ex-fling squeal was not something I wanted burned into my brain. Just imagining it was bad enough.

Kellan was visibly edgy as he walked to his front door. It was adorable; he so very rarely got nervous. But seeing his father was a really big deal to him. I wasn't sure exactly what he was feeling, but if it were me, it would be a mixture of excitement, apprehension, and terror. So much can go wrong when you hold your heart out to another person, especially one who is related to you. Kellan was being immensely brave right now, and I couldn't have been more proud of him.

Like he was mentally fortifying himself, Kellan let out another short burst of air as he arrived at the door. Slapping on his effortless grin, he pulled the heavy wood inward. I stood from the couch as Kellan's father came into view. Gavin was so much like Kellan that their lineage was undeniable. Same build, same height, same shade of sandy brown hair, same deep, midnight blue eyes, same strong, right-angle jaw. Looking at the two of them side by side was like being given a glimpse into Kellan's future. And from all I could see . . . Kellan was going to age very, very well. Gavin was hopelessly attractive.

From beside me, I heard my mother mutter, "Oh . . . my . . ."

Mom and I exchanged knowing glances as Kellan and his father shook hands. Elation on his face, Kellan gestured inside his house. "I'm glad you're here. Come on in."

Gavin nodded and stepped inside. Right behind him were his two children—Kellan's half siblings. I waved at Kellan's sister, Hailey. Giggling, she waved back at me. Hailey was close to my age, maybe a year or so younger. She had also inherited her father's deep blue eyes, but, surrounded in natural light, I could now see that her light brown hair was a just a touch blonder than the boys'. Close on her heels was Kellan's little brother, Riley. Cute as a button, Riley looked to be around ten years old, just a couple of years shy from the age Kellan was when he'd first experimented with the opposite sex. I really hoped Riley hadn't yet; he was far too young. With eyes the color of a spring morning, Riley looked up at Kellan with awe on his face. Obviously, Riley already idolized his rock-star big brother.

Kellan rumpled Riley's hair as he walked through the door. Once the trio was inside, Kellan indicated his small living room. "Please, have a seat."

I stepped away from the couch so Kellan's father could sit there. My parents stood so they could shake Gavin's hand. My dad gave him a firm, hearty handshake. My mother tittered, then tried to cover it by clearing her throat. Dad was frowning as he watched his wife shake hands with the older version of Kellan. He wisely moved over so that he was sitting by Gavin on the couch and my mother wasn't.

Riley plopped down on the floor, stretching out his legs as he looked around Kellan's home. I'd recently enlisted my best friend Jenny's help in painting the living room. It had been a drab, off-white color for as long as I had been here. She helped me paint it a warm, beige color with a deep, red focal wall. Along the corners of the red wall, Jenny had used her artistic ability to freehand music notes. She had also painted lyrics from one of Kellan's songs. In big, bold letters above the sliding glass door, it said: *Every single day I'll keep you with me, no matter how far from me you are.* Kellan thought it was a little pretentious to have his own words on his own walls, but I thought it was beautiful and wouldn't let him paint over it. It was my home now too.

Coming up beside me, Hailey wrapped her arms around me. By the delight on her face, it was clear to see that she loved me by Kellan's recommendation alone. I found it almost laughable now that I'd once suspected Kellan of cheating on me with her. But he had been pretty secretive about discovering his birth father and hiding it from everyone, including me. I think most girlfriends would have leapt to the same conclusion I had.

I thought Kellan's face might split apart, his grin was so big. As his eyes settled over his parent having a conversation with my parents, he smacked his hands together. "Well, I'll get started on brunch, since it's getting close to lunch time." Laughing a little, he held his palms up to his father. "I'm sorry I was so late in calling you."

Gavin's deep blue eyes took in his son, then swung my way. As I felt my cheeks heat under his gaze, it was easy to imagine how this man had seduced a married woman. Sure, it was an awful situation—just as awful as the situation I'd found myself in a couple of years ago—but it was easy to see *why* it had happened. Gavin's face was not one that many women would say no to. I was instantly grateful that Dad was acting like a buffer between Gavin and Mom. Not that Gavin was going to hit on my mom while he was here, and not that my mom would go there, but still . . .

A warm smile lifted Gavin's lips as he nodded at me. "Yes, I hear you got married last night. Congratulations."

My cheeks felt even hotter as Hailey squeezed me tight and squealed. "You're part of the family now, Kiera! Like it or not!"

My dad sighed.

Walking over to me, Kellan extracted me from his sister and gave me a soft kiss. His eyes drank me in like he'd never seen me before. The way he looked at me made my knees wobble, my heartbeat spike, my breath quicken. He was amazing.

"Like it or not," he murmured before kissing me again.

Feeling sappy and romantic, I breathed, "Like."

My dad sighed again.

Wrapping an arm around my shoulders, Kellan faced our families. "We'll be in the kitchen. Do you guys need anything?"

Grinning as she stared at Gavin, my mother muttered, "No, we're just fine here." Dad peeked over at her and leaned forward just a bit, blocking her view of Kellan's father.

Oblivious, Gavin shook his head. "We're fine, thank you, son."

Kellan was chuckling when we walked around the corner into the kitchen. Leaning down to my ear he whispered, "He called me 'son.'"

I smiled up at him, ecstatic for the bond that was growing between him and his father. Kellan stopped us in front of his refrigerator, and the smile fell off his face. His perfectly soft lips pulled down into a frown. "What the hell do I make them to eat?" He peered down at me, his face a mixture of panic and concern. "I'm not the greatest cook."

Releasing me, Kellan pulled open the refrigerator door and aimlessly looked inside. Trying to think of any meals I'd made that were half-decent, I tossed out, "I can make eggs?"

Kellan's bright smile returned as he found a carton in the fridge. "Yeah, okay . . . that will work." Handing me the carton, he closed his eyes for a second. "Please tell me we have bacon." I was just about to tell him that I'd picked some up the other day, when he opened the freezer door and spotted it. His face flooding with relief, he exhaled, "Thank God."

Amused at his nerves, I set the eggs on the counter and cupped his cheeks. "Hey, relax. They're here for you, not the food."

Kellan let out a long, cleansing breath. "Yeah, I know. I just . . . I don't want to mess this up." Shaking his head, he looked down at the floor. "I mess up everything, Kiera."

My stomach tightening at the painful look on his face, I wrapped my arms around his neck and pulled his body into mine. "No, you don't." With a serious expression, I pulled back to look him in the eye. "You haven't messed us up."

His lips twisted into amusement, like he was sure that wasn't true. It wasn't true, though. Our dark parts couldn't be contributed solely to him. No, our troubles had been a group effort.

His voice soft, he pointed to the cupboard under his sink. "No? I just threw away a sex tape, Kiera."

My stomach did a strange sort of twist. I was thrilled it wasn't still in his pocket, and horrified to know exactly where it was. Making myself smile in as natural a way as possible, I released myself from Kellan. Grabbing a pan for the eggs, I told him, "Exactly. You threw it away." Finding a fork in the drawer, I playfully poked him in the chest with it. "Now, if you had stashed it in a drawer to watch later, then you'd be an asshole."

Kellan chuckled at me as he swatted my bottom with the freezing cold package of bacon.

Just as I was cringing away from him, his sister walked around the corner. "Who's an asshole?"

Rubbing my backside, I automatically pointed at Kellan. He frowned, then shrugged. "Me . . . apparently."

Hailey gave him a wide grin as she pulled up a kitchen chair. Sitting in it backwards, she watched us try and prepare a decent meal. Kellan thawed the bacon in the microwave while I made a pot of coffee. The surging gurgle of freshly brewing java mixed with the pop and hiss of greasy fat as Kellan's bacon slices went into the frying pan. I got started on the eggs, cracking several into a pan, then waiting a few minutes for the white part to turn a solid color. When they looked ready, I attempted to flip them over. Kellan peered into my pan as I broke the yolk on yet another egg. "Uh, I think they have to sit longer," he murmured.

Glancing over at his pan of sizzling meat, I noticed an unappeal-ing dark smoke filling the air. Pointing at it, I retorted, "And I think you're burning the bacon."

He immediately went back to his own cooking while Hailey laughed out loud. "Good God, how have you two survived this long?"

Standing up, she walked over to where Kellan and I were butcher-ing breakfast. "I got it from here. You guys just go relax somewhere."

Kellan gave her an apologetic smile. "Thanks . . . sis."

She smiled back at him after flawlessly flipping an egg. "Not a problem, big brother."

I couldn't help but note the similarities in their smiles as they stared at one another. It warmed me that Kellan's grin seemed to be genetic. Maybe he would pass that unbelievable smile on to our chil-dren? When we had children. Many years from now.

Kellan slung his arm over my shoulder and let out a happy sigh. Looking down at me, he shook his head. "I've been cooking for my-self for years. I don't know why I can't this morning."

Grinning wide, I patted his stomach. "Welcome to the wonder-ful side effect of a really bad case of nerves, Kellan Kyle."

He frowned at my assessment. "I'm not nervous."

Hailey paused in her cooking to look back at him. "You're jok-ing, right? I can practically smell the fear coming off of you." Amused at herself, she giggled.

Kellan's frown deepened. "I'm so glad I have siblings now."

Loving the playful banter between brother and sister, I wrapped my arms tighter around Kellan. Hailey was right about his nerves, wrong about his scent. He smelled just as fabulous as he always did. That marvelous aroma that was his and his alone filled my senses as I leaned against him. He smelled better than the coffee and the bacon.

Riley came into the room a few minutes later, an excited expres-sion on his face. "Kellan, can you show me your guitar?"

Kellan smiled down at him. "Sure." He patted Riley's shoulder, then kissed my head. "I'll be right back."

I watched his backside as he left the room, feeling perfectly content. Then Hailey said something that cracked my contentment a little bit. Eyeing her little brother in the room with us, she asked, "Did Kellan really . . . make a tape?" Her eyebrows lifted meaningfully.

Hating that she'd overheard that, I cringed. Seeing my reaction, Hailey's eyes immediately widened and she returned her attention to the meal she was preparing. "Sorry, I shouldn't have asked. I'm sure you don't want to talk about . . . that." She looked a little embarrassed.

Riley, not really understanding what she was talking about, looked confused. "He's made lots of tapes, Hail." He looked up at me, pure innocence in his eyes. "There are tons of videos online."

I blushed and bit my lip. "Yeah, that's right . . . lots of tapes are out there." I sighed, knowing how true that statement was.

Hailey grimaced and mouthed, "Sorry."

I nodded at her. There was no point in worrying about all the footage of Kellan that was probably going to be leaked one day. It didn't matter. I could deal with it. The price was worth it. I could probably handle much worse to be with him. Not that I wanted to—but, push come to shove, I would take whatever crap came my way if it meant I got to be his wife.

Kellan came back into the room a few minutes later, the neck of his guitar in his hand. He was on a break from recording his album in L.A., and like always, he'd lugged his favorite instrument home with him. It was almost like a security blanket for Kellan, one he couldn't seem to part with for very long.

I smiled at him as he sat Riley in a kitchen chair and then gave him the cherished instrument. I thought Riley might pass out; he was so excited to hold it. There was a gleam in Kellan's eye as he watched the boy's exuberance, as if Riley reminded him of himself. I left the two to their bonding and tried to help Hailey with brunch. I found a fresh honeydew melon in the fridge and started slicing it into bite-size pieces as a disharmonious twang filled the air.

Kellan helped Riley adjust his technique, and as I listened to his instructions, I was reminded of Kellan's first attempt to help me play his guitar. The memory of his hands over mine and his breath in my ear made me smile. At the time, I'd felt really guilty over how much I'd enjoyed it. In truth, I did still feel guilty over it. I probably always would. What we'd done was wrong, and I knew it. I'd dressed up our flirting as nothing more than innocent caresses, but it had never been innocent. I'd wanted him, and he'd wanted me. I'd loved him, and he'd loved me. Nothing about what we'd done was right. But the memory still made me grin.

Over the sounds of Riley's strumming and bacon sizzling, I heard Gavin and my parents talking. Surprisingly, I heard my dad let out a mighty laugh. Gavin must be just as charming as his son— something else that ran in the gene pool. *Lord help the female population if Kellan and I have a boy one day,* I thought.

When the food was almost done, Gavin appeared in the archway that separated the dining room from the living room. He beamed as he looked over his three children. When he met my eye, I gave him a wide smile, happy that he was getting to experience the second chance with Kellan that he'd begged for. I knew all about the blessing of second chances, since Kellan had given me one as well. I nodded at Gavin as he sat in a chair next to Riley.

Riley glanced over at him. "Did you hear that, Dad? I finally got that section right!"

Gavin's prideful smile shifted to his youngest son. "Excellent! You're on your road to stardom already." His eyes shifted to Kellan. "Same as your big brother."

Riley returned to the instrument, but Gavin kept his eyes locked on Kellan. Lowering his voice, I heard him ask, "Can I speak with you a moment?"

Kellan's expression instantly turned guarded, but he nodded and indicated the hallway. Kellan gave me a kiss on the cheek as he walked by, then he disappeared with his father around the corner. I looked back at Hailey, but she only shrugged; she didn't know what Gavin wanted to tell him.

Finished with the melon, I hurriedly plopped the pieces into a bowl, then wiped the juice off of my hands with a towel. Curious, I left the kitchen and followed them.

Kellan and his father were just around the corner, near the doorway that held the laundry room and the downstairs bathroom. Standing close to Kellan, I heard Gavin say, "I didn't want to discuss this in front of Hailey and Riley, but—" He stopped talking when he noticed me. Kellan glanced up and gave me a brief smile, so I felt okay to walk over to him. Gavin looked unsure if he should speak with me nearby, but Kellan nodded at him to continue. "Um, well, Martin and Caroline told me about your visitor earlier. They said she was . . . sort of blackmailing you?"

Kellan sighed while my cheeks heated. Gavin looked between the two of us. "Is everything okay?"

Kellan grit his jaw and tightened his fists; his knuckles turned white. "Yeah, it's fine. This . . . is nothing. I'll take care of it before I leave tomorrow."

My heart dropped that Kellan was leaving so soon. I couldn't join him just yet. My parents were still in town for a few more days, and I had a job that I needed to quit. Pete had been good to me, so I wanted to do it right this time and give him a full two weeks' notice. I also had promised my flighty sister that I would go to her next doctor's appointment with her. So unfortunately, Kellan was returning to Los Angeles without me. But first, he was going to have to meet up with that . . . woman. *Bitch.*

Chapter 3
Honesty

Gavin and his children stayed at our house all afternoon. We spent the bulk of the sunny day playing board games in the living room; Hailey cleaned up in Monopoly, my dad kicked everyone's butt at Scrabble, and Kellan and I dominated at Pictionary, which sort of surprised me since I had no talent in drawing. Kellan was just an exceptionally good guesser.

By the time evening rolled around, Kellan seemed perfectly at ease with his newfound family, and the earlier incident with Joey was pushed to the back of everyone's minds. That was when my burgeoning-with-life sister showed up, baby-daddy in tow.

Without any sort of warning, Kellan's front door burst open and slammed back against the wall. I jumped off my seat, my heart thudding in my chest. Everyone's attention snapped to the entryway. I was positive that we were being attacked, and that a swarm of policemen were about to blaze into the room, weapons drawn.

Standing, Kellan protectively stepped in front of me. That's when Kellan's blond jackass of a bassist sauntered through the door. Relaxing when he realized who was here, Kellan glowered at his band mate. "Griffin? You ever heard of knocking?"

Griffin sniffed and tucked his chin-length hair behind his ears. "We're family, dude, I don't need to knock."

I sighed, not sure if Kellan could argue that point or not—not since Griffin had impregnated my sister. He really was family now. Lord help me.

Kellan opened his mouth to try and argue anyway, but Anna stepped through the door after Griffin and soundly smacked him across the back of the head. "Neanderthal," she muttered.

Mom and Dad rose from the couch to greet Anna. Dad's expression darkened as he examined his grandchild's father. By the way Dad looked at Griffin, I was sure that Kellan was suddenly perfect in comparison, the "golden" son-in-law who could do no wrong.

Recovering from the shock of Griffin's surprise entrance, I joined my parents in greeting my sister. Anna was one of the most beautiful women I knew. Her face dropped men to their knees; her body made boys follow her around like lovesick puppies. Even pregnant, her curvy figure still drew men's eyes. She had impossibly silky hair that rippled when she walked and eyes that were so green it was almost hard to stop staring into them. She was a knockout, and growing up with her perfection hadn't always been easy. But I was starting to be more comfortable in my own skin, and for once her absurd good looks didn't send a zing of jealousy up my spine. No, all I felt when I hugged her tight was happiness to see her. Even if she had brought the Neanderthal with her.

"Hey, sis." As I pulled back, my eyes roved over the clingy maternity top she was wearing. I wasn't sure how my sister had managed to find such provocative pregnancy clothes, but nearly everything she owned was designed to show off her ample cleavage. Griffin must be in hog heaven. God, I really hated having thoughts like that.

Anna was in the adorably cute stage of pregnancy, just rolling into her fourth month. She wasn't throwing up nearly as much anymore, and her energy level was returning. Not that you would know that by the way she waddled when she walked; Anna played up her condition whenever she got the chance. But I knew she was more active than she let on. I was pretty sure her evening with Griffin had been particularly athletic.

Anna looked over to where Gavin and his children were politely

waiting. Her brow scrunched in a way that only made her more attractive. "Oh, sorry, I didn't realize you had company."

Kellan met her eyes. "It's all right. Come on in."

Dad walked Anna into the living room, holding her by the arm
like she would fall if he didn't help her. Kellan gave her a brief hug
and then introduced her to his family. "Hey, Anna, I didn't get a
chance to introduce you last night. This is Gavin, my . . . biological
father." Scratching his head, he shrugged.

A flash of pride went through me that Kellan had admitted such
a profoundly personal thing so easily. He was really getting comfortable with the idea of having a parent in the world again.

Anna's eyes grew just a bit at Kellan's admission. She hadn't
known about Kellan's sordid past. As Anna shook Gavin's hand, Kellan introduced her to his half siblings. Her wide eyes opened even
more with each addition to his family. Gavin made a space for Anna
on the couch, and Dad helped her sit down.

Standing, one arm hooked over Hailey's shoulder, Kellan told
Anna, "Gavin, Riley, and Hails are visiting from back east. Pennsylvania." His focus shifted to Gavin. "Do I have any other family there?"

Gavin smiled; the grin was eerily similar to Kellan's. "My brother
and his family live there, and my parents as well."

Hailey elbowed Kellan in the ribs. "You'll love Grandma, Kellan.
She's feisty."

His face wondrous, Kellan looked over at me. "I have grandparents, Kiera." He looked back to Hailey. "I've never had living
grandparents, or an uncle either, actually." He chuckled, amused and
amazed by the information. My heart swelled as Kellan's family just
kept getting bigger and bigger.

Griffin, absorbing the conversation but not understanding any
of it, looked around the room. "Wait. Dude, I thought your dad was
dead. Who the hell *are* these people?"

Everyone ignored him.

Anna's gaze lingered on Gavin just as much as Mom's did. Griffin, either oblivious or indifferent, didn't notice. Then again, he was

still trying to puzzle out who Gavin was. A pleasant smile on her lips, Anna asked, "So, Gavin, is your wife here as well?"

Gavin looked down at his children sitting on the floor finishing out a board game. "No, I'm not . . . I'm not married." He looked back to Anna, a sad smile on his lips. "Widower . . . since Riley was two." Hailey glanced up at her dad, her expression equally glum.

Anna's small smile fell. "Oh, I'm sorry."

There was a moment of silence as everyone reflected on Gavin's statement. Griffin broke it by walking over to Kellan and whispering, "Dude, seriously, who are these people?"

Chuckling, Kellan socked Griffin in the shoulder. "Come on, I'll get you a beer and draw you a diagram." Laughter eased the tension in the room as Kellan led his bassist into the kitchen to tell him the truth about his origins. Griffin would be the first band member to officially know that Kellan's deceased father wasn't actually his father. Hopefully the imbecile could grasp the concept.

By the time everyone parted ways, it was late into the night, nearly morning. Anna and Griffin headed off to her apartment to make the most of their limited time together. Gavin and his children went back to their hotel; they had a flight in the morning. My parents shuffled off to the guest room to spend yet another night on my old, lumpy futon. Dad sighed when Kellan and I waved good night from the doorway of our bedroom.

Reluctant to waste what little time we had left together sleeping, Kellan and I stayed up the remainder of the night. Still dressed, we cuddled together in bed and talked until the gray, early morning light filtered through the window. Kellan stroked my hair as I rested my head on his chest, listening to his heartbeat and his soothing voice. The comfort I felt in his arms was palpable. His embrace cocooned me in a warmth that would hold back the deadliest ice storm, I was sure.

Wishing he didn't have to leave me in a few hours, I clenched his shirt and hugged him tight. He stopped speaking and kissed my hair. After a moment of silence, he whispered, "Kiera?"

I peeked up at his face. His eyes were dark in the faded light, but glowed with happiness. A small smile curving his lips, he asked, "Will you marry me?"

My heart raced against my ribcage as I sat up on my elbows. "What?"

His smile widened. "Will you marry me?"

I glanced at the ring on my left hand, then the ring on his. "Didn't we already get married?"

Kellan's chest under my arms rumbled as his amusement bubbled up in a deep laugh. "Yes, but I just realized that I never actually proposed to you." Sighing, he brought his finger up to tuck a strand of hair behind my ear. When he was finished, he stroked my cheek. "And you deserve a proper proposal."

After he said that, his face shifted into an expression of contemplation. Before I could answer his question, he gently pushed my body away from him. I tried to pull him back, to eagerly tell him yes, but he slid out from under me and stood up. Walking around to the other side of the bed, he stared at me for several long seconds. Just as I was about to ask him what he was doing, he let out a slow, controlled breath, and slowly sank to one knee.

I'm not sure why, but just watching him move to the floor made a sob rise up my throat. My vision hazed and I swiped my fingers under my eyes to clear away the tears. I wanted to see every part of this.

His eyes glossy in the dim light, Kellan stared up at me. "Kiera Michelle Allen, will you do me the absolute honor of being my wife? Will you marry me?"

I was nodding long before he finished speaking. Reaching down, I grabbed his face. "Yes, of course, yes." I kissed him over and over as I pulled him back into my arms.

His body settled over mine and we kissed, laughed, and even cried a little, until the faded morning light turned into brightly streaming rays of sunshine. I heard my father exiting the spare bedroom that had once been the room I'd shared with Denny. Kellan and I paused in kissing each other to stare at our closed bedroom door.

Dad took an inordinately long time about it, but he eventually shuffled downstairs to make some coffee. An ecstatic grin on his face, Kellan looked back at me. Lacing our fingers together, he whispered, "Why do I feel like I should be hiding in the closet?"

He ground his hips into mine and leaned down to kiss my neck. I closed my eyes and angled my head, perfectly content. Kellan's attentions started waking my body up. I wrapped my legs around his, wondering just how quiet Kellan and I could be. Silent sex with him was difficult, but not impossible. As his lips wandered farther down my neck, I murmured, "Mmm . . . because you're a villainous boy who is only using me to satisfy his baser instincts."

Kellan pulled back from kissing me. "Is that really what your dad thinks of me?"

Caught off guard by his abrupt change of pace, I blinked and stammered, "Uh, I don't . . . no . . . I don't think so."

Kellan shifted to the side of me, and I twisted my body to face him. "Yeah, he does. He thinks all I want from you is sex, and that I have a different version of you in every city that I visit."

I pursed my lips, trying to think of some tiny falsehood in Kellan's assessment. Unfortunately, I was pretty sure that was the bulk of Dad's problem with Kellan. He just didn't trust him, not with his lifestyle. I shrugged. "I'm sure he doesn't think it's *every* city."

Kellan frowned, then hopped out of bed again. Sitting up, I let out an exasperated grunt. "Now what are you doing?"

Kellan walked over to his dresser and started stripping. My objection left my lips as his boxers hit the floor. Kellan watched me watching him with a smirk. Slipping on fresh underwear and jeans, he rummaged for a shirt as I blatantly stared. As enticing as his bare body was, there was something overly erotic about him standing there with his jeans unfastened. Especially with the intriguing lines of definition on his perfectly sculpted abdomen stretching and flexing as he moved. I really wanted that body lying on top of me again.

Amused by my intense inspection, Kellan found a shirt he liked and slipped it over his head. I smiled as that fabulous body was encased in deep red cotton. Even dressed, he was stunning. Zipping up his pants, Kellan shook his head as he walked over to me.

"You do know that if I stared at you the way you stare at me, I would get yelled at."

I gave him a light kiss when he leaned down to me. "I would never yell . . . but yes, I know." His face was a mixture of amusement and irritation when he pulled away. Giggling, I told him, "Life is full of unfairness." I frowned. "Like you leaving me right now. Where are you going?"

Kellan smiled as he ran his fingers through his hair, effortlessly arranging the longer layers into an irresistible mess of bed-head. "I'm going to go show your dad that there is more to me than he thinks. My *only* interest isn't sleeping with his daughter." He winked, then turned to leave. Hand on his doorknob, he twisted back. "Although, that really is what I would like to be doing right now." His eyes trailed down my body, igniting me. Kellan sighed as I squirmed under his scrutiny. Meeting my eyes, he added, "See the sacrifices I make for you?"

He smirked and left the room before I could comment.

I thought of joining Kellan and my father, but decided against it. Dad needed to get to know Kellan one-on-one if he was ever going to bond with him. And besides, I didn't want to distract Kellan with my sexy allure. Yeah, right, sexy. Smiling at my own ridiculousness, I hopped out of bed. Kellan was the alluring one in the relationship, which was a perk for me. I was . . . the lucky one.

I bumped into Mom in the hallway as I made my way to the bathroom. Kellan's place was a little on the small side. The upstairs only consisted of two modest bedrooms with a bathroom tucked in between them. Running into people in the hallway was almost unavoidable. It was how I'd first officially met Kellan.

Mom smiled as she listened to her husband having a civil conversation with mine. I gave her a brief hug as I listened as well. Dad was asking Kellan if he could really make any money off his band "thing." As Kellan started to explain that he would probably make out "okay," Mom focused her attention on me. "We should hit some wedding boutiques while I'm in town. Find you a dress before I head back home."

I cringed at the idea. "Mom, I really don't need a big production. I just want to keep it simple."

Mom swished her hand. "Even simple, you'll still need a dress."

I contained the sigh of defeat stirring in my lungs. I really couldn't argue with that. "Okay, sure thing."

Before she could comment further, I popped into the bathroom and quickly locked the door behind me. I just knew that ninety percent of my wedding would be mapped out before Mom left. Who knew she was so obsessed with weddings? We'd certainly never discussed it before this. It just hadn't really come up when I was with Denny.

Maybe Mom saw the connection between Kellan and I, and knew, just like I did, that I'd found *the one*. My soul. My better half. My reason for being. Nothing in this life would ever fill me with as much joy and peace as Kellan did. I really didn't know what I would do without him.

When I came out of the bathroom after my obscenely long shower, Kellan was back in our bedroom, but he'd changed into his track pants and he was lacing up his running shoes. My expression must have been an odd one, for he did a double take when he noticed me. Of course, that could have been because all I was wearing was a thin, white towel that barely covered my body. I really needed to do laundry.

An amused smile on his lips, he finished tying his shoes.

"What?" I asked, closing the door behind me.

Kellan shook his head, his grin growing. "Nothing." I started to again ask what was entertaining him so much, but he finished with his shoes and stood up. "I'm going to go for a quick run."

"All right." Wondering if my dad had been hard on him in my absence, I added, "Everything okay?"

His deep blue eyes drifted down my nearly naked body. I was instantly aware of the fact that I wasn't wearing any underwear. When his eyes returned to mine, there was a definite edge of heat in them. "Everything's fine. Just need to do a little maintenance." Switching his expression to a casual smile, he ran his hand up his shirt and patted his rock hard abs. *Lucky hand.* Walking over to me, he withdrew his hand from under his shirt, then reached down to pinch my butt. "Wouldn't want to get all flabby now that I'm married."

I giggled and batted his hand away when it started drifting up my towel. Slinking my arms around his neck, I let myself get a little lost in his physical perfection. "I'd rather have you flabby than gone."

Kellan held me close to him; he looked a little lost himself as he gazed at me. "I just need . . ." He paused for a second and then told me, "I need a little fresh air." He gave me a quick kiss and seemed perfectly at ease, but I swear he'd just altered what he was going to say to me. Or maybe I was just being paranoid. Our relationship hadn't always been the most honest one. But we'd sworn that we were going to hold nothing back from each other anymore, and I trusted him.

Nodding, I released him. His smile never faltered, but I thought the light in his eyes dimmed a little as he turned away from me. Opening my dresser, I watched Kellan as he started to open the door. He stopped before he did, though. Laying his head against the door jamb, he muttered, "Damn it, I can't do this."

Ignoring my clothes, I twisted to him. "Kellan?" Was I right just now? Had he lied to me?

Inhaling a deep breath, Kellan stared at me in silence for several long moments. The tension in the room tripled as each second ticked by. The cool air washed over my damp skin, chilling me, and each drop of water that fell from my hair felt like an icicle piercing my body. I started to shake as my nerves amplified the sensation.

Seeing my fear, Kellan took a step toward me. "You said complete and total honesty, right?"

I nodded, not able to talk yet. Kellan looked away. His mind was clearly spinning over some problem. I just didn't know what it was. Swallowing the lump in my throat, I managed to ask, "What is it?"

He looked back at me. "I'm sorry. I purposely misled you right now. I'm not leaving the house because I want to exercise, or because I want air. I need to do something . . . and I need to do it alone."

The ice settling over my skin instantly burst into flames; I swore I could hear the sizzle. "You . . . lied to me? About what? What exactly do you need to do alone?"

Kellan cringed and held his hands up. "See, I wanted to avoid this reaction, that's why I lied. But we're trying to do the honesty thing, so I changed my mind and decided to tell you the truth. So don't get mad."

So hot with anger that I felt like my hair was going to dry by itself in the next five seconds, I bit out, "But you haven't told me the truth. You haven't told me anything. You're being vague and mysterious . . . and I don't like that."

Kellan closed his eyes. "It would have been easier to just keep walking." I started tapping my foot, and Kellan slowly reopened his eyes. "Joey called while you were in the shower. I'm going to go meet with her, and I want you to stay here with your parents."

My jaw dropped. "No! I don't want you to meet her without me. I'm coming with you!"

Kellan shook his head. "I don't want you anywhere near her. I want you to stay here." His tone was firm, commanding. It really pissed me off.

"You're not the boss of me. If I want to go—" Sighing, Kellan turned away from me. I grabbed his elbow and swung him around to face me. "Hey, I wasn't done talking to you."

Mouth set in a firm line, Kellan retorted with, "I know I'm not the boss of you, Kiera. I got that loud and clear when Denny walked back into your life and you didn't say a word to me. But you're not the boss of me either, and if I want to do this on my own, then I will."

With that, he turned and left. And I let him.

Tears were stinging my eyes as I sat on the bed. Absolute honesty wasn't all it was cracked up to be.

I fumed for a long time after he left. My dad tried to make me feel better by telling me that maybe Kellan wasn't the right person for me. He stopped talking when my cold glare turned deadly. My mom was suspiciously quiet as she flipped through a wedding magazine; I had no idea where she got the magazine, but by the delight on her face as she scanned the pages, and her silence at my obvious displeasure, it was clear she was hoping Kellan and I would patch things up soon. And I wanted to. I didn't like being angry with him. I didn't like it when we snipped at each other.

I knew disagreements were inevitable, though. It was finding a way through the disagreements that made a relationship work, or broke it apart completely. Kellan and I had fought many times before, but it seemed like most of our fights were over the big stuff. We hadn't had the tiny spats. Not really. This was all sort of new for us, and I really didn't know how to handle it.

All I kept thinking about while he was gone was what he might say or do with Joey. Well, no, I didn't really think he'd do anything with her. He loved me, considered us married. He wouldn't break that for some floozy he'd had sex with years ago.

So was I scared over what he'd say? Well, no, I pretty much knew what he'd say. He'd call her names, tell her she was a huge mistake, and throw a wad of money at her, hoping to shut her up. I smiled at the image of him all ticked off. He was absurdly attractive when he was angry.

My tiny smile thawed my nerves. No, I wasn't worried or concerned about *Kellan* in all of this. It was the unknown element. It was Joey. I didn't know what she would do or say to him, and that made me anxious. And that's exactly the reason Kellan didn't want me to go. He did know her, used to live with her. He knew she had a fiery temperament. He was trying to protect me by meeting her alone, and I'd bitten his head off for it.

My anger faded as I considered Kellan's view of the situation. He must be embarrassed. Not for the tape, but for the way it was exposed—in front of my parents and me. He wanted Joey appeased so she'd move on. He must have known that bringing me along would only drag out the process, or possibly even halt it all together. Surely Joey would say or do something that would offend me, and I'd end up going off on the woman. Kellan was probably right about having me stay behind. If I were him, I think I would have wanted me to stay behind too.

When Kellan finally came home about an hour and a half later, my anger had vanished. Everyone looked over at Kellan when he entered the house. He inhaled a deep breath as he shut the door. He cast me nervous glances, not ever fully turning to look at me. His hair was dripping with sweat and his arms glistened. I figured he'd decided to go for a hard run after all. Maybe he'd needed it after dealing with that trollop.

Knowing I needed to apologize, I set down the notebook that I'd been writing in and cautiously made my way over to him. He looked away from me and murmured something about needing a shower before heading out to the airport. A slice of pain went through me at the thought of him leaving, but right now, his avoidance was concerning me more. As I walked into the entryway, he turned and bounded up the stairs.

"Kellan?"

He disappeared around a corner, but tossed out, "I'll be right back . . . just need to clean up."

I tried not to interpret that in any way other than honesty; he was sweaty and wanted to be fresh for his trip. Briefly glancing back at my parents, I followed Kellan up the stairs. He was examining himself in the bathroom mirror when I caught up to him.

"Kellan?" I asked again.

He looked over at me and I gasped. In the mirror I could see an angry red line of torn and bloodied skin. It started at his cheek and stretched down to his jaw. That's why he wouldn't look at me downstairs—that bitch had attacked him.

"She hit you?" My heart surged as I rushed up to him.

Kellan glanced at his injury in the mirror, then sighed when he realized I could see it in the reflection. "I'm fine, Kiera."

Grabbing his face, I carefully twisted his head to examine the wound more closely. "She drew blood. That bitch drew blood!"

"It's fine." He smirked. "It's not the first time a woman has cut me."

I ignored his provocative reference to our steamy tryst in an espresso stand, my eyes watery. His smile slipped away from him as he examined my face as surely as I was examining his. "Things . . . didn't go very well. Maybe you should have tagged along after all."

I cupped his uninjured cheek. "Maybe it's better that I didn't. I probably would have gotten arrested for assault."

A faint smile lifted Kellan's lips, but it quickly faded. "I'm sorry I was sort of an ass to you. I just didn't want you involved in her ugliness."

I stroked his moist skin with my thumb. "I'm not involved with her, I'm involved with you, and I wanted to be there to support you. "

Kellan looked down, his face a mixture of appreciation and concern. "I know. I just . . . I know her, and I knew how she'd be." He glanced up at me. "Especially now that she knows what you mean to me. I wanted to protect you."

I gave his chin a light kiss; his skin was slightly salty. "I'm not weak. I can handle it."

Kellan's smile was peaceful as he sat on the bathroom counter. "I know you're not weak. I think I'm the weak one. I needed to know you were safe, protected. I didn't want you to have to hear . . ." His voice trailed off as he let his thought die. "This was all about me, Kiera . . . and I'm sorry."

I could easily imagine just what Joey would have said to me— every intimacy she would have described, every bad behavior she'd witnessed from Kellan. She would have tried to drive a wedge between us, just because she hadn't been able to turn Kellan into one of her boy toys. It only reaffirmed to me just how dangerous jealousy could be.

Straightening my shoulders, I laced my arms around Kellan's neck. "You can stop apologizing, you know. I forgave you a while ago."

His smile broad, Kellan wrapped his arms around my waist. The jagged line along his jaw didn't look quite as bad with his eyes glowing with happiness. "Yeah?"

Stepping closer to him, I shrugged a shoulder. "Of course. You and I aren't always going to agree; we're not always going to get along." Careful to avoid his cut, I grabbed both of his warm cheeks. "And . . . I am so proud of you for telling me the truth when you really wanted to lie. That means more to me than . . . well, that means everything." My throat closed up on me, and I had to swallow to relieve the pressure.

Kellan's eyes searched mine as he nodded in my hands. Moisture pricked my eyes as I thought of the many lies that had speckled our relationship. Honesty, while painful at times, was the best thing we could do for each other.

Before the emotion of the moment could sweep me away, I made my mood brighten and asked him, "Do you want to tell me what happened?"

Kellan gave me a long, drawn-out sigh, reminding me that neither one of us slept last night. I stifled a yawn after that realization. "She wanted to meet here at the house, but I told her I'd meet her around the corner. I wanted to beat her there so she didn't show up here anyway, so I didn't have time to go to a bank. I didn't have enough cash, and she freaked out when I wrote her a check for the rest. I offered to drive with her to a bank, but she smacked me, and I told her to fuck off. I went for a run after that to blow off some steam." *Bitch.* He rolled his eyes while I narrowed mine. "She's a touch crazy. I don't know how I ever lived with her."

I was more wondering how he'd ever slept with her. But he was already irritated, so I didn't say it. Kissing my head, he murmured, "I just want to shower now, get ready to go."

I stepped back so Kellan could step away from the sink. I hated that he was leaving today and I wasn't. I wished he could stay. I wished I could leave. But wishing doesn't change anything, and we would both have to be patient. Kellan turned on the water as I shut the bathroom door. I took over his spot on the counter and watched him adjusting the temperature of the shower. Hopefully the hot water had refilled since my epically long shower earlier.

When the water was perfect, Kellan took off his shoes, socks, and T-shirt; the damp shirt clung to his skin as he removed it. Once it was visible, my eyes fixated on the tattoo over his heart. It was a good thing Joey hadn't seen my name etched into his skin. Kellan might have received more than a bloody line across his face. But Kellan didn't often show his tattoo to the world. It was ours, private. I would really miss seeing the scripted letters when he was gone. Just one of a thousand things I would miss.

Kellan's fingers paused on his track pants. Roused from my melancholy thoughts, I glanced up at his face. He was frowning. "Am I making a mistake?" he whispered over the sound of the shower.

With no frame of reference, I wasn't sure what he meant by that. Seeing my lost expression, Kellan clarified. "Making an album, going on tour . . . am I making a mistake?" The room filled with steam as I hopped off of the counter. Kellan grabbed my hand when I stepped in front of him. "All I want is a quiet life with you," he continued. "What I just signed up for . . . isn't exactly a quiet life."

Wondering how to comfort him—when I often thought the same thing—I reached up and ran my thumb over his healing wound. "Kellan, your life will never be quiet, no matter what you do." He laughed at my reference, the confusion on his face lifting. I placed my hand on his chest and looked him square in the eye. "You belong on a stage. It's what you were born to do."

Even though it was contradictory to the peace and quiet we both wanted, I knew without a doubt that my statement was true. Kellan was doing what he was supposed to be doing. He was living out his destiny. But that didn't have to mean that we would give up on a peaceful life together. It just meant we had to be flexible. Giving him a soft kiss, I murmured, "We will just have to find moments of quiet in the chaos, and we're pretty good at that."

Kellan returned my soft kiss. "Yeah . . . we are." Tilting his head toward the shower, he raised an eyebrow in question. I knew what he was asking: *Want to join me?* A large part of me wanted to say yes, but we had important things to do today, and I had two ever-watchful parents downstairs that we were trying to impress with our restraint. And I was pretty sure there wasn't near enough hot water left in the tank.

Shaking my head, I gave him a final kiss, then gathered up his laundry. He frowned at me, then shucked off the rest of his clothes and put them in my arms. "Thank you for the pep talk," he said, leaning over to kiss my cheek.

I tried to keep my eyes on his face, I really did, but I couldn't resist a peek or two at his body. "You're welcome."

My cheeks flushed as I watched him step into the shower. He swished the curtain into place and started humming a song. I paused with my hand on the doorknob, listening to him; I could listen to him all day. Suddenly, he sucked in a sharp breath and swore. I glanced back at his shadow through the pale curtain. "You okay?"

He stuck his head out; his messy head of hair was completely slicked back and looked darker than it usually did, almost as dark as Denny's. "Yeah . . . damn scratch stings."

I wanted to frown at the pain that bitch had given him, but the petulant look on his face was so adorable that I ended up giggling instead. He wasn't amused by that and ducked back into the shower. "I could set some bandages out for you if you like?" I asked, a merry lilt to my tone.

Kellan let out a loud exhale. "I'm good, thanks."

"Big baby," I mumbled, opening the door.

Mom was coming up the stairs when I emerged into the hallway. Her face brightened as she saw me. Her long, elegant finger pointed to a section of the glossy magazine that she had in her hands. "I just found the most beautiful bouquet in the world. You have to take a look at this."

Arms full of Kellan's sweaty clothes, I tossed on a smile. "Sure, Mom . . . no problem. Let me just get these in the laundry first."

She nodded enthusiastically as she followed me into the bedroom.

When were she and Dad leaving again?

Chapter 4
Goodbye for Now

I was in the guest room with my mom when Kellan finished in the shower. She was explaining the pros and cons of having an all-white bouquet. Mom was so absorbed in her debate, she didn't notice Kellan walking into our bedroom with only a tiny towel around his waist. Then again, seeing him wouldn't have changed the conversation any.

For a moment, I wondered if I should ask Kellan to come in here so he could give his opinion on the floral arrangement. I didn't, though. For one thing, he needed to get ready to go. And secondly, I didn't think Mom really cared about his opinion. She certainly hadn't asked him anything about it so far. For some reason, all of the wedding details were being heaped solely on me, like only I had a say.

That wasn't true, though. I didn't have a say. I'd told Mom multiple times that I wanted a simple, short, private ceremony . . . if I had to have one at all. My impromptu marriage at Pete's was perfect, and I was fine with going to the courthouse to casually sign the papers that would make it official. Then we could have a small, quiet reception with a few friends and family. Mom wouldn't hear it, though. She was deadset on a gigantic shindig.

Kellan came into the guest room when he was dressed. He was reading something on his phone and grinning ear to ear. Mom stopped telling me that wildflowers weren't really classy enough for a wedding and looked up at Kellan. The scratch from Joey looked better now that his skin was clean and full of moisture. The red line was unmistakable, though, and Mom looked over at me after spotting it.

Ignoring her silent question, I asked Kellan, "What is it?"

His smile still huge, Kellan tucked his phone in his pocket. "That was Gavin. His plane is just about ready to take off. He wanted to thank me for meeting with him . . . finally, and let me know that I could visit him anytime I wanted." He let out a small laugh and looked at the floor. "He said he . . . he loves me."

Kellan peeked up at me and his brows were furrowed, like he couldn't comprehend why anyone on this earth would love him, especially a parent. Being loved was still a new experience for him. Or at least, accepting the fact that he was loved was new. Kellan had known love—his band certainly loved him, Denny loved him—but Kellan's view of himself was so skewed for so long, he hadn't recognized the love right in front of him. It took me entering his life and turning it upside down for him to see it, for him to really feel it. But a lifetime of feeling unwanted was hard to shake, and he still struggled with it on occasion.

Standing, I wrapped my arms around his waist. "Of course he loves you. You're his son."

The small smile slipping off of his face, he whispered, "That doesn't mean anything."

My heart breaking, I brushed a damp strand of hair off of his forehead. Leaning up, I murmured into his ear, "I will always love you, Kellan. Your heart is safe with me."

Kellan pulled me into a hug and let out a long, shaky breath as he held me. "Promise?" he whispered.

I squeezed him just a little bit tighter. "I promise." Pulling back, I rested my forehead against his. "Not loving you isn't possible. Trust me, I tried." Kellan smirked, then gave me a soft kiss. Our tender moment was interrupted by someone clearing their throat. Kellan and I both glanced over at my dad standing in the doorway, watching us.

"Something going on?" he asked, trying to keep his voice casual. But I could hear an undertone of disgruntlement.

Kellan let go of me and shook his head. Answering Dad, he locked gazes with me; the midnight blue depths were warm and untroubled. "Everything's fine . . . just getting ready to leave."

Dad brightened and clapped him on the back. "Well then, anything I can help you with?"

Kellan chuckled at his answer as he kissed my head. "No, I'm good, thank you."

He clapped Dad's shoulder as he walked around him and back into our room. I raised my hands at my father in disbelief. Seemingly perplexed, Dad glanced back at Mom. "What? I can't offer to help my future son-in-law?"

Sooner than I would have liked, the four of us were driving to Pete's bar. The band was meeting there for their send-off. Kellan refused to let me see him off at the airport anymore. He said watching the plane pull away with him inside was too dramatic.

Kellan sighed as he shut off the engine to his beloved Chevelle. He even gave the steering wheel a loving caress before glancing up at me. Eyes narrowing, he handed me the keys with clear reluctance on his face. He opened his mouth to speak, but I beat him to it. "I know. Be good to her, use the best gas, go slow. I got it." I snatched the keys out of his fingers, and Kellan frowned.

He cracked open his door. "We'll have to see about garaging her when you come join me. I don't want to leave her alone in the driveway for that long."

I cringed at his comment and looked back at my dad. I hadn't told him I was leaving Seattle. Dad's eyes were as wide as saucers. "Join him? Join him where?" he asked me.

I quickly opened my door. "I'll fill you in later, Dad."

"Wait, Kiera . . ."

I shut the door on Dad's argument. Kellan gave me an apologetic shrug over the top of the car as Dad popped out of the back. "For how long, Kiera?"

I sighed, really not wanting to discuss it with my parents right at that very moment. Luckily, an excellent distraction pulled up. Griffin's Vanagon parked in the spot right next to the Chevelle. Anna climbed out of the passenger's side. She held on to the doorframe like she was going to explode if she moved too fast. The rear door slid open, and Matt hopped out. He waved at us, then extended his hand back into the vehicle and helped his girlfriend, Rachel, out of the van.

I still found it hard to believe that Matt and Griffin were related. Matt was more like me: quiet, reserved. Griffin was more like . . . a genuine d-bag. I sometimes wished my sister had hooked up with Matt instead of Griffin. Okay, I often wished that. But Matt was happy with Rachel.

Matt greeted me with a courteous nod, then clapped Kellan on the shoulder. Griffin walked around the van to join where our group was congregating behind the vehicles. He sidled up behind Anna, grabbed her hips, and pulled her into him with an unmistakable thrusting motion. Dad's face turned an unflattering shade of red, and he immediately forgot all about the conversation he'd been trying to have with me.

As he walked over to stop Griffin from dry humping his eldest daughter, Evan's car pulled up. The engine shut off, and both doors opened simultaneously. Hand in hand, Evan and Jenny walked over to where we were gathered.

Evan and Jenny were Kellan's and my best friends. Kellan loved all of his band members, even Griffin in an odd way, but Evan was the one he opened up to the most. The tatted, pierced, and buzz-cut rocker was one of the sweetest men I knew. We'd bonded from the very beginning. Jenny was my closest friend and confidant. She was cute as a button, blond, and perky, the kind of girl men noticed. She also had the biggest heart; her sweetness rivaled her boyfriend's. Out of all of the couples I knew, Evan and Jenny were the ones I didn't have to worry about. They were going to make it together; they were too perfect not to.

I told Jenny everything, even things I probably shouldn't tell her.

But she'd always accepted me, good and bad, and she'd stuck by my side through all of the ups and downs in my life since I'd moved to Seattle. I was going to really miss Jenny when I was on the road with Kellan.

As she approached me, I suddenly realized that I hadn't told her the good news yet. I was beaming as she and Evan joined us. Her lips compressed when she noticed my elated expression. I usually wasn't peppy when Kellan left me. I was usually sullen, downcast, depressed . . . a real buzz kill. And I *was* a little sad about him leaving soon, but my news was too exciting to keep me melancholy. I was bursting at the seams with joy.

I didn't say anything to Jenny, just held up my left hand. She saw my ring and understood immediately. She squealed, startling my parents, and left Evan's side to wrap her arms around me. We were both hopping up and down while the men looked at us like we had suddenly lost our minds. Curious, Rachel peeked her head over. The girl was shyer than even I was, but she gasped and hugged me too when she figured out what all of the fuss was about. Anna joined our circle, and they all examined my wedding ring. It sparkled in the sunlight, its glimmer matching my cheery disposition.

Rachel sighed as she held my hand. "You're engaged." Her eyes drifted over my shoulder to Matt, before quickly refocusing on my ring.

I shook my head. "No . . . we're married."

Jenny snapped her head up. "What? You got married? Without me?" Jenny's hurt expression matched my mother's, and I was sure I now had two wedding planners.

Anna snorted. "Relax. They exchanged rings at the bar. They're not really married."

My parents were a little behind Anna, and I could clearly see a tiny smile form on my dad's lips. Kellan was next to them, and he frowned at Anna's assessment of our relationship status. I did too. "We're married in our hearts, where it matters. The legal stuff will come later."

Griffin broke away from a suddenly pale Matt to join our conversation. Just like Anna, he snorted. "Please, you guys aren't married." He crossed his arms over his chest and glared at Kellan. "No
bachelor party, no marriage. That's the law."

I matched Griffin's posture. "That is *not* a law, Griffin."

He swung his head around to look at me. "Well, it should be.
No T and A, no ball and chain." There was an annoying smirk on his
face, and I really wanted to smack it off of him. I resisted, though.

Anna helped me out by smacking the back of his head. He narrowed his eyes at her. "What? It's a fair sacrifice. If you've got to be
with one chick for the rest of your life, then you should at least get to
go out with a bang. Or two. Or three."

Anna raised a perfectly arched brow. "Really? Would you want
some jackass to do that with our daughter?" Her hand caressed her
belly, and Griffin's eyes shifted to where his child was peacefully
growing.

"Fuck no. I'll chop the little bastard's balls off if he tries that kind
of shit on my girl," he scowled.

"Hmmm." Smiling, Anna kissed his cheek and let the conversation die. I could tell Griffin was still pondering what she'd said,
though. And he clearly didn't like the scenario he'd imagined for Kellan when it was applied to his child. I shared a secret smile with my
sister. Maybe there was hope for Griffin yet.

Our group headed inside the bar to have a congratulatory toast
for the band before their taxi arrived to take them to the airport. The
night crew wasn't on yet, but a few familiar faces were around: Hun,
Sweetie, Emily, and Troy, the bartender with a never-ending crush
on Kellan. He perked up considerably when we walked in together.

When we all turned to head to the band's usual table, I stopped
in my tracks. A man I knew very well was sitting at the table, waiting
for the band. Denny Harris, the ex–love of my life. Kellan noticed
who had my attention and stopped too. Denny stood up, hands casually tucked in the pockets of his jeans.

Denny had changed a bit since coming back to Seattle. He seemed older, more mature. There was a confidence in the way he carried himself, and his dark brown eyes simmered with self-assurance. He just seemed to know who he was and what he wanted, and that wasn't me anymore. He was hopelessly in love with his girlfriend, Abby. It had hurt at first that he'd moved on—but I had too, and I couldn't be happier for him now.

Denny grinned at us as Kellan scoffed in astonishment. We crossed over to him, and Kellan immediately pulled him in for a one-armed hug. "You came to see me off?"

Denny shrugged. "You guys are about to hit it big. This might be the last chance I get to see you."

Kellan looked away, a small smile on his lips. "I don't know about that." He looked back at Denny. "But I'm glad you're here."

I stepped up to give Denny a hug after the two friends pulled apart. Since I was sure Kellan was still a little uneasy about me being too friendly with Denny, regardless of how many times he'd told me he was fine with our friendship, I kept the hug as brief as politely possible.

Denny turned to the other band members once he'd greeted me. As everyone squished around the table, I took a seat catty-corner to Kellan. When Denny was finished congratulating everyone, he took the only empty spot, next to me on the end of the table. Ironically, Denny, Kellan, and I were sitting in the exact same seats as the first time Denny and I had joined the band for a beer.

Denny looked over at me as Kellan ordered the table of round of shots. I saw a soulful expression pass over my ex's face. Maybe he too was pondering how drastically things had changed for us. I raised an eyebrow at him in silent question, and his contemplative mood evaporated. With a slight chuckle, he shook his head and turned to watch Emily approaching our table with our drinks.

Kellan was watching me as shot glasses were set in front of everyone. I didn't feel the twinge of guilt I used to feel when we were all together. Instead, I grabbed Kellan's hand and kissed his fingers, letting him know that I was his, bound in my soul.

Kellan gave me a smile that was loose and easy. He understood. My mom watched the dynamic between the three of us with a crease on her brow. I think it still blew her mind that we were all friends, especially since she now knew exactly what had transpired between Kellan and me.

When everyone had their shots—except my sister, of course, who was at the other end of the table staring at a cup of apple juice like it was toxic—we lifted them to make a toast.

Matt opened his mouth to speak, but his loudmouthed cousin beat him to it. "To fame, fortune, and scores of loose women!" Griffin downed his shot while the rest of us stared at him; Dad glowered, but then again, he usually did around Griffin.

When Griffin smacked his empty glass on the table, Matt continued with his toast like nothing had happened. "To good friends and good music. May we always have both."

"Here, here." We all clinked glasses, Denny and I stretching across the table to reach Anna and Rachel, then we downed our potent drinks. It burned, but Matt's well-wishes made the sting worth it.

We all talked, reminisced, and enjoyed each other's company until a sullen Troy walked up to the table. Eyes on Kellan, he told the group, "Your cab is here." My heart sank a little, and I fortified my stomach. Goodbyes were just a way of life with Kellan, and I had to get used to them.

Matt glanced at a clock on the wall and smiled; being the pseudo-manager of the group, he had made all of the travel arrangements. Keeping his motley crew on task and on time made him happy. Kellan helped me stand up, and we all headed out to the parking lot. Sure enough, the taxi Matt had arranged for them was there.

The band began their goodbyes. Kellan gave me a quick kiss before turning to say goodbye to the people he wasn't sure when he'd see again. He hugged my mom, shook hands with my dad, and rubbed Anna's belly. He gave Rachel a friendly hug, lifted Jenny a foot in the air while she giggled, and clapped Troy on the shoulder. Troy's grin was glorious after that. While Kellan was busy, I said my goodbyes to

Evan and Matt. Evan gave me a huge, lung-crushing bear hug, Matt a gentle, reserved squeeze. I kept my distance from Griffin, waving at him from the other side of the group. Then Kellan was standing by my side again.

Lacing my fingers with his, he looked over at Denny and extended a hand. "Watch over my girl for me?" Denny's expression blanked as he glanced between Kellan and me. Kellan smirked and added, "But not too well, okay?"

Denny let out an amused grunt. "Wouldn't want that . . ." He grabbed Kellan's hand, shaking it firmly. "Yeah, I'll keep an eye on her. She'll be apples." I giggled at Denny's saying and he gave me my favorite goofy grin. But when he released Kellan's hand, his face turned serious. "I hope things work out for you, mate."

Kellan grinned and looked down on me. "Yeah, me too." By the look in Kellan's eyes, I couldn't tell whether he meant hitting it big, or not hitting it big. I got the feeling that, as long as we were together, either scenario was fine. Wrapping my arms around his waist, I laid my head on his shoulder.

Kellan gave me one final squeeze and whispered, "See you soon." I nodded as I watched him sprint over to his car to get his only piece of luggage—the black case holding his prized guitar. Slinging it over his shoulder, he sauntered back to the taxi. The driver packed it in the trunk for him while Kellan slipped into the backseat. I had to bite my lip to stop the sadness from building. I would join him shortly . . . I could wait.

After every band member was tucked into the taxi, it pulled away. Kellan was by the window, and he stuck his hand out of it to wave at me, his wedding ring gleaming in the afternoon sun. Grinning like an idiot, I waved until the taxi turned a corner and disappeared from sight.

Denny looked over at me when I let my hand fall to my side. "So, how's married life treating you, Kiera?" His accent wrapped around my name in a wonderful way. Despite how our relationship had changed, the sound of his voice was still fascinating to my ears.

I studied his dark eyes, looking for any sign of pain. There didn't seem to be any as he casually stood beside me. As I considered everything that had happened in the very short span of time since my impromptu wedding, I shrugged. "Good . . ." Remembering Joey's unexpected visit, my voice gave out on me.

Denny caught the uncertainty. "You don't seem so sure about that."

A part of me really didn't want to talk about my marital problems to Denny. After everything that had happened while we were a couple, it felt wrong to confess my hardships. Didn't I deserve them? But Denny was an exceptional human being, and once he'd forgiven someone, he let go of the pain and resentment and moved on. Well, he tried to anyway. I'd seen him struggle with being around me. I'd heard the pain of betrayal in his voice. But he hadn't fled. He was still in my life. He was still my friend. And I owed him an honest response.

"There was an incident at the house," I muttered, looking back at my parents, who were talking with Anna, Jenny, and Rachel.

"Kellan's jaw?" I returned my eyes to Denny. "You do that?" he asked.

I smirked at him. "No. His ex-roommate came by . . ."

Denny, his mind a steel trap at times, remembered who she was. "Joey? The girl who took off after she slept with him?"

A twinge of something awful stirred in my stomach, but I pushed it down. "Yeah, Joey. Anyway, she came back for her stuff, but I sort of tossed it a while ago. Kellan had to pay her for it."

"Well, that seems reasonable, considering it *was* hers." He paused, then added, "I'm guessing there's more to the story. What else happened?"

I really didn't want to tell Denny about this, but I had to tell someone, and aside from Jenny, Denny was my best friend. "She gave him back their . . . sex tape . . . then made him pay her for it."

Denny didn't answer me for a long time. I could tell his mind was spinning, and he wasn't sure how to answer. As a gust of warm air swirled my hair around me, I wasn't sure what I wanted him to say. Maybe nothing was best. I stared at my feet and kicked a pebble on the cement while I waited for some sort of response.

"If she gave it back before he paid her . . . then it wasn't her only copy. You'll hear from her again," he said.

My eyes shot up to his. I hadn't considered that. I knew that other sex tapes were out there, but I hadn't thought about Joey duping Kellan. She'd brought it to the house to return it before she'd known about me. She'd acted like it was the only copy she'd had, and that she despised Kellan so much that she didn't want it near her anymore. Of course, maybe that was an act, her way of showing Kellan that she didn't need him, that he was beneath her. She seemed like the type to hold on to trophies of her conquests, and what greater trophy could she have than video footage? Denny was right; she had multiple copies. She hadn't ever intended to give Kellan the only recording.

Denny looked apologetic and sympathetic. "I don't know her so I can't say for sure, but if he does make it big, I wouldn't be surprised if she tried to make some money off of it. It could be everywhere someday, Kiera. Sorry."

Sighing away those future troubles, I told him, "It's okay. It doesn't matter, not really." Denny raised an eyebrow at me, and I laughed. The release felt good and lifted a bit of the apprehension from the air. "She doesn't have the only movie of him like that, so she won't get a very good price. Oversaturation and all." I wanted to grimace over the thought of multiple sex tapes on the market, but the look on Denny's face was priceless, and I laughed again.

Denny shook his head. "You *have* changed."

I smiled and shrugged, trying to be as okay with this as I could be. Kellan's life wasn't private anymore, and parts of it were going to be uncomfortable for both of us. But I knew his heart, and he knew mine, and together we would work through the rough patches.

As I pushed away the bad and focused on the good, Denny rolled his eyes. "I can't believe he filmed himself." Closing his eyes, he added, "Actually, yeah, I can." Denny's cheeks suddenly flushed with color, and his eyes shot open. There was a clear question in the dark depths, one he didn't want to ask. But the curiosity was eating at him.

Knowing where his head was at, I smacked his shoulder. "No! I didn't let him . . . we didn't . . . No!" I stammered, not able to put into words that I didn't—and wouldn't—make a sex tape with Kellan.

Denny chuckled and backed away from me. "Sorry, it slipped into my head before I could stop it."

Anna came up to us while Denny laughed even harder. "What's going on?"

Anna gave Denny a cool glance, not unfriendly, but not warm either. She still hadn't gotten over Denny's vicious attack on Kellan, and, inadvertently, me. Denny straightened, his laughter stopping. "Nothing. Just catching up."

Anna narrowed her eyes, like she thought Denny was going to try and woo me away from Kellan or something. I don't know how many times I'd told her that nothing but friendship was between us, but I don't think she would ever really believe me. "I'm going to go, Kiera. I need a nap." Her eyes focused solely on me. "The girls and I are sore."

I twisted my lip, knowing she was *not* referring to the child in her belly. "Yeah, okay."

As she waddled over to Griffin's van, Mom and Dad ended their conversation with Jenny and started heading toward me. By the look on Dad's face, I was sure he wanted to talk to me about my plan to join Kellan.

I sighed, and Denny looked at me. "You ready for them to head home yet?"

I grinned. "Yeah." As I waited for my parents, I pondered telling Denny that I was leaving. I suppose that should be an easier thing to tell him than confessing about Kellan's sex tape, but somehow, it felt harder.

Mom got distracted on her way over to me by a coin on the ground. Mom gathered every coin she could, even pennies. She kept any coin she found that was dated earlier than the seventies. She had dozens of containers at home, full of old currency.

While Dad groaned at Mom to let it go, I quickly blurted out what I didn't really want to say. "I'm joining Kellan in Los Angeles soon, and then I'm going on tour with him. I'm leaving Seattle."

Denny's mouth opened and his face paled. He looked like I'd just socked him in the gut. A ripping pain went through me. I had never left Denny before. He'd always been the one leaving me. As part of my soul ached, I reconsidered my belief that leaving was easier than being left. This didn't feel easy, and I wasn't even gone yet.

Denny averted his eyes and composed himself. Once he was more or less put back together, he shifted his attention to my parents. A sly grin lightened his face, but not his eyes. "I remember when we told your dad we were leaving Ohio." He looked back at me. "Good luck. You'll need it."

I nodded and rubbed Denny's shoulder. A moment of grief passed between us. Grief over what we'd had together. Grief over what we'd lost. We were both in a good place now, relationship-wise, but that didn't mean we'd forgotten, and sometimes missed, what we'd once been.

Denny gave me a small, understanding smile that broke my heart a little. As much as I was going to miss Jenny and Anna, I think I was going to miss Denny even more. Not sure if I should confess that to him or not, I gave him as convincing of a smile as I could. "But I'll be coming back a lot, to check on Anna, to make sure she's okay."

Denny nodded as my parents finally joined us. "That's probably a good idea. I would offer to keep an eye on her for you, but, uh . . . you know how she feels about me."

With my parents in earshot, I only gave Denny a slight nod in response. I didn't want to talk about why Anna had problems with Denny in front of my parents. They didn't know what Denny had done, what I'd pushed him to, and I would prefer it if they never knew. Dad would insist I cut Denny out of my life forever, and I didn't want to. He was part of me.

Dad looked exhausted, ready to take a vacation from his vacation. Crossing his arms over his chest, he stood tall and straight and tried to be imposing. "Kiera, I think we should sit down and have a discussion about you joining Kellan." By his expression, it was clear he thought the idea was ridiculous. "Are you really going to go to Los Angeles? Because I'm not okay with you being in a city that size." He paused, then added, "Surrounded by a bunch of rock stars."

I smiled at Dad and started to respond, but Jenny overheard Dad and bounded to my side. "You're really going down there? To be with them while they record the album?"

I hadn't had time to tell Jenny about it either. So much had been sprung on me so fast . . . I was still a little dizzy. I grabbed Jenny's arms and answered her and my dad. "Kellan really wants me there, and since I'm done with school, I've got lots of free time."

Dad frowned. "You shouldn't waste any time before applying for jobs, Kiera. It will look bad on your resume."

I cringed as I looped my arm around Jenny and held on to her; I suddenly needed her support. "Um, actually, Dad . . . I'm not going to be applying for a job. When Kellan is done with the album, he'll be touring again to promote it . . . and I'm going to go with him."

My voice came out in hushed tones. For a second, the only noise was the traffic zipping down the road. Then Jenny and my father spoke at the same time. Surprisingly, they both said the exact same thing, only in completely different ways.

"No way!"

Jenny's outburst was an exclamation of surprise; Dad's was an order. I looked between them both, giving Jenny an excited squeal, and Dad an empathetic smile. "I know it's sudden, but it's what I really want to do."

Jenny hugged me. In my ear, she told me, "I am so stinking jealous of you!" She pulled back, her pale eyes glossy. "I'm going to miss you . . . but you are going to have so much fun."

I giggled at her, her energy feeding my own. Then Dad's voice broke through my joy. "No, Kiera. That's not acceptable."

I looked back at him, my buzz fading. His frown deepened. "We didn't put you through four years of school so you could throw it all away to follow some *band* across the country." He said the word band with a sneer, and irritation shot up my spine.

I wanted to sullenly tell Dad that my scholarships had paid for the majority of my schooling, that his contribution had been pretty minor in comparison, but that wasn't really the issue being argued. "It's not 'some band,' Dad. It's my *husband's* band."

Dad rolled his eyes. "You're not really married, Kiera."

I ignored his comment. "And he needs me with him."

Dad snorted, like he didn't believe that, like he believed Kellan preferred to be on his own on the road. But Dad hadn't seen how hard Kellan's last tour was on him. True, a lot of the turmoil had been because of his father, but I think a large part was also because of me, because he'd wanted to be with me and couldn't be. I know that's how I'd felt about him.

Before Dad could voice his objection, I added, "And besides, I'm not throwing away my education. I'm going to be a writer, and I can do that on the road with Kellan."

Dad gave me a blank stare. "A writer? You can't make a living being a writer."

Mom elbowed Dad in the ribs, and he glanced over at her. "What?"

Ignoring him, Mom turned to me. "I'm sure you'll do very well, honey. Your father is just concerned about you struggling . . . just in the beginning, of course."

I frowned at Dad. That wasn't entirely his objection. Unless I was, say, a journalist writing for a major newspaper, Dad considered writing to be as frivolous as making music. A real job consisted of set hours, a set location, and a set paycheck. Dad liked things he could depend on. I did too, but I also knew that Kellan's life was about to explode. Dad may not believe it yet, but he would soon. Kellan was too talented for the world not to take notice.

Switching my scowl to a placating smile, I assured him, "Kellan and I will do just fine. You don't need to worry."

His irritated expression turned concerned. "I'll always worry about you, Kiera."

My anger softened. Sighing, I released my hold on Jenny and walked over to Dad. Throwing my arms around him, I told him, "I'll be fine, and I love you too."

I heard him sniff as he wrapped his arms around me. I figured then that Dad would eventually come around. He may not ever fully support my decision, but he wouldn't hold it against me either, just like he didn't hold Anna's poor decisions against her. My parents loved us through all of our ups and downs. And while this was a down for them, it was an up for me.

Pulling back from Dad, I brightly told him. "Let's go home, and I'll tell you all about it."

Dad nodded, then sighed.

Chapter 5
A Proper Sendoff

A week later, the whole family made the trip to the airport to see off my parents. When we got to the drop-off area, I couldn't help but longingly stare at the planes waiting outside. I wished I was getting on one to be with Kellan. I already missed him. He missed me too. I'd received a postcard in the mail from him the day before, a picture of the Hollywood sign. On the back he'd written, *Hurry up and get here so I can stop daydreaming about you.*

Mom gave Anna a warm hug while Dad explained that I needed to check in with him every day. "I'm serious, Kiera. And, if I don't hear from you for a couple of days . . . then . . . I'm flying out to get you." His face was stern, but his eyes belied his true concern for me. He really didn't like the idea that I was leaving.

Wrapping my arms around his neck, I gave him a quick kiss on the forehead. "Dad, I'll be fine. Kellan will be with me the entire time." Dad was scowling when I released him. My words of comfort weren't so comforting for him. Dad hadn't entirely warmed to Kellan yet, and he wasn't exactly the ideal bodyguard in Dad's eyes.

Anna distracted him from his misery by engulfing him in a playful hug. "Bye, Daddy."

Dad's frown shifted to a wide smile as he patted her back. I turned to say goodbye to Mom. After she kissed my head and told me she loved me, she asked, "So, have you decided between a winter or spring wedding? Because we've got a lot of work to get started on."

I contained my sigh as I stepped from her embrace. I'd heard this question about a hundred times already. "I'll let you know, Mom."

She raised her eyebrows. "Don't wait too long. I need to get the announcements out."

I did sigh that time.

Once our parents were safely tucked onto the plane, Anna turned to face me. With a long sigh, she asked, "Is it just because I'm pregnant, or are they always this taxing?"

I laughed at her and shrugged. I couldn't speak for the pregnancy part, but I had to imagine that her condition only added to the problem. Well-intentioned or not, our parents could be draining.

As eager as I was to see Kellan, I was also a little reluctant to leave Seattle. I had anchors here. A place was just a place, as I'd told Kellan before, but places came with people, and there were a few that I was really going to miss. When Jenny and I closed up the bar the night before my last shift, it felt surreal to me. Tomorrow was the last day I'd ever work at Pete's. Jenny grabbed me in the parking lot and pulled me in for a tight embrace; there were tears in her eyes. "I'm going to miss you so much, Kiera."

I held her back just as tight, holding in my own tears. "Stop, you're going to make me cry," I warbled. She released me, and I rubbed her shoulder. "And I'm not going anywhere yet. I still have to work tomorrow, remember?"

Jenny sniffed and swiped her fingers under her eyes. "I know. I just . . . I hate goodbyes."

I swallowed the lump in my throat as I watched Jenny let out a slow, controlled exhale. "It's not goodbye yet. And I'll be back."

Jenny brightened as she swished her hand. "Oh, I know you will. Besides, I'll be visiting you guys whenever I can." Her sudden grin was exhilarant; it matched the glow of her platinum hair. "There is one good thing about you leaving Pete's, though."

Not quite sure what that could be, I gave her a blank expression. Jenny bounced on her toes and exclaimed, "We get to throw you a party tomorrow night!"

I cringed. I really didn't want to be the center of attention at a going-away party. Seeing my reaction, Jenny schooled her features. "Oh, don't worry. We'll keep it real low-key. Just some cake in the back room."

Somehow, I was sure that wouldn't be the case.

Driving back to my empty home in Kellan's Chevelle, I was suddenly struck with loneliness. Kellan had only been gone for a couple of weeks, but it felt like forever. Our little white two-story house looked cold and uninviting as I approached it. There was just something about Kellan being here that made the house seem alive. His energy filled it with life, with music.

As I unlocked the door, I dug in my bag for my phone. It was late, but it probably wouldn't be too late. Kellan was sort of a night owl. He was also an early riser, so if I did miss him, I wouldn't have to wait too long to hear his sultry voice.

I closed and relocked the door as I dialed his number. He picked up almost instantly. "Hey, you. How did you know I was thinking about you?"

I laughed at his greeting. "Because you're always thinking about me."

"Very true," he husked. "I miss you. Are you coming up soon?"

My smile was blissful as I hung up my bag and jacket. "Anna and I will be on a plane Friday morning." Anna had taken the Fourth of July holiday weekend off of work so she could safely deliver me to Los Angeles. Surprisingly, it had been Dad's idea. But Anna was up for any sort of adventure and had eagerly agreed. In fact, she would have put us on a red-eye right after I finished at Pete's tomorrow, but she had a very important doctor's appointment the next day.

"Good. I've been prepping our room. You're gonna love it."

My grin got even wider. "Our room?"

"Yep." I heard the sounds of other people laughing and wondered who else was awake at this hour. "And, I'm not sure if I mentioned this or not, but bring your suit. The house has a pool."

Kellan and the band were staying at a house that the record label owned. From what Kellan had told me about it so far, it was nice, so I wasn't too surprised that it had a pool. It seemed like pools were a lot more common in California than they were in Washington. We had espresso stands on every corner; they had pools in every backyard.

Trudging upstairs, I told Kellan how excited I was to join him. Staying at this house by myself was a little scary at times. I'd even gotten into the habit of writing in bed until the early hours of the morning; immersing myself in my romantic memoir stopped me from thinking about the possibility that a boogeyman was lurking in the closet. Having Kellan verbally tuck me into bed also helped to ease those late-night fears. His voice always had a soothing effect on me. Well, perhaps "soothing" wasn't the best word. While his voice always affected me, there were definitely times when the sultry sound that came out of his mouth was anything but relaxing.

With the phone glued to my ear, I got ready for bed. Because I missed him, I threw on a shirt that I didn't typically wear. It was saturated with Kellan's scent, and I didn't want that to fade. Slipping on the black shirt with the word "Douchebags" in bright-white bold letters, I crawled into our bed.

As Kellan gave me the rundown on his schedule, I brought the fabric of my T-shirt up to my nose and inhaled the smell of him. It was incredible—manly, yet clean. I still wasn't sure what combination of products he used to create that scent, but it was the most sensuous smell in the world. I supposed it was possible that it wasn't a manufactured scent. Maybe he just naturally smelled amazing; his bare skin was quite edible, after all.

I giggled a little at that thought, and Kellan stopped talking. "What are you doing?" he asked, a clear smile in his voice.

"I just crawled into bed—"

He immediately cut me off. "Are you naked?"

I flushed all over and felt a stirring in my body by his words alone. I could still hear faint noises in the background, so I knew Kellan wasn't by himself. But maybe he could be . . .

"No . . . I'm wearing the shirt you gave me a long time ago. It's my favorite shirt. I don't usually wear it, though." I closed my eyes as I confessed just how obsessed with him I was. "It smells like you, and I want it to stay that way."

Kellan chuckled in a low tone; it ignited the spark of heat in my belly that he'd stoked earlier. I ran a hand over my body as the ache of loneliness within me grew. I missed him so much—his touch, his smile, his eyes, his tattoo . . . his heart. Everything.

"Really?" he asked. "Do I . . . smell?"

A low purr escaped me. "Yes, you do, and it's the best smell in the world. Better than coffee."

Kellan groaned. "God, Kiera, you're turning me on."

I smiled, imagining him as restless as I was becoming. "Are you alone?" I whispered, afraid that somehow, someone would hear me . . . or Kellan. He wasn't exactly opposed to intimate public performances.

"Hold on," he muttered instantly. After another second, I heard him addressing the room. "Night, guys, see you in the morning." There was some murmuring in the background, and then it faded, and all I heard was Kellan telling me, "Now I am. Did you want something?"

I ran a hand down my face. I still struggled with this part—forwardly asking him what I wanted, what I needed. But I remembered what he said the morning after our wedding night; he wanted me to feel comfortable asking him for anything, talking to him about anything. I shouldn't be embarrassed. Kellan loved me, heart and soul, and he'd never intentionally hurt me. He may tease me on occasion, but I didn't think he would tonight.

"Kellan," I murmured, my voice doing that groan-growl thing that had turned him on before. "I miss you, and I want to make love to you." Before I could comprehend what I was saying, I quickly added, "Take your clothes off."

I slapped my hand to my forehead after I said it—it wasn't exactly the sexiest request. I expected Kellan to chuckle and give me a smart-alecky line, but he didn't. Sucking in a quick breath, he groaned, "God, that was hot. I'm so hard right now. I wish you could see."

My heart thumping in my chest, an image of him flooded my head. A thought popped into my mind and I repeated it to him without exactly meaning to. "Send me a picture."

I clamped down on my lip so hard, I thought I might draw blood. Did I seriously just tell him to send me a d-pic? I really never thought I'd ever ask him that. Then again, there were a lot of things I'd never expected myself to do with Kellan. He opened me in very unexpected ways.

Just as I was wondering if Kellan really would send a picture, he told me, "Hold on." Maybe I was imagining it, but I thought I heard his jeans unzipping. Oh. My. God.

I wasn't sure if I could handle the erotic image he was about to send to me. My body was already aching for him to touch me. Seeing how much he missed me, how much he wanted me . . . might undo me.

The phone went silent, then his heavy breath returned to my ear. I wasn't sure if he'd done it or not, then my phone chirped at me. I closed my eyes for a second, nerves and excitement washing over me. God, I missed him so much. "Kellan," I murmured, as I pulled my phone away from my ear.

Careful not to hang up on him, I checked the message he'd just sent me. My jaw dropped when I opened it. He did it. He actually did it. He sent me a picture of himself in his most exposed and vulnerable state. True, Kellan wasn't nearly as reserved as I was, and this probably wasn't as monumental for him as it was for me, but still . . .

I couldn't stop staring at the photograph. Oddly enough, considering the subject, it was artistic and beautiful. Kellan's pictures usually were. He was bold and proud, the lighting was flattering, and his left hand was arranged in such a way that his wedding ring seemed to glow at me, as if to say, *This is yours, wife, and yours alone.* It was fascinating, breathtaking, sweet, and hot, all at the same time. The fire tingling me before shifted to a full-on blaze. I needed him . . . immediately.

"Kiera? You still there?"

I quickly brought the phone back to my ear. "I need you to touch me, Kellan . . . right now."

This time, he did chuckle. "Needless to say, I need you to touch me too."

The image of his body permanently etched in my brain, I moaned his name . . . and it wasn't the last time his name left my lips that night. . . .

I had a dopey smile on my face as I walked into work the next evening. It fell from my lips when I noticed what Jenny had done to the bar. Against my wishes, Jenny had decorated for my going-away party. Every archway and table was highlighted with twisting pink and white streamers. Balloons in every color of the rainbow dotted the ceiling. Long strings were tied to each one, dangling low enough so that people could grab them; the customers were having a great time yanking them down and watching them float back up. A huge banner was attached to the black wall behind the stage, right above the band's drawing. In embarrassingly tall letters, it screamed: GOODBYE, KIERA! GOOD LUCK! WE'LL MISS YOU!

It warmed and mortified me. Low-key, my ass!

Jenny trotted up to me as I stood gaping in the doorway. She gave me a swift hug as I exclaimed, "Jenny! What happened to having a small cake in the back room?"

Her smile big and beautiful, she shrugged as we pulled apart. "Don't worry, there's still a cake in the back room for you." Her pale eyes flicked around the bar, then back to me. "I just felt like your send-off needed a little . . . pizzazz. This is a huge moment for you, after all. You're not just leaving the bar, you're leaving Seattle." She frowned.

I sighed but couldn't really argue with her, especially as I watched her eyes mist over. So even though I really wanted to tear down all of the streamers and pop every balloon, I enclosed her in another hug instead. I guess I could put up with a few decorations for one evening; I drew the line at the party hat that she pulled out for me, though. I may have to feel like an idiot tonight, but I didn't want to look like one as well.

Nearly everyone I knew in Seattle came to Pete's to wish me well on my upcoming journey—my sister, my study buddies from school, the regular customers that I'd served almost every night, a couple of friends that I'd made in art class. Denny came in and sat at the band's table, joking and laughing with the bouncer, Sam.

It was comforting to have everyone that I cared about so close to me. I couldn't imagine leaving them all in a couple of days. The change almost seemed too monumental, and a part of me didn't think I could do it—but I remembered my phone call with Kellan the night before and what was waiting for me in L.A., and I knew I could do it. It would hurt to leave, but it's what I had to do. Besides, growing pains were supposed to hurt a little.

Later in the evening, one of my closest friends at school, Cheyenne, arrived. She was warm and outgoing, one of those girls that everyone liked. She had taken an instant liking to me and had saved my butt in our poetry class. I was sure I wouldn't have graduated without her. Well, okay, I probably would have graduated, but she definitely helped smooth the process.

Cheyenne was followed into the bar by her girlfriend, Meadow, and the rest of the members of Poetic Bliss. I was surprised to see the band there; they weren't scheduled to play tonight. As Cheyenne gave me a hug, Sunshine, Tuesday, and Blessing plugged in their instruments. Rain took her spot behind the lead microphone, while Meadow ducked behind the drums. Yeah, all of the members of the band had strange names. Saying their names directly to them had been a challenge at first. It's just a little hard for me to call someone Tuesday with a straight face.

As an energized hum filled the bar, I looked between my two

blond, perky pals. Cheyenne was gazing up at the girl band with an expression of adoration that I knew very well—I tended to look at the D-Bags the exact same way. Jenny was bouncing on her toes, giddiness over her successful party overwhelming her.

"Are they playing tonight . . . just for me?" I asked, surprised.

Cheyenne looked back at me, her grin wider than her home state of Texas. "Sure are! I asked Meadow if they could give you a proper goodbye." She sighed as she looked back to her girlfriend. "They had to rearrange a couple of gigs, but they were happy to do it. Anything for my girl Kiera!"

I blinked, wondering if I'd be that cool if Kellan wanted to give a former crush such a thoughtful gift. Then again, Meadow knew me, and she knew that I was with Kellan . . . and straight. I suppose that tempered the jealousy, if there even was any; Cheyenne and I had cemented our friends-only status before they'd even started dating.

I found it difficult to concentrate on my waitressing duties once the band was in full swing. Friends kept chatting with me around every corner, and several customers that were not there for me were a little irritated by the whole thing. Eventually, Pete came out of his office and let me go several hours early. There were loud cheers and whistles as I handed him my apron. Pete patted my shoulder, thanked me for my time here at the bar, then handed me an apple-flavored sucker. I tried to not get teary-eyed, but when my coworker Kate gave me a hug, I lost it.

Kate, teary-eyed herself, walked me up to the bar. Rita was tending, as she did almost every night, and she poured us shots while Jenny grabbed the cake from the back room. For the first time since I'd known Rita, she didn't mention my rock-god husband. She usually bragged about sleeping with him, or made some vague remark that reeked of innuendo, but tonight she seemed almost respectful as she ate some cake and chased it with a celebratory shot.

By the time the group of us had finished the cake, I'd had about six celebratory shots. They just kept miraculously appearing in front of me, and someone—usually my sister—kept encouraging me to drink them. My head was fuzzy when someone else pulled me out onto the dance floor . . . Cheyenne, I think. When I was pulled into the middle of the band's fans, I let go of my inhibitions and danced my heart out. I'd always found dancing freeing, a way to get out of my head. The alcohol surging through my system helped there too, of course. I felt like I was floating as I twirled around.

After an eternity of dancing mixed with drinking, I was sweaty, insouciant, and feeling no pain. I bumped into a familiar, athletic body, and turned to peer up into Denny's warm, dark eyes. He smiled down on me as he steadied me. The music, the crowd . . . it reminded me of dancing with Denny on a much different occasion. Examining my face, Denny asked, "You all right there, Kiera?"

Looking around the bar, I wondered if Denny's girlfriend was with him. She and Denny worked for a prosperous advertising company. Denny was sort of her boss. "Is Abby here?" My question came out a little slurred. As Denny started to answer me, a random thought popped into my head and shot right out of my mouth. "You guys work together . . . so, since you're in charge during the day, is she your boss at night?"

His cheeks red, Denny mumbled something about her being out with friends tonight while I giggled at the image now firmly etched in my head.

While I was chuckling, I noticed a friend of mine holding out another shot for me. I eagerly took it, reaching over Denny's body to grab it. We were flush together with my arm draped over his shoulder as I tipped it back. Giggling, I handed the empty glass to my friend and wrapped my other arm around Denny; a feeling of familiarity flooded through me as our eyes locked.

Even though Jose Cuervo didn't really care about personal boundaries, I knew in the back of my head that we were too close together. While Denny frowned at me, I gently pushed him back so that our chests were no longer touching. Well, I meant to push him. I ended up forcing *myself* back a step. I bumped into the guy behind me and almost lost my balance. Denny's frown deepened as he grabbed my elbow to keep me upright.

"You're drunk, aren't you?"

My answer came out in a high-pitched laugh.

Denny rolled his eyes and shook his head. "I was just about to head home, but I can't leave you here like this all alone. Did your sister leave already?"

I pursed my lips, trying to remember through the fog. Was my sister still here? Had she ever been here? I couldn't quite recall . . . and then my hazy brain pulled out a memory from just a few minutes ago. Anna had started feeling a bit run down, and had wanted to go home and crawl into bed. She'd tried to get me to leave with her, but I'd wanted to keep dancing and refused to let her move me. Irritated, Anna had grabbed Jenny as she'd walked nearby and told her to take me home before she waddled out the doors. It had shocked me a little. Anna had never been the first one to leave a party before.

I shook my head. "Nope, she pooped out . . . left."

I giggled, and Denny sighed. "Well, then, I guess I'm driving you home."

Touched by his offer, I squeezed him tight. "You're the best, Denny." A slight sob came out of me. "I'm so sorry I cheated on you."

Denny started moving me toward the back room. "Yeah, I think it's definitely time for you to go. Come on."

I clung to him like a lifeline as grief and giddiness battled within me. A part of me hated that he was taking care of me after I'd been so horrible to him, and a part of me loved that we were still such good friends that he needed to make sure I was okay. We ran into Jenny in the back as I was grabbing my stuff.

"What's going on?" she asked cautiously. She didn't seem happy as Denny explained that he was going to take me home. "Oh, well, I told Anna I would drive her after work."

Denny looked over at me. I couldn't stand straight, and I wobbled a bit . . . which made me laugh. "I don't think she can wait that long, Jenny."

Not wanting her to worry, I tossed my arms around her and told her I loved her. She seemed even more worried as I left.

Denny helped me to the Chevelle with a hand on my back. The band was still playing as I dug in my bag for the keys. I felt a little bad that I was missing the end of my going-away bash, and a part of me still wanted to be dancing—but my head was starting to spin. Eyes half-closed, I handed Denny my keys. As he opened the passenger door and helped me sit down, I asked, "What about your car?"

He buckled me in with a smirk on his face. "Don't worry about it right now. I'll get it later. What matters is getting you home safe."

He closed my door then walked around the back to the driver's side. Again, grief washed through me. Why was he so nice to me? I'd done horrible, horrible things to him. I was a horrible, horrible person. Did he really feel so strongly for me that he could look past all of my flaws . . . and still love me?

As he sat down beside me, I immediately asked him just that. "Are you still in love with me? Is that why you're taking care of me?"

Denny's fingers paused on the way to the ignition. He looked over at me, blankness in his eyes. "I don't know how to answer that, Kiera. And I really don't think I should right now." He shook his head and started the car.

I put my hand on his arm, not understanding. "Why?" My world started to tilt, and I exhaled in a long, slow breath.

Denny's eyes studied me for a second before he backed the muscle car out if its space. "Because you're wasted, and I don't want you to get the wrong idea."

Removing my hand, I ran it back through my hair, undoing my hasty ponytail. "I have no ideas . . ." I murmured, closing my eyes.

I heard Denny sigh, and thought I heard him say, "Yeah, I know you don't."

Denny called Abby on the drive home. His face lit up as he talked to her. From the half of the conversation that I could hear, she didn't seem worried about Denny being with me. He told her that I'd had too much at the bar and he was taking me home. I wasn't sure what her reply was, but he laughed, and his eyes were clear and untroubled. Even though I was starting to feel a little queasy, seeing him happy made me happy.

The longer I sat still, the worse I felt. By the time Denny stopped the car, my stomach was churning. Feeling flushed and disgusting, I whimpered and leaned my head against the window. Denny shot me a concerned glance. "You okay?"

I shook my head and slapped my hand over my mouth. No, I was definitely *not* okay. Denny cursed and quickly exited the car. He sprinted back for me and helped me get out and stand up. My stomach lurched when I moved. "Denny," I murmured, "I don't feel good."

I stumbled and Denny swooped me into his arms. I clamped my mouth shut, begging for the nausea to stop. It didn't, though. Instead, it got stronger and stronger. Denny hurried us to the house, telling me, "I know you don't, Kiera. It will be okay, just hold on." Tears were leaking from my eyes as he squatted down to unlock the door—I really hated being sick.

Closing the front door with his foot, Denny rushed us upstairs. He set me down in the bathroom right as I lost control. Sinking to my knees, I noisily lost my stomach into the toilet. Denny sighed and patted my back. He removed my bag from my shoulder while I heaved a couple more times. As I laid my head on the seat, I could hear him moistening a towel. He handed it to me and I gratefully wiped my mouth with the warm cloth. "Thanks," I murmured, then I threw up again.

I felt like I was sick for hours. It never seemed to end. I was a sniffling, blubbering mess, but Denny stayed by my side. When there was nothing left in my stomach, I lay down on the cool bathroom tiles. They felt wonderful. As I closed my eyes, Denny whispered, "Kiera?"

I was so tired, I couldn't respond.

He let out a long, slow exhale as he tucked a strand of hair behind my ear. I wanted to open my eyes to see his expression, but my eyelids felt like lead. I felt Denny's strong arms scooping me up again, then he slowly walked me into Kellan's and my bedroom and laid me on the bed. After he removed my shoes and socks, I buried myself into the covers; nothing had ever felt so incredible in all my life.

Denny leaned over me, tucking me in, then he hesitated; I could feel his presence above me. I again tried to open my eyes, but it was like they were glued shut. After another pause, I felt his lips lower to my hair. The tender gesture made me smile. He pulled away and I felt like he was going to leave me. I weakly reached out and grabbed his hand. I didn't want him to go. I didn't want to be alone like this.

"Stay," I croaked out. "Please."

Denny sighed again. "Yeah, I'll have to call Abby and let her know, but it's fine. I'll stay here if you need me to. I'll be in the next room if you need anything."

I nodded and released his hand. I could feel sleep creeping up on me, but Denny was still hovering, so I tried to push the feeling back. He watched me in silence for a long time, then he whispered, "I don't know what I feel for you, Kiera . . . other than . . . I care about you. I care if you're happy. I care if you're sad. I care if you're safe. And if that's love . . . then, yes, I guess I love you. I love you, but I'm not *in* love with you. . . . Does that make sense?"

It took a great deal of effort, but I twisted around and opened my eyes. He was giving me a soft smile . . . all three of him. I shut my eyes and nodded. It did make sense, even to my fuzzy brain. I loved him too, I just wasn't *in* love with him. He wasn't my heart and soul. He didn't consume every part of me. He wasn't Kellan.

Denny patted my leg, then left me. Just as sleep started claiming me, my phone rang. My bag was still in the bathroom, and I heard Denny stop and dig through it. Seconds later, he said, "Uh, Kiera . . . it's Kellan. Should I answer this?"

My eyes sprang open. Denny answering my cell phone late at night wouldn't look good. But not answering Kellan's call on the last night of my shift wouldn't look good either. Not only that, but Kel-

Ian and I were giving total honesty a try . . . so I really didn't have a choice. Gritting my jaw, I squeaked out, "Yes . . . please."

I heard Denny pick up the line. He said a few words in a low voice, then he came back into the bedroom. With a hand on my shoulder, he rolled me over. My stomach tilted again. "He, um, wants to talk to you."

I nodded, inhaling through my nose, out through my mouth. My shaky fingers brushed against Denny's as I took the phone from him. In an almost inaudible voice, I said, "Hello?"

"Kiera? Are you okay? Denny said you were sick."

There was a weird tone to Kellan's voice when he said Denny; not quite pain, not quite anger, but somewhere in between. "I'll be fine . . . I just . . . had a few too many shots at Pete's." My insides tightened even more just saying the word "shots."

Kellan let out an aggravated exhale. "I don't like you getting drunk when I'm not there to take care of you."

Without thinking, I told him, "It's okay, Denny's taking care of me."

Voice tight, Kellan replied, "Yeah, I know."

"Kellan, please don't worry," I murmured. "You know I love you. I married you, didn't I?"

Kellan laughed, the tension easing from his voice. I heard Denny leave the room, shutting my door behind him. I tried not to worry if that remark had hurt him. It shouldn't have. He'd just said he only felt friendship for me, after all.

I groaned into the phone as my stomach flip-flopped. "Kellan, I feel awful."

Kellan chuckled again. "Serves you right, drinking without me. And when I can't even take advantage of you too."

I smiled, wishing he could do to me what he did last night . . . Then my stomach lurched and I thought I might lose it in bed. No, no sexy time tonight. Breathing loudly through my mouth, I whimpered, "I think I'm going to be sick again."

Kellan's voice was calming as he told me, "No, you're not, sweetheart. You just need something else to focus on besides your stomach. Would you like it if I sang you to sleep?"

My grin was huge as I clenched my tummy tight. "I would love that," I told him.

A minute later, I could hear Kellan's guitar. Then his voice filled my ear, and Kellan started performing an acoustic set of all of my favorite D-Bags songs . . . just for me. The sensuous sound eased the distress in my belly, and my stomach suddenly felt a million times better. I wanted to listen to him all night long, but I succumbed to sleep and alcohol and nodded off into oblivion.

Chapter 6
Girl Time

I was parched when I woke up. Parched and confused. I couldn't remember leaving the bar. I remembered imbibing way too many drinks last night, then I remembered dancing to the band's music . . . but I couldn't remember how I'd gotten home. God, I really hoped I hadn't driven home. Kellan would be furious with me. *I* would be furious with me.

Thinking of Kellan sparked a vague memory of him singing to me, of the light twang of his guitar lulling me to sleep. I had no idea if that was a real memory, or if I'd dreamed it. It was peaceful, though, and I smiled as I rolled onto my back.

My stomach didn't like that—my head either.

I groaned and curled myself into a ball. I felt like I'd been brought back from the brink of death, and I silently swore to never drink again. I heard the sounds of someone else in the house and alarm shot through me. Who was here? I relaxed as I realized that Anna must have driven me home last night. There was no way she would have let me drive drunk.

Feeling disgusting, I made myself get out of bed. I just wanted to take a shower. I smelled like vomit. I stumbled a couple of steps as I yanked off my red Pete's shirt. Begging my stomach to stay at a tolerable level of nausea, I unbuttoned my jeans and pushed them down. I had to steady myself against the wall to kick them across the room, toward the general vicinity of the laundry basket. Seeing hard strands of dried gunk in my hair, I groaned again. So gross.

I could hear my sister clunking up the steps as I unfastened my bra. I flicked it toward the basket and prayed that she was bringing me a glass of water—I desperately needed one. I tried to shimmy out of my underwear and flick them into the laundry, but part of the fabric got stuck under my foot. Too tired and sick to be coordinated, I lost my balance and fell on my ass. Hard.

As I let out a loud curse, my bedroom door rapidly swung open. "Anna!" I exclaimed. Surprised and embarrassed, I tried to cover myself with my hands. "You're just as bad about knocking as Griffin! I'm not dress—"

I stopped talking as I stared up at the person standing in my doorway. It was not my sister. It wasn't a girl at all. "Denny? What are you—"

Denny's face was bright red and he immediately averted his eyes from my naked body. I felt red-hot. Oh my God, I'm such an idiot. Definitely done with drinking. Memories flooded into my brain as Denny stammered an apology and closed my door. Anna hadn't come to my rescue last night, Denny had. Anna hadn't watched me get sick, Denny had. And Anna hadn't tucked me into bed and stayed all night, just to make sure I was okay. Denny, my spectacular ex-boyfriend turned best friend, had done all of that. And I'd just flashed him. Damn it.

My stomach and head paling in comparison to my pride, I scrambled to my feet and grabbed a towel lying on the dresser. I opened the bedroom door and found Denny on the other side of it. He was still red, still not looking at me, but holding a glass of water in my direction. "Sorry," he muttered. "You sounded like you needed help."

I took the glass, grateful and mortified at the same time. "Thank you." I inhaled the water, and Denny cautiously peeked over at me. He was still dressed in the clothes I vaguely remembered him wearing last night—nice slacks and a sharp dress shirt. There weren't a lot of wrinkles in the shirt, so he must have taken it off before climbing into the lumpy futon that was in our spare room.

I handed him the empty glass, wishing I had more. Denny read my mind. "I have to go to work, but I'll get you another one before I leave. How do you feel?"

I closed my eyes. "Really, really embarrassed." I cracked one eye open. "I'm so sorry you walked in on that."

A tiny smile lifted Denny's lips, and he turned his head away from me. "I meant your stomach."

The heat in my cheeks flamed a little hotter. *Right. Duh.* "Oh, um, much better . . . thank you."

Denny nodded and started heading back downstairs to get some more of the cool, clean water from the fridge. As he walked away, I told him, "Thank you for watching over me last night. I really . . . I really appreciate it."

Turning his head, Denny gave me his signature grin. "Anytime, mate. I'm sure you would have done the same for me."

I gave him an enthusiastic nod. "I'd do just about anything for you, Denny."

The smile on his face fell some, and I immediately knew exactly what he was thinking—*anything but remain faithful to me.* He didn't verbalize it, though. Instead, he nodded and turned away to finish taking care of me. Closing my eyes, I laid my head against the door. Someday I would stop feeling guilty for betraying him, right? No, probably not.

I brushed my teeth while Denny returned with more water. Even though I left the bathroom door ajar, he knocked on it. After drinking my second glass, I felt a lot better. Well, I felt like I could shower without slipping or heaving. As Denny turned to leave, I asked him, "How are you getting your car?"

He shrugged. "I called Abby. She should be here in a minute."

Nodding, I again told him, "Thank you, Denny."

He told me it was nothing and gave me a small wave before turning to head downstairs. I thought I heard a car honking "goodbye" while I luxuriated in the steaming warm shower. I wasn't sure what Kellan would think about Denny spending the night with me, but then I remembered that he already knew. The thought made me smile. It felt good to be honest with him, to not have any secrets for once. And as I remembered Kellan singing me to sleep, I felt even better. He hadn't flown into a rage and hopped the first flight back into town. He'd trusted me, even in my drunken state, to remain faithful to him. And I had.

I felt pretty proud of myself as I washed slime out of my hair. Not for overindulging on free shots—that wasn't one of my finer moments—but for not letting alcohol sweep me away into a remembered moment of passion with Denny. I felt like I'd been tested, and I'd passed.

Figuring I should check in with Anna, let her know I was alive and well and still coming to her appointment, I ransacked the bed for my cell phone. I found it buried in the covers; the battery was long dead. Kellan must have sung me to sleep until my phone disconnected. I couldn't remember when I'd dozed off, but I could easily picture Kellan keeping the line open while he listened to me sleeping. Maybe he'd fallen asleep that way, pretending that we were in bed together. God, I hope I hadn't snored.

When I plugged the phone in, there were several missed calls from Jenny, Kate, and Cheyenne. I let them all know I was fine, then texted Anna and let her know I was on my way.

It took twice as long as usual, but I eventually made it to my old apartment. Anna was bright-eyed and bushytailed when she got in the car. She was excited for the upcoming news—the sex of her baby. She was having an ultrasound today, and if my niece or nephew cooperated, we'd find out whether to decorate the nursery pink or blue. Of course, Anna had "known" it was a girl from the moment she'd accepted the pregnancy, and she'd already loaded up my old closet with dozens of outfits in pale pinks, light purples, and deep reds. It looked like Valentine's Day had thrown up in there. And that thought did *not* help my stomach.

Anna smirked when she noticed the color of my face. "Good night?" she asked, in an unaccommodatingly loud voice.

I cringed as I glared at her. "Not really." Well, that wasn't exactly true. I'd been having a great time until my liquid friends had decided to leave the party in the most uncomfortable way possible.

Anna laughed as I focused on the road. "I feel a little bad for petering out on you. That's so unlike me. Jenny get you home okay?"

Remembering the look on Jenny's face as I'd left the bar with Denny, I frowned and answered my sister without considering just who I was talking to. "No, she didn't take me home . . . Denny did."

"What? You went home with *Denny*?" she snapped.

I mentally smacked myself. I really hadn't planned on mentioning that to her. "I didn't 'go home' with him. . . . He dropped me off at the house, made sure I was okay." I stopped myself from telling her that he'd spent the night; I didn't want to send her into early labor.

When I glanced over at her, Anna narrowed her emerald eyes. Framed in hormonally lengthened thick eyelashes, her gaze was even more imposing than usual. "Yeah, I bet he made sure you were okay." Her eyebrow lifted in a clear accusation. "You sleep with him?"

My mouth fell open so far, I was sure my tonsils were visible. "Oh my God, Anna! No, I didn't . . . and thanks for your faith in me."

Pursing her lips, she snipped, "I have plenty of faith in you, Kiera. It's the massive amount of alcohol you consumed that I doubt. So, you really didn't bang him?"

Not answering her crass question, I studiously kept my eyes on the road. After a moment of silence, Anna finally said, "Okay, if you say so, I'll believe you." I could tell by her tone that she didn't completely believe me.

Relaxing my expression, I sighed in defeat. "I really didn't do anything with him, Anna. We're just friends now, I swear. And in case you're wondering, yes, I told Kellan. He called last night while Denny was taking care of me."

She considered my words for a moment, then said, "I thought Denny dropped you off?"

I glared at her out of the corner of my eye, and Anna chuckled. "Okay, Kiera. I believe you. If you say nothing happened, then nothing happened." Almost instantly she added, "Besides, you're a terrible liar anyway." I gave her my most wicked expression. She laughed again.

At the doctor's office, an ultrasound technician in faded yellow scrubs cheerfully walked us into a low-lit room. There was a faint antiseptic smell, and a computer nearby whirred and hummed, filling the silence. The woman instructed Anna to lie down on an examination table lined with paper. With a wonder-filled smile, Anna carefully reclined her plump body and adjusted her stretchy pants so that the bulk of her belly was exposed.

"Okay, let's get a look at my little girl," she merrily exclaimed.

"Oh," the technician said, "you already know the sex?" She squeezed some gel onto Anna's belly. As an afterthought, she told her, "This will be cold."

Anna sucked in a quick breath as the gel touched her skin. "No, this is my first ultrasound." She looked up at the woman spreading the gel around with a taser gun—I swear that's what it was—that was attached to the computer. "I just know I'm having girl, is all."

The woman smiled at her but didn't comment. I supposed she'd heard every wives' tale in the book from pregnant women claiming to know the sex.

When the image of Anna's belly appeared on the monitor, it was a blob of indistinguishable gray shapes. The technician seemed to know what she was looking at and pointed out several body parts to us. Anna and I looked at each other, then shrugged. Neither one of us was really seeing anything that resembled a human being. But then the spine came into view. It was distinct, defined . . . unmistakable. My eyes teared up as I saw something on the screen that I could relate to. Then a hand drifted into focus—a perfect, five-fingered hand. The fingers curled a little as the technician held the wand still.

"Oh my God, Kiera . . . look at that," Anna murmured, tears running down her cheeks. "My daughter waved at me."

I hugged my emotional sister, a little emotional myself now. After finishing up with the measurements and still shots, including one that was a perfect profile of the face, the technician frowned. "Hmmm."

Panic shot through my body. Was something wrong with the baby? Anna tried to sit up but couldn't around her stomach. The technician frowned more and moved the wand around to find whatever she'd been looking at. "Hold still, please."

"What is it? What's wrong?" Anna's voice had an edge of fear to it.

The technician relaxed her face, then smiled. "Oh, there's nothing wrong, it's just . . ." she trailed off, searching the screen again.

"Just what?" I asked, leaning in to see what she saw. I didn't see anything remarkable. The technician did, though.

"Yeah, that's what I thought. I'm sorry, but . . . you're having a boy."

Anna propped herself up on her elbows. "I'm what?"

The technician cringed. "I hope you haven't bought too many pink things."

"No, there must be some mistake. Check again. I'm having a girl." Anna scowled.

She did, then repeated, "Sorry . . . definitely a boy."

Tears started running down Anna's cheeks again, but for a completely different reason this time. "No, no, no . . . I'm having a girl." She snapped her head to mine. "I was supposed to have a girl!"

I rubbed her shoulder. "It's okay. You'll do great with a boy."

Anna nodded as she sank back to the table. "I know . . . I just really wanted . . ." She bit her lip to stop herself from saying it. I understood, though. Anna was a girly-girl, and she'd gotten her hopes up that she'd have a little princess to dress up. I doubt she even knew where to begin with a boy. But I knew she'd figure it out.

The technician handed Anna a tissue. "Sorry about that."

Anna dabbed her eyes but remained quiet. She remained mute until we got back into the car. Then that fiery hormonal temper that

I knew and loved kicked in. Slamming her door shut, she snapped, "I'm going to kill that fucker when I see him tomorrow." I could only assume she meant Griffin.

Cringing at the harsh way Kellan's prized vehicle was being treated, I gingerly closed my door. "It will be all right, Anna. Little boys are fun." I really hadn't spent a lot of time around kids, male or female, so I wasn't sure if that was true. But that's what you're supposed to say, right?

Apparently not. Anna glared at me. She channeled all of her anger toward the technician, toward Griffin—hell, toward the universe—into her eyes. I was sure my internal organs were starting to boil as she stared at me.

"I don't know the first thing about raising a little boy. And look who's going to be his role model." She directed her stare out the window, choosing to melt the glass instead of my poor brain. "He'll be a self-righteous, womanizing Neanderthal, just like his father."

"I thought that's what you liked about Griffin?" I murmured that, but Anna heard me and redirected her ire back to me. I wisely said nothing further and started the car. Whatever Anna and Griffin had together, it was best to leave it between them.

When we got back to the house, Anna's irritation had dissipated some, and melancholy started to replace it; she even shed a few silent tears. She'd really had her heart set on a girl. Wondering if she would bite me, metaphorically or perhaps literally at this point, I put my hand on her shoulder. "You will love your baby boy just as much as you would have loved your baby girl. And don't worry about Griffin. You know that Kellan, Matt, and Evan won't let him corrupt his child . . . too much."

Anna gave me a blank stare for a moment then her face broke into a tiny smile. And even though her cheeks were splotchy, her nose was running, and her eyes were red, she was still drop-dead gorgeous.

I stayed with Anna for a while after that, making sure she was okay and helping her pack. Even though Anna was only going to be in Los Angeles for the weekend, she packed more stuff than I did. As I wrestled her bag closed, she told me that she wanted to be prepared for anything. I couldn't help but glance at her stomach after she said that. If my sister had been a little more "prepared for anything," she wouldn't be in the situation she was in now—about to bring a mini-Griffin into the world.

A surprise was waiting for me when I got home. Jenny's car was in the driveway, and she was standing beside the open driver's side door, waving at me. When I parked beside her, Rachel, Kate, and Cheyenne popped out of the other doors. I grinned ear to ear at seeing my girlfriends.

"What are you guys doing here?"

Jenny hopped over to me, a spring in her step. "We're here to help you celebrate your last night in Seattle."

I grabbed my head as the perky blonde wrapped her arms around me. "I think I celebrated enough yesterday," I murmured.

Cheyenne ducked back into Jenny's car. "Well, we'll have a much more subdued party." She reemerged from the car with an overnight bag. "We thought we'd all sleep over."

Shrugging, I grinned and indicated the house. "Sounds great."

Jenny, Rachel, and Kate grabbed their bags while I unlocked the front door. As I was trying to wrestle the key out of the lock that was starting to stick on me at times, Jenny came up to me and put a hand on my shoulder. "Hey, was everything . . . all right . . . last night?"

I could tell by the angle of her brow that what she really meant was, *Did anything happen with you and Denny?* She was nice enough to not say it directly to me, but she was wondering the same thing my sister had—if I'd cheated on Kellan. I shook my head at her, trying not to be irritated. It was my own fault, really.

"Nothing happened . . . except Denny watched me throw up in the toilet all night long."

Jenny cringed. "Ugh, sorry we got you wasted. That wasn't intentional."

I smirked at her. "You don't have to apologize for my bad judgment." I frowned as I remembered why I'd been so quick to drown the evening in alcohol. "Leaving Seattle is much harder than I ever thought it would be." My voice fell to a whisper and my vision hazed with unshed tears. God, was I losing it already?

Jenny hugged me. "Don't you dare start crying on me now! If you start, then I'll start, and we'll both be a blubbering mess all night long."

I laughed as I held her tight. Before long, the rest of my girlfriends enclosed us in a group hug. The moroseness of the moment made me chuckle. "Okay, enough of that," I told them, breaking apart from the circle. "Tonight is about having fun, not wallowing." I looked over each of them as I added, "And I'll be back. Seattle is as much of a home to me as Athens."

Kate ran her fingers under her eyes, then her face brightened. "I've got candy and popcorn."

Cheyenne looped her arm around Kate's. "And I've got every chick flick under the sun."

It wasn't too much later that we had a full-fledged slumber party going. I hadn't had a sleepover since the eighth grade, but childhood memories instantly assaulted me as the girls spread out their treasures. There were enough movies to last a week solid, enough candy to feed a small country, and enough beauty products to keep my sister stocked for a month. It gave me a serious case of the giggles to give myself a facial in my living room with four other girls. And it was so much fun I didn't care how ridiculous we all looked.

Halfway through the second movie, my doorbell rang. Even though I was in my pajamas with a green facemask on, I hurried to answer it. Dressed in a tank top and Kellan's black boxers, I pulled the door wide open. Hopefully it was our pizza. And hopefully the delivery girl noticed that I was wearing Kellan's underwear . . . since she'd seen them when Kellan had ordered food during our strip poker night.

My amused laughter died on my lips as I stared at the person standing in my doorway. It wasn't the pizza girl. Joey stood in my doorway. She ran her eyes over me and let out a derisive snort. I felt my cheeks heat, even under the layer of the cooling green tea mask slathered over my skin.

"What are you doing here? Kellan told you to never come back," I snapped, my good mood gone.

Joey ignored my attitude and tilted her head to look past me into the house. "Kellan here?"

I sidestepped to block her vision. "No, he's in L.A."

She grabbed a long lock of her black hair and twirled it around her finger as she absorbed my answer. Her fingernails were long, sharp, and painted bright red. Remembering the long scratch along Kellan's jaw, I ground my teeth together and considered slamming the door in her face.

She looked unaffected by my unhappiness. "Is he seriously recording an album? Or is that just some line he uses to pick up girls?" She smirked as her dark eyes drifted to the ring on my finger.

Even though I knew it shouldn't bother me, it really got under my skin that this woman was belittling our relationship. Kellan and I had gone through so much together. For her to demean it and dismiss it as some casual hookup boiled my blood. "Yes, he's recording an album." I started to close the door. "I'll tell him you stopped by."

She stuck her toes in the door's path. "Interesting. So . . . he's gonna be hot shit soon? Well, hotter than he already is, at any rate."

As she stood in my doorway chewing on her lip, an expression seeped into her features that reminded me of Ebenezer Scrooge in *A Christmas Carol*. I could clearly see the woman's mental image of herself counting large stacks of money, money she'd earned at someone else's expense.

I could feel my friends cautiously approaching the door as I sighed, "You have other copies of the tape, don't you?"

Joey removed her foot as she shrugged. "I was just returning *his* copy. I have plenty of others." As Jenny stepped to my side, her face equally covered in green goo, Joey sprightly asked, "You guys want to watch it? It's pretty freaking hot. Kellan did this thing where he—"

I put up my hand to stop her explanation. God, no, I didn't ever want to watch him having sex with someone else. And I definitely didn't want a play-by-play. "I don't want anything to do with you or your tape. Kellan paid you, and we're done as far as I'm concerned."

I heard some of the girls behind me gasp as they realized just what was going on. Jenny was the only one of them I'd told about the sex tape; she apparently hadn't passed on the information. Jenny was awesome that way.

Joey shrugged as she adjusted her short skirt. "Whatever, I was just offering you an advance screening to the movie of the year."

She spun on her heel to leave. Outraged, embarrassed, and mortified for Kellan, I stepped forward and blurted, "Are you really going to sell that? I mean, you're on it too. Do you really want a bunch of skeezy guys entertaining themselves with your private life?"

Joey stopped on the sidewalk and turned her dark head to glare at me. "If it means I'm set for life, then yes." Raising one edge of her lip, she added, "Besides, I'll be forever linked to a rich and famous rock star. I'll be famous, and what could be better than that?"

I shook my head, not understanding the desire to be famous, regardless of the price. Here I was, trying to find a way to stay out of Kellan's spotlight, while Joey was perfectly fine with selling her skin to find a way into it. How sadly desperate she must be to crave attention so much she'd do just about anything to get it. Oddly enough, my anger faded as I stared at her in stunned silence. While Joey waited for some response from me, all I felt for her was pity.

Retreating to the warmth of my home with Kellan, I told her, "I hope you find what you're looking for, Joey." Not expecting me to react that way, her brow was deeply pointed in confusion as I shut the door on her.

Chapter 7
So Long, Seattle

I woke up with a feeling in my chest that bordered on delirium. Today was Friday, my last day in Seattle. By this afternoon, I'd be in Kellan's arms in Los Angeles. I couldn't wait. I bounded out of my makeshift bed and nearly tripped over the girlfriends sprawled around the living room floor.

Jenny groaned when I bumped her elbow, but she didn't wake up. Giddy, I hurried upstairs to take a shower and get ready to go. Anna was picking me up soon, and I wanted to be fresh and sparkling clean for my reunion with Kellan. It had only been a couple of weeks since he'd left me, but it felt like an eternity. That always happened when he went away. Time's continuity seemed to depend on Kellan's proximity to me—the farther away he was, the longer time stretched.

When I emerged from the shower, I smelled the heavenly aroma of freshly brewed coffee. My mouth watered at the smell, and Kellan was instantly in my mind . . . not that he'd ever really left. He was usually somewhere in the back of my brain, but coffee always brought him right to the forefront.

After I was dressed and ready to go, I grabbed my bags and hurried downstairs to set them by the front door. Most of the girls were awake by then, rubbing their eyes, sipping on mugs of coffee while they started putting their stuff back together. Jenny gave me a one-armed hug as she held a travel mug of coffee out for me. "Anna just called. She's on her way."

I nodded as I took a sip—it burned my tongue a little but it was gloriously creamy. Jenny glanced around at the still-full living room. "I'll make sure the girls get home, then lock up the house before I leave."

Her words reminding me of something, I dug through my bag to find my key ring. After freeing it from the book I was hoping to read on the plane, I flipped through the keys until I found the one for the Chevelle. "Can you do me a favor today?" Jenny nodded as I handed her the key to Kellan's baby. "I made arrangements with the auto body shop below Evan's loft. They're going to garage the Chevelle for me until I come back. Can you drop off Babe-ette?"

Jenny smirked at my nickname for Kellan's car. "Sure thing. Rachel and I will drop it off this afternoon."

Rachel came over to stand by Jenny and rested a tired head on her shoulder. We'd stayed up way too late last night. The exotic beauty let out a loud yawn, and Jenny sympathetically patted her dark head. Her almond eyes blinked at me a moment, then she lifted her head. In a quiet voice, Rachel asked, "Would you mind saying hello to Matt for me? And telling him . . . I wish I could be there with him?"

The demure girl bit her lip, and a light flush tinted her tanned cheeks. I immediately told her I would. I knew exactly how it felt to be kept apart from the person you loved. It sucked. But Matt and Rachel seemed to have the long distance thing down pat, and I felt pretty good about them making it through the crazy lifestyle the boys had—or were about to have.

I also felt good about Evan and Jenny's relationship. Looking over to my best friend, I told her, "And I'll give Evan a great big bear hug for you."

Jenny gave me a wide smile, then reached into her back pocket. She pulled out a lime green box of candy that had been flattened and folded into thirds. With a mischievous grin, she handed it to me. "Can you give him this too?"

Curious, I unfolded what turned out to be a box of Jujubes. As I refolded the box, I asked, "You want me to give him your garbage?"

Jenny started giggling. "Don't worry, he'll get it."

I tucked the box in my bag, wondering just what inside joke I was being the messenger of. Well, however I could help was fine by me. Evan and Jenny were my rock star role model couple after all.

Cheyenne and Kate came over to give me goodbye hugs. As Kate pulled away, she said, "Hey, Justin is in L.A. right now. If you happen to see him, will you tell him I said . . . hey?"

She laughed, and her springy ponytail bounced around her shoulders. Justin was the lead singer of a band that was already pretty big—Avoiding Redemption. The five-man group had been the ones to "discover" the D-Bags, inviting them along on their sold out tour. Kellan's band got noticed by the industry while on that tour. In fact, Justin's label was the label that had scooped up the D-Bags. Kate had a thing for Justin, and I think Justin had a thing for her as well. Ever since the pair had met, they'd been texting each other on a regular basis. Her golden brown eyes sparkled with excitement when I told her I'd keep a lookout for him.

Just as the doorbell rang, Cheyenne wrapped me in a hug. "You keep your pretty little butt safe down there, ya hear?"

I chuckled at her as Jenny opened the door for my sister. My chuckle died as Anna stormed into the room. She dramatically tossed her bag onto the half-moon table in the entryway. "It's times like these that I really wish I could drink," she murmured.

"Problem?" Jenny asked as she shut the door.

Anna looked over her shoulder. "Besides the fact that I'm going to kill that fucker when I get to L.A.?"

No one needed to ask who the fucker in question was. Pursing her lips, Jenny asked, "What . . . did he do?" Her face was blank, like there was no answer on earth that would shock her. I understood that feeling. Really, a better question for Jenny to ask would have been, *What* didn't *Griffin do?*

Knowing what Anna's problem was, I sighed. "It's not that big of a deal, Anna."

She glared at me. The rest of the girls looked at me with shocked expressions. I didn't usually defend Griffin. "A boy, Kiera. He gave me a boy. All I asked out of this entire . . . *fiasco* was for him to give me a little girl, but the idiot couldn't even get that right."

Frowning, I told her, "It's not like he can control—"

Her icy stare stopped my voice. As the other girls caught on to the source of Anna's vexation, Kate gushed, "Oh my God! You're having a little boy—congratulations! Boys are so a . . . dor . . . able." Kate's voice faltered as Anna's glare shifted to her.

There was a moment of silence, then Jenny cautiously said, "I'm sure it will turn out fine." Anna started tapping her foot, and Jenny shrugged and gave up. "You're right, Griffin's a tool."

Anna immediately brightened. "I know! Right?" I had to shake my head at Anna as she went off on her boyfriend for a solid five minutes. Sometimes you just want someone to blindly agree with you, no matter what the problem is. And even if Anna was blowing her predicament *way* out of proportion, none of us was going to argue with the fact that Griffin was indeed a tool.

Eventually Anna simmered down enough to say goodbye to everyone and help me get my stuff into Denny's old Honda. Well, okay, she supervised while I packed my bags into the car. I had two of them, which I thought was pretty modest for an open-ended stay. Anna had three stuffed bags and a carry-on that pushed the boundaries of acceptably fitting into the overhead compartment.

Just as I was settling into my seat and the flight attendant told us to turn off our electrical devices, my cell phone buzzed. Thinking it was Kellan, since I'd just texted him to let him know we were about to leave, I discretely checked the phone. I smiled, seeing a message from Denny on the screen. *I'll miss you, mate. Good luck, and be careful.*

I had to shake my head at Denny's never-ending thoughtfulness. I almost showed the message to Anna, to maybe change her mind about Denny, but she would look at the text and immediately assume I'd slept with him the other night. Not wanting to defend my innocence again, I turned my phone off and tucked it into my bag.

The flight to Los Angeles wasn't long, but I bounced my feet, played with my guitar-shaped necklace, and worried my lip the entire time we were in the air. I even tried writing a little, but I couldn't concentrate enough and eventually put my notebook away. I just wanted to be with Kellan already. My heart was hammering in my chest when the plane touched down, and I think I was breathing harder when we finally taxied into position. Anna snorted and told me, "Calm down, horn dog." But I couldn't calm down. And I wasn't horny or anything, I just . . . needed him.

It was a free-for-all to exit the plane, so I grabbed my bag and darted for the door before Anna had even stood up. Even though we were seated near the middle of the plane, I was the second person to leave. Nerves skittered around my belly as I sprinted up the ramp. I wasn't sure how I'd spot Kellan in the sea of travelers and visitors in this massive airport. I supposed I could text him if I didn't spot him right away in baggage claim.

I burst through the corridor toward the waiting area for visitors. I took one brief sweep of the crowd eagerly waiting for friends and loved ones, then I started laughing. Kellan was standing front and center with his arms extended into the air like John Cusack in *Say Anything*. Only, he wasn't holding a boombox blaring Peter Gabriel. No, Kellan was proudly holding a sign that read—in embarrassingly large black letters—MRS. KELLAN KYLE.

I should have known that Kellan wouldn't be hard to spot. Even without the sign, he stuck out.

I let out a strangled laugh-sob as I rushed over to him. I just couldn't believe I was finally with him—and I wasn't leaving this time. Kellan barely had time to drop the sign and catch me as I leapt into his arms. I buried my head in his neck, wrapped my legs around his waist, and held on as tight as I could. His masculine, clean, intoxicating scent hit me as his warm hands caressed my back. My jittery nerves instantly evaporated. I was there. We were together.

I pulled back when I felt low laughter vibrating my chest. Kellan was beaming as he stared up at me. Maybe it was my imagination, but his midnight blue eyes seemed to be even deeper in color, his lashes longer. Even the curve of his amused smile was more sensual than I recalled. I didn't know it was possible, but he'd become even more attractive in my short absence.

"Miss me?" he murmured, leaning up in a gesture that clearly said, *I want to feel your lips.*

Grinning, I obliged him. Even his mouth was sweeter, more tender. When his tongue flashed against mine and his hand sneaked down to my backside, I suddenly remembered that we were in a very public place, a place swarming with young, innocent eyes.

Squirming, I broke free from his grasp and set my feet on the ground. He frowned at me; if it was possible, his pout was even more adorable than his smile. "Hey, I was enjoying that."

"Yeah, I know." I rested my hand against his stomach, and he reached up to grab my fingers; his frown instantly disappeared. He chuckled and bent down to pick up his welcome sign. I had to resist the urge to run my fingers through his impossibly sexy, shaggy, bed-head hair. When he straightened, I pointed to the ostentatious placard in his hand. "I like your sign."

He grinned. "I thought you might."

Reading it again as it dangled by his hip, I frowned. "But, just so you know, I'm not going by Mrs. *Kellan* Kyle. It's too old-fashioned."

Kellan glanced at the poster board by his thigh, then looked back up at me. "What? It's endearing to take your husband's full name, isn't it?" His thumb reached up to brush my wedding ring as he said *husband,* and the pride he felt at me being his wife was clear on his features.

"It's sexist, Kellan. I have my own name. I don't need to assume yours." I smoothed my hand over the soft, black cotton covering his pecs. To make my point, I traced the scripted letters of my name along the hidden tattoo above his heart. Kellan shuddered and his eyes started to blaze. "Just your last name," I whispered.

Kellan's sultry gaze drifted to my mouth. His lips parted, and as I watched, enraptured, he flicked his tongue over his bottom lip, then slowly dragged his teeth along the plump skin. It was distracting, to say the least.

Just as I was wondering how much PDA we could get away with before being carted off by the TSA, a loud voice erupted over the cacophony of the airport din. "Thanks, Kiera! I nearly gave birth trying to get my carry-on down!"

Kellan and I both looked back at my red-faced sister. As she stomped toward us, she huffed at a stray strand of hair that was dangling close to her eye. It was an exaggerated expression that screamed to everyone around her that she was put out. Kellan dropped my hand and took a step toward her. "I guess I should help."

"Is Griffin here?" I whispered, looking around for the bassist. I was sure he knew Anna was coming with me.

Kellan paused and ran a hand through his hair. "He . . . decided to wait at the house." He shrugged in apology.

I was irritated at first, but then I let it go. Griffin had never been an attentive boyfriend. Hell, Griffin had never been an actual boyfriend. He was an f-buddy. He'd said so himself. I thought he'd change once he knew Anna was pregnant, maybe grow up a little bit. But, as Kellan was always telling me, Griffin was . . . well, Griffin.

It took a while to get all of the luggage, but eventually we wrangled every piece and made our way to Kellan's car. The record label was letting him drive one of theirs while the band stayed at the house. It was a shiny silver Audi convertible. Anna openly fawned once she saw it, but I wasn't too impressed. Kellan looked much better in his solid, sleek Chevelle. Kellan let out a soft sigh as he got behind the wheel, and I could tell he felt the same way about the flashy car.

Anna was nearly buried in luggage in the backseat, since the trunk in this thing wasn't overly spacious. But she didn't seem to mind as we sped with the top down along the sun-soaked streets of

Los Angeles. Her smile was huge as her hair whipped around her. "I could definitely get used to this," she murmured, resting her head back on the seat.

It had been a drizzly, overcast day in Seattle, which the residents there had actually been happy about—less risk of your house catching on fire by a stray firework if everything was a little sodden. Here, the skies were a clear, bright blue. Well, I suppose the blueness was a bit tainted by the layer of smog hovering over the city, but it was brilliant and beautiful nonetheless.

The air running through my fingers as I held them in the breeze was also different than back home—warm instead of cool. I took in the expansive, sprawling city in absolute awe. Everywhere you looked, cultures and ethnicities were blended together. The lacing freeways and highways were more complex than any I had ever seen before, but Kellan seemed comfortable traversing them as he led us to the heart of the city. My eyes were everywhere as I tried to take it all in. Kellan laughed at my wonderstruck face. I couldn't help it, though. Los Angeles was iconic, legendary. The size and scope of it was intimidating. There was a reason people were drawn to L.A.— dreams were made there and they were destroyed there. You could almost feel the pulse of life in the tepid air.

Moving away from downtown, we began approaching residential districts. As we kept going, it was clear from the neighborhoods that we were getting into one of the more affluent parts of town. The properties were spacious, the houses absurdly large, the lawns ridiculously green and plush; they were even nicer than the yards in Seattle.

As the houses became farther and farther apart, we turned onto a street that was closed off by a gate. There was a paunchy, older man in a booth overseeing the gate, and for a moment I had the strangest feeling that we were crossing the border into a foreign country. If the man asked to see our passports, I wouldn't have been surprised.

Kellan reached into his back pocket as he stopped the car. "Afternoon, Walter," he said as he handed the man a card.

"Back already, Mr. Kyle? That was fast. And I see you picked up two beautiful young ladies while you were out." He tipped his hat to me as he handed Kellan back his card and raised the gate.

Kellan grinned as he revved the engine. "Careful, Walter. I might think you're trying to make a move on my wife."

Walter seemed abashed. "Wouldn't think of it, sir." He winked at me as he indicated the now-cleared path. Kellan was shaking his head good-naturedly as he pulled forward. Laid-back in his sporty car with dark sunglasses covering his eyes, he already seemed comfortable in his new place. Then again, Kellan had lived in Los Angeles for an entire year after high school, although he probably hadn't lived quite so nicely.

As we drove past monolithic homes that probably cost more money than most people made in their lifetimes, I hoped Kellan didn't want to settle down here. True, I'd follow him anywhere, but this city just didn't hold the same appeal to me that Seattle did. Everything here was just a little too flashy for me.

Like the house Kellan finally stopped at, for example. It was a contemporary, three-story home, with sandblasted white walls. There were large decks jutting out from the home, one on the right side, one on the left, so each floor received the most unobstructed sunlight as possible. All of the balcony railings were frosted glass and shiny chrome, and even from the parking area I could tell that the top floor had a pool on its deck.

It reminded me of a "party house." The kind that you would see in a crude comedy about spoiled teenagers throwing a rager while their well-to-do parents were "abroad." The fact that dozens of beautiful, scantily clad people were milling about the property—with drinks in hand, despite the fact that it wasn't even noon yet—didn't deter that image either. I frowned over at Kellan as a woman in a teeny weeny bikini walked past the front of the car.

He answered me before I could even ask him who all these people were. "It's the record label's house. Any artist on their label is welcome to come here, and some of them invite guests. Actually, almost all of them invite guests . . . at all hours of the day and night." He rolled his eyes.

That made me frown even more, because I'd always pictured him tucked away in a quiet, secluded spot, dutifully working on his album. I hadn't pictured him staying at a frat house while I'd been finishing up school. And I'd really thought that Kellan and I would have some much needed privacy here. It looked like I was wrong.

Giving me an apologetic shrug, Kellan returned his sunglasses to the clip attached to the visor. He hopped out of the car and started grabbing Anna's bags from the backseat. I helped him while my sister looked around with approval in her eyes; she was in seventh heaven. With a wide smile, she locked her eyes onto a blond, blue-eyed man sporting an eight pack. "Oh, yeah, I definitely could get used to this."

My eyes zoomed in on the blond man's counterpart. She was wearing a triangle top bikini that barely held in her curves; curves that were too round and perky to be natural. As she walked past the car, the curvy woman gave my husband a onceover and husked out, "Hey, Kellan."

Kellan nodded at her, then cast me a quick glance. By great effort, I kept my face smooth. It didn't matter if he knew a bunch of beautiful blondes. I was the only woman who would be sharing his bed. I did wish I couldn't see her entire ass as she walked away, though. I mean, really, with how little she was wearing, she shouldn't have even bothered with clothes at all. She obviously wanted to be naked, and I was sure she probably would be at some point today.

Loaded down with luggage, the three of us made our way inside the spacious home. Everything was first class—the overpriced art on the walls, the leather couches dotting the room, the Persian rugs lining the hardwood floors. Everything screamed money, and as a result, I was a little scared to touch anything. The half-dressed couples lounging around the home like it was their own didn't seem to share my reservations. They draped their bodies across armchairs, used coffee tables without coasters, picked leaves off of impossibly manicured trees. One was even smoking in the corner. Rebel.

Ignoring them all, Kellan led us upstairs. There was loud music blaring outside. But it was much more subdued the farther into the house we got. Large panes of glass in the curving staircase gave me a view of the central pool in the backyard, where the bulk of the people were loitering. I couldn't be sure, but I thought I saw Griffin in the mix . . . and that he had a bikini-clad ass on his lap. Too distracted by the fineries around her, Anna didn't notice where her boyfriend was. Not that she would care. Well, I didn't think she would care, anyway.

When we got to the second floor, Kellan led us to a large living room. The way it was set up, it reminded me of a dorm: the main room was the communal gathering area, the door to my left was a free-for-all bathroom, and the five doors along the perimeter of the curved wall were clearly bedrooms. A slider to the second-floor deck was straight in front of us. Evan and Matt stepped through it as Kellan and I dropped our bags to the floor.

The blond guitarist was laughing and juggling a water balloon in his hand as he said something to Evan that sounded like, "Nice toss." Evan shrugged, raising his tattoo-covered arms in an adorable display of modesty.

Anna brightened at seeing our boys and looked behind them for Griffin; he usually wasn't too far from his cousin. I didn't have the heart to tell her that I was pretty sure Griffin was waist deep in half-naked babes. Sneaking a quick peek around the space, a thrill of delight went through me that no one but D-Bags appeared to be on this floor. The revelers must have been keeping the party downstairs and outside. That was fine by me. Maybe Kellan and I would be able to have that privacy after all.

When Matt and Evan noticed us, their playful demeanors turned warm and welcoming. Matt gave me a brief embrace, then Evan scooped me up into a giant bear hug; my feet left the ground. After Anna greeted them, she asked Matt, "Where's Griffin?" A small pout graced her perfect lips as she rubbed her growing belly.

Matt glanced at Evan, then Kellan. I heard the question in his pale, blue eyes as he sought confirmation from his band mates: *Do we tell her?* It irritated me that there was a moment of "guy code" camaraderie going on, but I decided not to be mad about it. The band had been together a long time. They'd been through a lot of hard times together, I was sure. They were family, and family stuck by each other . . . even if one sibling was a jackass.

Finally seeing the answer he needed, Matt focused his attention on Anna. Indicating the deck behind him with his thumb, he told her, "He's by the pool."

Evan smiled and added, "Look for the annoyed one with sour milk dripping down his face."

Matt snorted and held up his hand to Evan. "Damn fine shot, man." The two boys high-fived and I glanced at the remaining balloon in Matt's hand. It was bright pink, and now that I was paying more attention, I could see that there was an opaque liquid inside it, not clear. Definitely not water, then. Milk? And not just any milk. Now that I was close enough, I could smell the balloon . . . and it did not smell good.

A milk stink bomb? Ew. Disgusting. Good thing Matt and Evan's victims were standing beside a pool. Even though it was wrong of me, I sort of hoped they'd nailed tiny-triangle-top girl who'd openly flirted with Kellan.

Anna's hand clenched over her belly as she realized just where her man was—partying with scantily clad women instead of helping her cart her bags upstairs. She looked infuriated for a moment, then a pleasant smile passed over her features. Hand outstretched, she turned to Matt. "Would you mind if I borrowed that?"

Laughing, Matt handed the milk balloon to her. "Be my guest."

Still sweetly smiling, Anna stalked out to the deck. Matt and Evan waited five seconds, then hurried after her. Kellan shook his head and looked down at me. "Want to see our room, or watch Griffin be assaulted?"

I bit my lip. "Wow, that's actually a really hard choice."

Kellan chuckled and grabbed my hand. Leading me to the first door along the wall, he murmured, "Well, I've had enough of Griffin lately and not nearly enough of you."

He opened the door wide and I gasped as I stepped inside. It was more like a studio apartment than a guest bedroom; it was about three times the size of our room back in Seattle. The walls were painted a surprisingly warm shade of gray, with furniture in a deep, contrasting dark cherry. The bedspread was black with intricate silver designs. The sheets and pillows were crisp white, with designs that matched the comforter, but in black. Silver and black lamps adorned the nightstands, and gray lounge chairs created a quiet space in the corner, perfect for reading or writing. A giant flat-screen TV was fixed to the wall opposite the bed.

All in all, it was a very manly room, but it did have some feminine touches. A crystal chandelier was hanging in the middle of the room. Deep purple throw pillows were artfully arranged on the bed, and a plush purple rug was lying at the foot of it. Tall pillar candles were positioned in clumps of three throughout the room, and a vase overflowing with white lilies highlighted an ornate lowboy dresser.

The room was stunning, but that wasn't what made me gasp. Kellan had taken bright red rose petals and scattered them over the floor and on top of the bed. The red seemed even deeper in color against the black bedspread. Over the top of the red petals, Kellan had carefully placed a layer of white petals. Those petals formed a heart, and on the inside of the heart was a box. A small, velvet box. My heart was surging as I stared at it.

Closing the door behind us, Kellan murmured in my ear, "Do you like it?"

I couldn't answer him. I could only nod as I laser-focused on the gift waiting for me. Kellan pulled me forward, and the smell of fresh flowers tickled my nose in a wonderful way. I slipped off my sandals as we walked so I could feel the silky petals under my toes. When we got to the edge of the bed, Kellan stopped and stared at the box with me. After another moment, he pulled it off of the bed, careful to not disrupt the artful white heart. My eyes followed his fingers. Without a word, Kellan dropped to a knee. Even though he'd done this before, even though we were already married in our hearts, the sight of him on bended knee made my eyes water.

Smiling up at me, he whispered, "Kiera Michelle Allen, will you be my wife?"

The tears in my eyes dropped to my cheeks as he opened the box. I was already nodding as I stared at the diamonds sparkling in the sunlight streaming through the window. The center diamond was a large round beauty that gleamed with life as it refracted the light. A "halo" of smaller diamonds circled it, amplifying its glow, while a similar strand of diamonds lined either side of the silver band. It was quite easily the most incredible ring I'd ever seen.

Kellan was calm and relaxed as he pulled the ring out of the box. My fingers were shaking as he slipped the new ring on my left hand, above the promise ring that I'd been wearing as a wedding ring. The two rings complemented each other perfectly, and I couldn't stop staring at them. Kellan was chuckling as he stood back up.

When I felt more composed, I looked up at him and said the first thing that popped into my head. "You didn't need to do that. My old ring was fine." I cringed at telling him that right out of the gate, but this ring looked pricey, and he didn't need to spend that kind of money on me. He didn't need to win me over—I was already won.

Kellan smiled and looped his arms around my waist. "Yes, I did."

I shook my head. "Don't get me wrong, this is . . . unbelievable . . . but I was content with the old band. You didn't have to do this."

Kellan's smile didn't change. "Yes, I did."

"Kellan—"

He cut me off with his lips on mine. "Yes, I did, Kiera," he murmured against my skin.

My eyes fluttered closed, and I dropped my pointless objection. It was his money, who was I to tell him how to spend it? As his arms tightened around my waist, my fingers tangled through his hair. Our kiss deepened as the emotion of the moment mixed with the ache of our weeks' long separation. It had been entirely too long since I'd been in his arms, and even though this house was swarming with people, I suddenly didn't want to be wearing anything but the new, shiny ring he'd just given to me.

Silently begging him, I pulled at his shirt. He understood and stripped it off immediately. I ran my fingers over his chest, delighting in the warm, smooth skin, the etched lines and valleys. Leaning down, I placed a soft kiss over my name drawn above his heart. Kellan sighed and held my head to his chest.

I peeked up at him, and his eyes were closed. His expression was peaceful, happy. Wanting to see his eyes sizzle, I ducked down and ran my tongue around his nipple. Then I closed my mouth over it and gently dragged my teeth across the sensitive skin. I was sure his chest wasn't as sensitive as mine, but I'd read somewhere that guys enjoyed a little stimulation there. Kellan's eyes flashed open, and his smooth face morphed into a devilish, one-sided grin.

The pads of his fingers trailed down my back, barely brushing against me on their journey down my spine; waves of heat radiated from each point of contact. When he got to the bottom of my shirt, he slipped his fingers under the hem and deftly pulled it over my body. His eyes locked onto my bra.

I was traditionally a very practical dresser, especially in the undergarment department. Your basic white or cream, full-coverage bras appealed to me the most. But my sister had started interjecting herself into my wardrobe choices. Telling me that no one married to a rock star could wear a bra whose slogan was *Finally a Woman,* she'd taken me lingerie shopping. I'd ignored her suggestions at first, since the scraps of material she'd tried to force upon me barely constituted a bra, but then she'd started showing me pretty, elegant pieces that I actually liked. The one I was wearing now was a lacy, light pink, push-up bra. I didn't have a whole lot of assets to begin with, but the bra took what I did have and squeezed them together in such a way that it looked like I had a whole lot more. I'd say I was stretching our honesty pact by wearing it, but Kellan already knew my body well. I was merely dressing up the package, or so my sister said. I couldn't wait for him to see the matching underwear.

It took him a solid fifteen seconds to return his gaze to my face. When he did, his eyes were burning with the passion I'd wanted to see earlier. He chewed on his lip a moment, then shook his head. "You didn't have to do that," he playfully told me. "I liked the old one just fine." His amused smile grew as he used my words against me.

Laughing softly, I yanked on the waistband of his shorts, pulling his hips closer to mine. "Yes, I did," I muttered, before attaching my lips to his.

He laughed in my mouth, but stopped when I unfastened the button of his shorts. He let out a low rumble when I slipped my hand inside. He was fully ready for me, his body hard against his silky boxers. I wanted to feel that soft skin directly, but Kellan pushed me back onto the bed. Lips parted, his hooded eyes scoured my body as I sat on a sea of petals. Bending over, he grabbed the bottom of my shorts and ripped them off of me. When he caught sight of the aforementioned underwear, he groaned. The light pink was slightly sheer, the straps over my hips embarrassingly thin.

Looking up at me with an expression that mixed both desire and irritation, he grumbled, "Are you trying to make this last about five seconds?" I laughed and his impish grin returned. "You're killing me, Kiera." He kissed my stomach. "You're actually killing me."

As his lips wandered down my stomach, I began to believe that *he* was killing *me*; the ache pulsing through me was bordering on painful. Dislodging the beautiful, artful floral arrangement, I scooted up the bed so Kellan could lie on top of me. Velveteen petals stuck to my skin as I reached out for him. His eyes softened into an expression filled with love and adoration. "You're so beautiful . . . do you know that?"

I felt my cheeks heat and I averted my eyes. I was . . . cute, sure, but a word like "beautiful" was reserved for my exotic sister. Kellan removed his shoes and shorts and crawled into the bed with me. Lying at my side, he grabbed my chin and turned my head toward him. "Do you know that?" he repeated.

Since I had no words in me, I shook my head. Kellan sighed and ran his fingers through my hair. "Well, I do," he whispered.

His lips returned to mine, soft, but fervent. He moved his hips over mine, and I cried out when we pressed together. The thin barrier of my panties between us amplified the sensation. Our kiss grew heated as the fire within us stoked even higher. Breath fast, Kellan ran his lips down to my ear and murmured, "I love you."

He rocked against me again, and I arched my back and closed my eyes. I wanted to tell him that I loved him too, but I was afraid that any noise I made right now would come out in a passionate scream, and a small part of my brain was still cognizant of the many people wandering around this home. Instead, I whimpered and dug my fingers into his shoulders.

When Kellan unclasped my bra and ran his glorious tongue around my nipple, mimicking what I'd done to him earlier, all thought of anyone else being around left my consciousness and I did cry out. Breathing so fast I was nearly hyperventilating, I discretely shoved his head down. He didn't need any more direction then that. Wrapping his fingers around the slim straps of my underwear, he yanked them off and continued exploring the southern region of my body. When his tongue swirled around my core, I screamed out.

He teased my body right to the edge of release, right to the point where I was panting and clutching at pillows, and petals were sticking to every section of my damp skin. He stopped before I crested, and I ached with the loss. Kellan didn't let me ache for long, though. Quickly slipping off his boxers, he moved over the top of me. He slid inside me at the same time he brought his mouth to mine. "Oh, God . . . I've missed you," I murmured as he filled me. Or maybe I shouted it, I wasn't sure.

Kellan rested his head in the crook of my neck as he let out a groan of relief. "You never have to miss me again," he panted. Then he started to move; there was nothing in this world more wonderful than the feeling of him moving inside of me.

My legs wrapped around his as I clenched him tight. The feel of his muscles stretching and flexing as he held himself above me was deliciously erotic. His skin was just as moist as mine, and somehow stray petals had found their way to his back. I wasn't too surprised. If I were a petal, I would find my way across Kellan Kyle's skin too. His breath was getting faster as his lips worked their way up my neck. Even though I could feel his body start to shake, he kept up the slow, steady rhythm that was rushing me to a soul-shattering climax. The scent of Kellan mixed with the light scent of sweat and flowers, filling my senses. I didn't think I would ever be able to forget this moment.

Nearing the end, even though a part of me didn't want to, I arched my back. I felt Kellan's body turn rigid, his shaking increase; he was nearing the end too, but by the look on his face, I could tell he was trying to hold off. I couldn't. Closing my eyes, I tensed as the burst of euphoria washed over me. I cried out in a long series of moans as I rode out the bliss. Somewhere near the tail end, I heard Kellan murmur, "Fuck," and then I felt his release as he groaned in my ear. It only added to the pleasure racing through me.

Drained and satisfied, we slumped in each other's arms. Once our breaths were somewhat normal, Kellan husked out, "Sorry, I was going to try to give you a twofer, but I couldn't hold out." He lifted his head and raised an eyebrow. "I blame it entirely on the underwear."

Giggling, I gave him a light peck. "If the first one is done right, I don't need two."

Kellan chuckled, and we languidly kissed as we cuddled, both of us now covered in stray petals. As Kellan picked off a few near my breast he murmured, "Give me a minute, and I can probably change your mind about that."

I was laughing at his answer when the door to the bedroom suddenly banged open.

I screamed and grabbed for anything that could shield my body. Kellan helped, moving over me so that all anyone would really see was him, which he didn't seem worried about. Horrified, I helplessly watched as my worst nightmare played out before my eyes. Griffin sauntered into the room. His expression was giddy as he beamed at

Kellan. Maybe I was misinterpreting it, but I didn't think his happiness was from catching us post-coital. In fact, he didn't seem to even notice that I was there.

Now I was positive I would never forget this moment.

Glaring at the person intruding on our very private moment, Kellan yelled, "What the fuck, Griffin?"

Bouncing on his feet, Griffin ignored him. "Kellan, you're not gonna believe who's here!" His shirt and hair were covered in white, curdled goo; he smelled awful, overpowering the perfect rose aroma that had filled my love nest until just a few seconds ago.

Irritated, Kellan tossed a thick purple pillow at him. "I don't care! Get the fuck out!"

Griffin took a step back as the pillow dinged him in the face. I felt red-hot, but Griffin still hadn't noticed me yet. "Dude, you're gonna care when you see her. Get the fuck out of bed, lazy-ass!" It was only then that Griffin seemed to notice that Kellan had company. His smile growing, Griffin drawled, "Hey, Kiera . . . it's good to see you."

He meant that in the most provocative way possible. I was sure that Kellan would've stormed over and decked Griffin if he hadn't been busy using his body to cover the bulk of mine from Griffin's sight. Realizing he was sort of stuck, Kellan yelled, "Matt! Get your cousin out of my fucking bedroom before I toss him off the fucking balcony!"

It took a moment, but eventually Matt and Evan stormed into the room to remove their bassist who clearly had a death wish. I groaned and covered my face. Damn it! Now this really was my worst nightmare. Matt and Evan were courteous enough to not look at us directly, but still, it was mortifying. As Anna peeked her head into the room, giggling, Matt and Evan dragged a protesting Griffin out. "Dude, they can bone later! He needs to see who's here!" Griffin returned his attention to us. "She's asking for you, dude. You!"

Matt smacked him on the back of the head. "Remember what we said about giving Kellan some space when Kiera got here . . . because of that *thing* he was going to give her?" When Griffin seemed oblivi-ous, Matt hit him again. "Fucking moron," he muttered, pulling him out of the room. "Sorry, Kell!" he yelled as he shut our door.

Mortified, I clutched at Kellan. "Oh my God! That did *not* just happen, did it?"

Kellan sighed and rubbed my back. "Unfortunately . . . it did. Sorry, I forgot to lock the door." He chuckled. "I was a little preoc-cupied."

I pulled back to glare at him. None of this was very funny. Remembering Griffin's words—because how would I ever forget them—I asked, "Do you know what he was talking about? Who's here to see you?"

Kellan shook his head. "No idea." He turned his head to the door, where we could hear Griffin and Matt arguing about Griffin's com-plete and total lack of common decency. "I suppose I should go see, though."

Chapter 8
An Offer

Thanks to the layer of rose petals we were both wearing, it took Kellan and me a few minutes to redress. Kellan laughed to himself as he pried a few petals loose from my hair—hair that I'm sure was a snarled, tangled mess that screamed to the world that I'd just had an afternoon delight—or late-morning delight, to be more accurate. Oh well, things could be worse. The entire band could have walked in on us completely naked and exposed. Oh yeah, that's right—they did.

I was frowning as I stood up and stared back at the rumpled bed. Kellan followed my gaze as he slipped on his shoes. Slowly standing beside me, he smiled, inhaled a deep breath, then kissed my forehead. "Stay here. I'm gonna go kill Griffin."

I instantly grinned and followed him as he stormed out the door. If Kellan was about to cause Griffin bodily harm, there was no way was I going to miss it. Griffin was on the other side of the living room, as far from our door as his cousin could get him. He was partially undressed, using his T-shirt to scrub sour milk out of his chin-length hair. Matt and Evan were telling him something, and Anna was tapping her foot. I was sure she wanted to berate him for giving her a boy but hadn't had a chance to tell him yet with the other annoyances that had cropped up. How one person got in so much trouble so fast was beyond me.

Griffin looked up when he spotted Kellan storming his way. A wide smile stretched his thin lips. "Dude—"

Griffin didn't get to say anything else. Kellan walked right up to him, placed both palms on his chest, and shoved him to the floor. He hit his ass hard, and the smile finally fell off of his face. "What the fuck, Kell?"

Lips in a hard line, Kellan stared down at Griffin. I'd seen Kellan ticked off before, at other people and even at me, but I'd never seen him direct that anger toward his band. Well, except for the one time that he'd gotten irritated enough at Griffin harassing me that he'd snapped at him to knock it off. This seemed different, though. He seemed . . . done, like Griffin had finally crossed the line with him.

When he didn't answer, Griffin rolled his eyes. "Relax, besides your ass, I didn't see anything."

Kellan pointed to the hallway that led downstairs. His voice low and cold, he told Griffin, "Grab your shit, and get out."

Matt and Evan stared at Kellan, shocked. Even Anna was speechless. Griffin snorted and stood up. "Oh, come on, Kell." He pointed back to our bedroom. "It's not like I knew she was here."

As I heard my sister mutter, "Did you think we flew in separately?" Griffin sniffed and crossed his arms over his chest. Griffin had a handful of tattoos across his body, but for some reason, I could not stop staring at one of a busty girl in a sailor suit straddling a sword. I guess it hit a little close to home at the moment. That, and I couldn't quite look Griffin in the face yet.

"Besides, you can't kick me out of the band, dude."

Kellan stepped toe to toe with Griffin, and the others tensed. Matt and Evan exchanged a brief glance, and I could almost hear the conversation in their eyes: *Okay, on three, you take Kellan, and I'll take Griffin.*

"Why the hell would I keep you?" Kellan seethed, his eyes hard.

Not looking intimidated, Griffin smirked and relaxed into his hip. "Because I'm the shit, and you know it." He gave him an innocent smile. "And we're best friends."

Kellan closed his eyes and took a step back. Matt and Evan both relaxed their stances. Inhaling a calming breath, Kellan finally opened his eyes. "If I am anywhere with my wife—*anywhere*—you knock and wait for permission to enter. Can your tiny fucking brain comprehend that?"

Griffin shrugged. "Fine, whatever, dude." Shaking his head, Kellan turned around and grabbed my hand. Even though my cheeks felt flaming hot, I forced myself to smile at Matt and Evan in a small token of appreciation for their earlier help.

Griffin, seeing that the heated moment was over, must have figured that all was right as rain again. Stepping up to Kellan as we walked away, he slung an arm over his shoulder. I could smell the sour stench of spoiled dairy even from the other side of Kellan. God, Porta Potties smelled better. "So, can I show you who's here now?" he asked.

Kellan grimaced at the stench wafting from the half-naked bassist and pushed him away. Maybe thinking Kellan was still angry, Griffin frowned. "Hey, come on, I'm sorry for barging in on you, okay? I just got excited." Grinning, he bounced on his toes, eager again. "I mean, how often do you get to meet a porn star!"

My heart sank as I began to get a really bad feeling about who was here. As Kellan furrowed his brow, Matt muttered, "She's not a porn star, Griff. Stop calling her that."

Griffin scowled at Matt. "Tomato, tomato, dude. She had sex on tape. I got off on it. Boom—porn star."

I closed my eyes and pinched the bridge of my nose. Just when I thought I couldn't possibly be more horrified by him, Griffin would find a way to prove me wrong. Ignoring Matt rolling his eyes and Anna looking intrigued, Griffin focused on Kellan. "And she's asking to see you . . . by name! Can you believe that shit?"

Kellan stopped walking and looked around the room. "Who the hell is he talking about? Who's here?"

Evan scratched his buzz-cut head. "Uh, Sienna Sexton."

Kellan's jaw dropped. So did mine. Sienna Sexton was a huge

celebrity—everyone knew her name. And not just for the reason Griffin had mentioned. Yes, an ex-boyfriend of hers had leaked a sex tape, and yes, the tape was widely available on the Internet, but all of that aside, she was actually a very talented artist. She'd grown up under the spotlight as a child actor. When she'd started maturing, she'd branched out into music. When the sex tape scandal had exploded, it could have killed her career, but she'd used the new provocative image of her to shift her music into a more adult sound. She was consistently on top of the charts. And she knew my husband's name . . . and wanted to see him. I couldn't believe it.

Kellan looked between Matt and Evan. "Are you serious? Sienna Sexton? *The* Sienna Sexton? Why does she want to see me? How does she even know who I am?"

They both shrugged, then Matt told him, "Don't know, man. She just came in with her entourage a few minutes ago and asked to see you." He pointed to the ceiling. "They're waiting upstairs for you." He glared at Griffin. "Which we were going to tell you about when you were done . . . giving Kiera . . . you know." His cheeks flushed with color as he gestured to my hand. "I like the ring. It's really beautiful on you, Kiera."

Mortified, I whispered, "Thank you."

Still stunned, Kellan shook his head. Delighted, Anna walked over and grabbed my hand. She gave my ring a cursory glance, then squealed, "Holy shit, Kiera! We're going to meet Sienna Sexton." Her emerald eyes sparkled so much I was pretty sure she'd forgotten all about the problem she'd wanted to kill Griffin for this morning.

I sighed, not sure if I was as excited about this as she was. Seeing that Kellan was finally listening to him, Griffin wrapped his arm around his shoulder again. "So, can we go now?"

Kellan made a face like he was gagging. "You smell awful. Could you shower first?"

Griffin scowled at Matt again, clearly blaming him—and only him—for smelling like a landfill. "Yeah, just give me two secs."

He dashed off to one of the bedrooms, and I heard the sound of a shower being turned on. I hadn't had time to investigate yet, but all of the rooms seemed to have bathrooms with showers in them. Kellan watched Griffin leave, then turned to Matt and Evan. "Let's go." He smirked, clearly amused at the small form of payback he'd just given Griffin.

As we were walking up the stairs that led to the top floor, Kellan picked a stray petal from my hair. I couldn't contain my smile as he handed it to me. Palming the red piece of velvet, I leaned over and whispered, "Were you really going to kick Griffin out of the band?"

Looking over his shoulder, Kellan murmured, "No, I just wanted to make a point." He turned back, his expression thoughtful. With an adorable half-smile on his face he glanced over at me and added, "Well, maybe. Do you want me to?"

I thought about that a moment, but then slowly shook my head. As big of an ass as he was, he belonged with the band. And besides, it wouldn't help my sister's situation any if her baby-daddy was suddenly unemployed.

When we got to the upstairs suites, a matching set of bodyguards blocked our path. Wearing corded earpieces and sunglasses, the pair looked more like secret service members than pop star guardians. Kellan looked between the two hulks blocking his path. "I'm Kellan Kyle, this is my band." He indicated all of us. "Ms. Sexton asked to see us."

One of the guards discretely squeezed something in his palm and told someone on the other end of the earpiece that Kellan was there. After a moment's pause, the guard moved away and let us all pass through. Walking between the mountains of muscle made me a little nervous. Tight security. I understood, I guess, since Sienna Sexton was pretty much on top of the world and must have fans coming up to her at every opportunity. It made me wonder if that would happen to Kellan someday. Would he need Thing 1 and Thing 2 watching over him? Watching over me?

Lana, the rep from the label whom I'd met before when I'd wrongly believed that Kellan was having an affair with her, stepped up to our group. The woman, who could have easily doubled for Halle Berry, nodded warmly at her recruits. "Kellan, boys."

Kellan acknowledged her with a charming tilt of his head. "Lana."

She swept her hand to indicate the looming space behind her. "Miss Sexton would like to speak with you, Kellan, if you're free?" Lana gave me a knowing glance and I fought back the flush threatening to creep up my cheeks. After being walked in on by Griffin, innuendo was suddenly a lot less embarrassing. Huh. Maybe he'd done me a favor after all.

The edge of Kellan's lip curled up before he schooled his features. "Of course."

Lana led us through a set of solid white French doors. I'd expected to see Sienna right away, but the only people in the room were a young couple pawing through a cabinet stocked with liquor and a man in a suit patiently sitting on a couch, shuffling some papers in his hands. A pair of ornate double doors led outside to where I knew a rooftop pool was tucked away. The doors were open, letting in the sunshine and a light, warm breeze. Another set of closed double doors led to what I assumed was the master bedroom. Was she in there? The thought of meeting a bona fide pop star had my heart racing, and I squeezed Kellan's hand.

As we approached the couch, the man in the suit stood and extended his hand. "Kellan, nice to meet you. I'm Nick Wallace, VP of Vivasec Records."

Shock flashed over Kellan's face as he shook the man's hand. I was sure he'd met a ton of important people by now, but it was clear from his expression that he hadn't met someone this far up the chain of command. "Nice to meet you."

As I was wondering just what the heck was going on, three people walked into the room from the outside deck. I didn't recognize two of them, but the person walking between them was unmistakable. Sienna Sexton. Physically, she was everything I would expect a celebrity to be—flawless olive skin, perfect bone structure, and from what I could see since she was wearing a bikini, zero body fat.

Her hair was smooth and straight, even in this heat, and fell past her shoulders in a perfect, black curtain. Her eyes were just as dark and were framed in expertly applied mascara and eye liner; they seemed huge, like they took in everything. Her smile was warm and bright as she held both of her hands out to Kellan.

In a charming British accent, she exclaimed, "Kellan, I am so excited to meet you. I'm a huge fan." Clasping Kellan's fingers with hers, she leaned up and kissed each one of his cheeks. She was standing so close to me that the hem of the sheer white robe she was wearing over her bikini brushed against my hand. She smelled like coconut suntan lotion, and her deeply tanned skin seemed to glow with health and vitality. I'd only ever seen skin like that in moisturizer commercials.

When she pulled back from Kellan, she stared up at him with an expression of adoration and interest. It was an expression I was used to seeing on his fans, so I figured her statement was true. I bit the inside of my cheek to stop myself from possessively leaning into his side. His fans could touch him . . . even the ones that were rich, famous, and drop-dead gorgeous.

Kellan seemed at a loss, which was an odd thing to see on him. He was usually so at ease. "Uh, thank you. I'm a . . . huge fan too." He smiled at her and I couldn't stop the momentary scowl that crept into my lips. *Huge fan?* I'd heard him sing along on the radio once or twice, but that was about it. Kellan's preferences tended to run more toward classic rock. But he was probably just being nice. He couldn't exactly tell her, *Thanks, your stuff is all right*.

Giggling, Sienna dropped his fingers and took a step back. I let go of the breath I hadn't realized I'd been holding. "Ah, love, aren't you a sweet one."

As Sienna's hangers-on flipped on a TV and made themselves at home, Kellan introduced the rest of his band, sans Griffin of course, who was probably screaming at the linebackers in the hall to let him in. Sienna greeted them politely, but only with a demure handshake. I guess her lips were solely reserved for greeting Kellan. Hopefully

that was a onetime thing . . . otherwise I may have to have a talk with
the pop princess.

When the introductions with the band were finished, Anna
stepped forward and grabbed Sienna's hand. "Anna Allen, mega fan.
You're practically my idol."

The two beauties smiled at each other, then Sienna patted Anna's
belly. "You due soon, love?"

Anna frowned for a second, then shook her head. "No, November . . ." Her voice trailed off, and I wondered if Anna was offended
that Sienna thought she looked so big that she was going to pop at
any moment, or if the idea of her upcoming birth still scared the
pants off of her. I figured it was a little of both.

Eyebrow cocked, Sienna looked back at Kellan. "Yours?"

Kellan glanced at Anna's belly and shook his head. Placing an
arm over my shoulder, he drew me to his side. "Mine."

I smirked at him as I extended a hand to Sienna; my fingers were
trembling, and I prayed she didn't notice. "Kiera . . . hi."

The smile slipped from Sienna's face as she looked between Kellan and me. It seamlessly returned as she shook my hand. "Nice to
meet you." Her accent reminded me a little of Denny. I made a mental note to call him soon, let him know that I landed safely. My dad
too, for that matter.

Once everyone was introduced, Kellan asked, "You . . . wanted
to see me?"

Sienna clasped her hands together. The move accentuated her
ample cleavage and I couldn't help but sigh; she was perfect there
as well, even more endowed than my hormonally enhanced sister. I
wondered if they were real.

"Yes! I have a proposition for you. One I think would be in your
best interest. Yours and mine." Kellan didn't seem any less confused.
Sienna smiled wider and pointed at him with her laced-together fingers. "I want you."

I was just about to politely tell her that she couldn't have him,
when Nick finally spoke. "As you know, Sienna is the label's largest

star." Sienna winked at Nick's praise. He smiled at her, then continued, "She's been listening to your finished tracks, and she's impressed, to say the least." Nick splayed his fingers out as he gestured to his "biggest star." "We've been looking for a way to rejuvenate Sienna's sound, add some kick to it."

Sienna nodded. "Something new . . . fresh."

"We've been looking for a collaboration that would blend well with her unique style." Nick brought his hands around to Kellan, his smile wide. "And that's where you come in."

Kellan blinked. "Me?"

Nick clapped his shoulder. "Yes. Your sound is exactly what Sienna's been looking for. And we have the perfect song for you—'Regretfully.' Sienna's already recorded her half of it." He shrugged. "We just need you."

Kellan stared at him a moment, then looked back at Matt and Evan. "You mean all of us, right?"

Sienna gave him a sweet smile. "Of course."

Matt and Evan tried to keep their composure, but I could tell they were bursting with excitement. A song with the hottest person on the charts—they'd be an instant sensation. My heart dropped as Kellan looked back at me. I always knew he'd be big one day, but I thought I'd have years to get used to it all. This would practically guarantee him stardom overnight.

Almost like he was reading my mind, Kellan chewed on his lip. After a few seconds, he looked back to Nick. "Our styles are very different. Can I hear the song first, make sure it's a good match . . . for us?"

Nick pursed his lips, clearly just wanting Kellan to do whatever he asked him to do. Smile tight, he told him, "Absolutely."

"Come, I'll play it for you." Sienna grabbed Kellan's hand and pulled him toward a piano in the back of the room. I tried to not be irritated with how comfortable she was touching him, or how little effort he made to get away. I also tried to ignore how much of her body was visible through her diaphanous cover-up. Shouldn't business meetings be conducted fully clothed? Not if you're a world-famous pop star, I guess.

Excited over a private performance, Anna giggled and grabbed my hand. Sienna sat down at the piano while Kellan stood beside it, arms folded over his chest. As Sienna began to play, Matt and Evan made their way over to Kellan. I reluctantly followed, not really wanting to hear how fabulously talented this provocative, beautiful woman was. But then her voice filled the air and I couldn't deny it—she was incredible. She was clear and powerful, sweet and sassy, all at the same time. The rhythm of the song was beautiful, not quite a ballad, not quite up-tempo. The lyrics were similar to something Kellan would have written. They were good, really good. Haunting, soulful, a touch profound, and . . . romantic. "Regretfully" was a song of loss. Of having everything with somebody, and then losing it all and trying to pick up the pieces.

Evan started tapping out a melody on the top of the piano, and Matt was nodding to a beat only he could hear. Kellan tilted his head, absorbing how the two styles would blend together. I could almost hear the D-Bags accompanying Sienna in my head, and the imaginary sound was incredible. The real sound would be unbelievable.

When the song was finished, Matt and Evan looked sold. Kellan still seemed unsure. Lana put a hand on his back and he twisted to her. "This is one of those once-in-a-lifetime moments that we talked about, Kellan. I would say yes, if I were you."

Kellan smiled and nodded at Lana, appreciating her advice. Being in this room, with people who knew Kellan in ways I didn't, made me suddenly feel very small and insignificant. Pushing back the feeling, I reminded myself that I wasn't. I had a voice, and it was an important one. To Kellan, at least. Looping my arm around his waist, I asked, "What do you think?"

"I don't know. What do you think?"

Not sure if I was telling him the right thing or not, I gave him my honest, impartial opinion of the song. "I think it's incredible. I think it would be a waste of your talent to say no." *And I'm afraid I'll lose you if you say yes.*

I didn't tell him that last part, though.

Kellan smiled at me, then looked over at Nick. "I guess we'll get to work on it first thing."

Nick smiled, clearly expecting that end result. Sienna squealed with delight and started playing another song on the piano. Surprisingly enough, she was playing a D-Bags song—she really was a fan. Even before she started singing, I recognized it as one of my favorites. It was the one that had first made me notice Kellan; it held a special place in my heart.

Halfway through the first verse, she told us, "This is my favorite of yours. I may have to cover it someday, with your permission, of course." She winked at Kellan. His corresponding grin was massive.

Holding me tight, he told Sienna, "That's Kiera's favorite too."

Sienna turned her radiance to me. "Well, don't we have a lot in common?" As her eyes drifted back to Kellan, I thought the two of us had more in common than I cared for.

Fifteen minutes later, we were back on the second floor. Matt, Evan, and Anna were all flipping out over the upcoming collaboration. Griffin was pissy, scowling as he sat by himself in the corner. Anna eventually cheered him up by sitting on his lap and nibbling on his ear. I guess meeting her "idol" had obliterated her irritation with Griffin. Of course, she never stayed mad at him for very long. Kellan was deep in thought as he sat beside me on the couch, stroking my hand with his thumb. I wasn't sure where his mind was, but I was pretty sure he was thinking about Sienna. I wanted to disrupt his train of thought, but I couldn't think of anything to say.

In the end, I decided to get out my notebook and work on my story. I would let Kellan keep thinking about . . . whatever he was thinking about. I wanted to be the supportive and encouraging type of person that he often was. Kellan would sort out whatever he was sorting out, and we'd be fine, because we trusted each other. Even though my head was spinning with a multitude of horrible scenarios, I wouldn't give them power over me by dwelling on them.

Sienna stayed at the house the entire holiday weekend. A group surrounded her wherever she went; I don't think I ever saw her by herself. It didn't take my sister long to become a member of her entourage. When Sienna came down to the main pool Saturday afternoon, my sister tossed on a bikini and joined her. And I swear, only my statuesque sister could pull off pairing a pregnant belly with polka dots.

Sienna continually struck up conversations with Kellan. Whenever he went out back to lay in the sun or take a dip in the pool, she was right there, telling him how great their single was going to be. I tried to ignore the light in her dark eyes when she talked to him. I tried not to notice how casually he carried on a conversation with her. And I really tried not to think about how much they had in common. Kellan and Sienna seemed cut from the same cloth, and I had to imagine that if I had never come into Kellan's life, he would have dated the superstar in a heartbeat.

But he never said or did anything inappropriate when he was around her. In fact, he was usually touching me in some way when he was talking to her—a hand on my thigh, his knee glued to mine, our bare arms brushing together. Some tiny bit of contact was almost always between us, like he was subconsciously letting me know that I had nothing to worry about.

On my sister's last day in California, Kellan and I were enjoying some sunshine by the pool. Most of the houseguests had gone home last night after the fireworks, and for once, Kellan and I were completely alone. He was relaxing in a lounge chair, wearing black swim shorts and nothing else. I was in the chair next to him, my left hand entwined with his right. Eyes closed, he played with my wedding ring while I gazed at the tattoo above his heart. I was in a near trance as I mentally traced the scripted letters of my name when my sister's irritated voice broke through my peaceful fog. So much for being alone.

"No, it's not a good thing. I wanted a girl!"

Anna passed through my field of vision and I followed her with my eyes. She stormed over to a table and set her juice down so hard she spilled some. Griffin followed her. Like Kellan, he was only wearing swim shorts. While Griffin was fit and could definitely pull off the look, he wasn't quite as well defined as Kellan.

"Well, I'm cool with a boy. I think it's awesome. Instead of Myrtle, we can call him Myrt or Mort . . . Mortimus." He paused for a minute while my sister made a face. I did too. *Mortimus?* I could *not* call a baby that. Suddenly, Griffin raised a finger into the air. "Maximus!" he exclaimed.

I looked over at Kellan and we both smiled and shrugged. Maximus was a heck of a lot better than Mortimus. My sister snorted, and I looked back at her. A wry smile on her lips, she shoved Griffin's shoulder back. "Maximus . . . like the gladiator?"

Griffin smiled and brought his hands to his hips. "Well, he will be a slayer." He thrust his hips forward and I stopped smiling. Anna laughed and trailed her hand down Griffin's chest. She tugged on his shorts, pulling him into her bare stomach. His lips were instantly attached to her neck, his hands immediately slipping down the backside of her bikini bottoms. I turned back to Kellan. I really hoped they didn't try to make another baby while they were ten feet away from me.

Kellan watched them for a minute more, then closed his eyes and laid his head back on the chair. Sienna's toned legs appeared on the other side of him. Shirking off her sheer robe, she frowned as she watched my sister being mauled by the D-Bags' bassist. "Are those two really a couple? He's hit on me about a dozen times."

Sienna seemed as confused by Anna and Griffin's relationship as I sometimes was. As I tried not to gape at the perfection of her sculpted body, Kellan looked over and smirked. "That depends on your definition of 'couple.'" Returning his eyes to my sister, he added, "We're all still trying to figure them out."

Sienna smiled; the brilliance of her white teeth nearly blinded me. "They're not as exclusive as the two of you then?" Her eyes drifted over Kellan's tattoo before shifting to my wedding ring.

Kellan smiled at her as he brought my ring to his lips. "No, definitely not."

Sienna smiled politely as she watched him. If she was disappointed over Kellan's commitment to me, I couldn't see it. But then again, she was a performer, and acting was a big part of that. As her entourage spread out around the pool, Sienna flipped onto her stomach. Her backside was impossibly perky, and I discretely adjusted the bottom of my modest tankini.

Pulling the sheet of dark hair off of her shoulders, Sienna unhooked her top. Resting her head on her arms, she told us, "I'll be heading back to London in the morning. Would the two of you like to have dinner with me tonight?"

Kellan was silent, leaving the answer entirely up to me. Not able to pass up a meal with number ten on the "Most Influential People in the World" list, I shrugged and nodded. "Yeah, sure . . . sounds great."

Closing her eyes, Sienna murmured, "Fabulous." I wanted to agree, but I wasn't entirely sure that I hadn't just made a horrible mistake.

Anna was upset that she wasn't invited to go to dinner with her new BFF. Griffin was too. His eyes barely left Sienna's body the entire time she sunbathed half-naked by the pool. His rapt attention didn't seem to bother my sister. She really didn't seem to care what Griffin did, so long as he was attentive to her and respectful to me. Honestly, I had no idea how those two were going to be as parents.

Standing in front of a full length mirror in the bathroom later, I debated if I looked good enough to be seen with Sienna Sexton. I hadn't planned on fancy dinners out while I'd been packing, and the only semi-dressy thing I had with me was a long, simple black dress made of soft cotton that swirled down to my ankles. It had wide straps, a v-neckline, and an empire waist. It was more comfortable than sexy, but it was all I had. Sighing, I ran my fingers along a wavy strand of my hair; I'd thought to offset the plainness of the dress with big, bouncy curls, but I'd only managed wavy.

Coming up behind me, Kellan kissed my bare shoulder. "You look incredible."

I looked at the reflection of him over my shoulder. He was wearing a fitted blue dress shirt worn loose over dark blue jeans. The color of his shirt brought out the depth of his eyes. He was stunning. As always.

A part of me wanted to tell him that I wouldn't look incredible standing next to a bombshell like Sienna, but I knew he wouldn't agree, so I didn't say it. Looking back at my reflection, I tried to see what Kellan saw when he looked at me. My eyes were "expressive," meaning they were large. They were generally a seaweed brown shade, but in this light, the green was a little more apparent. With the simple layer of mascara I had on, I'd say they were even pretty. I had nice cheek bones, a cute nose, full lips. Maybe my chin was just a tad too pointy, but all in all, I was well proportioned and symmetrical. I wasn't gorgeous, but . . . maybe I was beautiful.

Smiling at him, I pulled out my lip gloss and applied a coat of light pink. "Thank you."

Kellan blinked, surprised. "You're not going to argue with me? Make me convince you that you're attractive?" I shook my head and his lips curved into a small approving smile. "Well, that's new. I like it. Confidence is sexy on you." He flashed me a wicked grin.

I felt my cheeks heating as his bedroom eyes locked with mine in the mirror. God, we'd never make it to dinner if he kept looking at me *that* way. Twirling him around, I shoved him out the door. Kellan chuckled to himself while I gathered the rest of my things, then we headed out to the sitting area, where the rest of the band was lounging.

Evan came over and wrapped a tattooed arm around me. "You're a doll, Kiera."

I smiled up at him, then remembered the favor Jenny had asked me to do days ago. Embarrassed that I'd forgotten, I hurried back to my room and dug through my bag until I found the flattened candy box. Smiling in apology, I handed it to Evan. "Jenny says she misses you, wishes she could be with you, and asked me to give you this."

As Evan took it, I swear his cheeks flushed with color. Peeking up at me with his warm brown eyes he asked, "Did she tell you what this was?"

I shook my head and he laughed as he put it in his back pocket. "Thank you, Kiera." Digging into his other pocket for his cell phone, he headed for his bedroom. I could still hear him laughing as he shut the door. Hmmm, guess he wasn't going to explain the inside joke.

As Kellan pulled me toward the door, I relayed Rachel's message for Matt. He smiled, nodded, and waved goodbye. Griffin and Anna both pouted as we left. I'd have to make it up to my sister somehow. Griffin I wasn't too worried about; he could pout all he wanted.

Sienna brought Thing 1 to dinner with us. It surprised me a little bit when the massive bodyguard climbed into the driver's seat of the black Escalade. Maybe Sienna expected someone at the restaurant to approach her? Or maybe she was concerned about getting accosted on the walk into and out of the restaurant. I'd never spent time with someone at her level of fame before, so I wasn't sure what to expect. The idea of being in her spotlight made me more nervous than the idea of sitting at a table making small talk with her.

Maybe seeing my nerves on my face, Kellan discreetly handed me something. It was a pale pink rose petal. My mind instantly re-wound to the red and white petal–strewn bed he'd laid out for me. As I stroked the silky petal, I smiled at the words written with a fine-tipped Sharpie. Well, not words exactly. Very carefully, he'd drawn a picture of an eye, the symbol for a heart, and a drawing of an animal that I could only assume was a female sheep—*I love you*. Laughing a little as I peeked up at his amused face, I tucked the petal in my purse. It never failed; Kellan always found a way to ease my anxieties.

Twenty minutes later we were walking into a restaurant that I could tell was way out of my price range just by the entrance. A valet swept Sienna's car away as another man in a full suit held the door open for us. He greeted Sienna by name and smiled so widely at me that I could almost count all of his teeth. I felt like I wouldn't have been greeted nearly so cordially if I'd walked in there alone.

Sienna thanked the doorman and waited for Kellan and me to catch up to her. When Kellan was level with her, she wrapped her arms around his elbow. "Ready? I'm starving." She leaned around him to speak to me. "You're going to love this place. The food is to die for."

I tried to ignore how much of her body was pressed against Kellan's. And how much thigh was showing on her mini mini-skirt. And that her top was loose and billowy in the front, but almost backless, with a deep V that nearly reached to her skirt; it screamed to the world that she wasn't wearing a bra, and I figured clothes like these were exactly why she sunbathed with her top unfastened.

As Kellan politely escorted her toward the open restaurant door, I saw flashes of light behind us. Glancing over my shoulder, I noticed men with cameras snapping picture after picture, until Thing 1 stepped in front of them and firmly asked them to leave.

Did I just have my photo taken by the paparazzi? Really? God, I hoped not.

The restaurant was just as opulent on the inside, and I suddenly felt a little underdressed. The refined hostess took one look at Sienna and instantly started leading us to a secluded table in the back of the restaurant. Sienna confidently followed the waitress; the pop star's walk had a slight swagger to it that was impressive, considering the size of her heels. Kellan followed after her with a hand on the small of my back.

A white linen tablecloth was draped over an intimate round table with four place settings. The waitress deftly removed one setting, sweeping the silver cutlery into her pocket as she indicated the three remaining places. Looking around, I saw that Sienna's bodyguard hadn't come into the restaurant with us. Guess he figured she was safe enough in here. I noticed some other guests stealing a peek here and there, but no one gave any indication that they were going to bother us. When your meal cost as much as a week's worth of groceries, you probably want to savor it, even if a celebrity is sitting a few tables away.

Not long after we ordered, our cocktails appeared, and we sipped on them while we waited for our food to arrive. This was the first time I'd really had a chance to talk to Sienna one on one. She was surprisingly warm, pleasant, and friendly—down-to-earth in a way I wouldn't expect someone in her position to be. She was even remarkably funny. It was easy to see why the world was so in love with her.

When our calorie-laden food arrived, she put a hand on her stomach and moaned, "My trainer is going to kill me for this." Lifting a perfect brow, she added, "Being scrutinized as much as I am, I try to stay fit. The last thing I want to see is my rippled ass on the cover of some tabloid." Lifting her fork, she purred, "So basically I've been starving for a freaking decade." The pasta-coated fork slid into her mouth, and she made a noise that was almost too erotic for the dinner table.

Kellan chuckled at her and gave my plate a suggestive glance, like he wanted me to one-up her satisfaction. Rolling my eyes at him, I told Sienna, "That must be difficult, having complete strangers pick you apart all of the time."

She smiled as she ate. "You have no idea." Shifting her eyes to Kellan, she bumped his shoulder with hers. "Men have it so easy. You just have to have an amazing smile and you're golden." She gave him a dazzling grin as she studied his features.

I cleared my throat while Kellan asked her, "What was it like, growing up in this business?"

She paused between bites, then lowered her fork. "Not easy. I had the domineering, stage-mom type parents. Not a lot of sympathy if I wasn't perfect. That sort of expectation is . . . challenging . . . to say the least." She looked down. "There were many nights I just wanted normal, loving parents who didn't care if I flubbed a line or missed the high note." She looked back up and her eyes were glossy. "It just would've been nice to feel loved, no matter what."

Kellan was staring at his glass, his expression thoughtful. After a moment, he whispered, "I know just what you mean."

Knowing what he was referring to, I put my hand over his. He smiled, his eyes still on his drink. Sienna glanced between us, then her expression brightened. "Well, if I've learned anything in this business, it's that you either roll with the punches, or you simply roll over." She popped a bite in her mouth. "And I'm not rolling over for anyone."

Remembering just how Sienna had skyrocketed to fame—mainly her very private moment being exposed to the world—I fixed my eyes on my plate. I didn't know how she dealt with the entire world knowing so much about her. I couldn't handle that. I wondered how Kellan would handle it, once his intimate act was exposed.

Seeing my face, Sienna asked, "Wondering about the tape, aren't you, love?"

My head shot up. "No, I . . . maybe. I just . . . can't imagine anything more horrifying." I glanced at Kellan and he sighed; the apology in the sound was crystal clear.

Sienna studied us for a minute before answering. "Yeah, that was a moment in time I'll never forget. The media had a field day— *Sienna Sexton's Scintillatingly Scandalous Sex Tape.*" She rolled her eyes. "Alliteration junkies."

Pausing, she took a sip of her drink. "But, like I said, you develop a thick skin in this business, or it will eat you alive." She shrugged. "Was I thrilled that someone I once trusted betrayed me? No. But the genie was already out of the bottle, and before I knew it, the footage was everywhere, so what could I do? In the end, I did the only thing I could. I embraced it. I rode the hype, and steered my career down the path I wanted." A coy smile touched her lips. "It wasn't how I planned it, but it's been an incredible journey, and I haven't looked back." She gave Kellan a pointed look. "No regrets. It's the only way you'll survive in this town."

Chapter 9

Finishing Touches

The following morning Kellan and I took Anna back to the airport. Properly chastised for not being at the airport when we arrived in L.A., Griffin came with us to see her depart. It was weird to see my sister off. I kept feeling like I was missing my flight by not boarding with her. Even though I'd spent a few months on my own in Seattle when Anna had been back east with our parents, I'd gotten used to having her around. Watching my sister leave the city was hard.

But I still had Kellan, and that made things considerably easier.

After Anna left our sight, Griffin turned to Kellan. "Did you hear, man? She's having a boy . . . my boy." He lifted his chin up, pride evident in his light blue eyes.

Kellan smiled and tightened his grip around my waist. "Yeah, I seem to recall hearing that somewhere."

I contained my smile as best I could. Anna had found a way to mention the sex of her baby at every possible moment, most of the time with a perturbed scowl on her face. She still wasn't overly excited about Maximus, but I knew she would be when he arrived.

Kellan clapped Griffin's shoulder, then we made our way back to the car. As was usually the case with boys, whatever beef had been between them was over. Kellan and Griffin seemed just like they always did as they joked around while leaving the airport. I was starting to get over the embarrassment too—I could finally look Griffin in the eyes again.

As Griffin went on and on about how hot Anna and Sienna were when they lounged by the pool together, I thanked fate that Sienna was also leaving the city today. She hadn't done anything wrong, per se—and I did like her—but her interest in Kellan got under my skin a little. Sure, it was mainly a professional interest, but I wasn't naïve enough to think that that was all it was. She found him just as attractive as she found him talented. She knew he was taken, but would that stop her from making a play for him? I didn't really want to find out. Distance was a good thing.

We went straight from the airport to the recording studio. Kellan and the guys were finishing up their stuff so they could get started on the new song with Sienna. I was excited to see the recording process. I'd heard Kellan describe it a thousand times, but I was eager to see it with my own eyes. Plus, I hadn't seen Kellan sing in ages, and I'd really missed it.

Showing the proper credentials to security, Kellan confidently walked me back into the working area of the studio. True to form, Kellan had his preferred instrument slung over his shoulder, while a plethora of studio instruments were waiting for everyone else to use.

The "live room" was a large soundproof space designed to achieve the best acoustics possible, or so Kellan told me. In the back was a room-within-a-room holding a drum set. There was another room off to the side that only had a microphone in it. Different sections of the main room were separated by movable panels that isolated sound. Two guitars were amped and miked, while a third space was empty and waiting for Kellan's guitar.

Just being in there made my stomach buzz with excitement. Part of me wanted to pick up an instrument and start jamming away. Too bad I was astoundingly bad at playing everything. As the rest of the guys strolled into the room, Kellan waved at some people watching us though a large glass window. Setting down his guitar case, Kellan led me to the mixing room where the magic happened. Inside, I was introduced to about five different people who were the brains behind the album.

Eli was a highly respected producer, with a resume about as long as my arm. He'd worked on Justin and Sienna's award-winning albums, and those were only a couple of his accolades. He seemed way too young to me to be as prolific as he was, but he sure knew his way around the very confusing assortment of levers, switches, and dials.

The dark-skinned man gave Kellan a complicated handshake for a greeting. Waving a hello to me, he turned to Kellan and said, "Heard you said yes to Sienna's song?"

Kellan nodded, running a hand through his hair. "Yeah, it should be interesting."

Eli smacked him on the chest. "Interesting? It's going to be hot! Just wait until you hear what she's already laid down."

I sat on a chair near the door and stared around the room, feeling a little out of my element. Kellan gave me supportive smiles, but he was at work now, and his focus was on his music. Realizing I should get to work too, I asked one of the men in the room if I was in the way in the corner. He assured me it was fine, and I dug through my bag and pulled out my notebook and story notes. I made time every day to write a little, and I was well over halfway finished with my novel. I still hadn't shown it to Kellan. He was respectful, giving me my space. But I could tell he was curious.

As I tapped the pen cap to my lip, I tried to block out the world and remember how it felt when Kellan quietly pleaded with me to leave Denny and stay with him—when he'd given me the ultimatum that had seared my soul. Just remembering it brought tears to my eyes.

Just as I was about to write something, a voice intruded my thoughts. "Hey, Kiera. You okay?"

I glanced up, then did a double take. Justin Vettel, lead singer of Avoiding Redemption, was standing right in front of me. Having met him a time or two, the shock of who he was quickly left me. Giving him a warm smile, I nodded. "Yeah, what are you doing here?"

He nodded at Kellan, still talking with Eli. "Wanted to see how the album was coming along." With light blue eyes and blond hair in a layered cut that only a rock star could successfully pull off, Justin was definitely cute. He was wearing a collared shirt, and I could see part of the tattoo that stretched from one collarbone to another. I still had no idea what it said, but it was a beautiful piece. He smiled as I tried not to stare. "We're finalizing the next tour, and I want to get Kellan on it."

"He'd love that. He had a lot of fun touring with your band."

Justin smiled. "Yeah, it's a hell of a lot more fun if you're touring with guys you get along with." He paused for a minute, then added, "Do you think Kate would join me for a couple of weeks if I asked?" Sputtering a little, he immediately added, "Or would that be too forward, since we're not technically dating or anything."

His cheeks were a little rosy and I marveled that this celebrity—who could have just about anyone—was flustered over my friend. Famous or not, in the end, Justin was just a typical boy.

"I think she'd like that, Justin. Actually, she wanted me to tell you 'hi' if I ran into you . . . so . . . hi," I said.

I rolled my eyes at myself. Nice message delivering. Justin's grin grew, and he bit his lip. Remembering something Kellan had told me once, I asked him, "I thought girlfriends weren't allowed on the bus—only wives."

Justin scrunched his brows. "The label doesn't care who's on the bus . . . so long as *we're* on the bus." A mischievous smile crept over his face. "Who told you that?"

Pursing my lips, I glanced over at Kellan. He happened to look back at me, and when our eyes met I minutely shook my head at him. He'd been teasing about the whole wife thing. Kellan cocked a questioning brow at me, and I giggled. "My *husband*," I told Justin.

Justin laughed, then patted my shoulder. "Ah, well, congratulations."

Justin left to say hi to Kellan after another minute, and I got back to work on my novel. Within seconds, I was absorbed in the story and had blocked out everything else around me. I started when a hand caressed my knee. Kellan was squatting beside me, an amused smile on his sculpted face. "We're just about to start. You good here?"

I lifted my pad of paper and nodded. Kellan glanced at my bag full of notes and frowned. "You should get a laptop so you don't have to lug around all this paper." Twisting his lip he added, "I think when we're done here we'll go shopping."

Smiling at his thoughtfulness, I leaned over and kissed him. "I thought you would appreciate my old-fashioned approach."

His lips lingered against mine, warm and sensuous. "I do, but it's time to step into the twenty-first century, Kiera."

I made an unladylike noise of amusement, almost a snort. "That's funny, coming from you."

"Hmmm," he murmured against my mouth. "You know what's not funny?"

He pulled back and I pouted a little. *Your lips no longer touching mine?* His amused expression returned as he searched my face, then a small scowl formed on his lips. He tapped my pad of paper. "That I still haven't been granted access to your bestseller."

I sighed and discretely covered the top sheet with my arm. "You'll have access . . . when it's done. When it's perfect."

He shook his head; the long, shaggy layers on top were irresistibly tousled this morning. The shorter layers near the bottom slightly curled around his ears, hugging them. "I don't care about perfection." He touched my forehead with his finger. "I care about what's going on up there. I care about what you think." Averting his eyes, he added in a quieter voice, "I care about what you think . . . about what happened with us."

My heart broke when he looked back up at me. His deep blue eyes could hold so much pain sometimes. Not able to say anything, I nodded. It might hurt me, it might hurt him, but I'd stick to our pact of honesty and let him see the deepest, darkest corners of my heart, of my soul. It was only fair, since he constantly let me see his.

Kellan smiled, gave me one last kiss, then exited the control room to go record his masterpiece. Headphones were put on, instruments were plugged in, lights on the board lit up. Evan ducked into his private drum room while Kellan stepped into the vocal room. It was fascinating to watch, but after a while, it did get a little tedious. There was a lot of repetition involved in recording. The song was played several times so the best recordings could be used. By the fifth or six run-through of the song, I stopped listening and worked on my book. I got through the painful part just as Kellan and the guys were finishing up for the day.

"Ready?" Kellan asked, a gleam in his eye.

I nodded and stood up to stretch. Sitting for so long had made part of my butt fall asleep. Hazard of my chosen profession, I supposed. Kellan said goodbye to the guys in the room, who were intently listening to the song they'd just finished mixing. It sounded amazing—a million times crisper and clearer than the live version of it. Hearing Kellan's voice so pristinely gave me goose bumps. He was going to be so huge.

Eli clasped hands with Kellan, telling him, "We'll start on the new song after you guys have had a couple of days to practice. Cool?"

Kellan nodded, and my heart sank a little. If they were going to learn a new song that fast, then I wasn't going to see a whole lot of Kellan. But that was okay, since neither one of us was going anywhere . . . except shopping, apparently.

The next couple of weeks were relaxing and peaceful—for me, at least. I called my parents as often as I could. Mom started crying when I sent her a picture of my new ring. Dad, just slightly less emotional, told me things like, "Now, don't you go anywhere without Kellan, you hear me?" It made me smile that Dad now saw Kellan as my protector.

Kellan was pretty busy, though. The band learned the new song faster than I would have thought possible. Of course, they only had to learn it, not create it. Creating a fresh piece of music was a time-consuming process. I'd watched the boys debate about a thirty second song intro for three hours once. Every time I'd approached their table at Pete's, they'd been discussing it. Well, Matt, Evan, and Kellan had been discussing it. Griffin had been trying to convince anyone who would listen that the Starbucks's logo was kinky.

Once the band had the new song down, they started recording it. I went in every day with Kellan, new laptop in hand, and dutifully worked on my book while Kellan worked on his album. It delighted me to no end that our careers could coexist so peacefully. Kellan's actually helped mine. His band, his music, and his voice all opened up my mind, and the words poured out of me. In fact, there were several times when he was done for the day and I wanted to keep going. But Kellan was pretty good at persuading me to put away my computer and go home with him. The art of seduction always was one of his greatest talents. Right up there with music, really.

At the end of July, Kellan and the boys were done with their portion of the album; the mixing men would finish the rest. All the guys had left to do was have their photo taken for the album cover. Kellan was morose about it on the drive to the studio. "I don't see why we have to be on the cover. Couldn't it be some generic photo of . . . a duck or something?"

"A duck? Really?" I questioned as I tucked a strand of hair behind my ear that the wind was continuously whipping into my mouth. Darn convertible.

"What? Ducks are sexy . . . right?" Kellan gave me a sly grin. I rolled my eyes and he chuckled. "They've got those long, flat bills, plump bellies, wide, webbed feet." Still grinning, he brought his eyes back to the road. "What could be hotter than that?"

Staring at the way his dark sunglasses framed his face, amplifying his attractiveness, my immediate thought was, *You*. Smiling at his ridiculous suggestion, I laughed out loud. "Um, just about anything."

His perfect face swung my way. "We'll just have to agree to disagree on this one."

I was just about to tell him that he would be all alone on his side of the argument when my cell phone rang. Quickly digging it out of my bag, I glanced at the screen before answering it. "Hey, Denny. How are you?"

Kellan's eyes shifted to the front as he turned the radio down. I played with the guitar-shaped necklace around my throat while I waited for Denny's response. It was long in coming. "I'm fine. How are you?" The concern in his accent was clear, and confusing.

"I'm great. Why do you sound weird?"

As Kellan pulled onto a side street, he flashed me a brief questioning glance. I shrugged, not knowing any more than he did. In my ear, Denny's warm voice asked, "You're okay . . . really okay?"

"Of course." Dread started filling my stomach. "Why? Did something happen?" My thoughts immediately went to my sister and my unborn nephew. "Is Anna okay? Is the baby?" Fear seeped into my stomach, and I tried to squelch it. Surely Anna, Kate, or Jenny would have called me if something had happened to the baby.

Denny immediately sputtered, "No, no, they're fine. It's nothing like that. It's just . . . have you seen the tabloids recently? Been on any gossip sites?"

Relief immediately flooded me. I shook my head at Kellan's concerned face, letting him know that everything was fine with Anna. Focusing on the first part of his reply, I told Denny, "Oh good, you freaked me out." I frowned as I puzzled his question. Tabloids? "No, I've been way too busy for that. Why would I care about tabloids and gossip sites?"

Denny sighed. "Crap. I would've called you sooner, but I just noticed today. It's still pretty quiet around here, and I don't think anyone's put two and two together yet, but I thought you should know what's out there, so you could be prepared."

More confused than before, I tentatively asked, "Prepared for what?"

Denny paused again, and my anxiety started resurfacing. "You mentioned earlier in the month that the guys were doing a collaboration with Sienna Sexton."

His voice held a trace of awe and wonder in it, a feeling I completely understood; it sort of blew me away too. But I didn't understand why he was changing the subject, and my voice came out agitated. "Yeah, what does that have to do with tabloids, though?"

As I watched Kellan swerving his way through traffic, a slight frown on his lips as he listened, Denny said, "Does Kellan . . . hang out with her?"

My frown deepened. "No. She's not even here. She went back to London after recording her part of the song." Pulling my gaze from Kellan, I bluntly asked my ex, "What's going on, Denny?"

He sighed. "There's a picture of Sienna and Kellan that's circulating the Internet. It's all over the magazines too. No one seems to know who Kellan is yet. It's mainly his back in the photo, but there is some serious buzz about Sienna and her new mysterious . . . boyfriend."

My jaw dropped so far I thought it might have to be surgically reattached. "Boyfriend? Wait, what picture?"

Denny's exhale was sympathetic. "I don't know. Looks like they're walking into a restaurant together. She's holding onto his arm. He's smiling and looking down at her. It's all very . . . convincing. Are you okay?"

My mind blanked, then I remembered the photographers outside of the place we had gone with Sienna for dinner. They'd been snapping pictures of all three of us as we'd been walking into the restaurant. Sienna had invaded Kellan's personal space a bit before we'd walked through the doors, but I'd been in the picture too; Kellan was holding my hand the entire time. But of course they wouldn't show that. I was a nobody. Sienna was a celebrity. And Kellan was now her new mysterious boyfriend. They were already linked . . . and no one knew about the single yet. What would happen when they did know? My stomach dropped as the car pulled to a stop.

"It's not what it looks like. I was there, you just can't see me." As I whispered that to Denny, I felt irony wrapping around my throat, sealing it shut. Hadn't I wanted to be invisible, to not let Kellan's spotlight shine on me? *Be careful what you wish for.* I was now invisible. "I have to go, Denny. Bye," I mumbled into the phone.

"Kiera, wait, are you okay?"

I disconnected the line without answering him. No, I didn't think I was okay. As Kellan shut the car off, I stared in shocked silence at my phone. What the hell just happened? In the public eye, Sienna and Kellan were dating? Did this change anything for me? No, not really. It didn't matter what the public thought was real; I knew what was going on. It still churned my stomach, though.

"Kiera, are you okay?"

Kellan's concerned words matched Denny's. Feeling light-headed, I looked up at him. "I'm fine," I whispered.

He frowned. "Honestly, you're fine?"

I groaned internally, really hating our honesty-at-all-cost pact at the moment. "I don't know what I am."

Kellan nodded. "Okay, can you tell me what that was about? Maybe we can figure out what you feel together."

I bit my lip and held up a finger, so he knew I would speak when I could. Kellan grabbed my hand and patiently waited. As he rubbed his thumb over my wedding ring, the shock of Denny's revelation passed through me, and I truly did feel okay. Not great, but okay.

As I turned to face him, his brow furrowed even deeper. He'd taken off his sunglasses, and the worry emanating from behind his midnight blue eyes was nearly palpable. "Talk to me," he whispered.

Feeling a little silly, since I knew where his heart was firmly planted, I smiled and shook my head. "Denny was just concerned about me because there's a photo of you and Sienna running rampant on the Internet. Everyone on the planet thinks you're her new 'unknown' boyfriend. Apparently, the photo is convincing. Denny didn't directly say so, but I think he thought you were stepping out on me." I started to laugh, until the thought of Kellan actually cheating on me with her strangled the sound. I had to swallow three times to ease my throat.

Kellan's eyes unfocused as he looked over my shoulder. "Photo?" His gaze immediately snapped to me again. "You know I'm not, right? I'm not interested in her . . . at all. You know that, don't you?"

Nodding, I cupped his cheek; it was warm from the sun beating down on us. "I know," I whispered. Snapping myself out of the dark mood that had settled over the car, I asked him, "Should we go get this photo shoot over with?" I forced a smile to my lips and humor to my voice. "Maybe you can request a duck for the background?"

Kellan was frowning at me as I got out of the car. "Kiera—"

I put my hand up to stop whatever it was he felt he needed to say. "I'm fine. Honestly. Can we just . . . not talk about this anymore? It doesn't matter anyway. It's not true."

Kellan hesitated, then nodded and got out of the car.

We met up with the rest of the band in a large studio building. A huge backdrop of billowing white fabric covered the far wall floor to ceiling. People were buzzing around everywhere—adjusting lights, moving reflective panels, smoothing the backdrop, manning stations that were overflowing with hair and makeup supplies that rivaled my sister's.

As the five of us watched the chaos in stunned silence, a tiny man in skinny jeans and a turtleneck pointed our way. "Ah, the talent arrives." I couldn't tell by his voice if he was being complimentary or condescending.

Loosely holding a camera in one hand, he snapped his fingers with the other; a buxom blonde was instantly at his side. Staring at our group through slim rectangle glasses, he waggled his fingers and told her, "Fix them."

The blonde glanced over at a group of women hovering around the makeup stations. As if they were all silently being commanded by their queen, they instantly turned from their beauty supplies and started swarming our way. Kellan frowned. Griffin grinned.

As the busty blonde strode up to him, Kellan murmured, "I don't think we need—"

She thrust out her hand, silencing him. "Name's Bridgette. I'll be taking care of you today." Grabbing his hand, she yanked him toward the vanity.

"I really don't think we need—" he tried again.

Shoving him into the seat, she had her fingers through his hair before he could finish his second objection. Even though a gorgeous woman tangling her fingers through his locks wasn't my most favorite thing in the world, I had to smile at the look of petulance on his face. The photographer walked over to us while Bridgette debated how best to beautify my husband.

Running his finger and thumb along his goatee, the photographer told her, "Not too much on this one. He's fine as he is." His gray eyes traveled down Kellan's body. "Have him see wardrobe first, though."

With that, he shuffled off to inspect the rest of the band. Kellan sighed.

By the time Bridgette and her merry maids were finished with the D-Bags, I had to admit that they looked good. Every single one of them was stunning, even Griffin. But Kellan . . . was drop-dead gorgeous. Smoldering. My jaw dropped when he stepped in front of the plain backdrop. He'd come into the studio wearing loose, faded blue jeans and a white T-shirt. They'd dressed him in slim jeans that were frayed in all the right places, and they'd layered his basic white shirt with a dark brown leather jacket. It was tight to his body, so it looked more like a fitted shirt, and it was zipped open to his mid-chest. It stopped right above his waist, so that his entire studded belt was visible; a trace amount of skin was visible too. It was . . . hot. His hair was usually a rumpled, sexy mess, but Bridgette had flawlessly styled it so that every strand was in the most appealing place possible. There was this one strand hanging down by his eye that just about did me in.

He looked the part of the sexy, bad boy rock star that worried my father on a daily basis, but he was frowning as he walked over to me.

"You look great. What's wrong?"

"I'm wearing makeup. I feel like an idiot."

I examined his skin, but I couldn't really tell that he was wearing anything, maybe just some definition around his eyes; the blueness was popping out at me so much that my heart was beating a little faster. "I can't even tell. You're fine."

He started to run a hand through his hair, then stopped himself. I couldn't help but notice that his ring was gone. "I'm wearing eyeliner . . . and I'm pretty sure she put lipstick on me."

My smile was impossible to hide. "You look incredible . . . darn near delectable."

Cocking his head, Kellan wrapped his arms around me. "Yeah? Would you like a bite?" As I felt heat staining my cheeks, Kellan glanced around, then leaned down to my ear; the smell of the leather jacket mixing with his scent was intoxicating. "We could disappear for a few minutes."

His grin was decidedly inappropriate when I pushed him away from me. "I think Bridgette would have my head if I messed up her handiwork."

Probably ruining whatever Bridgette had done to his lips, Kellan sucked on his bottom one as his eyes roved over my body. "Yeah, but just think about it . . . every time you see the album cover, you would know, without a doubt, that *you* put that smile on my face."

His hands ran over my backside, gently squeezing, and as my eyes rolled back into my head, I briefly considered ducking into a vacant room . . . somewhere . . . but I heard the photographer snap his fingers, and my eyes flashed open.

"Let's do this, people!" he called out.

Kellan let out a low laugh as he separated from me. As he moved away, his hand trailed down my arm. I grabbed his fingers, leaned forward, and planted a kiss on his makeup-covered cheek. Feeling the absence of his wedding band, I asked him, "Where is your ring?"

He patted his pocket as he frowned. "Label doesn't want us to advertise that we're not single." He rolled his eyes. "Apparently sales drop twenty percent if we're off the market. Or so Frank says." He pointed at the photographer, who was tinkering with something on his camera.

Kellan hesitated a minute, then looked around. Giving me a devilish grin, he reached into his pocket and pulled out his ring. Glancing around like he was breaking the law, he quickly slipped it on his finger. "What the fuck do I care what people think, right?" His face sobered. "I do care about that photo with Sienna, though. I'll take care of it, Kiera."

I shook my head and was about to tell him that it didn't matter, when he was suddenly pulled from behind by one of Frank's "helpers." Once Kellan was manhandled into position, Frank started snapping away. It made me smile that in every shot, Kellan's ring glimmered just a little bit. It was his small display of rebellion against the system.

After about three dozen photos, the session was done. I was glad I didn't have to pick which one was going to grace the final cover; I was sure they were all going to be breathtaking. Looking relieved that it was done, Kellan kissed my cheek and murmured, "I'm gonna go change and wash this shit off my face."

As I was giggling at him, Griffin stepped into our circle. Smoothing down his leather jacket, he asked Kellan, "Hey, you think they'll let us keep these clothes?" He smiled over at me; my skin crawled. "I am *so* getting laid tonight."

The irritation inside me quickly boiled over into righteous indignation. Narrowing my eyes to pinpoints that would surely pierce his unfeeling heart, I bit out, "You make me sick!"

Griffin blinked; he looked both confused and annoyed. "What's your problem?"

Balling my hands into fists, I resisted the urge to clock him. "You're about to have a baby with my sister, and you're still putting your . . . Hulk . . . into anything that lies still long enough. It's disgusting!"

Hands on his hips, Griffin stepped in front of me. "I'm a rock star. I'll fuck anything I want to fuck. It's what we do."

Shaking my head, I looked from Matt, to Evan, and finally to Kellan. None of them acted like Griffin did. "No, it's not."

Griffin looked over his shoulder at Kellan and rolled his eyes. "Oh, please. Just because you pussy-whipped him doesn't mean you can pussy-whip me." He swung his gaze back to mine. "Besides, it's not like Anna isn't out banging every guy that she wants to. And do you see me getting all bent out of shape about it?"

I knew he had a point, and I knew I had no business saying anything, but he was just so . . . ugh! "She's not like that anymore. She hasn't been with anyone but you since she got pregnant. You're the only man she talks about now."

Griffin looked surprisingly astonished by that. "Really?" He seemed to mull it over for a second as he looked around at everyone staring at us. Then he returned his eyes to mine and tossed his hands in the air. "It's just fucking. What's the big deal?"

I could only shake my head at him. "You're both going to be parents, Griffin. That's a life-changing event, one that Anna is scared to death about. And here you are, living it up, still banging babes left and right. Do you even care about what she's going through? You enjoy having sex with Anna, but do you care about my sister at all?"

Griffin stared at me blankly, his face expressionless. After another pause he gave me a derisive snort. "I was just joking. Relax the fuck up, Kiera." With that, he stormed off to the changing rooms.

Matt, Evan, and Kellan all watched him leave, then Matt turned back to me with wide eyes. "I can't be sure, but I think you just gave him food for thought." He held his hand out to me, and I shook it with a laugh. "Nicely played, Mrs. Kyle." Matt winked at me then clapped Evan's back. Lightly chuckling, the pair strode off after Griffin.

After everyone was gone, Kellan slung his arm around me. "It's adorable that you still try."

I smirked up at him, then glanced down at his jacket. "Griffin did ask a good question. Think they'll let you keep the clothes?"

I let my gaze wander down to his strategically torn jeans. Breath warm in my ear, Kellan muttered, "I don't need to keep them . . . they're just in the way."

I closed my eyes, instantly picturing warm skin, light moans, and soft lips. When I opened them, Kellan was walking away from me, but still watching me. His eyes simmered with heated promise, and when I inhaled, my breath was shaky. God, he was attractive.

Chapter 10
Buzz

The release date of the album was set for the thirteenth of September. The first single was going to be the song they recorded with Sienna. There was already a huge buzz about it, especially once word got out that the mysterious man in the photograph was the lead singer of the band featured on Sienna's new song. I wasn't sure how it happened, but the tabloids figured out who Kellan was and ran with the story of two young musicians falling in love while recording their duet. Rumors of their relationship popped up everywhere. Now that it had been brought to my attention, I couldn't seem to escape it—TV, grocery store magazine racks, the radio. I'd seen or heard about the damn photo fifty million times already. Okay, it was an attractive photo. They'd captured the moment right when Kellan had been politely smiling down at Sienna, and she was smiling back up at him. I couldn't successfully pull off a profile shot, but Kellan and Sienna looked just as good from the side as they did straight on; it really wasn't fair.

For some reason, everyone was excited about this imaginary blossoming romance. And everyone was eager to hear what sound these two impossibly attractive people would produce, which instantly made me think that the label was the one that leaked Kellan's name. Hell, it wouldn't surprise me if they'd been the ones to tell the photographers where we'd been going to dinner that night. Anything to drive up interest.

Kellan had tried his best to squelch the rumors. After the photo shoot, he'd called Sienna on the drive home. It floored me that Kellan had Sienna Sexton's number in his cell phone. Weird. Even weirder, Sienna had Kellan's name in her phone; she instantly knew who he was when he called her.

"Hi, Sienna, this is Kell—" He paused. "Yeah, it's me. Hi." While he laughed, I tried in vain to hear her side of the conversation. All I got was Kellan's, though. "Have you seen that photo of us? Yeah, that one. Have you said anything yet? Made a statement or something?" He frowned as he listened. "People are linking us . . . romantically." His brows drew together. "Well, I think it's a big deal." He splayed his hand like she was in front of him. "Because I'm married, and I don't want this perception out there that you and I are—"

Kellan glanced over at me and shook his head. "No, not officially, but we still consider ourselves husband and—" His frown returning, he swung his eyes back to the road. "Look, can you just say that we're only working together, and our relationship is purely professional?" He smiled. "Okay, thank you."

Once he hung up, he told me, "She said she'd take care of it."

"And you think that she will?"

He looked over at me, his sunglasses hiding his expression. "Of course. Why wouldn't she?"

I didn't want to tell him, but we'd agreed to honesty, so, sighing, I did. "Because I think she's interested in you. Because I think she *wants* the two of you to be linked. Because I think it creates a stronger buzz for the single if the two of you are together. And because I think she is very good at manipulating public perception to get what she wants."

Kellan was silent after I said that, which made me think he, at least in part, agreed. After a long moment he said, "And you think what she wants . . . is me?"

Leaning my head back on the seat, I closed my eyes. *Who wouldn't want you?*

Surprising me, Sienna did release a statement shortly after Kellan's phone call, explaining that she was currently single and loving it, and that the man in question was "Merely a close friend who is working on a project with me that the fans are going to love!"

While she'd done what Kellan asked, I wasn't sure if that explanation helped anything or not. No one seemed to believe that "close friend" really meant "close friend." They all assumed it was code for "we don't want to announce our relationship yet." It certainly fueled the hype for the single. I'd known Kellan's first album would be exciting, but I had no idea there'd be so much energy around the release, energy fueled by rumors and speculation about Kellan and Sienna's personal life.

Jenny, Kate, and Cheyenne listened to my concerns with sympathetic ears. My sister told me not to worry about it. When I'd asked her if she'd seen the photo yet, she told me, "That? Oh, yeah, I saw it a week or so after I got back. Kellan looks superhot in that pic, by the way!" She sighed. "Too bad he's not turned more toward the camera. They really should have waited to get an exit shot."

Remembering that Thing 1 had cleared the sidewalk before we left the restaurant, I snapped, "Why didn't you tell me the minute you saw it?"

Anna let out a long, low exhale. "Because I knew you'd freak out, and I knew the picture was nothing."

"They're linking them as a couple, Anna." Lying on my bed, I stared at the chandelier above my head. "That's not nothing."

"Yes, it is. What do you care what the public thinks? You and I both know that he's not with her. Hell, I was there the entire time that she was there, and I know for a fact that nothing happened between them. This isn't a big deal, Kiera."

"It's weird." Seeing a rose petal on Kellan's pillow, I held it up and rubbed the silky petal between my fingers. This one was a coral color, from a fresh bouquet the maid had placed in the hallway yesterday. Kellan had gone for a run earlier, and left the petal in bed for me. He'd written the words *Back soon* on it.

Anna sighed again, but more compassionately. "It's only weird if you let it be weird. Don't get yourself tied up in knots over one harmless photograph. I mean, what's the worst that can happen?"

My sister was right, of course. But still, having the world at large hope for your husband to hook up with someone else was a little . . . heartbreaking.

A few weeks before the album dropped, the boys were slated to set off on a whirlwind promotional tour. They were hitting all of the biggest cities in almost every state in the continental U.S. Looking at their schedule was mind-boggling. It was a nonstop jumble of plane rides, radio interviews, and private performances. There were times when they were booked for appearances in three different cities in one day. I was exhausted just staring at the itinerary. If we could get through this, touring should be easy.

Their first stop on the promo tour was a popular radio station in Los Angeles. No, it wasn't just popular—it was the number one station in the city, and they were going to debut the single there while the boys were in the studio. My stomach was a swarm of butterflies. Even though I knew this song release was only going to fuel the flames of Kellan and Sienna's formulated relationship, I couldn't wait to hear Kellan's voice being broadcasted over the airwaves. It was such a surreal thought.

Knowing life was going to get very hectic very soon, Kellan and I savored every moment of quiet togetherness that we could. Kellan gave me a tour of the city, showing me some of the dive bars he and the D-Bags had played at during their time here. I could easily picture a fresh-out-of-high-school Kellan wowing the panties off of wannabe Hollywood starlets. It must have been very easy for him to line up "dates" down here.

Kellan showed me the touristy things too—Disneyland, Seaworld, the Walk of Fame—but my favorite moments were lounging by the pool at the record label's house. Especially when everyone else was gone and it was just the two of us. On a sunny mid-August morning, a few days before the chaotic part of Kellan's career kicked in, we were enjoying a private dip in the pool. I was leaning against the cool white steps that led down into the turquoise water, watching the tiny disruptive waves my legs made as I lightly kicked them in front of me. The smell of chlorine and sunblock filled my senses, and except for some birds squawking in a nearby tree, all was quiet. Knowing this peace wouldn't last, I savored it.

Under the water, a dark shape approached me. Hands ran up my legs, stilling them, as the submerged body swam right over mine. Stopping at my waist, Kellan lifted his head out of the water and crooked a grin at me. "Hey."

"Hey," I muttered, biting my lip. His hair was slicked back from his face, and beads of water rolled down his cheeks. The sunlight sparkled in his eyes, lightening the deep blue color. He was glorious, and for this one moment in time, he was all mine.

Sighing, I sat up and wrapped my arms around his neck; my legs automatically tightened around his waist. He sank to his knees, holding me in his arms in the shallow water. If contentment could be felt as a physical thing, like the warmth from the sun or a cool breeze on a hot day, then surely I was feeling it wrap around me right now as I laid my head on his shoulder and let myself be consumed by his presence.

Just as Kellan pulled back to look at me, the tranquility on his face matching mine, Griffin stepped out of the house. He walked over to the steps, frowned, and scratched his head, like he was trying to puzzle out how to do something. Then he shrugged and knocked on the railing that divided the steps.

Struggling to keep his face straight, Kellan peeked up at him. "Yes?"

"That dude from the record is here. Wants to talk to you."

Setting me down beside him, Kellan stood from the water. Rivulets ran down the lines and curves of his body. Beads of moisture were left in their wake; they clung to his skin like they were reluctant to leave him. I completely understood the feeling.

"Which dude?" Kellan asked.

Griffin shrugged, indiscretely checking me out. "I don't know. The uppity one in a suit."

Kellan stepped slightly in front of me. "Nick? The vice president of the label?"

Griffin raised his gaze to Kellan. "I don't know. Sure."

Kellan glanced back at me. The last time the VP of the label showed up, it had been to offer Kellan a major opportunity. I had a feeling that whatever he wanted now would be just as big. For some reason, though, my stomach dropped.

Quickly toweling off, Kellan threw on a shirt and I threw on some shorts. I'd prefer to meet with a bigwig fully clothed and fully dry, but my tankini top and wet hair would have to do for now. Best not to keep the man who controlled my husband's destiny waiting.

Griffin led us upstairs, to where we'd met with Nick and Sienna last time. As I was about to follow Kellan into the room, Griffin grabbed my elbow. I instantly tensed as I looked up at his face. A frown on his lips, he said, "Anna tells me you don't like me. That true? I thought we were cool."

Wondering why on earth Griffin wanted to talk about this now, I gently pulled my arm from his grasp. "We're . . . cool. Sure." *Stay out of my bedroom, don't touch me again, and quit fooling around on my sister, and we're great.*

His pale eyes hardened as he tucked some hair behind his ears. "You just totally lied." He folded his arms over his chest. "I'm not sleeping with you, so I don't really give a shit what you think about me, but I would like to know why you hate me, since I've been nothing but nice to you."

Nice? Is that what he's been to me? Stifling an eye roll, I glanced over Griffin's shoulder; I could see Kellan shaking hands with the "uppity one in a suit," Nick. I really wanted to hear what was going on in there, not engage Griffin in a pointless conversation. As I avoided answering Griffin's question, he added, "Is it because I said I wanted to get laid? Because I was totally kidding."

My eyes involuntarily narrowed into slits as I looked back up at him. "No, you weren't kidding. You're crude, obnoxious, and you're a bigger man whore than Kellan ever was!"

Griffin gave me a "yeah, right" face, which I forcefully made myself ignore. "You represent everything I hate about rock stars. The partying, the women, the sex. You're everything that I'm afraid Kellan will become!"

Griffin poked me in the shoulder. "So your problem isn't really with me. You're afraid of what Kell might do when you're not around, so your problem is *you*." He spread his hands out. "Anna's never asked me to not dick around. We've never been exclusive. She doesn't care who I have sex with . . . so why should you?" Raising his chin, he added, "And I'll have you know, I've only fucked about five people this year, and nobody since Anna told me she was knocked up. So, yeah, I do fucking care about her. I think I may even fucking love her."

He spun around and stormed into the room after that, and I could only stare at him in shock. Did I just get schooled by Griffin? That had to be one of the signs of the apocalypse. But . . . he did have a point. I mainly disliked him because I didn't want Kellan to be like him. And Kellan wasn't like him. They were night-and-day different. Griffin was just so crass. But so was my sister, and I loved her to pieces. Well, crap. Now I had to make an actual attempt to like Griffin. And, wow, he just said he loved Anna. That blew my mind.

I finally walked into the room, thinking that nothing Nick told me could shock me more than what Griffin had just said. Kellan was sitting on one of the couches across from Nick. Evan and Matt were sitting next to him, but there was just enough room for me. Feeling like I was completely disrupting the conversation, I walked in front of Matt and Evan to sit by Kellan. Griffin threw his weight down in a chair opposite us.

Nick paused in his pleasantries to wait for me to settle myself into Kellan's side. My cheeks heated as the blond, blue-eyed man tapped his thumb on his crossed leg. Even though it had to be ninety degrees outside, Nick was in a full suit. And an expensive one at that—Armani probably. His tie was bright red, a power color. He seemed pretty young to be a VP, mid-thirties at best, so I figured he was confident and driven, a man who was used to getting his way.

When I was situated, Nick gave me a brief smile. His calculating eyes took in my appearance, and he said, "Making good use of the home's amenities, I see." His eyes shifted to Kellan. "That's good. You'll need your rest now to get you through the launch."

Kellan eyed me and nodded. Before anyone in the room could ask what Nick wanted, he told us, "I have good news. Great news." Leaning forward, he clasped his fingers together. I noted the lack of a wedding ring. "Diedrick Kraus just agreed to shoot the video for 'Regretfully.'" When no one said anything, Nick smiled. "You have no idea who that is, do you?"

"Sorry, no," Kellan told him.

He waved off Kellan's apology. "Diedrick Kraus is the genius behind some of the greatest music videos of our times. He's exclusive. Hard to come by. We gave him a sample of your song, and he wants to direct it." Nick clapped his hands together. "No, he fucking insisted on it."

I blinked at the use of profanity by such a high profile person, but Nick quickly moved on. Pointing at Kellan, he said, "Diedrick's got a couple days available at the end of the month, Sienna's got a tiny break in her schedule, and we'll squeeze it in for you during the promotional tour." He lifted his hands to the sky. "I swear the stars aligned for this."

Kellan's mouth opened as he glanced at his band mates. "We're making a music video?" He looked back at Nick. "Do people even still watch those?"

A small frown turned down the executive's lips before he righted them again. "Yes, they do." His smile widening, he leaned forward so much I thought he might topple off of the couch. "And we've got an opportunity here to stir the hornet's nest."

Confusion marred Kellan's features. "I have no idea what that means."

Nick shook his head. "It means we're going to cause some serious buzz with this video. Ever since the public caught wind of you and Sienna in that photograph, there has been a firestorm of interest. Everyone is curious about Sienna's new man."

"I'm not her man," Kellan interjected.

Nick ignored him. "We're going to fuel the flames of Kellan and Sienna madness, and ride the hype to the top of the charts."

My heart sank as I looked at the eager expression on Nick's face. I wasn't sure what he meant by that, but I was sure I wasn't going to like it. His demeanor radiating caution, Kellan asked, "What do you mean?"

Excitement on his face, Nick spread his fingers. "We're going to play up the romantic portion of the song, make the video seriously hot. Naked bodies, deep kisses, moaning and groaning, whatever we can get away with." Winking at Kellan, he added, "Anyone who watches it will immediately need to take a very cold shower. The buzz around you and Sienna is going to skyrocket."

I wanted to stand up and tell this scheming moneybags that Kellan would be doing no such thing, but knowing it wasn't my place right now to say anything, I grit my jaw tight. Kellan's face went the opposite way; his mouth dropped open. "The song is about a breakup," he sputtered, mystified.

Nick nodded, steepling his fingers under his chin. "Yes, and what great breakup didn't start off with a fiery romance?"

The room was silent for a moment. Evan and Matt were staring at me, making my cheeks heat. Griffin was ear-to-ear smiles. I wasn't sure if he was happy about filming the music video in general, or about watching Kellan film a scene with Sienna that would make him need "to take a very cold shower." Probably a little of both.

Finally, Kellan told Nick, "I'm married. I can't do that."

Griffin volunteered immediately. "I can!"

Ignoring Griffin's outburst, Nick gave Kellan a hard stare. The look on his face made goose bumps break out on my arms. Definitely a man who was used to getting his way. "I'm not asking you to have an affair with the woman. That part is entirely up to you." He smirked and flicked a quick glance at me. As I glowered, his eyes returned to Kellan's. "I'm merely asking you to film a *fictional* video with her to a song that you've already recorded, a song that we own, by the way." He pointed at Kellan with laced fingers, and a chilly smile touched his lips.

Leaning back, he placed his hands on his thighs like he was going to stand. "Entertaining the masses is part of your job description, and sometimes that includes acting. If we'd known you were . . . unwilling . . . to do that, we wouldn't have signed you." Standing, he narrowed his eyes and took an intimidating stance above Kellan. "All I'm asking for here is for you to buck it up and do your fucking job. And in case you couldn't tell . . . I'm not really asking." His voice was ice cold; it raised the hair on the back of my neck and filled my stomach with lead. Shifting his focus from Kellan, Nick walked out of the room.

There was a thick layer of silence in the room after Nick left. You could have heard a pin drop. Not surprisingly, Griffin was the first to pop the stillness with a loud exclamation. "Dude! You get to film-fuck Sienna Sexton! High five!" He held his hand up in the air, palm exposed to Kellan in congratulations.

Still shocked at this turn of events, I had no comment to Griffin's statement. Kellan glared at the bassist, then seemed to realize that was pointless and shifted his gaze to the floor.

He was silent one moment longer, then abruptly stood. Staring at the door Nick had strode through, Kellan's face hardened. "This is bullshit."

He stormed out of the room, harshly brushing past my legs in the process. Evan stood in his wake. "Kellan?"

Kellan didn't answer him. Hands clenched into fists, he disappeared without a backwards glance at his band. We all stood and stared after him. "What's he gonna do?" Matt asked the room. No one had an answer, and a feeling of dread pricked my skin. I knew exactly what he was going to do. What he always did when things got too hard. He was going to run.

I took off after Kellan, the guys following after me. Kellan wasn't on the stairs, and for once the stunning view didn't impress me. Nothing was impressing me at the moment, because I was pretty sure I was going to have to do something I did *not* want to do. I was going to have to convince Kellan to make out with another woman. No, not just make out. Simulate a love scene. Somehow, that made the whole thing ten times worse.

I found Kellan in our room. Face stormy, he was shoving shirts in his bag. My empty bag lay beside his. A part of me wanted to start packing up my stuff in silent concession. That would be an infinitely easier choice. Instead, as Evan, Matt, and Griffin trailed into the room behind me, I asked, "What are you doing?"

Kellan glanced up at me, his eyes blazing. "Pack your stuff. We're going home. I'm done."

Griffin immediately burst out, "What the fuck, Kellan?"

Evan put a hand on Kellan's shoulder, trying to calm him down; Kellan shrugged him off. Matt quietly countered with, "We signed a contract, Kellan. We can't just walk away."

Kellan glared at Matt, snapping, "Then they can fucking sue us! I'm not whoring myself out for them. I'm going back to Pete's. Are you guys coming with me or not?" Knowing that all of this was ultimately because of me, my heart thudded in my chest in a painful staccato rhythm.

Griffin gaped at him. "You are the biggest fucking pussy—"

Kellan took two aggressive steps toward Griffin, silencing him. Evan stepped between the pair, his hands on Kellan's shoulders. Matt put a hand on Griffin's chest, keeping him back as well. There was suddenly so much tension in the air that I knew nothing constructive was going to happen while everyone was present. Kellan needed to be calmed down, not confronted. And, at the moment, I was the only one who could do it. I hated that the power was in my hands. Especially when going back to Pete's sounded like a fabulous idea.

Keeping my eyes locked on Kellan, I told the guys, "Could you give me a moment with my husband, please?"

Kellan snapped his eyes to mine, his expression still searing. Evan stepped away from Kellan, squeezing my arm before he left. Matt dragged Griffin out of the room, but not before Griffin shouted, "You talk some fucking sense into him, Kiera! *This* is bullshit!"

When I heard the door close, I took a step toward Kellan. With no one else in the room, Kellan's anger and frustration turned solely toward me. I was prepared for it, though; I'd been on the receiving end of vicious snarls from Kellan more than once. "You gonna call me a pussy too? Think I ought to go ahead and fuck Sienna, just to prove a point?"

I cringed a little, but let it slide off of my back. His anger wasn't really directed at me. Walking over to him, I grabbed his hands; they were still clenched into fists. "Kellan . . . you can't give up now."

Kellan pried a hand loose and pointed at the door. "Were you in that meeting? Did you hear what they want me to do?"

Grabbing his hand again, I nodded. "Yes, and it's okay." Just saying the words made my stomach tighten, but it had to be done.

Kellan gaped at me. "It's . . . okay? How is me 'film fucking' someone okay?"

Stepping into his body, I trailed my fingers up his arms and wrapped them around the back of his neck. He was rigid at first, but he gradually relaxed as I held him. "Well, all right, maybe 'okay' isn't the best word. The thought of you being with her is actually a little horrifying." Kellan's body started to tense again and I immediately told him, "But it's a necessary evil."

Kellan shook his head, his arms wrapping around my waist. "No, it isn't necessary." His anger draining, he rested his head against mine. "I don't want to hurt you. And I don't see how any of this won't hurt you."

Pulling back from him, I said, "And I don't want you to give up on your dream because of me." He shook his head, looking away from me, and I grabbed his cheek. "You're so close, so very close. Just do this one thing to jumpstart your career, to jumpstart the guys' careers. Then, when you've completed your contract terms and you're the most sought-after band in the industry, find another label. *That* will prove your point much better than . . . you know."

Kellan smirked at me, and I smiled at seeing some of his humor coming back. But the seriousness in his face returned as he exhaled a long breath. He didn't say anything for several seconds. I could see that his mind was churning, debating, and I gave him a moment to process everything that had just been thrown at him. When he did finally speak, his voice was quiet. "I don't want to let the guys down, I really don't, and I see what you're saying. But when I said I was through with other girls, I meant it. You're it for me. I don't want to touch her."

Stroking his skin with my thumb, I murmured, "I know. And I love you so much for that. But this doesn't have to affect us if we don't let it. You're still my husband. I'm still your wife. Acting like you feel differently on camera doesn't change any of that. Okay?"

Kellan slowly nodded, then sighed. "I'm not even sure if I can film a love scene with someone other than you."

Running a hand through his still slicked back hair, I husked, "Sure you can. Just pretend she's me. It wouldn't be the first time."

I gave him a wry smile so he would know I was teasing. He gave me a devilish grin in response. His face sobered instantly, though. "You really want me to do this?"

I bit my lip. Did I want this? No. I didn't want his body anywhere near Sienna's. But I wanted success for him, and for him to walk away now, over . . . *this* . . . seemed too great a price for him to pay. I nodded. "Yes, I do." Kellan closed his eyes, nodding once. I gave him a light kiss, hating that someone else would be touching that miraculous mouth soon. "And, Kellan"—his eyes cracked opened—"if this is really going to happen, I need to be there. I need to watch it."

His eyes sprang all the way open. "No."

I nodded, kissing him again. "I have to, Kellan."

"Why?" he murmured against my lips. "Why would you want to see that, Kiera?"

Because I'm a glutton for punishment. "Because it will be so much worse in my head if I don't."

"Kiera," he pleaded. "I don't want this, but if I have to do it, then I want you as far away from it as possible." Pushing my shoulder back, he squatted to look me in the eye. "I don't want to hurt you, and if our roles were reversed, I couldn't handle watching you with another man."

I gave him a sad smile as I whispered, "You already did."

Kellan's mouth parted, and a wave of sadness swept over his features. It broke my heart. "I love you," I told him, bringing my lips to his.

Doing my best to erase his sadness, I tasted his lips over and over. His breath eventually picked up as the passionate fire inside him sparked under my administrations. His hands came up to tangle in my hair, holding my head tight to his. His tongue passed over mine, teasing me, and a low moan disrupted the stillness of our bedroom. An erotic noise burrowed up from Kellan's chest, mixing with my breathy exhales. My impatient hands ran up and under his shirt. I needed all of the barriers between us gone. *Now.*

Kellan broke apart from me to help my eager fingers remove his shirt, then instantly sought my lips again once the material was free. I traced the lines and valleys I knew and loved so well. My fingers found the deep V of his lower abdomen, and I tugged on the waistband of his damp shorts, needing those off as well. Kellan helped me there too, and before I could really comprehend it, he was standing before me, completely bare and not the least bit self-conscious about it.

His eyes were hooded as mine roved over his body. He was mine, heart and soul. Sienna may have a brief moment with him—a very tiny, tiny, taste—but she would never have the full magnificence of this stunning man. I almost felt a little sorry for her. Almost.

Breath fast, I wrapped my arms around his neck and pulled him onto the bed. As soon as my back hit the mattress, he started stripping away my clothes. My damp shorts met up with his on the floor, my tankini briefs immediately following. His hands slid up my sides, taking my top with it, and I groaned when my chest was free. His mouth enclosed a nipple, and I delighted in something I knew he wouldn't be able to film with her. Not for a PG-13 music video.

Kellan, also reveling in what was his and his alone, moved my leg up his hip and immediately sank himself into me. I clutched him tight, groaning "Yes" a lot louder than I probably should have.

Kellan sucked in a breath through his teeth. "God, Kiera . . ." he murmured, before he began to move.

Maybe it was the wildly swinging emotions we'd been experiencing just before this moment, but every cell in my body felt energized, alive, and tingling with sensation. And I didn't hold anything back as Kellan and I rocked together. This was ours, and Sienna would never share in it. And even though she was nowhere near us, I let out my joy as if she could hear it.

Kellan did too. And it wasn't too much longer before we were both approaching the crest, our bodies lightly shaking, slightly damp from the exertion. As my climax burst through me, I raked my nails down Kellan's back. Not strong enough to draw blood, but strong enough that he would feel it for a while. My little reminder of who we were and what we'd been through. Kellan buried his head into my shoulder. He cried out as his body tensed, then released. I groaned as I felt him, heard him, was one with him.

No, Sienna would never have this. Her pale imitation of this moment wouldn't even come close.

Breath heavy, Kellan rolled to my side. I kissed his cheek and he smiled with his eyes still closed. I watched him as he recovered, mesmerized by him. His smile never faded, but his breathing slowed and evened. When his face relaxed and his breathing turned shallow, I realized that I'd relaxed him right into sleep. That gave me a strange feeling of euphoria. But then I started thinking about Wednesday, and my earlier bravado faltered. Maybe Sienna wouldn't have *this* moment with him, but was I opening a can of worms by giving them a taste of each other? Was I making a monumental mistake by allowing this to happen?

Stealthily sliding out of bed, I folded the comforter around Kellan so he was covered. After putting on some clean, dry clothes, I picked up Kellan's phone from his nightstand and silently left my sleeping husband. When I got back into the main lounging area, I was expecting to see the other D-Bags waiting around to hear what Kellan had to say. But then my mind replayed the last few moments and I realized that Kellan and I had both been quite vocal, and they probably already knew that I had successfully changed his mind. My cheeks heated, but I ignored the embarrassment. At least no one had walked in on us this time.

Griffin came out of the community bathroom as I was making my way to the deck. I froze when I saw him, wondering what obscene comment he was going to make. With a look of pride on his face, he pointed at my closed bedroom door. "Did you just fuck him into submission?" He held his knuckles up to me. "Nice."

My initial reaction was to scoff, call him a pig, and storm off in a mortified huff. But I'd promised myself that I'd make an attempt to be nice to him, so I shrugged and made myself talk to him. "I changed his mind about doing the video, but . . . now I'm worried that I made a mistake."

As Griffin ran a hand through his hair, I realized that this was the first conversation I'd ever really had with him. It was odd, and I had no idea what he would say, or if I would find it offensive or not.

He made a dismissive sound with his lips. "Nah, don't worry about it. You guys aren't into sharing, so he won't really do anything with her." He winked at me, and I strangely found it charming instead of creepy. "Kell knows what side his dick's buttered on."

Feeling oddly reassured by his absurd expression, I muttered, "Thank you . . . I think."

Griffin laughed as he left the room. "Anytime, Kiera."

Shaking my head, I began to wonder if I'd just entered into some strange sort of opposite world, where I encouraged Kellan to make out with other women and found advice from Griffin comforting. What else was going to happen? Anna and Denny hook up and decide to get married and raise Griffin's baby as their own? That made me laugh as I walked outside. No, no way would those two ever get together. Anna would eat Denny alive.

Palms sweaty, I started pacing near the railing. I had a view of the backyard pool and could see Matt and Evan near the edge, both of them chatting on their cell phones, most likely to Rachel and Jenny. Probably telling them the exciting news about their music video with Sienna Sexton. Internally groaning, I pulled up Kellan's contact list and scrolled through until I found Sienna's number. Kellan was mine, and I wasn't just going to roll over and let somebody else nab him from me.

She picked up almost immediately. "Kellan, what a wonderful surprise. What can I do for you, love?"

I bristled at her charming term of endearment, but tried not to think too much of it. She called everyone "love." "Um, actually, this is Kiera. I'm borrowing Kellan's phone."

"Oh, well, what can I do for you, Kiera?" There was a small trace of disappointment in her accent, but she covered it well with bubbly politeness.

"I just wanted to let you know that I talked Kellan into doing the music video with you," I said.

She couldn't hide the disappointment this time. "He didn't want to do the video?"

I sighed, hating that I had to placate both sides. "He wasn't okay with the direction the director wanted to take it, filming a love scene with you. But I told him . . . it was fine."

"He had to ask for your permission? How . . . quaint." Her amusement was evident. Sienna Sexton probably didn't ask permission for anything.

I hesitated, not really wanting to defend Kellan's actions. And that wasn't really the point of my phone call anyway. "Well, the fact that he's agreed to do it is all that's important. But, I just wanted to know . . ." I inhaled a deep breath. *Here goes nothing.* "Did I make a mistake encouraging him to film an intimate scene with you? You're used to getting what you want. Woman to woman, be honest with me . . . do you want my husband?"

There was a long pause on Sienna's end. My stomach twisted into a knot that I was positive I would never be able to untangle as I waited for her to say yes. When she did, it came as no surprise. "Yes, I do . . . but not in the way you think." I blinked. That *did* surprise me. Call me naïve, but what other way was there?

Sienna continued before I could ask. "My career has hit a . . . stalling point. I need Kellan to refuel it. Being in the tabloids with him just this short while has done wonders for me. I've already received collaboration offers from other musicians, and just yesterday, I was handed a movie script." As her words sank in, she added, "So, yes, I want him . . . desperately . . . but only for the buzz."

"Oh," I murmured.

"Did you need anything else from me, love?"

My mind still spinning, I told her, "No . . . that was it. Thank you for being honest."

"Sure thing. Ta-ta!" She clicked off the line, and I stared at Kellan's phone for long seconds. Did I believe her? Could I trust her? Only time would tell.

Chapter 11
The Madness Begins

There was an energy in the air the night before the single was to be released; it even alleviated Kellan's qualms about his upcoming sex scene with another woman. It was a tangible feeling that invigorated the band. Like kids waiting for Christmas morning, they were all giddy, excited, restless. As usual, the guys burned off their excess energy by tormenting Griffin. While I feverishly worked on my book, the boys played one of the Halo games. Without verbalizing it, Griffin somehow became everybody's "target." There were a lot of swear words flying around as Griffin slowly lost his cool.

"Quit fucking killing me, Matt!"

Eyes glued to the screen, the blond guitarist did his best to not smile. "Sorry, didn't mean to."

"Evan, dude! You nailed me in the head!"

Evan also tried not to smile. "Oops, my bad."

"Kellan, Jesus Christ! Learn to fucking aim!"

Kellan wasn't as successful at hiding his glee as his band mates started laughing. Griffin threw down his controller. "You guys suck!"

He stormed off to his room, and everybody started laughing. They stopped when Griffin reappeared a minute later with two full-sized Super Soakers. "Die, fuckers!" he yelled before letting loose on the four of us.

I screamed and covered my laptop as best I could. The guys let out surprised exclamations and took off, each one darting toward a different point of retreat. Griffin let out a maniacal laugh, then took off after Matt, who'd dashed downstairs. Evan emerged from his room, bucket of water balloons in hand. At least, I hoped they were water balloons this time. He chased after Griffin, letting out a fierce battle cry as he went. Laughing, Kellan followed after him, eager to join the assault. I shook my head as I listened to the chaos. *Men.*

There was yelling, banging, cursing, and at one point, Griffin loudly exclaimed, "The hose is cheating, Kellan!"

When they finally resurfaced forty-five minutes later, each and every one of them was soaked. Setting my laptop on the table beside me, I crossed my arms and murmured, "If you think I'm cleaning up the mess you just made downstairs, you're dead wrong."

Smirking, Kellan shook his head. Water droplets fell from his hair, shirt, and his pants. "Don't worry, the maid comes in the morning."

With that, he twisted his body and revealed the bucket behind his back. I had just enough time to tell him, "Don't you dare!" before he flung the contents at me, drenching me with ice cold water.

Screaming, I shot up off the couch. "You are so freaking dead, Kellan Kyle!"

Griffin pursed his lips as I ran past him to get to my soon-to-be-deceased husband. "Oh, she gets feisty when she's angry. That's hot!"

Needless to say, we all stayed up much too late, considering the boys had a radio show interview at the crack of dawn the next day. Then after the interview, we were immediately getting on a plane to start the first leg of the D-Bags' chaotic promo tour for their album. *Ready or not, let the madness begin.*

When we all ambled downstairs in the morning, bags in hand, Nick was already there waiting. Lifting an eyebrow, he asked, "All ready?" Kellan nodded, yawning. His yawn contagious, I yawned too. Nick smiled at us, then indicated a woman to his right. She was a tall, leggy blonde who was dressed as posh as he was. Her face was stern, cold, impassive, not much in the way of warmth. "This is Tory. She'll be your handler for all of the media interviews."

Tory extended her hand to Kellan. "Nice to officially meet you. Nick has told me many nice things," she said. While her face remained expressionless, her eyes darted down his body.

Kellan shook her hand, asking Nick, "A handler?"

Tory answered his implied question about what a handler was and why he needed one. "I'm the one that lined up all of your interviews. I'll be checking you in for each one, and letting the interviewers know which questions you won't be allowing. I will also end the interview if I feel they are not respecting the label's wishes."

Kellan frowned. "The label's wishes. Not mine, then?"

Tory cracked a smile. "Nick has requested that you not talk about your personal life." Her steely blue eyes shifted to mine, and the implication was all too clear. *Do not mention that you're married.*

Kellan snapped his head to Nick. "You don't want me to talk about my wife? So when they ask what's going on with Sienna and me, I'm supposed to say . . . ?" He raised his hands in the air to punctuate his lingering question.

Nick gave him a calm smile. "You tell them no comment, and let them stew on that any way they want to."

Kellan dropped his hands. "'No comment'? I might as well tell them I'm screwing her brains out on a daily basis."

Nick shrugged. "I'm not asking you to lie, I'm merely asking you not to respond, and not to divulge any . . . unnecessary information." His brow arched in challenge. "Think you can handle that?"

The guys all gave Kellan cautious glances while I grabbed his hand. If Kellan didn't deny the rumors that were already beginning to run rampant, then he would be, in essence, confirming them. He was already bothered by the risqué music video he'd agreed to shoot with Sienna. Even though abstaining from talking about his personal life was nowhere near the realm of him sticking his tongue down another woman's throat, somehow this seemed just as intrusive. I wasn't sure what he would say to Nick.

Nick seemed unsure as well, adding, "We're expecting this single to reach number one. When your album releases in a few weeks, I wouldn't be surprised if it debuts in the top twenty. All of that is due, in large part, to the fact that the public has a soft spot for you and Sienna together. You've become a couple in their eyes, and that sort of publicity cannot be bought. When your video hits the market, the buzz around you two will be out of this world. And if we don't take advantage of that, ride the tidal wave while it lasts, we'll lose the momentum and your album will sink like a rock to the low hundreds. It's a very crowded market, jammed-pack full of talented, gorgeous individuals, such as yourself. Do you want to start your career on top of them, or on the bottom of them . . . crushed into the oblivion of obscurity?" His face smug, he raised a shoulder in a seemingly unaffected way. "The choice is yours."

While he looked like he didn't care, his tone of voice made it very clear that he did. It was also very clear that the choice wasn't Kellan's at all. The choice was Nick's, and he'd already decided Kellan's fate.

Jaw tight, Kellan said nothing. Not sure what Kellan should do, I gripped his hand tighter in silent support.

Belongings in tow, we headed outside to where a pair of gigantic, solid black SUVs with dark tinted windows were waiting. I thought the twin vehicles looked a little conspicuous, like we were spies or government agents . . . Men in Black. If the company was going for subtle transportation, they would have been better off hiring a stretch limo in this town. But if they wanted everyone to wonder who was inside, then I guess they made the right choice.

One of the drivers greeted us and opened the rear door of an SUV before leaning over to pick up our bags. Kellan tried to help him, but was politely shooed away. Our driver was wearing a crisp suit, and even though it was early in the day, he had on dark aviator sunglasses. He and the other driver stuffed bags and instruments into both vehicles while we climbed in. Griffin immediately grabbed the front seat while Matt and Evan took the middle row. Kellan and I climbed into the third row; it was a little cramped, but still comfortable. The inside of the vehicle was luxurious—digital controls on everything, tan leather that was soft as silk, and light and dark wood inlays along the dash, console, and door frames that created an eye-catching pattern when taken in as a whole. It had that new car smell, like it had been detailed recently. Despite its size, it was a nice ride.

Thankfully, Nick and Tory got into the matching vehicle in front of us. When all of our stuff was packed away and settled, the driver climbed into the car and we were off. The vehicle buzzed with excitement, and not just because of the upcoming radio interview—the guys were stoked about what Nick had said in the house, that the album could debut in the top twenty.

Matt and Evan twisted to face Kellan. "Do you think he's right? Do you really think we'll debut that high?"

Kellan shrugged, his face impassive. "I don't know, maybe." His voice was small as he turned his head to stare out the window; he was right beside me, but he seemed a million miles away.

From the front, Griffin shouted, "Hell, yeah, we'll debut in the top twenty! Number one with a bullet, baby!"

Matt and Evan turned back around and leaned forward to have a conversation with their more eager band mate. Kellan sighed and laid his head against the glass. Concerned, I rested my chin on his shoulder. "Hey, you all right?"

Lifting his head, Kellan wistfully gazed at his friends. "I just . . . I wish I could be as excited about this as they are." He looked down at me, his brow furrowed. "I feel like I'm letting them down, because I'm not enjoying this."

I clasped his hand with both of mine, clicking my wedding ring over his. "It's different for you than it is for them. The label is asking you to do uncomfortable things. They understand. Well, Matt and Evan understand." I gave him a small grin, hoping to lighten his mood.

The corner of his lip twitched up, then he frowned. Scrunching down so our heads were closer together, he lowered his voice. "It's just so . . . fabricated. I don't see why there has to be all this hoopla-

crap about some sordid imaginary romance. I just wish that the record and the music were enough to stand on their own. If we're going
to make it, I want it to be because we're good, not because people are
enamored with . . . my personal life." He frowned, like the idea of him
being this ideal, desirable, rock-god dreamboat was absurd, like he
still didn't see why anyone would want more than a fleeting moment
of passion with him. It wasn't absurd. He *was* a desirable boyfriend,
a desirable husband. But I did see Kellan's point.

"And it *will* be about the music, Kellan. The high debut may be
because of your celebrity status, but the album will stay there because you guys are amazing—one of the best bands I've ever heard."

Kellan cocked his brow. "One of?" I rolled my eyes at him and
Kellan glanced up at the other D-Bags. "They've stood by me through
so much." He looked back at me, sorrow in his eyes. "They were my
family when I had . . . nobody. Literally nobody. And when I left
everything in Los Angeles to move back to Seattle, they gave up everything we had down there to follow me, to stand by my side." He
ran a hand over his face. "I owe them so much."

Dropping his hand, he stared at his lap. "We would have gotten signed ages ago if we'd stayed in L.A. I took this life from them
once. I won't do it again." Sighing, he looked up at me. "I owe them
the chance to be big, to really make it in this business. And Nick is
right about one thing. It's a packed industry, and Matt, Evan, Griffin—they don't have anything else to fall back on. It's this or nothing for them, so . . ."

Seeing where he was going, I murmured, "So . . . no comment?"

Kellan nodded. "I don't want you to be offended, or worried, or
hurt. And I'm not having an affair, or even interested in having an
affair. If all I have to do to make a . . . splash . . . is film a video and
keep my mouth shut during interviews, then I owe them that much."

Inhaling a big breath, I considered the ramifications of Kellan's
silence. The world would think he was with Sienna. There would be
so much gossip about them, I probably wouldn't be able to escape
it. I'd be bombarded with tales of elicit rendezvous, endless secret

weddings, and a plethora of pregnancy rumors. But they would just be rumors. And Kellan wouldn't be anywhere near her. Ignoring his scandalous public persona but still getting the warm, affectionate man behind it all seemed like a fair compromise. I'd never wanted to be in his spotlight anyway.

"I understand, and it's okay."

Kellan blinked. "It is? If someone asks me if I'm married to Sienna," he lifted our laced together wedding rings for emphasis, "and I say nothing, that's okay?"

I shook my head. "Being a celebrity isn't as simple as it once was. It used to be that you had a talent, people liked it, and you excelled accordingly. Now, it's almost more about being adept at traversing the social waters. You need talent, and the ability to sway the public. Nick is good at the manipulation part, and you're really good at the talent part. You let him do his thing, you do your thing, and I'm sure everything will work out fine."

Kellan gave me a grin that finally looked happy. "I can't tell if you're wise . . . or still naïve."

I lifted my chin. "I'm gonna say wise." Kellan laughed while a thought struck me. "Oh . . . will we still be able to get married? With a ceremony and everything?" I chewed on my lip. "Because my mother will have an aneurism if I try to back out of it."

Leaning in, Kellan kissed my cheek. "We're still getting married, Kiera. He only told me not to say anything to the public." Cupping my cheek, he whispered, "And I plan on saying 'I do' just to you." He grinned. "And a few hundred friends and family."

Groaning, I laid my head down on the seat. "Oh God."

Kellan poked me in the ribs. "You'll be fine. If I can do all this, then surely you can manage pledging your undying love, devotion and fealty to me in front of a small crowd."

Pulling back, I snorted. "Fealty?"

Kellan gave me an innocent smile. "What? Isn't that one of the vows?"

When we arrived at the radio station, there was a swarm of people waiting outside. They were being contained on the sidewalk by thick velvet ropes while a couple of fresh-faced college kids wearing colorful lanyards around their necks walked back and forth along the other side of the rope—interns for the radio station, probably.

We all gaped at the assemblage as we watched Nick's car pull up and drop Tory off. A second man exited her vehicle, grabbing two guitar cases from the back; the boys were going to play one of their songs live this morning, after the station debuted their single with Sienna.

"Are all those people here for us?" Evan murmured.

Nobody knew, so nobody answered him.

When our car pulled up and let us out, the crowd of women started screaming. It hurt my ears from inside the car. I couldn't believe that so many people were hanging around a radio station at this hour of the day, just hoping to catch a glimpse of the D-Bags. When Kellan stepped out of the car, the earlier outburst was silent in comparison. My ears were ringing when I stepped onto the sidewalk.

Kellan held his hand out for me, his small act of rebellion since Nick hadn't given him any warnings on PDA, but Tory pulled him forward before I could grab his hand. The front doors of the station opened at the same time, and Sienna walked out, flanked by her two bodyguards. Not realizing she would be at this interview, I was surprised to see her. I guess most of this crowd was here for her then. God, she wasn't going to be on the entire promo tour, was she?

Kellan seemed surprised as well. Especially when Sienna flung her arms around his neck and kissed each one of his cheeks. Glancing around, I noticed the scores of cell phones capturing every moment of the "lovebirds" reconnecting. The crowd of girls jumped up and down in their excitement of watching this breathtaking couple in action. Farther back in the crowd, I noticed a man with a high-end camera. He had to be paparazzi or with an entertainment magazine; he had a satisfied smile on his face as he clicked photo after photo of Kellan and Sienna.

And Sienna, ever aware of her surroundings, gave him the money shot. Swishing her long dark hair away so her face was clearly visible, she leaned up and finished her greeting with Kellan by placing a light kiss on his lips. Kellan pushed her away as he stepped back from her, but the damage was done—I was positive the photographer had captured the moment. As Kellan started to scowl, Sienna pulled him into the building and away from the tittering public's sight.

Feeling more like the band's forgotten assistant than the lead singer's wife, I hurried after the group. Kellan broke apart from Sienna in the lobby. "What was that?" he snapped at her.

Sienna patted his cheek. "That, love, was marketing." Kellan's frown deepened and Sienna's full lips turned down. "Relax. It's a harmless photograph to titillate the masses."

Kellan shook his head. "Not on the lips. They belong to my wife."

Sienna smirked, and maybe it was my imagination, but I swear she was thinking, *They won't be in a couple of weeks when you're rolling around in bed with me.* "Fine. How's your voice? Ready to do an acoustic set to kick off our single?"

That took me back. I hadn't realized that they'd be performing the new single this morning. By the blank look on Kellan's face, he hadn't been told about it either. The plan had been to play one of their album cuts once the station played the official recording of the duet. Guess Sienna had decided that she wanted a flashier debut of her sure-to-be-hot song.

Before Kellan could answer her, Sienna swept him away. Kellan looked back at me as I followed behind the entourage. I gave him a warm smile, letting him know I was fine. Sienna and her bodyguards practically shoved him into an elevator while the rest of the D-Bags got into a second one. When both sets of doors closed before I could get into either one, I sighed and waited for an empty car with some of the interns. They giggled and I heard one intern whisper, "Holy crap, Sienna's boyfriend is hot!"

Not seeing Tory anywhere around, I told them, "They're not dating." Nick hadn't told me that *I* had to be silent, although it was implied in every stare he gave me. I didn't want to spoil anything for

Kellan by outing that we were married, so I didn't say anything else, but it didn't matter anyway. The interns looked back at me with humoring eyes; they clearly didn't believe me.

When I finally got up to the floor of the building that the radio station recorded from, Kellan and the boys were already in the room with Sienna, wearing headphones and making small talk with the disc jockeys. Their instruments were brought in and set up, and I quietly sat on a stool in the corner, absorbing it all.

The boys all introduced themselves. After Kellan said his name, the female DJ told him, "It really is a shame you are so unattractive, Kellan. It's a good thing we're on the radio, ladies, because you would all genuinely feel sorry for this man." By the sarcasm dripping off her voice, the entire listening audience had to know she was joking.

Kellan smiled and shook his head. She groaned. "Dear, God . . . you're killing me."

Her male counterpart held his arm out like he was holding her back. "Easy, there, let's not's mount the artists before they've even had a chance to play."

The female DJ let out an exaggerated sigh. "I'll try, but you know me and good-looking men."

The male DJ immediately added, "The whole city knows about you and good-looking men." Kellan and the guys chuckled and he added, "Sienna Sexton is also here in the studio, and, on behalf of men listening everywhere, can I just say . . . you are smoking hot!"

Sienna flashed him a smile as she brushed her dark hair away from her shoulder. "Ah, thank you . . . so sweet," she cooed in her charming accent.

Pointing a finger between Sienna and Kellan, the woman asked, "So, Sienna, Kellan, rumor has it the two of you are an item?"

Sienna looked at Kellan right as he looked at her. Kellan grit his jaw. Sienna shrugged and said, "Well, he is quite . . . edible." She looked back at the woman jockey with a conspiratorial grin. "I would have to be an idiot to pass him up, right?"

The woman leaned in, like she and Sienna were best buds. "Is that a yes, then?"

Sienna gave her a coy smile, but didn't answer her. Probably hoping for something juicy that she could talk about later, the woman turned her attention to Kellan and said, "So, come on, give me the scoop, Kellan. What's going on with you and Sienna?"

Looking very uncomfortable, Kellan scratched his head. Tory was standing beside me, but she looked like a coiled viper, ready to strike out at the DJs if they asked just the wrong question, or at Kellan, if he answered in a way that the label didn't want him to. Just standing beside her pent-up energy made me nervous. Finally, Kellan murmured, "Ah . . . our single is out today . . . the album drops in September."

Both DJs laughed at his sad attempt to change the subject, knowing smiles on their faces. I felt a sharp sting jolt through my body, like a Band-Aid had just been ripped off of my soul. He'd done it. By dodging their question, Kellan had just confirmed his relationship with Sienna. Where that was going to go from there, I didn't know, but I knew it had just started. The match had been struck with Kellan's answer; I just prayed the resulting fire was small and easily contained.

Kellan looked over at me, an apology in his eyes. I kept up my encouraging smile. It didn't matter what the public thought. We knew the truth.

The DJs spent the next few minutes talking with each boy in turn. Evan seemed completely at ease as he gushed about Jenny. Matt seemed like he hated every second of being interviewed, and was even vaguer about his life than Kellan. Griffin ate up the attention like a starving dog downing its bowl of kibble. He told all of Los Angeles about his "availability" should any of them want a private performance. But then he went on to mention that he was about to have to kid with his girl. I had no idea if he was being serious about his single status, or if he was just playing up the rock star image. Either way, I was surprised that he mentioned Anna and his soon-to-be child.

The boys set up to play after that. Griffin and Matt both grabbed acoustic guitars while Evan sat behind a compact drum that one of the assistants must have brought in. Kellan stood at a microphone, looking comfortable and relaxed. I would be sweating bullets if I were him, about to perform to thousands of people, maybe hundreds of thousands if they broadcasted online. And performing acoustically was even more of a challenge; no searing electric guitar to hide your flaws. But Kellan was pretty flawless, so I knew he'd do well.

When the DJs gave them the go-ahead, Evan started the intro. Griffin and Matt joined in on their part with Kellan a few beats after them. The first portion of the song was quiet, but Kellan's smooth voice still filled the small space. When the song switched to a more emotional section, his voice was powerful, commanding, and yet heartbreaking too. As I knew he would be, Kellan was perfect. What the audience was now discovering about him was something that I'd known from the very beginning—Kellan was so much more than a pretty face. He had genuine talent.

Equally talented, Sienna nailed her part when it came up. The two singers were standing side-by-side, each lightly keeping time to the music with their bodies, but when the song switched into a battle of wills, the pair turned to sing directly at each other. Maybe it was the moment, maybe it was the song, maybe it was the look on Kellan's face as he sneered at Sienna, but I had goose bumps by the end.

I felt like clapping when it was over, but the DJs immediately started in on the praises, so I didn't. I wanted the whole world to hear how amazing the D-Bags were. And it looked like the world *was* hearing it. A computer screen in front of the male DJ showed a never-ending stream of text messages from listeners. The feedback was unbelievable. *"Wow! I can't believe that was live! Who are these guys, because I need to buy their album! Sienna was great, but Kellan . . . good God! If he looks half as good as he sounds, I might die right on the spot! D-Bag fan for life!"*

The accolades went on and on and on. Everyone was blown away. My chest was bursting apart, I was so damn proud of him!

The guys packed up, then said their goodbyes. Kellan was all smiles as we left the studio. Scooping me up, he twirled me in the air as members of our assemblage passed by. Sienna eyed us with a strange expression, but didn't say anything. He set me down by the elevators just as a car dinged open. Ducking us inside, Kellan hit the "close door" button before anyone else could enter. He waved at Sienna and Tory through the crack, then twisted to me.

A little boy grin on his face, he asked, "How was it?"

I shook my head, wondering if he was aware that my answer to that question was always going to be the same. Tossing my arms around his neck as the falling elevator made my stomach shift, I told him, "Amazing! Perfect! Wonderful! I could go on and on."

Pressing me against the back wall, Kellan murmured, "Maybe later," as he leaned in to kiss me. He stopped right before our lips met. I think I whimpered. Pulling back, he seemed concerned. "Sienna kissed me . . . I feel like I should bleach my lips before I kiss you."

Smirking at him, I pulled his mouth to mine. "I think I'll live."

As our mouths moved together, I silently wished that we were on the top floor of a very tall building. As Kellan's tongue brushed against mine, his hips pushing me against the wall as his fingers slipped under my shirt to caress the indentation of my lower back, I knew that no building on earth could have possibly been tall enough.

When the car stopped, Kellan released me. Face contrite, he whispered, "I'm sorry."

Feeling a little drunk from our short, heated moment, I responded with a laugh. "You don't ever have to be sorry for that."

Pulling me past the small swarm of people trying to enter the elevator, Kellan shook his head. "No, for earlier, in the interview . . . when I didn't say anything about you." Stopping us, he twisted to look at me. "I really wanted to."

Cupping his cheeks, I firmly told him, "Don't do that. Don't turn this moment into something you feel guilty about. I told you that I understand, and I meant it. You have to do what you have to do right now." Grinning wide, I added, "And did you hear the reaction? The listeners loved you for you in there. Once your album is released, you can do and say whatever you want, and it won't matter . . . because they'll love *you* . . . not you and Sienna."

My eyes watered as I stared at him. "You just gave an acoustic performance at one of the biggest radio stations in the city. Your single is going to be all over the airwaves soon. I am so incredibly proud of you right now."

Kellan's smile was glorious. "Will you marry me?" he whispered.

I laughed at his oft repeated question. Before I could give him my answer, the other elevator car arrived and Tory marched over with the rest of the guys. Wedging her way between us, she informed Kellan that he had more interviews to give and a plane to catch, so there was no time to dawdle. She did give him a few minutes to greet the fans outside, though.

Kellan was in his element as he chatted and signed autographs. Watching him talk to his fans, it was easy to see Kellan's genuine affection and appreciation for them. He laughed as they screamed and giggled, agreeing to sign anything they threw his way, and posed for pictures with as many of them as he had time for. There were parts of this business that Kellan didn't care for, but meeting his fans wasn't one of them.

Just as Tory snapped her fingers and told him it was time to wrap it up, a limo pulled up to the curb. For a minute, I thought it was there for us, but then Sienna emerged from the building. The gathered fans erupted as she waved and signed a few CD covers on the way to her car. When she passed by Kellan, she gave him a long, lingering kiss on the cheek. "See you later," she husked, just loud enough for everyone around to hear.

Kellan only had time to nod at her before she was whisked away. Kellan looked back at me and I shrugged. At least she hadn't kissed him on the lips again. Maybe she actually would respect his wishes.

The next several days were a blur of traveling, fans, interviews, acoustic performances, and Taskmaster Tory. I couldn't decide if having a handler was helpful or a gigantic pain in the ass. Everywhere we went she was right there, keeping everyone in line and on focus. Remembering some of the troubles Matt used to have when he'd solely managed the group, I did appreciate how difficult her assignment was—just wrangling Griffin was a full time job—but she had an edge of bitchiness about her that got on everyone's nerves.

And she was constantly interrupting tender moments between Kellan and I. Consciously or subconsciously, she found ways to keep us apart while we were in public. Our short second of PDA in the lobby of the L.A. radio station was the last moment we had for a while. We didn't even get to sit on planes together. But through the chaos, we still found time to appreciate each other. Kellan said we had to, otherwise none of this was worth it. I agreed. We passed romantic notes back and forth, and Kellan slipped me rose petal messages when Tory wasn't looking. I wasn't sure where he was getting the flower petals—hotel lobbies, street vendors, green rooms—but whenever he handed me one, it brightened my day. *You're hot, I love you, I want you,* and my personal favorite, *Marry me.*

It wouldn't surprise me in the least if Nick had instructed Tory to keep us apart on purpose. He wouldn't want anyone catching on to the fact that Kellan and Sienna weren't really an item. And that's what the world firmly believed after Kellan's L.A. radio interview. Combined with the photo of their momentary lip lock, the general consensus was that Kellan was "doing" Sienna; the gossip sites were smoldering with completely fake details of their hot relationship.

The buzz around them was so intense, I could almost feel the vibration in the air everywhere we went. Luckily, Sienna parted ways with the D-Bags after Los Angeles, so no more fuel was being added to the fire, but Kellan was still asked about her at every interview. Every time she came up, Kellan dodged the question as best he could. A week into the promo tour, the are-you-or-aren't-you question was so predictable, that Kellan and I started laughing about it when we did get a chance to be alone. It was all we could do at that point. Roll with it, or roll over.

Leaving the last interview for the day, Kellan laid his head back on the headrest of the rented SUV we were traveling in. "I'm so tired," he murmured. We were halfway through the tour, making our way up the east coast.

Resting my head on his shoulder, I grunted some sort of agreement. Endless shuffling around was surprisingly wearisome. I just wanted a hot bath, a good book, and a long nap . . . all with my very comfortable Kellan-pillow, of course.

Everyone else in the car was exhausted too. Matt and Evan were quiet as mice as they sat behind us, Griffin was sitting by the driver, snoring from what I could tell. Eyes closed, I halfheartedly listened to the radio. When a familiar song came on, I quietly started singing along. When I realized what I was singing, my eyes shot open and I stared at Kellan in shock. He looked over at me with a furrowed brow. "What . . . ?"

His voice trailed off as he heard it too. It was *his* voice coming through the speakers. Kellan twisted to the driver, leaning forward on the seat. "Hey, man, can you turn that up?"

The driver turned the knob and Kellan's voice boomed throughout the car. I squealed into my hands as I bounced on my seat. Matt and Evan started freaking out in the backseat. Griffin snorted awake, heard his bass line playing, and instantly joined in the ruckus we were making. I couldn't even hear the song anymore over everyone laughing and hollering.

Tory had told us that the D-Bags' song with Sienna was in heavy rotation all over the country, but we'd been so busy flying here and there and everywhere, that we hadn't heard it on the radio before. There was something surreal about hearing Kellan's voice coming through the speakers.

I turned to Kellan. "You're on the radio!"

Wide-eyed, he shook his head. "I know! What the hell?"

Tossing my arms around him, I squeezed him as tightly as I could. He was doing it. He really was doing it. And I couldn't have been happier. Seconds later, everyone was on their cell phones, calling someone to let them hear the tail end of the song. I was sure most everyone but us had already heard the song on the radio before—I knew my mom, Jenny, and Anna had, since they'd called me squealing about it afterwards—but this was the boys' first moment, and they wanted to share it. Matt called Rachel, Evan called Jenny, and Griffin called my sister. Kellan called his dad, and I . . . called Denny.

"Hey, Kiera," he answered, his accent warm. "You at a party or something?"

Plugging an ear so I could hear him, I shouted into the phone, "Can you hear the song on the radio?" I held the phone up to the front of the car, then pulled it back to my ear. "It's Kellan's song! He's on the freaking radio!"

I started laughing and could just make out Denny saying, "Yeah! I've heard it. They're playing it nonstop here."

As the song ended, the driver turned the radio back down. Cell phone conversations quieted to soft chuckles and exclamations of wonder. Kellan clasped my thigh as he talked to his family. I could see the glow in his eye, and could just imagine his father telling him how proud he was . . . and how amazing those words probably felt to Kellan, since he'd never heard a parent say them.

Now that I could hear better, Denny's words struck me loud and clear. "I saw the latest pictures running around. You, uh, okay with it?"

Wondering if Denny knew the public perception of Kellan and Sienna was unfounded, I told him, "They're not together, you know. The gossip sites are wrong."

Denny sighed, and I could easily picture him running a hand through his chunky, dark hair. "Yeah, that's what Jenny says too, but, uh, she's . . . in the minority. Most of the people I've talked to think Kellan and Sienna are hooking up. Sorry."

I frowned at this news. "Why would I still be with him if he was with Sienna?"

Denny hesitated, clearly not wanting to answer. Eventually, he did, though. "Kellan's . . . on the fast-track to becoming rich and famous . . . a celebrity. They assume you put up with it because of his status."

I scoffed. "That's not me. I don't care about any of that. If anything, it just makes everything harder!"

"I know, Kiera," he said soothingly. "That's why I don't really buy the rumors. Because I know you, and I know you wouldn't put up with him cheating on you." As guilt flooded me, he added, "We're a lot alike in that way."

Everyone else was finished with their conversations while I sat with my mouth open, not sure what I was supposed to say. In the end, I simply told him, "Yeah, I know." After a moment of silence, I added, "I have to go, but I'll call you later, okay?"

"Okay. Tell Kellan congratulations for me."

"I will."

Kellan was staring at me when I ended the call. Wrapping an arm around my shoulders, he said, "Gavin hadn't heard it yet." He let out a deep laugh. "I think he was just as excited as me. Hailey too." He wiggled his finger in his ear, like it was ringing.

Smiling, I held up my phone. "Denny says congratulations. He heard it the other day."

Kellan was all smiles, so I didn't mention the rest of the conversation I'd had with Denny. I'd tell him later. For right now, I wanted him to enjoy his moment in the sun. He deserved it.

Chapter 12
Video Lovin'

Two weeks into the promo tour, we flew back to L.A so the guys could shoot the "Regretfully" music video with Sienna. There was a feeling of melancholy in the air when Kellan and I returned to our room at the record label's house. And it wasn't just because we were dead tired. We'd been so busy promoting the album that the video had happily slipped our minds, but now it was all we could think about. Neither one of us was excited about it. Kellan had to pretend to make love to another woman. And I had to watch it, so that my mind didn't blow it up into some crazed, passionate porno. I'd always heard that filming love scenes was antiseptic and clinical. I hoped that was true.

On the morning of the shoot, I tried to alleviate the tension by waking up before Kellan and surprising him with a heart-pounding lovemaking session, but the reason behind the attack was all too obvious for both of us, and the intimate moment was laced with a fine layer of desperation.

Kellan was quiet on the ride to the studios. The rest of the guys were a bundle of energy and ceaselessly chatted about how excited they were to have an official video being produced. I was torn on the matter, both excited and full of dread.

The limo that Sienna had arranged for us took us right into a movie studio lot. Huge, long rectangular buildings were stretched as far as the eye could see. Each building had a number on it, and as the driver slowly made his way through the maze, I couldn't help but wonder what masterpieces were being filmed all around me. Just the thought plastered a huge grin on my face that made Kellan chuckle. That made my smile even wider; being amused by me was far better than being sullen.

We stopped at a building labeled B7. The driver let us out and pointed over to where we should go. It was unnecessary, since Sienna was standing in the doorway, waving at us with a glowing smile that could probably light up a small city. Dressed in a white tank top and skinny jeans that must have been molded onto her body they were so tight, Sienna looked flawless. Did she come in looking like that, or had she already been to hair and makeup?

Her long black locks sparkled in the sunshine as she approached us. Tossing her arms around Kellan, she kissed each one of his cheeks in greeting. "So good to see you all again," she cooed.

Holding his hand out for me, Kellan gave her a polite nod. Not at all bothered that Kellan and I were physically connected, Sienna looped her arm around his elbow and pulled him into the building. People in headphones were everywhere. There was so much activity that I instantly felt out of place just by standing still. I felt like I should be doing something, I just had no idea what it was.

As the boys gawked at the production before them, Sienna started showing us around. There were multiple sets inside the studio building, but we'd only be using a few of them. Really, we'd mostly be using two. There was a set that was dressed up like a stage. That one filled me with warmth and comfort—there were few things on this earth more natural than Kellan on a stage. The stage set would be used for filming the band all together. Their scenes would be small snippets that would be tucked around the heart of the video. And the heart of the video centered around set number two—a wide room with a huge bed as the main focal point. Seeing that set made my stomach churn in unpleasant ways.

Giving me a concerned glance, Kellan squeezed my hand harder. As Sienna sat on the bed, giggling in a coquettish way, I began to be filled with doubt that I could watch this. Just seeing her sitting on the mattress made me want to lose my stomach. But it wasn't real, and I could handle it. I'd handled much worse already.

Just as Kellan was about to say something to me, we were approached from behind. Dressed in his trademark impeccable suit, Nick strode into the room with a tall man with hair longer than my sister's. Pulled back into a neat ponytail, the blond locks almost reached his backside. Nick gave Sienna a snake oil smile, holding his arms wide open. "Sienna, baby, you look fantastic."

She melted under his praise, leaping off of the bed to give him a kiss on the cheek in greeting. "As do you, Nicholas."

Wrapping an arm around his pop star prodigy, Nick turned to Kellan. "Good to see you, Kellan." He lifted an eyebrow; the look oozed triumph, like he'd known all along that Kellan would agree to this.

Jaw tight, Kellan nodded. Ignoring the heat in Kellan's gaze, Nick indicated Ponytail Man. "Boys, this is Diedrich Kraus, visionary genius." He indicated the D-Bags. "Diedrich, this is Kellan, Matt, Evan, and Griffin." He squeezed Sienna's waist. "And you already know Sienna."

Trying to ignore the fact that I was completely skipped over in the introductions, I watched Diedrich smile at Sienna and then address Kellan. Reaching out for his hand, he spoke in a thick accent that I couldn't quite place. Swedish, maybe? "It is very excellent to meet you." Clasping both of his hands around Kellan's, he exclaimed, "The camera is going to love you! You and Miss Sexton are going to sizzle every piece of equipment in this place."

He was laughing to himself when a man in a clipboard came up to the group and announced that everyone needed to get to wardrobe, hair, and makeup. Sienna sauntered off in one direction while the boys were ushered a different way. Kellan kissed my cheek, telling me that he'd be back in a minute. I couldn't help but wonder just what his wardrobe would consist of. Hopefully he'd at least get to keep his underwear on.

While I wondered what to do with myself, Diedrich was called away and only Nick and I remained. Blue eyes hard, he turned to me and asked, "Are you going to be a problem?"

Lifting my chin, I tried to be as confident as possible. It was challenging, but I managed to pull off a firm, "No."

Nick gave me a lopsided grin. "Good. Because I'll have your ass tossed out of here if you mess with this production." Leaning in, he whispered, "And I'm pretty sure I could toss you all the way back to Seattle if I needed to. Just something for you to keep in mind, in case you find any of this . . . distasteful." Seeming like he didn't have a care in the world, Nick suddenly smacked his hands together. "Now, let's do this!"

Needing to do something with my nervous energy, I headed for the snack table. I was munching through my weight in carrots when Griffin strolled into the room. He was fully dressed—tight black pants, fitted gray shirt, loose leather jacket, and a studded wristband. I'd always found Griffin's personality distracting, but physically, he was a cute guy, and looked really good today. Standing by the set, he had a deep frown on his face. Looking around the room, he spotted me and started heading my way. Wondering if I wanted to talk to him right now, I popped another carrot in my mouth and debated moving on to the chocolates.

Grabbing a peppermint disc, Griffin quickly unwrapped it and popped it into his mouth. "This sucks," he murmured.

I sort of agreed, but I was surprised by his reaction, so I asked, "Aren't you excited to film your first video?"

Looking a little surprised that I'd acknowledged his existence, Griffin took a second before answering. When he did, he turned toward me, giving me his full attention. I had to fight the natural urge I had to take a step back. "Oh, yeah, I'm totally stoked. But they're filming the band scenes at the same time they're filming the love scene," he pointed over to the pristine bed, "so I won't get to watch Sienna Sexton roll around half-naked. It's not fair."

Wondering if maybe I should watch the boys instead of Kellan, I sighed, "Yeah . . . not fair."

Griffin seemed even more surprised that I agreed with him. I didn't necessarily agree with him, I just wasn't enjoying much of anything right now. Forgoing the vegetables, I grabbed a Kit-Kat and moodily chomped into it. Griffin watched me while he chewed on his candy. "You still freaked out about Sienna and Kellan?"

Wondering how on earth Griffin had become my confidant, I shrugged and nodded. "Yeah. I'm really not looking forward to this."

Swallowing the last bits of his candy, he nodded as he looked back at the bedroom set that filled me with dread. "Don't worry about it. It's just tonsil hockey . . . maybe some grinding." He looked back at me while I grimaced. *Grinding?* "Kellan's in such a pissy mood today, I doubt he'll even get a half-chub." My eyes widened. I hadn't even considered Kellan becoming aroused during this whole nightmare. But of course that was a possibility; blood flow wasn't exactly something a person could control.

Griffin rolled his eyes. "You should have heard him complaining in wardrobe." His voice went up an octave in a poor imitation of Kellan's. "Oh, poor me, I have to make out with a hot superstar. Women fawn over me wherever I go. I have fucktastic hair and an eight pack. Boo-hoo."

Twisting his lips in a look of contempt, he made an obscene gesture over his privates. I couldn't help the small smile that crept onto my face. He was rude and crude and said things I didn't want to hear sometimes, but somehow Griffin was also amusing in a comforting sort of way, and I actually did feel better. Lord, help me.

Griffin was dragged away a few minutes before Sienna showed up. Wearing a fluffy white robe, she looked incredible. As I wandered closer to the fake bedroom, Diedrich approached her. He indicated the crowd of people in the room, probably asking her if she wanted a closed set. Sienna looked around, shrugged, and shook her head. Nothing bothered this woman. Slipping the robe off of her shoulders, she handed it to an aide hovering nearby. My jaw dropped at the skimpy underwear set she was proudly wearing. Even though I'd seen her in a bikini that was about as revealing, there was something about underwear that made it ten times more provocative.

Someone in the back of the room whistled, and Sienna flashed a grin that way. Diedrich frowned and snapped something to another aide. I figured somebody just got fired. The bed on set only had a thin, silky sheet for a cover. An aide pulled the sheet back for her, and Sienna seductively crawled onto the firm mattress. As she settled into place, Kellan made his appearance. Like Sienna had been, he was wearing a robe. I stopped halfway across the room and watched him. He was looking down at Sienna sprawled on top of the satin sheet. There was a look on his face that was close to sadness. It made me want to hug him.

Sienna frowned at his expression and patted the bed beside her. Diedrich started talking to Kellan, maybe giving him pointers on how to make love to a woman—like Kellan needed pointers. I noticed that Diedrich didn't seem to be asking Kellan if *he* wanted the room cleared. I guess that consideration was only for females. Kellan was nodding as he started removing his robe. I chewed on my lip as his beautiful skin came into sight. He was wearing underwear, thankfully, but not boxers like he normally wore. Instead he had on low slung boxer-briefs. They looked . . . good on him. Some of the female members of the crew stopped and stared, but none of them were stupid enough to whistle.

Even from the distance between us, I could see that his chest was flawless . . . no tattoo. I guess the makeup department had covered it up. They probably didn't want my name all over the video since they were trying to promote a Kellan/Sienna love fest. His wedding ring was most likely gone too.

Before he crawled into bed with another woman, Kellan looked around the room. He spotted me instantly, and gave me a brief, troubled smile. This was hard for him. It made me feel better that it was. Griffin was right; Kellan didn't want this.

I nodded my encouragement and forced myself to step closer, to show my support. Kellan sidled up to Sienna in the middle of the bed and she eagerly wrapped her arms around him. I wanted to tell her that she didn't need to canoodle with him when the cameras weren't rolling, but Nick was eyeing me warily, so I kept my mouth shut.

Another assistant adjusted the sheet so it just covered the couple's hips. Lights were adjusted, and reflective panels were put into place, giving the pair of lovers mood lighting. Cameras whirred to life, red lights on the top of them indicating that they were ready. Large screens beside them showed just how the recording would look in the finished cut. My gaze flitted from the real couple to the couple on the screen. I found it easier to stomach if I watched the television. Somehow that seemed less real.

On the screen, Kellan seemed nervous as he lay on his back beside Sienna. She was propped up on her elbow, leaning over him, her dark hair brushing his shoulder. She didn't seem nervous at all. She seemed . . . ecstatic. Before I was ready, the director yelled action and the room silenced.

Kellan didn't do anything, he didn't even move. Sienna did. Leaning over, she touched her lips to his. I bit my cheek so hard I tasted blood. Kellan tentatively kissed her back, but it was nothing that anyone would constitute as hot. Awkward would be a better description. Every move of his lips against hers was clearly forced. Looking a little frustrated, Sienna climbed onto his stomach, grinding her hips into him as she did. Again, Kellan didn't react like someone in that situation actually would. All he did was lay there while she attacked him. Slightly frowning, Sienna tossed her hair over her shoulder, and dove in for his mouth. Thanks to the close-up on the screen I was watching, I could see her tongue dart between his lips. I could also tell from how little his jaw moved, that he wasn't letting her in. He was resisting; it was clear as day that he wasn't into this woman ravaging him.

"Cut!"

The sudden voice in the stillness made my heart skip a beat. I unfurled my hands and rubbed out the indents of my fingernails on my palms. I hadn't noticed, but I'd almost drawn blood there too.

Sienna rolled off of Kellan while he sat up. "He's not giving me anything to work with!" she yelled.

Kellan sighed and looked over at her. "I'm sorry. I'm trying."

"No, you're not, Kellan," I muttered. Worrying my lip, I hated the fact that I may have to give my husband a pep talk so he could successfully make love to another woman on film. Which was doubly strange, considering the fact that Kellan had already filmed a love scene or two in his lifetime. In retrospect, filming fake sex should have been a walk in the park for him. But he was clearly struggling.

As Nick bellowed at Kellan to get with the program, Kellan searched for me. Standing near the monitors, I nodded at him and mouthed, "It's okay." He sighed again and looked away.

Nick was shooting bullets into me with his eyes, like Kellan's tepid mood was entirely my fault. It made me think that maybe I should leave so this would be easier for Kellan. Just as I was considering going to watch the other D-Bags, Diedrich took a more proactive approach to his temperamental actor's reluctance. "Remove the bra, sweetheart." Much quieter, he added, "We'll get his blood pumping one way or another." Some of the men around him laughed. Staying put, I clenched my fists again.

Sienna shrugged and then removed her tiny black bra. She handed it to an assistant, not even bothering to cover herself up. How does a person get so much confidence that exposing their chest to a roomful of strangers didn't even faze them? It boggled my mind. As did the perfection of her bountiful breasts.

Tearing my gaze from her, I looked down at Kellan. His eyes were averted and he shifted on the bed like it was the most uncomfortable place he'd ever laid down in. Even though he was in a spot that most men would willingly chop off their right arm to be, I couldn't help but feel bad for him. He looked miserable.

Sienna either didn't notice or was choosing to ignore it. Climbing on top of him again, she pressed her bare chest into his. Someone on the set made sure none of her unmentionable parts were showing while Kellan stared up at the ceiling and exhaled in a long, even breath. What I wouldn't give to know what he was thinking right now.

After one last nipple check was done, an assistant grabbed Kellan's hand and placed it on Sienna's ass. Then they took his other one and placed it on the low ridge of her back—one of Kellan's favorite spots. Sienna smiled and whispered something to him. Kellan looked down at her face and gave her a tight smile in return. Everything about him seemed tense, like he couldn't relax . . . or he was afraid to.

Diedrich yelled action again, and Sienna leaned down to kiss him again. My heart instantly started beating harder, and I had to practice deep cleansing breaths. Kellan mildly kissed her back, his rigid hands glued into position on her body. It went on for a seemingly endless amount of time—Sienna trying her damnedest to turn him on, Kellan barely responding. He was so different than the passionate man I knew him to be.

Just when I thought Diedrich was going to yell cut again and Nick was going to evict me from the premises, Kellan sucked in a deep breath, closed his eyes, and started coming to life. It began with his hands, traveling over her skin, playing with the indent of her low spine. Then he started kissing her with genuine fervor. Before I knew it, there were flashes of their tongues meeting on the mega-sized screen right in front of my face. Lip smacking had been clear in the air for a while, but now that Sienna was getting a response from him, her light moans punctuated the silence. I felt warmth trickle down my palms as my fingernails finally cut through the skin.

Oh. My. God. What did I agree to let him do?

Now that his "actors" were getting into their roles, Diedrich started barking out commands—feel this, touch that, lift your head, kiss her there, roll her over. By the time Kellan had her on her back, he was completely and totally immersed in what he was doing. Tears stung my eyes, but I made myself continue to watch.

There was a camera at the foot of the bed as well as one beside the bed. The one at the foot was getting an impressive view of Kellan's defined back. The thin bed sheet was strategically placed low on Kellan's hips, just enough to cover his underwear, giving the viewer the illusion that he was naked. The sheet was so thin that it outlined his body, and every thrust he gave Sienna was completely obvious, and disturbingly graphic.

The camera beside the bed was the one getting a close-up of their faces. That one almost disturbed me more, because the expression on Kellan's face was one I'd seen before . . . when he was with me. Eyes closed, he was breathing hard in between frantic kisses. Sienna was squirming and groaning beneath him; it wouldn't surprise me in the least if she wasn't acting, if he actually *was* pleasing her. Was she pleasing him? Was he aroused? I had no idea, and it drove me crazy not to know. I think knowing would have driven me crazy too, though.

Kellan's lips played over hers. His tongue ducked into her mouth, then slid over to trace the outline of her ear. Upon request of the director, Kellan's fingers trailed up her side, stopping right over the breast closest to the camera, cupping it. I thought I'd seen enough to give me nightmares for a month, but then Kellan ran his nose up her throat, his tongue stretching out to lightly taste her skin.

An irrational jealousy swept through me. That was *my* favorite move! And he was using it on this . . . bitch! True, we hadn't set any boundaries on what he could and couldn't do today, but, out of re-spect for me, couldn't he stay away from moves that were used in *our* bedroom?

Words that my mother had spoken to me last Christmas leapt to life in my brain. *It takes a special person to be able to handle all of the attention he'll receive. Are you sure you're that woman?* I'm sure my mom hadn't anticipated this level of attention, but her point was suddenly a valid one. Could I handle this?

I started to turn away from him, disgusted, but then I remem-bered the look on his face when this all started. And I remembered the pressure he was under to do this—by his band, by the label, even by me. And then I remembered what I'd told him when I first talked him into this, when he said he couldn't do it. *Just pretend she's me.*

My eyes snapped back to him on the monitor. Was that what he was doing? Pretending she was me?

The director yelled cut, and Kellan froze and immediately rolled off of her. He kept his eyes closed as he laid his head back on the pillows. I could see his chest heaving, and as he swallowed, I swear I saw his jaw tremble. My concern for him instantly shot past my brief moment of jealousy. God, was he okay with this?

Sienna sure was. She was fanning herself like Kellan was the greatest thing since sliced bread. How could she be so oblivious to his turmoil? Was I the only one that noticed how tightly he kept his eyes closed, like he was afraid to open them? I wanted to run over to him, to tell him that I wasn't mad, but after some quick adjustments, Diedrich yelled action again, and the making out continued.

When the camera was rolling, Kellan seemed fine—he smiled, teased, tasted, appeared like he loved her—but the minute there was a break, he went rigid stiff, and kept his eyes sealed shut. I don't think he'd opened them once since he'd finally caved and kissed her. He must be terrified of what I thought, of what he thought he'd see on my face.

The filming took hours, and I was exhausted by the time they wrapped. Looking pleased as punch, Diedrich profusely thanked his stars and announced that he'd see everyone tomorrow. Kellan shot up off of the bed, grabbed his robe from a crew member nearby, and darted off the set before I could even call his name. For the first time since it began, Sienna looked sad as she put her robe on over her still-bare chest.

Ignoring her melancholy, I set off in search of my morose husband, but I couldn't find him. The place was a maze of hallways and people. I ran into the other D-Bags before I ran into him. Back in street clothes, a boisterous Evan wrapped me in a bear hug. "Kiera! You are not gonna believe how badass we looked!"

Setting me down, Evan searched the hallway. "Where's Kellan?"

As Matt gave me concerned eyes, and Griffin chatted with a nearby blonde that I recognized as Kellan's robe holder, I shrugged. "I don't know . . . he kind of took off."

Matt shrugged. "Maybe he needed air? Maybe he's waiting in the car?"

Not knowing where else to look for him, I nodded and let the guys escort me outside. Sienna waved as I passed by her dressing room. She was back in her street clothes as well, but her fit body was still seared into my brain. As was the image of Kellan's tongue running up her throat. My stomach was churning a little bit when we got outside, and I inhaled the fresh air like I'd been in a stagnant cave for decades.

Evan patted my back, then pointed at a black limo waiting for us. "Car's here. Let's go see if Kellan's waiting for you." Eyes moist, I gave him a weak nod.

The driver opened the door as we approached. My heart was thudding as all of the boys hopped inside. I heard Evan greet Kellan. So he *was* hiding in the car. I heard Griffin ask him how it was, and I felt faint. *It was awful. That's how it was.* I hesitated at the car door, not sure if I could stomach seeing Kellan yet. It was all just too . . . fresh.

Hating myself, I ducked into the car and purposely avoided looking his way. I stared out the window as the car started moving. I could feel Kellan's eyes on me, but I couldn't bring myself to look at him. It was the oddest feeling I'd ever had. I recognized how difficult it had been for him, I realized that he'd pretended she was me so he could get through it, and I wanted to comfort him, because I'd seen how badly he'd been bothered by doing it. And yet, at the same time, I didn't want to see his face. I knew if I did, I would see hers too. And I just couldn't handle it at the moment.

As the conversations in the limo died down, the tension built. Eventually, it was so thick I had to believe that even Griffin felt it. In fact, he started to ask, "Are you two fighting?" but someone elbowed him before he could finish saying it. Good thing, too, because I wasn't sure if we were or not. All I knew was I still felt ill, and I still loved Kellan more than anything.

I got out of the car the minute the driver opened the door and dashed upstairs, slamming our bedroom door shut. I had to see him. I couldn't possibly avoid him. I just needed . . . a minute. Grief welled in me, followed immediately by guilt. This was my idea, and I'd requested to watch it. All of this self-inflicted pain was unnecessary. I couldn't stop feeling it, though. Hearing the guys in the lounge area, I quickly walked into the bathroom and turned on a faucet so I could cry in peace. As I wiped a knuckle under my eye, I noticed my bloody palms from where I'd cut myself. Eyes wide, I scrubbed my hands under the cool water.

That's when the bathroom door was tapped on. "Kiera . . ."

There was so much pain in his voice, I shut off the water. I hic-cupped back a sob and stared at myself in the mirror, willing myself to calm down. This was only as big of a deal as we made it. I remembered the look of horror on his face, the clear reluctance in his first few kisses. Those images helped burn away the heated, passionate kisses that had happened later. I could do this. I could handle being with him. I could handle being his wife.

When my breathing returned to normal, his voice called to me again. "Kiera . . . please."

His voice hitched, and I heard a sound I'd never wanted to hear from him again. He was crying. Wiping my hands dry, I opened the bathroom door. He had his head in his hands, and his shoulders were shaking. I immediately wrapped my arms around him. He buried his head in my neck, murmuring, "I'm sorry. I'm so sorry. Please don't hate me . . . please don't leave me."

I held him tight to me, my tears threatening to resurface. Stroking his hair, I shushed him, whispering, "It's okay . . . I'm not mad . . . it's okay."

Eventually, he pulled back to look at me; his eyes were red, his cheeks wet. "How can you not be mad after what you saw? How can you not . . ."—his voice hitched—"hate me?"

I held his cheeks in my palms. "Who were you kissing today?"

He scrunched his brows, confused, then his expression softened. "You . . . I was kissing you. I was thinking about the first time we made love . . . after you told me that you loved me." His smile was radiant, even under the layer of pain still on his face.

I nodded, my smile matching his. "I know. I could tell . . . and that's why I'm not mad. I know you were with me . . . and I love you so much."

Kellan sagged in my arms as relief filled him. "God, thank you. I was so scared I'd just lost you. You wouldn't even look at me in the car . . ."

I held him to me, nestling against him. "I'm sorry. I just needed a minute. That was . . . intense."

Kellan pulled back to look at me. "Never again. I don't care what's at stake. I don't care who I have to let down. I won't ever do that to you again. You . . . or me. I'm done playing their game."

I sagged against him, my relief equally palpable. Kellan started bringing his lips down to mine, and I bristled. His eyes were wide when I pushed him back, the fear and tension instantly returning to his features. Cringing, I told him, "You . . . smell like her."

Kellan clenched his jaw, anger flooding his features. "Not for long."

Walking over to the shower, he turned it on high and stripped off his clothes. I smiled at seeing his familiar black boxers. I never wanted to see him in briefs again. Stripping those off, he climbed into the shower. I quickly added my clothes to the pile and climbed in after him. He gave me a brief smile as he handed me a bar of soap. "I want every trace of her off of me." Nodding, I got to work on cleaning his back.

When I got to his front, I scrubbed extra hard over his tattoo until the industrial strength makeup finally dissolved and my name sprang back to life. When it was visible again, I smiled and kissed the indelible ink. Kellan gave me a charming grin as he started working on sanitizing his hair. Locks full of suds, he gazed at me while I scrubbed his legs clean.

When I worked my way between his legs, his eyes fluttered closed and he told me, "That's the one part she didn't touch." He cracked an eye open, "But I do appreciate your thoroughness." Giggling, I reached up to kiss him. He put a hand out to stop me. "Wait. One more spot."

While I wondered what spot on him I'd possibly missed, Kellan grabbed the bottle of shampoo and squirted some in his mouth. I dropped the bar of soap as I gaped at him. "Kellan!"

Holding up his finger, he swished the horrid liquid around his mouth, then he made a face like he was about to vomit, and leaned over to spit it out. While he choked and sputtered, I started laughing. My eyes watered with merriment, and it felt so good. "I cannot believe you just did that!"

Kellan held his face up to the showerhead; bubbles foamed from his mouth and traveled down his chin. The tears ran down my cheeks as I laughed. Spitting and choking, Kellan scrubbed his tongue with the top of a loofah sponge. I had to hold in my stomach; my sides were starting to cramp.

Turning off the water, Kellan twisted his lips in disgust. "God, that was nasty."

Getting my breathing under control, I wiped the happy tears off of my damp skin. "That was *not* necessary, Kellan."

Kellan grinned as his adoring eyes searched my face. "Yes, it was."

Loving him more than I ever believed possible, I wrapped my arms around his neck and hopped up so I could wrap my legs around his waist. "I love you . . . even if you are insane."

Kellan was chuckling as he opened the shower door. "Good, because I think I'm going to be burping soap bubbles for a week." Tangling my hands through his hair, I gazed at him until I thought my heart might burst. He unwaveringly met my eyes. "I love you too, Kiera. Just you. You're my always."

Chapter 13
Plans

The rest of the video shoot was a lot less traumatic. Kellan shot his part with the band and finished up his scenes with Sienna—fully clothed, this time. The band footage was amazing. It was like being back at Pete's as I watched them rock out on the makeshift stage. Kellan was incredible as he poured his heart and soul into the microphone. And even though the audio recording wouldn't be used for the video, they were spot on each time they played.

The remaining bedroom scenes were actually interesting to watch this go round. Now that the painful, naked part of filming was over, I could stomach Sienna being around Kellan, even if she did still feel the need to greet him with a kiss on the cheek. The entire song was essentially one long ode to a romance gone south. Diedrich's vision of it was Kellan and Sienna reminiscing and arguing about their doomed relationship while walking around the bed where their naked bodies were in the throes of a "passionate embrace," as Diedrich called their sex scene.

The passionate part was already in the can, thank God, so they spent an entire day filming the breakup scenes. It was fascinating to watch. Kellan would lean down by one side of the bed, singing his line as he stared at nothing. In the final version, though, he would be staring at the image of himself making out with Sienna. At one point in filming, they had a couple wearing lime green jumpsuits hop into bed and simulate what Kellan and Sienna had done yesterday. It blew my mind that *that* was actually someone's job. Then they had Kellan drag his fingers down the Green Sienna's arm. In the final cut, one version of Kellan would be making out with Sienna, while the other version of him would be longingly running his hand down her arm. If I could look at it without revulsion, the video was going to be haunting and beautiful, much like the song.

During the angrier portion of the duet, Kellan and Sienna sang their parts directly to each other, both purposely ignoring the bed in the background, where their entangled bodies would be digitally added later. I had to say, I much preferred watching Kellan sing to Sienna with a sneer on his face than watching him run his tongue over her chin.

The song ended with Kellan and Sienna exiting the shot in opposite directions. Diedrich explained that he was going to use the portion of the love scene where Kellan rolls off of Sienna and lays back on the pillows with his eyes tightly shut and his jaw lightly trembling as the last frame of the video. He said the look on Kellan's face right then was a picture-perfect foreshadowing of the impending breakup, thus creating a never-ending video that could be watched in a continuous loop and still make sense. I would have to take his word on that, but thinking back over the pain on Kellan's face at that pivotal moment, I knew the scene was going to be emotionally powerful.

Looking like a proud father, Nick approached Kellan after the final day of shooting. Patting him on the shoulder, he proclaimed, "See, now, that wasn't so bad, was it?" Not waiting for Kellan to answer, he immediately added, "This video is going to be smoking hot! Scorch everything else out of the water." He rubbed his hands together and I could practically see the heaps of money in his mind.

Putting his arm around my shoulder, Kellan held me tight to his side, and said to Nick, "I'm glad you're happy with it . . . because I'm never doing anything like that again."

The smile instantly fell off of Nick's face. "Never say never. You're awfully new in this business."

His tone implied that Kellan and his band were also replaceable. I disagreed. Their single with Sienna was skyrocketing up the charts, and I was positive their album would do the same when it was released in a couple of weeks.

Kellan looked down at me, then back up at Nick. "No, I'm never filming anything like that again. I'm done. I made a promise, and I'm keeping it. I'll help you promote the album in any way I can, because I owe that to my band mates, but my wife comes first, and you need to accept that."

Kellan stared Nick down, and I felt a crackle of tension in the air. Nick didn't like being told no, but Kellan was done towing the company line. Maybe seeing Kellan's determination, Nick sniffed, then asked, "*Any* way you can?"

Kellan nodded. "Within reason . . . of course. I won't let you play with my personal life anymore. I prefer to be private, but I'm not staying quiet. If someone asks me about my relationships, I'm going to give them an honest answer." He leaned in, his voice dropping. "And I reread my contract. I know what my job entails, and I know what I have to do and *don't* have to do for you."

Nick smirked, like he knew something Kellan didn't know. After another moment, he shrugged and smiled like nothing was wrong. "Well, it's good to know where you stand."

Nick left with Sienna soon afterwards; both of them seemed a little pissy as they hastened off the lot. I felt great. Even when Taskmaster Tory returned and shuffled us off to the airport so the D-Bags could finish promoting their upcoming album, I was pleased. Kellan had put his foot down, he wasn't staying quiet anymore. I asked him to not mention me specifically, because I did *not* want that level of attention, but he told everyone who asked that Sienna was no more than a colleague he worked with and he was "in a relationship." Tory really didn't like that he was answering a question that Nick had given him specific instructions not to answer, but Kellan didn't care what she thought, or what Nick thought, and only smiled at her when she berated him after every single interview.

While the frantic pace of shuffling from one city to the next was chaotic and exhausting, no longer having the strain of filming a provocative music video hovering over our heads was refreshing. It was like a weight had been lifted, and Kellan and I both felt lighter. And since Sienna was starting her own cross-country tour, we probably wouldn't even see her for a very long time. Eventually the rumors would die off, and I wouldn't have to hear about how great a couple she and Kellan were. I was looking forward to that day.

At the end of the promo tour, the band had a bit of a break before their tour with Justin and Avoiding Redemption started, so we all flew home to Seattle. The last several weeks had been draining, and we all needed to rest and recharge. Being in my own bed had never felt so good; I slept for twelve hours straight the first night back, and Kellan slept even longer.

As Nick predicted, their single with Sienna skyrocketed to number one right before the D-Bags' album dropped—the album debuted at number nineteen. Even though Kellan had talked a big game with Nick, he was a little shocked by the album's success. I wasn't. I knew he'd be big once the world knew about him.

We all decided to go out to celebrate the band's success, and when we were in Seattle, there was only one place to go to celebrate—the place that had started it all: Pete's Bar.

Kellan and I held hands as we stared up at the bar sign glowing in the windows. It was almost hard to believe that it was just a little over two years ago that I'd first lain eyes on Kellan here. He'd seemed like such a player, and I suppose he was back then, but there was a surprising amount of depth to this ex-player.

As I was reminiscing, Kellan bumped my shoulder. "Did I ever tell you that I noticed you the second you walked into Pete's with Denny?"

I looked up at him, surprised. "Really? While you were playing? With all of those people in the bar?"

Walking backwards, Kellan pulled me toward the double doors to the large, rectangular building. "Yep. It was like an electric current zipped around the room when you stepped through the doors. Like I knew I'd never be the same from that moment forward."

He gave me a crooked grin. I rolled my eyes. "That did *not* happen. You noticed Denny. I seriously doubt you noticed me."

Kellan stopped walking, and I stepped into his chest. Being here, in the parking lot of Pete's with him, felt just as much like home to me as our cozy little love nest up the road. He said, "I could barely pull my eyes away from you. Just glancing at you made my head feel lighter, made my stomach . . . tingle. Watching you was life-changing."

I couldn't help but be moved by his words. Then I remembered his very suggestive performance. I gave him a sly grin. "And yet, you still managed to mentally undress *every* female in your audience."

Kellan laughed as he resumed walking. "Yeah, okay, I'll give you that one." He cocked a brow at me. "I did notice you, though. How could I not?"

As I mulled over his question, Griffin stormed in front of us. With as much dramatic flair as he could muster, he burst through the front doors. As I was usually on the inside of the room when Griffin made his grand appearance, it was a little strange for me to walk in *after* the egomaniac. Kellan let out an amused laugh as he grabbed the swinging door and held it open for me. I kissed him on the cheek as I walked through.

The bar erupted into a chaotic melee of cheers, shouts, and whistles. The volume made me cringe. Rachel too, as she walked in with Matt. Within seconds, the boys were surrounded by a cluster of new fans and old regulars. Kate and Jenny gave Rachel and me a warm greeting while the boys were swarmed. Standing away from the guys, by the bar with the girls, I marveled at how familiar and different Pete's was. This used to be a quiet place of solace for Kellan, but his newfound fame had followed him here, disturbing that peace some. Amid the noise circulating around the front doors, I heard whispers of Sienna's name while people gave me strange, confused glances. Guess she had followed us here too.

I caught up with Rachel, Kate, and Jenny until the hullaballoo around the boys started to dissipate. Then Jenny went over to wrap her arms around Evan. The gentle giant scooped the tiny woman up into a huge hug, holding her thighs as she wrapped her legs around his waist. I heard Evan call her his "Jujube," and smiled at whatever their private joke was.

Rachel quietly walked away with Matt as soon as he could politely escape the limelight. Griffin was pulled over to a table of fresh-faced college girls, and eventually only Kellan was left in the swirl of eager and curious patrons.

Turning to Rita, I decided to order the boys some beers while I waited for Kellan. Not surprisingly, Rita already had several bottles of their preferred beer on the counter. Nodding over at Kellan, the bleach-blonde asked, "So what's really going on with Kellan and Sienna? Because by the looks of that video, that wasn't their first roll in the hay . . . or their last."

Surprise washed through me at her question, not because she'd asked it, but because I hadn't realized the video had been released. That must be why Sienna's name was being spoken in hushed tones around me. Looking over at Kellan frowning as he scratched his head, I shrugged. "Don't believe everything you see." I returned my eyes to the appraising bartender. "He's barely seen or spoken to Sienna."

Rita smirked. "Honey, when he was in his prime, he barely saw or spoke to *any* of them."

I lifted my hand to show her my ring. "We're still together."

Rita whistled as she grabbed my hand. "Damn!" She glanced over at Kellan. "Boy does have good taste." As I watched the middle-aged woman lick her collagen-injected lips, I didn't think that was entirely true. There had been points in Kellan's life when his taste was quite questionable.

Once Kellan broke free from the inquisition, he made his way back to the band's traditional table. Sam had cleared it upon our arrival, and the displaced customers didn't seem too angry since bona fide rock stars were in their midst. Denny and Abby were at a nearby table having dinner. Kellan yanked their chairs over, making them sit with us, while Abby laughed at the move.

Now seated on my right, Denny and I clinked glasses and toasted each other. We took a moment to catch up on our time apart while the boys at the table bragged about the success of their album. Flicking a quick glance at Kellan, Denny leaned over to me and asked, "You guys still okay?" His tone was laced with concern.

Knowing he'd probably seen the video too, I contained a sigh. "You mean because of the music video, don't you? Yeah, I'm fine."

"You've seen it?" he asked, his voice hesitant.

"Not the final version . . . but I watched the boys film it." The memory of seeing Kellan grinding with Sienna threatened to overtake the present, but I pushed it back. We had a lot to celebrate, and I wanted to enjoy it. I wanted to stay in the moment.

"Oh." Denny seemed genuinely shocked. I could understand his reaction. I could only imagine how hot the final video was, and combined with the sordid gossip about Kellan and Sienna running like wildfire across the countryside . . . Well, my being okay with the situation, and even being a watchful participant in the filming of it, must seem a world away from the timid, jealous, and selfish girl I'd been a few years ago.

"I'm sure it looks more intense than it actually was. It was pretty . . . tepid during filming." *Well, at least for the first few takes, it was.*

"Oh," Denny said again. "It's just . . . very convincing."

Setting down my drink, I looked over at Kellan on my left. "We're great," I reiterated to Denny. He nodded, but I could tell by the look in his eye as he glanced at Kellan that he'd ask me again if I was all right. He probably would every time he saw me.

Anna showed up when she was finished with work. Wobbling over to our table, she plopped herself on Griffin's lap. He'd pulled himself away from the coeds' table once I had started doling out beers. Griffin choosing beer over women had surprised me some, but with the smile on his face as Anna nibbled on his ear, I began to wonder if maybe women didn't hold the allure for him that they once did; he sure seemed content with my sister wriggling around his privates.

As it was a Friday night, Poetic Bliss showed up not too much later and took to the stage. Rain made a huge deal about Kellan being in the audience. While he laughed, she rushed to his table and dragged him to the stage. The awaiting crowd starting screaming with excitement. Holding his hands up, Kellan playfully batted the spunky rocker chick away from him. She dodged his mock blows, holding her hands into little fists; the pleated skirt she wore was so short that I could see the edge of her underwear when she crouched down. Even though I hated that the pair had a history, I had to laugh at the cute display they were putting on.

After another minute of playful pretend fighting, Kellan finally caved and grabbed her microphone. Twisting to the crowd, he muttered, "Hey." His one word caused an ear-splitting shriek to rip around the bar. It made my ears ring. Kellan laughed. Holding a hand up, he told the crowd, "It is so fucking good to be back here at Pete's!"

More shrieking. My sister held her fingers up to her mouth and whistled. It had always made me a little jealous that she could do that; I couldn't whistle with my fingers to save my life. Kellan looked out over the bar, his deep blue eyes sparkling. "You guys mind if the D-Bags take over for a song or two?"

There was no doubt by the crowd's reaction that they didn't mind in the slightest. Kellan looked back at the other members of the girl band. They were all nodding, clapping or whistling, willing to share their spotlight. Kellan smiled, then indicated for his band to join him.

Griffin wasted no time hopping up out of his seat. He nearly toppled my sister to the ground in his excitement, but Denny caught her and helped her into a chair. She grudgingly thanked him while Matt smacked the back of Griffin's head. The table next to us chuckled at the familiar sight of the cousins fighting.

Once all the boys hopped on stage, the girls handed them their instruments. Griffin frowned as Tuesday handed him her bright pink bass guitar. Blessing handed Matt her teal guitar, while Evan tucked himself behind Meadow's drums; the band's logo on the drum had a giant purple flower in the background. The girls shifted to the sides of the stage to give the boys room, while the crowd sniggered over the guys playing such feminine instruments. Rachel got such a bad case of the giggles that she started hiccupping.

Shaking his head, Kellan's amused expression made my heart beat harder. Kellan on stage. Nothing on earth could compare. The crowd agreed with me. Their eruption of noise when Evan started the intro vibrated the windows and created rings of distortion in Anna's glass of water. Running a hand through his hair, Kellan began to sing a popular D-Bags song. Every one of the old fans in the crowd started singing along, while the new fans continued shrieking.

Pulling the microphone from its stand, Kellan began his "strut." It was a seductive back and forth saunter across the front edge of the stage that let every woman watching know that he was aware of them. He locked eyes with every single one of them, giving them half smiles and cocky grins between the words he was singing. At various points along his path, he would stop, put his foot up on a speaker, and lean over to extend his hand to a few fans. They always reached back for him, squealing as their fingertips brushed his.

It used to send tiny bolts of jealousy through me, but seeing his amusement and their joy, all I felt was happiness watching him. He had a beautiful, almost symbiotic relationship with his fans; they fed off his energy, he fed off theirs. As the song neared its climax, Kellan stopped in the center of the front of the stage. Face full of playful expectation, he sang the crowd a question, "Is this all you want?" They passionately shouted back their answer.

When the song ended, the D-Bags immediately moved into another one. I wasn't sure if they were using a set song lineup, or if Evan just randomly decided which song to start playing next and the rest of them went along without hesitation. They'd been playing together for so long, maybe it was a little bit of both.

Their next song was fast and catchy, and Jenny and I dragged Rachel onto the floor to dance with us. Anna joined in, bumping and grinding despite her growing curves. I noticed Denny pulling Abby to the side of the crowd; they danced with bright smiles on their faces—no pain, no jealousy, just peace, which is what I'd always wanted for him.

When the song was over, Kellan took a quick bow, thanked the crowds, and then jumped right into the midst of them. He waded through a sea of wandering palms to get to me. Our arms wrapped around each other and eventually the friendly fingers of fans backed off. Kellan gave me a few light kisses as Rain's voice broke over the microphone. "Thank you, boys, but it's the girls' turn to kick ass now!"

Kellan looked back at her, laughing as they started one of their driving beats. Jenny headed back to work while Rachel slinked off to join Matt at the table. Anna meandered to a stool to sit down. Griffin headed over to nibble on *her* ear for a while. Denny gave me a small wave as he headed toward the doors with Abby. Kellan and I stayed in the thick crowd, dancing to Poetic Bliss's infectious beat. It had been a while since I'd danced with Kellan; the boy had moves. Sliding up behind me, he swayed his hips with mine in such a seductive way that I suddenly wanted to stop this public celebration and have a much more private one instead. Breath hot on my neck, he ran his nose up the side of my throat. Closing my eyes, I laid my head on his shoulder and reveled in the feeling of his body against mine. With a soft kiss on my jaw, he said over the music, "Wanna go somewhere with me?"

Boy, did I ever.

His hands slid down my hips, subtly pulling them back into his. I didn't need to feel his body to know what he was in the mood for, but feeling the outline of him through his jeans sparked a fire in mine. Twisting my head to look at him, I gave him a playful half smile and nodded. His corresponding grin was as devilish as the sudden gleam in his eye.

Biting my lip, I tugged him through the crowd of people until we got to the hallway. People tried to stop us as we moved along toward the back room of the bar, where only employees were supposed to go, but I expertly weaved us around them. Sliding around a couple of girls coming out of the bathroom, we slipped into the back room, quickly closing the door behind us.

Kellan pressed me into the door, turning the lock on it as he did. "New lock still works," he whispered, leaning in for my mouth. I chuckled as I drew him into me. It might have been the dancing, or the few beers I had, or seeing him on stage, or just the novelty of showing affection for him in public—something we hadn't been able to do much while on tour for the single—but I desperately wanted him.

While our mouths frantically worked together, my fingers slid down his chest to unfasten the button of his jeans. Groaning, his hands started in on mine. As I unzipped his jeans, I looked over his shoulder, just to make sure we were alone. The room was fairly open, I didn't see anyone hiding anywhere, so I found his lips again and closed my eyes.

As Kellan started to shove my pants down my hips, I slipped my hands into his jeans. He was so ready for me, hard and straining against my palm. He whimpered a bit as I squeezed him. My breath was fast as I fed off of the fiery passion I felt from him. It was like he was going to explode if he didn't have me. I was sure he was already on the edge, and just the slightest touch would send him right over. Remembering something Kellan had said once, to Denny, of all people, I stopped his hands from removing my clothes. He made a noise that sounded close to a growl as his fingers curled around my jeans. Well, we *were* celebrating, perhaps I should give him a present, something I didn't typically do for him—but maybe I should, since most guys like it. Or so I'd heard.

Pushing him away, I slid my back down the door. Kellan watched me descend with clear confusion on his face. "Kiera . . . ?"

When I stopped at his waist, he stopped breathing. The look on his face was as clear to me as if he'd begged: *Please do what I think you're going to do.* His finger slowly reached down to trace my jaw, and I felt more powerful, more desirable, and more beautiful than I ever had before. Not able to pull myself away from his intense eyes, I adjusted his clothes so he was exposed. The anticipation grew as we stared at each other. Kellan started breathing again, faster than before. He didn't say anything, didn't pressure me in any way, just continued to beg me with his eyes. When I noticed he was trembling, maybe fighting back the urge to bring my lips closer to him, I lowered my mouth and took him in. Kellan gasped, then groaned. I heard a thud as his forehead hit the door. I had tasted him before, on several occasions, but usually just a small lick or two when we were both rolling around naked. Nothing like this. Nothing that was so blatantly just for him.

As Kellan's erotic breaths picked up the pace, his hand cupped my cheek. He stroked my skin with his thumb while I did my best to relax as I moved over him. Faster than I thought it would take, I felt him tense and knew he was close. It was a now-or-never sort of moment, and I wasn't sure what I wanted, but I knew I wanted to satisfy him, and I knew what *I* would want if the roles were reversed. Kellan had his own thought on the matter, though. Murmuring my name with a light groan, his hand moved to my shoulder and he tried to push me back. I grabbed his hips and pulled him deeper into me. I'd committed to do this, and I would see it through to the end.

My aggressive move pushed Kellan over the edge. Crying out, he grabbed the door handle and squeezed it as he released; I could hear the metal rattling in the lock. It was enough to distract me from the taste . . . which wasn't quite as bad as I'd imagined.

After he slowly came down, I adjusted his boxers and slid my way up the door. His head was still resting against the wood, his eyes closed as he breathed in and out of his mouth. His face, his look, his reaction . . . I don't think I'd ever been so turned on in all my life. Slinging my arms around him, I nestled into his chest.

He shifted to bury his head in my neck. "Holy . . . oh my . . . fuck," he muttered.

His body sagged against mine and I giggled at his complete lack of coherency. I think I satisfied him. Stroking his back, I whispered, "Don't swear."

He chuckled and shook his head. "Sorry." His voice was groggy, like he'd just woken up.

My body was blazing with need, but Kellan was still slumped against the door; he didn't seem to be in any shape to help me with my situation. And I didn't really want him to. I loved the fact that I'd completely overwhelmed him, and I wanted this moment to just be about him. Reaching down, I slowly zipped up my pants, then moved my fingers over to zip up his. Still breathing deeply, Kellan pulled back and glanced down when he felt me fastening his jeans.

"What are you doing?" he asked.

Giving him a soft kiss, a kiss that a part of me really wanted to deepen, I told him, "I'm making you presentable, so we can finish celebrating with our friends."

Kellan seemed even more confused by my answer. "But you didn't . . . don't you want me to satisfy you?"

Just the inquiring angle of his head made me want to tear off his jeans and beg him to take me against the wall. But smiling at him, I shook my head. "You did satisfy me."

Kellan cocked his eyebrow. "I did? Are you sure? Because you're usually more vocal when you're satisfied." He gave me a provocative grin.

Biting my lip and rubbing my legs together, I debated changing my mind. Pushing him back a smidge, I told him, "I may not have . . . finished . . . but you definitely made me happy." I swept a strand of hair away from his eyes. "I want to give you this." Grabbing the doorknob behind him, I muttered, "You can return the favor later." I could hear him chuckling as I stepped into the hallway.

With the tour with Avoiding Redemption starting soon, the D-Bags dropped off of the face of the earth as they hid away with their significant others. I didn't see or hear from my sister for the next five days. When I wasn't visiting with old friends in the area—mainly Denny and Cheyenne—Kellan and I spent most of our dwindling free time tangled up in our sheets. I was very happy for my laptop; I could get some much needed work done while spooning with Kellan. And what greater writing inspiration could there be than that?

Needing a break from the drama of my past, I closed my manuscript file and started surfing the Internet. Kellan lifted his head from the pillow and kissed my shoulder. "You finally done with that?"

"No, I'm just taking a break. And no, you can't read it yet." Smiling, I typed in the name of his song with Sienna—"Regretfully." Maybe I was crazy for wanting to watch it, but the curiosity had been eating away at me ever since Denny had called it "convincing." Sienna wasn't why I wanted to watch it anyway. I wanted to support Kellan. He'd released his very first video, and I still hadn't seen it. That didn't sit right with me.

Kellan sat up, the sheet over his chest sliding to his waist. "Well, good, because I didn't want to read it right now anyway." I gave him a hard look, and he threw on an innocent smile. "I *was* finding the ceaseless typing relaxing, though." He glanced at the screen and frowned when he noticed what I was about to watch. "You sure you want to see that?"

There were dozens of titles on the screen that were close matches to what I'd typed in, but a still shot of Kellan's face was staring at me on the very top of the list. "No, not really . . . but it's your first official video. I feel like we should watch it. Maybe it won't be so bad if we do it together?"

Kellan nodded and grabbed my hand. He tenderly kissed my wedding ring, an apology already on his face. I reached up to stroke his cheek, then turned back to the laptop. It felt hotter as it rested on my legs, like it was slowly burning a hole through the thin sheet covering me.

After I clicked on the link for the video, a short ad for perfume started playing. I read some of the comments below the video while

I waited. "Kellan and Sienna are so hot together!" "OMG, I love these two!" "They need to be together! Are they getting married?" "I heard they already were!" "OMG, Kell-Sex forever!"

I frowned. Kell-Sex? The fans had already combined their names. Fabulous. And the moniker they'd given them was downright God-awful. Couldn't they think of something a little more . . . poetic?

The video started playing, and I clenched Kellan's hand. He didn't complain about how tightly I was gripping him. I could feel his eyes on me as I watched him and Sienna rolling around in a bed together. I'll admit, it was painful to watch at first, but after a while, I got sucked into the beauty and artistry of the video and I almost forgot that the man cringing in ecstasy was my husband. By the time the video ended, I saw what the fans were attracted to—Kellan and Sienna sizzled on screen.

Kellan cleared his throat, and I twisted to look at him. He was searching my face for any clue of what I was thinking. Giving honesty a shot, I told him before he could even ask. "The two of you look amazing together. I can see why the fans are so in love with the idea." Kellan started shaking his head, and I cupped his cheek to stop him. "Were you really thinking about me throughout that entire thing?"

He nodded, his face intense. "It was the only way I could get through it."

My heart swelled as we stared at each other. He really did only have eyes for me. Pushing aside what the world wanted for him, I focused solely on what *he* wanted, what I wanted. Feeling languid and content, I asked him, "Kellan Kyle, will you marry me?"

Moving the computer off of my lap, he gave me a teasing smile as he climbed on top of me. "I thought you'd never ask," he murmured, lowering his lips to my neck.

"Is that a yes?" I asked, giggling.

He ground his hips into mine as he brought his lips to my ear. "With you, it's always yes."

As he ran his lips down my skin, I thought about my mother . . . which was sort of a strange thought to have at the moment. But she'd called me that morning asking about wedding invitations; she desperately wanted to get some ordered. She'd tried to hide it over the phone, but I'd heard the uncertainty in her voice as she talked about my future. She wasn't sure if the wedding was still on. She watched TV. She noticed the magazines at the store. She heard the gossip just as much as I did, and I'm sure she had heard all about how hot and sweaty Kellan and Sienna were getting. If I were her, I'd wonder if Kellan and I were still together too. I'd reassured her that we were still getting married, but I hadn't given her a firm date.

Before Kellan's lips found their way to my chest, I pushed him back. He looked up at me, eyes blazing with desire. I had to swallow twice before I could remember what I'd wanted to ask him. "How long is the break in the tour schedule for Christmas?"

Kellan looked over my shoulder, thinking. "Ah, I'm not sure. Four or five days, maybe a week?" He looked back at me, a small smile on his face. "Why?"

Shrugging, I looped my arms around his neck. "Want to go to a wedding with me in Ohio?"

Rolling to my side, Kellan sat up on his elbow. "Anyone I know getting married?" he asked, amusement in his voice.

Smiling, I shrugged again. "Just some annoying wishy-washy girl that half the world hates."

Kellan raised a brow, then lowered his lips to mine. "They don't hate you." He chuckled against my lips. "They don't even know about you. And you're not annoying or wishy-washy. At least, not anymore."

He laughed and I smacked his shoulder. *Jerk.* Then I frowned. He was right about the "Kell-Sex forever" fans not knowing about me. And it was probably a good thing that they didn't. If they did . . . they would certainly hate me. Kellan kissed the corners of my mouth, erasing the worry lines. "I would love to marry you in December . . . in Ohio . . . in front of your entire family." Pulling back, he gave me a wide grin. "In front of my family."

I ran my hand up his chest, fingering his tattoo. "Can you find out the exact dates of the break? So I can tell my mom?"

He nodded and turned away from me, like he was going to do it right this second. I stopped him by pulling his shoulder back to me. His eyes flashed to mine as I placed a light kiss over his heart. "Could you do it a little later though?" I peeked up at him from under my eyelashes. "I'd like to have sex with you first," I matter-of-factly stated. Pride leaked into my smile; I'd asked him for sex unsolicited, and I hadn't even stumbled over the words.

Kellan's mouth opened in mock surprise. "Why, Mrs. Kyle, I am shocked at your brazenness." Then he beamed at me like I was his star student. His sexual protégée. His sextégée. His lip curved up into a wicked grin. "I'm also incredibly turned on."

He started to lean over me, but I pushed him to his back. Kellan laughed as I straddled him, but only for a minute; the sounds that came from him after that were anything but amused.

Chapter 14
Putting on a Show

It seemed like we went from leaving Seattle to hopping on a tour bus with Avoiding Redemption in a blink of an eye. The transition happened so fast, that I had a horrid feeling that I was forgetting something as we stepped onto the bus that would be our home for the next several months. I was pretty sure I wasn't forgetting anything—I had my clothes, my toothbrush, my laptop, my notes, and my rock star husband—what else could I possibly need, besides some privacy? All of the bands were sharing two busses this tour, so there was going to be a lot of people around us; privacy would be hard to come by in the coming weeks.

The first venue was the House of Blues on Sunset Strip in Los Angeles. I thought it was the perfect place for the boys to kick off their tour. It was well-known, iconic, yet still intimate; everyone in the audience would have a great view. Fans were everywhere I turned backstage, screaming and hollering, giddy over all of the rock stars in their midst. It was a little chaotic, which only added to the anticipation in the air.

Kellan and Justin were signing autographs with some of the other musicians while I wandered the area. It was fun to see everyone in D-Bags shirts. On the tour before this, Kellan had been a last-minute addition and still relatively unknown. He wasn't anymore. I was positive that everyone here had heard their single with Sienna; most of them had probably picked up the album too. This time around, people experiencing Kellan on stage wouldn't be a happy accident. No, a lot of these fans, the majority of them from what I could tell, were here specifically for the D-Bags. It made this moment feel so much bigger and so much more exciting. Even though Justin was headlining this tour, it was definitely Kellan's show.

Besides the D-Bags and Avoiding Redemption, there were three other bands on the tour. The first one started off the show and the music reverberated through the walls. The crowd loitering backstage didn't lessen any now that the concert was in progress. If anything, it ramped the party up a notch—some people in the center of the room even started dancing as they lifted their drinks in the air.

While I watched Kellan from across the room, smiling and talking to a fan in bright red pigtails, I listened to the people around me. Most of them were talking about Kellan's looks. "Holy crap, he's hot! How the hell does he look even better in person?" "Fuck, look at that body. You can tell he's cut . . . but we should go rip off his shirt, just to be sure. Research, you know."

I snorted into my drink after hearing that line, and subtly turned away from the girl who had said it. He *was* cut, but hell if I was going to let her strip him. Her "research" would just have to be imaginary. Walking away from the girl who thoroughly wanted to examine my husband, I started picking up conversations that I found a lot less amusing. "He's dating Sienna, right?" "I don't know, I heard he said he wasn't in an interview." "They always say that, it just means they don't want to talk about it." "They're such a hot couple, have you seen the video?" "So jealous, but they're perfect together!"

I heard that sentiment repeated about three dozen times as I worked my way over to Kellan. When I finally got to him, I was already sick of Sienna . . . and she wasn't even here. Grinning at me, Kellan leaned down to kiss my cheek. "Thanks," he muttered in my ear as he stole my beer from my fingers.

I glared at him as I watched him tip it back. "Just so you know, I totally backwashed."

Kellan paused mid-gulp, then shrugged. Smiling wide once he was finished, he husked, "That's all right . . . I like your fluids."

Justin was staring at us with his nose crinkled. Lightly smacking Kellan in the stomach, I muttered, "You've been hanging out with Griffin too much." Kellan just chuckled and continued drinking my beer.

Justin laughed at our banter, then turned to face a fan when she stepped right in front of him and let out an ear-piercing squeal. It drowned out the music pounding around the room. "I love you, Justin!" she screamed.

Justin's expression shifted into the courteous, professional one that Kellan's often did when he talked to fans. "You're so sweet, thank you." She squealed again and forcefully shoved a CD case into his hands; she almost made him spill his beer. Not at all fazed by the outpouring of excitement in front of him, Justin nimbly signed his name across the hard plastic.

The girl fanned herself, then glanced over at Kellan. Her eyes practically popped out of her head. "Oh my God, Kellan Kyle! I am your biggest fan!" Justin looked offended for a minute, then laughed as he rolled his eyes behind her back.

Kellan's biggest fan plowed past Justin to get to her favorite rock star. I bit my lip to contain my grin; the girl was shaking. Kellan gave her a polite smile as he smoothly told her, "Thank you, I appreciate that."

Whipping out another CD case, she shoved Kellan's album in front of him. I glanced at the cover of the D-Bags' CD as she held it in her trembling fingers. The picture the label had ended up using was one that had all of the guys standing in a line, Kellan slightly in front of the others. Kellan's head was down and he was looking up at the camera with a seductive half-smile. It was an incredibly hot shot, but it conveniently cut off Kellan's hands so you couldn't see his wedding ring. The lengths Nick would go to to create the illusion that Kellan was single were as amusing as they were annoying.

"Can you sign this, *To the girl of my dreams*?" She sighed after she said it. Justin sniggered, then walked away.

Kellan covertly looked my way as he answered her. Lip in an

amused curl, he said, "I don't think my *girl* would appreciate that." I hid my smile. Even though we were married in our hearts, Kellan was respecting my wishes by not publicly clarifying our relationship. He usually just said he was "seeing somebody," or he "had a girl in his life."

Fan-girl waved her hand. "Oh, I know you're with Sienna, and I don't really have a shot, but—" She giggled. "—it's fun to pretend."

Kellan snapped his gaze to the fan. "I'm not with Sienna. She's not my girlfriend. We only worked together on an album . . . and a music video." Remembering the video, he frowned. I subtly put my hand on his back.

The fan smiled and nodded, but it was obvious that she didn't believe a word he'd just said. Kellan flicked a glance my way and opened his mouth. Knowing what he was about to do, I pinched his back. While Kellan was being obscure about me to the masses, he probably wouldn't think twice about explaining things to fans on a one-on-one basis. I'd rather he didn't, though. When it came to his job, I'd rather be as anonymous as possible.

Kellan flinched and snapped his mouth shut. Just signing his name to the album, Kellan handed the CD back to the uber fan. She held it to her chest, cradling it like a baby. Even though the moment was over, she didn't move away. I thought she might hang out with us for the remainder of the concert, but she spotted Griffin emerging from the bathrooms and dashed off yelling, "Griffin! I love you!"

I could only shake my head in disbelief. Justin, Kellan, and . . . Griffin? Really?

Turning to face me, Kellan asked, "What was that?"

I blinked, not following. "What was what?"

He rubbed his back. "The Smurf bite. I was only going to tell her *you* were my girl, not Sienna."

Cringing, I massaged the spot I'd probably bruised. "Sorry. Yeah, I know you were. I just . . . I don't want to be paraded around your concerts and introduced to fifty thousand curious people. I don't want them all looking at me, talking about me. I don't want one of them mentioning something to all the press around here. I don't want them catching wind of me. And I *really* don't want to be front page news, and since everyone wants you with Sienna, that's exactly what would happen. I would be a breaking news story. And I just . . ." I shrugged. "Let's stay vague about us, okay? This craziness will die off soon."

Kellan set down his drink and looped his arms around my waist. "So, should I not be doing this then?"

I laced my arms around his neck. "This is fine. We don't need to stop living our lives, we just don't need to go into detail about it. We can be private. We're good at private."

Kellan smirked, then pulled me into him for a hug. "Well, people are watching me right now, so they're probably figuring it out that you're my girlfriend."

Laughing, I pushed him back. "No, trust me, they're most likely trying to figure out where the 'Get a Hug from Kellan' line forms." Kellan just laughed, but I knew I was right.

While we waited for the D-Bags' turn on stage, Kellan and the boys visited with fans and band members. I stayed close to Kellan's side, laughing with him and enjoying the mixed company. Several of the other band members had been on the last tour and knew the guys well. A couple of band members even recognized me from Kellan's scrapbook, and made a point of saying hello. Aside from a few jealous glances, the fans didn't comment much on my "flirty" relationship with Kellan as he put an arm around me or held my hand. Since a couple of other fans did successfully tackle him into a quick hug throughout the evening, maybe they just assumed that he was a friendly, give-the-fans-what-they-want kind of guy. And he was. To a point.

The D-Bags were slated to perform right before Justin's band. Before he headed off to the staging area, I leaned up and gave Kellan a soft peck. "Good luck."

The excitement in his eyes was evident as he grinned at me. He loved this. "Thank you. Back in a bit."

He hurried off to start his show, and I couldn't help but notice that a large majority of the crowd backstage had already disappeared—everyone wanted to see the D-Bags perform. Making my way to the side of the stage, I found a spot where I wouldn't be in the way, but I'd have a killer view. That's when I fully realized just how packed the house was. The floor before the stage was crammed with people. They were jammed in so tight, I almost wondered if the club was in violation of some city ordinance; surely they were over capacity. But no one in the audience seemed to care that they were squished like sardines, especially when Kellan strutted onto the stage.

Guitar slung over his back, Kellan raised a hand as he walked to the microphone stand. The room erupted into shrieks. While the other guys bounded into position, Kellan leaned into the mike and murmured, "Evenin'."

Hearing the reverse of his typical greeting made me chuckle. It made the crowd jump up and down. When the screaming diminished somewhat, a section of the crowd simultaneously yelled out, "We love you, Kellan!"

Kellan shielded his eyes from the bright lights beating down on him and scanned the audience. "I love you guys too." He laughed, and the girls in the front row looked they might hyperventilate—if they could breathe to begin with, that is.

Removing the guitar from his back, Kellan asked the crowd, "Is everybody having a good time?"

My ears rang a little after the shrieking response. Kellan cocked his head as he flipped the guitar around and slipped the strap over his shoulder. The body of the guitar was now resting right in front of his pelvis, and there was something insanely erotic about that. "Hmmm, I don't know. Doesn't really sound like you guys are having fun."

Jumping and screaming, the crowd tried to prove to him that they were indeed having a good time. The display made me laugh. Kellan shook his head. "Let's try that again. I said, is everybody having a good fucking time!" He shouted his question this time, and the crowd went nuts. They even started stomping their feet; it sounded like an earthquake was rolling through the building.

Satisfied, Kellan glanced back at Evan and nodded. Taking that at his cue, Evan started the intro to the first song. There were some things in this life that I would never get tired of. Watching Kellan perform was one of those things. He just had that spark that made it impossible to take your eyes off of him. And unlike a lot of singers I'd watched, Kellan didn't just stand behind his microphone and belt out his songs. No, he actively engaged the crowd, making them a part of the show. I was positive that everyone in that audience felt a connection with him at some point during his set. Kellan's ability to sound amazing, while still being fun and playful, was one of his greatest attributes. When it came to music, at least. I could think of several other highlights that had nothing to do with being on stage.

When the D-Bags were done, they each bowed and darted off the stage. Kellan scooped me into his arms right away, and I could tell he was flying high, energized from the performance. Nuzzling my neck, he murmured, "Let's go back to the bus."

My eyes fluttered closed as I considered it. Justin was up next, and a lot of the other band members were still mingling and celebrating backstage. We'd probably have a little bit of privacy if we left right now. After the final performance wrapped up, the boys would all filter back to the busses and we'd hit the road, so alone time would be out of the question.

I was grabbing the belt buckle loops of his jeans and pulling his hips into mine when I heard a warbled chant coming from the crowd. I opened my eyes and strained to understand what I was hearing. Kellan lifted his head and turned his face to the stage. He was sweaty from performing, and his hair was damp around the edges. It was a distracting sight, so I turned to face the stage as well. "What are they chanting? I can't make it out."

Kellan bunched his brows as he listened. It wasn't the band's name, it was too long. After another couple of seconds, the crowd's chants lined up and the word they were saying finally made sense. Twisting back to me, Kellan said, "They're saying 'Regretfully.' They want to hear the single."

I nodded, since that's what I was hearing too. Kellan frowned as his gaze returned to the stage. "We don't have her vocal track.

We can't perform that song without Sienna . . . unless . . ." When he looked back at me, there was such a devilish gleam in his eye that I knew exactly what he was thinking. I shoved him away and tried to scramble out of his arms. Laughing, Kellan held me tight. "Sorry, babe. You know I don't like disappointing the fans, and you're the only one here that can fill in for Sienna."

I had twisted in his arms and my back was to him; he had a vise-like grip around my waist and I couldn't break free. "No way in hell, Kyle! I am not going up there!"

Still laughing, Kellan started backing me up onto the stage. "I'm sorry, but you're gonna have to sing with me tonight."

I started screaming and kicking like he was mugging me until he finally let me go. Tears of laughter in his eyes, he asked, "Don't you want to live out your girl band fantasy? I'll help you through it, and if you get sick, there's usually a bucket in the corner."

Killing him with my eyes, I very firmly informed him, "You're sleeping in your own cubby tonight."

His expression changed so fast I had to turn away to hide my smile. "I was joking, Kiera." Pretending like I didn't hear him, I stormed away. "Kiera? You know I was kidding, right?"

Not able to maintain my fake anger anymore, I tossed a smile over my shoulder. His corresponding grin was so delicious that I knew my bold statement wouldn't end up happening. No matter where Kellan went, my body, my heart, my soul, would automatically follow him. Except onto that stage.

A week into the tour, all of the bands had fallen into a comfortable routine: travel, setup, play, takedown, travel. Sometimes band members shuffled from one bus to another, but generally the D-Bags shared a bus with the five members of Avoiding Redemption; the rest of the bands shared the other bus. Immediately after the first concert, Kellan had claimed the only bed on the bus. He'd stretched a couple lines of yellow Do Not Enter tape across the doorframe and taped a huge sign in the middle of the crisscrossing X that read: *Reserved for*

Mr. and Mrs. Kyle. Stay Out. That means you, Griffin. I was so grateful that Kellan nabbed the bedroom before Griffin had a chance to sully it. He may be practicing monogamy right now, but I still didn't want to share bedding with him.

Griffin pouted, but the rest of the band members thought it was funny and let us have the bed, since we were the only couple on the bus.

Aside from the fans asking Kellan about Sienna each night, and chanting for their single at the end of the show, the hype around the two was starting to taper off. I'm sure Nick just hated that. Sienna too for that matter. But she was off doing her thing, and Kellan was off doing his. With no more leaked photos and risqué videos, there just wasn't anything interesting to keep the pseudo-couple at the top of the gossip news.

That didn't stop the questions, though.

"So, Kellan, what's really going on with you and Sienna Sexton?" A radio personality was leaning over her microphone, beady eyes intent on Kellan's answer. I don't know why she looked like she had just asked him a life or death question.

Kellan smiled, but I could see the sigh behind his eyes. He was really getting sick and tired of answering the same thing city after city. I thought he might go back to saying "No comment," just because explaining his life was driving him crazy. "We're colleagues. We worked together on a project, but that's it."

Kellan paused and waited for the question that always came next.

"So, you're single?" By the look on the DJ's face and the tone of her voice, it was obvious that she totally thought Kellan was blowing smoke up her ass.

An easy smile still on his lips, Kellan shook his head. "No. I don't want to go into detail about it, but I'm in a relationship." I was standing behind the DJ while Kellan was in front of her. His eyes shifted to just over the DJ's shoulder, and locked onto mine. "And I love her very much." He shifted his gaze back to the DJ before she noticed that he'd directed that statement to me.

God, I really did have the best husband on earth. I schooled my features as best I could, but I just couldn't remove the small smile on my lips. The DJ pursed hers. "Okay, well, how about you boys play us a song?"

Kellan seemed confused about why the DJ looked so apathetic over his answer. She'd asked him a direct question, he'd given her one. It may not have been what she wanted to hear, but, well, too bad.

Matt and Griffin strummed their guitars while Evan beat out a rhythm on a lone snare drum. Kellan's voice filled the studio, pitch-perfect, and the mood instantly lightened. No one could deny that the D-Bags were good. No, not just good . . . amazing.

Afterwards, the group of us slipped into a couple of waiting cabs and headed back to the tour bus. The driver of the cab Kellan and I were in was listening to the radio station we'd just left; I recognized the DJ's high-pitched voice. Evan was riding in the cab with us. Leaning forward, he said, "Think they'll talk about us now that we're gone?"

Kellan and I shrugged, then started paying closer attention to what she was saying. I instantly wished I hadn't. "Kellan's a liar, that's all there is to it. Just colleagues. Right. I'm supposed to believe that that freaking hot music video was fake? Sorry, sweetheart, Sienna's not that good of an actress. Those two are swapping a lot more than lyrics! In a relationship? Yeah, tell us something we don't know, Kellan . . ."

Kellan groaned and dropped his head back on the seat. I completely understood the feeling. Guess I know why no one was really hearing what he was saying now.

The station started taking callers after that, and every single one of them were diehard Kell-Sex supporters who helped twist everything Kellan had just said into something else entirely: "He loves Sienna! And did you hear his voice when he said it? Sigh. Best boyfriend ever!"

Best boyfriend ever? God. Not only had the fans stolen Kellan and given him to Sienna with a big red bow around his middle, they'd even stolen my praise of his significant other skills.

While Evan shook his head in disbelief, Kellan looked over

at me, "Remind me to never do another interview for that radio station."

Duly noted.

Raising an eyebrow, he added, "Are you sure you still want me to be vague?" I bit my lip, but nodded. The hype would die off sooner or later. If I could keep my privacy, I wanted to.

The boys were playing at another House of Blues tonight, but in Dallas this time. I'd never been to Texas before. For some reason, I kept picturing Kellan in a cowboy hat everywhere we went. It gave me the giggles, which Kellan found adorable. When I told him why I was laughing so much, he shifted his weight to his hip, put his hand up to his hairline like he was wearing a Stetson, and drawled, "Well, hello, little lady."

Griffin immediately beaned him in the back of the head with a Hacky Sack. "Dude, grow some balls. You're an embarrassment to penises everywhere."

A tight smile on his face, Kellan reached down, grabbed the sack, and tossed it across the bus. He nailed Griffin right in the junk. As Griffin's face turned bright red and he doubled over in pain, every boy nearby cringed in sympathy and let out a long, "Oooooh."

Justin shook his head as he patted Griffin's shoulder. "Wow, ouch. Guess you won't be having anymore kids there, huh, Hulk?"

Griffin weakly lifted his hand and flipped him off.

As everyone onboard chuckled, Justin's bassist, Mark, rushed onto the bus. Looking around, he searched for his band mates. Spotting Justin first, he told him, "You are not going to believe who's here."

A really uncomfortable feeling started sizzling in my gut as I watched Justin's cute face contort into confusion. "Ah, okay, who's here?" I locked eyes with Kellan and I could see the same expression on his face that was in my heart. *Please let it be anyone but her.*

Filling me with dread, Mark's gaze swung around to Kellan. "Sienna Sexton, man."

Kellan and I both exhaled at the same time. *Damn. It.* Kellan twisted around to face Mark. "She's here? Why?"

Mark shrugged. "I don't know. She's got some uptight blond bitch with her who told me to find you, stat. Who the hell actually uses the word 'stat'?"

Kellan sighed again. "That would be Tory." He looked over at me. "I guess we should go see what Sienna wants." Wishing I could do anything other than agree, I nodded.

Maybe for moral support, or maybe just out of morbid curiosity, Evan and Matt followed us to where Sienna was waiting. Griffin stayed behind. He still couldn't sit up straight. Sienna was in a private office of the club that someone had hastily converted into a green room. Thing 1 and Thing 2 were guarding her door, keeping all the looky-loos away. Since no one was here yet besides the staff, I thought that was a tad unnecessary.

Both of the men looked at Kellan like they didn't know who he was. When Kellan moved between them to grab the doorknob, they each put an arm in his way. Irritated, Kellan told them, "I'm Kellan Kyle, remember? You've seen me before?" No muscles in their faces moved, neither did their arms. Irritated, Kellan raised his hands. "Sienna asked for me." One of them spoke into a headset, waited a few seconds, then opened the door for us.

"You can go in. Ms. Sexton is expecting you." Kellan rolled his eyes as he reached back for my hand.

Sienna turned to the door the minute we stepped through it. She was just as breathtaking as the last time I'd seen her—flawless, glowing skin, perfect body wrapped in tight, revealing clothes, and long, dark shimmering hair. Much to my disappointment, no sudden deformations had struck her down since we'd parted ways. Damn. Tory was behind her, leaning against a wall with a scowl on her face as she flipped through a planner bursting with colorful Post-it Notes.

"Oh my God, Kellan! It's been so long." Sienna moved to embrace him and Kellan held his finger up. She didn't toss her arms around him, but she did peck his cheek lightning fast. "It's absolutely lovely to see you." I hadn't missed the fact that she hadn't even acknowledged me yet, or Matt and Evan either. All her focus was on Kellan.

As Kellan swished his hand behind him, she finally glanced at the rest of us. "What are you doing here? Shouldn't you be on your tour?" he asked.

In a shy, yet flirtatious way, Sienna raised one bare shoulder and averted her eyes. "I'm playing nearby, and had the night off." She looked back up at him. "I just couldn't miss out on an opportunity to see you perform."

Kellan slowly nodded. "Well, it should be a good show."

Sienna clasped her hands together, pure joy on her face. "It's going to be fabulous. I can't wait!"

Looking confused, Kellan asked, "Did you want to see me, just to tell me you were watching the show tonight?"

A look flashed over Sienna's face that reminded me of Nick. It was an expression of annoyance, of someone who clearly didn't like to be talked to in any way but with the utmost deference. It vanished instantly as she gave Kellan a broad smile. "Actually, I had a brilliant idea, and I wanted to run it by you."

Kellan deliberately placed one arm over the other. "Yeah? What's your idea?"

Sienna frowned at his posture, then immediately brightened again. Watching her emotions flip back and forth was like playing with a light switch on a wall. "Well, I don't know about you, but I'm being hounded nonstop to perform the new single at every show."

She lifted a brow in question. Kellan nodded. "Yeah, I'm getting that a lot too."

Biting her lip, she poked a well-manicured nail into his chest. "I can't really perform it without you."

Kellan looked down at her finger, then back up at her. "Nick can give you my vocals, or you can hire another guy to sing my part."

Irritation flashed in her eyes before she cooed, "It's not the same. I'd like to perform it again with you. Really wow the fans. Blow the lid off this place."

Raising his eyebrows, Kellan looked around the room. "You

want to perform the song tonight? Here?" I understood his confusion. It was a hole in the wall compared to the arenas Sienna played at.

Sienna seemed overjoyed by the idea, though. Vigorously nodding, she told him, "Wouldn't that be wild? Nobody would expect it. What do you think?"

Kellan seemed unsure, and looked back at Evan and Matt for guidance. Evan was frowning; he'd heard and seen just what the media was doing with Kellan and Sienna. Matt—ever the manager— was smiling; he knew how huge this would be. The place would go absolutely crazy if it happened.

Seeing that he still needed to be persuaded, Sienna leaned in and told us, "Just imagine the headlines tomorrow, and what that could do for your friends' careers. 'Sienna Sexton surprises the audience on Avoiding Redemption's sold-out tour . . .'"

Kellan worked his lip while he gazed down at me. Not seeing any harm in this, I nodded. Looking back up at her, he asked, "All you want from me is one song?"

Giggling, she nodded. "This is going to be great. For all of us." I sighed, and hoped that was true.

It was decided that the D-Bags would go up last, by whom, I don't know. It made sense I guess. Sienna coming in last would be a great topper to the evening, and her coming in right after the D-Bags performed would make the night flow better. And, I hated to say it, especially to Justin, but the bulk of the crowd was here for Kellan. The D-Bags closing out the show made sense. Kellan didn't agree, and fought to keep Justin as the closer, but he was overruled.

Sienna stayed hidden away while all the bands performed. Not a single one of the fans had caught on to the fact that she was in the building. I had to admit, being in on such a huge surprise gave me a buzz. I had to share the knowledge with someone, so I texted Anna and Denny. He immediately responded with, *Really? Wow.* A couple of minutes later he added, *Wait, she left Montana to do a show in Dallas?* Anna just texted back, *Jealous!*

That took me back. She was in Montana? How was that in any way "nearby"?

I didn't have time to worry about it though, because the D-Bags were up. Maybe it was the extra electricity in the air, but they killed it on stage. Everything about the performance was perfect. Just listening to them stirred my creative juices. I'd been on a bit of a holding pattern with writing lately. I tried to fit it in during quiet moments on the bus, but there were so many people and so much activity, it was challenging. And backstage was no better. It was like one neverending party, which was fun, but not very conducive to writing heartbreaking romance.

When the boys walked off the stage, the chanting for the crowd's favorite song began. From the angle of where I was watching, I could see a few Kell-Sex shirts in the crowd. They were going to freak when Kellan and Sienna took the stage. I instantly saw a downside to this plan and wondered if maybe it wasn't such a great idea. We were trying to squelch the rumors, not help them grow. It was too late, though. Sienna was already primed and ready for action.

Everyone waited near the stage for the clamoring to reach a near-frantic level. I thought the crowd might bring the house down if the boys didn't go back out there. Kellan laughed as he stood beside me, waiting for the most opportune moment to reappear and announce the surprise to the fans. I squeezed him tight while the noise from the audience vibrated my chest.

When I was sure ceiling panels were about to break loose, Kellan gave me a long, lingering kiss. When he pulled away, his eyes were blazing. "I better go up there, so I can get this over with and take you to bed."

Feeling better already, I grinned. "I like that plan."

Kellan swatted my butt, then turned and dashed onstage. The noisy chaos of stomping and clapping switched to shrieking. Kellan held his hands out as he reached the mike. The noise didn't stop, so he had to speak above it. "What are you guys still doing here? It's over."

Kellan shooed his hands at the audience, like he wanted them to leave. I laughed at the display, and several people in the crowd did too. As he was doing that, Sienna came up beside him. The outfit she was wearing was not the one she'd arrived in. Before, she'd been wearing tight jeans and a tight sleeveless top. Now she was wearing a sheer white top with a black bra underneath. A black bra? With a sheer top? And with the way the lights hit her shirt, she may as well have *only* been wearing the bra.

The crowd went nuts and Kellan peeked behind him. This was not the plan. Kellan was going to play with the crowd, then verbally announce Sienna. She was supposed to wait for her cue. While Kellan straightened as he stared at her, dozens and dozens of cell phones were whipped out. Waving to the crowd, Sienna beamed as she walked right up to Kellan. Her arms slid around his waist as she playfully kissed his shoulder, then rested her head against it. The crowd gobbled up the affection. Kellan spun around, discreetly getting away from her. A seamless smile plastered on his face, he told the hollering crowd, "Ladies and gentlemen, Ms. Sienna Sexton."

By the tight way he said it, I could tell he wasn't pleased. A staff member handed Sienna a mike while the rest of the D-Bags took their positions. Ignoring Kellan for a second, Sienna bowed and thanked the crowd. When she was done speaking, Kellan signaled Matt to start the song. The fans went absolutely ballistic when Kellan started singing, and Kellan's irritation fell away as his professionalism kicked in. Kellan was a showman through and through, and regardless of his feelings about his singing partner, he'd give the crowd the best performance he could.

After singing a duet with Kellan that nearly brought the house down, Sienna brought both hands to her lips and blew a steady stream of kisses into the mass of enraptured fans. While she basked in their plentiful praises, Kellan gave the audience an appreciative wave, then he looked over his shoulder to where I was waiting offstage. When we locked gazes, he shook his head, then discretely shrugged. Like it or not, there was no denying the fact that that song was a gargantuan hit, and Kellan and Sienna performing it together was electrifying.

Chapter 15
No Hard Feelings

After Dallas, the tour meandered through the Midwest. It was just as flat, open, and spacious as Kellan had told me. I found the monotony of the environment relaxing, it allowed my mind to drift. And, like it so often did, my mind drifted to Kellan—my past with Kellan, to be exact. The bus was noisy and boisterous with so many boys on it, but I found small pockets of time throughout the day where I could hide in the back bedroom and write a paragraph or two.

This bus was a lot like the last bus Kellan and the guys had been on, more designed for capacity than comfort. The "bedroom" in the back was basically a larger version of a cubby—a thin mattress shoved up against the back portion of the bus. It constantly smelled like engine exhaust. The flimsy door cut out some of the sound though, and the bed was large enough for Kellan and me to sleep side by side, so I was satisfied. It wasn't as nice as our place back home, but it was better than the bunk beds.

We'd left Sienna about a week ago. She'd headed back to her tour with a smirk on her face, and we'd packed up and moved on to the next location. The headlines the next morning were huge—*Sienna Sexton Surprises Boyfriend on Tour!* Even though I should have expected it, the gossip shocked me. It just didn't seem to matter what

Kellan said or did; everything was twisted around in the media to make it seem like he and Sienna were deeply in love.

The still shot of Sienna kissing Kellan's shoulder that night was everywhere. I'd even seen fans ask Kellan to sign copies of it backstage. He never did. Saying that Sienna wasn't his girlfriend, and the photo was misleading, he always asked them if he could sign something else. And the fans always looked at him like his devotion to keeping his relationship with Sienna quiet was endearing. They loved him all the more for the way he protected her, when in reality, Kellan was protecting me.

"Irritated" didn't even begin to describe how I felt about Kell-Sex being the number one gossip story again. At least it would eventually die back down, now that they were apart. And Kellan wouldn't agree to another duet if she happened to "show up" for another publicity stunt; he'd already told me as much. Kellan would just have to keep doing his best at squelching the rumors while we patiently waited for another celebrity couple to pull at the world's heartstrings. And I was sure it would eventually happen. People loved to hear about power couples, especially when the power couple had problems.

We were in South Dakota today, to do a promotion for the tour that cracked me up every time I thought about it. The radio station that was sponsoring the event called it "Darts with D-Bags." They had rented out a local pool hall for the afternoon to host the band and a few dozen contest winners. Kellan was looking forward to throwing darts, but he wasn't the best pool player. Me either. The other D-Bags were decent though; Griffin in particular had a true talent for it. As we drove to the hall in one of the radio station's vans, Griffin started to give Kellan some pointers.

"Now, if the girl is bending in half to make her shot, that means she totally wants you to grab her ass."

"Griffin," I groaned, closing my eyes. *What the hell did my sister see in him?*

Griffin looked around Kellan to scoff at me. "What? That's what it means. There's no shot on earth that a chick has to bend over that far for. It's obviously code for, 'Grab me now and do naughty things to my no-no places.'"

Looking over at Kellan, I asked him, "Would you mind?"

Smiling, he answered, "Not at all," then reached over and smacked Griffin on the back of the head.

"God, just trying to help, man," Griffin muttered, rubbing his skull.

While Griffin switched his conversation to Evan in the front seat, I leaned my chin against Kellan's shoulder, silently thanking him for understanding what I wanted. He kissed my head as he softly laughed. True, I was trying to be nicer to Griffin, but some comments deserved a good smack. Even Anna would have thwacked him for that one.

We arrived at the pool hall and were ushered through the back doors by the radio personnel. Kellan and the boys posed for photos with the DJs while I waited with a group of interns. One girl chewed on her lip while she watched Kellan flash the cameraman a heart-stopping grin. Maybe it was my imagination, but I thought I heard her groan.

Playing with my wedding ring, I debated if I wanted to try my hand at darts. I wasn't all that coordinated, and there was a distinct possibility that someone could get injured if I threw a pointy object across the room. The intern switched from watching Kellan to watching me. I glanced over at her with a puzzled expression.

"You came in with the guys," she said as her eyes darted to my ring. "You married to one of them?" I could tell she was silently praying that I said no. Nerves clenched my stomach. I hadn't anticipated someone asking *me* about *my* relationships. True, this was a one-on-one conversation and not an official interview, but this girl had the ears of the DJs. Saying something to her was akin to saying something to the whole city. Well, maybe it wasn't that dramatic, but I still didn't like the idea.

Not knowing quite what to say, I simply told her, "No. Not married." That was the truth, since legally I wasn't. She looked about to ask me more, but, getting uncomfortable under her scrutiny, I excused myself and walked away.

The contest winners were divided up into four teams, and each team was assigned a D-Bag as its captain. The girls on Kellan's team were very excited. More than a few girls on the other teams seemed a little jealous, but quickly got over it; they *were* shooting pool and throwing darts with rock stars, after all. I weaseled my way onto Kellan's team. I wouldn't do much good in helping him win, but I could at least give him moral support when we lost. *If* we lost. I suppose I should start thinking positively. Go Team Kyle!

Each D-Bag had ten contest winners on his coed team. The team was then subdivided into a team of five that would play against another team of five. Plastered on a wall nearby was a complex bracket system that would eventually tell us which "Bag has the largest D." There was even an ostentatious D-shaped trophy for the winning team captain to take home. But the scoring process was more complicated than any statistics assignment I'd ever had at school, and I couldn't figure out how it all worked. All I knew was that even though Kellan and I were on the same team, he insisted on trying to distract me so much that I botched almost every shot.

During the dart game, Kellan would reach over and pinch the back of my thigh right as I was about to shoot. I missed the board three times in a row. One time when he did it, I'd been concentrating so hard on hitting the target—any target—that I hadn't noticed him behind me. Right as I was getting ready to throw, he nonchalantly ran his hand around my hip and into my front pocket. It scared the shit out of me. I twisted as I tossed, and flung the dart into a clump of pool players. It hit Griffin in the ass. Fortunately, or unfortunately, we were playing electronic darts, and Griffin wasn't injured. He did retaliate, though, by flicking a blue cue chalk at Matt, whom he'd incorrectly assumed had tagged him.

Kellan laughed so hard he had to step away from the game. A crowd of girls hovered around him like cats circling an open can of tuna. But again, the people around didn't seem to think it was weird that Kellan flirted so much with me. Probably because they all shamelessly flirted with him. It was like Pete's on crack. Kellan spent most of his nonplaying time swatting touchy-feely palms away, and politely redirecting wandering fingers. Even I had to admit, it was pretty amusing.

When our group switched over to the pool tables, the team's rankings were: Griffin's team, Evan's team, Matt's team, and then Kellan's team. I wasn't surprised that we were dead last. Nobody on our team was focusing very well, except maybe the three male contest winners. Although, even those guys found it hard to shoot pool with so many flirtatious girls around.

While two of the men on our losing team hit on a tall redhead who clearly only had eyes for Kellan, I leaned over to him and whispered, "Twenty bucks says I sink more shots than you."

Kellan scoffed at me. "Forty bucks says you just lost twenty bucks." I laughed at his remark and stuck my hand out to shake his. Kellan's lip curled into a smile that sent my heart soaring. "No, let's make this interesting. If I win, we have sex backstage tonight. If you win, we have sex backstage tonight."

I wanted to laugh again, but the way he said *sex* froze my brain for a second. "Um . . . I don't think you understand how betting works."

Moving in close to me, he breathed his response into my ear while he rested his hand on my stomach. "Don't I?"

"Okay," I muttered, wanting him to slide his hand down a little. "Deal." I had no idea where we'd find privacy in the circus that was the backstage area, but I didn't really care at that moment.

Kellan and I both proceeded to miss shot after shot after shot. I was beginning to wonder what the rules of our bet were if we tied with zero, when the sun shone down upon Kellan and he finally sank a ball in a pocket. He seemed just as surprised as me. Throwing his fist in the air, he shouted, "Yes!"

Since our team was still dead last, everyone around looked at him like he was slightly off-kilter. Kellan didn't care, though. Grinning like a little boy, he started playing his pool cue like it was a guitar. I rolled my eyes, but the girls watching him flew into a giggling fit.

While they fawned over how adorable he was, he told me, "I win." I knew I'd probably have one more chance to sink a ball, and I also knew the odds of me doing that were pretty slim. And I also knew that it didn't really matter who won this game—we were having sex backstage tonight.

As for who won the D-Bag cup, that honor eventually went to Evan. It was an upset heard around the pool hall. Mainly because Griffin let out a *Braveheart*-worthy yell of defeat when his team lost by four points. Who knew a kitschy plastic trophy was such a point of pride?

Evan proudly displayed his giant "D" on his lap the entire ride back to the radio station. By the time we all headed out to the venue, Griffin was so bent out of shape, he wouldn't even look at Evan anymore. "You cheated," he muttered.

"How could I possibly cheat?" Evan countered.

Sniffing, Griffin murmured. "I don't know, but you definitely cheated."

"If you mean I cheated by being better than you, than yes, I totally cheated."

Kellan chuckled at his band mates while Griffin scowled at Evan. As the conversations shifted to less combative topics, Kellan looked over at me with pure, undiluted desire in his eyes. "I'm really looking forward to the show tonight. I can *hard*ly wait."

I felt my cheeks heating as his innuendo hit me full force. Wanting to match his playfulness, I murmured, "Yeah, I know. I think it's going to be a real rager." *Oh my God, did I just say that out loud?*

Kellan's eyes widened, along with his smile. "I think I'll be drenched by the time I'm done."

I immediately looked away. Oh God, this was so embarrassing . . . and hot. Looking back, I smirked and told him, "Yeah, you'll probably be completely drained." I couldn't believe I said it with a straight face. Kellan either. He looked away, his lips twitching.

Just as he composed himself, we arrived at the rear entrance to the theater where the guys were playing tonight. Before Kellan opened his door, he told me, "I hope I have the stamina to plow through it."

Following after him as he exited the car, I tossed out, "I'm sure you'll reach your climax."

All of the guys were staring when I got of the car. Matt and Evan looked surprised by what I'd just said; Griffin looked a little turned on. Kellan was barely containing his amusement. Feeling red-hot, I locked eyes with Kellan. "That wasn't subtle enough, was it?"

He shook his head, then fell apart as he started laughing hysterically. I covered my eyes with my hands. God. Guess I'm still an idiot. When I heard Matt and Evan start chuckling, I peeked through my fingers. They were giving me such affectionate smiles that I couldn't help but start laughing too.

Everyone walked into the theater in a really good mood. Especially Griffin, who was a few steps behind us, simulating thrusting while he was walking. When he started getting left behind the group, he moaned out, "Wait for me, I'm coming." I bit my cheek and made a mental note to leave the provocative talk for times when Kellan and I were alone, or at least, nowhere near Griffin.

As Matt and Evan headed over to help out with setting up the show, Kellan stepped behind me and wrapped his arms around my waist. "Where shall we go?" he asked as he bent down and nuzzled my neck.

I glanced around the room already buzzing with fans and rock stars. There really wasn't any privacy here; even the bathrooms were constantly opening and closing as people used them. Looking over my shoulder, I asked him, "Were you serious about that bet?"

Kellan spun me in his arms. A couple of fans stopped and stared at him; they obviously wanted a turn being held by Sienna's flirty boyfriend. "Was I serious about the sex? Always." Leaning down, he whispered in my ear, "And I'm pretty sure I have a favor to return." His lips brushed against my ear as he said it, and a jolt of electricity shot down my spine. I could feel the heat retuning to my body, but it had nothing to do with embarrassment this time.

Grabbing my hand, Kellan started pulling me through the throngs. I had no idea where he was taking me. Storage closet, maybe? People we passed by murmured that Kellan sure was friendly with his fans, but they said it in an excited way. I even overheard one girl saying, "I hear Sienna's really cool about his flirting, so maybe we'll get to cuddle next!"

I almost couldn't believe how dense some people were, but it really wasn't their fault. They didn't know him, they didn't know me. They only had money-hungry gossip magazines to believe. It really made me wonder what celebrity stories I'd firmly bought into that had actually been complete crap.

Kellan was making a beeline for a hallway. He had to stop and sign something every five steps, but he always resumed his path when he was finished. His determination made me giggle. "Shouldn't you be helping set up the show, rock star?" There weren't a lot of roadies on the tour, so all the guys helped out with setup and teardown. Kellan was being a slacker by slipping away with me.

Kellan smirked at me over his shoulder. "When I can concentrate properly, I'll—"

His comment was cutoff when Justin bumped into him. Eyes glued to his cell phone, Justin had been walking on a perpendicular path to us and hadn't noticed Kellan in time to avoid him. Justin looked up when he was jostled, and the small smile on his face turned sheepish. "Oh, hey, sorry, wasn't watching where I was going." He flashed his phone at us, and I noticed Kate's picture in the corner. I wasn't too shocked to see it there; last time I'd spoken with her, she'd told me that Justin texted her every couple of days. She always giggled after she mentioned his name. It made me happy that Justin and Kate were frequently talking; he was a good guy, and she was a sweetheart.

I smiled at him while Kellan said, "No problem, we were just . . . running an errand."

Justin scrunched his forehead together like he was trying to figure out just what errand we could possibly be running backstage. I had the sudden urge to pinch Kellan again. He was usually much better at making up stories.

Kellan clapped Justin's shoulder, then started to move around him. Justin let us walk by, then called out, "Hey, I just wanted to let you know, I totally understand, and there's no hard feelings. We're cool, dude."

Kellan stopped in his tracks and looked back at Justin. "What are you talking about?"

Justin took a step toward us. "You leaving the tour. I just wanted you to know that I get it. You guys are bigger than this. Even I'll admit that."

Kellan's jaw dropped. "I'm . . . leaving . . . what? What the hell are you talking about?"

Justin's expression was a strange combination of horror, shock, and confusion. "You don't know? I just assumed you knew. Fuck, sorry, man."

Kellan's face clouded over. "Know what? What the hell happened since this morning?"

Justin sighed as he ran a hand through his choppy hair. "Ah, crap. Well, it went down while you guys were doing the thing with the radio station. Some, ah, bigwig from the label showed up and started barking orders at people. He said that he'd be sending people over after the show tonight to 'collect' your things, and if anybody else touched your stuff, there'd be hell to pay."

Kellan's grip on my hand tightened, and I subtly stroked his forearm. "And where exactly are they sending our stuff? Where the fuck are we going?"

Justin shifted on his feet, clearly uncomfortable with being the bearer of bad news. "Uh, back to L.A. You're playing Staples Center tomorrow night . . . with Sienna Sexton. The label's putting you on her tour."

For just a fraction of a second while Justin had been speaking, I'd thought Kellan had somehow done something really wrong, and he was being tossed off the tour as a punishment. Maybe he'd even be sent home. I wasn't sure. But after Justin said *her* name, it all started making sense. Sienna wanted her spotlight amplified, and Kellan was just the extra wattage she needed. "That bitch!" I exclaimed.

Justin looked over at me, then back to Kellan. "I don't think it was her. It's just, you know, you guys are huge now. I mean, you could be selling out venues ten times as big as the places we're going. The label knows that. They're just doing what makes sense, and they're right. It really doesn't make sense for you to be on tour with us. I knew that the minute Sienna showed up for the duet." He clasped Kellan's arm. "You're beyond this, man. We're holding you back."

Clearly not agreeing, Kellan shook his head. He tried to say something, but he didn't have any words. Understanding, Justin smiled, gave him two congratulatory smacks on the back, then walked away. Kellan turned to me. "What the fuck just happened?" he asked.

Sighing, I told him, "Sienna and Nick. That's what happened."

Kellan dug in his pocket for his phone. "I don't think so." He scrolled through his contact list until he reached Nick's number, then he started the call and brought the phone to his ear. While it rang, he murmured, "This is bullshit, and this is *not* how this is going down."

Kellan's eyes hardened and I could tell Nick had picked up. "What did you do?" Fuming, Kellan listened in silence for a moment, then surprise washed over his features. "You're where?" Kellan looked back at the hallway that we'd been approaching earlier. "Fine, I'll see you in a minute." I guess we were going down there after all, just for an entirely different reason now.

Kellan shoved the phone back in his pocket and stormed forward. Since he was still holding tight to me, I had no choice but to follow him. I didn't want to miss this anyway. Nick couldn't do this. He didn't own Kellan. He couldn't just dictate where he went and who he went with. That seemed completely out of line to me, and way beyond the scope of Kellan's contract.

There were a few rooms along the hall that people were stumbling into and out of. But there was only one room with a man standing in front of it, arms crossed over his chest. Kellan headed straight for that room. The man glanced at Kellan coming then rapped on the door behind him. "He's here."

Nick must have responded to the man because the guy opened the door for us right as we got there. Kellan didn't even look at the bodyguard as he barged through the door and strode into what appeared to be an office for the theater. Nick was patiently waiting for Kellan behind a desk littered with paperwork. "Why the hell did you pull us from the tour?"

Nick smiled at us in a perfectly calm and composed way. It irritated me. Indicating a couple of chairs to our left, he said, "Why don't you have a seat?" I started to walk over to one, but Kellan held my hand tight and snapped, "I'm not sitting, and I'm not leaving Justin's tour."

Nick sighed and placed his hands in his lap. "You seem to be under the impression that you have a choice on the matter. You don't. I decide where the acts play, and who they play with." He splayed his hands. "Now, I'm usually a very flexible man, and I strive to give my artists as much free range as possible." I snorted at that, and Nick shot me a hard glance. "But in some cases," he continued, "when my talent is being wholly underrepresented, I feel the need—no, I feel it's my *duty*—to step in and make things right."

Standing, he casually tucked his hands in the pockets of his slacks and strutted our way. His demeanor was laid-back, but yet somehow also intimidating. "The hard fact here is that you're too big of an act. You belong in stadiums. It's a waste of our money and a waste of your talent for you to be playing anything smaller. And I'm not a man to waste . . . anything."

Sitting on the edge of the desk, he shrugged his shoulders. "Sienna's tour is where you belong. That was made quite clear to me after that duet she performed on stage with you. It's magic whenever you two are together, and we're going to capitalize on that magic."

Kellan inhaled a deep breath, then stated, "No. I'm staying."

Nick continued like he hadn't just spoken. "Sienna's been informed, and she's graciously made room for you. Your stuff is being moved over tonight, which I'm assuming you already know. A car will be picking you up and taking you to the airport the minute your set is over. When you arrive in L.A. a limo will be waiting, courtesy of Ms. Sexton."

Releasing my hand, Kellan crossed his arms over his chest. "I said we're staying."

Nick slowly stood up. He was shorter than Kellan, but that didn't seem to matter. "And I said you didn't have a choice. If you read your contract, like you said you did, then you should know that the label has final say over your schedule. If we want to pull you from one tour and put you on another, we will. If we want to send you on an over-fifty singles cruise in Alaska, we will. And you'll go, because, what you still don't seem to grasp is . . ." Standing toe to toe with Kellan, he leaned in like he was telling him a secret. "We own you."

When Nick pulled away, he patted Kellan's arm. "And besides, you told me, and I do believe this is a direct quote, 'I will help you promote the album in any way I can . . . within reason.'" He sniffed and straightened his jacket. "I think asking you to perform in the hottest concert tour on earth is very . . . reasonable." He lifted a brow. "Don't you?"

There was nothing Kellan could say to that. Nick had him and Nick knew he had him. He'd always known it. That's why there hadn't been a bigger pissing match the last time Kellan had stood up to him. Nick had been in control all along.

Kellan was trembling when Nick left the room. I could see the thick veins along the sides of his neck and knew he was absolutely livid. Silently standing next to him, I gave him a minute to calm down. It didn't seem to help. Letting out a frustrated grunt, Kellan snatched one of the chairs beside us and flung it at the wall; it left a couple of circular dent marks in the drywall.

I flinched, then tentatively put a hand on his arm. "It will be okay, Kellan."

He snapped his head to me. "I thought I was done being ma-nipulated, but every turn I take another string gets pulled."

I nodded as I cupped his cheek. His skin was warm, and his eyes were fiery. And damn if it wasn't attractive as hell. "I know this sucks. Believe me, I know. But . . . Nick may actually have a point."

Kellan furrowed his brow, but his anger dissipated a little. "What do you mean?"

Glad that he was calming down, I laced my arms around his neck. "As much as I love Justin and the guys, you are bigger than them. I mean, you've already replaced them as the closing act. You do belong in a stadium." Smiling, I threaded my fingers through his hair. "And Staples Center, Kellan. That's . . . as large as it gets."

Kellan frowned at me. "I like small." A delightful curve appeared on his mouth. "I like intimate."

Reaching up to kiss that delicious mouth, I murmured, "I know. But you might like this too. You won't know for sure if you don't try." I shrugged. "Maybe this will be a good thing."

Kellan shook his head at me. "I think you're being naïve again."

My mind ran through a million horrible scenarios, some probable, like Sienna being a constant thorn in our side, some highly improbable, like the record label lacing Kellan with some designer drug so that Sienna was able to seduce him for a night. Their drug-induced one-night stand would then result in Sienna getting pregnant with the world's most anticipated child. Nick would name her "Platinum."

I frowned at my imagined scenario. "I'm trying to look on the bright side."

Kellan let out a long sigh. "Guess we better go tell the guys the 'good' news."

We were all escorted from the venue the very second the D-Bags were done with their performance. The crowd clamored for "Regretfully" just like they always did, but the guys weren't given time to do an encore. They weren't given time to do anything. In fact, they were swept away so fast that Kellan wasn't able to grab his prized guitar. He worried about his instrument the entire time we were in the air. I briefly considered joining the mile-high club with him, just to get his mind off of it, but in the end I just told him that his baby was in good hands.

The limo waiting for us in Los Angeles was impressive. It wasn't a typical limo, it was a stretch Hummer, a fact that Griffin was nearly epileptic about. After he eagerly climbed in we all heard, "Oh my God, Kell, you gotta see the bar in here. And there's totally room for a stripper pole! I'm so getting one of these someday."

Kellan rolled his eyes at his bassist as he helped me into the gargantuan symbol of affluence—wealth on wheels. The guys had been torn on the news when we'd broken it to them. They liked Avoiding Redemption and the rest of the bands, but touring with Sienna was a big deal and could open even bigger doors for them. The exposure was going to be off the charts.

Much to my surprise, Sienna was inside the car. She had an open bottle of champagne in her hands and was pouring some into a pair of glasses that Griffin was holding. "Welcome, loves," she brightly exclaimed as we took our seats.

Matt and Evan warmly acknowledged her while Kellan only gave her a brief smile. Indicating for Griffin to start passing out the glasses of champagne, Sienna let out a morose sigh. "I am so very sorry that you were all yanked from your tour like that. Yes, Nick has the right, but as a professional courtesy to the other bands, he shouldn't have done it." Looking like she didn't understand Nick at all, she shook her head as she finished pouring everyone's drinks. "I told him he was making a mistake, and he should leave your band alone, but . . . well, Nick gets carried away sometimes."

She tossed on a charming, sympathetic smile, but I wasn't entirely convinced. Her words sounded great, but this benefitted her just as much as Nick, so I would be hard-pressed to believe that she hadn't had a hand in it. When we were all holding glasses, Sienna lifted her drink high into the air. "This may not have been the ideal start to our union, but I say we make the best of it." She extended her glass out to the middle of the car. "To making this the greatest tour anyone has ever seen."

Kellan sighed, but he clinked glasses with everyone. After accepting the toast, he seemed lighter. Like me, he probably didn't believe Sienna, but he agreed with her sentiment. Leaving Justin sucked, but it was done, and we all might as well move forward.

After taking her sip, Sienna squealed like a little girl. "I can't wait for you guys to see your bus. You'll love it. It is *so* much nicer than the one you were on."

Kellan looked around at the opulence that he was already surrounded in, but didn't seem impressed. If Sienna really knew him, then she would understand that her statement didn't mean much to Kellan. He didn't need *things* to be happy.

Even though it was really late—or really early—Sienna insisted on showing us the busses. The lights were off when we approached, but Sienna said the tour had pulled in the night before and the guys were sleeping at a nearby hotel. That brightened my spirits. Would we get to sleep in hotels from time to time? That was one luxury that Justin's tour didn't have.

Nearly glowing with glee, Sienna gave us a tour of our new home away from home. Walking down the main aisle, she ran a hand over some plush chairs surrounding securely anchored tables. A curved couch took up a large portion of the "lounging" area, and there was a flat screen TV bolted to the wall in front of it, along with a cabinet nearby overflowing with video games. Sienna was right, this bus was *much* nicer than the one we'd been on. Showcasing every amenity on the bus in a charming accent that made even the drollest words sound sublime, Sienna led us to the sleeping area. This bus had cubbies in the wall, just like the last bus, but there weren't nearly as many, so there was a decent amount of room in each one. I'd say two people could fit comfortably, if they snuggled.

Since Sienna was squeezing us into a tour that was already in progress, I wondered which bunk Kellan and I would be sleeping in. As I debated if the top bunk was better or worse than the bottom bunk, Sienna grabbed Kellan's hand and pulled him through the open curtain that led to the back. Frowning at Kellan's abduction, I followed them. Past the sleeping cubbies was a bathroom—with a shower and everything—and a closed door that I had to assume was the back bedroom.

Sienna was standing by the door like Vanna White. Her smile effervescent, she twisted the knob and pushed the door open. "For the happy couple," she murmured, her eyes lingering on Kellan's back as he stepped inside.

Kellan reached out a hand for me, and I joined him. The first thing I noticed, besides the fact that this was a hundred times nicer than the glorified cubby we'd slept in on Justin's bus, was the windows. All three walls of the back section of the bus were covered in huge, black, one-way glass panels. At least, I hoped they were one-way glass. I could see everything in the parking lot. Once I got over the openness of the room, the huge bed in the center of it got my attention. A bed . . . we'd be sleeping on an actual bed with a decently supportive mattress! There was a cabinet near the door for our clothes, and even a TV bolted to the wall. It was almost like our own private studio apartment. I could have hugged Sienna for rearranging things so we could have this room.

Still dazed at how comfortable Kellan and I might be here, I twisted back to our benefactor. "Thank you, Sienna."

She waved off my gratitude. "Anything I can do to help." Lips pursing, she added, "I want this arrangement to work . . . for all parties." The look on her face radiated sincerity, and I wanted so badly to believe her. I just . . . didn't.

Chapter 16
Spectacle

I was a bundle of restless energy as I waited for the boys to take the stage. Staples Center. They were playing at Staples Center! This was no small-to-moderately sized venue. This was an arena, and from what I could tell as I snuck a peek at the audience from backstage, it was sold out. I had no idea how many people that equated to, but I was sure it was in the tens of thousands. It boggled my mind.

Kellan was fine as he lounged in a chair beside me, sipping on a beer; you would think it was just another night at Pete's from his breezy attitude. As I played with my necklace, yanking the guitar pendant from left to right in a repetitious pattern that was surely weakening the thin chain, Kellan had a lazy conversation with Deacon, the lead singer of Sienna's other opening act, Holeshot. They'd been the only act until Nick had appropriated the D-Bags from Avoiding Redemption's tour.

Kellan's eyes were amused as he watched me while shooting the shit with Deacon. Since my nerves where slowly eating holes through my stomach, I jumped to my feet and started pacing. Kellan and Deacon both watched me, entertained expressions on their faces. Deacon's band had a song on the radio too, but it wasn't doing nearly as well as Kellan's single with Sienna. Deacon didn't seem too upset that the D-Bags had been added onto the tour at the last minute, cutting into his set time. If anything, Deacon just seemed happy to have some guys to hang out with. Good thing, since the two bands were sharing a bus for the next several months.

I watched Kellan and Deacon as they chatted about music. The pair were night-and-day different. Kellan had light brown, shaggy, bed-head hair. Deacon's was black, and longer than mine, nearly to his waist. Kellan had dark blue eyes, like the evening sky. Deacon's were so light blue they were almost white. While Kellan kept himself clean-shaven, Deacon had a neatly trimmed goatee. But about music, the two seemed equally matched.

Luckily, I had plenty of room to pace, and I made the most of it. One thing I'd noticed right away on this tour was that the security here was much tighter than the last one. On that tour, the backstage area had seemed like a frat house—women, booze, and rock and roll. This was a lot more regimented. A group of fans had met with the boys earlier after the sound check. Tory, handler extraordinaire, had been there to give the fans strict instructions on what they could and couldn't do with the rock stars. While the boys were busy onstage, Tory had barked at the group of radio contest winners like a drill sergeant until they were all docile and submissive. Listening to her go off on them had shocked me, and honestly, her "rules" made the whole affair awkward, for Kellan and the fans. In my opinion, if Tory had just let the bands and fans mingle organically like the other tour, it would have been a much more rewarding experience for both parties. She didn't seem to understand that the boys needed the fans just as much as the fans needed them.

The only people backstage now were press, staff of the venue, roadies for the tour, and band members. In the dressing room where we were waiting, it was just the three of us. For some reason, the lack of people around was making me even more anxious for Kellan.

Deacon pointed at me with a long finger. "Is she always this nervous?"

Kellan smiled at me around the beer bottle he held to his mouth. "Pretty much," he answered after he swallowed.

The door opened to the room, and a man wearing a headset popped his head in and looked at Deacon. "Show's starting, sir. You're up."

Deacon nodded at him, then stood and stretched. "Catch you guys on the flip side."

Kellan nodded at him, then turned his attention to me once he was gone. "Would you sit down, please?"

I pressed the palms of my hands over my stomach, trying to stop the butterflies from taking flight. "Aren't you nervous? Even a little bit?"

Kellan took another swig of beer. "Well, watching *you* is making me a little nervous." Setting his drink down on a nearby table, he patted his lap. "Come over here and help me relax."

Smirking, I walked over to him. He didn't have a nervous bone in his body. Not about this, anyway. This, Kellan could do naked in front of a million people and be just fine. There was something seriously wrong with him.

I straddled his lap, tangling my hands in his hair. Maybe his calm would seep into me, if we got close enough. I placed a light kiss on his lips and Kellan let out a soft laugh. "There, I feel better already."

Loving the fact that we were surrounded by people and yet completely alone inside this dressing room, I ground my hips into his, and let my soft kiss turn into a deeper one. He let out a low groan and ran his hands up my back, under my shirt. I pressed my chest against his, delighting in the smell of him, musky and manly, the taste of him, slightly bitter from the beer, the feel of him, warm, hard, and yet soft too. Feeling lost and carefree, I let the world around us melt away.

Kellan's fingers rubbed my back in soothing patterns while his tongue lightly brushed against mine. Then those tricky fingers of his unhooked my bra. Pulling back, I gave him an admonishing glare; we may be alone for now, but this place wasn't exactly private. His grin was cocky as he murmured, "Oops."

As I was reaching around to fix my bra, the door to our room opened again. I leapt off of Kellan's lap, twisting so that my back was to the far wall; I incorrectly latched the hook of my bra and had to try again. As my cheeks heated to flaming hot, Sienna sauntered into the room.

Glancing between the two of us, she asked, "Sorry, did I interrupt something?"

Smiling over at me, Kellan told her, "Don't worry about it. We're getting used to it."

Sienna laughed and sat down in a plush chair. "That's a story I'd like to hear."

My bra finally back in place, I took a seat beside Kellan. My nerves started returning, and I bounced my heels to dissipate the energy. Holeshot had started to play, and their music filtered through the speakers. They were pretty good. Not as good as the D-Bags, but good. Kellan looked back at Sienna when she asked him, "You ready for this?"

Kellan picked up his beer, showed it to her, then took a swig. "All set." Sienna grinned and shook her head, amused by him; I sort of hated her being amused by him.

Kellan and Sienna fell into a lively discussion about music. While he didn't enjoy the games Sienna played, I don't think he minded her as a person. When she started talking about her parents, Kellan got quiet. Her face void of emotion, Sienna told him, "They would be screaming in my face right now, if they were still allowed at my shows. A little terrified . . . that's how they liked to send me out on stage."

Kellan's expression turned thoughtful. "I'm sorry you had to go through that."

"Thank you." Sienna reached over and put a hand on his leg. My nerves about the show suddenly vanished as I watched her flirt with him. "What are your parents like? Warm and fuzzy?" she asked with a smile.

Politely, but firmly, Kellan picked up her hand and placed it back on her own lap. She frowned, but didn't say anything. Leaning back in his chair, Kellan took another drink of his beer. "No, definitely not." Setting his beer down, he shrugged. "But, I don't have to worry about them anymore."

I laid my hand on his chest and Kellan smiled down at me. I knew that casual sentence was filled with more pain than Sienna could possibly imagine. I lifted my lips to his, in comfort, and as a reminder to Sienna: *He may sympathize with you, but his heart is with me.* As Kellan gave me a brief peck, Sienna commented with, "Family. It's not all it's cracked up to be."

Thinking of my flighty sister, over-protective father, and wedding-obsessed mother, I tossed out, "My family is great."

Sienna's sad smile turned humoring. "I'm sure it is." Her dark eyes flicked between Kellan and I. "So, will you two be creating a family of your own? Any kids in your future?" Her gaze locked onto my stomach.

Pulling my legs up onto the chair, I hid my body as much as I could. "Someday, sure."

Kellan bumped my shoulder with his. "Maybe after we're officially married." He hesitated, then looked up at Sienna. "Which, just so you know, is happening on December twenty-seventh, when the tour is on break for Christmas." Luckily Sienna's and Justin's tours were breaking for the holiday at the same time. If I'd had to change the wedding date after Mom had already sent out the invitations, she'd skin me alive.

Sienna's lips twitched, but she very smoothly told us, "Well, I suppose congratulations are in order." She looked like she wanted to hug Kellan to congratulate him, but the way Kellan and I were cuddling really wasn't giving her the opportunity.

The same man who'd come for Deacon came to usher Kellan onstage. Sienna stood up with Kellan. Extending her elbow to him, she demurely asked, "Can I show you the way?" Maybe it was my imagination, but the question seemed laced with dual meaning.

Kellan didn't take her elbow, but gave her a polite nod of his head. I followed them out the door, my fingers loosely held in Kellan's. A group of men and women wearing lanyards sporting the name of one of the local radio stations spotted Sienna instantly. Of course, she wasn't hard to miss. She was in her stage outfit—a one-piece seventies-inspired jumpsuit littered with rhinestones that sparkled in the lights. It tied around her neck in a halter and had absolutely no back on it; it was so low that I could see the dimples beside her tail bone. And I'd been trying very hard to ignore how deeply cut the V was in the front while we'd been talking in the back room. I'm assuming that a hefty amount of double-sided tape was keeping everything in place.

"Sienna! Can we have a quick interview? Maybe some photos?"

The bodyguards that seemed to flank Sienna everywhere she went didn't let the people through until Sienna spoke. "Sure thing."

"With Kellan?" A blonde in super tight jeans asked. The suggestive smile on her face was very unprofessional.

Kellan jerked his thumb toward the stage. "Sorry, I have to go."

The blonde pouted at him, holding up a camera. "Just a quick photo of the happy couple?"

Kellan rolled his eyes as he looked back at me. I was standing a little behind him, so the blonde probably couldn't tell that we were holding hands. Locking eyes with the blonde, he pointed at Sienna and firmly told her, "We're not together."

The blonde gave Kellan a knowing smile. It was so clear to me that she was thinking, *Got it, you don't want to talk about your relationship with Sienna yet. Your secret is safe with me.* Kellan looked like he wanted to set her straight, but I tugged on his arm. He'd have to point out who I was to effectively set her straight, and I didn't want to be a part of this spectacle. Besides, the man wearing headphones was frantically waving at us to hurry.

As we turned away from the press, I noticed Sienna blowing Kellan a kiss. Before we were out of earshot, one of the radio personalities pointed at me and asked, "Who's that?"

Her smile still bright and charming, Sienna immediately answered, "Just an old friend of Kellan's." She smirked a bit after she said it, then all of her attention was given to the interviewers.

Kellan didn't hear, but I glared daggers into her back, not sure if I should be angry or not. She *had* called me an old friend when she

could have just said "nobody," and left it at that. I just wasn't sure
what to feel for Sienna. One minute she wasn't so bad, then the next
she was just as manipulative as Nick. I couldn't tell what her deal was.

Thinking of old friends and sorting through my feelings got
me thinking of Denny. The All Access pass around my neck let me
go anywhere I wanted backstage, so I took out my cell phone and
snapped a few pictures to send to him. Making my way to where
I could watch the boys play, I snapped a pic of the massive crowd
jumping up and down. Right after I sent the photo with a message
that read, *Can you believe the size of this crowd?* I noticed a huge sign
that a fan was holding high in the air—Kell-Sex forever! God, I really
hated that nickname.

Denny texted back while I was looking around the dimly lit
arena for more signs. *Damn, I'd be crapping my daks if I were him. I
suppose he's not the least bit nervous, though, is he?*

I laughed as I texted back that he was fine. Phlegmatic, even.

The stage was dark as the lights dramatically danced across the
crowd in haphazard patterns. The fans roared in delight and lifted
their arms in the air. Then all of the lights simultaneously swung
toward the stage, and the mob screamed. Kellan and the boys had
stepped out while they weren't looking. Once the people realized
they were standing there, waiting, they went nuts; it was easy to see
that the fans were losing their minds over the fact that the D-Bags
had been added to the tour. The noise vibrated my chest. I covered
my ears as I laughed. From my vantage point, I could see Kellan
shaking his head a little bit, completely blown away by the swaying
mass of bodies before him. Even though I'd seen him do this a thousand times before, excitement flooded through me as I watched him
approach the microphone.

"Good evening, Los Angeles!"

The answering squeals vibrated my skull. Adjusting the guitar
strapped over his chest, Kellan flashed the crowd a panty-dropping
grin. I saw someone in the front row fall back into her friends; guess
her knees gave away.

As the rest of the boys got into position, Kellan raised his hand in the air. The crowd silenced . . . sort of. "We're the D-Bags, and we're honored to be playing for you tonight." The silence evaporated into shrieking. Kellan put both hands up to quiet them. "Now, we're only going to play for you if you've been good." Unhooking the microphone, he walked up to the edge of the stage and looked down on the crowd at his feet. "So . . . have you been good?" he asked, his voice dripping with sensuality.

The crowd's response was so loud that I almost didn't hear Evan start the intro. I was sure that Kellan and the guys only heard it because of the earpieces they were all wearing. Giving the audience a glorious view of his backside, Kellan sauntered back to his microphone stand. Sliding the equipment back into place, Kellan started playing his guitar. It was miked as well, and the twang echoed around the arena.

They were playing a song that was classic to me, but new to most of the fans here. The crowd ate it up. Kellan's voice was perfect and powerful; it made a shiver run down my spine. He really was so good at this, so inspiring to watch. As he played, words and storylines filtered through my head. Even though I hated to turn away from Kellan, I decided to not let this creative spark get away from me. As quickly as I could, I dashed away to find some paper. By the time I got back to my spot, the D-Bags had switched songs. Kellan's guitar was resting near his empty microphone stand, and Kellan was strutting back and forth near the edge of the stage, tantalizing the crowd with his proximity.

Words were tumbling through my brain as his voice drifted past my ears. Watching a movie play out in my head, I jotted down everything I saw. It was a completely different story I was seeing than the tragedy of my past that I had been working on. Switching to something new brought a huge smile to my lips. Writing was so rewarding. And writing while listening to Kellan perform live was darn near euphoric.

Kellan found me after his set was over, and I practically leapt into his arms I was so proud of him. He was giddy as he swung me around in a circle. Just like after their other shows, the audience was shouting for the D-Bags, shouting for Kellan. Setting me down, Kellan peeked out over the crowd.

Evan and Matt were awestruck. Griffin looked like he'd expected nothing less. Smacking Kellan's shoulder, he told him, "We gotta give 'em an encore."

Kellan looked back at the bassist and shook his head. "We don't have time to play another song. It's Sienna's show, and she's big on structure."

Griffin pursed his lips then grabbed Kellan's arm. "What the fuck do I care about Sienna?" Shoving Kellan forward, he smirked, "It's our time to shine, baby."

Matt and Evan pushed him forward too. Matt said, "Just pop your head out and wave." As Kellan shrugged, Matt looked back at me and laughed. "Plug your ears, Kiera."

Grinning at the group as they dashed back onto the stage, I did as Matt suggested. Good thing too. My eardrums may have burst if I hadn't. A panicked staff member frantically waving his arms at the boys finally got them to come down from their spotlight. They were all laughing as they joined me again. I couldn't help but be caught up in their excitement.

Kellan wrapped his arms around my waist as the hollering from the crowd died down. "We have to stay close by to join Sienna for the final song, but the guys and I were thinking about running across the street to the bar. Wanna come?"

A part of me wanted to stay where I was so I could work on the new novel that had sprung to life during Kellan's performance, but Kellan's grin was contagious, and there was no way I could say no. Besides, there would be countless live performances in my future to draw inspiration from. As I nodded, Kellan pointed at the notepad I was hugging to my chest. "Were you writing?" My emphatic nod continued and he asked, "While I was singing?"

"You're very inspiring to watch," I stated.

His face was incredulous as he ran a hand through his slightly damp hair. "I . . . inspire you?"

Stars in my eyes, I sighed, "Daily."

Kellan looked at me like I'd just grown another head. "And you say I'm absurd." I laughed until he pried the notebook away from me. I tried to snatch it back, but he handed it to the man in a headset who'd retrieved him from the dressing room. "This is priceless, literary genius, and you need to guard it with your life."

The man's eyes went wide as he held it close. "Yes, sir." I almost thought he was going to salute us.

Satisfied, Kellan told him, "Make sure it ends up inside my guitar case, please."

"Yes, sir," the man said again before he took off.

"Did he just call me sir . . . twice?" Kellan laughed as he slung his arm around my waist.

I lightly smacked his stomach. "Don't let it go to your head."

He looked down at me with a grin. "Wouldn't dream of it."

The group of us headed toward the exit after that. Matt and Griffin were leading the way, sneaking around corners like we were robbing the place. "Are we allowed to leave the arena while the show is going on?" I asked Kellan.

He laughed as he looked around. "We have no idea . . . hence Spy vs. Spy up there."

Avoiding every person that we could, we crept our way to a set of doors marked with an Exit sign. We stealthily made our way down a hallway that Matt said let out by the busses. We weren't going to the busses, but no one around needed to know that. When we got outside, a guard was stationed outside of the door, keeping an eye on things. The guys nodded at him, walking past like they owned the place. Either the guard recognized them as rock stars, or saw my go-anywhere pass. Either way, he didn't question any of us as we left the arena. I suppose he was more concerned with people trying to get *into* the backstage area than people leaving it.

When we got onto the regular street, that one security guard was the only person who knew we were gone. That sort of freedom gave us all a buzz; there was a lot of giggling and playful ribbing. I loved being included in it. Griffin scoured the street, trying to figure out where we were in relation to the nearest bar while Kellan nudged Matt's arm. "You know what time we should be back, right?" Matt nodded as he tapped the watch on his wrist. I hoped he did. It would not be good if the boys were late.

Suddenly, Griffin pointed to his right and shouted, "Bar, ho!"

He immediately started sprinting toward his alcoholic haven. Matt and Evan took off after him, both of them laughing. Kellan looked over at me. "Last one to the bar has to sit by Griffin." I darted away before he even finished his sentence.

I had a serious ache in my side when I stepped on the rubber welcome mat, but my foot came down a half-second before Kellan's, so I considered that a victory. Hands on my knees, I struggled to catch my breath as I peered up at him. It had been a while since I'd sprinted. "Beat 'cha," I panted.

Kellan was breathing heavier too as he pulled the door open. "I let you win. I liked the view." He winked at me as I ducked inside.

I expected every sound in the bar to stop when the D-Bags walked in, but nobody here seemed to know who they were. I loved that they still had some anonymity. Kellan was the only one who caused a stir, but I didn't know if that was recognition, or if it was just his looks that were causing a ripple of whispers to float around the small circular tables.

Griffin made his way to a table in the back and we followed him. When we all arrived, his face turned oddly serious. "Same rules as last time."

Matt rolled his eyes while Evan laughed and shrugged. Kellan frowned and glanced at me. "We're not playing that game tonight, Griff."

Griffin eyed Kellan up and down. "Uh, yeah, we are." His smile turned arrogant. "What? Afraid you'll lose?"

Evan turned to Matt. "When has Kellan ever lost?"

Curious, and wondering if I wanted to know what game they routinely played at bars while on tour, I asked, "What game?"

Kellan turned to me. "It's stupid . . . Griffin came up with it." He said it like *Griffin* and *stupid* were synonymous.

Griffin snorted. "You're a pansy. All intimidated 'cuz your girl-friend's here?"

"Wife," Kellan corrected.

"Whatever, we're playing. Turn out your pockets." He instantly pulled the innards out of his jeans. They were empty.

Kellan looked over at me and, too curious to say no, I nodded. Kellan turned out his pockets, which were also empty. After all the guys did it, Griffin looked satisfied. "Good. Now, numbers count as one point, condoms count as five. The person with the least amount of points picks up the tab. The stud with the most gets a shot from every-body . . . and top shelf shit too." He pointed at each guy in turn. "And cheating in any way is grounds for immediate ass-kickery." His fingers pointed at his own eyes, then Matt's. *I'm watching you.* Matt sighed.

Still trying to wrap my head around the point system—condoms?—I asked, "Wait, what game?"

Griffin squatted in front of me. "The dude who fills his pockets with the most chick's phone numbers wins." He said it slowly, like I was already drunk so I couldn't possibly understand him.

My eyes widened, and I turned to Kellan with an eyebrow raised. "And you haven't ever lost this game?"

Kellan lifted his hands in the air. "Completely unsolicited, I swear." I pursed my lips at him and Kellan scratched his head. "You, uh, want a drink?"

I gave him a tight smile. "Mmm-hmm."

Kellan immediately tucked tail and headed for the bar. I had to laugh a little as he waded through the crowd with his head down. Evan wrapped his arm around my shoulders. "He really doesn't ask for any. He doesn't have to. Girls tend to . . . shove things Kellan's way." His raised his eyebrow, and the ring pierced through it sparkled at me; it nearly matched the amused gleam in his eye. "Just you watch."

Curious, I turned around to observe my husband. As he waited at the bar for our drinks, he was approached by a couple of girls. They hadn't talked to him for more than five seconds before one of them was sliding a napkin his way. My jaw dropped. That was so fast! Griffin was apparently just as shocked as I was.

"You've got to be fucking kidding me!" He raised his hands in the air. "You're a whore!" he yelled at Kellan. Some girls, maybe thinking he meant them, looked back at Griffin with scowls on their faces. I figured none of them would be approaching him with their numbers tonight.

Kellan looked back at our table. Seeing my amused smile, Kellan teasingly waved the napkin at Griffin, then stuffed it in his pocket. Griffin's scowl grew. "No way that cocksucker's pulling one over on me again." He disappeared into the packed bar, and I had the distinct feeling that every one of his phone numbers would be "solicited." Heavily solicited. Perhaps bribed.

I knew the game should have disgusted me, but aside from Griffin, none of the guys actively tried to get phone numbers. Their natural good looks and charisma did it for them. Their quickness to laugh and easygoing personalities drew a circle of people around them. It was almost like we were back at Pete's. I even had to stop myself from clearing off a table once or twice. But, unlike Pete's, Kellan merely had to walk by a woman to get her to discretely shove a finger in his pocket. He didn't acknowledge the slip, or the girl, and I began to wonder if maybe I was wrong. Maybe this was *exactly* like Pete's and I just didn't realize it. Maybe Kellan got slipped numbers at our bar back home and I had never noticed. Well, if he did, he was quick to discard them.

It also helped that all of the guys treated the game as a big joke. Whenever Kellan grabbed a drink at the bar, or went to the bathroom, someone asked him how many names he'd nabbed when he returned. When Griffin sulked his way back to the table with an irritated expression, Matt gave him an exaggerated, sympathetic, "Ah, no luck?" to which Griffin responded with grace by flipping him off.

Drinks and merriment abounded at our table, and I grew to love my decision to roam around the country with D-Bags more and more. When everyone was feeling no pain, the alarm on Matt's watch went off. We all stared at it for a second, then remembered that there was still a show going on.

"Shit, Sienna's set is almost over. We have to go." Matt looked a little panicked as he downed his beer.

Everyone started to leave the table but Griffin threw his hands out. "Wait! We need a winner. Pockets."

As I stifled a drunken giggle, I wondered which guy would be breaking the most hearts tonight. My bet was on Kellan. I eagerly leaned into his side, like he was laying down a winning poker hand, not phone numbers from girls. Evan started the process, slapping down a single phone number scrawled on a wadded up piece of paper. "Just one." He shrugged, not really caring.

Exalted, Griffin tossed down a napkin, a business card, and . . . I swear . . . a section of toilet paper. "Ha! Three! Read 'em and weep." He crossed his arms over his chest and glared at Kellan.

Knowing he had to have way more than that, I nudged him in the ribs. Kellan shook his head at me, then pulled his prizes from his pockets. He had to unfold them all he had so many. "Uh . . . five," he muttered, throwing them on the table.

Griffin slammed his hand on the table. "Damn it, Kellan! I fucking hate you."

Evan raised an edge of his lip. "Just five? Slow night, Kell?"

Kellan laughed at Evan, while Griffin muttered, "Fine, prick, what shot do you want?"

"What about Matt?" I asked, looking over at the quiet guitarist; he was watching the exchange with a secretive smile on his lips. "How did you do?"

Matt was about to answer when Griffin interrupted. "Pfffft, no way Matt beat Kellan . . . it's over." He raised a pale eyebrow. "Unless . . . someone slip you a condom?"

Matt slowly shook his head. "No . . ." Reaching into his pocket, he slowly pulled out a flat credit-card looking thing. His cheeks brightened with color as he tossed it on the table. "I got a motel key."

By the whooping and hollering the guys did, you would think Matt had just won the lottery. "Holy shit!" Griffin exclaimed. "That's an instant win!" Bouncing on his feet, Griffin grabbed Matt's shoulders. "Oh my God, you beat Kellan!" Turning Matt around, he showcased him to the bar. "Everybody! This is my cousin right here, and he just dethroned God's Gift to Women!" He rubbed Matt's head with his knuckles while Matt turned about a bazillion shades of red.

Slipping away from him, Matt hurried out of the bar. Griffin raised his hands. "Dude? Your shots?"

Evan was laughing so hard he had to wipe tears out of his eyes. I couldn't stop laughing either. When Evan could talk, he mumbled, "I guess I lost," and started reaching for his wallet.

Kellan stopped him and handed the waitress a folded up one hundred dollar bill, or maybe two of them. I wasn't sure. "I got it, Evan."

Evan clapped his shoulder. "Thanks, Kell," then stumbled after Matt and Griffin.

Kellan grabbed my hand and pulled me after them, leaving the motel key and the stack of phones numbers sitting on the table. It made me smile that not a single member of the band kept any of the numbers . . . not even Griffin. When we got outside, Kellan asked me, "So, you're really not mad?"

I gave him a sarcastic smile. "I'm furious." Kellan raised an eyebrow at me, and I laughed again. "It only would have made me mad if Griffin had beat you."

Kellan looked over at where Griffin was announcing to the street that his very embarrassed cousin's "balls had just dropped." Shaking his head, Kellan murmured, "Never would have happened."

Under Matt's insistence, the very buzzed D-Bags stumbled their way back into the arena with me. Getting past the security guard near the back entrance was a little trickier than leaving it had been. It was a different guard than before, and he kept asking for proof that the boys were really in the show. Kellan, Matt, and Evan had their clearances with them, but Griffin had forgotten his. Everyone was too drunk to come up with anything logical sounding; Griffin just kept showing him the pass around my neck, but that only allowed *me* access. Luckily Deacon was relaxing in the bus, overheard the argument, and grabbed Griffin's missing credentials for him.

Once inside, the boys made a beeline for the stage. An over-wrought person with a clipboard hurriedly pulled them toward the rear entrance of the stage. Before Kellan disappeared, he grabbed my face and kissed me. The alcohol on his breath was strong; hopefully he remembered all of the words to the duet he was about to do.

I moved back into my favorite place to watch Sienna announce her special encore to wrap up the evening. The crowd went nuts, already suspecting what it was going to be. Light-headed and giddy, I tried to whistle along with the crowd. It came out flat and airy, more like I was blowing up an inner tube.

Sienna's arm swished to the back of the stage. "Ladies and gents, please put your hands together again for the D-Bags, led by the out-standing Kellan Kyle!"

Maybe it was because I was tipsier than before, but the screams seemed extra piercing. The boys hobbled out, only half stumbling as they switched places with Sienna's band. Kellan walked up to stand be-side Sienna, and she grabbed his hand then leaned over to kiss his cheek. I really wished she'd stop doing that. Kellan discretely pulled away from her as he acknowledged the crowd. Wondering if any of the forward girls at the bar tonight realized just whose jeans they'd been shoving their numbers into, I watched Kellan and Sienna start their number-one hit.

Even though Kellan had stumbled and fallen onto a streetlamp on our walk back to the center, he seemed completely with it as he sang about his imaginary heartbreak. When Sienna stepped to his side to sing her part to him, she was so close I was sure she could smell the fumes wafting from him. Instead of facing the audience, Kellan and Sienna kept the song insular, singing toward each other, virtually ig-noring the crowd. It amplified the pain in the song. Flashbulbs went off like crazy, capturing every heated moment. When the song ended, Kellan made like he was going to storm off of the stage, like he was so angry he couldn't stand to be near her anymore; that matched the way the video ended. Sienna changed it up, though. Grabbing his arm as he walked past, she yanked him into her body. Too drunk to resist, Kellan collided with her. Quickly reaching up, she pulled his head down to hers. Their lips collided next, and then the stage faded to black; only the flashes of cell phones lit up their bodies.

The response from the crowd was thunderous. I was so stunned, I couldn't move.

So much for Sienna respecting Kellan's wishes.

Even though I was sure Sienna had mainly kissed him in front of the audience for the photo op, I had the overwhelming sensation that she was also declaring her personal interest in Kellan. Her dramatic affirmation hit me like a wrecking ball in the gut. Well, of course she wanted him. Who wouldn't? But he was *my* husband, and she couldn't have him.

Knowing I was probably about to get myself kicked off of the tour, I stormed to the rear entrance to the stage where the performers would just now be stepping down. I felt my hands balling into fists and wondered if I was about to clock a superstar. I wanted to. She'd gone too far.

As I worked my way to the back, Kellan was stomping down the stairs and shoving people out of his way. His face matched my fiery mood. Evan was a step behind him, calling his name. Sienna was on the top of the stairs, her hands on her hips. "You're overreacting, love," she called after him.

Lips tight, Kellan closed his eyes. I paused and watched him. That was usually the face he made when he was about to rip someone's head off. Turning back to Sienna, he pointed up at her. "I told you, not on the lips!"

A sweet smile on her face, Sienna breezed down the stairs past Evan; he tensed as he noticed Kellan's expression. Sienna stopped at Kellan's side and put a hand on his rigid arm. "I got carried away by the heat of the moment. Won't happen again." She shrugged, her long, sleek ponytail bouncing around her shoulders.

Seeing right though her, I stepped forward. "Hell right, it won't happen again!" Maybe it was the liquid courage in my belly, but I suddenly wanted to give this woman a smackdown. Yeah, definitely the booze talking. "He doesn't belong to you!"

Someone grabbed my shoulders as I lurched forward. I thought it was Kellan at first, but looking behind me, I saw one of Sienna's ever-present bodyguards holding me back—Thing 2, I think. Face serene, Sienna stepped in front of me. "He's a person, love, so he doesn't *belong* to anyone."

She gave everyone watching a cool glance, like all of this drama was beneath her. When her eyes returned to mine, there was fire in the dark depths. "And in case you didn't notice, he didn't exactly pull away from me." Her challenging eyes swung to Kellan; his jaw tightened, but he didn't say anything. Satisfied, Sienna stalked off, and Thing 2 let me go.

I huffed as I straightened myself. She had a point. I locked eyes with Kellan. The people around us resumed what they were doing now that the mini-fight was over. Evan patted my shoulder as he walked away with the other D-Bags. Matt tore Griffin away. Thankfully, or maybe unthankfully, no one from the media had witnessed the "lovers'" spat. I didn't know what to think of my husband at the moment. Part of me understood—he was a performer, he was on stage, he wouldn't have made a huge spectacle in front of so many people. The rest of me had Sienna's words wrapped tight around it like a vice. He hadn't pulled away. Had he kissed her back?

Not able to stomach looking at him anymore, I turned on my heel and stumbled away. He was behind me a second later. "I'm drunk, Kiera. It happened so fast, I didn't have time to—"

Spinning around, I lifted my finger to his face. "I know!"

I turned back around, and he continued following me. "Then why are you mad?"

Sighing, I turned around again. It made me a little dizzy. "Because I'm drunk too!"

When I attempted to spin around again, Kellan grabbed my arm.

"Would you stop walking away from me, please?" Irritated, I gazed at him as best I could. "Are you mad at me?" he pointedly asked.

My feelings still swirling, I countered with, "I don't know. Did you kiss her back?"

Kellan's mouth dropped open, and I saw the struggle in his eyes. He could lie as seamlessly as he could sing. I'd seen him do it. It was one of the many issues that had held back our relationship for so long. It's hard to trust someone who was so comfortable being duplicitous. But I had absolutely no room to talk on the matter, so I tried really hard to never use that fact against him. We were both capable of horrible things. Which is why honesty was so important to us now.

Mouth in a firm line, he told me, "Just for a micro-second." As my eyes misted, he started rambling. "I'm drunk, she caught me off guard. It was instinct. I moved my lips once, just a tiny fraction of an inch, but I didn't do it again. I pushed her away when I realized what was happening, but the lights had already blacked out by that point." He tossed his hands up. "Griffin's gotten more action out of me, but I have to say yes to be honest with you."

I wanted to be angry at him, I really did, but I understood him too well, and I was actually sort of proud of him for telling me a painful truth when a white lie would have been so much easier. Sniffling, because it did hurt a little bit, I slung my arms around his neck and pulled him tight.

"It's okay," I murmured in his ear, "I'm not mad at you. I'm mad at her."

His body relaxed against mine. "So am I."

I had no idea how long I'd been on the road at this point, but I was getting used to the constant traveling. Sleeping had been difficult at first; the motion of the bus kept waking me up, especially when it turned or slowed down. But now I barely noticed it. The bus could probably slam to a stop, dumping me to the floor, and I wouldn't wake up. Well, okay, *that* might wake me up.

As was typical most times I opened my eyes, the bus was moving. It took a while to tear down Sienna's shows—they were much more theatrical than Justin's small tour had been—so the busses usually started their journey to the next venue late at night or early in the morning. Some of the stars and members of the crew utilized the hotel rooms provided to sleep for a few hours, but Kellan and I liked our private room on the bus, so we stayed if we could.

As I looked over at the world rushing past the wide window on the far side of the bus, I noticed that it was early in the morning; a rosy glow was still in the sky. Kellan's toy muscle car that I'd given him last Christmas was perched on the ledge, gently rolling back and forth with the rocking movement of the bus. As was also typical first thing in the morning, I was alone in our bed. Kellan was on the floor of the bus, doing pushups. It was something he routinely did when he first woke up—push-ups and sit-ups. He said it was to keep his body conditioned, but I think it helped clear his mind too; Kellan didn't always sleep well. I was usually asleep while he was exercising, but occasionally I'd hear him, wake up, and secretly watch him while I dozed on and off. I usually had some pretty fantastic dreams in that half-awake state.

Peeking over the edge of the bed, my smile was unstoppable as I mentally traced the lines of his bare back. Kellan's arms were shaking as he fluidly moved up and down. I wondered how long he'd been working out while I slept. He really pushed himself sometimes, almost like he was punishing himself.

I hoped his fervor this morning had nothing to do with Sienna. She hadn't kissed him again on stage, but the fan photos of that moment were everywhere. *True love sealed in a kiss,* was the tagline often used with it. The gossip magazines were having a field day with Kellan and Sienna now touring together. I'd seen more stories about how they "couldn't stay away from each other" than I cared to count. Headlines like, "Kellan Kyle Ditches Tour with Avoiding Redemption to Rush to His Lover's Side" were all too common. Everyone was enamored with the fact that, regardless of his abject denial of their relationship, Kellan seemingly couldn't stay away from Sienna.

Wondering if Kellan was all right this morning, I whispered, "You okay?"

He paused an inch from the floor and looked up at me. Then his arms gave out and he crashed to the ground. Laughing a little, he mumbled, "Yeah, I'm good." Standing up, he swung out his arms; his muscles flexed and released as he stretched them out. "I just missed feeling sore, so I was doing a few extra today. I didn't mean to wake you up."

My eyes drifted down to his signature black boxers. "You didn't. I was ready to get up."

Lifting up the covers, Kellan crawled back into bed with me. His skin was warm from working out; slightly moist, but not yet tacky. I cringed back from him anyway. "You're sweaty."

Laughing, he clamped his legs around mine. "Well, we'll just have to make you sweaty too, so it doesn't bother you."

I laced my arms around his neck and pulled him into me; it suddenly didn't bother me anymore. As his lips lowered to my neck, I looked out the closest window. We were speeding down an urban freeway in an early morning commute. A car was right beside us, and the driver was singing along to something like *he* was the lead singer of a rock band. I froze as I wondered again about the glass. It had a dark tint to it, but could that guy see me?

Kellan didn't notice I was distracted and started moving his lips down my neck. His fingers started bunching up my shirt in preparation to remove it. I groaned and half-closed my eyes, but somehow managed to stop Kellan's fingers. Intense bedroom eyes peeked up at me, and I swallowed as I nodded toward the glass. "Kellan, can they see us?"

Kellan glanced over at the car, not looking like he cared if the guy could or not. "No," he quickly answered, bringing his lips back to mine.

Believing him, I let myself relax into his arms. There was something incredibly erotic about making love in a place that had the illusion of being very public. As cars buzzed around three sides of us—each one of them with a stunning view, if only they knew—my body heated to a boiling point.

Breath intense, I helped Kellan strip off all of my clothes. When I was bare beneath him, his warm palm molded to my breast, gently squeezing. Wanting to return the favor, I slipped my hand down the front of his shorts. He was fully ready for me. As I moved my hand along him, Kellan stopped kissing me. His breath started speeding up as he closed his eyes. He was gorgeous to watch, and I ramped up my efforts. He dropped his head to my shoulder, slumping his chest against mine. "God, I love it when you touch me," he groaned in my ear.

His words sent an ache straight to my core, and I suddenly wanted to do a lot more than touch him. I wanted to reduce him to a pile of incoherent rubble again. I wanted to make him cry out so loud, that surely someone in a car zipping past us would hear him. Knowing that I *could* do all of those things made me feel both beautiful and seductive, and made me love being with him even more.

Kellan didn't give me a chance, though. Before I could make my move on him, he pulled his body out of my reach and started working his way down my skin. His fingers slid between my legs right as his mouth closed over my breast. Clutching my pillow, I cried out like I'd wanted him to. As his fingers stoked the fire raging within me, I arched my back and glanced at the car behind us; the driver following the bus looked so bored. I moaned and closed my eyes. If they only knew.

Kellan's lips quickly trailed over my stomach, leaving tingling goose bumps in their wake. When he neared my waist, I started mumbling his name. I was gripping the pillow in my hands so hard, I was sure it would tear any minute. Kellan reached where I needed him, but he didn't do anything. I felt like I was going to die while I waited. He stilled my squirming hips, then he lightly blew on me. I gasped, and commanded myself to not climax. It took a lot of willpower.

I thought I heard him laugh, but his tongue was on me then, so I didn't much care if he was amused or not. Reaching down, I tangled my fingers in his hair. As I clenched and unclenched, he alternated patterns up, over, and across my tender flesh. I couldn't take anymore. As a burst of euphoria flooded through me, I cried out. Kellan gently brought me down, then worked his way back up my body.

When I was taffy beneath him, soft, warm, and pliable, and now a little sweaty, he murmured, "I can never get past H with you."

I had no idea what he meant, but I was reeling from my explosive release and didn't really care. "What?"

I languidly ran my hand up his back as he started grinding his hips against mine. He was turning me up again, and it was working, the fire was rekindling. His lips followed my collarbone. "The alphabet . . . I can never make it past H before you . . . finish." He peeked up at me with hooded eyes.

"What . . . are you talking about?" I muttered.

He ran his nose up my throat, lightly tasting my skin with his tongue. That miraculous tongue worked its way over to my ear, and that's when I finally caught on to what he was saying. I looked over at his amused face. "You're drawing the alphabet while you . . . ?"

He smiled, placing a light kiss on my slightly damp cheek. "It's been a goal of mine to make it through the entire alphabet, but I've yet to do it." His grin turned cocky. "I'll keep trying, though."

Kellan removed his boxers, then ground his hips against me again. The very tip of him moved into me and I gasped and clenched his back. When he pulled away, I groaned; he was killing me. "Has anyone done it to you?" I asked, restraining myself from grabbing his hips and forcing him to bury himself inside of me.

Kellan paused in kissing my neck. "The alphabet? No, I don't think so."

It was only then that I realized just what I'd asked him. Was that a strange question? Could that be done on a guy? Would he like that? Just the thought of doing that to him made my earlier desire resurface full force. He'd just satisfied me. If I could give him just a fraction of that . . .

Before he could say anything else, I pushed him back and started working my way down his chest. His breath hitched as he caught on to what I was planning to do. "I know it's not your thing, Kiera. You don't have to do something you don't like to please me." His eyes met mine as I peeked up at him. "I like tasting you, that's why I do it."

His words made an ache surge through me. Smiling into his belly button, I murmured, "No, it's not my favorite thing. But I like the way you react to it." I playfully bit into the lean muscle of his lower abdomen, and Kellan's eyes fluttered closed as he laid his head back on the pillow.

"Uh . . . 'kay," he mumbled.

His hand threaded through my hair as I kissed the tip of him. Not really sure what I was going to do, I gently took him into my mouth. This really wasn't my favorite thing, but hearing Kellan's reaction, the deep groan he made as he clenched my hair tight *was* one of my favorite things, and I focused on that. Working my hand over the long part of him, I alternated bringing him deep into my mouth and letting him go so I could run my tongue over the top of him. I drew a different letter each time I swirled around the tip. Around G I could tell that I was seriously driving him crazy. It drove me crazy too. I lost myself, getting more and more into it. Kellan's hand wrapped in my hair started shaking, like he was restraining himself from holding me down on him. On the letter L he was squirming around the bed, moaning my name. I nearly lost it, but I kept going with the elaborate tease. When I swirled my tongue around him in a giant O, he sat up and pulled me off of him as he moved to his knees. Before I knew what he was doing, his lips were on mine, hard, needy, and he moved me so I was straddling him. Without a word, he pulled my hips down, sinking me onto him—it stole my breath, it was so intense.

We held each other tight as we began to move together in a near frenzy; I'd never seen him so riled up. With cars still zipping past us, oblivious to our passion, I skyrocketed right over the edge. Kellan stiffened a fraction of a second later, plummeting as well. When we were both spent, we slumped in each other's arms. The driver behind us still looked apathetic, poor soul.

Carefully lifting myself from Kellan's lap, I collapsed onto the bed with a content sigh. Kellan snuggled up next to me, his breath erratic. As I twisted to cuddle into his chest, Kellan let out a low groan. "Oh . . . my . . . God . . . that was amazing."

Containing my smile, I murmured, "Well, looks like I didn't get to finish the alphabet either."

I felt a little wobbly when I made my way to the shower later. I could hear snoring on the other side of the curtain separating our room and the bathroom from the rest of the bus. Good, probably nobody had heard us. *Wow, what a way to wake up.* My mind and body were completely energized and the creative juices were flowing. I kept my shower brief so I could get started on writing.

Kellan was absent from our room when I went back to it, but it didn't take me long to find him. The bus was only so big, after all. Creeping past the people still slumbering, I made my way to the lounging area of the bus. The driver nodded at me and I waved, hoping he hadn't heard anything. I sometimes forgot about the drivers of our busses. This one was a sweet older man named Jonathan. Oh well, Jonathan was a professional bus driver for rock stars. I'm sure he'd heard and seen a lot.

Kellan was seated on a plush chair near a table, strumming his guitar. He peeked up at me and smiled, and I took a moment to just appreciate him before making my way over. He nodded his head at a steaming cup on the table. "Coffee? It's instant." He cringed. There was a small kitchen area near the bathrooms, with a microwave and a mini-fridge, but that was about it.

I graciously accepted the cup anyway. "Thank you."

Kellan watched me set up my notes and laptop, then returned to his guitar. We worked side by side for a while, with Kellan's guitar and my keyboard making the only sound. Then Kellan started humming a song. It wasn't a melody I'd heard before, and I paused the story in my head to listen to him work on something new. I guess I wasn't the only one who'd been inspired this morning. I loved that we could be together, but could be doing our own thing too. We each had our own lives, our own joys, our own friends. We weren't dependent on each other for happiness, but being together sure amplified the feeling.

As the minutes stretched on, I thought I could peacefully live out the rest of my days this way. Then an exclamation of surprise sounded from the back of the bus. Kellan and I both turned to look, but the curtain was still in place, and we couldn't see anything. We heard it, though. Or rather, we heard *him*.

Louder than was necessary, Griffin was repeating, "Oh my fucking God!" over and over. Other people grumbled, while a few more loudly shushed him; it was still pretty early. Dread bubbled in my stomach. I was really apprehensive about anything that could shock Griffin.

Kellan set down his guitar and stood up. "Why don't you stay here?" he said to me. For once, I did as he asked. My heart was beating harder as I watched the curtain swish closed behind Kellan.

I heard a slew of excited whispers and mumbled complaints. I really had no idea what was going on. The longer Kellan stayed back there, the more curious I became. I half-stood a handful of times, only to sit back down again. Did I really want to know? Yes . . . and no.

When I finally couldn't stand it, Kellan remerged. Maybe it was my imagination, but he looked a little paler. As he approached me, I thought I heard my cell phone going off in the very back of the bus. After it silenced, it went off again.

Kellan quietly sat in the chair next to me while Griffin peeked his head out of the curtain. I couldn't tell if the look on his face was incredulity, excitement, or just uncontainable curiosity. He was pulled back into the sleeping section seconds later. My eyes were wide and fearful, my belly full of dread as I locked gazes with Kellan. "What?" I whispered.

Kellan scrunched his brow, almost like he was at a loss for words. My cell phone was still incessantly ringing. While he thought, I murmured, "Maybe I should get that. It could be my sister."

Kellan's expression darkened. "I wouldn't be surprised."

"Kellan?"

Sighing, he placed a hand on my knee and said, "Joey leaked the tape. It's all anyone is talking about this morning."

My heart sank, but it quickly evened out. I'd been expecting this bombshell. "Oh, you had me worried for a minute." Kellan chewed on his lip, and I instantly knew there was more. "What?" I muttered.

He rubbed his thumb around the temple of his skull, like he had a headache. "Joey's camera was . . . fucking fabulous." His tone was harsh and sarcastic. Pausing his mind massage, he looked up at me. "It's so grainy that she's hard to make out, so, because of Nick shoving me onto this tour, and all of the stories, photos, and speculation, everyone is just assuming that I'm doing—"

My heart stopped. "They think you made a sex tape with Sienna."

Kellan nodded. "They look enough alike that it's a really easy mistake to make. Plus, the angle wasn't that great, and there's no date on the tape. The only clear thing about it is that it's definitely me." He rolled his eyes. "There is this one clear shot of my face, since I . . . started the recording . . . and Joey says my name a lot."

A wave of nausea rolled through me, but I pushed it back. He'd made that tape a long time ago. "Oh, should you say something?"

"Yes, absolutely, but . . ." Kellan shrugged. "I'm not so sure that it will matter. People will believe what they want to believe." He closed his eyes that suddenly looked very tired. "Even Griffin believes it's Sienna on the tape." Reopening his eyes, he cupped my cheek. "I'm sorry, but I think I just unintentionally gave them the irrefutable proof they were looking for. I don't think it's possible to stop this now."

Knowing he was probably right, I let out a weary sigh. We couldn't just make a statement and think that everyone would suddenly understand what was really going on. The public was too in love with the idea of Kellan and Sienna as a couple. No one had really believed Kellan before this tape exploded in our faces. They definitely wouldn't believe him now. With Kellan's very first "No comment" response, we had unwittingly helped fuel up a locomotive. Nick and Sienna had then taken control and sent it barreling down the tracks, and this sex tape had just snapped the brake lines. The gossip train was out of control now. All we could do was wait for its inevitable crash and hope we all survived the wreckage.

I pushed my computer away, no longer inspired.

I fielded phone calls after that, a lot of phone calls—my sister, Jenny, Cheyenne, Kate, and horrifyingly enough, my parents. They thankfully hadn't watched the videos or seen any still shots, but even my mom and dad couldn't escape the global gossip of Kellan and Sienna's sex tape. I don't think my mom believed me when I told her the wedding was still on.

I finally calmed my parents down, but every single one of my friends had to be "convinced" that the video was years old. Eventually it came down to the tattoo. I gave all of them the assignment of watching the video and looking at Kellan's chest. If my name wasn't engraved above his heart, then they would know without a doubt that it was filmed before we were a couple. That fact wouldn't help me with the general public, since not a lot of people knew about his tattoo as it had been cleverly covered up for the music video, but it swayed my friends. By the time I hung up with them, they grudgingly believed me.

Denny was the last phone call of the day—and the one I'd been dreading the most. I was sitting on the bed I shared with Kellan when my phone rang. The bus had stopped a while ago, and the numerous roadies were out in force, setting up tonight's show. I had no idea what city we were in; I'd already lost track.

The boys were all out exploring, probably introducing Holeshot to their little drinking game. The two bands meshed together well, which didn't surprise me; the D-Bags were an easy-going group, they got along with most people. Kellan had asked me to go out with him, but I didn't want to. Then he'd offered to stay in with me, but I didn't want that either. I wanted to be alone, staring at the rain streaking down the windowpane and contemplating the strangeness of my life. After he'd gone, I'd found a flower petal taped to the bathroom mirror with the words *I'm sorry* on it. I knew he was. I was sorry too.

I stared at my ringing phone in annoyance. I almost didn't have it in me to explain to yet another friend that Kellan wasn't having an affair with Sienna Sexton. It was a little irritating how quick they all were to jump on the "He's a D-Bag" train. But with the music video, the photos, the tour changeup, and now the sex tape, the evidence against him was pretty damning, and I didn't blame them too much. If I weren't here with Kellan, I might have believed it too.

Seeing Denny's name on my screen, I hesitated, then picked it up. "Hey, Denny," I answered, feeling sleepy.

"Hey . . . I bet you're tired of people calling you."

I smiled for what felt like the first time in hours. "You have no idea. But I'm glad *you* called me."

"So . . . do I ask?"

"It's Joey's tape, the one I told you about. She finally leaked it . . . and everyone thinks it's Sienna. It's kind of sad, really. Joey wanted to be in his spotlight so badly, and even with documented proof, she still can't get there." A humorless laugh escaped me.

Denny exhaled a long breath. "I figured that's what it was. Are you holding up okay?"

Relief flooded through me. It was so nice to not have to convince someone. "I'm as okay as I can be, considering Kellan is making front page news with another woman. Regardless of who that other woman is or isn't, it still sucks. I'm afraid to even turn my computer on."

"Give it some time. They'll move on to something else soon."

I shifted my gaze to a raindrop running down the window. Watching the rain was so peaceful. My life used to be peaceful. Wasn't it, just this morning? "I know, but it's entirely possible that the next story they move on to will also include Kellan." I sniffed, hating that this was getting to me. "I just miss . . ."

My voice trailed off. I was about to say that I missed nobody knowing who he was, but that was never true. Kellan had always had a swirl of notoriety around him. He was always a star. It was just on a much smaller scale at Pete's. Sharing him was nothing new, it was just more expansive now.

Denny answered my open-ended statement. "I know." Silence stretched out between us, then Denny added, "You could always come home, Kiera. Let that world go for a while?"

Holding my knees tight to my chest, I considered it. I could stay home in an empty house, writing all day and night. I could visit my sister, my friends. I could even fly home to see my parents—briefly— and I could spend time with Denny. It sounded nice, familiar, comfortable, but . . . my heart was anchored to Kellan. Being apart from him stretched my soul in opposite directions. It was painful. No, it was torture. He was everything to me, and I didn't want to miss a moment of his journey just because parts of it were unpleasant. No. When I'd agreed to be his wife, I'd also been agreeing to stand beside him through thick or thin. And if I could stand by his side during the filming of that damn music video, then I could stand beside him while he dealt with the consequences of his reckless youth. I wasn't running, I wasn't avoiding—not anymore.

"No . . . I belong here with Kellan. But thank you for listening, Denny."

When I ran into Sienna that night, she was all smiles, loving the attention. Of course, she acted mortified when she spoke with anyone who interviewed her. She even walked away from a gossip site reporter, throwing her hands into the air and stalking off like she was offended to the core of her being that something so private was being brought up in casual conversation. By her actions alone, the rumors were confirmed: Kellan and Sienna had made a sex tape together. The world went into a gossip mongering frenzy, and the glorifying of them as a couple exploded into the stratosphere.

Kellan tried to put out the fire. Physically, he stayed as far away from her as possible, even going to the extreme of singing their duets on the other side of the stage as her. He told everyone who would listen that Sienna was not the girl in the video, and he was not, nor had he ever been, in a relationship with her. It was all too little, too late, though. Nothing could stop the gossip train.

Two weeks after the tape's release, the sordid gossip was still going strong. We were in Atlanta, Georgia, a place I had always wanted to visit, and the boys were doing an early afternoon in-studio radio interview. I was sitting on a stool against the wall by Tory, who was always present when Kellan and the boys spoke to the press. While I was slumped against the wall, Tory sat ramrod straight, slightly leaning forward, ready to pounce. Her eyes watched the DJs like a hawk—or like a mama bear protecting her cubs.

"So, Kellan . . . rumors are going crazy. Anything you want to say about the lovely and quite *talented* Sienna Sexton?" The DJ stressed the word talented, and everyone in the room knew he wasn't talking about her music.

Kellan shifted on his seat. "I've said this about five million times, but she's an acquaintance of mine. We work together, nothing more." Tory's eyes tightened at Kellan's admission, but she knew, just like Nick and Sienna, that nothing Kellan said at this point really mattered—a fact the DJ confirmed seconds later.

"Right . . . work." He turned to his partner. "That's a gig I wouldn't mind getting."

They both let out hearty laughs while Kellan's expression darkened. "I am not, nor have I ever been, in a relationship with Sienna."

The men turned incredulous eyes to Kellan. "So, that's not her on the tape with you?"

Kellan closed his eyes and seemed to count to ten before answering, "No."

The second male DJ responded with, "Sure looks like her. Even freeze-framed."

My stomach churned and my hands balled into fists. I hated that the odds were very good that everyone in this room had seen the tape of Kellan having sex. Well, everyone except for me. There was no way on this green earth that I was watching that. Some things can't be unseen, and Joey and Kellan going at it like porn stars was one of those things.

Staring the DJ down, Kellan straightforwardly told him, "I don't see what any of this has to do with my music, which is why I'm here. The woman in the video was a girl I dated years ago, long before I ever met Sienna. While she happens to sort of resemble her, it's *not* Sienna Sexton."

Both male DJs glanced at each other. "It's sort of strange that no girl has come forward then, right? I mean, if this 'not-Sienna' you dated leaked the tape . . . where is she?" He used air quotes, like he still didn't believe Kellan.

This was unfortunately a sticky point for us. Joey hadn't made a peep. She hadn't come out to fight for her right as the proud participant in the video. She hadn't basked in the glow of Kellan's spotlight. She hadn't snatched her claim to fame. The only thing she'd done so far was stay quiet as a mouse and let Sienna take all her "glory." It seemed completely unlike Joey to me.

Kellan stammered on his answer. "I don't . . . I don't know." Knowing he was digging himself into a hole, Kellan turned around and glanced at Tory, silently asking her to shift the conversation.

A female in a back booth chimed in with her thoughts. "I think it's sweet that he protects Sienna by denying it. It's chivalrous." She pointed at the two DJs. "You guys could learn a thing a two." I wanted to stab the girl with a pen. How much clearer did Kellan have to be?

Tory stepped forward and made a cutting motion with her hand over her throat. The implication was clear to the DJs: *End this line of questioning, or I pull my talent.* They quickly redirected the interview toward the band's concert that night, and Kellan visibly relaxed.

When the interview was over, Kellan walked over to me, his expression glum. He really hated that he couldn't steer the public's perception of him. He was a puppet, along for the ride, but not really a part of it. No, this show belonged entirely to Nick and Sienna. I patted his arm in sympathy, then I dropped my hand to my side. I was keeping public affection to a minimum. Not only did I still not want the world's attention focused on me, but things with "Kell-Sex" were just too crazy at the moment. And if Kellan couldn't control what people thought about *him,* then he definitely couldn't control what people thought about *me.* If the gossipers figured out who I was, they'd never leave us alone. They would paint me as the other woman in the Kell-Sex love affair. I would be hated, reviled, possibly even egged. Being in an across-the-globe scandal freaked me out so much that I had even asked Kellan to switch his wedding ring to his right hand when we were out. I just didn't want to cause unnecessary problems for myself. T̶   ̶l̶m̶ ̶a̶ ̶l̶i̶t̶t̶l̶e̶ ̶b̶i̶t̶. And they would, as soon a

In an absurd way
turbingly familiar fee
were going to keep o
could. Marriage licen
one searching deep e

Since we had roll
until tonight, the ba
and I had decided t
with a Jacuzzi. As a
Bags and company
through my bag, I fo
I was trying to rea

would have had more luck reading an entire novel if Kellan read it to me. Actually, that wasn't a bad idea.

Glancing at the screen, I answered with, "Hey, sis. What's up?"

"Where are you?"

Looking out the window, I told her, "Atlanta, why?"

My sister huffed. "I know you're in Atlanta. Where in Atlanta are you right at this very second?"

"We're on the road. We just left the radio station and we're heading to the hotel, some swanky place in Buckheel, Buckhead, something like that. Why?"

My sister's tone brightened. "Oh, good! I'm coming to the show tonight. Can you flip a bitch and swing by the airport to pick me up?"

It took me a minute to register what she was saying. "You're in Georgia?"

Twisting around from the front seat, Griffin echoed my question. "Anna's in Georgia?" His eyes damn near sparkled with the news. "Awesome. Where is she?"

I answered Griffin with "Airport," while my sister answered me. "Yep! My flight just arrived."

Dumbfounded, my only thought was, "Why are you in Georgia?" My second thought was *Swing by?* The airport was nowhere near our hotel. In fact, our hotel was a bit north of the heart of Atlanta, where the concert was tonight, while the airport was south. Going to get her was way out of our way. But I wouldn't abandon her the airport. Neither would Griffin; he was already telling the driver n around.

snorted before she answered my question. "I just told you me get me. Love you!" Then she disconnected. I shook ed the phone back in my purse. Of course my sister lfway across the country on a whim to watch a

Chapter 18
Company

My spontaneous, erratic, fly-by-the-seat-of-her-pants sister arrived with a half-dozen pieces of luggage. Just by the look of her, I had a feeling she was staying for more than *one* concert. And her belly had grown so much bigger since the last time I'd seen her. Her waddle had turned genuine. As I wrapped my arms around her, the baby pressed against my stomach. Giggling, I leaned down and placed a hand over the protrusion. "Hi, Max," I cooed.

"It's Maximus," Griffin interrupted, brushing me aside to collect Anna into his arms. Grabbing her face, he greeted her with his tongue. It was a little over the top on the PDA scale, but I'd been watching Griffin ever since his admission that he hadn't been with anyone else since Anna told him she was pregnant, and from all I'd seen, he was telling the truth. And that was a lot of abstinence for the horn dog; he had to be practically dying on a daily basis.

When they pulled apart, my sister's deep green eyes scoured Griffin's body like she was starving and he was a prime rib dinner. She'd been "abstaining" too, and had a sex drive just as insatiable as Griffin's. Great. Unless I locked myself away somewhere, there was no way I'd be able to avoid hearing, and possibly seeing, their sexploits. This was going to be a long visit.

The two of them were all hands and lips in the car. Grimacing as he sat beside the pair, Matt asked, "We *are* going straight back to the hotel, right?"

Kellan and Evan laughed while I did my best to ignore the fact that Griffin and my sister were panting. I was keeping my gaze strictly on the scenery flying past, but I could hear clothes rustling. God, I hoped they were both still fully dressed. If I heard a zipper, I was out of the car, regardless if it was speeding down the freeway or not.

The behemoth of an SUV finally arrived at the St. Regis Atlanta. The posh hotel was a tall, stately building that screamed elegance and opulence. A fountain in front highlighted a covered drop-off area paved with what looked like slabs of slate. Everything about the architecture was designed to intimidate and impress. But the beauty of the building was lost on me at that moment; I didn't care how nice the hotel was, I just wanted out of the car. When the vehicle stopped, band members poured out of it like something toxic had been released inside. Evan and Kellan were still chuckling as they started gathering Anna's luggage from the back. Matt looked ill. Anna and Griffin didn't get out of the car.

A bellhop magically appeared with a luggage rack, and our driver took over the unpacking job from Evan and Kellan. We had a handful of drivers available to us whenever we went anywhere. All of them were arranged by the label. This one's name was Paul. He was polite, competent, and most of all silent; he only spoke to us if we asked him a direct question. I was sure that was why the label employed him. Who knows how many nondisclosures he'd had to sign.

Evan and Matt walked away with the bellhop while Paul went back to the driver's side and climbed inside. I stood by the back with Kellan, waiting for my sister to get out of the car. Seconds turned into minutes. The weather there was beautiful for late October. While back home it would be starting to bluster, rain, and turn frigid at night, here it felt like a perfectly breezy spring day. Still, I did not feel like spending the entire day waiting for my sister to get out of the damn car.

Paul was sitting behind the wheel, politely waiting for the rock star to finish . . . whatever he was doing to Anna. Not wanting to interrupt them myself, I twisted to Kellan. "Can you . . . ?" I indicated the backseat of the tank in front of us.

Kellan smirked, payback in his eyes. "I would love to."

He strutted over to the door, swung it wide open, and reached inside. God, I really hoped they were still dressed. A second later, Kellan reemerged with a disheveled Griffin. Griffin glowered at Kellan, pushing his hands away from him. His jeans were open. The sight made my stomach tighten. Griffin was just about to launch into a curse-filled rant when my sister slid out of the door. She kissed Griffin's cheek as she readjusted the clingy maternity dress she was wearing. Griffin's objections immediately died off. Anna walked over to me and looped her arm around mine like she hadn't just been rounding third base in the back of an occupied vehicle.

"This is going to be so much fun, Kiera!" she squealed, squeezing me tight. As she pulled me toward the hotel, I looked behind us. Griffin's eyes were glued on her ass; he still hadn't zipped up his pants.

The bellhop was waiting for us when we entered the lobby. I had to give this hotel high scores in the Wow department. The lobby looked straight out of *Gone With the Wind*—sweeping grand staircases, crystal chandeliers, hardwood floors, and exquisitely detailed rugs. While Anna gaped at the luxury around us, Matt and Evan made arrangements for her at the front desk. It warmed me that the boys so easily accepted girlfriends and wives joining them, whether for short or long bursts. As far as twenty-something rock stars went, the guys weren't your stereotypical hotel-room trashing, groupie-banging, party-all-night divas. Well, most of the guys weren't, and they kept Griffin in line.

When the bellhop got the okay to lead Anna to our rooms, we made our way to the elevator. Kellan and Griffin were back by that time, but they had to wait for the next car. This hotel was plusher than any hotel I'd been in back home, ten times nicer than my honeymoon suite with Kellan. The inner doors of the elevator were made of burnished brass, and Anna's and my reflection stared back at us.

Anna preened while I examined her belly. "I'm thrilled to see you, Anna, but should you really be traveling in your condition?"

Anna stopped running her fingers through her board-straight, dark brown locks. "Condition? I'm not diseased."

The bellhop's lips twitched. His head was facing straight forward, but the reflective doors made it pretty obvious that his gaze was blatantly fixed on Anna's ample chest. Sort of wanting to block his view, I told my sister, "Yeah, but what if you went into labor early, on the plane or something?"

Anna gave me a humoring smile as she wrapped her arm around me. "You worry too much. Besides, how awesome would that story be?" Her fingers spread in the air like she was reading a headline. "'Baby Boy Delivered at 30,000 Feet.' Film at eleven."

The bellhop snorted, switching it to a cough. Anna flashed him an award-winning smile. I couldn't help feeling just a tiny smidge of jealousy. Ah, to be as breezy as my sister. Somehow, the I-don't-give-a-crap gene had skipped me. The elevator dinged to a stop, and the bellhop politely indicated for us to go first. I wasn't sure if that was his training or if he wanted a peek at the backside that had Griffin poised for action.

As we walked along the thick carpet, I glanced at the copious amount of luggage my sister had decided she couldn't live without. "You sure brought a lot of stuff for one concert," I murmured.

Grasping my hand in hers, Anna giggled. "Actually, I'm staying."

All of the muscles in my jaw stopped working. "You are? But, what about your job?" Anna worked at the "family" restaurant, Hooters. Her manager had spent a lot of time and energy mentoring her on the business side of the restaurant. Up until, well, yesterday, Anna's plan had been to get into management after the baby. Had she up and quit her job? Actually, that would not surprise me in the least.

Not a care in the world, Anna shrugged. "I decided to go on maternity leave."

We arrived at the end of the hallway where the rock star's rooms were. The D-Bags and I had two rooms on one side of the hall, and the three members of Holeshot had one room on the other side. Sienna had the entire penthouse suite. I had a feeling that Anna and Griffin would be confiscating one of the D-Bags' rooms, and the rest of us were going to be very cozy for a while. Maybe Kellan and I would return to our bus sanctuary quicker than I thought.

Still a little shocked, I sputtered, "But you have a month left," as I used my key to unlock one of the rooms.

Anna walked through like she owned the place. "I know! Just one month to be wild and crazy and completely carefree." Walking over to a crisply made bed, she sprawled herself across the elaborately brocaded cover. "Why would I want to waste my last chance at freedom being shackled to a restaurant when I could be touring the country with a bunch of rock stars?" She raised an eyebrow at me, like I should completely understand. I did. I just also understood the reality of her situation.

I sat beside her as her luggage was wheeled into the room. "But what about the baby? Where are you going to have him?"

Her face turned droll. "Call me crazy, but I was planning on having him in a hospital."

I shook my head. "What if we're not near one when you go into labor? What if we're in the middle of nowhere?" Oh God, was I going to have to deliver my sister's baby? On a tour bus? I felt a little sick just thinking about it. I was not a blood, mucus, and gore-friendly person.

She waved my concerns away. "It will be fine, Kiera. Don't stress so much."

I knew that the delivery part of having a baby actually did worry my carefree sister, and I started to wonder if that was the real reason for her escape from Seattle. My sister could do denial better than anyone.

Griffin and Kellan popped into the room a minute later. Kellan tipped the bellhop while Griffin lay down on the bed next to my sister. His hands were under her dress before I even had a chance to turn away. Feeling my cheeks heat as the sounds of lip-smacking filled the air, I hurried over to Kellan. He was lightly laughing at the frisky pair of reunited lovers. Grabbing his hand, I pulled him from the room and tossed over my shoulder, "Catch you guys later."

Anna mumbled some response, then let out a low moan. I quickly closed their door and headed over to the other room reserved for the D-Bags. Anna and Griffin could have that room all to themselves. That was just fine.

Just as she'd said, Anna stayed with us after the concert. When the busses packed up and left Atlanta, my sister packed up and headed out with us. Griffin was in seventh heaven now that Anna was with him again. A part of me wanted to believe that it was just because he was having regular sex again—a *lot* of regular sex—but there were brief moments of tenderness in between the sex that made me wonder if Griffin really did love my sister, and if she really did love him.

I certainly enjoyed having some more feminine energy on the bus while we traveled, and I loved having my sister close to me again; it was nice to have someone to talk to about all the craziness going on. The only thing I didn't love was the loss of my marriage bed. Griffin and Anna evicted Kellan and me from our bedroom the minute she climbed on board. And I couldn't even really complain about it because she was pregnant—very pregnant. Making her sleep in an uncomfortable cubby would be cruel.

So I grudgingly squished myself between Kellan and the bus wall every night and tried to ignore the lack of privacy, space, and comfort. *It's okay, I love my sister and she needs the room more than I do* became my new bedtime mantra as I attempted to fall asleep amidst the snoring, shuffling, and chatting of my many rock-star bunk mates.

Waking up with a kink in my neck after another restless night, I debated if Kellan and I could rent a motor home for the remainder of the tour. The hole-in-the-wall bunks even made me miss our thin mattress on Justin's bus. It was dark in our cubby, and the bus was unusually quiet. I figured it was still early, or late. I didn't know. Time was meaningless when alternating between packing up late at night and heading out early in the morning. And crisscrossing over time zones only added to the confusion. My internal clock was all sorts of messed up. I only knew that I was awake while others appeared to be asleep.

The sleeping portion of the bus had no windows, and the thin gray curtain that gave us the illusion of privacy was fully extended. It was peaceful, if cramped. My eyes quickly adjusted to the lack of light, and blocky shapes sharpened into distinct objects. A smiling set of lips were the first thing I noticed.

"Mornin'," Kellan whispered.

I stretched my tight joints and carefully turned my neck; it ached badly. I was going to have to invest in a therapeutic pillow soon. "Good morning . . . is it morning?" I yawned.

His hand on my stomach shifted to my side, pulling me into him. "No idea."

Kellan was tall, a bit too tall for the cubbies, and his knees were pressing into my thighs. As we scooted closer together, I wrapped my legs around his. Coincidentally, our bodies lined up right "there." Kellan's grin widened as he leaned in to give me a soft kiss. "Sleep well?" he asked.

My neck complaining, I shook my head. "Not really. I miss our bed."

Kellan frowned as he shifted around; his head bumped the top of the cubby while his feet kicked the side and his elbow brushed the curtain. "Me too, I feel like a sardine in here."

Sighing, I laced my arms around his neck. "I suppose we don't always have to sleep together. We might sleep better apart."

Kellan hugged me to his bare chest, his long arms wrapping over and under my ribcage. "I'd rather go without sleep than without you."

As we lightly kissed, Kellan's hands slid under my tank top. Loving the feeling of his skin dancing over mine, I melded my body into his. Maybe being cramped wasn't such a bad thing after all, although it did lend itself to intimacy problems. We hadn't been together much since my sister had joined the tour a couple of weeks ago. I was sort of dying to make love to him.

I could tell that Kellan was dying too, as one of his hands followed the curve of my spine and darted beneath my underwear to rest on my backside. I stifled a groan and pressed my hips into his. Cramped or not, we could make this work. Our kiss picked up as his hand massaged my skin. My fingers tangled in his hair, drawing him into me.

With some shuffling, cursing, and light banging on the sides of the cubby, we resituated so that Kellan was on his back and I was on top of him. There was not a lot of room, and my back almost touched the top of the cubby. It gave me a weird feeling to know that Evan was sleeping just a few feet above me. Kellan's knees were raised as I straddled him, and he pressed against the back of the cubby to lift his hips. I shoved aside the thought that Matt's head was essentially right next to Kellan's feet.

Now that our sensitive parts were crushing together unimpeded, the rush of desire blossoming in my core spread throughout every nerve in my body like a wildfire. Not wanting to cry out, I clamped my teeth around Kellan's shoulder. He sucked in a breath and started pulling down my lounge pants. Damn clothes. They were difficult to get off in such a tight space, especially with covers wrapped around us, and both of us were panting with exertion and excitement as we tried to shove them down my hips. God, why didn't I sleep naked? With more curse words and scuffling, we finally managed to get them around my legs. Kellan reached down and looped them off of my foot. I kicked with my other foot, not caring where my clothes ended up at this point. I thought I saw them disappear out the cubby curtain.

I attacked Kellan's mouth while ripping at his boxers. I wanted him so badly, I might just tear the damn things off. Stilling my needy hips, Kellan lifted his and shoved his clothes down, but not off. That was fine with me; I just needed them out of the way. Positive I would explode any second, I pushed myself onto him once he was free. Kellan groaned and I clamped my hand over his mouth. It was still quiet in here, and as long as it was still quiet, I could pretend that we were completely alone.

We moved together with forceful determination. I didn't need foreplay, I didn't need teasing. I just needed him. I was all too aware of the creaking sound we were making, the unnatural rapidness of our breath, the seductive sound of skin on skin. There would be no way to deny what we were doing, if someone did happen to wake up. I didn't care anymore though—the look on Kellan's face, the fire raging at our point of connection—that was all I let fill my mind.

As the coiling in my body started to reach an apex, I moved my fingers away from Kellan's mouth and clamped my lips over his. Kellan's hand came up to the back of my neck, securely holding me in place. We whimpered between our fierce kisses. Just as I was sure I couldn't take anymore, I felt the glory of my release as I crashed over the edge. Kellan stiffened below me, and I knew he was feeling his own climax. I loved that we were experiencing it together. My body shook as I quietly contained the explosion shivering through me in waves. Kellan squirmed underneath me, his eyes squeezing closed as he contained his. Somehow, the self-imposed silence made the moment even more intense.

When we finally broke apart, we were both breathing heavily. I slumped in his arms as he let out a long, steady exhale. I listened for the telltale sound of movement as our breaths evened, but I didn't hear anything, thank God.

I cuddled with Kellan for as long as I could, but my body was fully awake now and I needed to use the facilities. I looked around for my pants before remembering that they had fallen into the aisle. Awesome. Carefully scooting over Kellan, who took the opportunity to tickle my sides—not helping my bladder *at all*—I peeked my head out of our curtain. Since we were on the bottom of the stack, my pants hadn't fallen too far. As I reached out for them, I noticed that the curtain was pulled back on the cubby directly across from me. Deacon was partially sitting up, reading a book with a soft night-light.

All of the blood drained from my face as he glanced over at me retrieving the bottom half of my pajamas. Thankfully, I was still wearing the top half. Now I remembered exactly why I didn't go to bed naked. As I stared in horror, Deacon lifted his hand in a small wave. It was too dark for me to know for sure if he was embarrassed or not, but his smile was appropriately sheepish.

I opened and shut my mouth like a guppy that had been yanked out of its fishbowl. What do I say? Should I apologize? Should he? What was the proper etiquette in this situation? What would Miss Manners do? As I was floundering for something to ease the awkwardness, Deacon reached up and removed a small speaker from his ear; his long, dark hair had been hiding them from my sight. The tinny sound of loud rock music drifted over to me as he whispered, "Did you say something?"

I instantly relaxed. He hadn't heard anything. But Deacon wasn't an idiot. He'd seen my pants falling to the floor, and he was staring at me picking them back up. He knew. And I really didn't know how long he'd been awake, reading and listening to music. We may have stirred him from sleep, and he may have turned on his music to tune us out once he realized what we were engaged in right next to him. At least he was polite. If Griffin were across the aisle from us, he probably would have grabbed his cell phone and started recording.

Clutching my pants, I quickly shook my head and darted back into the solace of my Kellan-filled cubby. When I buried my head in his chest, Kellan asked, "Problem?"

I peeked up at him. "I *really* miss our room."

Kellan gave me a lopsided grin. "We'll start getting our own room at the hotel when we can."

I took what comfort from that as I could; brief moments of privacy were better than none at all. Dressing hastily, I accidently kneed my love in the privates, making him scrunch in pain. He glared at me as he clutched himself. "Sorry," I whispered, kissing his cheek.

"Definitely getting our own room," he muttered, closing his eyes.

Feeling bad and amused, I quickly left Kellan and made my way to the back of the bus to use the bathroom. I purposely kept my eyes on the tiny LED lights in the floor. I didn't want to see any other open cubbies. Ignorance was bliss.

By early afternoon, we were pulling into Charlotte, North Carolina; the concert tonight was at Time Warner Cable Arena. Anna was using my laptop to surf the Internet as everyone on the bus relaxed in the lounge section. Kellan and Evan were playing poker on one side of the room with Deacon and the bassist from Holeshot, David. Thankfully, Deacon hadn't said a word to me about our awkward exchange this morning. Matt was having a quiet conversation on his cell phone, most likely with Rachel. The other Holeshot band member, the drummer, Ray, was playing Guitar Hero with Griffin. Griffin was winning hands down. Like I had been for the past hour, I was impatiently waiting for Anna to finish with my computer so I could write a paragraph or two before the show. Every time I'd asked for it back, she'd given me the "just a minute" finger. She was visiting a parenting website, though, so I didn't push her too hard. I could go back to my old-fashioned notebook for a little while longer.

Looking up at the thick, dreary clouds hanging low in the North Carolina sky, Anna pouted and murmured, "I miss Florida."

After Atlanta, we'd spent some time in the Sunshine State. Miami was a big hit with my sister; even bursting at the seams pregnant, she'd had a good time. She'd been delighted that she could sunbathe in the middle of autumn, and was even up for some club-hopping after the boys' show. I reminded her that she was due in a couple of weeks, so maybe bumping and grinding at a night club wasn't the best idea. The band's concerts were loud enough, no need for baby Maximus to be born deaf by dancing the night away in bass-thumping nightclubs. Anna had scoffed at me, but with a big yawn had finally conceded. She'd gone on to bump and grind the night away privately with Griffin.

Giving my sister a humoring smile, I tapped my pen against my pad of paper while I thought about the way Kellan and I had reunited. I was approaching the tail end of our story, my favorite part of it, truly, when I'd stopped living in fear and had finally accepted the fact that we were meant to be together. The moment flooded back to me, absorbing me, and my mind began to spin faster than my pen could keep up.

Anna's attention refocused on the computer in front of her while I whipped through an especially emotional segment of my life. After a brief moment of peace, Anna loudly snorted, completely breaking my concentration. "What?" I asked, a little perturbed. Between her talking to me every five seconds, the loud twang of poorly played rock songs, and the good-natured ribbing going on at the poker table—usually at Kellan's expense—I probably would have had better luck concentrating in the comparatively quiet, but cramped, cubby.

"Did you know there are websites solely dedicated to proving Kellan's sex tape is with Sienna?"

That question got my complete and total attention, and I set down my pad of paper with a long sigh. Well, of course there were. Seeing that she'd sucked me in, Anna twirled the laptop around on the table so I could see the screen. Sure enough, someone had created a blog that centered around proving—without a doubt—that Kellan and Sienna had filmed themselves having sex. What the hell?

The page was plastered with still shots of Joey's movie. The dark, grainy images were enlarged and out of focus, but objects in the photographs were circled, and fantastical theories of the objects' significance were explained in detail beneath them. Seeing Kellan's bare back while he was plunging into another woman was way more than I'd ever wanted to see. It brought the horror of watching him film that music video fresh to my mind. Only this was worse. This was real. And I didn't want to see anymore.

Grimacing, I swung the screen back around toward my sister. Her jade eyes glanced Kellan's way and then she leaned forward, like she was spilling top secret information. "They're comparing still shots of Sienna's original tape, looking for similarities. They're pointing out a mark on Joey's inner thigh that sort of matches a birthmark on Sienna." She rolled her eyes while I tried not to think about the angle needed to get a still shot of Joey's thigh. "And even more absurd, they're claiming that an alarm clock in the room exactly matches one in a hotel nearby where the video for 'Regretfully' was filmed. They're saying they 'rehearsed' for the music video." She lifted her eyebrow at me, amused. "What a stretch, huh?" She pointed at the screen I refused to look at again. "It's so obvious that it's Joey's room they're in."

My veins suddenly felt like I'd injected ice water into them. Oh. My. God. Kellan and Joey filmed this in *her* old bedroom at his house. *My* old bedroom. The bedroom I had shared with Denny. The furniture I had shared with Denny. Kellan and Joey had sex on the same mattress Denny and I had sex on. The thought made my stomach roil.

I looked over at Kellan shaking his head at Evan as he tossed down his cards in defeat. Did he realize the six degrees of separation that had occurred on Joey's mattress? Well, he knew that we'd all had sex on that bed, sure, but I doubt he'd thought too much about it. I mean, he'd taken plenty of girls on his *own* bed, and being with him *there* didn't bother me, so why would him being on my old bed matter? It didn't, not really. I guess it was just the knowledge of Kellan and Denny both using the same mattress that disturbed me some. Regardless of the horrible things I'd done, I'd never crossed the line and invited Kellan into the bed I'd shared with Denny. It was an arbitrary line, I know, but at least I'd had one.

Blocking out the mental image of Kellan screwing someone on Denny's and my bed, I shifted my attention back to my sister. "How can you tell it's *my* old room from these blurry photos?" Narrowing my eyes, I instantly came up with the obvious answer. "You watched Kellan's sex tape?"

Anna waved her hand at me dismissively. "You told me to, remember?" Her manicured nail tapped the spot just above her heart. "And you were right, no tattoo."

I wanted to be irritated at that, but I *had* told all of my friends to watch the tape so they would know without a doubt that it wasn't

Kellan. I guess I couldn't really complain. I'd just never really thought my friends would watch it. I thought they'd be swayed by my unwavering declaration of Kellan's fidelity and take my word for it without actually viewing the triple-X footage. I should have known better. At least when it came to Anna. She'd probably hunkered down with a huge bowl of popcorn and eagerly watched Kellan in action. The frown on my face was irremovable.

Anna pursed her lips. "Oh, come on. If you weren't dating Sex on a Stick, you would want to watch the tape too. It's freaking hot."

"Anna!" I reached over and smacked her arm. "I don't want to hear stuff like that!"

She cringed, looking apologetic. "Sorry, but, well, look at him."

She swished her hand in Sex on a Stick's direction, and we both twisted to stare at Kellan. Our synchronized movement caught his attention and he looked over our way. He paused mid-laugh as his eyes darted between us. Looking for all the world like he'd just gotten caught with his fingers in the cookie jar, he mouthed, "What?"

Still eyeing Kellan, Anna muttered, "Anything he filmed would be freaking hot." Not answering Kellan, I glanced back at my sister. Her grin was lascivious as she told me, "*Your* tape with him would melt this computer."

My annoyance evaporated after her comment and a tension-relieving giggle escaped from me. When Anna and I looked back at Kellan, he was still watching us with a bewildered expression. Anna and I both broke into laughter. Was I really amused that my sex tape with him would be more explosive than Joey's? When did my life get so surreal?

Our amusement died down by the time we pulled into the venue. Shutting my laptop, Anna finally gave me back my computer. As I listened to the busses' brakes squeal and groan, Anna spoke in an oddly serious tone of voice. "Have you talked to Mom recently?"

The genuine concern in her question made my heart rate quicken. Was Mom okay? Had something happened? She'd been cancer-free for years, but maybe something had cropped back up?

But surely Dad would call me if that were the case. And she hadn't sounded upset when I'd last spoken with her, a few days ago. "A little while ago, why?"

I chewed on my lip, not liking the look on Anna's face. "You need to call her immediately." I was preparing my body to sprint to the back of the bus to get my phone when she added, "Since your wedding is a little over a month away, and you put her in charge of everything, which makes me think you're crazy . . . she picked out a dress for you. She sent me a picture." Anna wrinkled her face in disgust.

I completely relaxed as I fell back into the plush seat. Good, wedding drama I could deal with. As I laughed at my sister, the bus groaned to a stop. "I'm sure it's fine, Anna."

Anna leaned forward again, face intent. "No, you haven't seen this thing. It's got puffy sleeves, Kiera. Puffy. Sleeves. You need to do something about this ASAP!"

I sighed. There wasn't much I could do about it on the road. And I really didn't feel like flying home just to demean my mom's fashion choice. Sure, puffy sleeves didn't exactly sound fabulous to me, but since this ceremony was mainly for her anyway, did I really care what I wore? Not really. All I cared about was Kellan. Everything else seemed . . . insignificant.

Playing with my sister's head, I smirked and told her, "I can't wait to see what she picked up for *your* dress, Maid of Honor."

Anna flashed a wide grin, happy that I'd given her the top spot in my bridal party. Then her face fell. "Holy shit! She wouldn't . . ." I kept my gaze level and my smile even. Yeah, she would. Holding her belly, Anna sprang from the table and shuffled her way toward the back of the bus, surely to go inform our mother that there was no way in hell she was wearing anything with taffeta.

With practiced ease, the crew traveling with the bands sets up the stage. Unlike Justin's tour, the "talent" didn't help with the equipment. They didn't really need to; there were more than enough people around to take care of it. After a brief sound check, Sienna,

Holeshot, and the D-Bags spent an hour or so with the fans doing a very formal type of meet-and-greet. While the majority of the fans won the right to meet Sienna and the boys, some of the uberSienna fans had actually purchased the VIP treatment. As always, Tory and Sienna's bodyguards were on hand to help corral the crowd of nearly hyperventilating devotees. Our necks adorned with our All Access passes, my sister and I waited in the room buzzing with expectant energy.

Tory was laying down the ground rules for the fans—no one was allowed to hug the band members, and everyone only had ten to fifteen seconds per person before they would be forcefully moved on down the line. It was all so mechanical, like a rock-star assembly line. Kellan's attentiveness to his fans had bothered me at one point, but it was preferable to the standoffishness being presented here—*Look but don't touch* was practically being shouted from the rafters.

But it didn't really matter what Kellan's wishes were. This was Sienna's show, and Sienna's rules, and she preferred a little space between her and her admirers. Made me wonder if she'd had some bad run-ins in the past. Probably. Idly, I wondered if Kellan would attract a few crazies. Thinking of Candy and Joey, I considered the fact that maybe he already had.

There was an electric buzz in the large, rectangular room as the fans waited for their moment in the sun with the rock stars. Sitting on chairs in the corner of the room, Anna and I scanned the bizarre festivities with amused smiles. Knowing the people that were being adulated was surreal. As always, there were a lot of D-Bags fans in the bunch; I could tell by their shirts. Unfortunately, there were also several people wearing Kell-Sex shirts. The Kellan/Sienna supporters had started springing up everywhere recently. There were huge banners at every show now, and even fan-made montages of them online. While artistically beautiful, I hated those damn videos.

Blinking in disbelief, I stared at a Kell-Sex fan in front of me who was holding a pair of underwear. Was she really going to ask Kellan to sign her skivvies? Then I noticed what was *on* the underwear and my mouth fell to my chest. "Oh my God, Anna"—I indicated the young girl showing the panties to her friend—"check those out."

Anna looked over and started laughing. Some forward thinking woman had embroidered a pair of lacey briefs with the letters *KK* on the front, and the words *Rock God* on the back. Laughing into my hand, I imagined wearing those for Kellan. He would flip out . . . in a good way.

Anna must have been thinking the same thing. Working her way to her feet, she sniggered, "I have to have those." She sauntered up to the girl and flashed her pass. Then she said something and jerked her thumb back at me. The fan started hopping up and down on her feet, and immediately tossed Anna the underwear. She and her friend were squealing when Anna walked away.

"What did you promise them?" I asked, knowing full well it involved me somehow.

Handing me the underwear, Anna crooked a Kellan-worthy smile. "That you were Kellan's personal assistant, and you would get them a private meeting if they handed over the goods."

I rolled my eyes at her. How was I supposed to do that? Tory was all over getting the fans into and out of the building as quickly as possible. She'd never let one stay behind for a private get together. Grinning at the fabric in my hands, I decided I would find a way, even if I had to seriously piss off Tory. These panties were too freaking awesome to not give the girl something in return.

As I stood up and stuffed the underwear in my pocket, the rock stars finally showed up. I plugged my ears until the screaming died down. Holeshot came in first, Deacon, David, and Ray waving as they made their way to their assigned area along one long wall of the room. The fans clustered in the center of the room naturally shifted toward the band members. I had to smile at Deacon; he had his long hair pulled back into a sleek ponytail. He always did this when he met with fans. He'd told me once that he'd lost a good chunk of hair to some over-eager admirers, so he was a little more careful now with his locks. David and Ray didn't have that issue. David shaved his head completely bald, and Ray's blond hair was about a quarter inch long.

The D-Bags appeared not long after Holeshot. I cringed and plugged my ears again for longer this time. Anna joined in with the fans' catcalls as our boys took their spot on the wall next to Deacon and his band. Matt was blushing and looked horribly uncomfortable as he ran his hand through his spiky, blond hair in an obsessive-compulsive fashion. This part never was a favorite of his. I sympathized. I didn't like being put on display either.

Evan was laid-back and comfortable as his warm brown eyes scanned the room packed with people. The flames on his forearms lined up perfectly as he crossed his arms over his chest; his grin was contagious. Griffin looked like he was the self-proclaimed ruler of this arena, and everyone in his presence was his faithful servant. He huffed into his hand, checking his breath, then rubbed his palms together and flashed a predatory smile, like some poor girl was about to lose her virtue tonight. I didn't buy the act, though. Anna had somehow tamed the beast, at least for now.

Last but not least, there was Kellan. My husband was dressed for comfort, like he always was, in a plain black shirt and loose jeans that hugged him where they needed to. The simplicity of his outfit amplified the attractiveness of his face. Once a person recovered from the hint of an amazing physique hiding beneath his clothes, his eyes and smile commanded their attention—along with his hair. Couldn't forget the impossible sexiness of his shaggy head of bedroom hair. Kellan's face wore a look of simmering seduction as he scanned the crowd. I knew he was looking for me, but the fans between us seemed to think his intense blue eyes were scouring the throngs for a potential mate. And many of them looked more than willing to volunteer, even some of the really young ones, which was a little disturbing.

I giggled as I watched him look for me. I couldn't wait to show him the surprise in my pocket.

With a small entourage swarming around her like bees following a pollen-filled flower, Sienna breezed into the packed room. According to Tory's earlier speech, Sienna was supposed to be standing near the doors, the last stop of the fan locomotive. But Sienna didn't seem to care about Tory's carefully laid plans and purposely strode over to stand between Kellan and Matt, making a flushed Matt now the end of the line. Kellan looked over at Sienna, his expression blank. She smiled and bumped her shoulder against his in a display of friendly camaraderie. Cameras started snapping, eating up the playful antics of the beautiful couple that were madly and deeply in love with each other. *Yeah, right.*

I held my irritation in check as best I could. Sienna just couldn't pass up a photo op with Kellan, and since he'd started rejecting formally posing with her, she'd started satisfying herself with candid shots. Anything to keep the public's interest in her up. Obviously, Kellan hated the game she was playing and kept a polite distance from Sienna as she stood beside him.

Tory and the security team ushered the fans into a somewhat orderly long line, then started them moving in a wedding-style greeting with the band members, starting with Holeshot. Wanting to speak with Kellan about Underwear Fan, I ducked into the massive line with Anna.

. The energy of the fans around me made me a little nervous as I approached the rock stars. That was ridiculous of course, since I'd seen all of them in their snoring, burping, and farting glory, but there's something to be said for mob mentality. Deacon gave me a swift smile as I passed by him, and a small sliver of embarrassment flashed through me as I again remembered this morning. Oh well. It happened, no point in dwelling on it. When I got to Evan, he looked like he wanted to sling his arms around me and pull me into a bear hug. He didn't, though. The tittering girls around me would take that display of affection as a free-for-all on the bands. Someone would surely get trampled—probably me.

Griffin was next in line and my nerves went up in smoke as he licked his lips, then kissed the air in front of me. I had to laugh at the display. He was crude as always, but not as bad as I'd once believed.

When Anna stepped in front of him, bumping me into the crowd of people waiting for Kellan, Griffin held his hands out. "Whoa, hot pregnant chick, I need a pic with you."

Anna rolled her eyes at him, but played along and pulled a small camera out of her bag. "I did come prepared," she murmured.

Griffin raised his eyebrows at her in a suggestive way that used to make my skin crawl. "I bet you always come . . . prepared."

Letting out a husky laugh, Anna rubbed her belly. "Except for one time."

Griffin's eyes softened as they shifted to his child. "Lucky fucker, whoever the father is."

With a snort, Anna told him, "He *is* a fucker"—she shrugged nonchalantly—"but I love him."

No one else in the crowd understood the enormity of what had just transpired but me. My heart was pounding in my chest as I watched my sister stare down Griffin. He met her gaze, swallowing uncomfortably. He was about to answer her when the fans behind Anna started getting restless. "Just take your damn picture!"

Shrugging, Anna sighed, handed me her camera, and stepped beside him. Griffin seemed a lot less cocky as he looked down at Anna. He didn't even put his arm around her, or stick out his tongue and make devil's horns, like he had with some of the other fans. He just gazed down at her, shocked into silence. I never thought I'd see the day.

I was still stunned by the time I got to Kellan. He was doing joint photographs with Sienna, which surprised me some. The pair weren't touching, but Sienna gazed at Kellan while the fan squished between them beamed into the camera. Then, at the very last possible second, Sienna scooted over and laid her head on Kellan's shoulder. Kellan jerked away immediately, but it was too late; the lucky fan had already captured the moment.

Stepping away from Sienna, Kellan let out a frustrated sigh. When he noticed that I was the next person in line, he blinked in surprise. "Hey," he said, his expression playful. "Is there anything you'd like me to sign?"

Glancing at Sienna, I shook my head. Brow furrowed, Kellan told me, "A fan begged. I didn't want to be rude."

I nodded, understanding. These fans had been in line a long time and were being herded past the rock stars like cattle. Kellan was just being nice, and Sienna had used that to her advantage. Flicking a glance at Tory, who was busy ushering the fans that had completed the circuit out of the room, I motioned for Kellan to come closer. He leaned down to me, and I paused a moment to absorb his captivating scent. When we were close enough, I pointed out the fan who'd given me her special memento. She was a couple of spots behind me, giggling as Evan showed off some of his tattoos.

"She gave me something special. Can you thank her for me?"

He arched his brow in a delicious way. "What did she give you?"

"You'll see later," I answered with a smile.

Kellan nodded at me as I was pushed from behind by a rabid fan who had sneaked around my sister to get to Kellan. "I'll see what I can do," he murmured, his eyes brimming with intrigue as I walked away.

My grin faded as I stepped in front of Sienna. Her smile was wide and polite as she acknowledged me. "Kiera," she laughed, "you don't have to wait in the line to talk to me, you know."

I know. And you don't have to try and convince the world that you're sleeping with my husband.

Even though I wanted to, I resisted the urge to say my thoughts out loud and instead smiled at her and politely left the room. I couldn't talk to her. Not here anyway. Maybe if I could get her alone, I could talk to her about how we could all work together to turn down the fire on her imaginary romance with Kellan. What the public believed was beyond ridiculous, and her fans' devotion to this fake relationship was nothing short of zealotry. If Sienna would just say something, I was sure the heat between them would start to dissipate. But both albums were soaring up the charts, so I knew she wouldn't open her mouth. Wrong as it was, the gossip around them was financially benefitting them both, and Sienna was keeping her comments as ambiguous as possible: "He's a remarkable man," "I love spending time with him every day," "I'm in awe of his art," and "He's the entire package—looks, brains, charisma, talent, and a body that would stop traffic."

It was frustrating. I'd like to hold my husband's hand in public without fear of some paparazzi person catching the moment and the fans going ballistic. I'd also like to feel good about Kellan wearing his ring everywhere he went. And I'd really like to not have to worry about some obsessed Kell-Sex fan crashing my wedding next month.

Chapter 19
Denial

After the meet-and-greet was over, Kellan pulled aside Underwear Fan and her friend. They both looked ready to pee their pants. Tory looked upset by the interruption to the flow in her scheduling, but then again, the statuesque blonde always seemed a little upset. Flashing her an I-don't-care-if-you're-mad smile, Kellan ignored Tory's displeasure and treated the pair of fans to a private backstage tour.

Since I was Mr. Kyle's "personal assistant" and had arranged this little tour, it would seem odd if I didn't tag along, so I followed behind the fans. They were amusing to watch. As Kellan walked in front of them, highlighting different areas, instruments, and people, the pair of fans clutched at each other like life preservers. And every limb on them was shaking. I nearly expected one or both to drop to the ground in an overload of endorphins. Whenever Kellan looked at them directly, tiny squeaks escaped their lips, followed by a burst of uncontrollable giggles. Was I ever *that* nervous around Kellan? I didn't think so.

Kellan ended the tour by hopping up onto the stage from the front of it. He extended his hand down to help the fans up and they both turned a sickly shade of white. I tensed, preparing to catch one if she fainted. Good Lord, he was just a man—an incredibly attractive and talented man, but a man nonetheless.

Laughing at their reaction, Kellan pulled them onto the stage and then reached down for me. Lower than they could hear, he asked, "Need a hand, Mrs. Kyle?" His eyes sparkled with mischief.

Shaking my head, I hopped up on the stage by myself. "I got it, Mr. Kyle." Standing beside him, I added, "Besides, I think you need to keep both hands free in case one of those girls passes out and falls off the stage. I wouldn't want you to get sued."

I pointed behind him at where the girls were giggling, hands over their mouths, as they openly ogled Kellan's backside. He looked back at them, and two harmonious high-pitched squeals filled the stage as they started hopping around like jumping beans.

Kellan looked back at me, cocky amusement infused into his lopsided grin. "I'm glad you don't squeal when I look at you." He leaned in, his arm brushing mine. "I like having to earn it," he whispered.

He turned his attention back to the fans as my lips parted and my cheeks flamed. I had to fan myself to cool my heated skin. Written or spoken, Kellan sure had a way with words.

Just when the private tour was wrapping up, Sienna popped onto the stage. I noticed her bodyguards nearby, watching her from a respectful distance. The two fans went into a swirl of excitement as the megastar approached them. Sienna was already dressed for the show, wearing the skintight jumpsuit that exposed most of her tan back. Her hair was slicked back into a sleek ponytail, highlighting her slim neck and perfect cheekbones. She seemed like a Greek goddess as she stepped near my Adonis—a pair of beautiful, mythical creatures brought to life.

The fans whipped out cameras from their pockets as the golden couple came close enough to each other that they were in the same frame. Sienna flashed them an Oscar-worthy smile as she motioned over to a couple of the arena's security team that were waiting nearby. "It's time, love." Her accent, warm and husky, hinted at all sorts of things that it could be time for.

As Kellan opened his mouth to respond to her, the fans finally found some courage. Babbling, they gushed, "We adore you so much, Sienna. You're amazing. And we think it's so awesome that you and

Kellan fell in love while recording a song together. They should make a movie about you two."

Sienna beamed and immediately replied, "I would love that! I could even play myself!" Flashing Kellan a mischievous grin, she giggled with the girls like they were all at a sleepover together.

As Kellan was politely informing the fans that he was not in a relationship with Sienna, the security team arrived and ushered the girls off of the stage. They pouted like preteens as they were escorted away from the superstars. I thought I even saw tears in the eyes of one of them. And it was clear by the fans' faces that they hadn't believed Kellan's oft-repeated denial. Two more victims of the Kell-Sex publicity machine.

Rolling my eyes, I followed Kellan down the back of the stage as he left it. Members of the crew were milling about with final preparations for the show in a couple of hours, but no one paid us any attention. The thrill of being amongst rock stars was lost on these professionals. I found their presence grounding.

Kellan rounded on Sienna. "We need to talk," he snarled, his face stony.

Looking unaffected, Sienna responded with, "Sure thing, love." She motioned with her finger for us to follow her. Then she started heading toward her dressing room without even bothering to see if we were. Definitely a woman used to people obeying her.

Still not looking at us, she disappeared into her assigned room. I put a hand on Kellan's chest when we got to her door. His jaw was tight when he looked down at me as I told him, "If you don't mind, I'd like to speak with her alone, woman to woman."

Kellan frowned, but nodded. Tilting his head over his shoulder, he murmured, "I'm gonna go blow off some steam. Find me when you're done." A tight smile graced his lips. "And don't feel like you need to go easy on her either."

I put my hand on his cheek, and Kellan swiftly kissed my wrist. My skin was tingling as he walked away. How he could still physically affect me after all this time, I'd never fully understand. But I was very grateful.

Steeling my nerve, I walked into Sienna's dressing room and shut the door behind me. Standing with her back to me, she started to twist around with a dramatic sigh. "What is bothering you now, Kellan, dear?" When she finished her circle and her dark eyes noted the lack of my husband, she murmured, "Just you, then?"

"I asked Kellan if I could speak with you alone."

Sienna seemed amused by my statement. Placing her hands on her slim hips, she asked me, "Are you going to threaten me with bodily harm if I don't *stay away from your man*?" Her charming accent shifted to a deep Texan drawl.

Honestly, I hadn't fully considered what I wanted to say to her. But variations of those exact words may have filtered into my brain in the last few seconds, only to be immediately discarded. Violence wasn't the answer here.

Knowing that any response to her question would put her on the defensive, I decided to ignore it. "Have you ever been in love?" I asked, my voice soft and disarming.

Sienna blinked, her long, fake eyelashes nearly brushing her cheeks. "I don't have time for love . . ." The way her voice trailed off, I highly doubted her answer.

Feeling like I had something to work with, I took a tentative step toward her. "Well, Kellan and I *are* in love, *deeply* in love. We've been through a lot together, and he's been through a lot alone. And this 'relationship' that's been produced between the two of you is very unsettling. He loves what he does. He adores the fans and the music. But this hoopla is making him miserable. Don't you care that he's unhappy?"

Sienna stared at me impassively. I couldn't gauge whether she cared about Kellan's well-being or not. I liked to believe that she did. After all, they were friends sort of. Finally, she raised a cool eyebrow. "I'm not hurting him in any way, nor have I crossed his line about kissing him on the lips."

I sighed. She was going to make this difficult.

When I opened my mouth to speak, Sienna beat me to it. "I respect you for coming in here. I do genuinely like you and Kellan, but

make no mistake about it: My career comes first, and I will do whatever it takes to stay on top, even harmlessly flirt with a married man."
She rolled her eyes. I wasn't sure if that was because of the harmless
part, or the married part. Both concepts seemed ridiculous to her.

I grit my jaw and prepared myself to storm out of the room. I
knew that talking to her wasn't a viable option. She didn't care if Kellan felt manipulated and used. She cared that her album hit number
one. It had been released just a few weeks before Kellan's, and had yet
to reach that elusive goal.

"I'm sorry I've wasted your time. I just wanted to have a civil
conversation with you about Kellan. Maybe come up with a solution
so that everyone can be happy, since you did say you wanted this arrangement to work. But I see that you only care about what *he* can
do for you, so I'll leave you alone so you can bask in your own glory."

I spun on my heel and Sienna grabbed my elbow. Her dark eyes
bored into me. "You're both overreacting," she snapped. "It's the reality of being in the public eye. At least I'm trying to help Kellan's
career as well as my own. If I were truly as selfish as you believe me
to be, than Kellan would be in *my* bed right now, not yours. But I
haven't made a play for him because I respect your relationship."

I scowled at her, hating that she thought she could win him so
easily. She couldn't. Kellan's heart was fixed on me.

Releasing my arm, she relaxed and her tone softened. I found
myself relaxing as well. "This media circus that he hates so much
is going to happen regardless of my interference." She smiled, and
a trace of warmth finally appeared on her face. "In case you haven't
noticed, Kellan is very attractive. And on top of his looks, he's also
very talented. That combination has the uncanny ability of reduc-
ing the most sophisticated woman into a trembling teenager. I think
even a happily married woman would consider shucking it all for
one night with him."

A soft laugh escaped me. Yeah, I had to agree with that one. Kellan was just . . . desirable.

Sienna put her hand on my arm, almost in comfort. "Get used to it now, while he's safely in my hands, because he's going to be linked with every female that he comes in contact with from here on out. It's just how the business works."

My heart sank, but I knew she was right. "But it's different with your fans. More intense. They've turned you into a power couple . . . Kell-Sex."

Sienna rolled her eyes. "God, that nickname. It's awful, isn't it?"

I smiled, feeling relieved for the first time. Since I felt we were being honest, I told her, "I'm afraid to touch him when we're around other people. I'm afraid we'll be discovered, and the fans will turn on me." Sighing, I asked her, "What do you think they would do if they knew about me?"

She shrugged, not too worried. "Bitch, moan, and crucify you online. I seriously doubt they would come after you with pitchforks or anything." Her expression turned thoughtful and a knot formed in my stomach. With a wave of her hand, she told me, "I doubt it would affect your relationship as negatively as you think." Rubbing my arm, she gave me a best-friend smile. "The fans would get over it. They love Kellan too much to dwell for long."

She winked at me and then twisted to walk over to a vanity that had been set up for her. Picking up a tube of lipstick from the table, she leaned over and stared at her reflection. "I'll ease up on the cuddling, if it really bothers you that much." She looked at me in the mirror, her gaze questioning.

"We would appreciate it . . . thank you." She was consenting to our wishes, but it didn't feel like a victory. I hesitated, then decided to ask her what I really wanted to ask her. "Will you please say something to your fans? Tell them that Kellan is in a relationship? Don't mention my name or anything," I quickly added, "just help us try and stop the rumor mill?"

Sienna took an inordinately long time applying a layer of deep red around her plump lips. When she was finished, she rubbed her lips together. "Sure thing, love."

Thinking our meeting was over, I turned to leave as she gave herself one last look over. Her voice stopped me, though. "I've seen you writing backstage. How is your book coming?"

Not realizing she'd seen that, I told her, "I'm just about done with it."

Twisting to me, she sat on her vanity and stretched her arms out behind her. The mirror gave me a full shot of her outfit; the counter was pulling down the already low back of her jumpsuit, so I could see the top of her ass. "I know people in the industry. Perhaps they could look at it when you're finished?"

I sort of felt like accepting any help from Sienna would come with huge strings attached—cable-sized strings—and all of them would be tied to Kellan. So I only smiled and said, "Thank you. I'll keep that in mind."

Sienna dismissed me with a friendly wave, and I left her room not quite sure if that conversation had gone well or not.

Shoving her to the back of my mind, I set off to find my favorite rock star. When I did find him, what he was doing surprised me a little. The crew hadn't finished setting the instruments up on the stage yet. In the prep area behind the stage, there were various lonely instruments in and out of their cases—a guitar here, a microphone there. A full drum set was resting peacefully in the organized chaos. Kellan was behind them, attempting to play a D-Bags song while Evan laughed at him mercilessly.

I'd never seen Kellan behind the drums before. The sight was both odd and natural—a beautiful blue jay gliding across a lake instead of soaring through the clouds. It was clearly something that was not his specialty, and he was biting his lip as he concentrated on the complicated rhythms. Watching him focus so intently on something was intoxicating, and I wasn't the only one who felt that way. A small circle of people were gathered around us, listening to him play—rather, try to play.

Evan spotted me and came over to wrap his arm around me. He was still laughing, the corners of his eyes crinkling as he watched Kellan fumble over a beat and nearly drop one of his sticks. "It's nice to know I'm better at something than Kellan," he told me.

I laughed as I watched Kellan curse and shake his head. He was losing the rhythm fast; I could barely recognize the song I knew he was trying to play. "His talent lies elsewhere," I murmured. Evan chuckled at me, squeezing me tight, and I realized my statement could be taken as dirty talk. "You know, singing and such."

He laughed a little harder. "Yeah, I figured that's what you meant."

When his attention shifted to Kellan again, I asked him, "What's with the Jujubes box?" I hadn't been going to pry, but darn if I hadn't been curious for months.

Evan looked down, a touch of embarrassment darkening his cheeks. "Oh, that. Ah, Jenny and me, the first time we . . . you know, we'd been snacking on those and the box . . . got squished . . . in the process." He peeked up at me. "I didn't know she kept the box." He smiled, a wide, lovesick, satisfied smile. "Sentimental girl."

My heart warmed for my friends. "Most of us are."

"Fuck! I give up!" Kellan called out.

The crowd around us started laughing as the awkward drumming ended. I twisted my head back to Kellan. He'd tossed the drumsticks out onto the floor and was resting his head on the snare drum in defeat. Evan clapped my back. "I think I broke him. You may need to console him before the show."

I was laughing as I walked up to my dejected husband. When he felt me beside him, he glanced up. "I suck," he muttered, his lips curving into a full-blown puppy dog pout.

Resisting the urge to suck on that lip, I extended my palm and helped him stand up. "You can't be a pro at everything, Kellan," I told him, fingering his wedding ring before letting go of his right hand.

Kellan's eyes turned heated as he stared at me. Voice as husky as his eyes, he responded with, "You're right. I'll just stick to what I'm really, really good at." His vision traveled down my body, the fire in his eyes tingling my skin like a Fourth of July sparkler.

I wanted to remind him to behave, but he instantly switched moods. Expression now curious, he asked, "What did Sienna say?"

Walking with him around the people busy working, I recounted my confusing conversation. "She said we were overreacting." I watched him as I continued. His gaze was speculative and disbelieving; he didn't agree. "She also said she'd ease up on the cuddling."

Kellan smirked. "She's said that before. But then a camera gets pointed in her direction and she . . . forgets." He rolled his eyes. "Gotta give the fans what they want. She's a performer to the core."

"It's how she was raised. It's how she survived the transition from child star to superstar." I blinked at my words. Did I really just defend her?

Kellan seemed surprised as well as he held open the door to his empty dressing room. "I get that. I think the only thing I really *do* get about her is that her childhood sucked just as much as mine did."

The door closed behind us, and I looped my arms around his neck. My face serious, I told him, "No, her childhood was nothing like yours, Kellan. Not even close."

Ancient sadness filled his eyes as he nodded, and I squeezed him tight in an attempt to prove to him that my love was stronger than their hate.

Later, when the D-Bags were on stage, Anna came up to me as I watched Kellan singing his heart out from my behind-the-scenes vantage point. I usually used this time every evening to work on my newly conceived book. Writing two books at the same time probably wasn't the best way to finish *one,* but whenever I watched Kellan play, my creative juices started flowing and I had no choice but to pour it out onto my laptop screen. He was my own personal muse.

I paused mid-sentence and glanced up at my sister. She looked a little uncomfortable as she rubbed a spot on the lower left side of her belly. Her green eyes shimmered a little in the stage lights. I didn't know if that was because she was feeling emotional or just really tired. Supporting a life had to be exhausting, not to mention dealing with Griffin. Remembering Anna's monumental admittance during the meet-and-greet today, I wondered if she was okay.

Closing my laptop and setting it on the floor, I stood and pointed at my straight-backed chair. "Do you want to sit down?" It wasn't the most comfortable thing in the world, but at least she could rest her feet.

Her eyes glued on the stage, Anna muttered, "Thanks," and worked her way onto the hard metal. As she tilted her head to keep the boys in her sight, or maybe just one boy in her sight, I noticed the dark circles under her eyes. She covered them well with concealer, but I could see just a smidge of purplish-black. She would never admit it, but she was worn. She really should go home and rest up while she had the chance.

Putting a hand on her shoulder, I asked, "You okay, sis?"

She immediately lifted her chin, her liquid eyes drying. "Of course, why wouldn't I be?"

There were so many things I could point out, but instead I focused on the one aspect that seemed the easiest for her to talk about—the physical discomfort of being pregnant. "You keep rubbing your side."

She grimaced and looked at the spot that she was now firmly holding. "Maximus keeps kicking me in the exact same spot." She sighed when she returned her eyes to mine. "I think he's bruised a rib or two."

The remark left my mouth before I could stop it. "Well, he wouldn't be part Griffin if he wasn't a pain in your side."

Anna smirked at me. "He's not as bad as you think he is."

Remembering the few surprising conversations I'd had with Griffin lately, I nodded. "I know."

Anna opened her eyes wide, like I'd just admitted to something so preposterous she could hardly believe it. I flicked my fingers across her shoulder, and she giggled. Seeing more humor in her demeanor, I asked the question I really wanted an answer to. "Are you okay with what happened earlier . . . with Griffin?"

The humor immediately vanished. "What do you mean?"

I contained a frustrated sigh. Those two were both so damn pigheaded, worse than Kellan and I ever were. "You told him you loved him, and he froze up like you just dipped him in carbonite."

Anna scowled and returned her eyes to the stage. "No, that doesn't bother me, Kiera. We don't have the hearts and flowers relationship that you and Kellan have." She shot me a quick glance out of the corner of her eye. "Which is fine. I don't need that romantic crap." She shrugged. "I was just joking around anyway. I didn't mean it."

She clamped her mouth shut and swallowed three times in a row. A new layer of moisture amplified the depth of her eyes, and I knew my sister was lying. She did mean it. She did love him. It did bother her. She did want more from him. But she wouldn't let herself admit it or feel it. When all else fails, deny, deny, deny.

Not knowing what else to do for her, I leaned over and kissed her cheek. "I love you, Anna." Griffin may not be able to say it, but she should hear it from someone. Anna looked up at me, just as a tear dropped to her cheek. She immediately brushed it away and retuned her eyes to the D-Bags' stage. "He told me that he loved you," I added.

I thought my words would make her feel better, but all she looked was tired as she watched Griffin onstage. That could just be the pregnancy, though. "I'm gonna go back to the bus and lie down. Let Griffin know? If he asks . . ."

Heart heavy, I told her that I would.

Griffin didn't ask about her when the set was over, but I told him where she was anyway. He nodded at me, so I knew he heard me. But instead of heading out to the bus to be with his baby-mama, he sat in quiet contemplation until it was time for the D-Bags and Sienna to close the show with their number-one smash hit. For the first time ever, I found myself watching Griffin onstage more than Kellan and Sienna. Even smack dab in the middle of the limelight, Griffin seemed uncharacteristically pensive. I really didn't know what to make of it.

When the show was over and the crowd was roaring its approval, the guys rejoined me backstage. Sienna was a step behind them. I thought Griffin would surely want to go see Anna now. We were playing at this venue again tomorrow night, so we had some free time to kill and a peaceful night of sleep at a plush hotel to look forward to. I, for one, was eager to go crash, mainly because Kellan had lived up to his promise and secured us our very own room. But instead of collecting Anna, Griffin turned to Matt. "Let's go drink."

Matt nodded, then asked the rest of us, "You guys want to go out?"

Kellan was already answering "No" when I set down my laptop and told Matt, "Sure." Kellan's eyes were disbelieving when he looked back at me. Kellan and I hadn't joined the group much for drinks once the Kell-Sex explosion had happened. We'd both been keeping a low profile, much to the band's dismay—well, to Griffin's dismay. I wanted us to go this time, though. I didn't like the look on Griffin's face. Griffin rubbed his hands together eagerly, and I liked his look even less.

Sienna had joined us by this time and seemed just as elated as Griffin. "Drinks sound bloody fabulous! I know just the place." She made a move like she was going to wrap herself around Kellan, but she surprisingly refrained. I was almost proud of her. Almost.

Kellan looked my way with a clear question in his eyes: *Wouldn't you rather be alone in a hotel room with me than out drinking with Griffin?* I forced myself to smile when I really wanted to frown. Yes, I would much rather be alone with him right now. But Anna was my blood, and I needed to look out for her.

Sienna was on the phone making arrangements while we walked toward the dressing rooms. I had no idea who she knew in North Carolina or what place she was taking us to. I wasn't even sure if I wanted to hang out with her, but it was too late now. Kellan and the guys took five minutes to refresh from their show; they pretty much just changed their slightly damp T-shirts and spritzed on some cologne. Griffin's was way too strong, burning the back of my nostrils.

Sienna took considerably longer, and when she reemerged, I wondered if I should change. She was in a bright coral dress that looked made for dancing. Loose and flirty, the bottom of it had wide panels that resembled a flower's petals. The petal layers were slit almost up to her waist, so every time she moved she flashed her tight, toned thighs.

I was wearing jeans and Keds sneakers. Hot.

Knowing I didn't have an outfit like that on me anyway, I ignored the plain feeling washing through my body and stepped up to Kellan's side. He glanced at Sienna, rolled his eyes, then looked down at me. "Even on her best day, you're still more attractive," he whispered.

Flushing, I suddenly felt like I'd just won the Miss America Pageant. His compliment made Sienna seem horribly overdone, like she was trying so hard to be noticed that she may as well have sprayed *I'm Sexy* on her chest. It brought her beauty down a peg in my eyes, and I felt more on equal footing with her as we stepped out into the chilly night.

Sienna looked freezing as she rubbed her hands over her bare arms. She didn't have to wait long, though. As if on cue, a limo pulled up to the back door, and we all hurried inside. I sighed as I looked around the twinkling interior. So much for blending in with the locals. This luxury also seemed to scream our "importance." It made me miss going to clubs with Kellan in Seattle. It made me miss hanging out at Pete's. It made me miss Justin's tour. *Simpler times.*

Kellan kept his arm around me the entire time we were in the limo. Sienna watched us, a strange expression on her face. It was a peaceful, supportive look, but there was wistfulness there too. And maybe a trace of sadness. No matter her bravado, I think she had loved someone before, and it hadn't ended well. For a moment her persona seemed cracked, and I almost thought I was seeing the real Sienna, not the celebrity. Then she noticed me analyzing her, and her mask of seductive confidence slipped back into place. She winked at me from across the limo.

When the driver pulled up to the front of a place called Poison, there was a swarm of photographers hovering around the entrance. Like they already knew who was in the car, they started snapping pictures of the limo the second it stopped. You'd think we were pulling up to a movie premier, by all of the photographers outside. Paparazzi in North Carolina? I was pretty positive that their being here wasn't a coincidence. Who the hell did Sienna call when she arranged this little outing? No wonder she had taken the time to make herself look like a million bucks.

With the car idling, the driver ran around to open our door.

While I watched the flashes in horror, a small smile lit Sienna's lips. This would be a big moment in the sun for her—a night out on the town with her rumored paramour. Even if they entered separately, there was no way they wouldn't be news tomorrow. And what would the fans think of me in this scenario? Was I a tagalong, perhaps one of the other band member's girlfriends? If Kellan and I walked in together, the speculation about me could be just as spectacular as the gossip surrounding him and Sienna. I did not want that.

As the driver opened the door, Sienna smoothed her dress in preparation for her grand entrance. The driver reached out his hand and helped her out of the car. The flashes went crazy. Sienna stopped and waited for Kellan while my body surged with adrenaline. Evan and Griffin started to stand, but Kellan held his hand up. Leaning forward, he told the driver, "We're not walking through that, take us somewhere else."

Nodding, the driver looked back at Sienna and asked her if she wanted to stay or go. Sienna hesitated, glancing at the crowd still snapping photos, then got back into the car. Pouting as she watched the light bulbs fading into the distance, she muttered, "Really? That was the best club in town."

Kellan leaned back in his seat and gave her a charming smile. "You were welcome to stay, if you wanted to."

Sienna rolled her eyes, then gave the driver the name of another club that she thought would be a "little less crowded."

Much to my relief, no one was hanging around the second club when we pulled up. Once we were inside, deep bass music made my ribs vibrate. An eager man in a suit led us to a private VIP area. By the look on his face, he was elated to have us here tonight and would probably get us anything we wanted. Maybe he was the owner. He had two girls in tight corset tops and black boy shorts beside him. They were either waitresses or strippers. I really couldn't tell.

Sienna ordered a couple of bottles of Cristal, and one of the scantily clad women took off to get them. Waitress, then. Her revealing outfit made me appreciate Pete's simple T-shirts all the more.

Smiling at the owner, Sienna sat sideways on a chaise lounge. The deep red cushion clashed with her outfit. It made me smile. No one but the band, the owner, and the one remaining waitress were in the room. All of the regular customers were on the other side of a thick glass wall. It ran along one entire side of the room, separating us from the main dance floor of the club. We had a perfect view of hundreds of gyrating, grinding bodies. I had no idea if the dancing couples had any idea that we could see them or not. It was clear that they couldn't see us, though. It was very voyeuristic. It made me blush as I watched some guy run his hand up some girl's skirt.

Griffin looked around the room, then at the wall of shifting bodies on the other side of the glass. "We need chicks," he muttered.

The owner instantly gave him all of his attention. Snapping his fingers at the remaining waitress, he asked Griffin, "Do you prefer blondes, brunettes, or redheads?"

Griffin smiled; it made me nauseous. "All of the above."

The owner returned Griffin's sickening smile. He lifted an eyebrow and glanced at Kellan. "I'm assuming nothing less than a perfect ten?"

Griffin nodded, his eager grin growing. The owner gave the "perfect ten" waitress beside him a quick glance and she turned to leave. Griffin called out after her, "I need at least a dozen!" She nodded and disappeared.

I narrowed my eyes at both Griffin and the sleazy club owner. I didn't realize you could order women as easily as you could order drinks. Kellan and I settled into a velveteen couch as I struggled to control my stomach. Kellan whispered into my hair, "We can leave any time." I nodded, but I knew that wasn't really true. I wasn't going to leave my sister's boyfriend here in Easy Hookup Land.

Chapter 20
Enough

Our champagne arrived and was dramatically poured into fluted glasses. Kellan and I clinked ours together right as the "entertainment" arrived. Much to Griffin's delight, a parade of hot women streamed into the room. They all seemed to be models in tight shirts, tight pants, or tight skirts. Maybe there was a convention in town? Tittering and giggling, the colorful assortment of eye candy floated around the room like cheap perfume. A handful stopped by Sienna's lounge chair, one or two sat with a disinterested Evan and a red-faced Matt, and a half-dozen flocked around King Griffin. The rest made a beeline for Kellan. In a rather aggressive move on my part, I hopped onto Kellan's lap, slinging my arms around his neck. *Back off, bitches.* They didn't, but they kept a greater distance than they probably would have if I hadn't. As the girls were handed glasses of alcohol by the waitresses, Kellan leaned in and told me, "I like you possessively sitting on me. Maybe we should hire the girls to follow us around everywhere?"

I made a face at his comment, but I couldn't hold onto it; his grin was just too darn provocative. In answer to his ridiculous proposal, I shifted my weight on his lap, grinding against him in all the right places. His eyes lit up. Grabbing my drink, he placed it on a waitress's tray as she walked by. "We need to dance," he stated. He stood up, and I had no choice but to stand up with him.

Several of the girls around joined us in the center of the smooth hardwood floor. Facing Kellan, I ignored them; he ignored them too. Hands low on my waist, he pulled our hips together until we were straddling each other. We moved together in intimate ways that spoke volumes about our true relationship. None of the visiting girls seemed to catch on that Kellan was taken though—at least, not by me.

Some of them kept looking between Kellan and Sienna, but since Sienna was merely watching Kellan with hooded eyes and not throwing a diva-sized tantrum at his seductive dancing, the girls felt just fine being flirtatious with him. As much as Kellan's hands were all over me, their hands were all over him. I had to remove wandering palms from his chest more than once. Kellan shook his head as he batted hands away from his ass. You would think he was a lucky charm by how often he was being stroked. Well, I suppose he was, in a way. I felt lucky being with him.

The thumping beat filled the low-lit room. While I melded my body to Kellan's, I kept an eye on the other boys. Matt and Evan weren't an issue. They were animatedly having a conversation between themselves. Matt was showing Evan guitar chords in the air, while Evan nodded, a wide smile on his face. It wouldn't surprise me in the least if the two were dreaming up a new song. The girls around them looked at a loss as to how to get their attention. I wanted to walk over and tell them to save their time and just enjoy their free Cristal. Matt and Evan weren't going to do anything to hurt their beloved girlfriends.

Slightly to the left of the two D-Bags was Sienna. When she wasn't staring at Kellan, she was flirting with a couple of boys that looked straight out of an Abercrombie ad. I guess the owner thought it was only fair to bring her a couple of treats too. She flicked her hair over her shoulder, exposing her elegant neckline. I could see her laughing, her eyes roving over the boys' bodies, as she fostered their hope that they had a chance with her. But her gaze always returned to Kellan. *Always.*

Threading my fingers through Kellan's hair, I pulled him a little closer to me; our chests were touching now too. Kellan's smile turned devilish as he focused solely on me. He smelled incredible, and his lips were so tantalizingly close. His hands were making patterns on my back—up the sides, around to my neck, down my spine, over my backside. I thought about having those hands on my bare skin and felt the rush of desire tingle me. Remembering that we had a hotel room waiting for us, I considered his offer of leaving this strange, private party. Then I remembered why I couldn't.

With trepidation, I looked around for Griffin. I found him tongue deep in some blonde. I immediately stiffened as pure venom seeped through my veins. Anna pours her heart out and this is how he repays her? What a prick! Kellan and I stopped dancing as I stared at Griffin cupping the girl's ass in front of him, while two more women hung off his arms. A vibrant redhead had her hands inside his pants. I was so pissed I could hardly see straight. I broke away from Kellan to give Griffin a piece of my mind, but Kellan yanked me back into his arms. My eyes bored holes into Griffin as Kellan's lips touched my ear.

"Making a scene with him isn't going to help anything. I'll talk to him later."

I pushed Kellan back, my mood frosty. "Later? What, after he's screwed them?"

Kellan shook his head at me and was about to respond when Sienna joined our group of gyrating bodies. Slinking up to Kellan's side, a beautiful man on each arm, she asked him, "Problem?" One of her guys was blatantly staring at her chest; the other was blatantly staring at Kellan. Of course. Everybody loved Kellan. Except me at the moment.

Kellan gave her a brief smile. "Everything's fine."

I was about to wholeheartedly object when Griffin walked through my peripheral vision. He had one arm around the blonde, the other around the redhead. He was striding them purposefully toward the VIP bathrooms, and I was absolutely certain that it wasn't because he had to pee.

"That son of a bitch!" I muttered, taking a step toward the restrooms. Damn if I was just going to sit back and watch him cheat on my sister. Kellan had a firm grip on my hand, though. I looked back at him when I was stretched to capacity. "Let me go, Kellan."

Shaking his head, he pulled me toward him. "You can't make him change, Kiera. He has to want to. And he's not going to stop . . . whatever he's doing in there just because you barge in yelling and screaming. Trust me. You'll just end up seeing way more than you want to."

Yanking my hand free, I pushed against his chest. "Then you go stop him. Drag him out of there like you dragged him away from those two girl-looking guys in New Jersey!" I was so irritated and hurt for my sister that tears were pricking the corners of my eyes.

Stepping into me, Kellan cupped my cheeks. "*He* has to make the choice, Kiera. It means nothing if I force him."

His eyes were soft with compassion. I knew he was right. Kellan and I couldn't watchdog Griffin every time he went out, but it hurt so bad to stand aside and let it happen. "He won't get away with it, Kellan. I'm not going to lie for him." I had a sudden, painful respect for Jenny in that moment. I felt sick for doing nothing while Griffin screwed around on my sister. She must have felt the exact same way when she'd done nothing while I'd been fooling around on Denny. I owed her a much bigger apology than I'd ever given her.

Kellan caressed my cheek. "Anna knows what he's like, Kiera. You don't have to lie."

Fighting back nausea and tears, I warbled, "I want to leave now."

Kellan nodded and held me close. I clutched him tight as he asked one of the waitresses to call a cab. After hasty goodbyes to Sienna and the D-Bags I *liked,* Kellan and I ducked out the rear exit. A yellow and black taxi was waiting for us, and holding hands, we darted inside. Kellan told the cab driver where to go, then twisted to face me. His expression was worried and apologetic. I searched his features as hot tears leaked out of my eyes. "I hate him," I seethed. And just when I'd actually been starting to like Griffin too. As irrational as it sounded, I felt like he'd just cheated on me as well as my sister.

Kellan grabbed my cheeks, giving me a soft, tender kiss. It took a moment, but as the cab started pulling away, his gentle touch finally eased my hardening heart. Not all men sucked.

I fumed as I lay in my spacious king-sized bed next to my sleeping husband. I wasn't even enjoying the fifteen hundred thread–count sheets or the ultra-warm down comforter. The silky silver tassels attached to the corners of my pillow were nothing more than stress-relievers as I repeatedly ran my fingers through them. Griffin was a certified, Grade-A asshole. If my father didn't first, I may put a hit out on him. I was sure I could talk Kellan into helping me hide the body.

Every sense I had was focused on the hallway, because the moment I heard Griffin's arrival at the hotel, I was going to pounce on him. And Kellan wasn't going to be able to stop me this time. Nothing would stop me this time. Even hotel security would have trouble containing me. Griffin had gone too far.

I knew Kellan was right. I knew the choice to be a decent human being was Griffin's alone, but Jesus Christ, Anna was about to pop out his child any day now. The least he could do was wait until *after* his son was born to resume banging random babes. And he wasn't exactly the brightest bulb in the box. Did he use condoms? What if he knocked one of the bimbos up? What if he caught something and spread it to my sister? It was all so disgustingly horrifying. It jacked up my already revving temper.

My feet were twitchy and restless as I waited. Kellan was peacefully sleeping beside me, which didn't help my anger any. How could he be so calm about the whole thing? Guys were weird. But, then again, Griffin and Anna were weird. They'd never really been committed to each other. I just thought . . . with the pregnancy, and Griffin's streak of monogamy . . . I had just hoped things were different. Maybe the only anger I should be feeling was toward myself, for assuming he'd matured.

No. Griffin was an asshole.

I leapt out of bed when I finally heard voices in the hallway. So help me God, Griffin was going to pay for this. Not even sure if it was him I was hearing, I yanked open the heavy outer door. Head down and hands in his pockets, Griffin was right in front of me as I stomped into the hallway. Smiling that fate *wanted* me to kick his ass, I pushed him into the far wall. Showing up out of nowhere and flinging myself at him got Griffin's attention. His face was pale white as he bumped into the hotel room door opposite mine.

Seeing the confusion on his face made my vision streak with red. Grade-A Asshole was going to get an earful, along with every other person on this floor who was trying to sleep. But I didn't care. My sister's honor was at stake. A small part of me noted the hypocrisy in my actions, but the inferno in me drowned that part out. "You are the biggest son of a bitch I have ever met!"

Being screeched at this early in the morning knocked the surprise off of Griffin's face. Scowling, he yelled back, "What the fuck's wrong with you?"

Matt had been walking in front of Griffin, Evan behind him. They both took a step toward me when I lunged for Griffin. Maybe seeing that I was going to throttle the bassist, Evan held me in his arms. "My sister is going to have your baby any second, and you're out screwing whores in bathrooms! I hope Anna finally wises up and kicks your ass to the curb!"

Griffin's face clouded over. "Yeah, like Denny kicked yours?" he snarled.

"Griffin!" Kellan was standing bare-chested in our doorway. My screaming may have woken him up, but it was Griffin's comment that had his blood pumping. His eyes were narrowed to icy pinpoints.

Griffin cast Kellan an annoyed, but cautious, glance. I took his moment of silence to shout back, "Minutes after Anna admits that she loves you, you find some cheap floozies to go down on you? What the hell's wrong with you?"

I could feel Evan's hands on my arms being replaced by Kellan's, but I didn't care. Kellan would have to gag me to shut me up at that point. Griffin stepped toward me, and the mood in the air shifted. Evan and Matt simultaneously put a hand on each of his arms, warning him to keep it together. Leaning into my face, Griffin yelled, "I didn't do anything with either of those girls, okay? So back the fuck off!"

Glaring, I spit out, "Right. And I'm supposed to believe that. I *saw* you."

His mood changing again, Griffin sighed. Voice still agitated, but quieter than before, he told me, "Yeah, we started going at it. I had both girls primed, panties on the floor, dying to jump me, but all I could think about was Anna." Raising his hands in the air, his voice picked up strength and volume. "I didn't want to fuck either of those girls because I'm in love with your fucking sister! Are you happy now, bitch! I'm fucking whipped . . . just like these other pussies." He indicated his band mates.

My jaw dropped. I couldn't even respond to that.

Someone else did respond, though. "You're in love with me?"

Every head shifted to the open hotel room door that Anna was leaning against. The energy in the air shifted again as Griffin locked eyes with her. Matt and Evan released him as he whispered, "Yes." Looking a little dejected, like he was admitting defeat, he muttered, "I'm in love with you, and I don't want anybody else." His brow furrowed, like he didn't understand how random hookups had suddenly lost their appeal.

Smiling, Anna strode out into the hallway to stand in front of him. "I love you too, and I don't want anybody else either." Cupping his cheek, she added, "You're enough for me."

That seemed to make sense to Griffin, and he finally smiled like he was happy. "You're enough for me too."

Grabbing his hand, Anna started backing toward her room. "Good, then come be enough for me right now. I'm horny as hell."

Griffin rushed up to her, grabbing her backside. "God, me too," he murmured before their mouths met.

My stomach twisting for a completely different reason, I turned around to flee back inside my room. Kellan was still blocking my path, though. Regardless of the sort of romantic moment we'd just witnessed, his expression was irritated. "Hey, Griffin!" I looked over to see Griffin reluctantly pulling his mouth from Anna's. Kellan's arm wrapped around my waist as he told Griffin, "Don't call my wife a bitch again."

Griffin smirked at him, then turned back to Anna.

Kellan and I went back to bed after the happy couple's breakthrough moment. Our slumber didn't last long, though. Kellan had a series of radio interviews that he had to call in for, which Tory reminded him about by mercilessly banging on our door. "Phone calls in ten minutes, Kyle."

Groggy and tired, Kellan sat up in our bed with slothlike speed. Scratching his chest, he kissed my cheek then nuzzled my neck. Giggling, I reached up and tangled my fingers through his hair. I'd been too upset to be intimate with him earlier, but I felt content and peaceful right then, and it was a shame to let this luxurious bed go to waste. Ten minutes wasn't a lot of time, but surely it was enough for a quickie.

As his lips worked their way up to my ear, I pulled his body down on top of mine. "Mornin'," he husked.

Wrapping my legs around his legs, I ground my hips against him, determined to wake him *all* the way up; it didn't take long. "Good morning," I whispered as I closed my eyes. God, he felt good.

Kellan didn't waste a second of his precious time; he pulled off my clothes while I pulled off his. When we were bare in each other's arms, I figured we still had over nine minutes left. Kellan's body was warm and soft, yet hard as steel as I clutched him to me. Enjoying our moment of freedom in our private suite, I held nothing back as his body sank inside of mine. The novelty of being completely alone with him had me climaxing at a minute and a half in. When Tory banged on his door at the five minute reminder, telling him she'd texted his interview itinerary to him, I cried out with my second release. When she came back around with her sixty second reminder, I experienced my third and Kellan finally allowed himself to join me.

We were panting, both well spent, when he slunk off of the bed, cell phone in hand to go make his round of appointed calls. With a satisfied smile, I wondered if he had anymore ten minute breaks in his lineup.

Deciding to be a little lazy, since today wasn't a traveling day, I ordered up some room and laundry service. Sienna's manager had booked the hotels for the tour, and Sienna had extravagant tastes— anything under five stars simply wouldn't do. Most of the hotels we'd stayed at would wash all of our clothes for us if we called and asked. This was a huge bonus for me, since laundry wasn't my favorite thing in the world. Life on the road with Sienna did have a couple of perks; I felt spoiled.

After throwing all of our clothes into a bag, including what we'd been wearing this morning, I grabbed a couple of plush robes from the bathroom. The long, white robe smelled of lavender and was softer than any robe I'd ever worn before. It made me feel like I was wrapped in a gigantic powder puff. I briefly considered stealing it.

Kellan was sitting at a table next to the doors that led to the balcony. The view of downtown Charlotte from our hotel room was impressive, with scores of beautiful skyscrapers reaching up to touch the clouds. I didn't give it more than a second's glance this morning though, because Kellan was sitting in the chair completely naked, and it was highly distracting. I tossed him a robe. It was a shame to cover up that body, but he might give the poor hotel employee heart failure if she walked in and saw him like that. Kellan smiled at me as he spoke to the DJ on the other line. He didn't put the robe on, but laid it over his lap. Good enough.

Just as I again was considering stealing both of the robes, our food arrived. Having food delivered straight to my bedroom was my favorite part about staying at hotels. There was nothing quite like propping yourself up on soft, plump pillows while a steaming plate of bacon, eggs, cinnamon rolls, orange juice, and coffee was rolled into position beside you. I liked it. It made me feel like a queen. In fact, I planned to find a way to continue the luxury when the tour ended. Maybe hire one of my friends to bring us breakfast in bed every morning, or maybe Rita. I'm sure she wouldn't mind swinging by each and every day for a chance to see Kellan shirtless. Hmmm, on second thought, maybe not.

As Kellan's food was placed in front of him at his table by a male employee, I handed a female employee the bag of laundry I'd scrounged together. It was so nice not have to look for Laundromats everywhere we went. The fresh-faced employee was very professional, but her eyes darted over to Kellan's half-naked body every few seconds. It almost made her seem like she had a nervous tic.

Kellan paused in his conversation to thank them both, then he gave me a quick smirk when he noticed what I'd ordered for him—a Denver omelet. Ignoring his enticing expression, I grabbed my purse so I could tip the employees.

The male employee politely took his bills and left as silently as he'd entered. The female lingered. Wondering if I'd have to turn her around and forcibly push her out the door, I glanced at her nameplate and said, "Thank you, Leanne."

Hearing her name snapped her out of her trance, and she pulled her eyes from Kellan. Cheeks slightly flushed, she smiled and told me, "Let me know if you need anything else," and darted out the door. I supposed the image of Kellan wearing only a fluffy robe across his privates would cause any woman to suffer from a moment of impropriety.

Kellan and I spent the day lounging in our room, enjoying the peace, enjoying the privacy. When it was time to head out for the show, we finally got dressed. Our laundry was clean, dry, and still a little warm. Reluctantly placing the robe on the bed, I slipped on my bra and the freshly washed KK underwear that Anna had gotten for me. Noticing what I was wearing, Kellan paused in zipping up his jeans. "What's that?"

I did a quick spin so he could see the words *Rock God* on my ass. "This is what the lucky fan gave me. Do you like them?"

Seemingly irritated, Kellan crossed his arms over his chest. "My initials are on your underwear. Of course I like them."

I frowned. "Then why are you scowling at me?"

His face instantly shifted into a devilish grin. "Because you could have been wearing those earlier today, and I could have ripped them off of you with my teeth." As my heart rate increased, Kellan sighed and finished zipping up his pants. "But it's too late now . . . you missed out."

"I'll still be wearing them later," I muttered.

Kellan heard me, and his eyes started burning with interest. I had as much difficulty pulling my gaze away from him as poor Leanne had.

As we all climbed into the dark SUVs that the label loved to rent, I looked around for my sister. I hadn't left my room at all, and I was curious to see how things were going with her and Griffin, now that they were finally exclusive. Matt was beside me in the car while I waited for Kellan. He'd been accosted by a couple of fans outside the hotel and was obliging them with autographs. No doubt Sienna was right by his side. "Have you seen Anna?" I asked Matt.

Matt shook his head. His pale eyes concerned, he asked, "Have you seen Griffin?" When I shook my head, Matt sighed. "If he misses the show I'm gonna kill him."

I patted his shoulder. "He'll be there. He's an idiot, but he's not stupid." Matt gave me an amused smile, and I laughed at my own summation. "How's Rachel?" I asked him.

Grinning, Matt leaned forward in his seat and started telling me all about her. Matt was generally more reserved when he spoke, but there was clear longing in his voice and I immediately understood his sudden openness. Matt and Evan hadn't had a chance to see their loved ones in a while. I knew how that felt, since Kellan and I had gone through it last tour. Matt seemed to need to talk to somebody, so I tuned the world out and gave him all of my attention.

We were stopping at the arena before it had even registered with me that we'd left the hotel. Security whisked us backstage and dumped us into a couple of dressing rooms with instructions that they would come collect everyone when it was time for today's meet-and-greet. Walking up to Kellan's back, I wrapped my arms around his stomach and kissed his shoulder. "I'm going to go look for Anna. Make sure she's okay."

Kellan nodded and flashed a grin. "I'm sure she's quite okay."

I rolled my eyes at his comment, then twisted to leave him. He called out after me, "See you later, KK."

I stopped in my tracks, my cheeks heating. Was he really referencing my underwear? We weren't the only ones in this room! In fact, Deacon was staring right at me, his face amused and confused. Oh well. If Kellan was talking about my under things, at least he'd used a vague reference. To the person not in the know, he could just be saying my initials . . . which I just now realized matched his. Amused by that sudden insight, I twisted back to him. "I look forward to it, KK."

Kellan's eyes widened and I knew he understood what I meant by that subtle innuendo. Feeling a little proud of myself, I set off in search of my hard-to-miss sister.

Oddly enough, I couldn't find her anywhere. And none of the crew had seen her either. Flitting from person to person, I asked everyone I came into contact with if they'd seen a very pregnant girl. Nobody had. I called and texted her about a dozen times, but no response yet. As the minutes stretched longer and longer, I began to get really worried. It wasn't like my sister to miss this. Even yawning and tired, she still showed up to the sound checks and fan greetings.

Thinking she was just waiting in the greeting room like we had yesterday, I started heading that way. All of the winning fans were there, waiting for their brief moment with the rock stars. I scoured their faces, but didn't notice Anna's among them.

To a surge of shrieks, Holeshot walked in, followed closely by the D-Bags. Griffin wasn't among them. Matt looked severely freaked out by the absence of his cousin and was snarling into his cell phone. Evan looked worried too as his gentle eyes swept the room. Kellan was frowning. When he locked eyes with me, he mouthed, "Anna?"

I shook my head. I hadn't found her yet. And apparently, no one had found Griffin yet either. God, what if something was wrong? What if she'd gone into labor this morning? She could be in a hospital right now, giving birth, and I wouldn't know. Surely she would call me. Why hadn't she called me? Where the hell was she?

Pulling out my cell phone, I stepped out of the room so I could start calling hospitals.

Fans filed past me as they completed their time with the stars. Anxious about finding Anna, I turned my back on them. By the time I put my phone back in my purse, I'd called every hospital, clinic, and veterinarian that I could get the number for. Who knows where Griffin would take my sister if she was having a baby. God, I hoped she wasn't in labor.

Hands clenching my stomach, I debated making the hardest phone call of all . . . to our father. He'd been so worried about my safety, I doubt he'd considered the possibility that something could happen to Anna. She'd always been so strong, so tough, so capable of taking care of herself. I doubt Dad even knew she was on tour with me. He was going to lose his mind. He'd call in the National Guard to help find her.

Pulling out my phone again, I sat in a hard folding chair and stared at the screen. Dad was going to officially disown me for losing her.

Kellan came up to me as I was contemplating what to tell Dad. Squatting down, he looked up at me. "No luck?"

I shook my head, tears in my eyes. "What if something happened to her?"

Kellan rubbed my thighs. "She's with Griffin. I'm sure she's fine."

I heard disgusted snorts and glanced over at two lingering fans staring at us. Kellan noticed them too and stood up. They glared at me with open dislike on their faces. As security forced them to move along, I wondered what that was about. Were the Kell-Sex fans so protective of the Kellan-Sienna relationship that Kellan couldn't even console a friend? Geez. They had bigger jealousy problems than I did.

Pushing them out of my mind, I looked up at Kellan. "What do we do?"

Running a hand through his hair, Kellan sighed. "Griffin won't miss the show. He'll be here, and he'll know where Anna is. We wait."

He extended his hand and helped me stand up. Rubbing my back, he led me to the dressing room so I could fret in private.

It felt like days passed while I waited for news of my sister's whereabouts. I tried her cell phone over and over, but she never answered it. Every time I asked Kellan if I should call my parents, he told me to wait another ten minutes. I was getting tired of waiting. So was Matt.

Pacing the room, he barked into his phone, "We're on in twenty minutes, Griffin! Wherever the fuck you are, get back here now!"

I'd never seen Matt angry before. It was a distressing sight. His cheeks were splotched with color, his temperament as prickly as his hair. I suppose part of his fiery behavior was being fueled by concern for his cousin. Even if they bickered like an old married couple, they still loved each other. Matt had to be just as worried as I was.

Stopping his friend from wearing a hole in the carpet, Kellan calmly told Matt, "Relax, he'll be here."

Matt tightened his grip on his cell phone, clearly blaming that inanimate object for Griffin's disappearance. "And what if he's not, Kellan? Do we bail on the show, or go up there without a bassist?"

Scratching his closely cropped head, Evan pointed in the direction of the stage, where Holeshot was finishing up their act. "David said he would play with us if Griffin didn't show."

Matt snapped his head to Evan. "Does he know any of our songs?"

Evan shrugged. "He said he'd fake it."

Matt threw his hands into the air. "Fake it? Wonderful!" Unfurling his fist, Matt took his aggression out on the touch screen of his cell phone while he flicked to Griffin's number. I was sure Matt was damaging the sensitive device and was about to offer to call Griffin for him when Griffin finally walked into the room. Seeing his cousin,

Matt lost the final hold on his temper. He chucked his cell phone at him, almost hitting Griffin in the cheek. "Where the fuck have you been!"

Griffin managed to dodge and catch Matt's phone at the same time. Juggling it for a second, he exclaimed, "Jesus, Matt! You almost nailed me in the face!"

Anna walked in right after Griffin. There was an aura about her that I'd never seen before. If I didn't know any better, I'd say my wanderlust sister was completely and totally at peace. Seeing her alive and well made *me* completely at peace. Shoving my phone in my pocket, I rushed over to engulf her still-with-child frame. "I was worried sick. Where were you?"

Pulling away from me, Anna bit her perfectly plump lip. "Well, don't be mad, but I sort of . . ."

She looked over at Griffin and he smirked back at her. That's when I noticed Griffin's fingers around Matt's phone. One of them was adorned with a very shiny gold ring. I immediately grabbed my sister's hands. Sure enough, she had a freshly placed ring as well. "Oh my God! You got married?"

Anna started giggling while Griffin put his arm around her shoulder. "We did!" Letting out a squeal, she lifted her hand to show all the guys in the room.

Everyone was too shocked to comment. Except me. I was too shocked to say anything other than, "You got married?" again.

Not getting the reaction she wanted, Anna pouted. "Yes."

I pointed at her new husband. "To *him*?"

Anna put her hands on her hips, her pout now a hard, angry line. "Yes."

As I struggled to not shake her and scream, *Why on earth would you do that?* Kellan came over and gave her a hug. "Congratulations, Anna."

Anna's frosty mood melted into excited giggles. "Thank you!"

Shaking his head, Kellan patted Griffin's shoulder. "You too, I guess."

Griffin raised his chin, pride on his face. "Thanks." Leaning over, he added, "The bachelor party is at the next stop."

Recovering, Matt and Evan finally offered their congratulations. Then Matt grabbed Griffin's elbow. "We have to go."

All of the boys left the room. When the dull thud of the background rock music was our only noise, I turned to my sister and again asked, "You married . . . *Griffin*?" She smacked my arm so hard I felt it in my teeth.

While Anna told me all about her romantic day of hanging out at City Hall, trying to get married in one afternoon, I contemplated the fact that Griffin was now officially my brother-in-law. Holidays, birthdays, family reunions . . . he would be there for all of it, cursing like a sailor. And, oh God, if Kellan and I ever had kids, he would be their uncle. *Uncle Griffin*. Just the thought sent a chill up my spine.

I watched the show in a daze. My sister *married* Griffin. On a whim. Because he said he loved her. And even more shocking, Griffin, the biggest player I'd ever met, *married* my sister. I never thought I would see the day. It was like the world had screeched to a stop and started spinning in the opposite direction. How had Anna beaten me to the altar? Our parents were going to flip. Or maybe not. Things like this tended to happen with Anna; they'd both learned to go with the flow years ago.

Needing to share my utter disbelief with someone, I texted Denny. *Guess who decided to throw logic out the window this afternoon and officially become Mrs. Griffin I'm-a-God Hancock.*

Denny's response was fast in coming. *Anna married Griffin? Really? Wow. Your dad is going to lose his mind*. I laughed at Denny's reaction. We really were a lot alike.

Chapter 21
Party Time

A few days after my sister's impromptu marriage, the tour was in Washington, D.C. Kellan and I had spent a good chunk of the morning exploring the city with everyone and were resting up a bit before the show tonight. I could not believe how much heritage was crammed into our nation's capital. Everywhere we'd turned there had been some amazing historical artifact or monument that I'd just had to see. It was like a *School House Rock* video come to life. Kellan and I were definitely coming back here when we had more time to explore.

While Kellan scribbled down some song lyrics in one of his journals, I typed *The End* on my story, saved the file, then reached across the table and wrapped my fingers around Kellan's. A sense of relief and completion filled me as I leaned back in the chair. It felt really good to get all of that out of my head, to finally be done telling my story. Kellan lifted his head as he noticed my expression. "You're finished? Do I finally get to read it?"

I hesitated, then turned the laptop so that it faced him. There were parts of this he was not going to like. A lot of parts, actually. But he wanted to know them, and I'd given him my word that I would let him read them. His eyes remained locked on mine as he set aside his pen and paper and slowly sat up straight. He knew the amount of trust I was showing him by letting him read my deepest thoughts.

When his eyes went down to the computer screen, a horrible feeling filled my stomach; it was a bad case of nerves mixed with a hefty dose of fear. I suddenly wanted to be anywhere other than the bus. I'd rather be in a press conference admitting to the world that I was Kellan's girlfriend than be sitting across from Kellan while he read my torturous book.

As Kellan worked his way to the beginning of the story, I stood up. His eyes flashed to mine, and I shook out my trembling fingers. "I can't just peacefully sit here while you read it." I looked around the empty bus, not knowing where to go. Everyone was still gone. Some were at the hotel, some were still exploring the city. My sister had gone shopping with Griffin. She was starting to turn the back of the bus into a nursery, which made me wonder if she really *was* going to stay on the tour until she delivered.

Kellan started to close the laptop. "If it bothers you, I won't read it."

I shook my head, running my fingers through my hair. "No, I want you to. I just . . . can't watch you do it."

As Kellan reopened the computer, I headed toward the cubbies. I could grab his Discman and listen to some classic tunes for a while. There were a few fans hanging around the perimeter of the parking lot. From the corner of my eye, I saw them start to freak out. Cell phone cameras were recording, people were yelling. They reminded me of a pack of jumping, chattering hyenas. I had no idea why they were suddenly riled; things had been pretty quiet here for a while.

The bus door was lightly rapped on, and Kellan and I both twisted to look. Who the heck was knocking? Security? Someone from the crew? I was pretty sure all of the guys in the band were still gone. Besides, none of them would've knocked; they would just enter if they were back. Well, except Griffin; he was still making an effort to knock whenever Kellan and I were alone together. I couldn't tell if he was trying to be respectful or trying to be an asshole. Either way was fine with me, so long as he didn't walk in on us again.

While I stayed near the center of the bus, Kellan headed over to the door. I peered out the window to get a better look and rolled my eyes. *Sienna*. Of course it was Sienna. Who else could get the Kell-Sex fans in a tizzy? I stepped forward as Kellan opened the door. "Sienna? What are you doing here?" She didn't usually bug us on our bus.

Sienna gave Kellan an adoring smile. "Can I come in?"

Kellan stepped back, swishing his arm to indicate that she could. When Sienna walked by him in the doorway, she paused. "Thank you," she murmured, batting her eyelashes.

Kellan kept his face neutral as he closed the door on the crowd of prying eyes. The fans shouted out comments and questions the entire time until the door seal drowned them out. *How long have you been together? Are you getting married? We love you guys! Kell-Sex forever!* Hearing that, I couldn't contain my eye rolling. How one imaginary relationship had become such a focal point for some people was beyond me.

As Sienna entered the lounge area of the bus, she smiled brightly at me, like none of that had just happened. "Kiera! Lovely to see you."

"You too," I muttered, not really meaning it.

Coming up behind her, Kellan asked, "What is it?" He said it slowly, like he was sure she had a hidden motive for being here. I was sure too, but with all those pictures that had just been snapped, I think she'd already accomplished it.

Sienna twisted to him, a coy smile on her face. "Can't a girl drop in on her friends? I'm used to having people around me, but this tour it's just been my security and me on the bus. Gets a little lonely." Thinking of something, her face lit up. "Would you two like to ride the next leg of the tour with me?"

Kellan opened his mouth, but I beat him to it. "No, it's all right, we're fine here." The tabloids would proclaim Sienna to be pregnant by the next venue if she and Kellan shared a bus.

Sienna pouted like she was crestfallen. "Well, the offer stands if you change your mind." Her dark eyes flicked around our home-away-from-home. "My bus really is much nicer than this one."

Walking past her, Kellan scooped my laptop off of the table, then twisted to Sienna. "I was actually going to rest a little bit before the show. Hope you don't mind." Sienna shrugged as she shook her head. Kellan turned to me. "You okay?" He discreetly indicated Sienna, and I knew what he meant—*Are you okay being alone with her?*

I nodded. Feeling those butterflies return, I touched the laptop with my finger. "I'm more worried about you reading this."

Kellan kissed my cheek, then breathed in my ear, "It won't change how I feel about you." His breath on my skin raised the hairs on my neck.

As Kellan started walking toward the back, I turned to face Sienna. She was watching him leave with a small smile on her lips. "Kind of weird, wasn't it?" I asked her.

She tore her gaze away from Kellan's backside to look at me. "What, love?"

I smiled at her as genuinely as I could, but it felt fake to me. "All those photographers waiting at the club when we arrived?"

Sienna's perfectly painted lips curved into a smirk. "Not really. My location seems to be leaked on a daily basis. I can barely use the bathroom without a witness." She indicated the empty bus with her hand. "It makes me a little jealous to watch how easily the group of you can come and go. I mean, your sister is shopping at a mall right now, isn't she?" I nodded, and Sienna sighed. "I can't even step inside a mall without being mobbed."

As I considered what her life was like, what Kellan's life was quickly becoming, I told her, "You could give it all up, move somewhere remote?"

Sienna laughed as she twirled a dark lock around her finger. "Give up the stage? Sure, I could, but what's the point of life if you're not doing what makes you the happiest? And even though it has its setbacks, the perks far outweigh them. I'm on top of the world right now, and I wouldn't change that for anything. I like where I am."

Her eyes drifted back to where Kellan was hiding away and I thought there was *one* thing Sienna would change if she could—Kellan would be right beside her on her throne as she ruled the world.

Sienna stayed and visited with me for about an hour. She glanced back at the cubbies a handful of times, but Kellan never reemerged. Perhaps bored, perhaps disappointed, Sienna frowned and said, "See you at the show," loud enough for Kellan to hear. If he did, he didn't respond. Slapping on a flawless smile, Sienna proudly left the bus.

After Sienna left, curiosity got the better of me and I went to go check on Kellan. He had closed the curtain to the sleeping area behind him when he'd gone in there. I tentatively pulled it aside and stuck my head in. The light was on in our cubby, and the privacy curtain was open. Kellan was on his side, staring at the laptop. His expression was intense, absorbed.

Quietly walking toward him, I murmured, "Sienna left."

He started and peeked up at me. "I didn't hear you come in. You scared the piss out of me."

I smiled at his comment and sat on the edge of our bed. Chewing my lip, I pointed at the computer. "Do you hate me?" I whispered.

Kellan stared at me a long, silent moment. His face was still blank. Aside from that brief moment of surprise, I had no idea what he thought. Had he read about my feelings for Denny? God, had he read our sex scenes? I shouldn't have let him read the full manuscript. I should have edited. How did he feel about it? Not knowing anything that was going on in his head was killing me, but I waited for him to be ready to speak. When he sighed and closed the computer screen, I braced myself for the worst.

Climbing out of the hole we slept in, he moved to sit beside me on the edge of the mattress. Our heads rested against the bunk above us. Face softening into sadness, he finally whispered, "I'm so sorry . . . for all the pain I put you through."

My eyes watered. "For all the pain you put *me* through? I'm the one that cut out your heart, then handed it back to you in pieces."

Kellan smirked. "I haven't gotten that far in the story yet. I'm still at the part where I'm an asshole."

Smiling, I bumped his shoulder with mine. "I kind of like it when you're an asshole."

Kellan smiled at the ground. "I'll keep that in mind." He looked up at me again. "But I mean it. I really am sorry. I should have just been honest with you. I wanted to tell you how I felt . . . I just . . . couldn't. It was too hard."

Swallowing, I nodded. "I know. But you don't have to apologize. What I did to you was so much worse. Sorry isn't a big enough word to cover it." Kellan didn't argue with me. He just gave me a sad smile and wiped a tear off of my cheek with his fingers. Needing to say it now, while we were knee-deep in regrets, I added, "I'm so sorry about the scenes with Denny. I shouldn't have let you read those."

Knowing which scenes I was referring to, Kellan put his finger over my lips. "Don't. I understand. I knew going into this that a story about us was also going to be a story about the two of you. And it should be. He was a big part of your life, and I'm okay with your history. It made you who you are. And I happen to be in love with who you are." I gaped at him, amazed at the depth of his empathy. He laughed a little. "I couldn't read about it, though. I, uh, skimmed a few parts. I hope you don't mind."

Shaking my head, I threw my arms around him. No, of course I didn't mind. Clutching his shirt in my hands, I buried my head in his neck. God, he was amazing. Holding him tight, I released a few final tears of guilt and remorse. Once the feeling was gone, I kissed his neck. "I love you, you know?"

Holding me tight to him, rubbing my back, Kellan murmured, "I know you love my hair." I pulled back to look at his amused face; he could barely contain his smile. "I mean you *really* love my hair . . . almost obsessively so. I had no idea." His grin turned bright and boyish. "And my abs." He cocked an eyebrow at me. "Would you like to try etching them with a marker? I'll let you. Although, edible paint is a lot more fun."

Pushing his chest away from me, I stood up. Jackass. Laughing, Kellan grabbed my hips and pulled me onto his lap. I giggled as I crashed into his arms. Tangling my fingers into his remarkable hair, I husked out, "I'll etch you if you etch me."

Kellan twisted me around so I was straddling him. His eyes were bright with excitement as he brought his lips toward mine. "Deal," he mumbled before our mouths touched. Then his fingers darted under my shirt, like he was going to start the art project right now.

His fingers danced along my skin, tickling me as much as caressing me. I was laughing in between our playful kisses and wishing that we could somehow sneak off of this bus and escape into a private hotel room.

"Well, this is familiar," said a voice from behind me.

I broke apart from Kellan's lips to glance at the now-open bus curtain. Being walked in on didn't startle me as much as it used to, but it still wasn't something I enjoyed. When I saw who was here, shock washed through me. "Jenny?"

My blond best friend giggled as she bounced on her toes. "Surprise!"

I squealed in Kellan's ear and shot up off of his lap. I collided with Jenny and held her tight as new tears stung my eyes. It had only been a couple of months, but it felt like forever since I'd last seen her. After our exuberant greeting, I noticed who was behind her. "Kate? Rachel? Cheyenne?"

Seeing all of my favorite people from Seattle here in D.C. was beyond odd. They seemed stranger to me than all the hoopla surrounding Kellan and another woman. Jenny laughed at the look on my face as I twisted between my girlfriends and Kellan; a small, knowing smile was plastered on Kellan's face, so I figured he knew what was up. "What's going on?"

Griffin and Anna were back from their shopping excursion. Anna was standing behind Cheyenne, her expression joyful. Griffin was loaded down with shopping bags and dramatically collapsed into a chair; a sea of colorful bags fell around him, and a couple of blue onesies fell to the floor.

Looping her arm around Rachel, Anna handed me the only thing that she was carrying—a completely black plastic bag. A little nervous, I gingerly removed it from her hand and peeked inside. There were a plethora of things in the bag, but a giant penis staring me in the face was the thing that really got my attention. Cinching the bag closed, my eyes snapped to Kellan's. "Okay, seriously, what the hell is going on?"

Kellan laughed as he stood and put an arm around me. "We're officially getting married next month, and Anna and Griffin just tied the knot, so we"—he pointed at Anna and himself—"decided a little celebration was in order."

Anna held her belly while she bounced on her toes. "Dual bachelorette party, Kiera!"

I looked over all of my friends, shocked. They had all flown across the country with hardly any notice to help Anna and I celebrate our weddings? And, I suppose, in Jenny and Rachel's case, to visit with their boyfriends.

After hugging each friend in turn, I looked back at Kellan. "You arranged all of this?"

He smiled and shrugged. "Our lives are crazy. When moments to remember happen, you have to pause a second to appreciate them. Otherwise none of this"—he indicted the bus—"is worth it. And getting married to you is definitely a moment to remember."

I heard a dreamy sigh escape Kate's lips as my eyes misted. Griffin intruded on my romantic moment by doing what he did best. He opened his mouth. "And while you guys are drooling over dudes, we'll be swimming in a sea of half-naked babes."

Anna elbowed him in the stomach, but she laughed. I looked back at Kellan. He shook his head. "We're just going to a bar after the show tonight."

Griffin pouted. "I said I wanted a strip club."

Kellan gave him a flat look. "And I said I wanted a bar. If you want to do separate bachelor parties, then by all means, go to a strip club tonight. But I don't feel like celebrating my marriage with overpriced alcohol and glitter."

Griffin rolled his eyes and made a sound like a whip being cracked. Kellan only smiled at him. I faced my sister. "And what exactly are *we* doing tonight?"

Anna gave me a wide smile. "Oh, don't you worry about the details. I've got everything under control."

Hours later, I was staring at myself in the mirror contemplating whether I should kiss my sister or deck her. Her master plan to celebrate our nuptials was to dress all of us girls in matching outfits that were half Robert Palmer video chick and half Muppet. We were all wearing skintight, short, long-sleeved dresses. Jenny and Anna had done everyone's makeup—bright red lipstick and smoky eyes— and Cheyenne and Kate had pulled everyone's hair back into long, sleek ponytails. I thought we were going to leave the dressing up at resembling "Addicted to Love" fill-ins, but I should have known that wasn't flashy enough for my sister. Once we were all uniformly dressed, she'd pulled out the coup de grace—an assortment of neon colored wigs.

As I fingered the bright pink hair in my reflection, Anna joined me. Giggling at her own mass of electric blue hair, she exclaimed, "We look fucking hot!"

Turning around, I examined my sister's outfit. Even with a belly large enough to house *two* small children, she looked good. I had no doubts she would be hit on at some point. "I feel ridiculous, Anna."

Making a dismissive noise, Anna smoothed my short, pink bob. "Well, you look amazing."

"Do I really have to wear this?" I pointed down the bus, to where Kellan and the guys were waiting to see us before heading out for their show. "Kellan got a say in his night. Don't I get a say in mine?"

Smiling, Anna shook her head, a neon strand of blue hair stuck to her lip. "No." When I grimaced, Anna turned me back around to face the bathroom mirror. "Tonight, you are not Kiera." She leaned in so that our faces were side-by-side, and for the first time, I noticed something I really never had before—my sister and I looked a lot alike. "Tonight, you are Kiki, sex goddess!"

I groaned, but then immediately laughed. Sure, why not. I needed a short break from my life anyway. "Okay, Anna, you win."

She smacked my butt as she walked away. "Don't I always, Kiera?" She smirked at me over her shoulder. "I mean Kiki."

Feeling like we were about to film a live-action version of *Fraggle Rock,* the girls and I stepped into the main portion of the bus. Griffin let out an earsplitting catcall. Matt's face flushed with color, while Evan's broke into a wide grin. And Kellan, well, let's just say I was getting thoroughly examined, and he appeared to like what he saw.

A lime-green-haired Jenny collapsed into Evan's arms, marking his cheek with a bright red lipstick outline. Rachel, wearing a canary-yellow wig, put her hands over her face and giggled uncontrollably as Matt held her; at least one of the girls was as embarrassed as I was. Kate smoothed her deep purple wig with a bright smile on her face. And Cheyenne, her hair a flaming red color that reminded me of Meadow's, clapped me on the shoulder as Kellan stood to greet me.

Lip curved in a seductive half-smile, he growled, "I am not going to be able to concentrate on stage tonight with this image of you in my mind." His smile widening, he added, "You are unbelievably hot."

Resisting the urge to deny his compliment, I instead told him, "Thank you."

Kellan's face was full of pride at my growing level of confidence. As my girlfriends said their goodbyes and grabbed their stuff, Kellan leaned in close. In my ear, he murmured, "You're keeping the wig, right?"

His fingers slid through a pink lock as he sucked on his bottom lip. Heat, fire, and passion were burning in his eyes, and I suddenly didn't want to go anywhere but to a private hotel room with him. My lips against his ear, I told him, "It's the only thing I'll keep on when I get back."

Kellan made a strangled groaning noise, then slung his arms around my waist. Over his shoulder, he told the guys, "Change of plans, we're canceling the show tonight and staying in."

Matt glowered for a fraction of a second, then looked over at Rachel grabbing her purse and smiled. Evan shouted his agreement and pulled Jenny back into his lap. Griffin exclaimed, "Fuck yeah," and pinched Anna's ass.

I smiled back at Kellan. "Nice try, but you know you can't do that."

He gave me a forlorn sigh. "I know, but it was a nice thought."

I gave him a soft peck, then slid away from him and collected my girls. Anna started doling out the rest of our outfits, and I contained a groan. It was the penis-paraphernalia that I'd noticed earlier. She gave each girl an obscene necklace, straw, suckers, and feather boas that matched our wig colors. The boas had shiny, tinsel penises woven into them. We were all dressed like sex-starved maniacs. I think my cheeks matched Cheyenne's hair.

As we gathered around the front of the bus, I saw a modestly sized black limo arriving at the edge of the lot. Kellan and the boys brushed past us. "We're going to head in now," he said as he kissed my cheek. Seeing me staring at the fancy car, he added, "I rented you a limo for the evening, so you could relax. Have fun tonight. You deserve it."

He winked at me and I smiled at his thoughtfulness. "Thank you. You guys have fun too." As he walked away from me, I grabbed his arm. "Hey, if you really want to go to a strip club, I would be okay with it. I trust you." I swallowed, not thrilled about the idea, but comfortable enough to know that Kellan wouldn't do anything differently behind my back than he would do if I were right beside him.

Kellan smiled. "I'm glad to hear that. I don't need a club, though." He shrugged. "They never really did anything for me anyway." I gave him a sly grin. That was probably true. Kellan didn't need to pay for beautiful, naked women to hang all over him. If he wanted, he could have that in a heartbeat just by throwing a party at his house.

There was a burst of noise and camera flashes as Kellan left the bus; some of the fans were still waiting around, then. Well, tonight was their lucky night. Not only were they getting an up close view of rock stars, but they were about to get an eyeful of rather bizarrely dressed women. Damn my free-spirited sister.

The girls and I waited a few more minutes, then dashed to our car. I stayed in the middle of the group, head down and neon pink hair blocking my face. The driver held the door open for us as we approached. Anna exchanged a few words with him before joining Jenny, Rachel, Kate, Cheyenne and I in the spacious vehicle. Remembering the spectacle at the club, Poison, I kept my eyes open for anyone following us. I know I would be curious about a group of women dressed like colorful hookers exiting a rock star's tour bus and hopping into a limousine.

Anna elbowed me in the ribs. "Relax, Kiki, you're free."

Laughing at my paranoia, I shifted to the front. "Yes, I am. Let's go have some fun."

The girls laughed with me while the driver gave us amused, puzzled glances. Per my sister's instructions, he drove us to a restaurant. Even though I felt like an idiot as the group of us slid out of the car and walked into Red Robin—my sister was having a craving for seasoned fries—I was grateful that we were eating first. I was starving.

Funnily enough, with the chaotic ambiance of the restaurant, we fit right in, like a piece of living art. Every patron in the place turned their heads to stare at us, though. Pushing aside the feeling of everyone's eyes on me, I followed my sister up the stairs to the bar. The six of us scooted into a booth, with Jenny, Kate, and Rachel on one side, Cheyenne, Anna, and I on the other. The fresh-faced waiter who arrived seconds later was clearly impressed with our outfits. "Hi, I'm Gabe. I'll be your server this evening." Pointing his pen at our penis-inlaid boas, he smirked, "Bachelorette party?"

Pulling the boa off, I placed it on the seat beside me. Flaunting phallic shapes at a family restaurant probably wasn't the best idea, young eyes and all. On the limo ride over, I'd made my sister put her penis necklace in her purse and promise me that she wouldn't use her straw or sucker here. She'd grudgingly agreed.

Tossing her arm around me, Anna beamed at Gabe. "Yep, my girl's tying the knot, so we need to get her lit!"

Gabe turned his blue eyes to me. "Congratulations."

Surprisingly, his gaze shifted over my face. Wow, was he checking me out? "Thanks," I murmured. "We're celebrating her recent wedding too." I turned to Anna. "I still can't believe you married Griffin."

Anna rolled her eyes. "Let it go. You're worse than Dad." I had to laugh at that comment. It was highly unlikely that Dad knew about Anna's marital status. I doubt she'd even told him that she'd left Seattle yet.

Gabe's smile widened. "Sisters?" Leaning toward us, he gave everyone a grin, then focused solely on me. "I know just what you guys need. Mind if I pick your drinks?" He winked at me as he straightened, and my mind froze. He really *was* hitting on me.

"Uh, no, go right ahead." Not knowing what else to do, I gave him a polite smile.

Leaning around me, Anna told him, "It's been a while since I've *been* one, but make mine a virgin, 'kay?" She rubbed her expanded belly and Gabe pulled his eyes from me to glance at her.

He nodded, his eyes instantly returning to mine. "Will do." He stood back up and pointed his pen at us again. "You ladies don't go anywhere. I'll be right back."

After he walked away, all of the girls looked at me simultaneously. "He was so checking you out!" Jenny exclaimed.

I sank into my chair and fingered my bright hair. "No, he wasn't." I giggled at the end of my sentence. *Yeah, he was.* Well, unfortunately for Gabe, I wasn't single. No, I was about to formally marry my rockstar sweetheart, whose searing good looks were insignificant in comparison to the beauty inside his soul. He was as close to perfect as one human being could be, and he was mine. I was beyond blessed.

Gabe returned a few minutes later with huge, crazy-shaped glasses full of something fruity and strong; I cringed a little after taking my first sip. Gabe winked at me again. "That should properly prep you for your evening."

I thanked him, then ordered some chicken strips. I was going to need a good base in my stomach if this drink was any indication of how the night was going to turn out. Gabe flirted with me throughout the remainder of our meal. Needless to say, I received the most attentive service that I'd ever received at a restaurant. The girls teased me about it relentlessly. Gabe was cute, so I was flattered, but Kellan had my heart and I wasn't interested. When Gabe handed me the receipt when we were finished, his number was on it. My eyes were wide as I looked up at him. He shrugged. "Just in case it doesn't work out."

I was so surprised that he'd done that, my only response was, "Thanks." Collecting myself, I added, "I think it's going to work out, though."

Gabe looked disheartened as I stood to leave him. I was so used to seeing that expression of disappointment on female faces as Kellan walked away that it was bizarre to see it directed at me. A thought struck me as I showed the receipt to my sister outside. If we'd been playing the game Kellan and the boys played when they went out, *I* would have won tonight. Just the thought made me giggle while the rest of the girls let out loud hoots and hollers.

Wondering what he would say, I snapped a picture of the receipt and texted it to Kellan with the message *I won!* I hoped he would find that funny, and not worry about what I was doing. But if I was willing to trust him with strippers, than he'd have to trust me too. And he did.

He didn't text me back, but I didn't expect him to. He was in the middle of a show, probably just about done with his set. It was strange not to be there, listening to him play, but I was enjoying my girl time. I wasn't sure where we were headed next, but I was slightly buzzed from Gabe's drink, so I didn't much care. Anna gave our limo driver a swift kiss on the cheek, making the older man blush. Feeling benevolent, I kissed him on the opposite cheek.

Where we ended up going was a strip club. I frowned as the car pulled up to the bright pink neon flashing a pair of female legs so that it looked like they were kicking. I cringed at the name of the club—Pole Palace. Glancing over to Anna, I firmly told her, "I have no interest in watching a bunch of half-naked women flirt with married men."

Anna let out an exasperated sigh. "Where's your sense of adventure, Kiki?" With a sly smile she added, "You will like this, trust me."

Not sure if I should trust my up-for-anything sister, I hesitantly stepped out of the limo. At the last minute, I told the driver, "If you see me running from the building in terror, please take me home right away."

The driver smiled at me as he held the door open. "Absolutely . . . Kiki."

Once again dressed in our penis gear, the group of us gathered under the front awning. Jenny and Kate seemed fine with going somewhere else or going inside; Rachel seemed just as dubious about this place as I was. Cheyenne was smiling. When I glanced at the front door of Pole Palace, I noticed the huge sign propped on an easel beside it and shook my head. *Ladies Night! Come on in to see the hottest men in town!* I should have known.

For some reason, it did make me feel a little better to know that we were going to be watching half-naked men flirt with married women. It seemed more innocent. I still felt horribly embarrassed about the whole thing, though, especially since I was dressed like a Bratz doll. "Anna, are you serious?"

With an ear-to-ear grin, she turned toward the bouncer. "Yep."

Jenny, Kate, and Cheyenne giggled and followed after her. Rachel and I looked at each other, shared a moment of mortification, then sucked up our inhibitions and followed after our more gregarious friends. The place was jam-packed with women of all ages. They were hooting, hollering, and shouting at the greased-up studs on the stage. The men dancing were gyrating and hip thrusting in a suggestive way that made me a little uncomfortable.

Wondering if Kellan would be okay with me being here since we hadn't talked about me going to a strip club, I grabbed Anna's arm. "Do you think Kellan . . . and the boys . . . will be okay with this?" I indicated some shirtless male servers posing for pictures with some very friendly female patrons.

Anna quirked a smile. "I think they'll be fine with it."

I wasn't quite sure, and I felt a little guilty about being here. I didn't plan on doing anything with any of these beefy, well-cut guys, but Kellan didn't know I was here, and it felt dishonest that he didn't know. I pulled out my phone to call him, and Anna snatched it away from me. "He won't mind, Kiera, and I told him where we were going. He was cool with it." She indicated the stage. "He's the one that found a place with male dancers tonight."

Surprise washed through me, but only for a moment. Of course he'd arranged this. Kellan wanted me to have a good time with my friends, and by the looks of the tittering women around us, being here was a *very* good time. Kellan also loved embarrassing me, and when a man wearing pants so tight they left nothing to the imagination asked me if I wanted a drink, I was very embarrassed.

Laughing, I finally accepted that being here was okay and relaxed with my friends. Anna sat us at a table near the front of the stage, and a couple of drinks into it I was hollering along with the rest of the girls in the audience. The dances were amusing, and yes, sexy as hell. My favorite part about it was the costumes. We'd had a fireman, policeman, and a construction worker so far. It was beyond ridiculous, and I couldn't stop laughing. Then a man dressed like a cowboy stepped out onto the stage.

He was wearing a bandanna around his mouth like he was a bandit and a black cowboy hat pulled low over his eyes. One of his hands was holding the tip of his hat, the other rested by his side. He was wearing a vest with nothing on underneath it, and his muscles had a light sheen to them, like he was slathered in oil. Like any good cowboy, he was wearing chaps . . . over a pair of dark spandex briefs. He was hot, and a hush went over the crowd. Just the way he stood there while he waited for the music to start was seductive, and I had a feeling he'd be good at riling up the crowd.

A heavy beat filled the air. I recognized the song as one of Rhianna's provocative hits. When the beat started, the cowboy lifted his eyes and stared at the crowd. I sputtered on the drink coming up my penis straw. "Oh my fucking God!" I screeched that, and Jenny, Kate, Cheyenne, and Rachel all twisted to stare at me like I was insane. Anna was holding her sides, laughing.

I couldn't even answer my friends' questioning looks, because I recognized the pair of seductive dark blue eyes sweeping the crowd. As his hips started swaying and the crowd started yelling, those familiar bedroom eyes locked right onto me. I couldn't see his mouth, but I knew he was smiling at me. I wanted to crawl into a hole and die, but I couldn't stop watching him. What the hell was Kellan doing here, in a strip club, dancing?

As he really started getting into his act, I stopped caring. Kellan was a natural seducer and was intoxicating to watch as he moved across the stage—a stage he owned just as much as when he was singing. Sliding and shaking, he worked his way back and forth across the front. When he stopped at our table, he slowly and seductively removed his vest. My heart was going a million miles an hour. When he tossed the fabric at me, I almost didn't have the reflexes to catch it. With his perfect chest on display, the crowd went nuts. With his tattoo of my name across his heart on display, my friends turned back to me, wide-eyed; they knew about Kellan's tattoo. Astonished, Jenny asked, "Is that . . . ?"

Fearing being overheard, she didn't say his name out loud. She didn't have to either. We all knew who she was referencing. As I weakly nodded that, yes, it *was* Kellan up there shaking his booty, they all started laughing. Anna let out an earsplitting whistle. Yes, my husband was stripping.

Just like when the D-Bags played, Kellan worked the crowd. He let the girls touch him, but backed off when they got too close or too friendly. He ran his hands over his own slick skin, caressing himself in ways that I was sure most of the audience was fantasizing about touching him. Halfway through the song, he ripped off his chaps to thunderous applause. I buried my face in my hands, mortified *and* turned on. I could not believe he was doing this, and at the same time, I wasn't surprised; it was exactly something Kellan would do.

Toward the end of the long song, Kellan sauntered my way. He was now only dressed in cowboy boots, tight spandex shorts, his face-concealing bandanna mask, and his cowboy hat. Holding my breath, I hoped he got to keep the outfit. Kellan jumped off the stage to land right beside our table. Women leapt at the chance to touch him, but he grabbed me and pulled me to my feet. As nearby patrons cursed in jealousy and hollered in approval, Kellan finished his tantalizing dance by grabbing my leg and hooking it around his hip. I instinctively conformed to his body, and for a moment forgot that we were the center of attention. Kellan dipped me when the song was finally over. When he pulled me up, our faces were inches apart. I could see his fast breath under his mask; it matched mine. Not caring who was watching, I kissed him through the fabric. His eyes fluttered closed as his hands traveled over my ass. The crowd erupted into shrieks.

Remembering that we were being watched, I reluctantly pulled away from him. Laughing, Kellan told me, "You probably shouldn't turn me on in this outfit. I may get arrested."

Laughing, I pushed his slick chest away from me. "I cannot believe you just did that."

Bending over he kissed my hand. "I couldn't resist." He pointed over to Anna. "It was her idea."

I glared at my sister, and she flashed her hands up and down his body. "Sex on a Stick," was all she said.

As the MC announcing all of the dancers started in on the next act—a soldier in a crisp, white uniform—Kellan gave me a final hug. "I have to go finish my *other* performance or Matt will have my head." Looking down at himself, he added, "And I need to go wipe this oil shit off."

I laughed and kissed his cheek. "You're something else, you know?"

He tilted his head at me. "So are you. It's good to see you having fun. I'll see you back at the hotel."

Raising an eyebrow, I mimicked his seductive tone, "Yes, you certainly will."

Kellan's eyes crinkled at the corners and I knew he was flashing me a grin that would have these women weak in the knees. I wanted to pull off his mask so I could see it, but I didn't want anyone here recognizing him. Kellan dressed as a half-naked cowboy was definitely an image I didn't want to get out to the Kell-Sex fans; this was mine and mine alone—well, mine and a barful of unsuspecting women.

We pulled apart, and Kellan made his way back to the stage so he could change and return to his concert. Along the way he was stroked and pawed by several feminine hands. He waded his way through them, stopping a couple that were drifting to the low side of his body. He looked back at me after he climbed the steps on the edge of the stage and tipped his cowboy hat. I smiled, sighed, and felt myself falling even deeper in love with him.

The rest of the acts paled in comparison to Kellan, and I found myself daydreaming about *him* more than watching *them*. Seeing that Anna was quickly petering out, I suggested that we call it a night. Everyone agreed, and we made our way back to our awaiting limousine. I thanked the driver as he opened the door for us.

Amusement on his face, he asked, "How was it?"

"Wonderful," I sighed.

He shook his head at me, and I giggled. Anna handed me back my phone as she sleepily rested her head on my shoulder. Patting her electric blue hair, I checked my messages. There was only one, and it was from Kellan. In response to my photograph of Gabe's phone number, he'd texted, *No, I get you tonight and every night, so I'm pretty sure I won*.

Biting my lip, I asked our driver to hurry to our hotel. I'd probably have to wait for Kellan to get back from his boys' night out after the concert, but I didn't mind. My pink wig and I would happily wait all night for him . . . and hopefully he'd come back with his cowboy boots and hat to go with the vest safely tucked in my purse.

Chapter 22
A Favor

Kate and Cheyenne flew back home the next morning, both of them looking a little worn as they climbed into the taxi. It warmed my heart to see them again; I'd really missed my friends back home. Jenny and Rachel were staying a couple of extra nights, to visit with their boyfriends. Our bus was rowdy and packed, full of music and laughter. I was firmly convinced that Disneyland had nothing on this bus—which was truly the happiest place on earth.

When we rolled into Philadelphia, the City of Brotherly Love, people on the bus started making plans for the afternoon. Jenny, Rachel, Matt, and Evan were going sightseeing. Deacon, Ray, and David were originally from around Philly, so they went to catch up with some friends. Anna and Griffin were going out for ice cream and pickles—another craving my sister was having. Wanting to spend some alone time together, Kellan and I turned down every group that invited us out.

When we were completely alone, I turned to Kellan and gave him a suggestive smile. "So, now that it is just you and me, Mr. Kyle, what would you like to do?" Dropping my voice to a seductive level, I said, "Maybe return that favor you still owe me?" I was a little proud of myself. Not only had I said it without blushing or squeaking, but my voice had even come out a little on the erotic side. I was getting good at this.

Kellan, however, surprisingly frowned and looked down at his shoes. "Actually . . . I have a favor to ask of you."

Seeing the seriousness in his expression, I twisted to face him on the couch. "What is it?"

Kellan leaned forward on his knees. He was wearing a long-sleeved white shirt with a short-sleeved black shirt layered over the top of it. The two contrasting colors seemed to perfectly express his disposition—he was eager, he was reluctant. He was happy, he was sad. He was at peace, he was melancholy. I hated seeing the conflict on his face, especially when I wasn't sure what he was conflicted about.

He ran a hand through his hair and peeked up at me. "I've been debating doing something. I wasn't going to do it, so I didn't even bother mentioning it, but the longer we sit here, the more it eats away at me, and I just feel like . . . I have to do it. I need to do it." He swallowed, then slowly exhaled. "But I can't do it alone. I need you."

Not expecting him to say anything like that, I grabbed his hand and squeezed. "My answer is yes. Whatever the favor is, my answer is always yes. Whenever you need me, I'm there, Kellan . . . I'm always here for you."

His eyes watered as he swallowed again. It broke my heart. Brushing some hair off of his forehead, I asked, "What do you need to do?"

He tried to tell me, but his voice was so hoarse he couldn't. After clearing his throat, he tried again. "I need to visit someone." He clamped his mouth shut after that and looked away; the pain on his face was obvious.

I kissed his shoulder. "Okay." I didn't know who he needed to visit, and it didn't matter. My husband was asking for me, and I would be there.

Kellan called for a cab while I grabbed my purse and a thick jacket. The label would arrange transportation if we needed it, but that was generally only for official functions; we were on our own if we were running errands. Upon Kellan's request, our friendly bus driver, Jonathan, had started parking so that the door to our bus was hidden by the other tour bus. It gave us a modicum amount of privacy from the fans and photographers when we entered or exited the bus. It also prevented Sienna from attempting anymore "conjugal visit" photo ops.

When the taxi arrived and was cleared by security, it parked in front of the crack between the two busses. Kellan slipped on his leather jacket and gave me a sad smile as he walked over to me. "Thanks for doing this," he whispered, twisting me around and helping me put on my jacket.

Looking over my shoulder and wondering what it was we were doing, I told him, "It's not a problem, Kellan. You're not ever a problem."

Kellan's face was a stone mask when we settled into the taxi; he looked completely impassive. To the driver, he said, "Saint Joseph's Cemetery in Gloucester Township, New Jersey." That answer was about the last thing I'd expected him to say. I could not have been more confused about why we were going to a graveyard. Turning to me, Kellan clarified, "It's where my parents are buried."

Knowing just how difficult this day was going to be for him, I put my hand on his thigh. He immediately placed his hand over mine and laced our fingers together. While Kellan's gaze shifted to the cityscape blurring past us, I asked him, "Why are your parents buried here and not Seattle?"

Still not looking at me, Kellan shrugged. "My aunt brought them here after the funeral. She said there was nothing left in Washington for them, so why bury them there." He returned his eyes to mine then, and there was a distinct edge of hardness in them. "She buried them *here*, near where she and my mom grew up."

Sadness swept over me. He really hadn't had anybody on his side when he was younger—except Denny and his band. "Oh, does your aunt live here, then?"

Kellan eyes snapped back to the window. "Don't know, don't care. We don't talk . . . never have." Kellan clearly didn't want to talk about her, so I let the conversation die.

We made one stop on the way to the cemetery—for flowers. It just about broke my heart when he ran into a shop on the corner and came out holding two bouquets. It really killed me when he handed me a white rose petal with the words *I'm glad you're here* written on it.

The drive to the cemetery took less than twenty minutes, but the light rain outside had turned into a heavy downpour by the time we arrived. I didn't have an umbrella with me, but I didn't really care; Kellan needed to do this. He needed closure. The cab stopped on a road that looped around an island of grass with a gigantic concrete angel in the center of it. Kellan told the driver to wait for us, then hopped out of the cab. Clenching both bouquets of red roses in his hand, Kellan immediately started turning his head back and forth, searching the expansive grounds. By the time I exited the cab, he was soaking wet; he looked lost and lonely as he looked around the empty graveyard.

He shook his head when I was beside him and ran his hand through his hair, slicking back the thick, wet mess. "I don't know where they are."

There was sorrow in his eyes as the rain streamed down his face. He didn't know where his parents were buried. Grabbing his free hand, cool from the damp air, I looked around the sea of headstones. The space around us was huge, and a road to our left led to even more graves that I could see through the breaks in the dripping trees. We could search for days and never find his parents. We didn't have days, though. We had a few hours at best.

Squeezing his hand, I firmly told him, "We'll find them."

We were running out of time, so we hastily began our search for the needle in this gloomy haystack. We started systematically going down the rows. We walked down separate aisles, two or three rows apart from each other, so we could cover as much ground as possible. We finished the first lot in thirty minutes with no luck. I glanced at the cabbie reading a book in his dry car, wondering how much this trip was going to cost us in fares. But, much like the limo for my bachelorette party, this was one expense that Kellan would gladly pay for.

Shivering and teeth chattering, we made our way toward the second half of the cemetery. This section was at least twice the size of the other side; I felt fatigued just looking at it. But we had no choice but to keep searching, so we did. With the names John and Susan Kyle blazing through my mind, I scoured the markers of the graves before me. So many people were buried here, each with their own stories, their own loves, joys, and heartaches. It was overwhelming to think about how many lives each person here had touched, in good ways, and in some cases, bad ways.

I was so focused on finding the names of Kellan's parents that the letters almost escaped me when I did eventually see them. *John and Susan Kyle: Beloved Friends, Family, and Parents.* I stared at the black marble in shock. I'd found them. I'd actually found them. From the corner of my eye, I saw Kellan a few rows in front of me, still searching. The flowers in his hand were a sodden mess.

I tried to speak above the rain, but my voice felt hollow. "Kellan."

He heard me and swung his head my way. His eyes lowered to take in the dual headstone at my feet. I watched him inhale a calming breath, then step toward me. It could have been the cold, but he was trembling when he reached my side. He stared at the grave with blank eyes. Without a word, he squatted before them. He brushed his fingers over his mother's name, then his father's. Then he placed his hand on the wet grass right in front of their gravestone and closed his eyes.

Even though the rain was pouring around us, spilling down his cheeks, I saw the telltale tracks of tears leaking from his eyes. I placed my hand on his shoulder in silent support. When Kellan opened his eyes, they were watery, and I had to force down the knot in my throat. How long would these people continue to hurt him? Tenderly, lovingly, Kellan placed a bouquet of flowers under each name. The significance broke my heart. After everything they'd done to him, every hurtful word, every brutal attack, after making him feel unworthy of any sort of affection . . . he still loved them. I'd thought "Beloved Parents" was a strange sentiment to have on their head-stone, but maybe it wasn't. Right or wrong, deserving or undeserv-ing, their son *had* loved them.

In a voice almost drowned out by the rain, Kellan said his good-bye to them. "I'm sorry I wasn't what you wanted, what you needed." His eyes drifted to his mother's name. "I'm sorry I ruined everything for you." They shifted to his father's. "For both of you." He exhaled a shaky breath, raindrops exploding from his lips. "I wish things had been different for us, but . . . wishing doesn't change anything. So, I just wanted to say goodbye . . . and—" He swallowed; his face held so much pain, it took everything inside me to not start sobbing. "I love you both."

When Kellan finally stood, he sniffed and his jaw quivered. I wrapped my arms around his waist, comforting him as best I could while swallowing back my tears. He held me close, his eyes still on his parents. After another moment of silence, he asked, "Do you think they would be proud of me? Even just a little?"

His voice broke, and I squeezed him tighter. I considered break-ing our all-honesty pact and lying to him, because how could I pos-sibly tell him what I really thought about his asshole parents? But I didn't. Instead, I told him, "I don't know . . . but *I* am so proud of you. For everything you've done, for what you just did."

I couldn't stop the tears then as sympathy for him overwhelmed me. Seeing me fall apart made him fall apart. He nodded, trying to keep it together, but then his fingers went to his eyes, and a small sob escaped him. I drew his head down to my shoulder, and he clutched me tight. Burying his face in my neck, he cried—cried for what he'd endured, for what he'd lost, and for what he'd never had.

When we were both emotionally spent, Kellan rested his head against mine. The rain had eased along with Kellan's tears, and only a light drizzle was falling on us now. "I love you, Kiera . . . so much."

I brought my lips up to his, tasting his tears along with the rain. There was a peaceful solemnity around us as we kissed—no birds chirping in the sky, no cars driving by, just the light splashing of rain falling from sodden leaves that could no longer hold the weight. The silence was cathartic.

An unnatural flash of light got my attention. I thought it was the sun finally showing itself, maybe glinting off the metallic foil of a nearby bouquet, but there was a familiar whirring and clicking sound that went with this odd ray of light. Breaking apart, Kellan and I simultaneously looked over to see a man near a clump of trees taking our picture. Some ambitious paparazzi must have followed our cab out here, hoping to get the money shot. And he had. That photograph of Kellan kissing me in the rain would go for thousands, I was sure.

Kellan's face twisted into irritated disbelief. "You have got to be kidding me."

My compassion for Kellan's pain mixed with my feeling of isolated frustration. The combination shifted and morphed into a blazing inferno of anger. I was so done with all of this pseudo-drama. The Kell-Sex supporters, the media, and Nick and Sienna could kiss my ass! And so could this man who was interrupting a very private moment.

Hands clenched into fists, I started stalking over to him. He liked that. His camera clicked even faster. "Have you no common decency! We are at a freaking cemetery!" I tossed my hands in Kellan's direction. "The man is clearly grieving! Show some goddamn respect!"

I was only a few feet away from the man now. He was grinning ear to ear, loving every single second of me going off on him. I could practically see the dollar signs in his eyes. It boiled my blood. He wouldn't be so amused when I smashed that pretty camera into little tiny pieces. I started to lunge for him, but Kellan grabbed my arm.

"No, don't—"

The cameraman shifted his attention to Kellan. "You stepping out on Sienna? This your dirty little mistress, Kellan?"

Kellan swung me behind him and shoved his finger in the photographer's chest. "She is *not* my mistress! You watch your fucking mouth!"

Still snapping pictures, the man backed up a step or two. "Sure looks like you're banging this bitch behind Sienna's back. Can't hide your little secret anymore. I got you, man! Gotcha red-handed! Your little slut is about to make headlines!"

Kellan smirked. The photographer probably thought he was amused, but I knew better. He was ticked. He was beyond ticked. He was three seconds away from clocking the guy. Fists clenched, he swung his weight around and landed his knuckles along the man's jaw. Oops—make that one second away from clocking the guy.

The photographer lost his balance and landed on his hip, hard. His camera fell from his hands, but being attached to his neck, unfortunately it didn't break. Quickly recovering, the man scooped it up and resumed taking photos. "You just fucked up, man! I'm suing your ass for assault now!" Even though there was blood trailing down his chin from a cut on his lip, the man was smiling.

Kellan took a step forward, but I pulled him back. This could quickly escalate way past assault if I didn't get Kellan out of here. "Come on. He's not worth it, Kellan."

Kellan's eyes swung to mine. "He's got your picture."

I sighed and shook my head. "Then he's got my picture. It's not worth getting arrested over."

Reluctantly, Kellan let me pull him away from the man who was now giggling at our misfortune. Venom in his voice, Kellan snapped, "You're scum, you know that, right?"

The man shouted back, "I'm not the one dicking around on the hottest girl in the world! What the hell are you thinking!"

Turning away from him, Kellan muttered, "I'm married to the hottest girl in the world, and I would never dick around on her, asshole."

Even though my body felt numb with cold dread, I looped my arm around Kellan's waist and smiled up at him. "Maybe it wasn't the smartest move . . . but I'm so glad you decked that guy."

Putting his arm around me, Kellan looked back at the man still taking our picture. "Me too."

Holding our heads high, the two of us walked back to our taxi. All of my attempts to keep myself out of the spotlight were in vain; I was out now. Thanks to that jerk-off's high-grade telephoto lens, my intimate moment with Kellan was about to be front page news. They would all know my face. My anonymity was gone, along with a good chunk of my freedom. I couldn't hide in plain sight, not anymore. The crazy, obsessed Kell-Sex fans were all going to know about me. It was only a matter of time.

When we got back to the venue, I thought we'd be hustling into the warmth and safety of our bus. But Kellan had other plans. Holding my hand, he led us to Sienna's bus. I tensed—not sure if I wanted to go in there—but Kellan's face was as stormy as the low-hanging clouds in the sky, and I knew I couldn't miss this confrontation.

Calling Sienna's name, Kellan pounded on her door. Just as I began to believe that she was out, or waiting for the show to start at our swanky hotel, Thing 1 opened the bus door. After eying us for any visible weapons, he stood aside to let us in. Once I walked inside, I wondered why Sienna ever left this place. It was luxury on wheels. Smooth leather couches lined the sides of the front half of the bus. The back of the bus had plush reclining seats facing a giant TV. There was a full kitchen off to the side, and from what I could tell, no sleeping cubbies. I was positive that Sienna's room in the back was finer than most studio apartments. I suddenly felt like I'd been living in squalor these last few weeks.

Sienna was draped across one of the couches reading a fashion magazine. She looked up at our entrance. "Kellan, Kiera, what a nice surprise." Her eyes darted to the window, most likely checking for photographers. "What can I help you with this fine afternoon?"

Kellan stormed over to stand right in front of her. Thing 2 rose from his recliner in the back, clearly not liking the look on Kellan's face. "Did you set us up?"

I snapped my eyes to Kellan, not realizing he'd jumped to that conclusion. It was a completely plausible scenario, though, and I shifted my gaze to stare at Sienna. Had she set us up? Sienna tilted her head, confusion on her comely face. "What on earth are you talking about? And did the two of you take a fully clothed shower? You're absolutely soaked." She snapped a finger and put her hand over her shoulder. On command, her bodyguard brought her towels from a closet in the hallway. She handed them to us while Kellan answered her question.

"Kiera and I were ambushed by some asshole with a camera. I ended up clocking him, but not before he snapped Kiera's picture."

Sienna gave him a knowing smirk. "Those little insects can be quite intrusive, can't they? Well, don't worry too much about hitting him. I'll have my people take care it. Toss them enough money, and nine times out of ten the paparazzi won't seek legal damages."

While I squeezed the water out of my hair, Kellan narrowed his eyes. "You tip him off?"

Sienna pouted as her dark eyes searched his face. "I had no idea where you went. How could I possibly give someone your location, if I didn't know it?"

Kellan's eyes narrowed as he studied her. "I never know if you're telling me the truth, or if you're feeding me bullshit." I hid my smile. I never knew that either. And, just for that reason alone, I knew Sienna would never have him. Even if something happened to me tomorrow, and the pathway to his heart was clear, Kellan would never date someone that he couldn't trust.

Ready to leave, Kellan tossed our towels on the couch and pulled me toward the door. Seemingly irritated, Sienna reiterated, "I had nothing to do with this. I'm not some mastermind out to sabotage your relationship. I just roll with whatever life gives me, and I suggest that the both of you learn to do the same."

Kellan looked back at her, fire in his eyes. "If I find out you had anything to do with this, we're done. I will pack up my shit and walk away from this tour, and I don't give a fuck what Nick does to me. Let him sue me for breach of contract. I won't be played anymore."

Later that night, I stayed in the dressing room when Kellan took to the stage, choosing to listen to him through the speakers but not watch him. I had too much on my mind. The photo was going to be out in a few hours, by the morning at the latest. The buzz when the sun rose in the sky would be so loud, it would probably wake me up. My stomach clenched. God, I hated being the center of attention—this was worse than every first day of school, new job, interview, birthday party, and graduation jitter I'd ever had. Walking down the aisle suddenly seemed like a piece of cake.

The loss of my anonymity affected me physically. It was as if I'd been wrapped in a windproof, fleece-lined, down-filled, zero-temperature blanket, sheltered from the cold, protected, and safe—and then I'd had that blanket ripped from my skin. I felt bare, exposed, raw, chilled to the bone. Kellan was a private person too. Was this how he felt, talking about his life to complete strangers? Maybe, but he had the love and admiration of his fans to keep him warm. I wasn't going to get a rosy reception from them. I was a roadblock to Kellan, and from all I'd seen, the fans either wanted him with Sienna, or they wanted him for themselves. There was no third option.

I couldn't control how the fans reacted to me, but I knew that how *I* reacted to this was my choice. I could keep hiding away, never setting foot outside the bus, and hope that the drama died down soon. Or I could take a stand and proudly walk beside my husband. This kind of exposure was the last thing I'd ever wanted, but I didn't feel like hiding anymore. Kellan and I had worked too hard to get together, to stay together. I didn't want to go back to square one. I didn't want to feel ashamed over what we had. I loved what we had. I felt like screaming to the entire world that Kellan was mine, and he always had been.

Jenny and Rachel were watching the boys perform, since they were flying back to Seattle early tomorrow morning. Anna was keeping me company . . . sort of. Crashed out in a comfortable chair, her mouth was open and she was slightly snoring as she took a power nap. I guess her afternoon with Griffin had worn her out. Knowing that either way Kellan and I handled this shit-storm heading our way, tomorrow was going to be different than today, I nudged my sister awake.

She startled and looked around, murmuring, "I'm up, Mom." Blinking, she glanced up at me. "Kiera? What the hell time is it?" By the look on her face, you'd think it was three in the morning.

"It's still early, the guys are still onstage."

She laid her head back and closed her eyes. "Then why the hell did you wake me up?" She gave me a crooked smile. "Johnny Depp was massaging my feet."

I smiled at my sister, then remembered what I wanted to do. "Tomorrow is going to . . . well, suck. So I wanted to do something tonight, while I'm still relatively unknown." Anna cracked her eye open, and I added, "I need to do something. Will you come with me?"

Without hesitation, my sister started standing, or trying to anyway. Folding around Maximus was no easy task. I helped her to her feet, and the only question she asked me was, "Where we going?"

When I told her what I wanted to do, she put her hand on my forehead. "Who are you, and what have you done with my sister?"

I batted her hand away. "I'm someone who is done hiding. I want the world to see."

Anna smiled at me, pride clear on her face. "Then let's do this."

Anna and I slipped out the back, unnoticed, and twenty minutes later, a cab was dropping us off at a tattoo parlor in a questionable part of town. The cab driver had assured us that they were the best in Philly, and were open late most nights. Considering that they were situated across the street from what looked to be a biker bar, I thought their late hours was probably a smart business move.

A bell in the door chimed as we opened it. Anna's eyes lit up as she took in the photos of skin art around the room. As we both examined a photograph of a woman with a cascade of stars trailing up her side and bursting across her chest, Anna told me, "I can't believe you're doing this." Slinging her arm over my shoulder, she added, "My baby sister is growing up."

Rolling my eyes, I shrugged her arm off. As I turned toward the front counter, Anna brightly exclaimed, "I should get one too." Bending over, she pointed to her ass. "Griffin's name, right here. Then he can kiss it whenever he pisses me off."

"You would be bending over all the time then."

Anna gave me a highly inappropriate grin, and I quickly changed the direction of the conversation. That was one mental image of Griffin I did *not* need to have ingrained in my head. "Maybe you should wait until after Maximus arrives to get a tattoo."

Anna sighed, tucking her hair behind her ears. "I suppose that would be a good idea." She laughed. "Guess I should try being responsible every now and again."

I laughed with her, rubbing her burgeoning belly. "Wouldn't hurt."

Her fingers cupping the child in her womb, Anna groaned, "God, I hope he arrives soon. I'm so sick of being pregnant!"

I was about to ask my sister if she was finally going to fly home, or to our parents', when an attractive man came out of the back. Every square inch of his arms was covered in colorful tattoos that reminded me of Evan's. He had gauges in his ears too, just like our D-Bag drummer. "Just don't give birth in my lobby, please."

Anna smirked at him as he extended a hand to us. He had a tattoo on the meaty part of his thumb that read *No Regrets*. I couldn't have agreed more with the sentiment, and I considered getting that tattooed somewhere on me too, but not tonight. I had other plans for tonight.

"Name's Brody. What can I do ya for?"

After shaking his hand, I pointed to the inside of my right wrist. "I want my husband's name, right here."

Brody nodded. "Popular spot. What's the lucky man's name?"

My grin burned brighter than the sun. "Kellan."

When Anna and I left the shop, my wrist covered in a thick bandage, I reconsidered ever getting another tattoo. A needle digging into your flesh over and over wasn't exactly a wonderful experience.

And I was sort of a wuss about pain, anyway. It was far, far down on my list of favorite things. Truly, it was miracle that I'd sat through the entire procedure. The second that machine pierced my skin, I almost shot into the air and vanished out the door. I think I would have, if the tattoo had been anything other than Kellan's name.

We had another show in Philly tomorrow, so Anna and I took a cab back to the hotel instead of returning to Wells Fargo Center to finish up the concert. Anna was tired, and I just wasn't in the mood for listening to the thunderous reaction of Kellan and Sienna closing out the evening with the passionate duet that had started this whole mess. So Kellan didn't worry when he couldn't find me, I texted him and then lay down in our bed to wait for him, wearing only my underwear and a light T-shirt.

I was more exhausted than I realized and fell asleep not long after setting my head down on the pillow. A body sliding into bed with me stirred me back to life. His skin was cool and a little damp, and he smelled like the citrus body wash that the hotel provided. He must have hopped into the shower before hopping into bed. I shivered as his chest pressed against my back and his arms and legs wrapped around me. "I'm cold," he murmured. "Warm me up."

Wanting to help him out, I flipped around and cocooned him with my body. Pulling his head into my neck, I kissed his cheek. He groaned in delight. "You're so warm . . ."

I smiled as I ran my hands over his chilly back, warming him with friction as well as skin. His lips brushed over my neck, and the temperature of my skin stopped slowly decreasing as desire kicked in. His mouth found its way to the electric spot at the base of my neck near my collarbone, and I suddenly felt red hot. Instead of pressing against his body to warm him up, I started pressing against his body to *rev* him up. It didn't take long.

Rolling me to my back, he settled himself on top of me as he worked his lips across my throat and up the other side of my neck. In my ear, he husked, "I love it when you make me hot."

He pressed his hips into mine for emphasis, and a low moan

escaped me. He was ready for me. The hard length of him being teasingly out of reach was enough to fully ignite me. I'd had such an
emotional day that a satisfying release was exactly what I needed
right now. Kellan too, probably.

Feeling frantic, I found his mouth and started clawing at his
boxers. Kellan didn't question my enthusiasm. He just went with it
and started tearing off my clothes. I felt like crying out with every
place he touched me—his mouth over my chest, his hand sliding
down my hip, his finger sliding over my sensitive core. Back arched
and breath needy, I was ready for him to claim me. He was ready
too. Breathing heavy, he angled his hips so that just the tip of him
entered me. I grabbed the pillow under my head with both hands.
Knowing how much he loved it when I begged him, I exhaled, "Yes,
God, please . . . yes."

I was expecting him to plunge deep inside of me. I was expecting
to scream out in ecstasy. I was going to clutch his hips and encourage
him to take me hard and fast instead of his usual slow and steady. I
needed him to work me over, to satisfy the ache escalating with every
second.

But he didn't take me. He shifted to my side. I groaned as the
aching shifted to the edge of painful need. I kissed his chest and
threw a leg over his hip. I would take *him* if he wouldn't take me.

Kellan seemed distracted, though, as he held both of my hands.
"Kiera?"

I ignored the question in his tone as I got him back into position.
It was tricky, since he wasn't letting go of my hands, but I weaseled
my hips over his and shifted down so the tip of him was back where
I needed it.

Kellan let go of one of my hands to still my hips from pushing
down on top of him. His hand shifted so that his thumb slid against
the thick bandage of the wrist he was holding. "What is this?" he
whispered, voice tight.

I groaned as I forced more of him inside me. I'd forgotten all
about the tattoo once his hands and mouth had started riling me up,

and it was about the last thing in the world that I cared about now. "It's for you," I moaned, successfully pushing myself onto him.

Kellan hissed in a quick breath. I thought his hand on my hip might move me away, but he pulled me into him instead. "Oh God . . . what is it?"

Our joint hands laced fingers while our hips began to move. I could barely focus on his question as he filled me, absorbed me. I clutched him to me as short, erotic moans filled the air. "Your name," I murmured, when I could speak.

"What . . . why . . . ? Oh God . . . God, Kiera . . . you feel so good . . ."

Forgetting his question, he groaned and clutched me tight. Our lips found each other's and all coherency was lost as our bodies pressed and pulled against each other in a steadily increasing tempo. I could feel my crest approaching, and my short, quiet bursts of sound turned into long, needy cries. It hit me like a wall, and I squeezed Kellan tight. A deep, satisfied groan left him as he climaxed.

Panting, he rolled onto his back, pulling me onto his chest. "What . . . ?" he asked.

Giggling, I sat up on his now-warm chest. "What, what?"

Swallowing, he took a moment to collect his thoughts, then he grabbed my hand so he could examine my bandaged wrist. "What did you do?"

Sitting up, I turned on a small lamp by the nightstand so he could see exactly what I'd done. He cringed in the sudden brightness, then his eyes widened and his jaw dropped open as he understood just what the bandage was hiding. As I carefully peeled it back to reveal the shiny ink staining my skin, his face grew even more disbelieving.

As we both stared at the swollen, glistening letters of his name upon my flesh, Kellan was silent. I started to think that maybe he hated it, and he just didn't know how to tell me, but then he looked up at me. Eyes shining, he murmured, "You know that's permanent, right?"

Smiling, I reattached the gauze and told him, "You know *you're* permanent, right?"

He looked away, like he found that hard to believe. Then he looked back at me and smiled. "Yeah, I know."

I feigned surprise. "You're not going to argue with me, call me absurd?"

He cupped my cheek. "Well, I still think you're absurd, but I'm not going to argue with you about spending the rest of your life with me."

I lifted a brow in challenge. "Because you know I'm head over heels in love with you."

Kellan smiled. "Yes."

"And you know you're a good man."

He hesitated, then nodded. "Yes."

"And you know you're worthy of being loved."

He frowned, and I thought here was the point where I'd lose him, but after a long moment his lips evened. "Yes." His voice didn't even quaver, and pride shot through me.

I leaned in to kiss him, but Kellan pulled back. "And you know you're sexy, intriguing, adorable, and the only person I'll ever be in love with. You know you're the most beautiful girl I've ever seen."

I saw the dare in the depths of his midnight eyes, and my peaceful smile grew wider. "Yes, I do."

"Good." Flashing a triumphant grin, Kellan finally let our lips connect. "I love hearing you say I do." I giggled and he added, "And I really love your tattoo."

Grabbing his face, I pulled him back down to the mattress. "Good, because I really love *you*."

Chapter 23
Backache

The next morning started peacefully enough, but I knew it wouldn't last, not with my imminent exposure on the horizon. But as the sunlight streaming through the open window beside me caressed the bare patches of skin that Kellan and I showed as we lounged in our tangled, tousled sheets, that future concern seemed a far-distant event, one I didn't need to worry over just yet. Wanting to purr with contentment, like the fluffy cat I used to own as a child, I shut out the world and focused on the man in front of me. He was all that mattered anyway.

Kellan seemed equally content as he traced the tender rectangle covering my wounded wrist. I knew we both had things we needed to do today, and we would eventually have to get up and deal with the gossip explosion that was probably already happening, but a few more minutes of quality time wouldn't hurt anything. And I had a feeling this might be the last peaceful moment we had for a while.

That thought was confirmed for me about ten minutes later. Like reality was throwing a wet blanket over our serenity, my cell phone started going off, and Kellan's went off a few second later. I inhaled a deep breath as I locked gazes with Kellan. We both ignored the ringing for a moment, then Kellan whispered, "Why did we get cell phones, again?"

Laughing, I kissed his nose. "I suppose we should answer those. The photos must be out by now. People are probably worried." I cringed, wondering if my parents had seen the pictures yet. Dad was going to flip if he saw a picture of his daughter being called a whore.

Kellan sighed, then nodded. He started to turn away, but I cupped his cheek. Ignoring the incessant ringing in the room, I looked deep into his eyes. "Whatever happens from here on out, I want you to know that I don't regret anything. Being with you, loving you, experiencing this with you . . . it's all been worth it, and we'll get through this together." I smiled. "We're a team. It's us against the world."

Clearly moved by my declaration, Kellan murmured, "Us against the world? That sounds like wonderful odds." Our phones were silent a second then started ringing again.

I chuckled as I placed a light kiss on his lips. "It's better than no odds at all."

It took a minute for Kellan and me to disentangle ourselves. Somehow, we'd wrapped the sheet over us *and* under us. We were giggling when we finally got the mess sorted out. It made me happy that even though this chaos was being shoved down our throats, we could still find tiny pockets of levity. I quickly tossed on some fresh clothes while Kellan pulled on his boxers. Before hurrying to my phone, I took five seconds to fully appreciate the sight of Kellan's tight abs and lean legs showcased by the silky black material. He was perfect, inside and out, and I really couldn't blame the world for being obsessed with him.

Wondering which concerned loved one would get a hold of me first, I glanced down at the screen before picking up. I smiled when I saw Denny's name. No matter what, Denny would always be on my side.

"Hey, Denny," I said, bringing the phone to my ear. Kellan was across the room, also on his cell phone now.

"Kiera, you okay?" His accent around my name was just as warm, sweet, and caring as the first day I'd heard it. "Have you seen the news? Your face is everywhere. They know about you. They're all calling you Kellan's mistress."

I sighed as I sat on the edge of the bed. "I haven't seen it yet, but I knew it was coming. That creeper ambushed us yesterday when we thought we were alone." Cringing, I asked, "So, how much do the Kell-Sex fanatics hate me?"

Denny let out a long sigh that said it all. "Well, let's just say that some of them are very . . . passionate. And inventive. Just hope you don't ever find yourself in any dark alleys with them." I laughed at that, and Denny sighed again. "I hate to sound like a broken record, mate, but you could always come back home if it gets too rough." Laughing a little, he added, "Abby even said she'd hide you in our closet if things got too bad."

I let out an unladylike snort. "Yeah, fleeing back home and hiding out with my ex and his girlfriend—that wouldn't be awkward at all." Having heard my comment, Kellan smirked at me.

After a long stretch of silence, Denny quietly told me, "Fiancée. I asked Abby to marry me, and she said yes."

Even though I'd been expecting it, my stomach dropped. This must have been how he felt when Kellan and I "got married" right in front of him. Swallowing, I pushed down the microscopic amount of hurt in my belly and fully embraced the epic amount of joy I felt for my best friend. "Denny, that's . . . Congratulations. I'm so happy for you, for the both of you. You deserve a wonderful life, and I know Abby will give it to you."

He exhaled, relief in his voice. "Thank you. I was . . . nervous to tell you."

"Don't be nervous to tell me good news. You and I are past that point in our relationship. I hope we are, anyway."

"We are," he agreed.

The second I disconnected with Denny, my phone rang again. I had a feeling I would be fielding a lot of phone calls today. I was really sick and tired of fielding phone calls. I grimaced as I glanced at the screen. Hitting the connect button, I brought the phone to my ear. "Hi, Daddy."

I kept my voice as carefree as possible, but it didn't work. My dad's response was, "You need to come home now!"

Making myself comfortable on the bed, I spent the next twenty minutes convincing my father that I was fine, and Kellan was fine, and everything was peachy keen, so he had absolutely nothing to worry about. I hoped I wasn't lying.

Kellan let Jenny and Rachel into the room while I was frantically trying to get off of the phone with my father; he was three seconds away from coming to Philly to collect me. Once I successfully disconnected, Jenny gave me a hug. "Hey, Rachel and I are heading to the airport now. I just wanted to say goodbye before we left."

When Jenny and I pulled apart, I noticed that her normally bright face wasn't as chipper as it usually was. Beside her, Rachel looked equally distressed. "I hate what the media is doing to you. They're making you out to be some two-bit hussy."

Kellan's phone rang again, and sighing, he turned away as he answered it; he was still in his boxers. Rachel was purposely keeping her eyes averted from Kellan's sculpted body; Jenny didn't even seem to notice.

Sighing at Jenny's comment, I peeked over at the bed. Kellan had brought me my laptop last night, as well as my overnight bag. While I'd been busy convincing my dad that there was nothing to worry about, I'd hopped online to find the story about me. It hadn't been hard. The news page that the web opened up on was showcasing the drama in their "Top Story" section. There was something really weird about a couple of rock stars' dating woes being splashed all over a reputable news site.

There were three shots of Kellan and me highlighted in the article. One of the photos was a close-up of our faces, snapped while we were kissing. Kellan was grieving in that picture, and the distress on his face was as clear as my lips upon his. The second was a moment later, when we'd noticed that we were being filmed. We were both looking directly at the photographer, shock on our faces; even surprised, Kellan looked pained. The shots were so zoomed in that the graveyard was nowhere to be seen. Thanks to the emotion on Kellan's face, it really did look like he was cheating on Sienna, and was torn up about it. I'd been comforting him at the time, but in the photo I came across as a stone cold adulteress, seducing him into being unfaithful to the woman he loved.

The last photo, the money shot, was Kellan standing above the photographer after knocking him to the ground. Looking thoroughly pissed off, Kellan seemed like he wanted to continue pummeling the man—a guilty adulterer furious about being caught red-handed. It was a gossip goldmine, and it was all very misleading and very incriminating.

Following my gaze, Jenny pointed at the computer. "I feel so bad for having to leave you in the middle of this circus."

Watching Kellan run his hand through his hair while he talked with someone on his cell phone, I told her, "Being with him is always going to be a circus." Smiling, I looked back at her. "He's worth it, though."

Jenny gave me another hug. "We have to go, but call me whenever you need to. Okay?" We separated, and her hand rubbed my arm. "And have faith."

Swallowing back sudden tears, I told her I did. Faith was one of the few things I had right now. Rachel and I exchanged a brief hug next, and then my two friends disappeared from my life again. A brief surge of loneliness swelled in me; I'd really enjoyed my girl time. I quickly reminded myself that I'd get to see them again at my wedding, and in the meantime I had my sister to keep me company. I wondered if she'd seen this yet.

Kellan looked around the room when he finally got off his phone. "The girls leave?"

"Yeah."

Kellan nodded and lifted the phone in his fingers. Grim amusement on his lips, he told me, "My dad and Hailey called. They're both concerned about you. Hailey is worried that you'll be lynched by the fans before this is all cleared up." He frowned, like he kind of thought that too.

Running my arms around his neck, I told him, "We'll sort this out, but right now, you have that private performance to get ready for." I lifted my brow as I reminded him that he still had a job to do in all of this madness.

Kellan dropped his head back. "God, I'd forgotten all about that." Looking like he really wanted to call in sick, he said, "I was hoping to sit down with someone this afternoon, make a formal statement about that picture, but I'm not going to have time."

Placing my palm on the tattoo of my name over his heart, I leaned up and kissed him. As if to punctuate just what he'd said, both of our cell phones started ringing again and Tory pounded on our door. "Ten minutes, Kyle!"

I was done hiding our relationship. So, when the dark SUV the label hired dropped us off at the venue, I held hands with Kellan as we walked inside. The swarm of paparazzi waiting on the other side of the security fence was massive; I'd never seen so many cameras in all my life. They immediately reacted when they saw the two of us together. Flashbulbs blinked on and off in rhythmic, random patterns. The crowd clamoring for the best shot of Kellan and I looked like a wide, chaotic Christmas tree, its lights struggling to outshine the sun on this crisp fall afternoon. The tall man in the middle only needed an angel on his head to complete the effect. I was grateful for the warmth and strength emanating from Kellan's hand as he squeezed mine tight—I felt like my entire body was falling apart, I was shaking so much.

This was so far outside of my comfort zone that I was pretty sure I was bumping into someone else's comfort zone. But instead of cowering and hiding, I lifted my head and straightened my back. I wasn't doing anything wrong, and I had nothing to be ashamed or afraid of. The fans in the crowd took my resolve as arrogance. Words drifted over the lot. Hurtful words—*whore, slut, home wrecker, bitch,* and several others that I couldn't even repeat in my own head. Kellan was squeezing my palm painfully hard by the time we were safely behind closed doors. I shook my hand so he'd let some blood flow back into my fingers.

"Sorry," he murmured. "I had to hold on to you to stop myself from smacking a few heads."

I smiled up at him. "Considering that most of the bodies attached to those heads are young, female fans of yours, I'd say it's a very good thing that you didn't punch any of them."

He wrapped his arms around my waist. "Well, don't think I didn't want to."

"Don't think I didn't want to either," I joked. Well, half-joked.

Kellan and I found our way to the D-Bags' dressing room. The rest of the D-Bags were already there when we entered. Anna was too. Standing next to a small table overflowing with snacks, she was pouring a bag of M&Ms into a gigantic bowl of freshly popped popcorn. Plodding over to a chair, she eased herself down and balanced the bowl on her belly. As Kellan walked over to Matt and Evan, I sat beside her.

"Hey," I muttered, watching the bowl shift a little as Maximus moved beneath it.

Anna shoved a handful of popcorn and chocolate into her mouth. "Hey, heard you're a bitch whore for stealing Sienna's man."

Leaning my head back on the chair, I smiled over at my sister. "Yep. I officially, globally suck."

Anna chewed her food for a minute, then smiled. "Well, cunt or not, I still love you."

"Thanks, Mrs. Han*cock*, I love you too." Laughing, I reached over for some popcorn. Anna smacked my hand away.

"Loving you doesn't mean I'm sharing my popcorn." She pointed over to the table. "Grab your own goodies . . . bitch whore."

Exaggerating a grieved groan, I prepared myself to stand up. I paused when I noticed Anna cringing and pressing a knuckle into her back. "You okay, sis?"

She nodded. "Yeah, just a backache. It comes and goes . . . I'm fine."

She seemed pale to me, her face wan and weary. Maybe it was just because she wasn't wearing her usual expertly applied eye shadow and mascara. I was used to seeing my sister all done up. It used to drive my dad crazy that she rarely went anywhere without makeup. He'd often say, "Why do you need mascara if you're just going to sit in a dark movie theater?" Her answer was always the same, "Because I have to walk through the lobby to get there, Dad." Just the fact that she hadn't decorated her eyes today spoke volumes on how tired she was.

"Anna, maybe you should go back to the bus and lie down."

She shook her head; even her hair seemed a little lackluster today. "I want to listen to the show. Griff's going to do a little solo for me." Her smile, while still clearly pained, was full of love for her husband. God, I still couldn't get used to that word being connected with Griffin.

Tory came in a bit later to grab the guys for their meet-and-greet. Not wanting to disrupt Kellan's job by unnecessarily riling up his fans, I decided to stay in the dressing room. Anna looked too comfortable to follow Griffin, so she stayed behind with me. Or maybe she wasn't comfortable at all. I couldn't tell. She seemed fine on the surface, but every few minutes she would get a weird, focused look on her face, and she'd start inhaling and exhaling in a slow, controlled way. Then she'd be fine and she'd resume munching her popcorn. It was strange.

"Are you sure you're okay, Anna?"

Squishing an M&M between her fingers, she frowned. "No, actually." Tilting her head to examine her bowl of snacks, she complained, "All of the chocolate shifted to the bottom of the bowl."

Giving her a not-amused expression, I pointed to her back. "I meant physically. Everything all right?"

Anna waved away my concern. "It's just a backache. It happens when you're carrying around a hundred pound bowling ball. It will go away if I keep my feet up." To emphasize her point, she wriggled her toes, which were stretched out on a chair in front of her.

"I don't know, Anna, maybe you should see a doctor. When was the last time you saw one?" Anna hadn't exactly been keeping up on her checkups since leaving Seattle. I wasn't sure what they did at all of those doctor's appointments, but they probably had advice on backaches.

Anna rolled her eyes at me. "For a backache? What are they going to do at a hospital? Have me sit down, that's what. And I'm doing that, so . . . I'm following my doctor's orders before even receiving them." She smiled at me. "Because I'm *that* good."

I was about to answer her sarcastic comment when she whimpered and hissed in a sharp breath. The bowl of popcorn rolled off her stomach and crashed to the floor, scattering everywhere. Both of her hands clamped onto her back, frantically massaging the muscles around her hips. Seeing the pain on her face, I turned her and moved behind her. Pressing my thumbs deep into her lower back, I watched my sister lean forward and struggle to breathe calmly without groaning in pain. My heart began to race as I quickly started realizing that this was so much more than a backache. This was my nephew knocking, and he wanted out.

"Anna, you have to go to a hospital. You're in labor."

She shook her head. Voice strained, she reiterated, "It's just a backache, Kiera. I'm not due until next week."

I wanted to smack my sister over the head like Kellan sometimes smacked Griffin, but I couldn't bring myself to stop massaging her while she was in so much pain. "Hardly anybody actually gives birth *on* their due date, Anna."

Groaning, she muttered, "Then why the hell is it called a due date? It should be called an estimated date of delivery."

Controlling my smile, I told her, "Well, no matter what it's called, the baby decides when to arrive, and regardless of what you have to say on the matter, it looks like Maximus wants to be born today."

Anna simpered and pointed at the colorful sea of M&Ms resting at the edge of the toppled bowl. "But my chocolate . . ."

Massaging her with one hand, I grabbed my bag and rooted around for my phone. "Your snack will just have to wait, Anna."

I found my phone once again hiding inside the book I was only halfway through. Yanking it free of the pages, I scrolled through my numbers and dialed Kellan. He didn't pick up. I tried Griffin next. He didn't pick up either. Not expecting anything different, I tried Evan and Matt, then Kellan again. Nobody picked up. I wasn't too surprised. Tory had a strict no-cell policy when it was time to meet with fans. Deacon had answered his once during a greeting, and Tory had ripped him a new one once all the fans had left. She may place rock stars higher on the priority list than the general public, but she understood just who it was who bought the CDs.

"Damn, I'm going to have to go get them." Which also meant I was going to have to barge into a room full of Kell-Sex supporters. I really didn't have a choice, though.

Anna nodded, a groan escaping her. "Get Griffin . . . I want Griffin." She sounded like a little girl, lost and afraid.

I patted her back, then stood up to go find her husband. Her voice made me pause at the door. "Kiera!" she shrieked.

When I turned back to her, she was looking at me with panic clear on her face. "I think I just peed my pants."

I shot back over to her. Her black stretchy pants were soaked, and the chair beneath her was wet. My mouth dropped open. "No, I think your water just broke."

My sister officially started to freak out. "No, no, no! I am *not* giving birth backstage at a rock concert. I need to be in a hospital, pumped full of every drug that they can legally give me!"

I was so shocked, my only response was, "Well, he was *conceived* backstage at a concert, so it's sort of fitting for him to be born at one."

Anna smacked my arm, and not gently. I was going to be bruised tomorrow. "Get me to a fucking hospital, Kiera!"

Not wanting to endanger myself any further, I turned and fled the room. For the first time since this tour began, I couldn't find a single person. Not a damn roadie in sight. There were usually people running around, doing something, but nobody was backstage. It was like a ghost town. Cursing my bad luck, I ran to the one spot I knew held people . . . lots of people. It was where I needed to go anyway, since Griffin was in that room.

I could hear squeaks and squeals as I approached the room, and figured the parade past the rock stars had just begun. The doors were wide open when I got there, and a few excited fans were just starting to trickle out. Some had red cheeks, like they'd been crying. Needing to get to Griffin, I breezed past them. One gasped and exclaimed, "Is that Kellan's whore?" Another replied, "Yeah, I think it is. I can't believe her nerve. What is she doing here?"

I gritted my jaw and ignored them. I had much more important things on my plate right now than gossip. When I burst into the room, my eyes instantly locked on Kellan. His went wide when he saw me. Alarm spread over his features as clear as day. He knew I wouldn't come in here unless it was absolutely necessary. I knew the fans would take his alarm as panic—*Oh no, my mistress is in the same room as my girlfriend*—but I knew that Kellan sensed something was wrong, very wrong.

Standing beside Sienna, he tried to step forward to get to me, but the crowd of fans wasn't letting him move. He wasn't who I needed to see, though.

Ignoring him, I cut through the twisting lines of fans to get to Griffin. That got me a lot of unwanted attention. A silence fell around me that quickly turned into harsh whispers. I made out a lot of "It's her! She's here! What a bitch!" As people started realizing who I was, people started reacting. At first, they just wouldn't let me get through them. I asked politely, I nudged, but it was like the wall of fans had suddenly turned to stone; they all had questions, and they weren't moving until they got some answers. Panic set in. My sister was going to have a baby. She needed her husband. I needed to get through. That's all I could think about. In my haste, I started shoving through them. None too thrilled with me, they shoved right back. While the area around me started turning into a mosh pit, I did start making some progress . . . especially when they started shoving me from behind. Hey, whatever it took to get me to Griffin.

Just as I was almost to him, I was shoved up against some tough-looking girl sporting a bright pink fauxhawk. She also was wearing a Kell-Sex shirt. I wanted to sigh when the recognition flashed in her eyes. She didn't even give me a chance to politely excuse myself so I could move around her. No, much to the delight of everyone around her, she full on slapped me. I'd never been slapped before, and I had a newfound appreciation for how much it sucked. I vowed to never hit a human being again, even if they deserved it.

My left ear was ringing, but I clearly heard Kellan shout, "Hey!" There was commotion behind me, but I took the fans' moment of distraction to finally make my way to Griffin. His eyes were just as wide as Kellan's had been. "Holy shit, she actually hit you. You okay?"

Anger clouded Griffin's face as he glared at the fauxhawked fan. Not needing him to defend my honor right now, I grabbed his hand. "Anna's in labor. Her water broke. We have to get her to a hospital . . . now!"

His mouth dropped. "She's . . ." His eyes flashed to the door blocked by hundreds of fans no longer waiting patiently in organized lines. I could hear Tory trying to calm them down, and I could hear Kellan calling my name. I ignored it all as I focused on Griffin. His eyes came back to mine, concerned. "She okay?"

I shook my head and pulled on his arm. "No . . . she's freaking out, and I had to leave her alone to come find you."

Griffin nodded, then started shoving his way forward. He wasn't as nice or as polite as I'd been. "Get the fuck out of my way!" Still holding my hand, he pulled me through the sea of startled fans. Matt and Evan tried to follow, but they were swallowed up by the crowd closing in behind our wake. When I passed by Kellan, I yelled over the din, "Anna! Hospital!"

Kellan understood immediately and turned to Sienna. The poor, frazzled fans in the room had absolutely no clue what was going on, but they took the chaos I'd created as an opportunity to bypass social politeness and swarm their beloved stars. Kellan was crushed back into the wall by eager people wanting his attention. The fans not close enough to love on him hated on me. I was cursed at, tripped, and I'm pretty sure someone spat in my hair. Griffin pulled me through the mayhem and out into the relative safety of the hallway. Things 1 and 2 rushed into the room after we left. I hoped they took the time to free Kellan as well as Sienna. I quickly prayed his fans wouldn't hurt him, then rushed after Griffin toward my sister.

Anna was pacing the room when we got there, rubbing her back and exhaling loudly. Sweat beaded her brow as she glanced at the door. The pain in her face eased to relief when she saw Griffin. "Griff? This is starting to really fucking hurt."

Griffin ran his hands back through his hair. "Okay, no problem. We'll get you to a hospital, and they'll knock you out." He rushed over to her and supported her arm as he helped her from the room.

I didn't want to burst Anna's bubble that it was probably too late for drugs, but I did feel like I should mention one tiny little detail that they both seemed to be forgetting about. "What about tonight's show?"

Griffin immediately remembered where he was. "Fuck!" His eyes bored into mine. "You know our songs. You play for me."

"I can barely strum a guitar!"

Griffin patted me on the back as he walked past me. "You'll do fine. Good luck!"

I watched him walk away, wondering if I'd really just become the replacement bassist for the D-Bags. Shaking my head, I ran after Griffin. "No, I'm coming to the hospital with you guys. I'd probably get egged on stage anyway."

Griffin was beyond caring about his band's fate as he rubbed Anna's back. "Matt will handle it. He handles everything." I silently prayed Matt didn't have an aneurism tonight.

As we opened the rear exit, I wondered if I should call a cab or an ambulance. But it turned out that I didn't need to call either. A car from the label pulled up as Anna huffed and puffed her way down the stairs. The young driver looked startled at the sight before him, but swiftly opened the door for Anna and Griffin. As I climbed in, I remembered Kellan turning to talk to Sienna before they were mobbed. He must have asked for her to get a car here. I made a mental note to thank Sienna later.

As the driver hurried us along the streets of Philadelphia, the phone still clutched in my hand rang. It was Kellan. Grateful that he hadn't been crushed to death, I answered, "Hey, you're okay."

Kellan let out a long exhale. "I was going to say the same thing. I can't believe that bitch hit you."

"I'm fine." My cheek was still warm from the slap, and it wouldn't surprise me if I had finger marks on my skin, but I was doing considerably better than my sister. She was breathing hard, tears pricking the corners of her eyes as she clenched her jaw and struggled to contain the pain.

"How's Anna?" Kellan asked while I watched her from the front seat.

"She's . . . okay." Anna closed her eyes as a pained noise escaped her. More tenderly than I ever would have thought possible, Griffin held her in his arms and whispered words of encouragement in her ear. They were a heartwarming sight, and suddenly the idea of Griffin beside my family on Christmas morning didn't sound quite so odd.

In my ear, Kellan told me, "I wish I could be there with you, but Matt's freaking out about the show. David is going to fill in for Griffin, and we're having an emergency practice session to get him up to speed. But I'll tell Sienna I'm skipping the encore tonight and come after our set. I'm sure she'll understand."

I wasn't sure if she would, but I also knew she'd have to chain Kellan up if she wanted him to stay put. "Okay, I'll see you then. Good luck."

"Yeah, you too." He laughed dryly.

When we pulled up to the emergency room of one the many hospitals in the city, I quickly texted Denny. We had a plethora of friends back home who would want to know Anna was having her baby tonight, so I asked him to relay the message. Griffin was helping Anna out of the car so I hopped out and ran around to help him.

Between the two of us, we got her to the emergency room doors. She kept trying to squat, like she had to pee. Hoping she wasn't doing what I think she was doing, I urgently told her, "Don't push yet, Anna, we're almost there."

Her eyes flashed over to mine. "It's not exactly something I can control. You have no idea what this feels like!"

"I know, just try," I nodded.

Heads looked up when the three of us entered the peaceful room; thankfully it was a slow night. Griffin met eyes with a nurse at the desk. "We need help! My wife's about to pop."

A small bit of relief washed through me that Griffin had managed to state what he needed without cursing. The nurse hopped up and grabbed a wheelchair for Anna. She handed Griffin a clipboard of paperwork. "I'll need you to fill out these while I admit her."

Griffin looked at the stack of papers like they were written in a foreign language. "I'm not filling out fucking forms while my wife gives birth. Are you fucking crazy, lady?"

Exhaling in exasperation, I snatched the clipboard from Griffin. So much for him not swearing. "I'll fill them out. You go with Anna." To the nurse, I added, "We think her water already broke."

The nurse nodded and started wheeling Anna through the double doors. Griffin was right on her heels. Before he disappeared, he tossed over his shoulder, "Thanks, Kiera."

I sighed and sat down, knowing that my nephew was most likely going to be born while I was filling out the damn paperwork. But Anna and Griffin doing this alone seemed appropriate.

When I finished with the clipboard, I handed it to the nurse who'd admitted my sister. She told me where Anna had been taken. I passed by a gift shop on the way there and stopped to buy my sister a blue teddy bear. Feeling the silky blue ribbon wrapped around the bear's neck, I made my way up to the birthing rooms.

Walking over to the nurse's station, I started to ask for Anna's room when I spotted Griffin. He was walking down the hall in a daze. A stream of fear washed through me at the look on his face.

Walking past me, he slumped into a chair in the waiting room. Torn between talking to him and rushing to my sister's side, I tentatively sat beside him. "Griffin? You . . . okay?"

His face still blank, he looked over at me. His pale eyes were wider than I'd ever seen. "That . . . was . . . the most . . . disgusting thing . . . I've ever seen."

My fear vanished. She was okay. I patted his knee and his expression changed. Peace filled his face. "And the most incredible." His eyes filled to the brim and I felt my throat tightening. "You should have seen Anna, Kiera. She was so brave." I nodded and had the oddest desire to hug him. Before I could he added, "You can see her now. She's absolutely beautiful . . . perfect, just like her mom."

It took a minute for what he'd said to register. "She? Anna had a girl?"

Griffin nodded as a tear rolled down his cheek. "Damn tech was wrong. Anna was right . . . She usually is." My hands flew to my mouth as a sob escaped me. Then I tossed my arms around Griffin and held him tight. He laughed and cried in my arms, and I felt something for Griffin that I had never felt before—a deep, familial love.

Drying my cheeks, I hopped up out of the chair. "What room?"

Standing, Griffin pointed down the hall he'd just come from. "There. I'll take you."

My sister looked drained and radiant as we walked into the room. She was holding a tiny bundle wrapped in pink blankets and wearing a pastel striped hat. I started crying again. When Anna looked up at me, her cheeks were wet. "I did it, Kiera."

I leaned down to hug her, overwhelmed. "I knew you would do great." She adjusted the tiny person resting on her chest so I could see the baby's face. She was plump, pink perfection, with pudgy cheeks that begged to be kissed. Like she knew I was watching, she opened her slate blue eyes and gazed at me. Her mouth opened, like she was already trying to smile. Griffin was right, she was absolutely breathtaking, quite possibly the most beautiful thing I'd ever seen. No, she *definitely* was the most beautiful thing I'd ever seen.

One small hand was free of the blankets encasing her, and I gently reached out to touch her. Her fingers instinctively wrapped around my pinky, and I sobbed again. Lifting the blue bear in my other hand, I told Anna, "I guess I need to go exchange this for a pink one."

Anna nodded. "I told that cow I was having a girl."

As I stroked the baby's fingers, I asked them both, "So . . . Myrtle, huh?"

Anna scoffed. "No. There was no way I was naming my baby Myrtle. We picked something better."

I looked between the two of them. When had they picked out another girl name? They'd been dead set on Maximus for months. Griffin smirked, and I started to worry about just what they'd named my niece.

"Her name's Gibson." He gestured in the air like he was playing a guitar, and I understood the reference. Gibson was a brand of guitars. It was kind of a strange name for a baby, especially a baby girl, but it was the perfect name for a rock star's child. I immediately fell in love with it.

Smiling, I kissed her cheek. "Hello, Gibson, it's so nice to finally meet you."

A thought struck me, and I glanced up at my beaming sister. My mom had been calling my sister nonstop for the last two weeks, trying to fly out to Seattle so she wouldn't miss the birth. Anna had been delaying her, telling her it was too soon to fly out. Honestly, I think she just didn't want to tell her that she wasn't in Seattle like Mom and Dad thought. Mom was going to be furious that she'd missed her first grandchild being born.

"Anna," I piped up. "Mom's going to kill us."

Chapter 24

Cuteness and Cruelty

Anna and I both decided that we'd call our parents in the morning. They'd already missed the birth, so what was a few more hours of ignorance? And besides, Anna didn't want to think about what she was going to do yet, and our parents would want an answer. Anna just wanted peace and quiet with her new baby girl.

I read my book in the corner of the room while Anna slept and Griffin held Gibson. He stared down at her like he couldn't take his eyes off of her. He couldn't stop smiling either. I'd never seen Griffin so completely happy. Every once and a while, Gibson would do something cute and Griffin would giggle. I'd never heard him laugh like that. It was adorable, and my book-reading quickly faded into Griffin-watching.

Adjusting her cap, Griffin stroked her thin, fine hair. Smiling, he looked up at me. "I think she's going to be blond, like me." He looked down at her again, adoration on his face. "I hope she has Anna's eyes, though." They were a dark blue-gray now, but the nurse had told us that most babies were born with eyes that color. They settled into the color they were going to have for life within the first year. I'd found that really interesting, but I was a little surprised that Griffin had retained that bit of information.

It was late when Kellan showed up with Evan and Matt, just on the verge of it being too late for them to visit at all. But I'd been coming back from the vending machine in the waiting room, and I'd watched Kellan smile his way through the nurse's station. Of course they'd let him visit. He probably could have gotten them to find him a cot and give him a sponge bath.

All of the boys were dressed differently than I'd last seen them. Kellan had gone on stage in a plain, short-sleeved red shirt, but his shirt under his leather jacket was now white. It made me smile that they'd freshened up for this.

Intent on finding Anna, Kellan didn't see me as he walked away with the boys. Suppressing a giggle, I strode up behind him and pinched his backside. He jumped about a foot in the air and spun around. "Hey, stranger, come here often?" I asked.

Kellan relaxed when he realized it was just me attacking him. "Not if I can help it," he answered.

Even though he'd received directions, I pointed out Anna's room. "She's in there."

I bit my lip in excitement as the boys hurried to see the newest member of their family. I'd texted them after Gibson was born, to let them know Anna and the baby were okay, but we'd all decided to not tell them the sex. Anna wanted it to be a surprise.

Matt beat everyone through the door to get a glimpse of his newest relative. Evan was a step behind him. Kellan and I trailed in last. Anna was awake now, but still resting in bed. Griffin was still holding his daughter, angling her up so Matt could see her. "She's totally got my nose, right?"

Matt was in complete shock. "You had a girl?" He looked between Anna and Griffin. "Congratulations, she's beautiful."

Griffin beamed like he'd done all the work, when really he'd had the briefest part in Gibson's creation. "Thanks."

Anna smiled at the pride on Griffin's face, then pointed to the sink along the far wall. "Wash up and you can hold her."

Watching these normally jovial and carefree rock stars juggling the tiny person between them like she was made of nuclear material made me laugh. When Gibson finally made her way to Kellan, he wiped his palms on his jeans. "I'm so nervous right now," he whispered to me. "What if I drop her?"

I rubbed his shoulder as I whispered back, "Don't worry, you're good with women."

Kellan rolled his eyes at me and gingerly took Gibson from Evan's hands. The grin that came over him as he looked down on her made my eyes mist over. Kellan holding a child . . . I'd thought he looked completely natural on stage, but that was nothing compared to this. Kellan had so much love to give; it was written all over his face.

Turning to me, he murmured, "She smells good. Why does she smell so good?" Since I often wondered why *he* smelled so good, I could only shrug.

He lightly swayed with her as he made silly faces, trying to get her to smile. I wiped a tear off of my cheek as I watched him. When he leaned down to rub his nose against hers, and she tried to suck on it, I had to look away before I started sobbing. I could almost feel the I-want-a-child hormones kicking in. But first things first—I had a wedding to get through next month.

My eyes found my sister's. She had tears in her own eyes as she watched her child being loved on. She pointed at Kellan and mouthed, "He needs a baby." Then she pointed at me and gestured with her hands over her much smaller stomach. I shook my head at her and reiterated my earlier thought—*First things first.*

Matt was taking about a hundred pictures on his phone. I already had about a bazillion on mine, but I pulled it out again to get some of Gibson and Kellan. Grinning ear to ear, Matt looked over at Griffin. "I'm gonna send some of these to Mom and Dad. You call your parents yet?"

Griffin nodded. "Yeah, they want us to fly her out to L.A. as soon as the tour's over." Griffin and Matt were both originally from Los Angeles and still had family in the area, on the other side of town from where the record label's house was. They'd both visited their parents while we'd been staying down there, but had mainly stayed at the label's place. Griffin had told me once that it was, "Hella nicer than my parents' spread."

Wondering what they were going to do in the meantime, I thought about broaching the subject with my sister. Matt beat me to it, though. Face serious, he told Griffin, "The tour is moving on tonight. What are the two of you going to do?"

Griffin looked over at Anna, his face torn. "We have to be on the bus when it leaves. I have to go with them."

Anna nodded as she swallowed. "I know."

Looking over at Kellan, I told Anna, "I'll stay here with you, Anna." When Kellan swung his eyes my way, I looked over at my sister. "I'm sure you'll be discharged tomorrow if everything looks good. Then I'll take you home . . . to Mom and Dad. You can stay there and rest up until the wedding."

Anna looked forlorn as she contemplated staying with our parents for the next month. What else could she do, though? If she flew back to Seattle, she'd have to fly twice with an infant during the busiest travel season of the year. That sounded really silly to me. Best to just plop her down in Ohio now. And besides, having Mom around to help would be good for Anna . . . even if she did drive her crazy.

Anna bowed her head, not thrilled about it, but clearly accepting her fate. Griffin, however, wasn't accepting it at all. "No, I don't think so." Walking over to Kellan, he gently removed his daughter from his arms; Kellan seemed reluctant to let her go.

Anna snapped her head up; hope was in her eyes that maybe a better option was available to her. Crossing my arms over my chest, I wondered what option Griffin might come up with. As everyone turned their eyes to him, he locked gazes with my sister. "I don't want you to go. I want you to stay on the bus with me." Griffin turned to stare me down. "After they let her go, you bring her to me." By the heat in his expression, it was clear he wasn't asking.

I couldn't help my startled expression. "You want a newborn on a tour bus with you?"

Griffin shrugged and looked around the room. "Sure. Why not?"

Anna seemed conflicted. Her maternal instincts had kicked in, and they were fighting with her natural, carefree spirit. "I don't know, Griff. It seems unsanitary."

Griffin snorted. "I'm probably the dirtiest thing on the bus, and you sleep with me every night."

I tried not to laugh at that. And failed miserably. Kellan elbowed me as he shook his head in amusement. Anna still seemed uncertain. She looked from Gibson to me. "What do you think, Kiera?" Her eyes were wide, fearful. Now that Gibson was a tangible object, Anna was terrified of doing something wrong. She was desperately afraid of making a bad choice.

I could feel Griffin boring holes into me, and I could see the hope on my sister's face, but if I was going to honestly answer her question, I needed to put the two of them aside and think about Gibson. What would be best for her? If she were mine, what would I do? I really didn't know much about babies, but I knew a lot about the people on our bus. Aside from my parents, who both had jobs that they couldn't just abandon to help my sister, there was no one better on earth to help raise this baby than the D-Bags.

Turning to my sister, I told her, "I think in most cases, having a baby on a bus, living the life we live, is absolutely insane." Anna frowned, and Griffin started to protest. I held up my hand to stop him. "But in this particular case, I think it works." I focused on Anna. "Your baby was never going to have a typical childhood, and I can't think of anywhere else that she could possibly be loved more than that bus."

As Anna's face broke into a tearful smile, I added, "Besides, didn't the nurse say they mainly sleep, eat, and poop for the first few months anyway?"

Griffin nodded his thanks to me, then seemed to realize he'd placed quite a burden on the rest of his band. "You guys . . . cool with that?"

Kellan wrapped his arms around my waist as he kissed my neck. "I think it sounds great."

Evan nodded in agreement; nothing much fazed him. Matt smirked. "Loud crying coming from your room at all hours of the day and night"—he twisted to look at Evan and Kellan—"I think we're already used to that."

After light laughter went around the room, Kellan frowned and looked over at Matt. "We'll have to have a talk with Holeshot."

Matt nodded. "Deacon is pretty easygoing. I'm sure he'll be fine with it."

Twisting my head, I told Kellan, "They can always hop on Sienna's bus. Didn't she say she was tired of riding alone?"

Kellan let out a laugh that startled Gibson. "That is an excellent idea."

Griffin glared over at him. "Dude, keep it down. You freaked out my daughter."

Kellan grinned at his bassist. "Sorry." Then he made a whipping noise like Griffin frequently made. I had to bury my head in Kellan's shirt so *I* didn't laugh too loud and get yelled at by the overprotective new father.

Kellan and the boys left a little while later. The show was over, and the process of tearing it down and moving on was probably already underway. I waited in the hallway with Evan, Matt, and Kellan while Griffin said goodbye to his family. Kellan was hugging me while we waited. "I'm going to miss you," he said.

Resting my chin on my chest, I peered up at him. "I'm going to miss you too, but you're only going to East Rutherford. That's not far."

"Feels far." He smiled at me, then looked over to Anna's door. "Do you think Griffin will be a good father?"

Smiling, I looked over to the closed door as well. He'd been in there saying goodbye to his wife and child for over fifteen minutes. "Yeah, surprisingly, I think he'll be great." I was still shocked by that fact.

Kellan turned back to me. "Do you think *I* would be a good father . . . one day?"

Tightening my arms around his neck, I eagerly nodded. "I know you will be." Kellan smiled at the subtle promise of our future in my words. Kids wasn't a matter of *if* for us, just *when*.

When Griffin finally emerged from Anna's room, he was subtly swiping his eyes dry. I gawked at the raw emotion on his face. I'd never seen him look so distraught. He frowned as he glared at all of us. "What?" Then he moodily walked down the hall, away from the two people who had just become his entire world.

Matt and Evan hurried after him, Evan tossing an arm over his shoulders while Matt playfully punched him in the arm. Kellan watched them leave then sighed; his smile was a sad one as he gazed at me. "Guess I'm off to work. I'll see you soon." His brow bunched in concern as he twisted me to face him. "Please be careful."

Leaning up, I placed a tender kiss upon his lips. "I'm always careful. I love you."

"I love you too."

As he walked away from me, I tried to not think about how much I was going to miss him while we were apart. Watching the way his clothes molded around his body helped with that. He turned at the door and gave me a small wave before exiting. I noticed a young nurse nearby sigh as she blatantly stared at him. Laughing a little, I waved back. When he disappeared, I exhaled just as forlornly as the nurse had.

Twenty minutes after he left me, my phone rang. I hurried to answer it. "Miss me already, Kellan?"

"Of course." His happy tone fell as he added, "Hey, I just wanted to warn you, there was a group of fans forming outside of the hospital as we were leaving."

I immediately stood and looked out of the window. Anna's room overlooked a courtyard in the center of the hospital, though, and not the front doors. "Kell-Sex fans? Here?" I asked. "How did they . . . ?" My voice trailed off as I remembered stupidly announcing to a room full of fans that I was heading to a hospital. The more ambitious ones must have followed me in hopes to see Kellan there . . . or possibly to confront me . . . I wasn't sure.

Kellan sighed. "Yeah, I think so. We left out of the ER doors, so they didn't see me. They may think I'm still in there . . . with you. I've already called the hospital to give them a head's up, so I don't think you'll be bothered on the inside. But just be careful when you do leave, please? I still haven't had a chance to explain that photo."

"Yeah, thank you." Great. Was I really going to have to deal with a bunch of rabid fans who probably hated me while trying to get my newborn niece back to her rock star daddy? And just when I thought my life couldn't get anymore surreal.

I woke up the next morning with a knot in my back, not feeling rested at all. Someone had come in every few hours to run tests on the baby, and I'd woken up every single time. When I fully came to life, Gibson was gone. Guess I'd finally slipped into a deep sleep early this morning, if she'd been removed without me knowing. While I was pretty sure Gibson couldn't be taken out of the hospital without someone notic-ing—much like expensive merchandise, the babies all had bracelets around their ankles that sounded an alarm if they passed through the front doors—a slice of fear shot up my spine anyway.

Anna was gone too, so I figured she was with her daughter. Slip-ping on my shoes, I debated scouring the hospital room by room to find my niece. That was panic talking, though. The more rational part of me knew I could simply ask a nurse where she was. When I stepped into the hallway, I saw that it was completely unnecessary. Anna was walking toward me, dressed in a hospital gown, cooing to Gibson as she cradled her in her arms. Relief instantly replaced my fears. Then amusement swept over me. A male nurse was walking a few paces behind Anna, and he had his arms weighed down with a car seat, flowers, and two bulging duffel bags. Even hours past delivering a baby, my sister could still get men to do anything she wanted.

Smiling as she walked past me, Anna chirped, "Gibson just had her hearing tested. She's perfect, of course." Giggling at her daughter, Anna instructed the nurse to put the things on her bed. He looked quite happy to do so, and even asked Anna if she needed anything else. She shook her head, her eyes never leaving Gibson.

After the nurse reluctantly left, I twisted to Anna and pointed at her supplies. "You, uh, go shopping this morning?" We'd left for the hospital with only the clothes on our backs.

Anna kissed Gibson's cheek. "No, Sienna sent it by. She knew I ran out of there and probably didn't have anything . . . and figured none of the boys would think of those kinds of details." Anna laughed; her face was completely worry free.

I blinked as I examined Sienna's gifts. That really was very thoughtful of her. I hoped there were toiletries in the bag; I would do just about anything for a toothbrush. "That was nice of her," I said.

Anna nuzzled her face against Gibson, then set her in her clear plastic bassinet. "Yeah, she even had a car and driver stay behind, so they can take us back to the tour when Gibson and I are cleared to leave." Walking over to the bags, she started removing clothes for her, clothes for the baby, and surprisingly, an outfit for me.

Disbelief washed over my curiosity. "You know, when she's not trying to manipulate the public into believing that she has a steamy, album-selling relationship with my husband, she's actually pretty considerate."

Anna paused in her clothes sorting. "You still think she's after Kellan?"

I frowned. "I don't think she's actively pursuing him, but I don't think she'd turn him away either."

Not worried, Anna sat on the bed and resumed emptying the bag; she cringed a bit when she sat down, and I figured she was still sore. "Would anyone turn him away, Kiera?"

Grabbing the smallest pink and white onesie I'd ever seen, I told her, "Well, I hope *you* would."

Anna snorted as she rubbed a soft pink blanket against her cheek. "That's a given . . . same goes for you too, you know." She raised an eyebrow, her expression completely serious.

I choked on my own saliva and started coughing. "Griffin? You're worried about me and *Griffin*?"

Anna started laughing so hard she had to wipe tears from her eyes. "No, not at all. I just wanted to see that look on your face." Sighing, she shook her head in amusement. "That was priceless."

A pediatrician from the hospital came in after lunch to give Gibson a thorough physical examination. Slinging his stethoscope around his neck when he was finished, he told Anna, "Your daughter looks perfect, and every test has come back within normal ranges. She seems well-fed, but are you having any problems with breastfeeding?"

My mind replayed earlier this morning, when Anna had sworn like a sailor while trying to get Gibson to latch on. Apparently, it's not as seamless a process as you would think. But Anna had successfully attached her daughter . . . eventually. Anna didn't mention any of that though. She also didn't mention that she'd be raising the baby on a tour bus filled with rock stars. The doctors would probably put her up on the pysch ward if they found out about that little detail. "Nope, we got it."

The doctor smiled and nodded. "Then I see no problem with the two of you being discharged today."

Three hours later, after watching a very boring video about "Taking Care of Your Newborn," Anna and Gibson were officially released from the hospital. While I called Kellan to let him know we were about to head out, Anna finally called our parents. Dad didn't handle the news very well. Cringing, Anna held the phone about a foot from her ear. Every so often, she said things like, "Dad . . . but . . . I'm . . ." Dad never let her finish, so she stopped trying to explain herself. Rolling her eyes at me, she played with her daughter's fingers while she half-listened to Dad vent about her life choices.

Once Anna was done being chastised, she handed the phone over to me. As I was still talking to Kellan, I shook my head. I really didn't feel like getting an earful right now. Anna indicated that I should take it, and I sighed in Kellan's ear. "Hey, Dad wants to talk to me, so I have to go."

Kellan's laugh made me smile. I missed his chuckle. "Good luck. I'll see you soon."

"Yeah, bye." Hanging up with Kellan, I reluctantly took Anna's phone. Expecting the worst, I held it to my ear. "Hello?"

"Hi, dear." Surprise and relief washed through me. It was Mom, not Dad. There was a good chance that I wasn't going to get yelled at for being an accomplice to Anna's give-birth-on-the-road plan, then. "I was just wondering if I'd see you for Thanksgiving. I'd really love to see you, since we have so much to discuss before the wedding next month. And I'm dying to show you the dress I bought. It's absolutely stunning, Kiera. You're going to love it."

I glared at my sister, and she started laughing. Feeling bad for what I was about to say, I turned my back on my gleeful sister. "Actually, Mom, Kellan really wanted to see his dad for Thanksgiving, you know, since we'll be spending Christmas with you guys." In a quieter voice, I added, "I know we have a lot to talk about, but Kellan's never had a decent holiday with his family, and I really want to give him this. I'm sorry. Is that okay?"

Mom was silent for several seconds, then she sighed in defeat. "Yeah, okay. Of course, I understand. You're married . . . almost. I'll have to get used to sharing you." Her voice hitched, and I hoped she wasn't about to cry.

Putting on my perkiest voice, I told her, "I'm excited to see everything you've picked out. And I know it's going to be perfect. Thank you for taking care of everything for me, Mom. I feel bad that I couldn't help you with more of it."

"Well, I know you've had your hands full, sweetheart." I could hear the concern in her voice. She knew things were stressful right now. I was about to tell her for the millionth time that everything was fine, when her tone brightened. "I'm so excited to see you in your dress!"

We chatted some more, then I told her goodbye and handed the phone back to Anna. Her face was incredulous. "I can't believe you still haven't put a stop to the puffy sleeves, Kiera." She exaggerated bulk around her arms. "We're talking Elizabethan puffy. It's hazardous, really. You could accidentally turn around too fast and knock your husband out cold." She giggled. "Then I'd have to resuscitate him."

Smirking, I threw a plastic barf tray at her.

East Rutherford, New Jersey, was only a couple of hours away, so I knew catching up to the boys wouldn't be a problem. If we hurried, we'd probably make it in time for the meet-and-greet. Not that I planned on walking into a room full of fans and causing a stir again. No, thank you.

Anna called the driver that Sienna had left behind, so he could pick us up. When he arrived, he came up to the room to give us a hand with all of our stuff. Or Gibson's stuff, rather. It took us thirty minutes to secure Gibson in her car seat. Anna must have taken her out and readjusted her twenty times. She was nervous to put her in a car. My sister was a caring person, but she wasn't prone to worrying, so seeing her stressed was endearing. After the twenty-first adjustment, I grabbed Anna's hands when she moved to unbuckle another strap. "She's fine, Anna. It's perfect."

Anna frowned at me. "You sure? Are the straps tight enough? Too tight? What about that thing around her head? Is her neck secure?"

Anna's eyes were glossy as fear filled her. Grabbing her cheeks, I firmly told her, "She's fine, and everything is going to be okay. Have faith."

Anna took a deep breath, then nodded. "This pit of dread in my stomach sucks," she muttered.

I couldn't help but laugh at her. "Now you know how Mom and Dad must feel on a daily basis."

That made Anna pause in picking up Gibson's car seat. "Oh my God, you're right. I owe Mom and Dad the biggest apology ever. Fuck." I sympathetically patted her on the back.

The driver had long ago packed our bags in the car. He was dutifully waiting for us right in front of the main hospital entrance. I could see the sleek, black sedan as we walked through the hospital lobby. I could also see a swarm of ten to fifteen people that the driver was trying to keep away from the vehicle. Damn it. I'd forgotten all about the Kell-Sex fans that Kellan had warned me about. I was going to ask the driver to pick us up around the back, but it had slipped my mind. And honestly, I thought they would have left by now. I could tell by the pink cheeks and breathy exhales that it was frigid outside; it had to have been freezing last night. Did they come back this morning, or stay all night long? Either way, why would they do that? Surely they must realize that Kellan had another show and had long ago moved on from Philadelphia. Were they really here for me? Was I that interesting?

Luckily, the driver's imposing size helped keep the fans at bay, and there was a clear walkway to the car. Looking at the people outside, I suddenly felt like we were leaving a trial that had ended with an unpopular verdict, and we had to wade through the protesters to get away.

Anna noticed the crowd right as the first set of automatic doors opened. "What's with the groupies?" She twisted to me. "Are they here for you?"

"They're probably here for Kellan . . . I'm just a lucky happenstance."

Anna held the car seat a little tighter. "Maybe we should have the driver go around."

I was starting to think the same thing, but a couple of the girls saw us and alerted the rest. Every head swung in my direction. Every expression turned dour. It was quite clear that all of these diehards believed the gossip, and none of them were on Team Kiera. God, I hoped I wasn't about to get stoned.

"Too late now. We've been spotted." I met eyes with Anna. "We may as well get it over with."

Anna glanced at her daughter as she chewed on her lip. "Yeah, okay."

I waved at the driver, letting him know that we were coming and needed a quick getaway. The group hovering around the car started closing in on the door. I felt like we were in some old spaghetti Western as we stared each other down. Even though the girls were on the young side, if one of them had leaned over and spat out a wad of tobacco juice, I wouldn't have been surprised. Well, maybe a little surprised.

Seeing the tension brewing outside, a couple of burly guys from the hospital escorted us out the main doors. They politely asked the group to stop loitering, but they may as well have been speaking a foreign language. The crowd invasively pressed in around Anna and me once we were outside. The awkward sensation of having strangers in your personal space made me uneasy as I hurried forward. A couple of brave girls shoved me into my sister's side, but mainly the group was using their words to hurt me. And let me tell you, sometimes words cut as badly as knives.

"Leave Kellan and Sienna alone! They're meant to be together! You're nothing, a nobody! You're not even worthy of breathing their air, ugly bitch! You should have never been born! You should just do the world a favor and kill yourself!"

Anna's face turned bright red, but I squeezed her arm and helped her get into the car. I didn't need her fighting for me while holding her daughter. Since Gibson was going into the middle of the backseat, I had to walk around the car to get to my seat.

The driver and the hospital guys helped me clear a path, and I noticed something I hadn't before. A couple of photographers were in the crowd. They must have picked up on my location from the fans. The social media sites were probably buzzing with the news that I was here. While the photogs snapped every angle of my face that they could, the girls continued taking pot shots at me.

"You think you're hot shit? You think Kellan gives a rat's ass about you? He's in love with Sienna, bitch! You're just a worthless toy. Once he's done with you, he'll toss you aside with the rest of the trash. Disgusting little cunt!"

Tears were stinging my eyes, but I ignored their hatred and lifted my chin. They had no idea what they were talking about. They had no idea what the truth of the situation was. If nothing else, I could at least respect their devotion, although I would never condone verbally attacking a person with such malevolence.

I was shaking when I sat down in my seat. Some of the girls pounded on the glass while the cameramen captured it all. I discreetly locked my door. The driver said a few harsh words to the crowd and I turned my attention to Gibson. She was positioned backwards, and she was looking at me. She had the cutest, softest chubby cheeks. Ignoring the malicious girls outside, I placed my finger on Gibson's palm; she immediately closed her hand around it.

As the car pulled away, the fans smacking it a few final times, Anna murmured, "Jesus. Are you okay, Kiera?"

When I looked over at her, a tear fell down my cheek. I was still shaking from head to toe. Pushing away the confrontation, I nodded at Anna and looked back down at Gibson. "My niece is holding my hand. I'm perfect."

I felt Anna's finger drying my cheek. After a moment of silence, she said, "I love you."

I exhaled a long, low breath, and finally stopped shaking. "I love you too."

The drive took a lot longer than expected. We had to stop a couple of times for Gibson. Once she needed to be changed, once she needed to be fed. We also hit some heavy traffic along the way—some accident that narrowed the freeway down to one lane. As we passed by the wreckage, I noticed that Anna wouldn't look at it. Instead, she ceaselessly kissed her daughter's hand. I could only imagine that she was thanking fate that Gibson was safe beside her . . . and that she hadn't given her up.

By the time we got to the venue, the concert had already started. Anna and I were beat, so we didn't go into the arena. Once we got cleared from security, we immediately headed for the busses. I wanted sleep. Badly.

Since all of the guys were inside playing, no fans or photographers were outside to bother us as we emptied the car. A good thing, because I didn't think I could handle being yelled at again. It felt so good to be back on the bus, like we were coming home. All of the familiar sights and smells were there when we stepped through the doors—leftover beer bottles on the tables, crusty socks in the aisle way, Evan's giant D trophy hanging from a noose above a window, and a bowl of half-eaten . . . something . . . on the couch. It was the cluttered mess that I had grown to know and love.

Anna looked around with a scowl on her face. "These boys are pigs. They're going to have to clean up after themselves now that Gibson's on board." Her sudden concern over the cleanliness of our bus made me chuckle. Up until today, she'd contributed to the mess just as much as the guys had.

With Gibson still in her car seat, we made our way to the back bedroom. Like an overwhelmed cartoon character, my jaw dropped to my chest. The bedroom was . . . babified. There was a narrow, portable playpen crammed between the bed and the one-way window, and a mobile attached to the top had stuffed musical instruments hanging off of it. A couple of stuffed animals were on the makeshift crib, along with a pink blanket that looked plush enough for a princess.

On the other side of the bed was a slim dresser. The drawers would be impossible to open, but the top of it had a built-in tray that held a curved mattress with a belt, perfect for diaper changes. Attached to the ceiling above the table was a cute, fabric diaper holder, also decorated in musical instruments. As Anna giggled in delight, my eyes settled onto the bed. It was littered with shopping bags, and I saw nothing but pink spilling out of them.

Anna set the car seat down and rummaged through a bag. Squealing as she removed a soft pink, plush guitar, she said, "Don't I have the best husband ever?"

I was so shocked, I couldn't even respond.

I helped Anna put away the mountain of clothes that Griffin had picked up for his daughter. Since they'd already bought a bunch of stuff when they'd believed Gibson was a boy, there was nowhere near enough room for everything. We ended up cramming clothes and toys all over the bus. Every available cubby had something stuffed into it. We even stashed some burp rags in the pocket in the bus driver's door. Once Anna and Gibson were comfortable and crashed, I crawled into the cubby I shared with Kellan. It had never felt so wonderful. I sighed after I inhaled our blanket; it smelled like Kellan. As I drifted off to sleep, I wondered if I smelled like Kellan too.

Chapter 25
On Our Own

Arms wrapping around my body and legs tangling with mine woke me up. The bus was still, silent, but I had no idea if we'd reached our new destination, or if we were still in Jersey. Smiling, I stretched as best as I could, then cuddled into the chest behind me.

"What time is it?"

"Late," he murmured. "They're still tearing down the show. We'll leave sometime tomorrow. I missed you last night. I couldn't sleep without you next to me."

I turned around to face him. Due to the confined space, it took some effort. I bumped my elbow against the wall and almost kneed Kellan in the groin again. He was prepared for it this time though and nimbly backed away just in the nick of time. When we were facing each other, we melded back together.

Kellan cupped my cheek. "Hey."

Pulling him tight, I smiled against his lips. "Hey."

Kellan's lips danced against mine, his tongue lightly probing. Hoping we were the only ones on the bus, I clutched at his shirt, wanting it off. Leaning over me, Kellan helped me out and pulled it over his head with one hand. I shoved it in the corner and ran my hands up his bare back as he settled over me. "Hey," I said again, my smile brighter than before.

"Always so eager to undress me," he whispered, his lips traveling to my neck.

I suppressed a giggle as I closed my eyes and savored the feeling of his body over me, around me. I loved getting lost in him. As his fingers traveled under my shirt and across my ribs, he breathed in my ear, "Any troubles leaving the hospital?"

Hyperaware of his hips above mine, separated from me by multiple layers of clothing, I sucked in a ragged breath. God, I really hoped no one else was awake. "Aside from some fans telling me that they wished I'd never been born? No. No problems at all."

The tips of his fingers paused at the base of my breast. "What?"

He pulled back to look at me, concern in his eyes. I shook my head and tried to scoot down so that his hand would move up. Didn't work. "It was fine. I'm fine."

Kellan slid off to my side, his hand retreating. Knowing our moment was over, I sat up on my elbow. "They threatened you?" he asked, an edge to his voice.

I shook my head. "No . . . they just expressed their dislike. Nobody touched—" Remembering being shoved a couple of times, I changed my sentence to, "Nobody hurt me."

Kellan sat up as much as he could. It wasn't very much. He leaned over on his elbow as he rested on his hip. Even though it was dark, I could tell that he was deep in thought.

"Kellan, nobody hurt me."

He peeked up at me, his lips in a hard line. He was pissed. "This time. Nobody hurt you this time." Looking away, he muttered, "This is such bullshit. You're my wife." He looked back at me. "Tory had us doing this meet-and-greet/concert for a high school that won some contest to have us there. It took all goddamn day. I was so freaking busy that the only person I had time to talk to was you. I hate that this has festered for so long. My silence isn't helping anything."

He looked angry and frustrated that he couldn't stand up for me yet, that all of this was snowballing so fast and he just didn't have time to react. Kissing him, I pulled him back down on top of me. "It's only been two days, and it's not your fault."

Kellan didn't answer me, just tentatively kissed me back. I could tell he was still stewing over the problem, a problem that I knew would still be there in the morning. Being together was what was important, and I wanted to enjoy the current moment with him. Threading my fingers through his hair, I pulled him into me. He let out a soft groan and kissed me back with a lot more intensity.

When his hips were in line with mine again, grinding into me at a delicious tempo, I let out my own exhale of ecstasy. Damn, I didn't care if we weren't the only ones there anymore. The guys all had iPods, anyway. I needed Kellan, and he needed me too. His hand slipped down the back of my lounge pants, under my panties. I arched my back as much as I could in our confined space, silently begging him to touch me. In my ear, Kellan growled, "I want you."

That did me in. While the ache building in me pulsed to life, my hands slipped down to Kellan's zipper. Wanting to snuggle with me, Kellan hadn't gotten ready for bed yet. I was more than happy to help him finish undressing.

Groaning as I unfastened his jeans, Kellan husked out, "But I want you . . . safe."

I paused and looked at his face. His eyes were blazing with desire, his lips were parted, and his breath was fast. I knew he wanted me, but I also knew he was still concerned about me. "Kellan, don't worry—"

He cut me off. "I heard you talking to Denny about fleeing back home. You were joking, but . . . maybe that's a good idea. Maybe you should head home until I have a chance to set this straight."

I couldn't believe he was actually suggesting that. "No, I want to be with you. Home is wherever you are."

Kellan slid to my side again. "I want to be with you too, but I can't stand the way people talk about you. It makes me want to kick every single one of their asses. And I don't want you around me if it's dangerous for you." I started to object, but Kellan cut me off again. "I saw that girl slap you, Kiera, so don't tell me it's not dangerous."

I closed my mouth and changed what I'd been about to say. Voice calm, I told him, "You said we needed to carve out time for each other, otherwise none of this mattered. You remember telling me that?"

Kellan sighed. "I know, but that was before things got so messed up." He ran a finger across my cheek. "And who is to say that anything will change when I do make another statement. They're so curious about my life, they might still hound you. They might still hate you, call you names. I can't handle that. I can't do my job if I'm constantly worrying about you. I just want you safe, even if that means we have to be apart."

He looked really guilty at playing the job card, but I knew he was frustrated with the situation and was being totally honest with me, and I respected him for that honesty. My answer to him was just as forthright. "And I just want to be with you. I can handle being mobbed. I can handle being photographed. I can handle being ridiculed. And I can even handle being slapped . . . on occasion." I grabbed both of his cheeks. "What I can't handle is people forcing us to behave in a certain way. People forcing us to be apart. We're not playing their game anymore, remember? We've fought too hard to be together. It's us against the world, Kellan, and they don't dictate our relationship. We do."

A slow smile curved Kellan's lips. "This attitude you've got right now is very attractive."

I laced my arms around his neck and brought his lips down to mine. "Then stop trying to send me away, and make love to me."

Eagerly returning my kiss, he finally helped me take his jeans off.

When I woke up sometime later, I was naked. I felt around for my clothes, but couldn't find them anywhere. That was alarming, since there weren't a whole lot of places for clothes to hide in our small cubby. Opening my eyes, I looked around for my pajamas. It was lighter, so I could clearly see everything around me, and I still didn't see them anywhere. Sitting up on my elbows, I noted that the bus was moving.

Kellan was asleep beside me; if I'd woken up before him, then he really hadn't slept well the night before when I was away. His clothes were nowhere to be seen either. What the hell? I clearly remembered shoving our clothes in the corners, because I didn't want them falling in the aisle again.

I nudged Kellan in the ribs. He made a noise that sounded like, "What?" but he didn't open his eyes.

"Kellan? Are our clothes on the floor?"

Maybe we'd been so caught up in the moment last night that they'd fallen out despite my precautions. Kellan cracked an eye open, then yawned. "What clothes?"

I laughed at him. "The clothes neither one of us are wearing."

Kellan smiled and rolled over to put his head on my chest. "Those are my favorite kinds of clothes."

His hands started traveling up my body, and I closed my eyes. Mmmm, his hands felt nice. Feeling playful, Kellan grabbed the blanket with his teeth and exposed my chest. Before I could stop him, his mouth was sucking on my breast. *God, what was I missing?* Forcing his head away so I could think clearly, I glared at him. "Could you take a peek and see if they're on the floor?"

Kellan's eyes were locked on my chest. "You sure you want me to do that?"

Giggling, I pushed his shoulder away. "Yes, please find them."

Kellan peeked his head out of the curtain, then instantly returned. He was frowning. "There's nothing out there."

I sat up, looked at all four corners, and even under the sheet. There were no clothes. "Where's our stuff then?"

"I don't—" Kellan stopped talking, then sighed. "I'm gonna kill that fucker, new dad or not."

My eyes went wide as I tucked the blanket under my armpits, completely covering my chest. "Griffin stole our clothes?"

Kellan cocked an eyebrow in answer. I wanted to be mortified that Griffin had peeked in on me while I was sleeping, and I really hoped I'd been fully covered by the blanket, but Griffin being a jackass was so wonderfully normal that I ended up bursting out laughing. Normal was good. Normal was great. I almost wanted to kiss Griffin. Almost.

The look Kellan gave me made it clear that he thought I'd officially lost my mind. Maybe I had, but Griffin's mischief was so much better than a complete stranger telling me I was worthless garbage.

Giggling, I pushed Kellan's butt with my knees. "Go get some new clothes for us."

Kellan groaned as he stuck his legs out of the curtain. "You want me to go out there naked?"

I held the blanket tighter around me. I may think Griffin's joke was funny, but I did not want to sit here with no clothes on with only a thin fluttery curtain as cover. "Do you care if you're naked, Kellan?"

Kellan gave me a crooked grin. "Not really." He leaned over to kiss me, then hopped out of the cubby. "Back soon."

Covering my face, I laughed into my hands. God, I hoped he managed to get into our bags without too many people seeing him. He was gone longer than I thought he would be. If it were me, I'd be running. Curious, I peeked my head out of the curtain. I couldn't see anybody, but I heard them. Some of the guys were still snoring, and some of them were in the lounging section. I could hear Gibson crying too. Our things were in the other direction, in a closet near the bathroom. Just as I was wondering where Kellan was, he reappeared from the curtain separating the cubbies from the back of the bus. He was fully dressed, laughing to himself. I wondered why until Anna stepped out of the curtain a second later. Oh God, had she seen him naked?

Anna smirked as she walked by him. Leaning down when she passed me, she scuffed up my hair and murmured, "Your husband's got a nice package." She looked back at him, winked, then returned her focus to me. "Lucky girl."

My face filled with heat. Yep, she'd finally seen Kellan in all his glory. Awesome.

After Anna left, Kellan squatted in front of me, clothes in hand. "Here you go." He laughed. Where I would be mortified at being caught in my birthday suit, Kellan was just amused.

When we walked out to the lounge, Griffin was watching Anna discretely breastfeed Gibson. A few days ago, I would have expected him to have a scandalous gleam in his eye while watching an act like that, but he wasn't looking at Anna in a devious way. In fact, he wasn't looking at Anna at all. His eyes were locked onto Gibson, and a small, peaceful smile was on his face as he watched her eat.

Kellan interrupted his moment by smacking him on the back of the head.

"Dude, what the fuck?" Griffin scowled.

Kellan pointed back to the cubbies. "That's for nabbing our clothes."

Griffin laughed and turned back to Anna, who was giggling uncontrollably now. "Oh yeah, that was awesome." He held his hand out to Anna and she gave him a high five. Turning back to Kellan, who was studiously ignoring my semi-exposed sister, Griffin added, "Gibson wouldn't go back to sleep so I paced the bus with her. We couldn't resist when we saw your jeans poking out of the curtain."

Kellan gave me a dry look at Griffin's explanation. *We?* He and Gibson were partners in crime now? Still laughing, Anna murmured, "You're the best Dilf ever, Griffin."

Leaning back in his seat, Griffin looked like a king upon his thrown. "Thanks, Milf. You're not so bad yourself."

Their pet names made me cringe. "Ugh, couldn't you guys find words of endearment that were actually endearing?"

Griffin snorted as he looked up at me. "What, like Snookums?" Brightening, he twisted back to Anna, "Hey, Milfums, it's my turn next, right?"

Anna gave him her best seductive smile. "Oh, don't you worry, Dilfums, I'll be satisfying you later."

Feeling a little nauseated, I turned away from the pair. God . . . never mind, they could keep their pet names, so long as I didn't hear them say anything like that ever again.

Kellan sat down next to Evan while I went to get us some coffee. I was going to need a little pick-me-up to get through this day. When I got back, Kellan was holding Gibson. Seeing how natural he was with her made me stop in my tracks. He was standing in the middle of the bus, swaying as he rocked her. And he was singing to her. It was low, and I couldn't quite make out all of the words over the video game Holeshot was playing, but from what I could tell, he wasn't singing a lullaby. He was singing a D-Bags song. My favorite D-Bags song.

Kellan peeked up when he saw me. I'd never seen a more exalted smile on his face. My sister was right; this man needed a child to love. I felt a little shaky as I sat down next to Anna and put our coffee cups on the table. Was I ready to give him one? Every maternal instinct in my body was screaming *Yes, do it*! But I needed to use my head here. If we had a child, we would have to be apart. A baby on the road was one thing, but a toddler? A school-age child? That was something else entirely. It wasn't as if I wanted to spend my *entire* life on the road, but I wasn't quite ready to give it up yet. Aside from the Sienna drama and the cramped sleeping quarters, I liked my life with the D-Bags. And maybe it was selfish of me, but I wanted to be Kellan's only love for a few more years. Then maybe we could have a whole busload of kids.

Anna slung her arm around me as we both watched Kellan and Gibson. He was just beginning another song for her when he suddenly froze. His face contorted and he held Gibson a foot away from his chest. "Uh, she doesn't smell so good anymore."

Anna let out a yawn-laugh mixture and started to stand, but, shocking the hell out of me, Griffin popped up and beat her to it. Rescuing Gibson from Kellan, Griffin scoffed, "Wuss." Holding Gibson like a football, he walked into the back with her.

Twisting to Anna, I asked with all seriousness, "What did you do to Griffin?"

Twirling a dark brown lock around her finger, Anna gave me a lazy smile. "It wasn't me. That little girl has got him completely wrapped around her finger. I never thought I'd see the day."

I understood the feeling; I never thought I'd see the day either. A tame Griffin. I almost didn't know what to do with that.

I looked out the window to see that the bus was rolling through the packed streets of New York City. Skyscrapers were everywhere I looked. As I took in the size of the city, I began to imagine the millions of people living there. How many would come down to the venue just to torment me? I was positive that paparazzi would be there today in force. Kellan said everyone was curious about his life, but maybe it was really me they were curious about. I was the enigma. Was I a casual fling that Kellan had been playing with the last few days, or was I more? That's what everyone wanted to know.

While I debated what to do about that, Matt emerged from the cubbies and threw his hand up in a wave. As I waved back, Kellan got a phone call. He was reluctant to answer it, and I realized why seconds after he did. "Sienna," he coolly intoned. After a moment's pause, he furrowed his brow, then said, "Yeah, everyone but Griffin is here, why?" Rolling his eyes, he muttered, "Fine." Holding his phone out, he stared at it blankly, then asked me, "How do I put this on speaker?" I contained my smile at Kellan's lack of technical know-how. Sometimes he seemed more like a ninety-year-old man than a twentysomething rock star.

I adjusted the phone for him, then Kellan put it on the table. Griffin was still in the back with Gibson, swearing from what I could tell, but we motioned for Evan and Matt to join us. "You're on, go ahead."

Sienna's bright voice burst from the small device. "Well, first off, I just want to say how much I miss all of you! Things have been so hectic, I feel like I rarely see you."

Kellan and I exchanged dubious glances. While it was true that Sienna had been just as busy as Kellan lately, that wasn't the reason for her disappearance, and we both knew it. Sienna was playing up the "wounded lover" act. Whenever any camera was on her, she appeared sullen, teary-eyed. I'd even seen photos of her dabbing a tissue into the corner of her bloodshot eyes. Her duet with Kellan was now filled with longing and heartache, and while she stayed close to his side at the meet-and-greets, the band had told me that her demeanor laced the room with tension. That DJ who had so long ago told us Sienna couldn't act was wrong. She had the betrayed girlfriend role down pat. Of course, from what I'd gathered during the rare moments she'd been candid with me, it was a role she'd been in before.

She was perfectly happy now as she squealed, "I just couldn't wait until the tour stopped to tell you all the fabulous news!"

"What news?" Kellan asked, his voice weary. Sometimes great news from Sienna wasn't that great.

Sienna giggled like a little girl. "I just got off the phone with Nick . . . and your album shot to number two on the charts, right below mine." She squealed again.

Kellan and I looked at each other, then the phone. "You reached number one?" I asked, shocked that everything she'd orchestrated had actually succeeded in getting her just what she wanted.

"And the D-Bags are at number two! Isn't that fabulous?"

Kellan leaned back on his hip as he absorbed it all. His expression was as blown away as mine. Sienna and Nick had totally manipulated the public into believing a sordid, phony romance. In their desire to be on top, they had completely ignored anyone else who might have gotten hurt in their schemes, and it had ultimately paid off for them. It didn't seem fair, and it definitely wasn't right. Anna and the guys were squirming with excitement, and obviously wanted to act elated, but seeing Kellan's and my faces, they stayed quiet.

Closing his eyes, Kellan scrubbed his face with his hands, then ran them back through his hair. When he reopened his eyes, his emotions still seemed mixed—elated and frustrated. While Sienna waited for our group to explode with excitement, Kellan turned to me. "I really miss Pete's," he said.

Sienna heard him and seemed confused. "This is incredible news. You should all be jumping up and down, screaming your bloody heads off, not pouting like I just told you your best friend moved away."

Kellan frowned as he stared at the phone. "The public thinks my wife is a whore. I'm really not okay with that. And now that you got what you wanted, and Nick got what he wanted, it's my turn. And I want you to admit the truth. All of it. From the very beginning."

Sienna inhaled a deep breath. "Here's the thing, love. If we confess that we fabricated our entire relationship to bump sales, there will be a public backlash that will negatively affect us both. The scandal will stay with you for the rest of your career. Do you really want that monkey on your back?"

Kellan closed his eyes. "This *scandal* was your doing from the very beginning." He opened his eyes. "And now you're asking me if I'm okay with it? I was never okay with it!"

Her voice all business now, Sienna told him, "You went along with it, Kellan. No one forced you."

His jaw dropped. Mine did too. *No one forced us?* We'd been bullied and manipulated at every corner. Kellan had done what he could to persuade the public, but he'd been way outmatched in this game.

"No one forced . . ." Kellan couldn't even finish that statement.

Exhaling in frustration, like we were raining on her good-news parade, Sienna told us, "Look, I only said that the truth couldn't come out. I didn't say that Kell-Sex couldn't end. If you're so bent out of shape about it that you can't even enjoy being on top of the world, then we'll 'break up' after the tour. I'll be heartbroken, but I'll quickly move on, and when everyone sees how happy I am with my new beau, you and your wife will be free to date in peace. Problem solved."

My thoughts were so jumbled, I stuttered a few times before I could speak clearly. "How does that solve anything? I'll still be the other woman who broke you up."

Sienna sighed. "We'll be at the venue soon. I just wanted to call and . . . congratulate you on your success." With another forlorn sigh, the line disconnected.

Everyone at the table stared at the phone in silence. Anna was the one who spoke first. "She's really not going to help you guys at all, is she?"

Kellan shook his head. "No, she was never gonna help us. We have to fix this on our own."

Anna grabbed my hand and squeezed. She'd seen firsthand just how despised I was.

Griffin and Gibson finally rejoined our group while Evan and Matt exchanged conflicted expressions; our drama aside, the band's success was amazing, something we should be celebrating. "Why the fuck does everyone look constipated. Bad coffee or something?" Leaning over, he peered inside my half-full cup.

Kellan was contemplative as Evan filled Griffin in. Griffin flipped his lid when he heard the D-Bags' album was number two. Afraid he was going to drop his daughter in his exuberance, I quickly stood up and plucked Gibson out of his arms. She smelled like baby powder.

Griffin tossed his hands in the air as he jumped up and down. "Whoooooooooo! Number two, baby!" He ran down the aisle of the bus screaming. If any of the members of Holeshot were still sleeping, they weren't anymore. Laughing, our bus driver shook his head.

It was hard to not get caught up in Griffin's enthusiasm. Evan and Matt joined him in the center of the bus while Kellan stood up and walked over to me. The grin on his face was completely worry-free. Our drama could wait; the guys needed a minute to bask in their accomplishment.

As the boys jokingly pushed each other around, Matt looked back at Kellan. "Number two, Kell! We're number two!"

Seemingly at peace, Kellan laughed and took Gibson from my arms. "I know, man. It's crazy." Smiling at his band mates, Kellan bounced Gibson as he swayed from side to side. I swear she smiled at him.

Evan was clearly dazed as he shook his head. "Number two . . . right behind Sienna Sexton. Six months ago, I never would have pictured that happening."

Griffin started grunting and thrusting his hips in a provocative way that made me want to shield Gibson's eyes. "Not me. I always knew I'd be banging on Sienna's backdoor one day."

The members of Holeshot trickled into the lounge area of the bus while Griffin was simulating sex with Sienna. They each barely gave Griffin more than a cursory glance before sitting down; they were used to his antics. When Griffin started "climaxing," I quickly sealed my ears shut so I wouldn't have to listen to it. It was bad enough when I accidentally heard the real thing; Anna and Griffin were not quiet lovers.

Griffin bowed to all of us once his erotic performance was done. I couldn't help but laugh along with Anna and the boys. Anna clapped. Griffin's crudeness was beginning to grow on me. I kind of liked it, not that I would ever in a million years tell him that. It would only encourage him to try harder to gross me out.

Shaking his head, Matt clapped Griffin on the back. "It's nice to see that becoming a husband and father hasn't changed you in the slightest, cuz."

Griffin sniffed and tucked his pale, chin-length hair behind his ears. "Did you think it would?"

After the laughter died down, Kellan looked at each band member in turn. Seeing his expression, Evan and Matt gave him their complete attention. Matt smacked Griffin to get him to stop goofing off. Once they were all looking at him, Kellan said, "Tomorrow morning, we're going to a radio station to perform. We're scheduled to play two songs, pimp the album and the concert, and leave. I don't want to do that. I don't want to sing." Still bouncing Gibson, he looked over at me. "I want to talk, and I want to tell them everything."

I swallowed as my nerves spiked. "You want to go on air, behind Sienna and Nick's back, and tell the world what they did? How they manipulated you?"

Kellan nodded. "And I want to tell them exactly who you are to me."

A smile crept onto my lips at the same time that my stomach rose into my throat. "Then I'll talk with you. We'll do this interview together."

Kellan lifted an eyebrow. "Are you sure? It's one of the largest radio stations on the east coast."

My smile shifted to a frown as I thought of speaking into a microphone that would be heard by thousands of people. "Yes, I'm sure. If you're going to do something as reckless as throw your record label and the biggest pop star on the planet under the bus, then I'm going to be right beside you." I lifted my wrist to show him the tattoo of his name branded on my skin. "I'm done hiding. And now I have to go throw up."

Kellan laughed at me as he leaned over and kissed me. After we pulled apart, Kellan turned to the guys. "This affects you too. If I tell everyone what we did to boost sales, it could hurt us. Sienna was right about that—the stigma could follow us for years. Are you guys okay with that?"

I watched the other band members carefully. Kellan was right, this affected the entire band, and Kellan didn't want to see them suffer. That was one of the reasons Kellan had played along in the first place.

Walking over, Evan picked me up and squeezed the life out of me. "I hated hearing all that Kell-Sex crap, so I'm thrilled it's about to be over."

Kellan nodded, then looked over at Matt. Matt wasn't always as easygoing as the others, and he took the D-Bags' career very seriously. As much as I hated to admit it, Kellan and I were about to wrap the band in a scandal that could end up really harming them.

Matt held Kellan's eye, but didn't speak. Feeling the tension, Kellan shrugged, and told him, "I'm sorry, Matt. I really didn't expect any of this . . . and I won't come clean if everyone's not onboard."

Smiling, Matt slugged Kellan's shoulder. "You're doing the right thing, man. Don't worry about it." He pointed at every D-Bag. "We just have to make sure the next album rocks so freaking hard that all of this doesn't mean a damn thing."

Kellan clapped his arm. "Deal."

Chapter 26
Coming Clean

On the car ride over to the radio station the next day, my nerves were ablaze and anxiety sizzled every cell in my body. I was used to being in the background. I was comfortable there. Being shoved into the spotlight was going to burn a little. But I had to do this. It may not change the way some people thought of me, but I had to stand by my husband's side while he put himself out on a limb. If it broke, at least we'd both fall together.

The boys checked out the sights as we drove through the packed streets of the Big Apple. We'd briefly been here before during the promo tour, and one thing I'd never get used to about New York City was how many cars and taxis filled the busy streets. The city teemed with life. There was movement everywhere—the roads, sidewalks, buildings, even the windows. It was so active it gave me a little buzz. I felt like I had suddenly developed restless leg syndrome; I couldn't be still. Of course, that could just be my nerves flaring up.

Kellan watched me in the car, amusement in his eyes. I wanted to tell Mr. No Nerves to stow it, but I had a frog in my throat and couldn't speak at all . . . yet. Reaching into his pocket, Kellan grabbed something, then handed it to me. Curious, I looked down and saw a fuchsia rose petal in my hand. In Sharpie he'd written *You are a* and drawn a tiny star. I glanced up at him, confused. He pointed at the petal. "I finished your book. It's amazing, Kiera. You really should get it published."

Smiling, I looked back at the silky petal in my fingers. "Thank you. I wasn't sure how you'd feel about it after you read it all."

His arm wrapped around me. "I didn't think it was possible, but I'm pretty sure I love you even more. How you see me . . . I never thought anyone would ever . . ." His voice trailed off as his throat tightened with emotion.

Understanding, I looked back up at him. "That's because you don't see yourself as clearly as I see you."

Laughing, he pulled me tight. "God, we really are peas in a pod, aren't we?"

My nerves not quite so bad, I nestled into his side. While he played with my wedding ring, I again marveled at his ability to turn my emotions around. And at his ability to constantly surprise me. Looking back up at him, I asked, "Where the hell do you keep getting these petals?"

Eyes mischievous, he murmured, "I'm a man of many mysteries, Mrs. Kyle." Then he started laughing again.

When we arrived at the radio station, the crowd was massive. How people found us everywhere we went, I'd never understand; it was almost like there was a D-Bag warning alert that went off in every town we visited.

Some of the people in the crowd around the station had hand-made signs proclaiming their love for their favorite D-Bag. There were a lot of signs for Kellan, but the other boys were being loved on too. It was surreal to see people I knew being idolized at *this* level. I mean, some of the girls were sobbing as they waited for a glimpse of the band—red-faced, snotty-nosed sobbing. I was pretty sure that if the girl holding the sign that read—*Marry me, Griffin*—actually *knew* Griffin, she probably wouldn't be shaking like a leaf. Or asking for his hand. Well, maybe with the new, calmer, gentler Griffin. He wasn't so bad. But pre-Gibson Griffin? No way.

The car let us out right in front of the crowd huddling around the front doors. Tory was with us, of course, and tried to immediately steer the boys into the station. They didn't go in right away, though. Evan warmly met fans by the front door, signing autographs and even hugging a couple of them. Matt stood a bit behind him, looking a little uncomfortable by the size of the crowd, but happy to shake a couple hands. Griffin took off down the street. When he got to the end of the fans, he turned around and headed back to the front. He lifted his arms as he ran, encouraging the crowd to do the same. Screaming, they mimicked him, and that's when I realized what he was doing—he was making the fans do the wave. Dork.

Kellan laughed at Griffin's antics as he waited for me by the car. When we were together, he held my hand and pulled me over to the fans. I was hesitant to go for several different reasons: one, this was his job, not mine, and it felt intrusive to be included in it; and two, I didn't want to get attacked before I'd even had the chance to say my peace.

The fans didn't know how to react to my presence. They were so excited to be near Kellan that they were hollering, crying, and shaking. But somehow they still managed to give me dirty looks. I hoped none of them were brave enough to say anything to me with Kellan a foot away from them. He would most definitely lose his temper if that happened.

Kellan let go of my hand to sign a few autographs. I held my ground and watched Kellan with a prideful smile on my face. He really was so great at it. He made a point of saying hello and making eye contact with every person who handed him something. He was warm and open. He joked with them, and even made remarks that were just on the edge of being suggestive. Surprisingly, that didn't bother me in the slightest. I understood why he crooked a grin and told a tiny strawberry blond girl that he "was thrilled to see her too." He wasn't saying it in the hopes of hooking up with her later, he was saying it for her. He was giving her a memory that she could hold on to, making her day. The mild flirting was actually sort of sweet.

Only one person had the guts to ask him about me. Proudly wearing her Kell-Sex shirt, the frowning fan jerked her thumb at me. "Why is *she* here with you?" Somehow she made the word "she" sound profane.

Kellan kept his expression as neutral as possible. I didn't think he was going to respond, but in a calm voice, he told her, "She's my wife. She goes where I go."

With that, he grabbed my hand and walked away. The sound of a handful of people gasping simultaneously was the last thing I heard before we darted inside the building. He'd never called me that in public before. Kellan smiled at me once we were in the lobby. "It felt really good to say that."

My heart plummeting now that we were even closer to disclosing our private life, I grumbled, "Just think how good it will feel to say it to millions of people in a few minutes."

Seeing my nerves, Kellan wrapped his arm around me. "It's not millions." He pursed his lips. "I'm pretty sure it's not millions."

Discretely breaking us apart, Tory checked us in with security, then led us to the elevators. When we were all squished into the car, the intimidating blonde focused on Kellan and me.

Glancing at where we were holding hands, she told us, "You're primarily here to perform a song or two for them, but I've allowed them five minutes at the beginning of your set to ask you questions. Remember to keep the interview focused on the tour and your album. I've informed them not to ask you about your personal life, or anything about Sienna or the photo of Kiera, but they will probably try to sneak in a comment or two." Her cool gaze slid my way. "You should probably stay in the hallway during the interview, so as to not provoke inappropriate questions."

Face calm and composed, Kellan simply smiled. Taking that as an affirmative response, Tory twisted to face the elevator doors. Behind her back, Kellan flashed me a devilish smile, one that clearly said, *Hell if I'm doing any of that.* My heart surged with anxious adrenaline. God, I hoped I didn't pass out.

When we got to the studio, I could see that the light was on—they were live. I felt nauseated but gave Kellan a confident smile. We could do this. I could do this. An intern for the radio station let us in. Looking confident and intimidating, Tory walked through first. Her hawklike eyes took in everything around her, but I was pretty sure she wasn't going to see this coming.

A tall, middle-aged man standing behind a confusing board of switches and buttons smiled into the microphone when he saw our group entering. "The D-Bags have just arrived at the studio. Good to see you again, guys."

Kellan reached over and shook the man's hand. We'd been here before, during our whirlwind promo tour, and I instantly remembered something about this studio that I had forgotten about. They had web cameras set up in every corner of the room. Not only was the world going to hear our confession, they were going to see it too.

Indicating a group of chairs set up for the band, the DJ told us, "Have a seat."

As Matt, Evan, and Griffin sat down, Kellan turned to a grizzly looking DJ behind a laptop. "Can we get an extra chair?" He indicated me with his head.

The man looked confused, then surprised, like he recognized me. Hopping up, he told Kellan, "Sure, no problem."

As a chair was set up for me beside Kellan's, I risked a glance at Tory. She was glowering; she hadn't wanted me in the room. She wasn't putting a stop to it yet, but she might when we started speaking.

An attractive brunette behind another laptop beamed at the boys. "It's so nice to have you back. How have you been?" Her eyes focused on Kellan first, locked on me, shifted to the rest of the boys, then locked back on me. I could feel the curiosity emanating from her.

As headphones were set up on the guys, a microphone was handed to Kellan. He wasted no time in starting the conversation that I was both dreading and looking forward to. "Not so great, actually."

All of the DJs' eyes lit up as they stared at Kellan. People generally did not speak the truth when asked that question. It truly was just a nicety to smooth the path before the real questions were introduced. The woman flicked her gaze between Kellan and me, like she knew everything that had been going on with Kellan—in the gossip-verse, at least. By the eager expression on her face, it was clear that seeing me in the studio at Kellan's side, but not being able to say anything about it, had been driving her crazy; she was hoping for some answers. And she wasn't going to be disappointed.

She cautiously indicated me. "I can imagine things have been . . . rough . . . lately?"

She flicked a glance at Tory, who was already giving the DJs a "cut" gesture. Kellan looked over at Tory, held a finger up to her, then glanced back at the DJ. "I need to clear the air about a few things. I know we were supposed to perform for you today, but I would like to do an interview instead. Do you mind?" Every radio person in the room shook their head. Kellan pointed at me. "Can she get some headphones?"

Several people jumped at once to get me some, but, seeing our resolve and knowing what we were doing, Evan handed me his. With trembling fingers, I took them, thanked him, and put them on. God, I was going to throw up.

Tory stepped forward and leaned into Kellan's side. Pulling back his headphones, she heatedly told him something. I couldn't tell what she was saying, but I had a feeling it was a warning to shut the hell up. Kellan shook his head and snapped, "No! I won't be quiet. I'm done with this." I thought he might shove her away, but instead, he just turned back to the DJs and ignored her. Tory was livid. Pulling out her phone, she darted from the room. I figured Nick would be calling us in about thirty seconds.

As Kellan grit his jaw, I was handed a microphone. The room filled with tension and anticipation as I tried to ignore the many cameras around us. Palms sweaty, I grabbed Kellan's hand. When he glanced at me and our eyes met, I instantly flashed back to the first time I'd really looked into his eyes. His intense gaze framed in that perfect face had been so intimidating back then, but now it was a source of peace. I drank him in as the world waited for us to speak.

Still looking at me, Kellan lifted the microphone to his mouth. "I'd like to formally introduce you to this beautiful girl at my side, Miss Kiera Michelle Allen." He turned back to the DJs. "My wife."

I didn't think it was possible to simultaneously floor so many people, but everyone looked stunned. Timidly bringing the microphone to my lips, I murmured, "Hi." Everyone's eyes flashed to our hands. I'd been wearing my wedding ring the entire time, but in an attempt to avoid speculation, I had asked Kellan not to wear his. He was proudly wearing it now, and the matching bands sparkled in the studio lights.

The female DJ recovered first. "Oh, well . . . congratulations. Is this . . . recent?"

Smiling ear to ear, like a huge weight had been lifted from him, Kellan told them, "No. We actually got married last June, before any of this craziness started."

Knowing he was leaving something out, I clarified. "Well, we aren't technically married yet. We had a small ceremony . . . sort of, but we haven't legally gone through the proceedings." My throat felt so tight I was sure I sounded like a frog.

Kellan shrugged. "I married you in that bar. That's all that matters to me."

The scruffy-looking DJ was all over that news. "You got married in a bar? Nice. That's my dream wedding location. Not that I'm ever getting married."

A nerve-releasing titter escaped me, and I felt my throat relaxing. Feeling more confident, I kissed the back of Kellan's hand. "We married in June, but we've been together . . . well, it will be two years now in March."

Brows knitted, the woman asked Kellan, "If you've been engaged this whole time, why has nobody heard about Kiera before now?" She gave me playful smile. "Where have you been hiding?"

Laughing a little, I told her, "I was hiding right by his side. We've been almost inseparable this entire time. I was even in the room during interviews when Kellan mentioned he was 'in a relationship.'"

The DJ looked back at him. "Why didn't you just point her out? Say, that's my girl, right there?"

I meekly raised my hand. "That would be because of me. I'm not . . . comfortable being the center of attention. Kellan was trying to keep me out of the spotlight." I indicated the room with my finger. "All of this makes me want to either vomit, pee my pants, or some horrible combination of the two." While the room laughed, I resisted the urge to slap my hand over my eyes. Did I really just say that out loud to thousands and thousands of people? Oh well.

Giving me a wide smile, the brunette grabbed her microphone and leaned in like she was telling me a secret. "It's okay. This makes me want to pee too."

Kellan laughed, then added, "Once all the hype over Sienna and me started, I couldn't keep quiet about it. I told whoever would listen that I was in a relationship, but everyone twisted it around to mean that I was talking about Sienna. I couldn't give them specifics about Kiera, because she didn't want that, and I wasn't about to throw my wife to the wolves against her wishes." He kissed the back of my hand, and I swear someone in the room sighed.

Eyes apologetic, Kellan locked gazes with me. "I was as vague as I could be about you. Maybe I was too vague. I should have at least said I was engaged."

I shook my head. "You did what you knew I was comfortable with, you don't have to feel bad about that." Laughing, I added, "And you know Sienna just would have started wearing an engagement ring anyway."

Kellan smirked as he shook her head. "Yeah, I can see her doing that."

The DJs picked up on what we were insinuating instantly. Leaning in, the female asked, "Are you saying that Sienna Sexton orchestrated the Kell-Sex phenomenon?"

Kellan slowly looked back at the DJ. This was hard for him. Regardless of how Sienna had manipulated us, she'd given the D-Bags their start. She'd put them on the map; they sort of owed her for that. And she wasn't all bad. I'd seen glimpses of her generosity, like her arranging a car to get my sister to the hospital, and her showering Anna with things for Gibson. There was a soul inside of Sienna . . . buried deep under her incessant need to be on top. I wondered how much of that drive had to do with her pressure-filled childhood.

Sighing, Kellan told her, "It's not entirely Sienna's fault, but yes, she definitely did her part to make sure the fans saw us together."

All of the DJs looked confused. "Why?" the unkempt one asked.

Kellan looked back at his band sitting slightly behind us. This was it, the point of no return. But we'd gone too far now. If people were going to really understand what had happened, then the *entire* truth needed to come out.

Evan reached over and put his hand on Kellan's shoulder. Squeezing, he nodded. Kellan returned his eyes to the DJ who had asked the question. "To boost sales. The record label decided early on that Sienna and I as a couple would create a buzz that would help us both. It was their idea to make the music video so . . . explosive." He frowned as he looked over at me. "And I'll never really forgive myself for doing it."

"I talked you into it," I reminded him.

Nodding, Kellan inhaled a deep breath. Looking back at the DJs hanging on our every word, he said, "I was encouraged by the label to let the rumors grow, to hold my tongue. I didn't want to let my band down. These boys are my family. I wanted the success for them, so . . . I went along with it in the beginning." He let out a weary sigh, then shrugged. "By the time I changed my mind and started speaking up, it was too late. Nobody believed me."

Seeing his forlorn expression, I told the DJs, "The label pulled the D-Bags from the tour with Avoiding Redemption. The label put them on Sienna's tour, trying to drive the hype up. Sienna made sure they were constantly photographed together. Kellan was being evasive to protect me." Shaking my head, I turned to Kellan. "It's no wonder that the fans didn't believe what you were telling them. No one's at fault there."

The female DJ scoffed. "No one but your label and Sienna. You were green to the business, probably overwhelmed, and they completely walked all over you. It's disgusting, and I for one am outraged for you."

Kellan and I both smiled at her. Finally, someone understood. Someone believed us. And having someone on our side felt better than I ever thought it would.

We spent the next several minutes answering any question they asked, including a lot of questions about the confusing sex tape. Kellan told them, "No, that wasn't Sienna. That was an old roommate of mine. We made it several years ago. She leaked it for money, and since she's never once spoken up about being the girl in the video, I'm assuming that she got paid a great deal of money." I thought he made a very good point. So did the DJs.

After the DJs' questions were satisfied, we took additional questions from callers. It went really well, although several of the callers sounded shocked, angered, and saddened that Sienna and Kellan weren't real. One was even crying. I hadn't meant to break the hearts of the Kell-Sex fans, but Kellan and I couldn't keep this under wraps anymore. In the end, I hoped they understood that.

The minute we stepped from the studio, I felt higher and happier than I had in a while; our relationship being out in the open was both terrifying and liberating. Even if we were going to get heat from the label and Sienna, at least things would be honest from here on out. For the first time in the last few weeks, I felt really hopeful. And proud. Hard as it was, Kellan and I were doing the right thing.

Tori was livid when she met up with us in the hallway. She wasn't the only one. We didn't even make it to the elevator before Kellan's phone started ringing. He cringed when he saw the screen, but he opened it. "Hi, Sienna."

She screeched so loud I could hear her. "What the bloody hell did you just do?"

Kellan was cool but collected when he answered her. "Something I should have done a long time ago. I said my peace."

"You just admitted that we manipulated the public for money! Are you trying to ruin both of our careers?"

Tory was red-faced, and I couldn't help but think that she absolutely agreed with Sienna; I was a little surprised she hadn't gone off on us yet. She was probably waiting to do it in the car. The rest of the band was quiet as Sienna's heated, tinny words rang in the air.

Kellan pulled the phone away from his ear. "Our albums will speak for themselves. And that's the way it should be. If our music isn't good enough to stand on its own, then we shouldn't be at the top. And if we fall . . . I'm fine with it."

"You are the biggest bloody fool I have ever met! Get your ass back here. Now!"

The line went dead, and Kellan tucked the phone back in his pocket. As the elevator dinged and the doors opened, Kellan leaned down to me and whispered, "You think she's mad?"

His lip curled up in an expression that was both sexy and adorable. I had no choice but to wrap my arms around his neck and thoroughly start kissing him as we stepped inside the elevator. Pausing for only a microsecond, I murmured, "I don't really care if she is."

Kellan's phone rang the entire time the car descended, but we both ignored it as we held each other. My good feelings diminished a bit when we stepped onto the chilly, gloomy New York sidewalk. The fans who had been outside before had grown in size during the interview. Their temperament was also different. The range of reactions was all over the place, from shock, to anger, to grief. But curiosity seemed to be the underlying factor. It was obvious that they'd all been listening to the interview. It was also obvious that they all still had questions.

There was also a fair amount of press in the crowd now. They hovered around, microphones ready, cameras blazing. The fact that news crews were already there reiterated to me how fast things happened in New York. I wasn't thrilled about being broadcasted

on TV, but after the interview, this didn't faze me as much as it once
would have.

Kellan and I had handed the media a story that was a little more
in depth than just juicy are-they-or-aren't-they gossip. We'd openly
admitted being used by our label. That sort of scandal got noticed.
The reporters tossed out questions as the assemblage pressed in on
us: "Kellan, Kiera, any comment on what the label did to you?" "Will
you sue?" "Will you leave the tour?" "Did you violate your contract
by speaking out?"

Those were good questions, but they weren't ones we had answers for yet.

The fans also had questions, but theirs were on a more personal
level: "You're really not with Sienna?" "That was really fake?" "The
video looked so real though, are you sure you don't have feelings for
Sienna?"

Tory and the staff from the radio station were trying to keep the
crowd under control so we could leave. I thought maybe we should
have stayed and answered everyone's questions, but the way they
were trying to close in around us made me feel really claustropho-
bic and uncomfortable. There were too many, they were too close. I
didn't like it. We'd said enough for now. I just wanted to get into the
car and get back to the privacy of our bus.

There was a brief space between the large clusters of fans and
press hovering around the doors. Security was holding people back
just enough that Matt, Evan, and Griffin were able to squeeze through,
and I watched them hurry into the waiting SUV in relief. Kellan and
I couldn't press through the fans side by side, but he clenched my
hand tight as he pulled me through the sea of people.

I noticed several flashes of light as we waded along and realized
that not just press were in this mix. Paparazzi had shown up too, and
they were by far more aggressive than the fans and reporters. While
security merely had to stand in front of those groups to keep them
back, paparazzi pushed to get past them. A pair of tenacious photographers found their way through the swarm to step right in front of

Kellan and me. Kellan forced me back a step, and I shielded my eyes against the ceaseless bright flashes.

The people snapping our picture didn't seem to care in the least that we were trying to get to the car. They tossed out question after question, never even pausing long enough for us to answer—not that we were going to. Miffed, Kellan tried squirming past one; the portly man wouldn't budge, though.

Careful to not be too aggressive, since we'd just narrowly escaped an assault charge the last time we'd encountered these guys, Kellan politely said, "We're trying to leave; please let us through."

It was like they didn't even hear us. They just kept snapping away. Looking up at the safety of the SUV, I saw Matt and Evan watching us in concern. They looked just about ready to start pummeling people aside to get to us. I didn't want that. Kellan didn't either. When I was beginning to believe there wouldn't be another choice if we ever wanted to get out of this mob, a narrow path to the street opened up. It was far to the left of where we wanted to go, and it cut right through a pocket of excited fans, but it was our only option at this point.

Kellan saw the ray of hope at the same time I did. He pulled us to the right, faking out the paparazzi, then swung us around to the left, and we ran for the closing hole. Kellan pulled me through the break in the crowd just as it began to close back up. We were stroked and fondled by fans on the way through, but the aggressive photographers couldn't follow us.

Now that we were through the conglomeration, we were a little stuck. The label's SUV was a ways up the street, blocked off from us by a mass of people. The buzzing crowd was behind us, and the street was in front of us. Since the rest of the band was safely tucked away, Kellan and I were now the only point of interest. Over my shoulder, I could see them all shifting our way. Kellan stuck his hand out for a taxi, trying to get us away, but trepidation shot up my spine as everyone zoned in on us.

The reporters kept up their questions, holding large microphones our way, hoping for a response. The paparazzi were pushing through the fans, trying to get a better angle. And the fans were in a dither having their idol so close to them. They didn't even seem to care about what we'd said about Sienna, especially the ones who Kellan had brushed past as he was trying to get us away. Those ones looked elated, and they looked like they wanted to touch him some more. I understood that feeling, but the zealous energy growing in the crowd made me nervous.

"Kellan, I don't like this, let's get out here."

Kellan nodded at me. "We'll get a cab in a second."

Just as he said it, the fans started to realize that he was getting away and surged forward. They swarmed around us, all hands and giggling laughter. Arms circled Kellan, hands ran up his chest, pens were shoved in his face, and cell phones recorded every moment. They squeezed between us, separating us. I tried to keep a hold on Kellan's hand, but like a stretched rubber band, we eventually broke apart.

"We love you, Kellan!" rose above the din of the reporters and photographers shouting questions. Much to my surprise, just as many fans were clamoring for my attention as Kellan's. I guess I was just as much an attraction as he was—the woman who had the Golden Boy's heart. Some wanted to know what he was really like, some wanted to know how I felt about the music video, some even asked if I was pregnant. Overwhelmed, I instinctively backed up.

The press were behind the fans now, and they moved forward as more curious onlookers swelled the crowd. The curious, eager fans in front of us were pushed from behind, and with nowhere to go, they bumped into Kellan and me. Kellan held his ground, but I was pushed back so hard, I lost my footing. My heel slipped over the edge of the sidewalk. I hadn't even realized I was that close to the street. I was even more aware of my proximity when I stumbled and fell into a lane of traffic. A fan reached for me, but she missed; I landed on my ass, hard. Dazed, confused, I stared at a pair of headlights baring down on me. The only thought that flashed through my head was that I hoped being hit by a truck wasn't as painful as it seemed.

I started to get to my feet but was disoriented, and I knew I wouldn't make it in time; the truck didn't even seem to be slowing down. Then, like my own personal white night, or maybe, more fittingly, like a clearly deranged madman, Kellan recklessly rushed into the street. I was one hundred percent positive that I was about to witness my husband's death. I was about to become a widow before I even had the chance to officially get married. I stopped breathing.

Kellan's fingers closed over the tattoo of his name on my wrist, and he yanked me to my feet; I felt like my shoulder was being disconnected as pain torn up my arm. I heard the vehicle's brakes squealing as it finally noticed us, but it was too late. When I crashed into Kellan's chest, he shoved me behind him and put his hand up to the truck, bracing himself for impact. It was all he had time to do.

Oddly, even though I knew we were a microsecond away from something terrible happening, I couldn't help but notice that it was a floral delivery truck about to hit us. My mind snapped to Kellan's petal messages. I'd really miss them.

The truck veered to the left, trying to avoid us, but it couldn't. It smashed into Kellan, hitting him at stomach level. The truck's forward momentum caused it to hit me too. I crashed into Kellan's back, then fell to the ground. It hurt just as much as I was afraid it was going to. The blow knocked the wind out of me, and I felt like rubber. My head hit the asphalt before my hands could break my fall. I felt my scalp burning, saw stars, and then all I saw was blackness.

Chapter 27
That Did Not Just Happen

When I came to, someone was shining a light in my eyes. It hurt. I hurt. I couldn't remember where I was. My head hurt, and I felt so nauseated. Why did I feel nauseated? Hating the brightness piercing my brain, I tried to look away, but something around my neck made it hard to do. What was that? From the corner of my eye, I could tell that I was lying on a city street; there was headlight glass and debris around my head. And a jagged piece of metal covered in blood. Fresh blood. Why was I lying in a street? Was I blocking traffic? People must be so pissed at me. I should get up. I didn't want to move, though. I had a feeling that would hurt.

My mind in a fog, I felt hands lifting me, then placing me on a flat, white table. It did hurt to move, and I cringed and sucked in a sharp breath. Why was someone putting me on a table? Why was there a table in the middle of the road? A man in a reflective jacket was asking me questions.

"Ma'am, do you know where you are? Do you know what happened?"

My body felt so heavy. My mind felt so slow. Blood was dripping down my face. I could feel it in my eyes. "I . . . I . . . don't . . ."

Memories floating through my brain. Headlights coming toward me. Brakes squealing. Falling. "I was hit by a truck," I muttered.

"Yes, that's right." A bandage was placed on my head. My head. I remembered hitting my head on the ground. That's why I hurt. That's why I was bleeding. But my body hurt too. My shoulder ached. I felt bruised. Kellan pulled me to my feet. I hit him before hitting the ground.

I instantly tried to sit up. "Kellan!"

The paramedic pushed me down and tried to stabilize me. My eyes flew to where Kellan had last been. All I saw was glass and blood; no Kellan. "You have a nasty cut, ma'am. I need to bandage this and make sure you don't have any other injuries. You could make things worse by moving. Do you know your name?" he asked, his voice gentle.

"Kiera Allen . . . Kyle. Where's my husband?" I asked, my voice raw.

The paramedic's hands worked on my head. I tried to hold still for him, but all I wanted to do was run up and down the street screaming Kellan's name. "The other paramedics are working on him, Kiera. He's in good hands."

Even though my vision was a little blurry, I noticed the paramedic look to our left. My soul filling with trepidation, my gaze followed. Kellan was lying on a stretcher similar to the one I was on. He was covered in blood too, and I didn't know if it was his or mine. And not knowing scared the crap out of me. "Kellan!"

I shouted his name, but he didn't respond. He was shaking. He looked ill. Then, to my absolute horror, he leaned over and vomited blood.

Panic set in, and I tried to get to him, but the paramedic held me down and my stretcher was shoved into the back of an ambulance. "Is he okay? Is he okay?" I just kept repeating it. I couldn't stop myself.

Before I got an answer, the doors were closed and the vehicle took off. The sirens hurt my ears, but it was nothing compared to the ache in my chest. Why was he throwing up blood? Was he okay? He had to be okay.

Holding my hand, the paramedic told me, "They'll do everything they can for him. I promise."

His words didn't help me much. I started sobbing.

I felt numb when we got to the hospital. Words hit my ears, but I couldn't process any of them. Someone said I was in shock. Someone mentioned concussion. Head injury. Internal injuries. None of the words stuck, though, because a vision of Kellan heaving blood was all I could think about. I was poked, prodded, and my stomach was pushed and massaged. I was sore, my shoulder throbbed, but I wasn't hurt. Only not knowing Kellan's fate hurt.

He arrived at the ER right as a nurse injected a numbing agent into my head; I had to get stitches for the cut on my scalp. I saw him being wheeled past my room and hopped off the bed. Kellan wasn't vomiting, but he wasn't awake either. He looked completely lifeless. It scared the shit out of me.

My nurse hurried after me, telling me I needed her attention. The nurses hovering around Kellan were telling the doctor in their midst just what had happened to Kellan. I stayed back so I could listen without them seeing me; I did not want to be dragged away until I knew what was wrong. "Young male, early twenties, involved in a car accident. Was confused and light-headed at the scene, vomiting blood. Abdomen is distended, he has tachycardia and is hypotensive."

The doctor nodded as he checked Kellan's vitals. He pulled up his shirt, and even I could see his stomach was bulging. He tenderly pressed on it and Kellan's eyes opened as he gasped in pain. "He's bleeding internally. Prep him for surgery."

That got my attention. Stepping forward, I asked the doctor, "Surgery? Is it bad? Is my husband going to be okay?"

The doctor gave me a polite smile. "I'll do everything I can." Blocking my path, he examined my head as Kellan was carted away from me. "You really need stitches for this cut."

He nodded his head at the nurse behind me. She gently grabbed my arms and pulled me back into the exam room. Kellan was already gone, and I knew there was nothing I could do for him by trying to follow. Tears in my eyes, I turned to my nurse. "Do you know what happened to him?"

The nurse sat me on the table and pressed some gauze against my head. "Most likely, something inside of him ruptured. He's bleeding. They need to remove or repair the damage as soon as possible."

She grabbed a needle and some thread and I fought against the sudden acidic bile in my throat. "Is he going to die?" The tears in my eyes spilled down my cheeks. It couldn't end like this.

The nurse didn't answer me right away, and when she did, her voice was professional and courteous. "We have the best doctors in the country here. He's in good hands." I knew she was giving me a stock answer. I wanted a real one.

Jerking my head up, I glared at her. "That's not an answer."

Turning my head back into position, she told me, "I know, but it's the only one I have for you." Her words were gentle and kind, but firm, and I understood: My question wasn't answerable.

They ran some tests on me after my head was sewn back together—X-rays, an MRI. They gave me a cold pack for the strain in my shoulder and told me to ice it twenty minutes every hour. Other than feeling sore and achy and having a headache, I felt fine, and I told them that repeatedly. When all of the tests backed up what I was saying, the hospital finally released me.

After filling out my paperwork, I shuffled out to the emergency room lobby to wait for news on Kellan. Nobody had been able to tell me anything yet. It was a busy day in the ER, and as I scanned the crowd, I wondered how many poor souls had had their lives altered today. Like me. Tears filled my eyes, but I held them back. I didn't have time to break down, and I didn't need to. Kellan was going to be fine.

My purse was strapped around my chest. It had miraculously remained attached to me throughout the entire accident. Setting down my cold compress, I dug through my bag for my cell phone. Hopefully it had also survived and still worked. I needed to be doing something. I needed to be active. If I stopped, even just for a second, I'd start to think, and I didn't want to think. I didn't want to worry.

Thankfully, the phone was intact. Scrolling through the list of people that mattered to me, I wondered who to call first when I heard somebody shout at the top of their lungs, "Kiera!"

I looked up and scoured the patients until I found the person who had yelled for me. Eyes wide and bloodshot, my sister was running across the lobby to get to me; Griffin and Evan were right behind her. Anna engulfed me in a hug that knocked me back a step. It hurt, but I didn't care. I tossed my arms around and hugged her back just as hard. "Anna," I croaked, trying not to sob.

Smoothing my hair, she whispered, "You're okay, you're okay, thank God you're okay." Pulling back, she cupped my cheeks. "Do not *ever* scare me like that again, you hear me?"

I nodded as I fought back tears. Griffin and Evan stepped up to us. I looked around for Matt, but I didn't see him anywhere. Both boys looked pale, somber. Griffin looked a little green as he held Gibson tight to his chest. "They won't tell us anything. Do you know what's happening to Kellan? Is he gonna be okay?" he asked, his voice breaking.

Stepping apart from Anna, I swallowed three times so I could speak. "He's still in surgery." Plastering on a fake smile, I added, "But he'll be fine."

Anna rubbed my back, "Kiera, I saw the accident on the Internet. The reporters caught every second of it."

Blinking away the collecting moisture in my eyes, I locked gazes with her. "He'll be fine," I reiterated.

Eyes shimmering, Griffin stared down at his daughter. Evan enclosed me in a warm hug. When he pulled back, I scrunched my brows; it felt weird with my partially numb head. "Where's Matt? Isn't he here?"

Griffin sniffed, then looked toward a set of automatic doors. "He's still outside. He said he needed to make some calls before he came in here . . ."

Giving Evan one last squeeze, I looked over to the doors. Sure enough, in the distance, I could see Matt pacing back and forth. He looked troubled, but that was to be expected. "I'm going to go let him know about Kellan."

Everyone nodded at me. Anna cuddled into Griffin's side. For once, the way the pair embraced each other was heartwarming and spoke volumes about how much they really did love each other. The way they looked at each other said even more. Turning from them, I made my way to Matt. He had to be just as worried as his band mates.

Halfway to the doors, the phone I was still clutching in my hand rang. Relief mixed with pain when I saw who was calling me. "Denny, I'm so glad you called, I—"

He cut me off. "I saw the accident on the news. Are you okay?"

"I'm fine."

Denny let out a long, relieved exhale. "I was so worried. The footage is scary as hell, they won't even show all of it on TV. God, I am so happy to hear your voice."

I closed my eyes as I walked through the doors that led to where Matt was still walking back and forth. "I'm fine, but Kellan—"

Denny's voice was so quiet, I almost didn't hear him over the hum of the doors. "Please tell me he's okay."

I pressed my lips tight together. God, I hated saying it. I hated thinking it. I hated everything about this moment. "He's in surgery. They aren't sure . . ."

"Jesus. Kiera . . . I'm . . . I'm so sorry."

Even though we were in the middle of New York City, it was quiet outside the hospital. Peaceful. I could hear everything going on around me—cars driving past, a couple talking as they walked down the sidewalk, a siren in the distance, and Denny sniffling in my ear. "I'm sure he'll be fine, Kiera." By the pain in his voice, I could tell that, regardless of what had happened between them, Denny was genuinely concerned for his longtime friend.

I leaned against a column supporting the overhang to the ER entrance. Matt stopped pacing and stared at me. The terror in his eyes matched the horror in my heart. "He has to be," I whispered. I couldn't picture my life without him.

I hung up with Denny after telling him that I'd call him the minute I had any news on Kellan. When I tucked the phone back in my purse, Matt approached me. "I'm so glad you're okay, Kiera. That was the scariest shit I've ever seen."

Walking over to him, I nodded. He had his cell phone in his hand, and he was squeezing it so tight, his fingers were bloodless. Placing my hand over his, I attempted to relax his death grip on the device. "Who were you calling?"

He stared at the doors over my shoulder. "My parents, Rachel . . ." When his gaze returned to mine, his pale eyes were glossy. "I'm scared to go in there," he whispered.

"I am, too," I told him. Successfully dislodging his cell phone, I grabbed his hand. It tightened around mine like a vice, like I was the only thing keeping him upright. "We'll go in together, okay?"

Looking like a lost little boy who had finally found someone to guide him home, Matt nodded at me. Together, we walked into the hospital to await Kellan's fate.

Deacon and the rest of the boys from Holeshot were waiting back inside the ER, as was Taskmaster Tory and some of the crew members. They all looked just as worried as we were. While everyone settled into a comfortable place to wait, I called everyone I could think of—Jenny, Cheyenne, Kate, my parents, Kellan's dad. Most of them had already heard the news by this point, but talking to them gave me something to do besides worrying about Kellan.

When I had exhausted the contact list in my phone, Anna pulled me into a bathroom to clean me up; I was still a blood-covered mess. She washed my face and my hands and tore off one of her layered long-sleeved T-shirts. It was a maternity shirt and way too big for me, but it effectively hid the blood splattered across my top. Still ripe with emotion, Anna lightly kissed the bandage on my head. "I never want to see your head wrapped in gauze again," she told me.

Looking at myself in the mirror, I nodded in agreement. "Me either."

"I'm so glad you're okay." Starting to lose it, she brought her hands to her face.

Knowing she needed to cry, I held her tight and let her. I stopped myself from crying along with her, though. There was no need. Kellan was fine.

When we got back to the waiting room, I noticed people staring out the window, pointing and whispering. I didn't really care what they were finding so interesting, I just wanted news on Kellan. But Deacon was with them and he motioned me over. "You gotta see this, Kiera."

Feeling stiff, sore, tired, and drained, I shuffled over to the wall of windows where people were gathering. Not knowing what to expect, I peeked outside. It was almost lunchtime, and there was a group of people across the street, leaning against a low wall by a parking lot. They looked like they were having a picnic. Fascinating. I was about to ask what the big deal was when I noticed the shirts under their jackets. They were all wearing D-Bags shirts, and the opaque cups they were holding as they stood in a line on the sidewalk weren't holding beverages, they had small candlesticks inserted through them that gave the cups a cheery glow on this dreary day. My heart swelled at the sight of even more people loving Kellan. He wouldn't believe this.

I knew the answer, but I had to ask the question anyway. "Are they here for Kellan?"

Deacon smiled as he stared at the growing crowd. "Yes."

Warmth filled me as I watched this silent vigil for Kellan. I could almost feel the healing, positive energy flowing from them. Kellan needed to see this. He needed to see how much he was cared about, how much he was loved.

"Mrs. Kyle?"

I turned around to see a woman with a stethoscope around her neck standing behind me. She was looking at every person in the waiting room, her face neutral. I didn't know what that face meant. This wasn't the doctor who had been with Kellan in the ER. I didn't know who she was or what she wanted. I'd already filled out the paperwork for both Kellan and myself with the nurse, so she had to be here to tell me about Kellan, about whether he was alive . . . or not. Why couldn't she smile, give me some ray of hope? My chest felt tight. Breathing was impossible. Stepping toward her, I nodded and raised my hand; it was all I could do.

Approaching me, she calmly said, "Your husband is out of surgery. Everything went well, and he's recovering in a room upstairs if you'd like to go see him."

My knees gave way, but Deacon caught me. "He's fine? You're sure he's fine?" I choked out.

The doctor finally smiled. "His spleen ruptured in the accident, which can be very dangerous, but my colleague and I were able to repair the tear and save the organ. He also bruised his hip, fractured a few ribs, and he'll be sore for a long time, but he was very lucky. I've seen much worse. He'll need to stay here for a few days so we can watch for complications, and then he'll need lots of rest . . ."

She kept speaking but I didn't hear a word of it. *He was alive.*

The assemblage waiting to see Kellan headed upstairs. Once we got to the nurse's station, a tall woman with her hair pulled back into a tight bun stopped our group. "Who are you here for?" she asked, eyeing our motley crew.

I looked behind me at the various band members and roadies. I could only imagine who the nurse thought we all were. Turning back to her, I spoke in a shaky, excited voice. "I'm here to see my husband, Kellan Kyle."

A small smile crept into her mouth, and I could tell she recognized his name. "Oh, yes, well he's still recovering so only one of you—"

I stepped forward, not letting her finish. "I need to see my husband, please."

She indicated with her head for me to follow her. While we walked down the crisp white halls, the nurse looked me over. "We've had a few celebrities over the years, but none quite as big as Kellan

Kyle. Half of the girls on the floor are in an absolute tizzy that he's here. So, you're really his wife?"

My eyes were frantically scouring the names on all the doors we were passing. *Where was he?* "Yes," I told her, only half-listening.

"Oh," she said, sounding surprised. "All that hoopla with Sienna Sexton must have been really hard on the two of you."

I looked up at her. She seemed youthful, but the crinkles around her eyes and mouth suggested that she was older than she appeared. The smile she was giving me was full of sympathy. "You have no idea." I gave her a wry smile.

She held her hand out to me. "My name is Carly. If you need anything, you just let me know."

I gave her hand a quick shake. "Thank you, I really appreciate that." I had a feeling I would definitely need her help while we were here.

I knew the minute we were at Kellan's room. I knew it because a swarm of young nurses were hovering at the open door, glancing inside. The smile on Carly's face vanished as she scowled at the girls. "If you all have nothing to do, I'm sure I could find something for you."

Tittering, the girls scampered off. Carly sighed as she indicated his door. "Like I said, we haven't had anyone quite like Kellan here."

A nervous laugh escaped me as I stepped into Kellan's private room. Leaving us alone, Carly closed the door as she left. The lights were low, the shades drawn. It was solemn and quiet. Kellan's eyes were closed and his head was angled away from me. The top of the bed was elevated some, so he was propped up, and the covers were tucked under his arms. His hands rested at his sides in an almost unnatural way. An IV pierced through the back of his left hand, pumped him full of medication and painkillers. His ring was missing; they must have removed it before the surgery.

Kellan was tall and well-built, but he looked tiny as he lay in the bed. The sight made my eyes sting.

The expression on his face was so peaceful as he slept that I almost wanted to stay where I was so that I didn't unintentionally disturb him. I couldn't stay that far away, though. Quiet as a mouse, I walked to his side. He had small cuts on his face, but other than that he looked perfect. He was wearing a hospital gown, the embarrassing kind that ties in the back, and a bag of his belongings was sitting on the nightstand next to the bed.

Careful to not hurt him, I sat on the edge of his mattress. I was a little scared to touch him, but I needed to, so I gingerly wrapped my fingers over his arm. He was warm. "Kellan," I whispered, "are you awake?" His head moved, but he didn't answer me. I ran my fingers down his arm, cupping his hand. "I'm right here, waiting for you." Tears clouding my vision, I ran a knuckle down his cheek. "I'm not going anywhere, baby."

Minutes ticked by as I waited for whatever drugs they'd used to knock him out with to wear off enough that he'd wake up. It felt like it took forever, and a little bit of guilt crept into me that the others couldn't see him yet. But I needed to be there when he woke up. I just . . . needed it.

I could tell when he was starting to come around. His eyes moved beneath his lids. Then he inhaled a deep breath and cringed on the exhale. I hoped he didn't wake up in too much pain. When he finally opened his eyes, I thought my face might split apart I was smiling so hard. "Kellan, baby?"

He didn't look my way, just slowly blinked and stared at nothing. He had to be confused. I wondered if he even remembered the accident. Tenderly, I stroked his cheek again. "Kellan?"

He finally turned my way, his expression blank. As his midnight eyes searched my face, I began to get the horrid feeling in my gut that he wouldn't remember me. The doctor hadn't mentioned a head injury, but what if he'd struck the concrete too? What if he had amnesia? God, would he still love me if we had to start over?

Kellan worked his mouth, then swallowed a few times. Forehead wrinkling, he said, "Kiera? What happened?"

Relief and amusement flooded through me. Of course he still

remembered me. "I got pushed into the street. You raced out to help me, and a truck hit you. You're in the hospital."

Kellan's eyes fixed on the bandage at the edge of my hairline. "Are you okay?" he asked.

Shaking my head that he was still more worried about me, I leaned down and gave him a soft kiss. "You're alive. I'm perfect."

Closing his eyes, Kellan looked pained as he breathed shallowly through his mouth. "I don't feel good."

I smoothed back his hair. "I know. They had to operate on you because your spleen ruptured. They were able to save it, but you're going to be sore for a while."

Kellan cracked an eye open, and a ghost of a smile crept into his lips. "Oh, good, I'd hate to be spleenless." He closed his eyes again. "What the hell does a spleen do anyway?"

A small laugh escaped me. His sense of humor was definitely still intact. "From what I remember in school, it's like the oil filter of your immune system . . . and it was once thought to be the source of anger. I'm not sure about that one though."

Kellan started to chuckle, then froze. "Oh, don't make me laugh."

I kissed his cheek. "I won't. We'll never laugh again, I promise."

Opening his eyes, he chuckled again, then cringed. "I said don't make me laugh."

Resting my head against his, I whispered, "I love you so much. I'm so glad you're okay."

Kellan tried to pull me into a hug, but he was so weak and so sore. I didn't want him hurting himself, so I stilled his hands and crawled into the bed with him. Carefully draping my arm over his upper chest, I gently squeezed the top of his shoulders. He sighed in relief. "I love you too."

Tears rolled down my cheeks as what nearly happened today crashed into me. I kissed his head as I held him tight. "You saved my life," I whispered, my voice warbling.

His words thick with sleep, he told me, "I was returning the favor."

He started to doze off again, and I thought to leave so others could see him. His hand on my back tightened when he felt me move away. "It's okay, I was just going to let the others come see you. They're all so worried."

"Stay . . . just . . . for a minute," he mumbled.

I kissed his shoulder. "As long as you want, Kellan. As long as you want."

He dozed off again after a few minutes. Knowing others needed to see him, I carefully climbed out of his bed. He stirred but didn't open his eyes. When I got back to the waiting room, a surprise was waiting for me. Justin was there, talking to Evan. The nurses who had been hovering by Kellan's room were openly gaping at the new rock star who had dropped into their midst. I figured this day would live on in infamy for them. For me too, I supposed.

Touched that Justin was there, I immediately threw my arms around him. "Justin, thank you for coming. This will mean so much to Kellan."

Justin patted my back in a friendly squeeze. "Our tour was close by. When I heard the news, I had to. Is he okay?"

I nodded as I stepped back. "Yeah. Groggy, but okay." I looked around the band members. "You guys can see him now."

Matt, Evan, and Griffin all looked at each other. The nurse had said one person could go in at a time; they were trying to decide who should go in first. Shrugging, Matt stuck his hands out with his fist on his palm. "Rock Paper Scissors?"

Griffin rolled his eyes. "We're fucking rock stars. When did we start caring about rules?"

Still carrying Gibson, Griffin strode toward the room I'd just left. Matt and Evan glanced at each other, then followed him. Giggling, Anna hurried after her husband. I watched the crowd descending on Kellan, then motioned for Justin and Holeshot to come with me, and we all followed the D-Bags. One for all and all for one.

Kellan was more like himself as the afternoon wore on. He was tired and in pain, but mostly in good spirits. Tory left soon after checking

on Kellan; she said she was immediately going to issue a statement
to the public that "It was touch and go, but Kellan narrowly escaped
Death's dark call, and he is slowly recuperating from his nearly tragic
accident." I thought her story was a little dramatic, but by the glow in
her eyes, I could tell that framing it that way was excellent publicity.
I found it really interesting that we couldn't get her to lift a finger for
us when we needed her to, but she was all over it when it benefitted
the label.

Rock stars and roadies loitered around Kellan's room as he recovered, much to the delight of the nurses who popped in every five
minutes. The doctors and the head nurse, Carly, were less happy
about Kellan's numerous guests, and eventually made everyone leave
Kellan's room but me. Since Holeshot and the tour crew members had
to go get ready for the show tonight anyway, they said their goodbyes
and grudgingly left the hospital. Justin stayed, since his band wasn't
playing, but he gave Kellan and me some privacy by hanging out in
the lobby with Anna and the other D-Bags.

When the sky began to darken, I wandered over to the window
to peek outside. I'd heard from the nurses that the crowd of fans outside had swelled considerably since earlier today. As I started to peer
through the blinds, Kellan asked, "Have you heard from Sienna? She
didn't come by. I'm kind of surprised by that."

I looked back at him in bed. He was sitting up higher with fluffy
pillows shoved behind his back, but still at an angle that was comfortable for his stomach. There was a tray of uneaten food hovering
over his lap, and he was frowning as he poked at a cup of Jell-O with
a plastic spoon.

"I'm kind of surprised by that too," I answered. It wasn't like Sienna to miss a photo op, and her rushing to the side of her fallen colleague seemed like a missed opportunity to me. Even if Kellan and I
had come clean about our relationship and no one believed that they
were dating—and I was really hoping that was the case now—visiting Kellan at the hospital would still make her look good. And after
what we'd said about her, she probably needed a little positive PR.

"She sent flowers." I pointed over to a modest floral arrangement that was resting between an elegant bouquet of lilies from Lana, and a monstrous vase overflowing with cloyingly powerful red roses from Nick. All the card attached to Sienna's said was, "I'm so sorry. S."

Kellan glanced at them, then frowned at me. "A subtle get-well bouquet isn't exactly her style. I was expecting her to hand deliver them to me in a sequined, floor-length gown."

I smirked at him. Yeah, something that outrageous that demanded people paid attention was much more Sienna's style than being virtually silent with anonymously delivered flowers. Shaking my head since I didn't understand it, I turned back to the window and pried open the slits. The sun had set not too long ago and it wasn't fully dark yet, but I could easily see the many pinpoints of lights as fans crowded around the hospital with cups of glowing candles. My throat was thick at the display of love before me. "Kellan," I whispered, "you have to see this."

I knew he wouldn't be up to standing yet, so I raised the blinds in a hope that he could see the lights from his bed. Since he was only a foot or two away, he had a pretty good view. I watched his face as he dropped his spoon to his tray. "What is that?"

"Those are your fans. They're here for you." I waved at the fans. Since the light was on in Kellan's room and it was dark outside, I knew they had a full shot of me. I wasn't sure how they'd react to seeing me here, but surprisingly the candles started moving in unison, like they were waving back at me. I took that as a good sign.

Kellan looked up at me, mystified. "That's for me?"

Walking over to his bed, I sat on the corner and ran my hand through his hair. "You're very loved. And not just because of what you are. Your fans see you. Through your music, they see you. And they love you." I cupped his perfect, right-angled jaw, and stroked his cheek with my thumb. "It's not just *this* that they love, you know? It's you."

Leaning down, I kissed his forehead.

I looked up when I heard a light tap at the door. When I saw the group of people who were watching us, I thought I was going to start sobbing. Standing just inside of the doorframe were my mother and father, and Kellan's father, Gavin. Hailey and Riley were peeking into the room from behind their dad. I was so surprised, I was at a loss for words. I had just talked with each of them a few hours ago, and none of them had mentioned hopping a plane and flying out here.

Kellan was just as much at a loss as I was. "Gavin, Caroline . . . Martin? What are you doing in New York?"

Gavin approached his son; the worry on his face was as clear as day to me. It warmed my heart. Even if he'd kept his distance for most of Kellan's life, he really did love him. "I'm sorry we're so late. We got on the first flight we could." Standing beside Kellan, Gavin put a hand on his shoulder. "We were all so incredibly worried about you."

Hailey and Riley came up to stand at the end of the bed while Kellan's eyes teared up. "You were worried about . . . me?" He still seemed stunned that they would care.

Gavin's face softened into a smile. "Of course I was, son. When I heard you were in an accident, I was terrified."

Reaching down, Hailey rubbed his foot through the blanket. "We love you, bro." Riley nodded in agreement.

While Kellan swallowed back both physical and emotional pain, my parents stepped up to the bed. My mom was cradling Gibson to her chest, but reached over and put her hand on Kellan's leg. "We came as soon as we could too." Her green eyes flashed to mine. "You're family, Kellan."

Kellan turned to me, and I could see the pain and joy in his eyes. This is what he'd always wanted. Family. A real family. I couldn't contain it anymore, and big fat tears started rolling down my cheeks. Dad looked like he was suddenly worried about my health as he stared at me. Mom simply walked around and gave me a knowing hug. Having my family fully accept my husband was the greatest gift they could have ever given me, and him.

When I calmed down, Kellan relaxed back into his cushions.

Even though he cringed in discomfort, he was smiling at me. "So adorable," he muttered.

Ignoring him, I watched my mom as she kissed Gibson's nose. "How is it you are all here together?"

Dad frowned as he gave Mom a pointed glance. "Your mother spotted Gavin in baggage claim . . . from clear across the room."

Ignoring him, Mom cooed at her granddaughter. I stifled a laugh. Yeah, like Kellan, Gavin stood out in a crowd.

As it grew late into the evening, I thought about the concert going on, and all the fans who would be disheartened that Kellan and the D-Bags weren't playing. But they couldn't play without their lead singer, and he was in no shape to be on stage. I was a little surprised that Sienna hadn't played up her distress over the accident by rescheduling the show. Everything about what she'd done today was surprising me.

I think my mom wanted to stay by Kellan's side all night, baby Gibson in hand, but I could see how tired she was, and I made the D-Bags take her and Dad back to the hotel. She promised to come back first thing in the morning. I didn't doubt she would.

Collecting her daughter from Mom, Anna asked me, "Are you coming with us back to the hotel?" I could tell from her tone of voice that she already knew my answer. I shook my head. No, I wasn't leaving Kellan's side. They'd have to drag me outside to get me to leave.

Justin and the D-Bags headed out with Anna and our parents. Gavin and his children went with them. The room felt a little bigger with everyone's energy gone, but the level of love inside it didn't lower at all. I gazed at Kellan for long minutes, just wanting time to stand still. Eyes heavy with drugs, pain, and sleep, Kellan stared right back at me. Then his face contorted into a strange expression. "Crap," he whispered. "I have to pee." He looked over to the bathroom and sighed, like it was so far away it may as well have been in another country.

Chuckling at him, I kissed his cheek. "I could help you?"

He pursed his lips. "Uh, no, I got it. I can do this." He let out a low, steady exhale. "The nurse said I should get up and move around anyway."

He leaned forward to stand and I placed my hands on his back in support. "She said tomorrow you should."

Kellan bit his lip as he tried to suppress a groan. It didn't work, and he let out a low rumble of pain. "It's just a couple of hours shy of tomorrow," he said through clenched teeth.

As he uncovered himself from the sheets, I hurried around to the other side of the bed, bringing the IV stand with me. Once he stood up, he gasped and clenched at the pole for support. I held it still so he wouldn't fall over. Pale and looking a little ill, he glanced out the window. His mouth dropped open as he got a clear view of the sea of candlelight in the darkness. "Oh my God, Kiera. They're still here."

Patting his hand on the pole, I urged him forward. "Of course they are."

Kellan seemed to forget about his pain until he took a step. Then he groaned and gingerly held his stomach. Feeling bad that I couldn't do anything for him, I merely held the bathroom door open. His face was tight as he passed by me. "Thanks."

Before I closed the door behind him, I couldn't help but check out the toned sections of skin showing between the ties along the back of his gown. Only Kellan Kyle could make a hospital gown sexy. Kellan started to chuckle when he noticed me watching; he instantly grimaced. "Stop making me laugh and close the door."

Letting out a hearty laugh, since he couldn't, I did what he asked. While I waited for him and hoped he didn't get light-headed and pass out, I meandered over to the window to watch the crowd of well-wishers. They were stretched along the sidewalk across from the hospital, almost as far as I could see; it really was an impressive sight.

A short knock followed by a polite voice disrupted my thoughts. "Mrs. Kyle, I'm sorry to bother you. It's after hours, but your brother is here?"

I turned to see the night nurse poking her head through the partially open door. I kept my face purposely neutral. Brother? I didn't have a brother. The nurse looked behind her, then back at me. "Normally, I'd make him wait until morning, but he says he flew across the country to see you?"

She looked at me skeptically, like she was sure the person behind her was not who he claimed to be. And she was right; he wasn't who he said he was. I let the surprise I felt show on my face. "Denny? Denny's here?"

The nurse seemed relieved and opened the door a bit wider. "I'll let him come in, but just for a few minutes, okay?"

I nodded, still absolutely stunned that he'd come all this way. The nurse stepped back and made a motion with her hand while opening the door wide with her other one. Denny stepped into the room, looking worn and weary. Abby followed a step behind him. Even more surprise trickled through me at seeing Denny's fiancée.

Respectfully, Denny turned to the nurse and told her, "Thank you for your help, Renae." For the millionth time today, I was shocked; he'd said that without any trace of an accent. Nothing.

Once she was gone, Denny turned back to me. I must have still looked shocked, because he started laughing. His accent back in place, he told me, "I couldn't be your brother if I didn't sound like you, and I wanted to make sure they let me in." My favorite grin formed on his lips. "And faking an American accent is not easy. I was positive she was going to see right through me."

Giggling, I rushed over to him and tossed my arms around him. "I can't believe you're here."

Sighing, Denny held me tight. "I'm only sorry I'm late."

The bathroom door swung open as Denny and I pulled apart. Kellan had a small smile on his face that fell when he noticed Denny. The same shock I'd felt flitted over Kellan's features as he wobbled a bit. He didn't seem angry, just massively surprised. Tilting his head, he asked, "Are you a figment of my pain meds? Or are you really standing right in front of me?"

"I'm really here. It's good to see you in one piece, mate." Smiling,

Denny walked over and gave Kellan a quick hug. It was pretty easy to see that Kellan was quickly losing strength.

As Denny helped him get back into bed, Kellan looked between Denny and Abby and stammered, "You're here? You both came all the way over here? For me?"

Once Kellan was lying down, Denny sighed and ran a hand through his hair. "Yeah, we came here for you." He glanced at Abby, then turned back to Kellan. "It scared the piss outta me, when I found out you were hurt. All I could think was that . . ." Swallowing, Denny looked away.

Realizing this moment had nothing to do with me, I stayed against the wall and tried to be inconspicuous. Abby moved beside me and gave me a soft smile as she patted my hand. I could tell by the look on her face that she was silently acknowledging all of the pain I'd gone through today, and offering me her support and friendship. I clasped her hand, grateful, and then the both of us turned to watch our fiancés.

When Denny could continue, he told Kellan, "We used to be close. We used to be like brothers. And if you died . . . it would be like a part of my family had died. And I don't think you realize that." His eyes returned to Kellan's. "I hate the idea of you dying without knowing how much I . . ." Closing his mouth, he sniffed, then said, "I don't know, I feel like, maybe I haven't been the greatest friend to you."

"Denny—"

Kellan tried to interrupt him, but Denny wouldn't let him. "I knew what was going on, Kellan, with you and your dad, and I didn't say anything to anybody. I didn't help you like I should have."

"You were a kid," Kellan muttered.

"So were you," he retorted. "And when I moved away, I didn't keep in touch like I promised." Clearly angry at himself, Denny shook his head. "You needed me, and I wasn't there for you. And I'm really sorry. That was pretty shitty of me."

"Are you kidding?" Incredulous, Kellan pointed over at me.

"I slept with your girlfriend . . . repeatedly." I flinched, and Abby squeezed my hand a little tighter.

Denny frowned. "Well, that was pretty shitty of you." A sad smile darkened his features. "But I left you alone in hell . . . and I almost think that was worse." He stuck his hand out to Kellan. "I know we've already put the past behind us, and I know we're friends, but I want you to know, without a doubt in your head, that we're still brothers. You understand me?"

Kellan still seemed shocked to his core, but he nodded and shook Denny's hand. "Yeah, yeah, okay."

Chapter 28
I Do

My mom was the first one to return to the hospital the next morning—bright and early the next morning. I was still sleeping on a chair in the corner of the room when she placed her hand on my shoulder. "Here, honey," she whispered.

Groggily opening my eyes, I noticed the steaming cup of liquid she was holding and smiled. Coffee. And the good kind too—it was in a paper cup from an espresso stand, not a Styrofoam one from a vending machine. God, I loved my mom. "Thank you."

Mom leaned against the windowsill, sipping her own cup of coffee, as she watched Kellan sleeping. Then her eyes drifted over to Denny, asleep in a chair on the other side of Kellan's bed. I'd called Evan last night and asked him to return to the hospital to take Denny and Abby to the hotel the band was staying at the night before, but after making sure that Abby was settled, Denny had decided to stay with Kellan. Maybe seeing that a crucial moment was happening, the nurse on duty had let him.

Mom's long brown hair was pulled back into a springy ponytail, giving me a full view of her expression. I couldn't tell what she was thinking, though. As I took a sip of my creamy caffeinated treat, I considered how odd it must seem to her to have my ex here. An ex I had cheated on with Kellan.

After another quiet moment of contemplation, Mom turned to me. Pointing at Denny with her pinky finger, she asked, "He really loves you, doesn't he?"

She seemed concerned, like somehow he was a threat to Kellan. I loved that she felt protective of my husband. My lips creeping into a smile, I shook my head. "No, he loves Kellan. He came here for him." My smile grew as I watched both boys sleeping. "He told Kellan they were still brothers . . . even after everything."

Mom's eyes widened as she took another sip of coffee. "That is a very forgiving friend that you both have. I hope you and Kellan realize how rare that is."

I nodded, my eyes stinging. I did. We did. And we'd never do anything to hurt him again.

The boys slept for another hour; we'd all been up late talking, and they had still been whispering when I drifted off to sleep. I think Kellan would have slept longer, but a nurse arrived to check on him and woke him up. The nurse asked him how he was feeling, how his pain was, if he was hungry, if he'd gotten up, if he'd gone to the bathroom; all the personal stuff that nurses don't seem to mind asking in mixed company. Kellan didn't seem embarrassed as he sleepily answered her, though. He actually seemed content.

Gavin, his children, and my father arrived at the hospital while Kellan was eating a watery-looking omelet for breakfast; it was the first thing I'd seen him eat since the accident. When Dad and Gavin walked into the room, they were having a lively discussion about the Pittsburgh Pirates and the Cincinnati Reds. I couldn't stop grinning as the two men went back and forth about which baseball team was better. No topic bonded my father faster to someone than sports. And my parents becoming friends with Kellan's parent was a very good thing.

Abby, Anna, and the D-Bags showed up with Justin mid-morning. That was still on the early side for the band members, and most of them were yawning when they raised their hands in greeting. Gibson wasn't in the room two seconds before Mom stole the bundle of pink out of Griffin's arms. He frowned at Mom, but he let his daughter go. Tossing an arm around me, Anna laughed and said, "No one else is going to get to hold her the entire time Mom's visiting."

I watched Mom rock Gibson as a thought struck me. "How long are you staying, Mom? I mean, Thanksgiving is coming up. Aren't you expecting company back home?"

Her eyes never leaving her granddaughter, Mom shook her head. "We canceled. We're staying here for Thanksgiving." She finally peeked up at me. "We'll fly back when Kellan is well enough to leave with you." She turned her smile to him. "Family sticks together."

I wasn't too surprised by Mom's news, but it was wonderful to hear. Hopeful, I looked over at Gavin. He pointed over at Riley playing a video game and Hailey flipping through a gossip magazine. The photo of Kellan and I kissing in the graveyard was on the cover. "The kids are on break from school, and I already told work there was a family emergency and that I wasn't coming back until Monday." His warm smile outshone his son's. "You're stuck with me until then."

Kellan grinned and looked down. "That means a lot to me. Thank you."

From the expression on the D-Bags' faces, I knew they were all sticking close to Kellan during the holiday, so I didn't even ask. I wasn't sure about Justin's schedule, though; I couldn't remember where his band was at. After I asked him, he told me, "We've got one more gig tonight, then we're free 'til next week." Leaning over, he asked Hailey and Riley, "Hey, you guys wanna see Avoiding Redemption tonight? Maybe hang backstage with some rock stars?" Gavin cleared his throat, and Justin snapped his head to him. "With your permission, of course."

Since Hailey and Riley were begging and bouncing up and down in their seats, Gavin really didn't have a choice but to say yes. Pointing at Hailey, he added, "You keep an eye on your brother. And no drinking."

Hailey rolled her eyes, then turned to Kellan. "See what I have to put up with."

Kellan gave her a crooked smile. "Yeah, he's a real brute." I raised my eyebrow at Kellan's comment, but his expression was amused, not pained, so I felt okay to laugh.

While light chuckles went around the room, my gaze shifted to Denny and Abby. "What about you two? When are you heading back?"

Denny put his arm around Abby, pulling her in close. "Well, this is Abby's first Thanksgiving in the states, and she wanted the full holiday experience. She even made me promise to watch the Macy's Thanksgiving Day Parade with her on television." He rolled his eyes while Abby gave him a playful scowl. I chuckled at the annoyance on Denny's face, but I knew better. He was probably looking forward to giving Abby a dream holiday, parade-watching included; there really wasn't much Denny wouldn't do for the person he loved.

Denny laughed at the look on Abby's face, then told me, "We talked about it on the flight over, and we've decided to stay through the holiday."

Abby patted his chest. Her engagement ring sparkled in the rays coming through the open window, matching her personality. "Denny's taking me to see the parade in person!" She giggled, and I could tell she was truly overjoyed about watching enormous balloons traversing through the city above elaborately decorated floats.

From across the room, Griffin discretely coughed, "Wuss." Anna giggled, but respectfully elbowed him. I thought defending Denny was pretty big of her, since he wasn't her favorite person. I guess his showing up here had really impressed her.

Smiling that everyone was staying for a few days, I stood up. "Well, I have a proposition then."

Walking around to Kellan's bag of belongings on the nightstand, I rummaged through it until I found the zip-top bag holding his promise ring. Kellan watched me with curious eyes as I removed the small bag from the larger one. Opening it, I fished out his ring and showed it to him.

Gingerly sitting on the edge of his bed, I reached across him for his left hand; my shoulder ached a little with the movement, but it was already feeling much better. Heart hammering in nerves and excitement, I told him, in a low voice meant only for his ears, "Kellan Kyle, you are the love of my life. You have my heart from now until the end of forever. Will you please make me the happiest woman on earth and marry me . . . Thursday."

After I slid the ring on his finger, Kellan cinched my hand. Eyes bright, he asked, "You want to get married on Thanksgiving . . . *here*?" He looked around the clinical room, the mechanical bed he'd only left a couple of times so far. It didn't exactly scream romance.

Content with my decision, I nodded. "The where doesn't matter . . . just the who. I can't wait another month to officially marry you, and what better way could we celebrate a day of giving thanks than by becoming husband and wife?" I indicated the people in the room staring at us. "The most important people in our lives are already here." I frowned. "Except Jenny and the girls. We'll just have to fly them back out to us. They should really be here for this."

Evan was leaning against a wall, his face bursting with uncontainable happiness. "Not a problem. I'll have Jujube gather the girls and head on over. She wouldn't want to miss this." He twisted his lips. "And I would never hear the end of it if she did."

And just like that, the entire moment felt perfect. I looked back at Kellan. "See? This is how we were supposed to get married."

Kellan's face shifted from surprise to wonder. "You'll really be my wife . . ."

Laughing as my eyes moistened, I gave him a soft kiss. "And you'll really be my husband."

From behind me, I heard my mother loudly exhale. "Here, Kiera? Really?"

I turned to look at her. She had a rigid frown as she looked around the room. "But we already sent out the invitations. We have family coming in from out of state, cousins you haven't seen in a decade or more. And everything is ready at our church. There's going to be a potluck after the ceremony. Polly is bringing her world-famous baked beans, and Gertrude is so excited to play the organ for you. She's ninety-eight, Kiera. She's only got a year or two left in her . . ."

Baked beans? Schooling my features, I risked a glance at Anna; she was quietly dying with laughter.

Standing, I walked over to Mom and grabbed her shoulders. "Mom, I almost lost my husband yesterday. I don't want to wait another minute to become his wife. Will you please help me get married on Thursday?"

A long, fat tear rolled down Mom's cheek. "Of course I will."

I dried her skin. "Good, then find someone who can marry us on really, really short notice."

Mom immediately went into active planning mode. "Okay, I'm sure somebody around here is qualified to marry people." She started pacing. "We'll need to spruce the place up a bit, get some flowers." She looked over at Kellan's many get-well bouquets, bouquets that had been steadily growing once fans realized he was here. "Oh, well, those will work." Gently bouncing Gibson, her face fell as she twisted to me. "Oh, your dress . . . I should have brought it with me. It was perfect."

I tried to look disappointed, but I'd heard all about the puffy-sleeved fiasco from my sister. Giving Mom a consoling smile, I shrugged. "Yeah, that is too bad. But Anna and I will find something, I'm sure."

Anna sprang to her feet. "And we'll get you your marriage license." She winked at me. I suspected that both people were supposed to apply for them at the same time, but Kellan was sort of bed-prone at the moment. I had no doubt about Anna's ability to persuade people, though, especially men. God, I hoped the person in the county clerk's office was a man.

Mom did the unthinkable and handed Gibson over to someone else. Griffin took his daughter back as Mom told the room that she needed a phone, a phonebook, a pad of paper, and another espresso—pronto! Gavin left to get my mom some coffee while Dad ransacked the room to get her everything else she needed to make my impromptu wedding a reality. I was elated as I watched her get to work.

Anna tugged on my arm. There was a glow in her green eyes that matched Mom's. "Let's go find you a dress today!"

Giggling, I skipped over to Kellan and gave him a light kiss. "We'll be back in a little bit. Will you be all right here?" Kellan looked just as euphoric as I felt as he nodded. In pain or not, I knew he was the happiest that he'd ever been. I knew, because that's exactly how I felt. *I was getting married!*

Griffin nodded at Anna when she asked if he could watch Gibson while we were shopping. From the way he was holding his child, it was pretty obvious that he hadn't been going to give her up anyway. Anna had just fed her not too long ago, but we'd have to make this outing on the short side. At least, on the short side for my sister; she could spend an entire day in just the shoe section.

After Kellan begged me for a final kiss, Griffin murmured, "Your wedding day is Thanksgiving. That's convenient." He pointed at Kellan. "You probably won't forget your anniversary." He looked over at Anna. "We shoulda done that. I already forgot ours."

Anna smirked at Griffin while Kellan's lip twitched. "Uh, it won't always be on Thanksgiving, Griff."

He looked horribly confused. "Huh? Yeah, it will."

Kellan bit his lip. I could tell he was trying really hard not to laugh, since laughing hurt. "Thanksgiving isn't on the same day every year. It moves around."

Griffin glared at Kellan. "Don't even try fucking with me, Kell." He tapped his finger to his head. "I'm on to you."

I heard Matt and Evan snigger with Justin and Denny. My dad stared at the ceiling as he shook his head. I couldn't contain my giggle; poor Kellan had to take long, slow exhales so he didn't laugh with everyone else. "Griff, I'm not . . ."

Still laughing, I patted Kellan's leg. "You should probably just let this one go."

A laugh escaped Kellan, and he lightly held his stomach. "Damn idiot," he muttered, his face scrunched in discomfort.

Feeling like Kellan was in good hands, I squeezed his leg and headed out of the room with Anna. Once in the hallway, she whispered, "Thanksgiving really isn't on the same day every year?" I almost stopped myself from laughing at her. Almost.

I explained to Carly what we were planning as Anna called a cab. The helpful nurse seemed a little surprised, since I'd told her that Kellan and I were already married, but a romantic smile lit her face as she agreed to help us out. When Anna and I exited the hospital, our cab was waiting for us near the front doors. I was surprised by the number of fans loitering around the hospital. The window in Kellan's room hadn't given me a full view of them. Not only were they directly across the street, but they were also along the side streets, huddled at the street corners and in large clumps around the entrances. The various groups started pointing and whispering when they noticed me.

Probably remembering the footage she had watched of me accidentally being pushed into the street by a mob, Anna was immediately on edge. "Let's hurry and get in the cab, Kiera."

I couldn't stop staring at the mass of people waiting, though. They looked genuinely distraught; some were even wiping tears away. Tears. For Kellan. It broke my heart. I was sure no one from the hospital had given these people any clue as to how Kellan was doing. They had probably only asked them to leave, or at least repeatedly asked them to stay out of the way. Tory had issued a dramatic statement to the press, but a blurb from a record label wasn't exactly comforting. Maybe *I* could be comforting.

Feeling every muscle in my stomach tighten, I locked gazes with my sister. "I'll be right back."

She narrowed her eyes at me. "What are you doing?"

Swallowing, I looked back at the crowd. What the hell was I doing? "I just want to let them know he's okay."

As Anna and I started to cross the street, the crowd along the sidewalk seemed to simultaneously shift in our direction. My whole body started shaking. I fought down my fear and anxiety and approached them with my head high. How did Kellan conquer his nerves when he first started going on stage? Do I picture the crowd naked? Unfortunately, *I* was the only one I could picture naked, and that wasn't helping my anxiety any. Instead of picturing them, or me, I imagined Kellan beside me, walking toward his eager fans with a charming half-smile on his face. I thought of the symbiotic relationship he had with these people, how important they were to each other, and how I could help bridge the gap between them today. My nerves vanished.

As soon as I got close enough, the fans started speaking. And all of them were asking me variations of the same question: *Is Kellan okay?* I held up my hands, and they instantly quieted.

In a more confident voice than I ever believed I was capable of using when addressing a swarm of people, I told them, "Kellan wanted me to tell all of you that he's fine." Remembering his pained face whenever he stood or laughed, I added, "Sore . . . but fine." As tears pricked my eyes, I brought my hands to my heart. "He is touched beyond words that you're here, sending out your love and well-wishes, and I know he would come down and thank each one of you individually if he could. Your support means a lot to him. To us. And we can't thank you enough."

The emotion of the last twenty-four hours caught up to me. It sealed my throat shut and forced the water in my eyes to run down my cheeks. As I hastily brushed tears away, I heard the crowd murmuring grateful thank-yous. As I turned to leave, someone in the back shouted, "Are you really his wife?"

A slow smile spread across my lips. *Yes, I will be.* Feeling close to this crowd of strangers, who deeply loved the same person I deeply loved, I told them the truth. "We've been married in our hearts for a long time, but . . . we're making it official this week." Not able to stop myself, I giggled as I said, "I'll be Mrs. Kyle by Thursday night."

Surprising me, the crowd erupted into screams and cheers. It made me laugh even more. And cry. Amazed that they were accepting me, my words escaped my mouth in an emotional jumble. "I have to go find a dress now."

Names and addresses of nearby stores were shouted at me. I was too overwhelmed to take it all in, but I saw my sister nodding as she absorbed it. She may not know when Thanksgiving falls on the calendar, but she was a savant when it came to memorizing sales.

I was still giggling about my very surreal life when Anna and I climbed into the cab. Anna pulled out her phone as she gave the driver the name of the store that was on top of her mental rolodex. I relaxed back into the seat, content. I was finally marrying Kellan. I couldn't wait. After a minute or so of silence, my sister nudged my arm. "Have you seen this?" she asked.

She showed me her phone. She was on a gossip site and, not surprisingly, the story about Kellan's accident was being featured. The still shots were horrifying. There were successive pictures of Kellan pulling me to my feet, shoving me behind him, holding out his hand, and the truck striking him. It made all of the fear from yesterday fresh in my mind. It made the injury upon my scalp burn anew, like it had just happened. If the truck had been going just a little faster, if Kellan had fallen back and smacked his head against the curb, if more internal organs had been damaged, I would have lost him.

As I swiped tears from my eyes, I noticed what my sister had wanted me to see. Below the photos were comments from fans. Hundreds of comments. And all of them were praising Kellan for his actions and proclaiming him a hero. Reading all of their heartfelt thoughts and prayers for his recovery warmed me. Reading about myself in the comments surprised me: *He stepped into traffic for her! He saved her life! That's true love. They belong together. They're perfect together. I never believed he was with Sienna.*

The outpouring of support for our relationship took me back. It was as if our accident had flipped a switch on the masses, and they were all announcing us as the new power couple. In the blink of an eye, I'd gone from the condemned other woman trying to steal Sienna's man to Kellan's soul mate. The change was so fast and drastic that my mind almost couldn't grasp it. And the fact that my head hurt and my stitches itched wasn't helping anything.

I looked back at Anna, floored. "They love us."

Anna gave me a humoring smile. "*Everyone* eventually falls for the two of you together. You're meant to be."

We had so much to do in so little time that I quickly put the mystery of ever-changing public perception out of my mind. When we were finished with dress shopping, I felt like I had run a marathon I was so tired. But I had everything I needed. Anna and I had even worked out the marriage license. I'd been worried about that one, but Anna had poured on the charm and the clerk had agreed to come to the hospital so Kellan and I could fill out the application together. Honestly, I think the female clerk just wanted to see Kellan in person. Her eyes had shone like the stars when she'd figured out just who was asking for permission to get married.

This was really going to happen.

Preparations began in earnest the following day when my numerous bridesmaids arrived. I squealed when Jenny, Rachel, Kate, and Cheyenne walked into Kellan's hospital room. My four friends encased me in a tearful group hug while the boys in the room shook their heads in amusement. Boys just didn't understand the power of girlfriends.

Overwhelmed and emotional, I sniffled as I told Jenny, "I can't believe you're here. Thank you for flying back out so soon."

Jenny's hazy eyes drifted to the healing cut along my forehead. "I wouldn't miss your wedding day for the world." Her gaze shifted to Kellan lying in his bed, smiling at us. "And I had to make sure you were okay. You scared the crap out of me, Kellan."

Kellan's lips curved up in a wry grin. "My apologies."

Jenny laughed at him, then walked over and gave him a quick hug while I thanked each girl in turn. Kellan and I had paid for their plane tickets and arranged for hotel rooms, but they'd each had to shift their lives around to make this happen for us. I was extremely grateful to them, to all of the people who were there.

After the greetings were over, Rachel cuddled with Matt, Kate nervously stood by Justin, and Cheyenne tried to get Gibson away from my mother. She failed. Jenny wrapped her arms around Evan and giggled. "While I'm thrilled to be here, I can't believe you're getting married in a hospital room, Kiera."

My mom sighed in agreement. I rolled my eyes at Mom as I faced my troops. "We've got a lot to do today." I indicated the stale hospital room around me. "We need to make this room suitable for a wedding tomorrow."

Standing beside me with Abby, Denny slowly shook his head as he took in the garish medical equipment and utilitarian furniture. "That is not going to be easy," he murmured.

I nodded in agreement. "No, but thank you for helping me."

Wide smile in place, he told me, "It's what I do."

Looking over at Mom, I asked her, "Did you find someone to marry us?"

Pleased as punch, Mom kissed her granddaughter's head as she beamed. "I did!" She pointed a finger at Kellan. "One of the nurses that helped sew him back together is an ordained minister. She said she'd be thrilled to marry a rock star."

Kellan laughed, then put a hand on his stomach. He still looked a little pale, and his eyes were still a little sunken, but he was slowly getting better.

Clapping my hands that everything was falling into place, I indicated all of the girls in the room. "Anna and I picked up my dress yesterday, but we'll need to get you all bridesmaid dresses."

Abby blinked in surprise. "Even me?"

I peered around Denny to smile at her. "Definitely you."

Abby flushed with color and seemed really touched that I would extend such a courtesy to her. She was a part of Denny though, and he was my best friend. They were as much of a unit as Kellan and I, so it was only right that they both be included. Glancing over all of Kellan's groomsmen, I frowned.

"Hmmm, will you guys be able to get suits today?" They were all dressed in holey jeans and threadbare T-shirts. I wasn't such a bridezilla that I needed them in tuxes, but a tiny step up from their typical wardrobe would be nice.

Grinning ear to ear, Griffin tucked his hair behind his ears. "Not to worry, I've got the suit I want all picked out."

My frown even deeper, I pointed at Matt. "Do not let him leave the store if he's wearing any sort of pastel color." I paused, then added, "Or anything assless."

After Matt wholeheartedly agreed, I shrugged. "That just leaves dinner."

Gavin raised his hand. "Martin and I did a little reconnaissance yesterday, and we found the perfect place. They serve traditional Thanksgiving dinners and are open on the holiday." A Kellan-esque grin spread across his lips. "They even agreed to deliver to the hospital for us."

I beamed at the two fathers in my life working together. Smiling at everyone, I shook my head. "Let's get to work, then."

The girls and I took off to find dresses, while the boys left to find suits. I felt a little bad leaving Kellan alone, but Carly assured me that he would be well taken care of, and he needed the rest anyway. I made sure to kiss him at least a dozen times before I left, though.

Instead of finding matching dresses for everyone, I let them choose their own styles. I didn't want anyone to be forced into something they found atrocious, like puffy sleeves. My only suggestion was that they all chose the same color—a rich deep red that reminded me of Christmas, and Kellan, and love.

Hailey chose something fun and flirty, Anna chose something so tight I doubt she could breathe. The rest of the girls' styles matched their personalities, demure and exotic for Rachel, playful for Jenny, sophisticated for Abby, and romantic for Cheyenne and Kate. Anna picked out a stunning red frilly dress for Gibson; she was going to outshine us all. Even my mom went with the red theme and found a nice cocktail dress that I was sure she'd wear over and over during the holiday season.

After dress shopping, we all brainstormed ways to romanticize the hospital room. Abby and Jenny were particularly good at decorating and came up with a plan that I thought would turn out nice. It was also going to stretch the nurse's patience, but hopefully they'd tolerate the slight disruption to their order. I mean, how often can you say a rock star got married at your workplace?

I was greeted with loud cheers from the ever-vigilant fans when we returned to the hospital. Their numbers weren't dissipating any, not even with the upcoming holiday. If anything, now that news of my nuptials was out there, the number of people was growing. Even a few photographers were in the mix. I didn't care, though. I held my head high as I waved to the group.

"We love you, Kiera!" was their response.

That still made me shake my head in disbelief. *They loved me?* Even if I disagreed with their statement—they didn't really know me, so how could they love me?—I appreciated the sentiment. It filled my chest with hope, love, and a general feeling that all was right with the world. And I supposed that was exactly how a person should feel when they were about to get married.

The boys were already back from their shopping trip when we returned to the room. Abby and Jenny laid out their decorating plan. The D-Bags looked confused by the explanations, but Denny nodded and instantly started getting to work. He had an eye for design and a knack for aesthetics. It was one of the many things that made him so good at his job.

Denny and Abby worked together seamlessly as they rearranged the room. There was an unspoken communication between the two of them that was adorable to watch. Denny would merely look at something with an eyebrow raised, and Abby would nod and say, "Yeah, I think so too." They really were a great match.

While Mom held Gibson and Anna supervised from the only

semi-comfortable chair in the room, a handful of us tried to hide some of the unsightly machinery. Riley and I were standing on step stools, awkwardly attempting to hang a superlong linen sheet from the ceiling; I was trying to keep my shoulder rested by not lifting my right arm too high, which made decorating a bit challenging. Kellan frowned while he watched me. "I feel completely and totally useless."

Dropping the sheet, I huffed a stray lock of hair out of my eyes and smirked at Kellan. "Well, that's what happens when you go and tear an internal organ. Maybe next time you should be more careful."

Kellan's lips curled into a sexy half-smile. "The next time we're hit by a floral truck, I'll be sure to do that."

My mother's face paled. "Not funny, you two."

The clerk from the city arrived when we were halfway done with decorations. She seemed flustered to be near Kellan, and even though he wasn't feeling all that hot, he did his best to put her at ease. Perhaps excited that there was finally something he could do to help, Kellan even flirted with the woman a little. Her cheeks flamed bright red, and Kellan shot me an amused glance. Just like the clerk, I had been a blushing mess when Kellan had first started flirting with me. There was nothing that I could have done about it, though. Kellan was just too sensuous for his own good.

By the end of the day everyone was tired, but everything was all set, and I was ready to marry the man of my dreams.

I couldn't sleep at all that night, especially since Anna had made me go back to the hotel with her and the girls. She said I couldn't spend the night before my wedding with my fiancé. When I told her she'd spent the night before her wedding with hers, she scoffed in my face. "Griffin and I are way different than you and Kellan." Pointing a finger at Mom holding Gibson, she'd added, "We did everything back-asswards."

The next morning, Abby disappeared for a few hours to go watch the parade with Denny while the other girls prepped me for my big event. Even though it was a holiday, we were able to get manicures, pedicures, and relaxing facials. New York City really did never sleep. Abby returned while Mom was getting my dress ready, and Jenny and Kate were curling my hair into long loose ringlets. Saying that the natural look suited me better than a fancy updo, they left my hair flowing down my back and across my shoulders. When they were content with my finished look, Anna went to town on my makeup. I reminded her that I was a pretty simple person, so my makeup shouldn't be too much.

Without skipping a beat, she told me, "Don't worry, I'll leave the whore makeup for your wedding *night*." Leaning in she added, "By the way, I asked a nurse for you, and you guys will be able to start knockin' boots again in four to six weeks."

Even though she'd just done my mascara, I closed my eyes in embarrassment as all the girls in the room tittered, our mother included. TMI, Anna. T. M. I.

Seeing my mortification, Anna giggled and merrily stated, "You're welcome." A laugh escaped me, and opening my eyes, I gave my sister a warm smile. I suppose that *was* information I needed to know.

Mom helped me slip into my dress when the girls were all done beautifying me. Anna and I had found a very simple satin, tank-top dress. It was a brilliant white color that had a bit of a shimmer to it— it was elegant and modest, but stunning too; Anna said it suited me to a tee, but I personally thought it suited Kellan to a tee. They were no frills on it—no lace, no beads, no ribbons, no elaborate sleeves. It was beautiful simply because it was beautiful. Like Kellan, the dress didn't need any enhancements.

I slipped on a pair of simple white shoes, then turned to look at myself in the mirror. I almost couldn't believe it was me I was looking at. With bouncing curls, moderately smoky eyes, and a gleaming white dress, I looked like something straight out of a fairy tale—the princess about to marry her prince. Except, instead of a crown, this princess had a sparkling guitar necklace draped around her neck. Even I had to admit . . . I was gorgeous.

Mom had tears rolling down her cheeks as she snapped pictures of me on her phone with one hand while juggling Gibson with her other. If she was crying already, she was going to be a wreck by the actual wedding. She might need a Valium. Good thing we were going to a hospital. Feeling my eyes start to fill, I warned her, "Stop it, you're going to make me cry and ruin my makeup."

Mom sniffed as she made a valiant attempt to control herself. "Sorry, honey, you're just so beautiful."

Grabbing her elbow, I inhaled a deep, calming breath. "I'm ready. Take me to my husband so I can finally marry him."

My dad had arranged for a limo to pick us all up. It was a plain one, clearly on the bottom of the rental scale. There were no real frills on the inside except a shelf in the wall holding bottled water. It was perfect, and I greatly preferred this simplicity to the overdone elegance of Sienna's limo.

The limo dropped us off right in front of the hospital. The fans outside went ballistic when they saw me. They tossed out such flowery compliments that my cheeks felt heated, but I smiled and gave them a gracious curtsy anyway. I even waved for the paparazzi. Let them splash my face all over the magazines. It would only give me more photos to use for my wedding album.

Our entourage walking through the halls had to have been a strange sight, but all I saw everywhere I looked were smiles. The nurses, the doctors, the other patients—everyone seemed as excited about this moment as I was. Well, maybe not as much as I was. I was nearly bursting at the seams as I clung to Mom's arm. When we got to Kellan's floor, rose petals were scattered along the ground. My eyes misted up just seeing the bright red velvet. My vision watery, I followed the path marked in flowers.

When I reached the hallway that led to Kellan's room, the moisture in my eyes grew disastrously thick. Dressed in gray slacks and a dark blue button-up top, my dad was waiting for me at the end of the hall. He looked ten years younger as pride filled his face. New tears spilling from her eyes, Mom handed me off to Dad. Whispering, "I have never been more proud of you," in my ear, he enclosed me in a warm hug. It took everything in me to not start crying.

Holding on to Dad for dear life, I looked down the hallway toward where the injured love of my life was waiting for me. The corridor was lined with at least a dozen nurses, doctors, technicians, and other staff members, and all of them were holding the softly glowing vigil candlesticks that the fans outside were using. Some patients' doors were open, with curious faces peeking through the cracks, but I didn't care one tiny little bit if strangers were watching this bizarre spectacle. *I was getting married today.*

The hallway floor was also littered with red rose petals, and at the end of the hallway, standing right in front of Kellan's door, was Deacon. He had Kellan's acoustic guitar strapped around his neck. The minute he saw me, his face split into a wide smile. "You're beautiful," he mouthed, then he started to strum my favorite D-Bags song. I just about lost it. My mother did.

Carly handed Anna and Jenny small bouquets that had been gifts from Kellan's fans; she gave Kate, Cheyenne, Rachel, Abby, and Hailey flickering candles. She handed me a bouquet of white and yellow Cala Lillies. I hadn't seen these in Kellan's room. Seeing my confusion, she shrugged. "I ordered them this morning."

Awed and impressed, I gave her a swift hug as each of my bridesmaids started drifting across the petal-strewn tile; their dresses perfectly matched the roses. Once they disappeared into the room, Deacon's song shifted to the traditional wedding march. I couldn't stop the tears then, and Mom quickly dabbed my eyes before running to the end of the hall so she could film my father walking me to my husband.

I had no idea how I did it, but I made it to the end of the hallway upright. I was shaking so bad, I was sure Dad could feel it. He patted my arm in reassurance as he helped me along. I gave Deacon a brief smile, then turned toward Kellan's room. Even though I'd helped set it up, the room marveled me. Long, silky tablecloths were hung from the ceiling all the way around the sides of the room, hiding the telltale signs that we were in a hospital. Strands of tube lighting were hung along the tops of each sheet-curtain and in between the seams. It bathed the dimly lit room in warmth.

The hospital had placed red industrial carpets from the door to the other end of the room where the minister, dressed in a sharp black pantsuit, was waiting by the wide window. Linens wrapped with tube lighting and flowers were hung in a way that framed the window, like an altar; outside the window, I could see the swarms of fans in the background. The floor was covered with the rest of Nick's ostentatious floral arrangement. The remainder of the bouquets lined the windowsill.

Except for Kellan's bed, all of the furniture had been removed from the room, creating space for the guests to stand. As my eyes drifted around the area packed full of witnesses who loved Kellan and me, each of whom was holding a flickering candlestick, I was overwhelmed with love.

The remaining members of Holeshot and Avoiding Redemption were here, clustered near the door. Still playing the guitar, Deacon moved into the room behind me. Jenny and Anna were standing to the left of the minister; both of their cheeks were wet. Evan was standing on the right side, and Denny was standing in a spot of great honor beside him. Grinning ear to ear, Denny nodded at me and minutely lifted his candle.

The rest of our massive wedding party was lining the carpet leading to Kellan's bed, boys on one side, girls on the other. Faces full of pride, Matt and Griffin were standing beside Justin, Gavin, and Riley. Opposite them were the rest of my girls, Rachel, Kate, Cheyenne, Abby, and Hailey. Griffin was rocking Gibson back and forth, the tiny baby fast asleep in her father's arms. And much to my relief, Griffin was dressed similarly to the other boys in a solid black dress shirt with matching black slacks that I'm assuming had a back to them.

My blurry vision drifted to my husband as my father and I passed by the bridal party and stepped to the foot of the hospital bed. Kellan's eyes were glossy as he stared back at me. "You're breathtaking," he murmured. While I'd been gone, someone had helped Kellan put on real clothes. He was lying on top of the covers and had on a loose, white button-up shirt draped over dark black slacks. And he was barefoot. Even a little banged up, I thought he looked pretty breathtaking too.

I stood at the end of his bed, fully prepared to climb in with him and get married lying down, but Kellan held his hand up to stop me. "Wait."

Preparing himself for pain, he started to sit up. I immediately took a step away from my father. "No, Kellan, don't. You're still weak, you can lie down. You don't have to stand for this."

Cringing in discomfort, he grabbed onto his IV stand with white knuckles. "I've been waiting my entire life to marry you, Kiera. I think I'll stand."

Gavin instantly handed his candle to Riley and rushed to Kellan's side. It almost made me laugh that *both* of our fathers were helping us to the altar, but I was too touched by Kellan's actions to do anything but cry—a happy, pride-filled cry.

After Kellan jerkily made his way to the nurse marrying us, his father stepped back. My dad kissed my cheek before letting me go. Fearful of Kellan toppling over, I rushed in to take the void left by Gavin. Kellan smiled down at me, then let out a low, controlled exhale. "I'm okay."

Wanting to match Kellan, I kicked off my shoes and tossed them out of the way; rose petals stuck to the soles of my feet. Aside from the IV stand Kellan was holding on to for support, we looked like we were getting married on a beach, and I could easily imagine the sound of the ocean in the background—although that could have been the rustling of all the people trying to pack themselves around the door so they could watch.

Kellan laughed as I curled my toes on the carpet, and he didn't cringe as much as he had yesterday. While the minister thanked everyone for being there, Kellan reached into his pocket and placed something in my palm. Discretely looking, I saw a rose petal with the words *Forever Your Husband* written in bold black letters.

I clenched it in my hand as the tears mercilessly rolled down my cheeks. I wanted to lean up and kiss him, but we weren't at that part yet, so I restrained myself. *Not* kissing Kellan Kyle is very hard to do, especially when he was looking at me like I was the most miraculous thing he'd ever seen.

I clasped Kellan's free hand with both of mine as the minister directed her speech toward us. "Kellan Kyle, Kiera Allen, your friends and family are gathered here today to watch your two separate lives merge into one. From this point forward, you will face the trials, tribulations, and triumphs of life as one being. You will be bound together, body and soul, and the desires of the one will be forsaken for the needs of the two. But there is strength to be gained from this bond, for each of you. Where one might break, two can stand tall. Where one might fold, two can hold firm. From here until the end of your days on earth, you will have someone to support you during times of weakness, comfort you during times of grief, encourage you during times of fear, and celebrate with you during times of joy. That is a gift, one that should never be abused or taken for granted. Cherish each other as God cherishes you, and you will both know peace."

I squeezed Kellan's hand as I glanced up at him. We'd been through so much already, but she was right—we were strongest when we were together. We lifted each other up, brought out the best in each other. We were better people together. From somewhere behind me, I could hear my mother sobbing.

Looking to the Best Man and Maid of Honor, the minister asked, "Do you have the rings?"

Anna nodded as she wiped her tears away with a knuckle. Kellan and I had handed over our rings while decorating. I was a bit relieved that Anna hadn't lost Kellan's. Motherhood had done wonders for her responsibility. Her eyes swimming with more tears waiting to fall, Anna handed me Kellan's promise ring. Evan's face was equally emotional as he handed Kellan my wedding ring.

As Kellan and I faced each other, the nurse leaned in and asked, "Do you want me to say the standard vows, or would you like to say your own?"

Looking deep into my eyes, Kellan immediately responded with, "I'd like to say something."

Lost in his dark blue depths, I deflated the encroaching ball of nerves in my stomach, nodded, and said, "I'd like to say something too."

Looking pleased, she indicated for Kellan to start. Letting go of his stabilizing IV stand, Kellan wobbled on his feet for a second. Evan looked ready to hold him upright, but, face pale, Kellan managed on his own. Grabbing my left hand, Kellan tenderly opened my fingers; the warmth of his touch shot up my arm.

Placing the circle of metal at the end of my ring finger, his soft voice filled the space between us. "Kiera Michelle Allen, my life was empty before you stepped into it. I thought I had everything I needed, but only because I didn't let myself want anything. And then I saw you, and you burned a hole straight through me. I have never wanted anything more in my life. And I have never been more terrified in all my life. In *all* my life," he repeated.

I swallowed; I understood how dire that sentence was. I felt like he was cutting me open and caressing me at the exact same time. I wanted to say something, but a look of absolute wonder filled Kellan's expression. "And then, beyond some miracle that I'll never understand, I got to keep you, and now . . . I'm only just beginning to understand what it means to *truly* want something. Because I want so much now. I want to make you happy. I want to give you the world. I want you to be proud of me. I want to comfort you. I want you to comfort me. I want to hold you when you're scared. I want you to hold me when I'm scared. I want to make you laugh. I want to make you blush." Leaning in, he whispered, "I want to make you scream."

I subsequently blushed, and Kellan chuckled. Sliding the ring over my knuckle, he told me, "I want to give you a home. I want to fill it with children. I want to take care of you. I want to grow old with you. I want you by my side, every day." Folding his hand over mine once my ring was in place, he shrugged and shook his head. "I just want you. Do you want me too?"

I could barely speak I was so choked up. Man, he had a way with words. Somehow, I managed to squeak out an, "I do."

The smile that blossomed over Kellan's face brightened his pallid cheeks. Wondering how on earth I could possibly follow up that speech, I inhaled a calming breath and swallowed a half-dozen times.

Gently grabbing Kellan's hand, I slid his ring onto his finger. "I never thought of myself as anything but plain and ordinary until you came along. The way you look at me, the way you see me . . . you pull something out of me. When I want to hide, you urge me forward. When I think I'm not good enough, you make me believe I am. When I feel anything but pretty, you convince me I'm beautiful. Just being around you makes me feel special. You don't think you're good at loving people, but you are. Your friends, your family . . . the level of love that you have for people astounds me. You don't think people love you back, but they do. They fiercely love you. *I* fiercely love you. I've never met anyone as passionate as you, as kindhearted as you . . . as amazing as you. You love with every fiber of your soul. You inspire me every day. And if you'll agree to be my husband, I'll do my best to make you proud of me, to inspire you."

A tear rolled down Kellan's cheek as he watched me. Realizing I hadn't technically asked him a question, I sputtered, "So . . . will you . . . do you? Take me?" Eyes widening, I quickly added, "As your wife."

Light laughter broke around the room, and Kellan laughed with them. It embarrassed me some, but these people loved me, so I let it go and laughed along with them. Stopping his chuckles, Kellan cringed and grabbed the IV stand. "I do," he told me, his face pained. Exhaling in a steady stream, he added, "So damn adorable. I never stood a chance."

As I grinned at him, the minister warmly told us, "By the power vested in me, I now pronounce you husband and wife." Leaning forward, she told Kellan, "You may kiss your bride now."

As another tear rolled down his cheek, he muttered, "Thank God, 'cause I couldn't hold out another damn second."

Letting go of his supportive stand, Kellan reached up for my face at the same time that I reached over for him. Careful to not knock him over, I laced my arms around his neck and poured my heart and soul into our kiss. Warm and soft, sweet and luscious, the kiss was full of hope, love, passion, and faithfulness. It was a binding promise of everything we both wished for the other.

Lost in the moment, I could have moved my lips against Kellan's all night long. Over the din of clapping, I heard the minister announce, "Ladies and gentleman, Mr. and Mrs. Kellan Kyle." The corresponding whistles and shrieks were as deafening as a D-Bags' concert.

We did it. We were officially husband and wife. And I could honestly say I had never been happier.

Chapter 29
Help

Once the cheers and shouts died down, Kellan and I pulled apart from each other. Looking overjoyed but tired, Kellan mumbled, "Can we lie down now?"

Seeing the discomfort on his face, the tightness in his jaw, I nodded and started leading him back to his bed. He started to follow me, then paused as something outside the window caught his attention. Hoping he wasn't too faint, since falling to the ground would not be good for his stitches, I glanced out the window too. The candle cups outside were frantically being waved back and forth as the fans celebrated our union. I could even hear faint cheering as our room quieted.

Smiling, Kellan changed his direction and stepped up to the window. Wanting to support him, I went with him. The faint cheers grew to loud screams when the people got their first unobstructed view of Kellan. He had tears in his eyes as he waved back at them.

"See how loved you are?" I whispered.

He turned his attention solely to me, and his gleaming eyes sparkled with unashamed adoration as they shifted over my features. "Yes, I do." In full view of his loyal followers, Kellan leaned over and gave me a tender, but passionate kiss. It was one that made my heart beat faster. One that reminded me of tangled limbs and glorious releases. One that made my breath quicken. One that made me curse the fact that I had to wait six weeks to officially consummate my marriage.

It was going to be the longest six weeks of my life.

When Kellan pulled back from our kiss, his eyes were simmering with desire, and I knew, without a doubt, that we would never make it the full six weeks. We'd just have to be very, very careful. Good thing Kellan was an expert at keeping things slow and steady.

Then he flinched, and I remembered his current situation. Putting steamy thoughts aside, I returned him to his bed. He exhaled in relief when he was back to his prone position. I crawled into bed beside him as people huddled around to congratulate us. I'm sure it was the oddest wedding any of them had ever been to. I also thought it was probably the most romantic. But then again, I was a bit biased.

My mom was sobbing as she filmed herself hugging me. Then she reached over me, nearly squishing me, to hug Kellan. My dad gave Kellan a firm handshake. I'd never seen my dad look so proud, and I knew that he'd finally let Kellan into his heart. He was family now, and my dad would protect him just as passionately as he protected his girls. I'd never cried while smiling so much in all my life.

Anna was next, engulfing me in a jiggling hug that rattled my brain. She dashed around the bed to give Kellan an equally loving, but far more gentle, hug. Griffin was behind Anna, and when he stepped up to me, he checked his breath in his hand; that made me nervous. I raised a finger at him in warning. Griffin smirked. "Relax, it's not for you." Laughing, he lunged over me and planted a wet one on Kellan instead.

Kellan couldn't do much to get him away, since every movement he made hurt him. The entire room burst into laughter as Kellan finally shoved his bassist back. "Fuck, man," he scowled at Griffin as he wiped his mouth.

Griffin chuckled as he smacked Kellan's thigh. "Congrats, dude." Pointing at Kellan, he laughed and said, "Hey, you took my advice. You're getting better at the tongue thing."

My parents looked horrified and mystified by the conversation. I was laughing so hard my stomach was starting to cramp. Shaking his head, Kellan smiled at me as he flipped Griffin off. Surprising myself, I motioned for Griffin to hug me. He seemed surprised by that too. When he wrapped his arms around me, I whispered in his ear, "You be good to my sister. I sort of love you two together."

Pulling back, Griffin gave me a devious smile. "You love me."

My smile faded some. "I didn't say that."

Nodding, Griffin released me. In singsong, he said, "But that's what you meant. You totally love me!" Standing, he put his hands up in the air so everyone would look at him. "Kiera totally wants me!"

Matt shoved him back as he took his place. As I gaped at Griffin, Matt muttered, "I think he was dropped a lot as a child." Matt gave me a modest hug while I agreed with his assessment. He gave me a light kiss on the cheek as he pulled away from me. "I'm glad you and Kell made it. I really have never seen him happier than when he is with you." He frowned. "Plus, he gets really grumpy when you guys are apart."

I smiled over at my husband. Three nurses were wishing him well on his marriage. By the seductive smiles they were flashing him, I highly doubted they meant it.

When Matt stepped away Evan took his place. Slinging his arms under me, he lifted me up off the bed and twirled me around. Jenny giggled from behind him. Stopping us when we were facing Jenny, he bent down a little so she could hug me too; her cheeks were just as tear-stained as mine. "I love you, Kiera," she gushed out.

I wanted to tell her I loved her too, but the boisterous pair were squishing me between them. When Evan set me down, finally letting me breathe, I gave each of them a kiss on the cheek. "I love you guys too."

When they left me to go say their congratulations to Kellan, Denny stepped up to me. I inhaled a deep breath as I stared at him. He seemed so much older, wiser. Our separation had somehow matured him from a boy to a man. I could only imagine the internal struggles he'd gone through while he'd being healing from our breakup. He'd been put through the fire, but it hadn't turned him brittle, it hadn't turned him hard. He was just . . . stronger. Looking at the man in front of me now, he seemed so different from the boy who'd driven me across country to start our new life together. I'd never imagined then that our relationship would crumble so fast. I'd thought we'd be together forever. But I supposed we still would be, in a way.

The smile on his face was peaceful as he stared at me. When he opened his arms, I wrapped him in a hug. He would always be my friend. We would always care about each other. Folding his arms around me, he whispered, "I really am happy for you, Kiera."

I nodded into his shoulder as tears streamed down my face. "Thank you. And thank you for being here. You don't know how much it meant to me, to us."

He rubbed my back. "I wouldn't miss my best friend getting married."

I wasn't sure if he meant me or Kellan in that sentence, and it made me really happy that I didn't know for sure. Pulling back, I smiled up at him. "Well, don't think I'm missing your wedding. When is it, anyway?"

His smile grew absolutely radiant as he looked across the bed at his fiancée giving Kellan a hug. "Abby picked Valentine's Day." He laughed. "She's really got a thing for holidays. She even made us go out to a nice French restaurant to celebrate Bastille Day . . . and neither one of us has even been to France."

I laughed at Abby's adorable quirk. Releasing him, I said, "Well, you know I'll be there for your wedding. Kellan and I both." I gave him a crooked smile. "And if you need a band, I think I know a couple of guys who would play for you."

Denny looked around the room, amusement in his eyes. "I might take you up on that." His expression more serious, he turned to me. "Before we leave, Abby and I want to talk to you and Kellan about something. Okay?"

Confused, I nodded. "What about?"

Denny glanced at the line of well-wishers behind him. "Later." He started to turn away, then looked back at me. Voice low, he told me, "For the record, I always thought you were gorgeous. I'm sorry if I didn't make you feel that way."

His frown broke my heart a little, and I gave him another quick hug. "It wasn't you. It was my hang up. It was always my hang up. A by-product of having a perfect ten sister." I shrugged.

Denny gave me his world-famous grin. "I always thought you were better looking than Anna." His eyes flashed to Kellan. "And I'm not the only one." Heat flooded my face as Denny laughed and walked away.

Justin congratulated me next, then Kate. Incredibly flirtatious glances were being passed back and forth between the pair, and I was pretty sure they'd be an official couple by the time Kate flew back home. After them, Rachel, Abby, Cheyenne, Hailey, and Riley gave me big hugs, and Hailey made Kellan promise to visit Pennsylvania soon. Deacon, along with the rest of Holeshot and Avoiding Redemption, gave us well-wishes next, and I thanked Deacon for playing so beautifully.

After he stepped away from our bed, Kellan and I were approached by Gavin. Kellan's father was clearly touched by the level of emotion in the air. His deep eyes, so similar to Kellan's, were brightly shining. As I watched Gavin struggle to keep it together, I wondered if Kellan's emotional, passionate nature was hereditary.

"I'm so happy for the both of you. Savor this moment. Remember this feeling, because it won't always be like this. You'll have ups, you'll have downs." He laughed. "You'll drive each other crazy. But it's worth it if you stick through it. I had so many good years with my wife before she died."

His amused smile settled into a peaceful one; it was also eerily similar to Kellan's. I didn't condone what Kellan's mother had done to him, but I could understand how being around Kellan had been difficult for her—he looked so much like his natural father.

Kellan grasped Gavin's hand with both of his. "Thank you, Dad."

Gavin's eyes widened. Kellan had never called him anything but his name before. Maybe not wanting to break the moment, Gavin simply nodded his head. Or maybe he was too choked up to speak. I know I was.

For the reception part of our wedding, chairs were brought in for everyone to sit on, and we had a traditional Thanksgiving dinner. Even though it was my idea to get married on Thanksgiving, it was humorous to me, and I had a serious case of the giggles when the nurses started bringing in trays of turkey dinners complete with stuffing, mashed potatoes and gravy, cranberry salad, and green bean casserole. And for our "wedding cake," we had pumpkin pie. I guess a potluck with baked beans wouldn't have been so far off the mark after all. But the food didn't matter—just the company did.

Gavin and my father had done an outstanding job with securing the meal. The turkey was tender and moist, the potatoes were rich and buttery, and the pie was to die for. Everyone was celebrating as they ate—celebrating our marriage, and celebrating a day for thanks. Mom and Dad were chatting with Anna and Griffin, Mom securely holding Gibson. Gavin was alternating between catching up with his son and talking to Carly, who seemed very interested in everything Gavin had to say. Evan and Jenny were cuddling in side by side chairs while they ate. Rachel and Matt were sitting next to each other, both of them all smiles. Abby and Denny were discussing something in the corner, while Cheyenne asked Hailey and Riley about the Avoiding Redemption concert. Kate and Justin were sitting on the windowsill with their heads close together as they talked and flirted; their food looked like it hadn't even been touched. Kellan wasn't eating much, but in between giving me a peck or two, he was taking small bites of the potatoes.

It was the perfect ending to a perfect day.

But eventually the good feeling and camaraderie had to end, and people started filtering out. Gavin gave Kellan a warm hug before he left with Hailey and Riley. "As I've said before, son, my home is always open to you. Maybe after your tour is over?"

Hailey bumped his leg. "You promised," she reminded him.

Kellan laughed at his sister. "That would be great. Kiera and I would love to do that." I nodded in agreement when Kellan looked at me. A quiet vacation sounded nice after all of the craziness we'd had lately. Gavin looked happy and at peace as he left Kellan's room. I couldn't be sure, but just outside Kellan's door, I swear I saw Carly writing down her number for him. It made me laugh a little. He was so much like Kellan.

My bridesmaids were next to leave. Giggling, Jenny, Rachel, Kate, and Cheyenne descended on Kellan and me all at once. We were swarmed by arms, hair, laughter, and tears. Jenny gave me a kiss on my head. "Don't you wind up in a hospital again, got it?" She looked over at Kellan. "Either one of you."

Kellan's lips curled up in a devious smile. "Guess you're having the baby on the bus, babe."

Jenny's eyes bulged so far I thought they were going to pop out of her head. I immediately reached over and smacked Kellan's arm. "I'm not pregnant! He's joking!" Nobody believed me, and I spent the next several minutes convincing them I was not going to have a baby in nine months. Mom even threatened to make me take a pregnancy test right there at the hospital. Kellan was in a lot of pain as he struggled not to laugh. Served him right. Jackass.

Evan and Matt eventually pulled the girls away. Just as they started ushering them toward the door, Justin said, "Hold up, guys. I'll come with." Kate's topaz eyes sparkled with delight at the idea of spending a few more moments with her rock-star love interest.

Walking up to Kellan and me on the bed, Justin extended his hand to Kellan. "I'm glad you're doing all right, man." As they shook hands, Justin's face grew more serious. "What the label did to you with Sienna was crap. Pure crap. I wouldn't blame you if you dropped 'em." Kellan didn't answer him; I don't think he'd decided what he wanted to do yet. Seeing an answer in Kellan's non-answer, Justin smiled and added, "Next tour, when the D-Bags are headlining arenas, we'll open for you." He pointed over at Deacon and Holeshot as they were leaving the room with the other members of Avoiding Redemption. "We'll both open for you."

Kellan smirked at him. "I'm all for going on tour with you, but we're not going to be headlining stadiums anytime soon."

Justin laughed as he ran a hand through his wildly layered hair. "You sure about that? The D-Bags are on top of the world right now. I'd say your days of playing anything *but* the large venues are long behind you."

Kellan shook his head, but told him, "Yeah, let's make it happen." Satisfied, Justin headed out with Evan, Matt, and the girls; his fingers were entwined with Kate's as they left the room.

Yawning, exhausted from the day and probably the tryptophan in the turkey, my parents left next. Anna and Griffin went with them. They really didn't have much of a choice, since Mom wasn't relinquishing their child. Anna complained about it as she tried to get Mom to put Gibson into her car seat before they headed downstairs. "Mom, if you hold her nonstop, she's going to get used to it, and I'm never going to be able to put her down!"

Mom rocked Gibson back and forth, clearly not going anywhere near the car seat yet. "She'll be fine, Anna, and I have to hold her. I just have to. I don't get to see her as much as you."

Griffin nodded as he agreed with my mom; I never thought that would happen. "Babies should be held. It helps them form bonds and shit."

Aside from the swearing, I thought he made a good point. But Anna's point was good too. For the first time maybe ever, I wasn't sure which one of the two parents was right. Grinning at Kellan, I was grateful that I didn't have to deal with any of those kinds of questions yet.

After the five of them left the room, closing the door behind them, Denny and Abby were the only ones remaining. Noticing how late it was getting, I asked him, "You guys heading back to the hotel soon?"

Relaxing back in a chair, he nodded as he grabbed Abby's hand beside him. "Yeah, in a minute. Now that everyone is gone, there is something that Abby and I wanted to talk to you guys about."

Remembering what he'd said earlier, I sat up on the bed. "What is it?"

Denny opened his mouth to answer me, but Kellan's phone started ringing. I was going to ignore it, but I recognized the personalized ringtone that meant Sienna was calling him—it was the song "You're So Vain." I'd programmed it into Kellan's phone after the last time Sienna had called him, when she'd ticked us off by refusing to help quell the rumors. Kellan thought it was funny, so he'd left it that way. Plus, I'm pretty sure he didn't know how to change it.

We all looked over to the nightstand where I'd stuffed Kellan's belongings. "Sienna," Kellan muttered. "I wonder what she wants."

Standing up, I hurried around to the other side of the bed. I wondered what she wanted too. Finding the phone in Kellan's plastic bag, I quickly answered it before it could go to voice mail. "Sienna?" I asked.

"Oh, is this Kiera?"

A little bit of heat seeped into my voice upon hearing her accent. Aside from the flowers, this was the first we'd heard from her. "Yeah, Kellan's a little out of commission right now, so I answered his phone for him."

Her voice was instantly remorseful. "I am so sorry. So very, very sorry. I never meant for anything bad to happen to him, to you." She sniffled, and my anger faded a bit.

"You played with people's heads, drummed up a juicy story that wasn't even real. What did you think would happen?"

I heard the light sounds of crying, and my heart softened. "I just wanted to make a splash. I just wanted a little bit of a spotlight. I never wanted him to be chased or hounded. You have to believe me. I never wanted this."

I sighed. I did believe that she didn't want him hurt. I did *not* believe that she "never wanted this." The circus that we'd found ourselves in was just what she'd wanted. "Hold on, Sienna. I'm going to put you on speaker."

I switched the sound setting on the phone as I placed it on Kellan's lap. "Go ahead," I told her.

Her tinny voice immediately started gushing. "Kellan, love, I'm so sorry about what happened to you. I feel awful, just awful. I don't even know how to fully express how horrid I feel."

Kellan smirked at the phone. "Yeah, I got your flowers," he deadpanned.

Sienna sighed. "Look, I know you don't understand, but everything I'm doing, I'm doing for you, for the both of you."

Denny looked thoughtful while Kellan narrowed his eyes. "You're right, I don't understand."

Voice soft, she told him, "You will never have to worry about being manipulated by me again. I give you my word. And you won't have to worry about Nick either. My contract was up after that last album. I've threatened to walk if he bothers you again."

Shocked, Kellan looked between Denny, Abby, and me. "You . . . what?"

Sounding more put together, Sienna added, "I also spoke with the president of the label, Nick's father. He's none too happy about how his son has been handling things lately. He doesn't want the label associated with scandals. You calling the label out on the radio got his attention. My admitting to him what Nick helped orchestrate . . . well, let's just say that Nick will probably have to get permission to take a piss from now on."

Denny laughed at her comment; Kellan was still floored. I was just . . . confused. "Why would you do that?"

Sienna took a moment before answering. "Because I wronged you—both of you. And I'm trying to make it up to you. I've been stewing about this for days, but I'm going to give a public apology. I'm going to confess my part in what was done to Kellan."

Sitting on the edge of the bed, I stared at the phone, shocked. "You'll lose fans. They'll turn on you. Your career . . . ?"

"I'll bounce back. I always do." Her tone was so sure that I believed it.

"Well, thank you for helping us," I murmured.

In a quiet voice, she confessed, "If you knew everything I did to hurt the two of you, love, you may take that back."

I shook my head. "It's probably better that you never tell me, then."

A throaty laugh escaped her. "Agreed. But I give you my word that I will completely leave your relationship alone from now on."

Kellan frowned at Denny, and I knew the two boys were wondering what I'd already wondered. Had she orchestrated every seemingly random event that had led us to where we were now? I didn't want to give her that much credit, but I knew she was behind a lot more than she'd led us to believe. I highly doubted that any of those photographers who had randomly found us were really random.

As the room processed that, Sienna said, "Is your book done, Kiera? May I give it to my agent?"

I bit my lip. That was a really big question. One I'd been pondering during my brief moments of peace when I could think about my life and what I wanted to do with it. Did I want help from Sienna? She probably could get me places, and it was all about who you know, after all. But, like before, I wondered if that would bite me in the ass. She said the games were over, and she wasn't playing us anymore, but for how long? Walking away from her help felt like the right thing to do. Like Kellan, I wanted to succeed or fail on my own merits. With a knot in my stomach that was surely causing internal damage, I told her, "It's finished, but I, uh . . . I want to do it on my own."

Kellan and Denny both beamed at me. Sienna seemed genuinely shocked. "Really? You think you'll get anywhere that way?"

Happy with my decision, I laughed and said, "I don't know . . . guess we'll see." Maybe I was making a mistake by not letting her crack open a door for me, maybe not. But either way, success or failure, at least I would feel good about the journey.

Clearly not understanding why I would turn down her help, she murmured, "All right then. Well, if you change your mind . . ."

"I know where to find you," I finished for her.

Still clearly mystified, she said, "Good luck, Kiera."

"Yeah, you too."

She said her goodbye to Kellan, then he disconnected the call. Smiling at me, Kellan murmured, "Look at you, turning down an offer from one of the biggest stars on the planet."

My stomach felt so tight I was sure I'd never be able to eat again. "Crap, did I just make a huge mistake?" I looked between the two men whose opinions I valued the most.

They both glanced at each other, then simultaneously said, "No."

Kellan laughed once then sucked in a quick, pained breath and bit his lip. Denny gave him a sympathetic smile, then turned to me. "You'll get there your own way, Kiera, and you'll feel great about how you did it. I may not have read your story yet, but I've read your papers, and you're brilliant. I *know* you'll get there."

I gave him a soft smile. I'd need to let Denny read it before I did anything with it. It was too personal for both of us to not get his permission before I published it. But just having his support meant the world. "Thank you. That means a lot to me."

When the room quieted, a sense of expectancy filled the air. Kellan and I looked at each other, then looked over at Denny. He'd wanted to say something before Sienna's interruption, and by the look on his face, I was pretty sure he still wanted to say it.

Releasing Abby's hand, he leaned forward on his knees and clasped his palms together. For a second, he reminded me of how Nick looked when he'd made us an "offer of a lifetime." Unlike that moment, though, I had no qualms or terrors in my stomach. Not when it came to Denny. Aside from Kellan, he was the one person I wholeheartedly trusted.

Denny's dark brown eyes took in Kellan and me sitting very closely together on the bed. "Abby and I have been discussing something recently. We've been discussing it a lot actually."

Brows knitted, I tried to read Denny's expression for some clue as to what he was thinking about. I had no idea. I couldn't read him anymore. "Discussing what?" Kellan asked.

Denny smiled and looked over at Abby. Not missing a beat, she pointed at Kellan. "You, mate."

Kellan looked bewildered by that, and Denny laughed. "You and your band," he clarified. His amusement faded away and seriousness darkened his features. "Abby and I both feel that you are being poorly represented. The band isn't being looked out for. The people who are supposed to be protecting you aren't." He gave Kellan's hospital bed a pointed glance. "That much is clear."

Indicating himself and his fiancée, he continued. "We both have a lot experience in marketing things, people, brands, creating positive PR." Pausing, he leaned back in his chair. "If you're interested, we would like to manage you. We would speak for you, be your voice to the world. We would protect you." He jerked his thumb behind him at the large window showcasing the dark world outside. "And crap like what happened with Sienna wouldn't ever happen again. Not to that extent, at any rate."

Kellan looked like Denny had just confessed that *he* was actually his biological father. I understood the reaction; I was pretty shocked myself. "You want to be the band's . . . agents? You would do that for us?"

Denny's lips curved up into a warm smile. "Yes, of course we would."

I shook my head at them, amazed. "But, your jobs . . ."

He shook his head. "The D-Bags would be my only clients, and I don't anticipate you needing my help full time." He indicated Abby with his head. "As long as we're able to, we would continue with our jobs on some level." Leaning forward again, Denny set his hand on Kellan's arm. "But you would be my top priority, and if you needed me, I would be there for you. I would be honored to be the one standing up for you."

Kellan feebly nodded his head. "Yeah, okay. I mean, I'll need to run it by the guys, but . . . yeah, let's do it. I'd be honored to have you guys represent me." He stuck out his hand and Denny shook it, then Abby did. Everyone was all smiles. It warmed my heart. "And we'll pay you, of course."

Denny laughed. "We'll talk about that part later." He indicated the IV dripping fluid into Kellan's body. "Maybe when you're not on drugs."

We all laughed, and I marveled at how far we'd all come. We were so different from the people we were when we'd all started living together—stronger, more confident, more secure in ourselves. And yet, we were still exactly the same. We cared about each other. We supported each other. We looked out for each other. And now that the sting of betrayal and guilt was only a dull ache in the background, the three of us were what I'd always hoped we would be—the best of friends.

Chapter 30
Success

When Kellan was released from the hospital, he was put in a wheelchair and instructed to take it easy for the next six weeks. He looked irritated that he couldn't walk out of the place on his own two feet. He was walking around much better now, and probably could handle the journey downstairs just fine, but I made him suck it up and keep his ass in the wheelchair. His internal organs were sewn up, and rest was what he needed, not some macho display of invulnerability.

Much to the delight of Griffin and the other D-Bags, Kellan frowned the entire time I pushed him down the hall. Because I couldn't help myself, I patted his head like he was an obedient puppy. He pursed his lips at me, not amused. I thought he'd try and bolt for the door once he saw freedom, but he surprisingly stayed in his chair and let me continue to take care of him. A couple of nurses trailed after us with carts full of get-well flowers and gifts. I had no idea what we were going to do with all the stuff the fans had sent him.

As I rolled Kellan outside, where a sleek black stretch limo was waiting for us courtesy of the groveling-for-his-job Nick, I considered just having Kellan sign the gifts and pass them out to his admirers. They were everywhere outside. Holding signs, candles . . . each other . . . they cheered in wailing shrieks when they finally got to see their recovering rock star.

Attendees from the hospital hurried to push them back and rush us to the idling car. Kellan held up his hand when a burly guy grabbed his chair away from me. "Wait, I want to talk to them."

The hospital staff seemed surprised that he would want to address "the little people," but I wasn't. Kellan had watched these fans hold a vigil for him night after chilly night. Thanking them for their endless dedication was the least he could do. Knowing Kellan, he probably wanted to give each person a warm hug and a personalized message of gratitude. There were a lot of them, though, and Kellan and I did have a plane to catch. Since Kellan was in no shape to continue the tour right now, we were going to take Gavin up on his offer and spend a few weeks recouping in Pennsylvania before visiting my parents in Ohio. It was a break I was really looking forward to taking—Kellan too.

Taking back the wheelchair handles, I steered Kellan toward a large cluster of people hovering near the corner; the other D-Bags respectfully stayed by the car, giving Kellan a moment alone with his fans. Well, most of them were respectful. Matt had to shove Griffin into the limo to keep him from trying to steal the spotlight.

The screams from the crowd were earsplitting, and I hoped nobody on this side of the hospital was trying to sleep. When Kellan was close enough, he reached back and put his fingers over mine in a silent thank-you. Holding up his other hand, he silenced the crowd.

"I can't thank you enough for your devotion and your prayers." He shook his head, and some of the girls directly in front of him sighed. "I saw you. Every night I saw you standing out here in the cold . . . for me. You don't know how much that means to me, how much each and every one of you means to me." His eyes scanned the crowd, a crowd that was struggling to act mature and not squeal like little girls. "I will never forget this." He squeezed my hand, and I knew he didn't just mean the fans. This place, this moment in time would live on forever for us. We were married here.

Kellan thanked the crowd, and I started to turn him away. A brave girl off to our side shouted, "Congratulations on your marriage!"

Kellan looked back at her with an achingly sexy half-smile on his lips. "Thank you." The poor girl looked like she might pass out, so I quickly wheeled him away.

Amid the screams of his leaving, I leaned down and whispered, "You just can't help it, can you?"

His expression innocent, he asked, "Help what?"

Smiling, I kissed his cheek. "Being ridiculously attractive."

He was shaking his head as I helped him into the limo. "I'm pretty sure you're the only ridiculous one here," he murmured, grunting in pain as he transferred his weight.

I rolled my eyes as I got into the car behind him. Nice try, but Kellan knew he was attractive. He may have doubted that anyone actually cared about him, but his looks had never escaped him. Being openly ogled everywhere you go will do that to you, I guess.

Everyone's bags were inside the limo as we headed straight for the airport; even Kellan's guitar was there. The D-Bags were parting ways, and that thought made me sad. I was going to miss my extended family. But the tour was over for them. By the time Kellan was healed enough to return, only a few weeks of Sienna's tour would be left. Instead of rejoining Sienna for the last leg, the boys had decided that they would take a break and work on songs for their second album. Well, that wasn't entirely true. It hadn't entirely been the boys' decision.

Sienna had made her public apology the day after our wedding. Showing up on a popular morning show, she'd tearfully confessed to her fans that she'd helped fabricate and prolong her relationship with Kellan. She told her fans that she "got swept up in the game, and let money and success override common decency." She apologized to all of the fans for misleading them, and begged for their forgiveness. She'd ended her speech by telling the world that she would be completing the remainder of her tour without the D-Bags, so Kellan had ample time to rest and relax with his wife.

The fans were naturally quite upset with her, and from what I'd heard, tickets sales for the remainder of the tour had dropped considerably.

Even though it seemed too small a gesture, I sent her a thank-you card.

Nick immediately started planning a new tour for the boys—a tour that, just as Justin had predicted, they were going to headline. He called Kellan while we were enjoying a peaceful evening together with Gavin, Riley, and Hailey. In as polite a way as he could, Kellan told Nick that any and all arrangements for the band would need to be made through their new agent, Denny Harris. When he hung up with Nick, he had a huge smile on his face. "That was fun."

As the official go-to person for the D-Bags, Denny negotiated all details of the tour. When he called Kellan a couple weeks later with the information, I knew without a doubt that Denny was the absolute right person for the job. He understood the band, and he understood their desires. He fought to keep the venues on the smaller side—larger than Justin's last tour, but smaller than Sienna's—so the experience could be more personal for the fans and the bands. That meant less money for all parties—but Kellan didn't care about the money, and Denny knew that. And money wasn't really an issue anymore anyway. After the accident, the D-Bags' album shot right past Sienna's to land in the number one spot. And it stayed there. Financially, the D-Bags were going to be fine for quite a while.

Denny also helped me out with my career. Four weeks after the accident, when Kellan and I were in Ohio with my parents for Christmas, I finally let Denny read my book. I was a wreck when I e-mailed it to him. It was so much worse than letting Kellan read it. What I did to Denny in the book, in real life, was inexcusable. I didn't see how he could possibly be okay reading it. When I didn't hear back from him for three days, I thought my chest was going to explode from the anxiety. Kellan repeatedly told me it was going to be fine. My mother told me I was going to give myself unnecessary worry lines. I couldn't help it, though. The book was so personal; a piece of my soul. Not getting a reaction to it right away was killing me. But maybe I deserved that.

On the day that I had originally been slated to get married, I was pacing the living room and wondering if Denny was ever going to call me when he finally did. I was so nervous about talking to him, I stepped outside. My parents' yard was covered in snow, and everything outside was muffled and insulated. It was still early in the day, mid-morning, and there wasn't a whole lot of movement in the neighborhood. It made Denny's voice that much clearer in my ear.

"Hey, it's me. I finally read your book."

I sat on a bench on the porch and remembered sitting there with Denny, ages ago. "And . . . ?" I cringed, not sure if I wanted to hear his answer.

He paused. "And I think it's great. I think you should publish it."

Relief washed through me. "Are you sure? It's so . . . personal. I don't want to hurt you anymore than I already have."

Denny sighed, and for once there wasn't any lingering pain in the sound. "I understand too, Kiera. Reading the book . . . I understand so much better what happened. I wish it hadn't happened the way it had, and I know you feel the same, but I'm okay now, and this doesn't bother me. Go. Publish it. Knock the socks off the literary world. You deserve it."

As I leaned back on the bench, I told him, "Thank you. That means a lot to me." Smiling, I added, "I guess I should get started on getting it published. So, Mr. Brilliant, you have any contacts in the publishing industry?"

I could hear Denny's smile when he answered me. "Actually, I know you'd probably considered going with a traditional publisher right away, but what do you think about releasing it yourself first? Garner some attention before you dive into the traditional route? The minute I finished reading, I started looking into it, and I found a ton of articles and websites about self-publishing. If you want, I can help you with the technical side. Then I'll help you market the book. That is my specialty, you know."

"No, I hadn't considered that, but I like the idea." I paused to think it over, and he had a point. A story about cheating might be hard for me to sell to a publisher. Releasing it myself seemed like a great way to prove the story's merits first. Still amazed by Denny, I shook my head. "You'd really do that for me?"

"Like you told me before, Kiera, I'd do anything for you. You and Kellan both."

I didn't even know what to say to that, so in the end I just thanked him. Then I ran into the house and tossed my arms around Kellan's neck as I kissed every square inch of his face. "I'm going to be published!" I squealed.

Lacing his arms around me and gently sitting me beside him on the couch, he murmured, "I know. And you're going to be huge." His lips curled into an adorable pout. "When you're famous and I'm a has-been, you're going to leave me, aren't you?"

Giggling, I threaded my fingers through his hair. "For one, thanks to you, I'm *already* famous. And secondly"—I tenderly placed my lips against his—"I'm never leaving you." Pulling back, I lost myself in his amazing eyes. "And lastly, you'll never be a has-been. Not to me." Nope, not ever.

Two weeks later, Kellan and I said our goodbyes to our families and traveled back home to Seattle. Kellan was damn near giddy when our plane came to a complete stop. He immediately bounded to his feet and pulled me to mine. I wasn't sure why he was so excited as we exited the first class section, a complimentary upgrade from Nick. I thought maybe Kellan was just happy to be returning to familiar stomping grounds, but after acknowledging a few fans at the airport, gathering our things from baggage claim, and climbing into a taxi, the real reason for his excitement became crystal clear.

Instead of giving the taxi driver our address, Kellan gave him *Evan's* address. Confused, I looked over at him. "Why are we going to Evan's?"

It wasn't that I didn't want to see the guys. I did. But Kellan and I had been living with family for the last six weeks, and I wanted a little alone time with my husband. We had had some privacy at Gavin's and at my parents', sure. Dad had even let Kellan and I share a room since we were legally married. And even though we'd been warned not to, we'd broken the doctor's orders about restraining from intimacy. We'd actually broken that rule on week three. Kellan is hard to resist, and when he'd told me he felt fine as he was running his tongue along my collarbone . . . well, will power still wasn't my strong point, I guess. But those brief moments hadn't been nearly enough, and I was ready to go home.

Kellan glowed as he answered me. "We're not going to Evan's, we're going to the shop."

I was confused for a minute until I realized what he was talking about—the auto body shop beneath Evan's loft, the shop that was garaging Kellan's Chevelle. I rolled my eyes at him as I laughed. *Boys and their toys*. When the taxi let us out, Rox, the female mechanic who "knew" Kellan "very well," was there holding his keys. Kellan was so excited, he picked the girl up. I cringed, and not from jealousy. I just didn't want him injuring himself. He'd been given the all clear, but still, he should be careful.

Rox was laughing when Kellan set her down. With grease-stained fingers, she indicated inside the garage, where I could see a huge Chevelle-shaped sheet on the far side of the room. It made me happy that they'd protected the car as well as store it. It made Kellan's eyes shine as he gingerly took the keys from her.

Walking up to his car, he lovingly removed the cover. By the look on his face, I thought maybe I should give him a minute alone with his "baby." His smile wide, his hand slowly ran up the edge of the shiny black vehicle, then caressed the top. And damn if it wasn't erotic to watch; it gave me shivers, and I wanted him to finish fondling his car so he could fondle me.

From beside me, Rox murmured, "He sure loves that car."

I had to laugh as I watched Kellan rest his cheek on the roof. God. Really? "Yeah, that he does."

As I started to walk away, Rox blurted out, "I never believed the rumors . . . just so you know."

By the strange expression on her face, I didn't quite believe her. But I knew she was trying to be nice, so I played along. "Thanks. That's good to hear."

Stepping up to Kellan, I extended my hand, palm up. Lifting his head from the roof, he frowned at my gesture. "What?"

Keeping a straight face, I told him, "Seeing as how you're still recovering from a serious operation, I don't think you should drive."

Kellan's jaw dropped, and his fingers possessively curled around the keys. "I'm fine, and you know I'm fine. Sex takes way more energy than driving, and we've been doing that for weeks." A playful gleam in his eyes, he added, "And it didn't hurt at all when you rode me this morning. It felt pretty amazing actually."

Widening my eyes, I slapped my hand over his mouth. Rox was laughing, so I knew she'd heard him over the din of the noisy shop. I could feel Kellan laughing under my fingers. I considered punching him in the gut, just to see if *that* hurt, but I'd vowed never to hit anyone again so I contained myself. I did make him unlock the door and get inside as quickly as possible, though. He was laughing when I climbed in the other side. "What?" he asked, starting the car. "Am I wrong?"

Giving him a sly grin, I shook my head. No, he wasn't wrong. This morning had been pretty amazing. Kellan's stamina was right back where it used to be. In fact, you wouldn't even know he'd been in such a scary accident by the looks of him. The only visible mark on him was a slightly pink scar running down the middle of his abdomen from where the doctor had cut him open to save his spleen. But he'd been stitched together very well, and given enough time, the slight mark would be nearly invisible. I didn't care if the scar remained visible for the rest of his life. Inadvertently, the scar had saved his life. And, in a way that couldn't fully be explained, it was kind of sexy.

Really wanting to be alone now, Kellan and I headed for home. When we drove up to our street, a sad fact quickly became apparent to us. Sometimes, you can't go back home. Kellan's narrow, car-packed street was now so full of vehicles and people, we couldn't pull into it. Stopping alongside the main road, we looked down the street where tons of people were milling about. I could just make out our two story home, and I was horrified to see people taking pictures of it.

"Please tell me your neighbors are having a block party," I whispered.

Kellan looked back at me; his face was resigned. "I don't think this has anything to do with my neighbors."

While we continued to stare, a couple of those neighbors stormed into their yards and started shouting at the loiterers. I'd already known Kellan was right, but that confirmed it. Somehow, Kellan's house had become a well-known tourist attraction. And even if we called the cops and had these people removed, it wouldn't matter. They'd just come back. Idly, I hoped our stuff was okay. The thought of someone breaking in and smelling my underwear, or Kellan's, instantly flooded my brain. God, I hoped that hadn't happened.

Sighing, Kellan pulled back into traffic. I understood. We couldn't go back there. It broke my heart some. I had a lot of memories in that home. Some good, some not so good. But a place was just a place. His heart was my home, and I wasn't ever leaving it.

Kellan drove us to Matt and Griffin's house. It was in the comparatively quiet burbs, and no one was around when we pulled up. I doubted the fans knew about this place, so we wouldn't be disturbed here. And since Griffin had moved into my sister's apartment, Matt had room for us. Although, not as much room as we'd thought; Rachel had moved in over the holidays. But the pair were quiet and reserved, so I knew living with them would be comfortable—for the time being, at least.

Matt filled us in on what had happened with Kellan's house. Apparently, Joey had spilled the beans about where he lived in an interview with a skeezy online tabloid. Showing absolutely no ethics, the magazine had actually posted his address, and it had spread like wildfire around the Internet in just a few hours. After Sienna's confession of manipulating the public, Joey had also finally confessed to the world that she was the real star of the inconclusive sex tape and that Sienna had paid her to keep quiet.

I was both shocked and not shocked by the interview. We'd suspected that Joey had been paid off. It made me wonder if Sienna had also squashed the release of any of the other sex tapes, since no one else had come forward. Or maybe the other girls just had more self-respect than Joey. It didn't matter too much to me either way now. Let them be released. I knew my husband in a way that no woman watching erotic, self-made porn ever would.

While Kellan and I looked for a new place to live, I published my book as an ebook. Denny helped me prepare the manuscript and put together a classy, romantic cover that would instantly catch people's eye. Releasing it was scary as hell. I had no idea how people would react. I had no idea what they would say. But I had to do it. This was my dream, my career, my passion. So, with great trepidation and excitement, I uploaded my baby into cyberspace to be judged, hopefully more positively than negatively.

After the ebook went live, a feeling of relief washed over me. I'd done it. I'd created a story, a piece of my soul, and I'd had the courage to share it. Even if it wasn't universally accepted, I was proud of myself for following through with it. When I made my first sale, another feeling washed through me—excitement! I felt like I was officially an author after that moment.

While the ebook started gathering a fan base, I put my paperback together. It pained me to have to wait to hold the physical book in my hands, and I anxiously checked for my copies to arrive on my doorstep every day. When they finally did, Kellan intercepted the package. I'd been at lunch with Jenny, Kate, and Cheyenne, and when I got back to Matt's house, a note was taped to the front door. It merely read, *Come find me.*

Grinning at Kellan's handwriting, I opened the door. On the ground were rose petals. Each petal had one letter written on it. I was laughing as I followed the trail that spelled out, *I can't wait for you to find me, so hurry up already.* The excessive trail of petals led in a loop through the kitchen and into the living room. Oddly enough, the trail ended at the bathroom. I was hesitant to open the closed door, but I was too curious not to.

"Kellan, what exactly are we doing in here?" I murmured as I pushed it open. He wasn't in there, though. Instead, I found a huge note taped to the toilet. In large letters it screamed at me, *We don't have time for mind-blowing sex in here. Focus, and come find me!*

Turning around, I started laughing. "Kellan, where are you?" A sign near the bathroom light switch pointed down the hall, so I figured he was in our bedroom.

Heading down the hall, I noticed Post-its stuck to the pictures. *Are you excited? Are you ready? Would you hurry up and find me?* Griffin's old room that we were using as ours had a bunch of petals taped onto it. They formed a heart. In the center of the heart, a sticky note read, "*I think I'm in here.*"

Giggling, I pushed our door open. "Kellan? What's going on?" He wasn't in there either, though. His guitar case was open on our bed, and the story notes for my next novel were strewn all over it. A bright pink note exclaimed, "Future bestseller!" I laughed harder and looked around for Kellan. When I still couldn't find him, I looked in the closet. I knew he had to be in this house somewhere. He wasn't in the closet, though. All I found was a piece of journal paper with song lyrics written upon it. The words were beautiful, and brand new. I could hear Kellan's flawless voice singing them in my head as I read them. *You'll never know how incredible you are to me, how desperately I love you. I would do it all over again if I needed to. I'd go back to the beginning for you.*

My eyes hazy, I again called out for him. He still didn't answer me. Wondering if his lyrics were clues, I went back to the beginning and headed to the front door. Still nothing. Just when I was sure I'd never find him, I opened the door and took a look outside. Standing on the welcome mat, resplendent in faded blue jeans and his black leather jacket, Kellan was holding a dozen long-stemmed roses in one hand and a copy of my paperback in his other. I didn't know what excited me more—finally finding him, the electric gleam in his eye, the smell of the fragrant flowers in his hand, or my name splashed all over the glossy six-by-nine cover.

Raising a brow, Kellan spoke before I could respond. "What took you so long?"

Laughing and crying, I flung my arms around him and pulled

him out of the frosty air and into the house. I urged his head down to mine and thrilled in the coolness of his lips. Kicking the door shut with his foot, Kellan managed to speak a few words around my eager mouth. "I have . . . something . . . for you."

I was dying to finally hold my book. Letting go of Kellan, I extended my hands like a small child begging for a treat. Kellan immediately placed the roses in my arms. I frowned at him as he laughed; the roses were gorgeous, but he knew that wasn't what I really wanted right now. A teasing smile on his face, he pointed to the book I was aching to flip through. "You can't see it until you promise to sign one for me."

I pursed my lips, but Kellan shook his head. "Nope. I want a signed copy. I want the *first* signed copy."

Groaning, I nodded and shook my free hand at him. "Fine, I'll sign whatever you want, just let me see it."

Intrigued, Kellan murmured, "Really? Anything I want?" as he took back his flowers and gave me the book.

I ignored his suggestive tone as I stared at the sexy black and white photo of a woman standing between two men. The title, *Irresistible*, was sprawled across the top and the pseudonym I was using as my pen name was in big bold letters along the bottom. I wasn't hiding who I was anymore, but people knew my real name now, and I didn't want the story to become a success just because I was a rockgod's wife. Like Kellan, I wanted to make it on my own merits, not because of the hype that surrounded my life.

Holding the book was . . . surreal. I actually did it. I actually wrote and published a novel. Crazy.

"I'm so incredibly proud of you, Kiera."

As I looked up at Kellan, I could see that pride reflected on his face. It warmed me in places I didn't know I could be warmed.

Kellan's new tour, with Holeshot and Avoiding Redemption as his opening acts, was starting in April. I wasn't sure if it was the label's doing or Denny's, but the boys were going international this time.

At the tail end of the U.S. tour, they had concerts set up in both the United Kingdom and Australia. I found it really humorous that the D-Bags were going Down Under. Life sure had a way of turning full circle.

But before Kellan could go on tour with the boys, something he was really looking forward to doing, he had to do something he was not looking forward to. But, shocking the hell out of myself, I *was* looking forward to it.

Zipping up my carry-on bag, I walked across my new bedroom to find Kellan. We'd moved into a new spacious home a couple weeks earlier. It was a lot nicer than any home I'd lived in before. It was almost too much for just the two of us, but Kellan insisted that when our family expanded, we'd eventually need the room. And the location couldn't be beat. Griffin had wanted us to get a place in Medina, right next door to Bill Gates if we could, but Kellan and I had opted to get out of the city instead. Traveling north, we'd found a private, secluded home on eleven acres. Our nearest neighbor was a sweet older couple who dropped by with pie when they saw our moving van driving past. Living in the countryside, our life was going to be a lot more reclusive than it had been in Seattle, but considering how crazy things became whenever we were out in public, a mellow home life with few distractions was exactly what we both wanted.

Retrieving our things from Kellan's old house had been a process. My friends had helped, and had braved their way through the throngs of near-constant visitors to get inside the home and pack it up for us. It was a little embarrassing having other people box up all of our belongings, but Kellan and I lived pretty simply, and there really hadn't been all that much stuff to begin with at the old house. And we still lived pretty simply. Our new home seemed a little empty with the scant amount of furniture we owned. I was going to have to get some help filling it up. Good thing Jenny and Denny were extremely good at shopping and decorating.

I did what I could to make our house feel like a home, though.

There were personal touches throughout each room that made me feel like we were right where we belonged. As I walked through our spacious bedroom, I had to smile at the familiarity—Kellan's comfortable chair was tucked in a corner next to a floor lamp, creating a perfect space for reading. The Ramones poster I'd given him was framed and held a place of honor on the wall beside the D-Bags' Bumbershoot poster. Kellan's cowboy hat from the strip club was hanging off of a peg on the footboard of our new bed. And copies of the D-Bags' CD were resting near copies of my book. It already felt like we'd been living here for years.

Walking into the bathroom, I glanced over at the jetted tub large enough to sleep in, the ginormous two-person shower, and the expansive granite countertops. I could live just in this bathroom and be happy. Dressed in a white long-sleeved shirt, the sleeves pushed up to his elbows, Kellan was leaning on the counter, staring at himself in the mirror. He was taking long deep breaths in and out. If I didn't know any better, I'd swear he was nervous.

"We need to go. You okay?"

Kellan glanced my way, flashing me a perfectly carefree smile. "Yep. I'm ready."

Hands on my hips, I clarified my question. "I asked if you were okay."

His smile turning seductive, Kellan turned and wrapped his arms around my waist. "I just made love to a beautiful, successful author. I'm fantastic."

A bright grin exploded onto my face. Then my mind shifted back to Kellan's big news. "And your band is up for Best New Artist tomorrow, so we better hop on that plane and get your butt to the Grammys."

The nominations had been announced at the end of November, a week after our wedding, but Kellan was still in denial about the whole thing. He just couldn't wrap his head around how fast everything was happening. I couldn't either sometimes, but I wasn't as surprised as he was. Kellan was the entire package—looks, talent, charisma. He had that "it" factor that caught people's attention. The Grammys were only the beginning.

Kellan sighed, his smile relaxing. "Do I really have to go to this thing?"

Laughing at his reluctance to accept praise, even from his peers, I nodded. "You're scheduled to perform, so yeah, you kind of have to be there."

Kellan closed his eyes. "Why on earth did I agree to do that?"

I gave him a soft kiss as I squeezed him tight. "Because you can't resist a stage, and the world is a better place because of that fact."

Kellan opened one eye in a dry expression of disbelief. Laughing, I kissed him again. "Off you go to rule the world, rock star."

Releasing me, Kellan started heading for our bedroom. Over his shoulder he told me, "Well, it's not like we're actually going to win anyway. Our album hasn't been out long enough."

I kept my mouth shut, but I knew that fact didn't matter in this case. I had no doubt in my mind that Kellan was going to win.

When we were in the limo being driven to Staples Center for the ceremony, I reconsidered my excitement about being there. Aside from the industrial matting at my hospital-room wedding, I'd never walked a red carpet before in my life, and the thought of stepping out in front of all of those photographers made my stomach feel like a tiny person was in there frothing up some egg whites for a lemon meringue pie. I was possibly going to be sick. Looking at Kellan beside me, he surprisingly looked the exact same way. I was sure he wasn't nervous about his entrance, though—it was more his impending win that was bothering him. Kellan didn't mind the spotlight, but he wasn't the best at accepting kudos. He'd even refused to write a speech, saying there wasn't a chance he was winning so why bother.

To calm my nerves I pulled out my phone and sent a quick message. Kellan glanced down at my screen. Looking like he also wanted a distraction, he asked, "What are you doing?"

Smirking, I told him, "Tweeting your fans." Holding up the

phone, I read him my message. "About to head into the Grammys. Wish me luck."

Kellan rolled his eyes at me. One of the first things Denny had done as Kellan's agent was to have him join some social media sites. He'd told Kellan that the best way to put rumors to rest was to directly interact with his fans. I agreed and wondered why we hadn't done it sooner. But the look of confusion, reluctance and irritation on Kellan's face had explained it all. "You want me to whatbook? And Tweet? Like a bird? Are you serious?" he'd said to Denny in exasperation.

Kellan had stayed as far from technology as he possibly could, for as long as he possibly could. He just wasn't into it. He didn't even own a computer. He either borrowed my laptop or Griffin's. He preferred to use mine. He said that Griffin's keyboard tended to be on the sticky side. I did *not* want to think about why. But Kellan was being forced into the modern age, practically kicking and screaming. His expression of resigned disgust when he'd agreed was so adorable that I'd taken a photo of it. Maybe someday I'd post it on his wall.

After my Tweet on Kellan's behalf, the well-wishes started pouring in. Kellan eventually laughed and got sucked into it. We stared at my phone for so long watching the comments coming in that we didn't even notice when we arrived at Staples Center. Kellan and the guys had already been there earlier, when they'd rehearsed, but that had been nothing compared to this. People were everywhere. Cameras were everywhere. Celebrities were everywhere. It was one of those surreal once-in-a-lifetime moments.

Staring out the window, Kellan murmured, "Fuck me," as the car pulled around to the drop zone. The rest of the people in the car started freaking out as we came to a stop. Not wanting to ride separately, our limo was pretty packed—Griffin, Anna, Evan, Jenny, Matt, and Rachel were with us. Everyone looked amazing too. Anna and Jenny had outdone themselves on our hair and makeup, and all of the boys had been approached by big name designers to supply our wardrobe. My dress was a stunning black one-shoulder piece that probably cost more money than I made in a year waitressing. I was being very careful not to stain, snag, or rip it.

The boys were dressed a bit more casually but still looked incredible. Evan was in gray slacks with a matching gray jacket and a black button-up shirt underneath. Matt was sporting fashionably frayed jeans with a dark blue blazer over a white shirt. Griffin . . . was rocking really tight leather pants. Everyone had tried to talk him out of it, but he refused to wear anything else. Anna had at least gotten him to change his mind about wearing a T-shirt that read *Muff Master*. Not because of what it said, mind you, but because she felt a T-shirt wasn't appropriate for an awards show. Kellan was decked out in black slacks, a white button-up, and a black jacket. His shirt was open for three or four buttons, and his jacket only had one button that met halfway down his chest. He was both fashionable and sexy as hell. It was hard to take my eyes off of him.

Before heading out into the spotlight, we all gave each other a round of encouragement, support, and gratitude. And then it was showtime.

My nerves evaporated about halfway down the red aisle. It's amazing how fast you get used to people shouting out questions as they snap photos of you. I didn't want to do this all of the time, but every so often wouldn't be so bad. Kellan's smile was seamless, his swagger seductive. No one but me would know that he was freaked out. And I only knew because he had a death grip on my hand. I wasn't sure what he would be more relieved about—winning or not winning. Playing would probably ease his nerves, but unfortunately the band was scheduled to be on stage after their category was up. He would have no reprieve from his anxiety until the moment of truth was over. But, like he did so often for me, I would help him through it.

While we sat through the ceremony, I tried to help him get his mind off of it. We joked about Denny and Abby babysitting Gibson over the weekend, about how Abby was going to want to have a baby of her own by Monday. That led to a discussion about which songs the band should play for their wedding ceremony in two days. Abby was a huge fan of "Islands in the Stream," but Kellan refused to cover that song or "Endless Love," which was Abby's backup song.

As the time approached for Kellan's category, he started talking less and fidgeting more. He also started obsessive-compulsively kissing the tattoo of his name on my wrist. It was so bad at one point, I thought he was going to wear away the permanent ink. When the two announcers stepped onstage for the Best New Artist category, Kellan's knee started bouncing up and down. I'd never seen him this frazzled.

Reaching over, I stilled his leg. Eyes wide, he turned to me and whispered, "I'm nervous. I'm really fucking nervous. I never get nervous. What the hell is wrong with me?"

Smiling, I told him, "You're human. And I think it's pretty safe to say that everybody in here is nervous on some level."

As the pair in front of the microphone tried to lighten the mood with really bad comedy, Kellan told me, "You're not nervous."

I stared at Kellan for a few seconds, debating whether or not to tell him something. I'd been planning on waiting 'til all the hoopla had died down, but I knew it would absolutely take his mind off of his nerves. It was going to blow his mind. It had sure blown mine. A short movie started playing clips of the nominated bands. When I heard Kellan's pitch-perfect voice filling the auditorium, I leaned forward and whispered my secret in his ear. His mouth dropped wide open as he stared at me in shock. Tears filled my eyes as I nodded at his unasked question.

A smile spread over Kellan's face right as the announcers spoke in unison, "And the winner for Best New Artist is . . ." When they paused for dramatic effect, Kellan leaned forward to kiss me. "The D-Bags!"

The room erupted in cheers and applause, but I was sure Kellan hadn't heard a word of it. Grabbing my face, he finished his descent to my lips. The other band members started standing, but Kellan was still sitting in his chair, plastering my face with light kisses. Cognizant of millions of viewers watching this on TV, I pushed him back and urged him to stand up. His face was exhilarant as he finally did. Evan and Matt clapped him on the back, urging him forward. I stood with the rest of the girls and clapped as they fumbled their way to the stage. Kellan looked back at me every five seconds, his euphoric face still in disbelief. Whether that was over winning or over my news, I wasn't sure.

The boys climbed up the steps to the stage and exchanged polite hugs with the celebrities who'd announced them. As if on cue, Evan and Matt stepped back and let Kellan take the microphone; Griffin was subtly restrained by both men with a "supportive" hand on each one of his shoulders. Shaking his head, Kellan clutched his golden gramophone statue as he walked toward the mike

"Oh . . . wow . . . I don't know what to say. I want to thank . . ." His voice broke and the tears in my eyes rolled down my cheeks. Bringing the back of his hand to his mouth, Kellan stopped talking. Shaking his head again, he slowly lowered his hand. "I'm sorry." His voice warbled with barely contained emotion. "My wife just told me she's pregnant." He had to step back again as the moment overwhelmed him.

People started hollering. The D-Bags jumped on Kellan, congratulating him. Every head in my vicinity swiveled my direction, including my sister's and my girlfriends'. I hadn't told anybody about this yet. I'd really only just found out about it. Last week to be exact. And surprised wouldn't even begin to describe my initial reaction. I was on birth control pills for one thing, so I hadn't even been worried about getting pregnant. I just thought I was late because I was stressed, or excited. A lot of big things had been happening lately. But I just felt . . . weird. I wasn't sick or anything, I just didn't feel normal. I was more tired than I should be, and I alternated between not being hungry and being hungry enough to eat two loaves of bread in one sitting. I'd made an appointment with my doctor just to rule out any illnesses. She'd assured me that I wasn't coming down with Spanish influenza, that I was pregnant.

When I matter-of-factly told the doctor that pregnancy was impossible, since I was a fastidious planner and I'd never missed a birth control pill in my life, she then informed me about a bad batch of pills that had hit the market. Apparently, the pills had been distributed in the packet incorrectly, so the dosages were wrong. Good to know. All of the mislabeled batches had been recalled, but I had apparently hit the birth control jackpot. Our baby was due in September.

While my sister and Jenny started quietly grilling me on details, Kellan finally composed himself. Approaching the microphone again, he let out a long exhale. "Well, I can honestly say that this is the best day of my life." When the cheers died down, he told the crowd, "I want to thank every single person who has ever supported us. Your dedication has meant the world, and we wouldn't be here without you. I may be overly emotional right now, since I'm about to be a father, but I really do love each and every one of you. From the bottom of my heart, thank you."

I couldn't tell from where I was sitting, but I was pretty sure tears were in his eyes when he waved and stepped away from the microphone. I knew this emotional moment was going to be replayed on every show playing Grammy highlights tomorrow. It was going to be talked about on every radio station. It was going to be mentioned around every water cooler. And for once, I was glad. I wanted this moment to live on. I wanted to be constantly reminded of this memory. I wanted to replay this video in twenty years so I could remember the look on his face when Kellan found out he was going to be a father. And I wanted to show it to our son or daughter—so they would know, without a doubt, that they were loved. From day one, they were loved.

Chapter 31
Epilogue

Denny spared no expense when it came to giving Abby her dream wedding. Everything was picture-perfect, straight out of a bridal magazine. It was breathtaking. The ceremony took place at the impressive Fairmont Olympic hotel in downtown Seattle. With twenty-foot ceilings, crystal chandeliers, arched floor-to-ceiling windows, white brocade linens, table skirts, and china place settings, the place was top-notch.

Kellan and I were both in the wedding party, him as a groomsman, me as a bridesmaid. Standing next to the altar wrapped in pink flowers and twinkling lights brought tears to my eyes. Of course, that could have been the pregnancy hormones kicking in. I didn't think so, though. It was watching Denny marry his sweetheart. It was the look on his face when he said, "I do." It was seeing Kellan just over Denny's shoulder, beaming at his friend. It was the trace amount of moisture in my husband's eyes. It was remembering my vows from my own simple ceremony.

After the lengthy nuptials, long lines formed to congratulate the happy couple. Dressed in an intricately embroidered, long-sleeved, gleaming white wedding gown, I'd never seen Abby look more radiant. And I'd never seen Denny more joyful as he proudly stood by her side. When it was finally my turn to hug him, I could barely speak through my emotions. I think I told him I was happy for him as I squeezed him tight. Wiping a tear from my cheek, he told me, "I'm so glad you're here. I love you, mate."

That did me in, and chuckling as I started falling apart, Kellan escorted me away so I could sit down, maybe get some water in me or something. God, if I was this emotional now, I'd never make it through the next seven months.

"Keep it together, you," Kellan murmured as he rubbed my back. This wedding was a lot fancier than ours had been, and all of the groomsmen were in full-on tuxedos. Kellan looked jaw-droppingly good. I'd spotted more than a few guests in the audience who had been watching *him* during the whole ceremony, ignoring the bride and groom.

Pulling out my chair, Kellan helped me sit down. He'd been doing that ever since the Grammys, like he thought I was already feeble. I let him, though. He was still reeling from my surprise announcement. I was too, but I'd had just a tiny bit longer to get used to the idea.

Each table setting had silver name tag holders with cards written in elegant calligraphy. Seeing my new name, *Mrs. Kiera Kyle*, spelled out made me tear up again. Anna and Griffin sat to the left of us at the table, Evan and Jenny to our right, and Matt and Rachel completed the circle by sitting across from us. The rest of the tables seemed to be filled with friends and colleagues of Denny and Abby's.

After a five-star meal, toasts, and the bride and groom slicing the wedding cake, the D-Bags performed. It had been a really long time since I'd seen the boys perform at a venue this size. It was like being back at Pete's. The feeling was more intimate than a concert, the sound crisp and clear; it was incredible. Kellan played with the crowd, riling them up and getting them to dance. By the end of the night, no one was sitting.

As a gift to Denny and a surprise to Abby, and also, I think, because Kellan didn't like her song choices, he wrote them a song for their first dance. It was an amazing piece about finding someone who opened you up, about falling in love with them more and more every day, about feeling breathless when they were gone and out of breath when they were near. Like Kellan, the song was scintillating, sexy, and also exceedingly heartfelt and romantic. Even though he'd written it for Denny and Abby, I knew the inspiration for it had come from us. It made me cry again.

The newlyweds headed off at the tail end of the evening, disappearing to their suite. They were catching a flight early in the morning. They were going back home to Australia to start their honeymoon and to have a second wedding ceremony for their friends and family there. I thought Denny was crazy for doing this soiree twice, but it was what Abby wanted, so he was more than happy to do it.

Kellan and I would also be heading over to Australia, but not for a few more months. The tour was kicking off in Vegas first, yet another place I'd always wanted to visit. Denny had managed to score Kellan and me our own bus for this tour. Our very own private bus! I could be as loud as I wanted, and no one but Kellan would hear me. Well, Kellan and the bus driver, who I often forgot about—and our bodyguard. After what had happened in New York, Kellan and I agreed to hire protection for the times we were out in public. It was still an odd concept for me. But the truth was that Kellan and I attracted attention when we went out, and sometimes that attention was a little too friendly. We didn't want to take any chances now that I was pregnant.

So, while we wouldn't be quite as alone as I'd originally thought, we had enough privacy that I was giddy and couldn't wait for the tour to start.

The first show that the D-Bags headlined was sold out. So was the next. And the next. Whatever city we rolled into, they created a stir. A frenzy of D-Baggery. But it was all positive, and it was all honest this time—no more duplicitous gossip. The tour was spending three months in the U.S. and Canada and one month overseas. That was a stipulation that Kellan had insisted on. He didn't want to be on the road for more than a few months out of the year—especially once the baby was born. After that happened, if I couldn't be with him for some reason, then the touring time might be cut back even more. Kellan just didn't want to miss anything, and I didn't blame him.

As the tour progressed, so did my stomach. It was astounding how I would seemingly double in size overnight. I went from flat stomach to moderate bump to definite bulge to cantaloupe-sized to looking like I swallowed a watermelon—just like that! Kellan loved being able to see the progression. He would stare at my belly some-times when we were in bed together, just watching my skin, like he was waiting for it to expand before his eyes.

After a few months of him unabashedly staring at my bare stom-ach, I told him one evening, "A watched pot never boils, you know."

Pulling his eyes to my face, he murmured, "I know. I'm just imagining how big the baby is. I'm trying to visualize it."

I smiled at his answer as I stroked his cheek. "I do that too."

Grinning, Kellan carefully laid his head against the bulge of our child. At five months along, there was a decent amount of room for his head to rest. He stared up at me while I resumed stroking his smooth skin. "What are you doing?" I finally asked him.

His content expression grew dreamlike. "Listening to her. Or him." We'd decided not to find out the sex. We wanted to be sur-prised. And besides, like what happened with Anna, sometimes the technicians made mistakes.

Laughing, I told him, "No, you're listening to the chicken par-mesan that I had for dinner." Looking toward the door to our private room on the bus, I murmured, "I wonder if there's any of that left."

Whispering "Shhh . . . I'm listening," Kellan resumed his intense scrutiny of my digestive system.

Then he started to lightly hum, like he was singing along to my internal noises. I felt a rolling sensation in my stomach as the baby moved. Kellan's eyes widened, and he looked up at me. I laughed at the look on his face. "Keep humming," I told him.

He did, and the baby moved again, then kicked. Kellan smiled as I sighed and said, "The baby likes Daddy's voice."

Lifting his head, Kellan crooked a smile. "Just like his mom. Or *her* mom."

For a minute, I debated what I wanted more, him or the chicken in the fridge. I ended up choosing what I always chose. Pulling Kellan to my lips, I reveled in the one perk of pregnancy that we were both enjoying—a ramped-up sex drive.

When I moved into my seventh month, the D-Bags went international. Kellan was worried at first about me continuing to be on the tour. He didn't want to run the risk of me giving birth backstage; he wanted me to be as safe as possible. I told him it was fine, we would be home long before I was due. Kellan didn't really want to be away from me then anyway, so my words easily convinced him. Plus, I told him we could finally become members of the Mile High club during the super-long flight to Australia. Since Kellan had never had sex on a plane before, he was intrigued, to say the least. Considering how far along I was, joining the club was a challenge. It took a lot of finagling, skill, and a hand clamped over my mouth. Airplane-bathroom sex made tour bus–cubby sex seem spacious in comparison, but we managed to pull it off. A giggling air stewardess even gave us wings afterwards. Kellan wore his pinned to his shirt the entire time we were Down Under.

So, while I was plump and full of life, I roamed a rock concert with a rock star. The band was playing in Perth first, then heading over to Sydney and Brisbane. The backstage area was full of contest winners, diehard groupies, radio personalities, the crew, and members of the bands. While security was present and watchful, Kellan insisted that the fans weren't confined to a meet-and-greet room and were allowed to roam and mingle with the rock stars. Clumps of them were even allowed to stay during the concert, something Sienna had never allowed. But Kellan still wanted some level of intimacy with his fans. That made writing more of a challenge for me, since just as many of his fans wanted to talk with Mrs. Kyle too. But laptop in hand, I found a spot to listen to him perform and work on my writing.

Since publishing my first book, I had really started focusing on my second book. Maybe it was the countless hours that Kellan had read *Pride and Prejudice* to me, but the storylines that filled my mind were all Jane Austen–style historical romances. I found that time period fascinating and engrossing, and now that my autobiographical story was purged from my mind, I loved the idea of doing something different and shifting away from contemporary novels.

Periodically while writing, I watched my man on stage. He was having such a good time on this tour. He loved hanging out with Holeshot and Avoiding Redemption. The three bands meshed well, personality-wise and musically. In fact, when the tour was over, Justin and Kellan were going to record a collaboration, a song they'd both been working on during quiet times. I'd heard the guys practicing the song together, and it gave me chills. I couldn't wait for the fans to hear it.

Kellan and the guys were planning on recording the album in Seattle this time, keeping it close to home, since I would be so much closer to delivering by then. Nick was fine with it, though. Truthfully, Nick was fine with a lot of stuff recently. After the scandal with Sienna, he'd been scared straight by his father. That man did *not* want to lose his two largest acts because of the manipulative way his son had been running things.

True to her word, Sienna kept her distance from us. She'd congratulated the boys for their Grammy win at an after party, but that was about all we'd heard from her. Her album had plummeted after her soulful, honest public apology, but she was slowly starting to bounce back. And I had no doubt in my mind that she would. If anything, the woman was tenacious.

By the time the tour was over, I was ready to go home. I was tired and very, very pregnant. I had a newfound respect for Anna for staying on the tour right up until the very end of her pregnancy. It was fun on the road, but it was a draining lifestyle. I was eager to see my sister again too. So was Griffin. Anna had decided not to join the boys on this tour. Gibson was getting into a stage where she needed more attention and guidance—absolutely everything went into that girl's mouth—so Anna had stayed home with her. I was very proud of my sister for putting the baby's needs first. That was leaps and bounds from the Anna I'd grown up with. She'd been worried about it, but she was a great mom. I hoped I'd be just as great.

When I hit my ninth month of pregnancy, I was done with it. I was huge. I was exhausted. My feet were swollen. My back ached. I could not find a comfortable sleeping position to save my life. And my amped-up sex drive had sizzled away to nothing. I wanted this child out of my body.

Kellan did everything he could to appease me. He drove a half an hour away just to get me one specific kind of ice cream. He gave me back massages every night. He even tried to give me a pedicure, which made me laugh so hard that my feet were shaking and the bright red nail polish ended up smeared all over my toes and his hands. It was sweet, though.

Just when I accepted the fact that I was going to be pregnant forever, I started having contractions. I immediately wrote down when they happened and how long they lasted. Kellan noticed me scribbling in one of his lyric journals and rested his head on my shoulder. "Whatcha doin'?"

Staring at a stop watch, I counted the seconds as I breathed through the pain. "I'm logging my contractions."

"You're what?" Kellan turned me to face him; his eyes were wide and panicked. "Is it time? Should I take you to the hospital now? I'll start the car. And I'll get your bag. Shoot, I need to put the car seat in."

He took off before I could answer a single one of his questions. "Kellan! It's . . . still early." My contractions were mild and still really far apart. Even I knew we had plenty of time.

He was a flurry of activity, though, so I didn't bother explaining that to him. I simply sat on the couch and waited to log my next contraction. Kellan dashed around the house grabbing things he thought we needed and muttering to himself about things he was sure he was forgetting. "Kiera, will we need diapers? I'm grabbing diapers. We should bring diapers."

Over my shoulder I yelled out, "Kellan! I'm sure the hospital will have some." He didn't respond to me, and I was sure the trunk of the Chevelle was going to be loaded with enough diapers to cover the bottoms of half the children in Seattle.

I glanced over at my mom, calmly sitting beside me. Not wanting to miss another grandbaby's birth, she had flown to Seattle pre-due date. Dad was going to join her once the baby was here. "He's a wreck," I said.

Laughing, my mom patted my knee. "They all are the first time."

Even though I was nowhere near giving birth, twenty minutes later I was stuffed into the Chevelle and Kellan raced me to the nearest hospital. Glancing at his speedometer, I firmly told him, "Slow down. We have plenty of time."

Kellan flicked me nervous glances. "Are you sure? How do you know? Maybe you're just having a really mild labor. Maybe this is as bad as it will get for you."

Amused, my mother started chuckling in the backseat. I did *not* find that comforting.

Hours later, I could have killed my husband, I could have killed my mother, and I could have killed the manufacturer of the mislabeled birth control pills. I was going to die, I was positive. I'd never felt something so painful in all my life. But then, some angelic nurse in cloud-covered scrubs gave me drugs . . . and things were much, much better.

It was still horribly uncomfortable, and hard. I'd never really thought about how difficult the act of giving birth was. You would think, since it happens all the time, it would be a much more seamless process. I mean, you don't see cats and dogs screaming, grunting, and writhing in pain. I've watched videos of whales giving birth before, and I swear those creatures didn't even notice they were delivering. And let me tell you, even partially numb from the waist down, I noticed.

Holding my hand, Kellan helped me as best he could. I could tell he felt completely useless and wished he could do more. He'd probably offer to give birth for me if he could. "You're doing great, sweetheart, almost there."

The doctor told me one more push should do it, and I nearly cried. I just wanted to be done. I hated this. I would rather be hit by another truck than ever do this again. Mom squeezed my other hand. "You can do this," she told me.

I knew I could too, and I gave it my all. The relief was nearly instant, and I knew I was done even before I heard the baby start to cry. Tears rolling down his cheeks, Kellan kissed my sweaty head. "You're amazing," he whispered.

Closing my eyes, I managed a small, thankful smile.

The nurse's perky voice stirred me from my stupor. "Congratulations! It's a boy!"

I heard my mom start to cry as I flashed open my eyes and stared up at Kellan. A boy? We'd had a boy. Kellan's gaze was fixed on the small bundle in the nurse's arms. His expression was a combination of awe and joy. "I have a son?" A shimmering tear fell off his cheek and landed on my shoulder.

No, I was wrong, I would do this a thousand more times to see that look on his face. Well, at least two or three more times.

The nurse nodded as she came toward me with my son. I was dying to see him, hold him, but I minutely shook my head at her and flicked a glance at Kellan. Understanding, she handed the baby to him. Kellan had been through so much crap in his life, he deserved to be the first one to hold his child.

Making a sound that was both a laugh and a sob, Kellan stared into his son's eyes. "Hey, little man," he whispered. "I'm your dad, and I love you . . . so much." Voice quavering, he added, "I'm so glad you're here."

I was sobbing long before Kellan handed him to me.

Several months later, I was wading through a sea of pink and white balloons. They were all over my house. And I mean *all* over my house. Clumps of them were attached to every lamp, vase, banister, doorknob, cabinet handle, and chair back. The ceiling was littered with them. So was the floor. People in the living room were having a blast, kicking them back and forth. Hopefully nobody took a swipe while Gibson was near. My fifteen-month-old niece was in hog heaven, trying to collect as many squishy balloons in her arms as she could carry. Anna was watching her like a hawk, making sure none of the balloons popped and scared her, or popped and became rubbery treats. That little girl still had oral-fixation issues. She would put anything in her mouth. *Anything.* Anna had already told me about Gibson finding her sex-toy stash. She'd saved Gibson from a lifetime of needing therapy by mere seconds. They now kept their assortment of adult toys in a locked box on the top shelf of their closet. And I'd give anything not to know that.

In my kitchen, a three-tiered cake was resting on the middle of the wide oak table. It was in the shape of a heart, and each layer was a different shade of pink. Even the plastic tablecloth was pink. And the plates. And the silverware. Surrounding the cake were cookies and candies in various colors and styles, all of them with a heart theme. And little conversation hearts were spread over the table as edible decorations. It looked like we were throwing a birthday party for cupid.

We weren't. The party we were throwing was a conglomeration of congratulations. A banner taped above the sliding door leading to the wraparound porch out back announced all the festivities: *Happy one year anniversary, Denny & Abby! Congratulations on publishing your second book, Kiera! Congratulations on your second album reaching #1, D-Bags! Happy Valentine's Day!*

Abby had arranged the party. Not only was she a huge holiday nut, but she was also an impossibly organized multi-tasker. When she saw on opportunity to combine events, she jumped on it! The only thing that was missing from the banner was the fact that my little man was five months old today. But that fact was really only significant to Kellan and me. Most people didn't throw a birthday party every month of someone's life. But we celebrated the smallest milestones with our son.

It was lightly snowing outside, but that wasn't stopping our group from having a barbeque. Evan was in front of our stainless steel grill in a fluffy jacket and a stocking cap, flipping burgers and rotating the hotdogs. Matt was with him, his arms securely around Rachel, who looked like she was slowly freezing to death. As I watched other people come into the house to take a break from the chill, ducking under the massive banner as they did, I felt someone standing beside me.

Turning my head, I smiled over at Denny. He was completely clean-shaven; it was the first time I'd seen him that way since college. Back then, he'd seemed so young with his baby face and youthful smile. But he'd grown over the years, and now he looked like someone who knew exactly who he was and where he was going. The peaceful smile on his face told the world *My life is good, and I'm content.* Seeing him look that way lifted my heart.

Pointing over to the table of holiday-inspired confections, I told him, "You really weren't kidding about the holiday fetish, were you?"

Denny laughed as he looked my way. "No, I wasn't. You and Kellan will have to come over for St. Patrick's Day next month. You will not believe the dinner Abby serves." He twisted his lip. "Ever had green potatoes?"

I laughed at that remark and instantly pictured my pink table transformed into a green wonderland, full of foods that shouldn't ever be green. Glancing at the ring on his finger as he sipped his fruity pink punch, I told him, "Congratulations on your one year anniversary."

He paused with the cup to his mouth. "Thank you." After taking another drink, he told me, "I have some good news for you too. Like we talked about, I gave *Irresistible* to every publishing house I could. One of them called me yesterday. They're impressed with how well the book has been doing, and they absolutely loved the story. They want to talk to you about publishing it professionally."

My eyes widened. A traditional book deal? Right now, my book was only available on the Internet. Having my title on bookshelves everywhere would be the culmination of all of my dreams. Amazed, I told him, "Thank you for doing that. I'd love to talk to them."

I was still reeling over the news when Abby came up to Denny. Seeing the look on my face, she asked him, "Did you tell her?" When he nodded, she turned to me. "Congratulations, Kiera, we're very excited for you. I wanted to change the banner but Denny told me it was too soon to announce anything."

I smiled at her adorable accent. That was one of the perks for me when I hung out with Denny and his wife—two accents for the price of one. "Thank you. I'm still . . . taking it all in."

Abby nodded as she looped her arms through Denny's. "Well, you deserve your success, you and Kellan both." An impish smile crossed her lips and she added, "And isn't your congratulations cake gorgeous?"

"Definitely. It's almost nicer than your wedding cake." Abby lifted an eyebrow at me, and I had to laugh. Her wedding cake had been something straight out of a Martha Stewart catalog. There had been seven layers to it. And a fountain. I'm not joking.

Denny laughed with me, but stopped when Abby pouted at him. Giving her an adoring smile, he murmured, "Happy anniversary, sweetheart."

She immediately perked back up and leaned forward to kiss him. Shaking my head at the lovebirds, I turned away to give them some privacy. From the room behind me, I heard a person speaking through a microphone and cringed. Damn, someone had just turned on the karaoke machine. I'm not sure why I ever let Kellan convince me that we should get one. I'd only used it once, when just the two of us had been home, and that had been mortifying. But it was pretty amazing when Kellan took over, so I wasn't entirely disappointed with the purchase.

Excusing myself from Denny and Abby, I twisted around to head into the living room. Lightly kicking balloons out of my way, I came upon a sight that both made me laugh and warmed my heart. Griffin, in all his attention-seeking glory, was standing in front of the fireplace with Kellan; Kellan was holding our little boy in a front-facing infant carrier. Adorable wasn't a strong enough word to describe him. There was just something about an attractive man holding a baby . . .

Our living room had a capacious, open layout with clumps of furniture spaced here and there to break the space up. I could easily see every person who was curiously watching the two D-Bags about to perform. Anna, Gibson, and Kellan's sister, Hailey, were among them. Much to the chagrin of Gavin, Hailey had decided to move out here after she'd finished college. Well, I suppose Gavin wasn't too upset about it; it just gave him yet another reason to come visit. In fact, last I saw, Gavin and Riley were in the band's "practice room," a soundproof building that the boys used to work on new material. Riley was quickly becoming just as adept with the guitar as his older brother. He was also becoming just as impossibly attractive, a heartbreaker in the making.

Clearing his throat, Griffin brought the microphone to his lips. "Ladies and gentleman, I want to thank you all for coming tonight to *The G and K Show.*" He licked his lips, then air-kissed the crowd. "It's our pleasure to entertain you." He started suggestively thrusting his hips, and I slapped my hand over my eyes.

Anna, sitting on an ottoman in front of them, busted out laughing. Gibson was sitting on her lap, giggling. Wearing a frilly red dress, white tights, and the cutest pair of Mary Janes, the adorable girl had her blond hair neatly pulled into symmetrical pigtails. Anna told me that Griffin had spent thirty minutes getting the pigtails to perfectly line up. When Gibson started clapping at her daddy's antics, everyone around started laughing.

Kellan, also laughing at Gibson, brought his microphone to his lips. "Can you just start the music so we can get this over with?"

Griffin frowned at Kellan, but pressed Play on the machine. When Debbie Gibson's "Lost In Your Eyes" started playing, Kellan lowered the mike and stared at Griffin in disbelief. "Are you kidding me? This is the song you wanted to sing?"

As my sister fell over backward she was laughing so hard, Griffin pointed at his daughter. "It's Debbie *Gibson,* dude. Gibson. It's for my daughter."

Kellan sighed as he closed his eyes. "If we're gonna do a duet, can we at least sing 'Electric Youth'?"

Griffin made an obscene gesture then headed back to the machine to change the song selection. Behind his back, Kellan started cracking up. When Kellan held the microphone back up, a tiny hand reached out to grab the cord. I smiled at our son, Ryder. Kellan had named him. He loved that the name was similar to his half brother's. I loved that it sounded a bit rock 'n' roll. The son of the lead singer of one of the hottest bands on earth should have an interesting name.

Ryder's face was just at the edge of the carrier; he was chewing on the end of it like a dog gnawing on his toy. His little fist curled around the microphone cord in triumph and he gave it a tug or two. Kellan smiled down at him and bounced a little on his feet. Those two were peas in a pod already. Ryder loved me without a doubt, but he was daddy's boy through and through. And he looked just like Kellan—thick light brown hair that stuck up no matter how hard I tried to keep it down, and deep, dark blue eyes that looked like the evening sky. Maybe I was a bit biased, but everything about him was perfect—his cheeks, his nose, his toothless smile, the cute little freckle on the back of his neck. Everything.

The boys had a tour starting for their successful sophomore album this summer. Ryder and I were going to go with the boys, just to see how it went. If it was too hard touring with him, then we would go home and work out something else out for future tours. Short visits, maybe. But Kellan and I were pretty easygoing, and

Ryder was a dream baby, so I was expecting this tour to be just fine. Keeping Ryder away from the public was my biggest concern. Kellan's too. That's why we had a team joining us—we'd bumped our bodyguards up to two, and we'd hired a nanny. I didn't really think we'd need the nanny, I was pretty on top of things, but Kellan thought the extra help would be worth it. "And besides," he'd told me, "with a nanny, we could have a night or two alone for . . . dates." I was sold after that.

As "Electric Youth" started playing through the speakers, Jenny wrapped her arms around me. She had an engagement ring on her finger that twinkled in the living room lights. She and Evan hadn't been in any great hurry to move their relationship along, but he'd finally proposed to her last week. That left Matt and Rachel. Rumor was, Matt was going to propose to her on the day the boys left for their next tour. Rumor also had it that Matt was sweating bullets about it. I was positive he had nothing to worry about; Rachel was going to say yes.

"Hey, Kiera. Great party."

Leaning in to her, I laughed. "Thanks. Abby did most of it, though." Sighing, I looked back at Kellan. He'd started singing along with Griffin, but he was laughing so hard he didn't sound very good. He looked good, though.

Jenny snorted. "Is this because Kellan lost that bet?"

Looking over at her, I frowned. "What bet?"

She grinned and pulled her long locks away from her shoulder. "You know, Griffin bet him that he could knock Anna up again before Kellan knocked you up again." Jenny rolled her eyes. "I don't think Kellan actually accepted the bet, but still, you know how Griffin loves to win . . . anything."

My eyes widened as far as they could go. Anna was pregnant again? Sitting herself up, Anna happened to glance my way. When she saw my face, then saw Jenny beside me, she instantly knew that I knew. Her lips curled into a smirk, and she merely shrugged at me. I was so floored, I could barely come up with words. When I did, they were laced with disbelief. "Those two are going to overpopulate the earth, aren't they?"

Jenny pursed her lips. "Yep. Probably."

Kellan had control over his chuckles by the second verse. Then he started getting into it. Always the performer, he gave the cheesy eighties teeny-bopper anthem his best. No one in the room had dry eyes. Not Cheyenne, Meadow, or the rest of Poetic Bliss. Not Justin or Kate, cuddling on the love seat. Not Troy, Rita, or Sam.

When Kellan and Griffin's song was over, Kellan and Ryder took a small bow. Then Kellan handed the microphone out to Rain. Just as eager to perform as Griffin, Rain jumped off the couch and ran up to the "stage." They had to pry the microphone cord away from Ryder, which made him start to cry. Bouncing him as he walked, Kellan reached into his back pocket and handed him a rattle in the shape of a guitar. He instantly started shaking it, a smile on his tiny lips.

Kellan walked over to me, pulling Ryder out of his carrier as he did. My face scrunched up into a "gimme" expression as I held my hands out for my baby. Kellan instantly handed him over, kissing his head before he did. Warmth and softness overwhelmed me as I held Ryder close. I inhaled a deep breath as he grabbed a fistful of my hair. He smelled like Kellan. Somehow, whether it was hereditary or just a by-product of being so close to Kellan all the time, Ryder always seemed to smell like his daddy. It was incredible.

Hours later, when the party was over, I wandered through my home littered with red Solo cups and half-eaten pieces of cake. I felt totally at peace. Even messy from a party, this place was my sanctuary. My journey here had been tumultuous at best, but it was worth every scrape, heartache, and tear. Kellan and I were who we are now because of it. We'd learned to open up to each other, to trust each other, to face the world together. I firmly believed now that there was nothing we couldn't tackle together. No hurdle, no obstacle, no setback was so large that it would break us apart, and there was comfort and confidence in that knowledge.

Shuffling past stray balloons that had somehow found their way upstairs—I'd worry about cleaning up my safe haven later—I made my way to Ryder's bathroom. I could hear splashing water and Kellan's voice. Oddly enough, he was singing "Electric Youth" again. The song must have gotten stuck in his head. Heading for the open door, I leaned against the frame and watched my husband bathe his son.

Ryder was lying in a small blue plastic tub inside the larger one, keeping him safe and secure. As Kellan gently poured a cup of water over his head, Ryder's mouth opened wide and his tongue shot out, like he was waiting to get a drink. He shoved his hand in his mouth instead. When Kellan noticed me watching, he turned his head my way. "You can go lie down if you want. I got this."

Smiling, I shook my head. "I like watching the two of you together."

Rubbing some soap in his hands, Kellan told Ryder, "Hear that? Mommy likes to watch. That's called voyeurism." He sounded the word out, like he was expecting Ryder to repeat it back to him. Instead Ryder pressed his lips together and blew out, humming his lips and getting spittle all over his little face.

Stepping up to Kellan, I nudged his butt with my foot. Jackass. Chuckling, Kellan got to work sudsing up Ryder's hair; there was dried frosting in it. Thanks to a moment of playful splashing by Ryder, Kellan was a little wet by the time the bath was over. Pulling him out of the tub, Kellan wrapped Ryder in a towel shaped like a giant yellow duck. As if a man holding a baby wasn't cute enough, a man holding a baby wearing a hood shaped like a duck bill was downright delightful.

I wasn't sure if it was normal or not, but just watching him take care of his son was putting me in the mood. Maybe I *should* go lie down, wait for him in bed with just my KK underwear on. But I couldn't stop watching him with Ryder, and I followed the duo when they headed over to Ryder's bedroom.

We'd turned Ryder's room into a stage. Jenny had helped me paint it, since she was the one blessed with artistic talent. One wall was painted black with thick red curtains on either side of it. Ryder's crib was positioned in front of the black wall, in the lead singer's position. My mother had flipped out when I'd told her that I painted Ryder's room black. But it was an homage to Pete's, the starting point of both Kellan's career and our relationship; we were even going to hang some guitars on the wall when Ryder was older. And besides, every parenting magazine I'd ever read said that babies loved the contrast between black and white. And every other wall in his room was white. Well, white except for the black five-line stave across the center of each wall. Jenny had done an outstanding job with those. And the notes sliding up and down the perfectly straight lines were to an actual D-Bags song, the sad song that Kellan had been singing when we got back together. His ode to me. The significance squeezed my heart every time I walked into this room.

Wading through a sea of books and toys, Kellan laid Ryder down on his changing table and quickly slapped a diaper on him. That was something we'd both learned right away: if you wait too long to put a diaper on a baby boy, you were going to get peed on. Kellan got it in the face once. I'd nearly passed out from laughing so hard. Once Ryder was safe, Kellan leaned down and blew raspberries on his stomach. My favorite sound in the world filled the room—the uninhibited belly laugh of a sweet little human being that knew nothing about feeling self-conscious. It was infectious, and Kellan and I were both laughing right along with him.

After a half-dozen kisses, one on each foot, one on each hand, and a few on his cheeks, Kellan finally got him into his pajamas. Ryder's belly was already full, and he was rubbing his eyes like a madman, so I knew he was seconds away from sleep. Kellan still held him and rocked him until his eyes closed, though. And he sang to him. He sang to him almost every night. And he always told him that he loved him, like he wanted to make sure that Ryder never doubted that, not for an instant.

My eyes were wet when Kellan put our sleeping child to bed. Glancing up at me, he crooked a smile. "Every time," he whispered.

"What?" I sniffled.

Grabbing my hand, he quietly pulled me from the room, shutting the door after him. "Every time I put him to sleep, you cry. Why do you do that?"

Because I love you more than any one person should be allowed to love someone.

"I just love seeing how much you love him." In my complete happiness, I felt a tear roll down my cheek.

Stepping in to me, Kellan grabbed my hands and lowered his forehead to mine. His thumb traced his name on my wrist. "I love you too, you know."

I nodded. "I do know. You show me every day." Pulling back, I indicated our bedroom with my head. "But why don't you show me again right now?"

The smile that crept over Kellan's face was so devilishly handsome that a rush of desire flooded through me. I loved that he still had that effect on my body. "I would love to show you, again and again and again." He bit his lip, then slowly dragged his teeth across them while his eyes scoured my body. It was such a hot move. I felt naked already. And sexy, and loved, and wanted.

Needing him just as much as I'd always needed him, I pressed my body against his and wrapped my arms around his neck. With my chest flush against him, I stood on my toes until my lips were barely brushing his. "Take me to our room and make love to me nice and slow . . . please?" Not a trace of embarrassment was inside of me as I asked for him. I could ask him anything. I could tell him anything. I could be anything with him. I could be *everything* with him.

Kellan pressed me against the hallway wall, making me gasp. As his lips lowered to mine, his hands reached down and, scooping up my legs, wrapped them around his waist. Hungry and passionate, his mouth worked over mine. When he paused, we were both breathing heavier. We were both ready and aching for the other. "I love it when you beg," he husked, before stepping away from the wall and carrying me to our plush bedroom.

He didn't set me down until we reached our bed. I felt on fire as he stripped my clothes off. He hissed in a breath when I removed his shirt and kissed over his tattoo. By the desire racing between us, you would think we hadn't been together in weeks, not twenty-four hours, but that was just the way it was with us—electric. Every time.

His fingers unfastened my jeans and my fingers ducked inside the waistband of his. I wanted him, so much. He whimpered as I felt his need for me. By the time we were both laid bare, I knew I was going to explode soon, but that's when Kellan's expertise kicked in. Instead of finishing what we both wanted as quickly as possible, he took his time. He dragged it out. He kept me on edge, wanting more and more. It paralleled our relationship—always wanting more of him, never having enough. Sure, we had our moments, just like any relationship, but being with him, in any capacity, was always satisfying. And I knew by his reaction as we both finally reached our climaxes that he felt the same way. He needed more and more of me. He would always want me near him. I would always be first in his eyes. We were a good match. A perfect match. Soul mates.

Passion, friendship, love, loyalty, trust . . . if you found the right person . . . you really could have it all.

Acknowledgments

First and foremost, I would like to thank all of the fans. Bringing this trilogy to you has been such a joy! I am awed every day by the outpouring of love you have for these characters. They are like my children, and to know that others care for them just as much as I do warms my heart. Thank you for your devotion!

To my four foundations, Rena, Lesa, Toni, and Amy, you are all a blessing in my life that I wouldn't give up for anything. To my family, in case I don't say it enough, I love you all very much! To Wayne, Robin, Tyson, and Dean, thank you for your never-ending support and encouragement, and for being so patient with me and my crazy schedule.

To my mentor, Nicky Charles, thank you for guiding me through the rocky road of self-publishing! You've always been there to lend a hand and an ear, and I'm forever grateful.

To K.A. Linde, the world's greatest muli-tasker, you have been such an incredible friend, and I am so honored to have started this crazy journey with you. I'm so incredibly excited to see your star taking off! You deserve it! I'm so proud of you!

To Jenny . . . where to begin. Thank you for being my rock! Thank you for being my cheerleader! And thank you for being my friend! I think I would still be huddled in a corner crying my eyes out if it weren't for you. I love you to pieces!

To Becky, Monica, Lori, Gitte, and Sam, thank you for your advice and expertise. My stories are better because of your help! Thank you for selflessly giving me so much of your time. A huge thank you to Lysa at Pegasus Designs for my beautiful website, and Sarah at Okay Creations for my D-Bags store. And to Francine, your logos are incredible! Thank you so much for letting me use them!

Thank you Jamie McGuire, Colleen Hoover, Tammara Webber, Tina Reber, Tracey Garvis-Graves, Jessica Park, Abbi Glines, Jenn Sterling, Rebecca Donovan, Tarryn Fisher, and all of the other authors who have supported me, encouraged me, and answered endless questions. I'm honored and humbled to be among such greatness.

Heartfelt thanks to Kristyn Keene at ICM, for being a fan as well as a super agent, and Louise Burke, Jennifer Bergstrom, and Kate Dresser at Gallery Books, for believing in these books and taking a chance on me.

And a great big thank you to the reviewers and bloggers who screamed their passion for these stories! You made your voice heard, and I wouldn't be where I am without you—Totally Booked, Maryse's Book Blog, The Indie Bookshelf, Lisa's Reads, Tough Critic Book Reviews, Book Snobs, My Secret Romance, Lori's Book Blog, Novel Magic, Flirty and Dirty Book Blog, Literati Literature Lovers, The Subclub Book Club, The Autumn Review, and many, many more!